Blond, beautiful, voluptuous, she gives the best years of her life to a cold uncaring family . . .

ROWELL

His marriage to Willow saves his family. Cold, snobbish, unprincipled, he keeps a secret mistress and disregards his wife . . .

TOBY

Rowell's brother, he falls in love with Willow the moment he sees her, unaware he is rousing her to feel the same for him . . .

PELHAM

Rowell's other brother, a handsome charmer, is also attracted to Willow . . .

DODY

The younger Rochford sister, abandoned to a tower, for her illness must never be allowed to disgrace the family . . .

GRANDMÈRE

She rules the Rochford estate with an iron will and a heart of stone . . .

SOPHIA

Willow's daughter, who is stolen from her at birth and raised in a horrible orphanage, while Willow is told she is dead . . .

THE
CHATELAINE

CLAIRE LORRIMER

BALLANTINE BOOKS • NEW YORK

Library of Congress Catalog Card Number: 81-20525

ISBN 0-345-29884-5

This edition published by arrangement with

Arlington Books

Manufactured in the United States of America

First Ballantine Books Edition: May 1982

For my sisters, Eve and Anne,
with love

CAST OF CHARACTERS

GRANDMERE, LADY CLOTILDE ROCHFORD Senior member of the Rochford family

GENERAL LORD CEDRIC ROCHFORD Grandmère's husband

THE HON. MILDRED ROCHFORD
THE HON. GRACE (née ROCHFORD) } Grandmère's sisters-in-law

LORD OLIVER ROCHFORD Grandmère's son

LADY ALICE ROCHFORD Grandmère's daughter-in-law

THE HON. JOSEPHINE ROCHFORD
THE HON. BARBARA ROCHFORD } infants of the above

IRENE BARTON the infants' nurse

ROWELL, BARON ROCHFORD Grandmère's eldest grandson

THE HON. TOBY ROCHFORD
THE. HON. PELHAM ROCHFORD
THE HON. RUPERT ROCHFORD } Grandmère's other grandchildren
THE HON. FRANCIS ROCHFORD
THE. HON. DOROTHY ROCHFORD

VIOLET GULLY Dodie's maid

THE HON. SOPHIA ROCHFORD
THE HON. OLIVER ROCHFORD } Grandmère's great-grandchildren
THE HON. ALICE ROCHFORD

PATIENCE MERRYWEATHER the children's nurse

WILLOUGHBY TETFORD American millionaire

BEATRICE TETFORD his wife

WILLOW TETFORD their daughter

NELLIE SINCLAIR Willow's maid

GEORGINA GREY (née FRY) Rowell's mistress

PHILIP, MARK and JANE GREY Georgina's children

AUGUSTA FRY Georgina's aunt

LUCIENNE, COMTESSE LE CHEVALIER Grandmère's niece

SILVIE, BARONIN VON SENDEN Lucienne's daughter

BERNARD, BARON VON SENDEN Silvie's German husband

DR. JOHN FORBES the Rochfords' family doctor

PEGGY FORBES Dr. Forbes' wife

ADRIAN FORBES their son

JAMES MCGILL Havorhurst village schoolmaster

MRS. MARY GASSONS his housekeeper

ALEXANDRA MCGILL his daughter

THE REVEREND APPLEBY Vicar of St. Stephen's Church, Havorhurst

MR. BARTHOLOMEW solicitor to the Rochford family

MR. FELLOWS bailiff to Lord Rochford

MRS. GERTRUDE SPEARS housekeeper
MRS. CONNIE JUPP cook
GEORGE DUTTON butler
HAROLD STEVENS footman
JANET UPTON head parlormaid
PETERS head coachman
JACKSON head groom
BETTY tweeny
LILY maid
} servants at Rochford Manor

MADELEINE VILLIER New Zealand girl

MRS. MEADOWS her aunt

DESIREE SOMNERS actress

BURROWS her maid

SIR JOHN BARRATT, BART. friend of the Rochford family

ANNABEL BARRATT his eldest daughter

GILLIAN BARRATT another daughter

STELLA MENZIES the Barratts' governess

LORD THEODORE SYMINGTON
LADY ESME SYMINGTON
} friends of Rowell

AGNES MILLER farmer's wife

MATTHEW MAYBURY Bishop's Chancellor

MR. and MRS. PALEY American businessman and his wife

NATHANIEL CORBETT Willoughby Tetford's partner

BARRY ADAMS Willoughby Tetford's junior director

MR. GORNWAY brain specialist

DR. GOUSSE French doctor

MARIE cook at the Château d'Orbais

FATHER MATTIEU French priest

MOTHER SUPERIOR of the *Convent du Coeur Sanglant*

PIERRE French artist

MAURICE French artist

MONSIEUR GRIMAUD Parisian modiste

MADAME GRIMAUD his wife

MADAME LULU owner of the brothel *Le Ciel Rouge*

YVETTE
BABETTE
NICOLE
FIFI
} four of her girls

JOSE maid in the brothel
ANDRE Yvette's boyfriend
BLANCHE *cocotte de luxe*
MAXIMILLIAN, GRAF VON KREUGE German count

Prologue

1864

FOURTEEN TIMES A DAY THE CHILDREN'S NURSE, Irene, stood for ten minutes in the center of the sickroom waving her rod through the air. On the end of the rod was a three foot square of flannel cloth moistened in Sir William Burnett's Disinfecting Fluid—a patented purifying agent. Dr. Forbes thought very highly of it and had recommended it yesterday as a precaution lest the two infants were suffering from an infectious disease. But this morning the young doctor had informed the anxious nurse and parents that in his opinion, the likelihood was that the baby and the little girl were suffering from brain storms.

It was four o'clock on a dark December evening. An oil lamp, turned low, stood on the table between the baby's cot and that of her eighteen-month-old sister. There could be little doubt now that the two-month-old baby was dying. She was wracked by convulsive fits, her tiny body contorting grotesquely as she struggled for breath. Beside her, Alice Rochford wept quietly, powerless to help her offspring. Every now and again she turned in mute appeal to the doctor and begged him to do something to save her children. But from the young man's anxious expression and nervous pacing between the two cots, she sensed that he, too, had little hope of their survival.

A huge fire burned in the grate. On a trivet a bronchitis kettle poured steam out into the room. The atmosphere smelled of balsam, camphor and carbolic despite the fact that both windows were open, the curtains blowing inward as drafts carried the freezing night air toward the chimney.

The door opened and the small, plump, erect figure of Lady Clotilde Rochford, the children's grandmother, came marching into the sickroom. Her dark, beady eyes swept

1

round to the windows, and, seeing them open, she ordered
the nurse to close them at once.

The doctor's feeble protest was drowned by her imperious command that she wanted none of his new-fangled
ideas in her house; that he was far too young and inexperienced to argue with her and that the windows were
to remain closed. As always when aroused, Lady Clotilde's
voice betrayed her French origins and her accent became
noticeable.

The young man bowed his head submissively. Lady
Rochford senior's reputation was well known to him. He
had been warned several times that she was autocratic,
ruled her large household with a rod of iron and totally
dominated her son's wife, Lady Alice Rochford.

John Forbes decided not to argue with this formidable
woman. He was appalled by the misfortune that his very
first visit to Rochford Manor should be for so serious an
illness. But at twenty-six years of age, he had only last
week come to Havorhurst to replace the old village doctor who had formerly been in attendance on the Rochford family. The old grandmother was perfectly correct
when she called him, John Forbes, inexperienced, for with
a sinking heart he knew that he had still not diagnosed
the infants' illness.

Alice Rochford's endless sobbing filled the room. Her
mother-in-law, barely glancing at her, walked over to the
cot and looked down at the baby. Perfectly in control of
her emotions, she said sharply:

"I can see the child is dying." She turned to the nurse.
"Irene, tell Burns to send one of the menservants to fetch
the parson. The baby should be baptized at once!"

The child in the adjacent cot now went into a convulsive fit as she, too, struggled desperately for breath. Blood
and mucus dribbled from her mouth. The young doctor
wiped it away nervously with a piece of cotton wool. This
child, Josephine, had been ill for nearly two days and
despite the nurse's repeated attempts to feed her, was
now suffering from starvation and dehydration, for she
seemed unable to swallow even sips of port wine.

"You're certain they do not have diphtheria?" asked the
grandmother in doubtful tones, her eyes boring into the
nervous young doctor's face.

"There is no sign of the membrane in the throat," he

reiterated the opinion he had given her that morning. "And neither child has been in contact with anyone who has the disease." He turned and stared at the pale, weeping woman by the bed. "Lady Alice assures me that no one but herself, the children's father, you and their nurse have been near the nursery since the new baby was born. The children cannot have contracted diphtheria without catching it from someone with the disease."

Lady Rochford nodded. One of her own two sons had died of the complaint during an epidemic in France and she had seen for herself the cruel white membrane growing over the windpipe until the unhappy child had suffocated. Mercifully her second son, Oliver, Alice's husband, had not then been born, for the disease had spread like wildfire through the local community and her own child's death was but one of many.

"You must try to resign yourself to God's will, Alice!" she said in firm tones to her daughter-in-law. "Be thankful that you are young enough to bear other children."

There was a knock at the door and as Lord Oliver came into the room, his wife flung herself hysterically into his arms.

"My babies are dying," she cried.

A soldier by profession, Oliver Rochford was ill at ease in the sickroom; moreover, he did not care for his wife's uncontrolled emotionalism although he was a kindly man and sympathized with her distress. Barely recovered from childbirth, she was not up to this ordeal, he told himself as he patted her head soothingly. He himself was not particularly stricken by the thought that he was about to lose his two first-born children. Both were girls and he, like his mother, had passionately hoped both babies would be boys. By the look of things, the new baby had already passed away, he thought as he watched helplessly while the doctor covered the child's face with the sheet.

Alice Rochford clung to her husband, staring up into his pale blue eyes in despair.

"She has not yet been baptized," she cried in an anguished voice. "Do you understand, Oliver? She cannot now be buried in consecrated ground!"

Baron, Lord Oliver Rochford pushed a lock of gingery hair from his forehead and cleared his throat noisily.

"Nonsense, m'dear," he said firmly. "Parson will bury

the infants where I want—where all the Rochford are buried—in St. Stephen's graveyard, and that's all there is to it."

"But—" Alice began when old Lady Rochford interrupted.

"Oliver is quite right. The Reverend Appleby will not want to lose his living. He will do as Oliver says," she said pointedly.

She looked at her son—a rotund short sturdy man with ginger side whiskers and mustache. He had the upright bearing of a military man and she was immensely proud of him.

"Better take Alice to her room, Oliver," she suggested. "I'll stay here until . . ."

Until the older child dies, thought John Forbes unhappily. Deep down inside, he was a little shocked by this aristocratic woman's seeming indifference to death. She was, after all, the infants' grandmother, and as far as he knew, there were no other children. The return of the nurse, Irene, together with the Reverend Appleby interrupted his thoughts. He stood in the shadows at the back of the room while the parson, in his white surplice, prayed for the dying child.

"We beseech Thee to have mercy on this child, Josephine Mildred, and whensoever her soul shall depart it may be without sin presented unto Thee."

To the young doctor's surprise, the parson turned and walked over to the cot where the dead baby lay and in barely audible tones began the Baptismal service. Briefly he named her Barbara Alice and committed her soul to God.

Not a little shocked for the second time that night, the doctor realized that Baron Rochford, the children's father, must have spoken to the parson regarding the baby's future burial place.

Old Lady Rochford must have read his thoughts for she now approached him, saying in a low, forceful tone:

"We would not want a family doctor attending our household who was in any respect inclined to tittle-tattle," she said, her dark brown eyes boring into his as she spoke. "Naturally, I do not imagine you, Doctor Forbes, would dream of discussing our affairs with anyone, for I am sure you know what village gossips are—especially regarding those of us who happen to be born in better circumstances than others. You take my meaning, Doctor?"

He understood her very well indeed and for a moment anger surged through him. What right had this autocratic old woman to lay down the law—alter the rules to suit her own convenience? Was it money or position that made such people so powerful?

Both, he thought bitterly. There had been many other applicants for the post left vacant by the late Havorhurst doctor and he, John Forbes, newly qualified, had badly wanted this employment. Lady Rochford could soon turn this country district against him, he reflected, for the family owned nearly every farm, public house, cottage, mill, and smithy for miles around. His patients were the tenant farmers or employees of the Rochfords and doubtless were well aware of their dependence upon the family—a fact he was himself now forced to appreciate.

Weakly he nodded, telling himself that the matter of the baby's baptism was really no concern of his anyway; that he could count himself lucky that he had not been asked to disobey his Hippocratic Oath, something he would never do. And who could say but that it might be right not to deny an innocent baby a Christian burial merely because it had died before it had been named.

But the relief he felt at such self-reassurance was short-lived. Within two hours the little girl, too, was dead, and left alone in the sickroom with the nurse, he realized he had now to complete two death certificates.

"Cause of death . . ." What should I write? he asked himself uneasily. The fact was he did not know what had killed them. *Could it have been diphtheria after all?*

He searched his mind for facts he had learned about the disease and tried to recall the few cases he had seen in the hospital. The various possibilities that had tortured his mind these past two days now crowded in on him again. Tumor on the brain, epilepsy, croup, hemiplegia— all of these would give rise to convulsions and could bring about sudden death. But the fact that both babies had been taken ill at the same time . . .

Suddenly, with chilling clarity, he recalled a lecture he had attended as a medical student. It had been given by an eminent German professor and the young doctor could remember little of its subject matter. But what he did now recall was the Professor's caution at the end of the lecture.

"Never discard the diagnosis of an illness on the grounds that not *all* the usual or more obvious symptoms are present. You will come across occasions when even the most predominant symptoms are absent. The patient may still have the disease you suspect, but in that particular individual, the symptoms may be invisible to the naked eye. The day will come—and I am convinced of it —when we shall discover the means to see inside a body. Then and then only can we be certain of our diagnosis."

Shocked, wearied beyond words by the long vigil in the sickroom, the young doctor covered his face with his hands. To admit his doubts *now* to old Lady Rochford was a terrifying prospect, for he had been so adamant in resisting her suggestion that the babies had diphtheria. Not that he could have saved either child's life—for they would most certainly have died, so swift was the onslaught of illness. But the woman had seemed content to accept his diagnosis of a brain storm due either to a tumor on the brain or some other weakness in the constitution. When he had questioned her about possible hereditary factors, she had told him quite readily that she was far from happy about her daughter-in-law's mental condition. Poor Lady Alice had had difficult pregnancies and births with both children, was frequently ill, and cried a great deal, she said. The old family doctor had had to attend Lady Alice regularly and had stated bluntly that such cases of melancholia during the childbearing period could unfortunately be hereditary, though were not always so.

"I am not in the least surprised to hear that she may well have passed on this weakness of the brain to those children," Lady Rochford said bluntly. Her voice had softened suddenly. "My poor son! He may never now achieve his dearest wish to have a healthy son and heir for Rochford."

John Forbes sighed as he wrote on each certificate the word "Convulsions" as the cause of death. He could foresee that he might himself be a frequent visitor to the Manor to attend the bereaved mother who no doubt would relapse into yet another bout of melancholia. But for the meanwhile at least, his work here was done and he could go home.

"See that the room is fumigated very thoroughly with sulfur after the bodies have been removed," he told the weeping nurse. He felt a moment's compassion for the red-eyed girl. She would almost certainly be dismissed from her employment, although she had worked tirelessly and without sleep, caring for the sick children whom she had obviously loved in her simple way. "Try not to distress yourself too much," he murmured. "There was nothing you or anyone could do to save them."

He picked up his black bag and, with a last quick glance at the two white-shrouded cots, left the room and made his way downstairs. Everywhere the maids were hurriedly drawing the curtains in all the rooms. The silence and stillness of death had already penetrated the big house. An elderly butler handed him his coat and hat and opened the front door for him.

The night sky outside was brilliant with stars, the air sharp with frost which had already laid its white covering over the lawns and trees. He shivered as he waited for the groom to bring around his gig. There was something oppressive about the big darkened old manor house which seemed inexplicably to threaten him. Not a single light showed through the curtained windows. He could hear the sound of wheels crunching on the hard gravel of the drive and the noise from nearby of his horse snorting with impatience to be off to its own warm stable. The doctor shivered again, his mind tormented by the suspicion that he had made a terrible mistake.

He shook himself as if to shrug off his misgivings. What did it really matter, except to his own peace of mind? His wrong diagnosis could harm nobody, least of all the two dead infants. Doubtless, before long there would be other children, hopefully healthy ones, and these two little girls would be forgotten. Diphtheria or convulsions? What did it matter how they had died?

He could not know that it mattered so greatly to the children's grandmother that never again would she show affection for her daughter-in-law, never accord her more than the barest civility; that she was now convinced that poor Alice had brought into the Rochford family the ugly strain of insanity.

"There must be no more sickly Rochford girls," she said to her sister-in-law. "We can but hope that next time,

Mildred, Alice manages to give poor Oliver a healthy son and heir."

It was a year before Rowell, the first of the five healthy, lusty Rochford boys was born; ten years before Francis, the youngest arrived. By then the untimely deaths of the infants were all but forgotten until, on Francis' sixth birthday, Alice Rochford produced her last child.

She died not knowing that it was a girl.

❦ *Part One* ❦

1864–1896

"And fair the violet's gentle drooping head,
The primrose, pale for love uncomforted . . ."

Oscar Wilde, *Ravenna*

Chapter One

August 1889

CONCEALED BY THE CURTAINS DRAWN ACROSS THE oriel window in the long gallery, Willow Tetford peered down into the hall below, her gaze concentrated upon the tall, elegantly-clad figure of the eldest of the Rochford brothers. Rowell was, as usual, encircled by a bevy of admiring females.

"He is far the most handsome of all the men here to-night," Willow remarked. "Do you not agree that he looks very beautiful, Pelham?"

Pelham Rochford turned to the fifteen-year-old girl with a mixture of amusement and jealousy.

"You don't call men 'beautiful,'" he corrected her not unkindly. He too stared down at his eldest brother but without the young girl's adoration. He did not deny Rowell's good looks which he, being six years younger, often envied. But in Pelham's opinion that brooding romantic appearance concealed a nature very far from enviable. Ever since their father had died and Rowell had inherited the title of Baron and become head of the family, it seemed to Pelham that his eldest brother had grown far too superior and self-opinionated and had lost what little sense of humor he had had in his youth. Although still only twenty-four years of age, Rowell had adopted the airs and manners of a far older man and was on occasions objectionably autocratic with his four younger brothers. Pelham greatly preferred Toby, whose twenty-first birthday was being celebrated this evening with a gala ball at Rochford Manor.

"Who is that red-haired lady Rowell is taking in to dance?" Willow asked urgently beside him. "I don't think I have ever seen her before. She is very beautiful, isn't she?"

Despite the warmth of the summer evening, the girl

11

shivered, drawing her nightgown more closely around her slim young body and pressing nearer to her companion. She was supposed to be safely tucked up in her bed, but her curiosity had got the better of her, and dear, fun-loving Pelham had offered to keep watch while she crept from her bedroom to her present place of concealment. It was nearly midnight, and the hall, drawing room, and dining room thronged with several hundred guests, all attired in their finest clothes and jewels.

"That is Mrs. Georgina Grey," Pelham answered Willow's question; and, without thinking, he added "Rowell's mistress!"

Only as he looked down into Willow's wide uncomprehending gaze did he remember that he was talking to a girl still young enough to be termed a child. Brought up by a strict Quaker mother, Willow's innocence was total and he deeply regretted his slip of the tongue. Now, to further his embarrassment, she asked him to explain his meaning.

"I'll tell you one day—when you are older," he prevaricated, his voice sharper than he intended in his confusion. "You are much too young yet to understand about such things," he added more gently.

Willow's lips pursed in a pout, and she scowled at him as she said, sighing:

"That is what Mama always tells me whenever I ask her anything important, especially if it is about love and marriage and having babies." She swept the silky curtain of fair hair away from her delicately boned face and sighed again. "Anyway, I *do* know about love. I love you and Toby and Papa and I'm not sure but I think I love Rowell best of all."

"Then don't!" Pelham said, this time the sharpness of his tone intentional. "My dear brother Rowell isn't the least interested in a child of your age!"

Unperturbed for she was well aware of her unimportance Willow merely nodded her agreement. Rowell rarely spoke to her, and it was one of the "Very Special Days" she noted in her diary if he so much as smiled at her once in the course of a week.

"Nobody seems to notice that I am growing up very fast," Willow remarked, able as always to talk to Pelham on equal terms. He was exactly as she, an only child, had always imagined a brother might be—teasing, affectionate, sometimes a little patronizing but never more than his three years' seniority warranted, and never unkind.

Pelham remained silent. He was disturbed by Willow's innocent remark which was unconsciously provocative. He was only too well aware of late that the young American girl had made the transition from child to woman during the summer she had been at Rochford Manor. She had lost the roundness of childhood and was now tall and slender; her natural beauty was the more remarkable for her somewhat unusual coloring. From her Scandinavian mother she had inherited her beautiful hair, which was almost white blonde, and her large, expressive brown eyes.

Through the thin lawn of her nightgown, her small pointed breasts were clearly visible, and now, when she pouted, he found himself longing to kiss those pursed lips and to touch the delicately curved body with his hands. But her immaturity was a barrier he had not yet felt able to breach. He was both afraid of spoiling her radiant, childlike trust in him, and yet drawn to her as to a magnet. Instead of hiding here with her in the long gallery, he could have been downstairs drinking champagne, dancing with a dozen or more eager partners. But he preferred to be alone with Willow—a mere child. It was a state of mind he could not understand.

It was almost with relief that he saw the tall, angular figure of his brother Toby approaching them. Toby was carrying a tray of food.

"We're over here, Toby!" Willow called in a low voice as the young man peered short-sightedly over his spectacles down the long gallery.

"Didn't realize Pelham was with you!" Toby said in his short, clipped speech—a mannerism caused by acute shyness. "Thought you might be hungry, Willow. You usually are!"

Willow took the tray from him, her dark brown eyes sparkling.

"You're dear and kind and thoughtful," she said as she viewed the delicacies eagerly. Although very occasionally she had been permitted to eat with the grownups, normally she had her meals in the old nursery with the younger Rochford boys, seventeen-year-old Rupert and fifteen-year-old Francis, where food was served that Cook considered more wholesome for growing bodies. Willow did not mind being classified as "nursery," although she always ate with her parents when she was at home. The relegation was more than offset by the delight of being a guest of the Rochford family for the whole summer while her parents were touring Europe.

They had come from San Francisco to England and rented Langham House for a year. It adjoined the Rochfords' estate, and her parents, Willoughby and Beatrice Tetford, had warned her that they might not be received by their aristocratic neighbors. Despite the immense wealth her father had accumulated through his investment in the railroads, Willow was led to understand that the English upperclass was very particular about breeding, and she must not be disappointed if they were snubbed. But this had proved far from the case. Old Lady Rochford, who was the senior member of the family, had made discreet inquiries and pronounced that the fifteen-year-old girl would provide a much-needed feminine influence in the lives of her five grandsons.

"Reckon the old lady considers our little Willow too young to be of interest to the boys *that* way," Willoughby Tetford had commented shrewdly to his wife. "A good thing we are paying for a real lady governess for the child. She won't be at a loss when it comes to manners and deportment."

The shrewdness that had made him a dollar millionaire was proven once more when old Lady Rochford pronounced herself delighted by the young girl's behavior and disposition, and it was she who proposed that Willow should remain at Rochford Manor while the Tetfords made their European tour.

The arrangement had suited everyone perfectly, not least of all Willow, who was delighting in the sudden acquisition of five "brothers." Although Rowell, being so much older and the head of the family, had little to say to her, she adored him from afar and was soon caught in the grips of a mute hero-worship for the elegant, graceful young Baron.

At first, she had felt ill at ease in the company of the second brother, Toby. His shyness communicated itself in such a way that she imagined herself rebuffed, until one day he invited her into the room he called his "laboratory" and haltingly confessed that he would really like to be a doctor. For the first time she saw him smile when innocently she asked why he could not study the medical sciences if he so wished. Patiently, he explained that his grandmother would not permit him to consider such a middle-class profession.

"Gentlemen in England do not have careers," he told Willow wistfully.

The youngest of the five Rochford boys, Francis, referred to Toby as "the professor." Willow had to admit that Toby did often take on the appearance of an absent-minded scientist when, spectacles slipping to the end of his nose, and his mane of dark chestnut-colored hair in disarray, he strode through the gardens in a torment of silent thoughts about "his work." More often than not he ignored the young girl simply because he did not see her.

Willow had had no difficulty, however, in forming an instant rapport with the friendly, laughing, mischievous, good-natured Pelham. But with Rupert, as with Toby, it had taken a little time before she felt at ease. Shorter than his brothers, delicately built, with large, dark-lashed violet blue eyes, he would have made a remarkably pretty girl; but the absence of masculinity in his appearance and nature had made him the butt of his schoolfellows as well as his brothers, and by the time Willow was introduced to him he had developed a surly, reserved manner that was at variance with his sensitive, artistic nature. He had taught himself to play the violin, and when he discovered that Willow was only too happy to accompany him upon the piano, she found herself welcomed to the music room, his special domain unused by any other member of the family.

Although Willow was obliged to study English history and botany with her governess in the mornings, she was excused afternoon lessons, and the whole summer had seemed to her to be bathed in a golden glow of sunshine and happiness. The beautiful old manor house had been filled with guests, many of them eligible young ladies who lived in nearby country houses and the young bloods who had been Rowell's friends at Oxford. There had been tea parties on the lawn, croquet, boating on the lake, rides in the landaus into the lovely Kentish countryside for luncheon picnics; dancing, charades, and other such harmless entertainments in the evenings. Rupert avoided such occasions, preferring to spend the time with the hero of his schooldays, young Alfred Douglas. Francis and Willow were shadowy figures on the fringe of their elders' daytime entertainments, permitted to linger there provided they remained unobtrusive and undemanding of attention.

If there were any blight upon this idyllic summer for Willow it was the thought of the poor young girl who had perforce to spend her life in one of the two chambers at the top of the spiral staircase that comprised the west tower of the manor. Willow had been living at Rochford for several weeks before she even heard mentioned the existence of the only Rochford girl. A servant inadvertently spoke of "poor Miss Dorothy," and when Willow questioned the maid, she was told that the little girl was mentally and physically subnormal and that no one but Lady Rochford, the doctor, and the nine-year-old child's nurse was allowed to see her. The household staff were forbidden to talk about her.

"So don't you ever let on I told you, Miss Willow," the maid said fearfully, "else I'll be dismissed as sure as you're standing there."

Her governess professed to know nothing, and Willow, with her insatiable curiosity, longed to ask Pelham or Toby more about their little sister; but she dared not do so for she was greatly in awe of old Lady Rochford. Although Grandmère, as she was called by her grandsons, treated Willow kindly enough, she was dictatorial, critical, and demanding, ruling even Rowell with a rod of iron. Her sister-in-law and companion, Aunt Mildred, lived in terror of arousing the old lady's displeasure, and Grandmère, who was nearly seventy, openly gave orders to the pour soul as if she were a servant. Aunt Milly, as the Rochford boys called her, never answered back and, uncomplaining, allowed herself to be bullied.

It disturbed Willow that the brothers seemed to take this domination of the elderly spinster quite for granted—as indeed did Aunt Mildred herself, Willow decided. Although they never defended her, at least Toby and Pelham always treated their aunt kindly; Rupert and Rowell ignored her and only Francis made fun of her.

Willow had not been long at the manor before she recognized that Francis was his grandmother's favorite.

Indifferent to this favoritism, Pelham informed Willow that it was due to his brother's uncanny resemblance to their late father, Grandmère's only surviving much-loved son. Willow had seen the portrait of Lord Oliver Rochford in the library and had to admit there was a singular likeness. Francis' ginger fair hair and blue eyes were replicas of his father's. Rupert, alone of the five boys, resembled his dead mother, Alice Rochford, a fair-haired, shadowy creature. Willow was certain Grandmère had never much liked her daughter-in-law, for she never spoke of her without a note of irritation in her voice.

Pelham, Toby and Rowell had inherited their grandmother's French blood and with it her dark Latin coloring. Rowell was by far the most handsome of the three, but Toby was the nicest, Willow thought. It was typical of him to think of her up here in the gallery supposedly alone and with nothing to eat.

"You ought not to be here," Toby said as he watched Willow sampling the food he had brought her. "If someone tells Grandmère or your governess, you'll be in serious trouble."

Willow smiled mischievously.

"I know, Toby, but it *is* your birthday, your coming-of-age birthday! I can see everything but the dancers from up here. I can't just go to bed and imagine it all. I saw Rowell go by. He is with a Mrs. Georgina Grey, who Pelham says is his mistress, but Pelham will not tell me what a mistress is. You will explain to me, won't you, Toby?"

"I'll do no such thing!" Toby replied with a sharp, angry look at Pelham. "You really should go to bed, Willow. One of the servants will see you and tell Grandmère, or your governess may already be looking to make sure you are safely in your room. And Pelham, you should be downstairs. I saw several girls without dancing partners."

"You're the guest of honor, Toby, you go and dance with them!" Pelham said quickly. "I'm going to dance with Willow."

He jumped up and pulled Willow to her feet as the strains of a polka wafted up from the ballroom. Toby stood suddenly silent, watching as, with a little murmur of excitement, Willow took Pelham's outstretched hands. As they gavotted down the length of the gallery, Toby turned on his heel and went downstairs.

"Enjoying it?" Pelham asked Willow as he looked down at her flushed, excited face. Her white nightgown was billowing around her, and her eyes were sparkling with laughter as he whirled her around and around. He too felt excitement mounting in him and he drew the girl closer. Her breath was warm on his cheek, her body even warmer, and he said softly:

"Close your eyes, Willow. Imagine you are wearing the most beautiful white satin ballgown. There are flowers in your hair and diamonds around your neck and wrist. You are the loveliest girl in the room, and everyone else has stopped dancing to watch us. You are Cinderella and I am your Prince Charming. We are falling in love . . ."

Pelham's voice, the music, the excitement of the evening, were overwhelming. Willow felt her body melting as she gave herself up to the dream Pelham was creating. This was the most magical moment of her life. Perhaps she really was falling in love, she thought, except that it should be Rowell's arms enfolding her, Rowell's voice whispering to her . . .

With her eyes closed, it was not so difficult to imagine that it really was Rowell's arm encircling her waist, the warmth of his palm penetrating the thin satin of her ballgown, Rowell's voice murmuring against her hair: "You are so sweet, my little Willow. You cannot believe how lovely you are, so soft, like a swansdown feather in my arms."

It seemed the most natural thing in the world when, as the music ended, she felt the strong, firm lips of her dream lover pressing against her mouth. She began to tremble as strange, sweet sensations spread through her body. Her eyes still closed, she returned the kiss. Only when Pelham broke away from their embrace and spoke her name did her eyes open, and with a gasp of dismay, she realized that it was not Rowell who had been kissing her but his brother.

"Pelham," she gasped. The hot color flooded her cheeks as she stared at him in an agony of embarrassment. Unaware of her inner turmoil, Pelham smiled.

"No one has ever kissed you before, have they?" he demanded. Mistaking her blushes for those of a young girl newly awakened to the emotions of passion, his excitement mounted. But as he tried to draw Willow back in his arms, with surprising force she raised her hands and pushed him away from her.

"No, Pelham, I don't want to be kissed again. You don't understand. I did not realize what was happening. I—" She broke off in confusion. Still convinced that her rejection of him was but the manifestation of maidenly reserve, Pelham caught her outstretched hands and pulled her back into his embrace. Feeling her body stiffen as she resisted him, he did not try to kiss her mouth but ran his hand gently down her back.

"You have nothing to fear, my little darling," he murmured reassuringly. "We are doing nothing wrong. Admit that you like to feel me touching you. You liked my kiss too, didn't you?"

Willow drew a deep, shuddering breath as she strove to unravel the melee of her feelings. She did not question how Pelham knew that she was indeed enjoying the sensation aroused deep within her by the gentle motion of his hand on her back; that his kiss had been a totally new, disturbing, but far from unpleasant experience. It seemed illogical that he could guess at her body's response to him and yet be blindly unaware that in her mind it was Rowell she wanted to touch and kiss her.

As she drew away from him, she said urgently:

"I think Toby was right and I ought to go back to my room before anyone sees us. Goodnight, Pelham. Thank you . . . Thank you for letting me enjoy a little of Toby's party. Let me go now, *please!*"

There was something in the girl's tone which warned Pelham not to try to detain her, although by now he was himself deeply aroused. He watched her disappearing down the long gallery, the white nightgown floating around her small, ghostly figure. What had started almost as a prank to please a child had ended with the discovery that the child was very much a woman; indeed, far more desirable than most of the pretty young girls who awaited his attentions downstairs. In their teens and early twenties, most had already been presented at Court. They were well launched on the social round of activities provided by their mamas to enable them to find suitable—and eligible—husbands. Flirtatious, pretty coquettes, they giggled and danced and schemed in a merry-go-round of activities that might enhance this search.

Pelham, even at the moderately tender age of eighteen, had amused himself throughout the summer holidays in the company of these young females and been quite content to do so, enjoying the harmless flirtations. For more down-to-earth pursuits, there were the young actresses—always available at the stage door—who were only too happy to be wined, dined, and then seduced by any young blood with money enough to shower them with gifts in return for their favors.

Rowell, of course, had a mistress, the exotic Georgina Grey, older than he by six months and already a widow. Disappointingly for her but fortunately for Rowell, her late husband had been in poor straits financially and left his young widow practically penniless. But for Rowell she would have had to return to the stage, where she had been a very indifferent actress with little hope of stardom. Nor could there ever have been any hope for Georgina of captivating a future king, as had the beautiful Lillie Langtry. But she was certainly beautiful enough to attract Rowell's attention and seemed very satisfied with her handsome young baron. Unfortunately for Rowell, Pelham reflected, other men were interested too, and Rowell was finding his lovely Georgina an expensive pleasure.

But Pelham was not thinking of Rowell or his mistress as he descended the wide staircase and joined the throng of merrymakers who were calling greetings to him. His mind was filled with the memory of Willow's soft lips, of her tiny, slender waist, of the warmth of her body beneath his hands.

Willow was relieved when, on the following morning at breakfast, Rowell announced he was leaving for Cowes where Queen Victoria and the Prince of Wales were entertaining the German Kaiser on an official visit.

"I will be away for several days," Rowell said, adding that he would be on his yacht at Cowes. Unable to forget the stupid trick her imagination had played with her the previous night, Willow felt unbearably shy in his presence and was pleased when he left.

Lady Rochford seemed equally happy about Rowell's departure, for she approved very much of the fact that Rowell was frequently admitted by the forty-eight-year-old Prince of Wales into his circle of friends. The Prince liked to have attractive people around him, especially if, like Rowell, they shared his own enjoyment of shooting, yachting, croquet, cards, and horse racing. Rowell kept an excellent stable at Rochford and had even lent the Prince one of his stallions at stud that had won several big races.

Grandmère was unaware that the Prince would be seeing Georgina, as well as Rowell, at Cowes; that he approved of Rowell's lovely red-headed mistress who reminded him not a little of his ex-mistress Lillie.

But no sooner had Rowell finally departed in his phaeton with a second carriage following with his valet and luggage, than Willow's relief turned to dismay. She felt as if all the sunshine had gone from her life; that these next five days would have no point, no meaning. Not even Pelham's suggestion that they should take a bicycle ride into the countryside, a pastime she usually much enjoyed, could cheer her flagging spirits. Pelham watched her anxiously, afraid lest he had forced himself upon her too hurriedly; that she was not, after all, ready to grow up, and consequently feared him lest he renew his advances.

Pleading a headache, Willow evaded his company and since her governess was nowhere to be seen, she went in search of Toby. He, as always, was in the turret room he called his laboratory. Despite the late hours he had kept the previous night, he was deeply engrossed in his work and did not at first hear Willow's entry.

When at last he looked up from his Bunsen burner, he was surprised to see her sitting silently in the window seat, staring forlornly into the sun-drenched garden.

"I beg your pardon, Willow. Never heard you come in," he said, pushing his spectacles further up his nose and peering at her vaguely. "Something you wanted?"

Willow shook her head. The kindness that always pervaded Toby's voice when he did remember to speak to her was now her undoing. The tears which had threatened all morning spilled down her cheeks. Short-sighted though he was, Toby saw them, and walking over to her, handed her his handkerchief. The creases which were already etched into his forehead by too much frowning now deepened into an anxious scowl.

"Pelham hasn't been upsetting you, has he?" he asked suspiciously. When he had found Pelham last night in the long gallery with Willow, there was something in his brother's flushed cheeks and bright eyes that had warned him Pelham was up to mischief. Throughout their long, shared childhood, Pelham had always had that look when he was about to misbehave himself. Toby had come upon him once with a giggling housemaid with just that same expression on his face and he had not needed Pelham to explain what he was about!

"If Pelham has done anything to upset you—" he began, but Willow interrupted him.

"No, Toby! He . . . I . . . it wasn't his fault. I was dancing with him and I thought . . . it was my fault—" She broke off as the tears choked in her throat.

Toby's long thin fingers curled into his palms as his hands clenched. This was one of the very, very rare occasions in his life when he was furiously angry. Willow was a guest, very young and totally trusting. If his brother had taken advantage of her even in the smallest way, Toby intended to see that he suffered for it.

"Perhaps you'd better tell me all about it," he said, keeping his voice as gentle as he could in the circumstances.

He waited patiently while Willow sniffed, blew into his handkerchief, and found her voice. Haltingly, she told him that she was afraid she had fallen in love with Rowell; that she knew such a love was ridiculous and quite hopeless; that she was far, far too young for him. She ended with a watery smile:

"But even telling myself so and believing it doesn't stop me thinking about him. Don't you see, Toby, what it means?" she said wistfully. "I'm doomed forever to love a man who could never love me. So now I'll never be able to get married and have babies like other girls!"

Despite his concern for her unhappiness, Toby only just succeeded in hiding his amusement.

"I don't think the situation is quite as serious as all that," he said, stroking her hair clumsily as if she were a dog or a horse that needed his soothing touch. "From what I've heard, most girls of your age fall in love a dozen and one times before they meet their future husbands. After all, Willow, you *are* only fifteen, aren't you? Or is it fourteen?"

Willow managed another watery smile.

"It was my birthday last month!" she reminded him.

"You gave me Rudyard Kipling's new book, *Plain Tales From the Hills*. Don't you remember?"

"Yes, of course!" Toby replied, although he had indeed forgotten. "Well then, fifteen, *just*. I think I'd forget all about falling in love for the time being if I were you."

"And forget about kissing, too?" Willow asked.

Once again, Toby's face darkened.

"What has kissing to do with it? I thought you said that it was when you were dancing with Pelham that . . . that you started thinking romantic thoughts about Rowell."

"Oh, yes it was!" Willow agreed. "But it was even worse when Pelham kissed me. If it had been Rowell, I don't think I'd ever have wanted that kiss to end!"

Abruptly, Toby turned his back on her and returned to the work table where he pretended to busy himself tidying some of the paraphernalia littering the surface. It was only rarely that he concerned himself with the activities of his four brothers. At a very early age, he had felt apart from them, different in some indefinable way; and although they continued on occasions to try to interest him in their schoolboy games, they finally left him alone to study the only thing that really interested him—medicine.

More than anything in the world, he would have liked to become a doctor, but Grandmère, of course would not hear of it. He had had to content himself at school and at college studying science, and in his spare time secretly learning about the old and the newest medical discoveries and diagnoses. He was now as knowledgeable as a physician—if not more so in some fields—for he was intent upon research of his own. His solitariness and self-seclusion were taken for granted by his family, and he was only vaguely aware of what they were doing while they neither knew nor cared about his work.

But the occasional contacts he did have with his brothers had given him a clear enough insight into their characters, and he knew Pelham was a born philanderer. He knew that this handsome younger brother was without a serious thought in his head, lived through his senses and enjoyed the easy pleasures of life without questioning the rights or the wrongs of them. Toby had decided that Pelham was amoral rather than immoral, cheerfully accepting the pitfalls if things went wrong along with the punishments if he could not manage to avoid them! Equally cheerfully, Pelham forgot his yesterdays while he pursued the pleasure of his todays. Never did he concern himself about tomorrow.

But not where Willow was concerned, Toby reflected. He would speak to Pelham, *make* him see that Willow was only a child and in need of his protection. If Pelham would not listen, he, Toby, might be forced to threaten to report him to Grandmère. So long as Grandmère doled out Pelham's monthly allowance, he would not ignore *her!* Pelham's extravagances were legion and he was nearly always in debt.

"I'm interrupting your work, Toby. I'm sorry!" Willow said contritely as she stood up to leave. She came to stand for a moment beside him, leaning her head against his shoulder with the complete naturalness of an affectionate child.

"One day will you tell me about your work?" she said. "Maybe I could help you wash up some of those dishes and tidy up a bit." Seeing the expression of horror on Toby's face, she laughed, her mood suddenly happy again. "Well, if I couldn't tidy up, I could take notes for you. I know you write a lot, because I've seen the piles of papers, and Mama says I have a very neat hand."

"Maybe one day!" Toby said, satisfied now that he had heard her laugh again. "Meanwhile, since you are feeling more cheerful, why don't you go and feed the swans on the lake? I saw two new cygnets when I walked by their nest yesterday morning."

Willow's face revealed her excitement. She had been waiting for the eggs to hatch for what seemed weeks and weeks. She stood on tiptoe and kissed Toby's cheek.

As she ran across the smooth lawns down toward the lake, she thought about Toby and how different it felt when kisses were on the mouth rather than the cheek. Despite what Toby had said about her being still too young to fall in love, she *had* felt different when Pelham embraced her. The sweetness of his kiss lingered in her memory, and she half hoped that Pelham might seek her out again. She might even have tried kissing Toby on the lips, except that he was too unromantic a figure to be considered in the same breath as love. His long hair was always untidy and fell over his forehead, while his spectacles were usually on the end of his nose. No matter how hard his valet tried, Toby's clothes never looked neat and clean, and even Grandmère had given up trying to make him pay more attention to his appearance. Toby simply did not care what he looked like.

Pelham, on the other hand, was by way of being a dandy, sporting the newest fashions and selecting the most outrageous of them to suit his extrovert nature. As for Rowell, he was immaculately tailored, as conventional in his attire as he was in his behavior. No female could feel less than proud walking with her arm through his, she thought, as she watched the tiny brown fluffy cygnets follow in the wake of their graceful parents toward the crust of bread she had thrown for them. She thought of the red-haired woman Pelham had named as Georgina Grey and how proudly *she* had walked with Rowell's arm through hers as they made their way toward the ballroom.

Envy swept over Willow with such force that she felt almost physically sick. What *was* a mistress? she wondered. A line from Shakespeare shot into her mind, *"I guie thee this for thy sweet Mistris sake because thou lov'st her."* It sounded very much as if a mistress were indeed loved since Shakespeare took the matter for granted, she thought unhappily. Her *Dictionary for the Young* gave no information on the subject. If only her parents would allow her to read the kind of book which might answer her questions more clearly! But they, like Pelham and Toby, considered her too young for such knowledge. If Rowell did love the beautiful Georgina, then she must try to be happy for them both.

But despite all her efforts, Willow's spirits remained low while Rowell was away and did not improve until his return at the end of the week. When he was once more seated at the head of the dining table she listened breathlessly to his every word as he recounted how magnificent had been the Naval Review at Spithead. She felt her own heart leap with excitement as he described in glowing tones the miniature fleet of twelve men-of-war that the Kaiser had brought with him, and how superb was the Kaiser's royal vessel *Hohenzollern* with its sleek, high-raked lines.

Suddenly Rowell turned his head and his eyes encountered Willow's rapt face. He smiled at her.

"It is a pity you were not at Cowes to see some of the

beautiful dresses and hats the ladies were wearing," he said. "When you are older you must come to England again, Willow, and I will insure that you are presented at Court. Then you will be able to see all the finery for yourself—and, indeed, wear some of it too!"

His promise, his thoughtfulness, should have made her happy, but instead her heart turned to stone. For Rowell had inadvertently reminded her that soon her Mama and Papa would be back from Europe, the summer would be over, and they would be returning to America. She had no way of knowing if she would ever see England or any of the Rochfords again.

Knowing that she could bear the parting from everything and everyone but Rowell, she continued to stare at him mutely, her eyes full of longing and of pain.

Chapter Two

June–November 1891

WILLOW SMOOTHED THE FOLDS OF HER YELLOW skirt over her narrow hips and surveyed herself in the looking glass as her young maid, Nellie, puffed out the sleeve tops of her chiffon blouse. It was a new outfit she was wearing for the first time, and since this was a Very Special Day in her life, she wanted to look as pretty as possible.

Rowell, Lord Rochford, Baron, and a Peer of the Realm of England, was calling upon her Papa this very morning to ask for her hand in marriage!

"Oh, Nellie," she gasped. "I am so excited I do not know how to contain myself. Do I look nice? Do you think he will be here soon? Do you think Papa will say 'yes'?"

Nellie smiled fondly at the sixteen-year-old girl.

"Don't you worry none, Miss Willow," she said reassuringly. "There can't be no one more eligible than the Baron and that's for sure."

Willow let out her breath in a sigh of relief.

"I know! I'm silly to worry, aren't I?" she confided. But a slight frown lingered in her eyes. Both Papa and Mama were still a little distant in their manner toward Rowell, despite the fact that he had been calling regularly ever since his arrival in San Francisco three months previously. Papa, who was usually so open and friendly with everybody, and who at first greeted Rowell with all the warmth she could have wished, seemed suddenly to withdraw his friendliness from the man she loved so passionately.

She could not understand this *volte face*, more especially when Rowell, who had come to San Francisco only for two weeks—to buy a brood mare for his stables, he said—decided to prolong his stay on *her* account. Willow, expected her father to be as delighted as she was herself at this marvelous news. But, although he made Rowell welcome in their big house on Nob Hill and proudly introduced him to all their neighbors and friends, he was never overly enthusiastic when Willow rhapsodized about the elegant, handsome, aristocratic Englishman.

It was now almost a fortnight since the miracle had happened and Rowell had confessed that he was in love with her. At first Willow had not been able to credit it. Rowell had never even noticed her two summers ago, when she had stayed at Rochford Manor.

"You were very young then, my dearest," he said, adding with a delightful smile: "And not nearly so pretty!"

Willow was immeasurably happy and she was convinced that her parents—indeed, anyone who came in contact with her—must guess how deeply in love she was with Rowell. Her girlfriends were openly envious and considered her handsome Englishman to be the most romantic of suitors.

"It looks as though you will be the first of us to get married," one of them said.

But Rowell had felt it best not to ask for her hand too soon.

"Let us give your parents a little more time to become accustomed to me," he suggested. "After all, you are still very young, and I am what you would call your first 'beau,' am I not?"

Then the day finally came when Rowell made up his

mind to ask her Papa for his permission for them to be married.

"I really must go home to England soon," Rowell had said. "And I mean to take you home with me, my dear, as my wife. I cannot delay speaking to your father any longer."

Nellie broke in on Willow's reverie.

"I think I heard a carriage arriving!" she exclaimed, running to the window to draw back the pretty frilled white organdy curtains. She peered down into the graveled drive and turned back to Willow with pink cheeks.

"Yes, it's *him*, Miss Willow. He's here!"

Willow caught her lower lip between small white teeth.

"Of course Papa will say 'yes,' " she murmured. "There is no reason on earth why he should not!"

It was fifteen long minutes before one of the maids knocked on Willow's door and told her that her father wished to see her.

"Good luck, Miss Willow!" Nellie said kindly.

There was no sign of Rowell as, without regard for propriety, she raced down the stairs and burst into her father's study. But she was too excited to appreciate the implications of Rowell's absence as she threw herself into his waiting arms.

"You have said 'yes' to Rowell, haven't you, Papa?" she cried.

Willoughby Tetford regarded his starry-eyed daughter with mixed emotions. He loved her better than anyone in the world, and it hurt him deeply to think that at any moment he must wipe that radiance from her face. But at the same time, he was her father, and it was his duty to protect her.

"Come and sit down, my darling," he said gently, leading her to a leather sofa by the windows. "I want you to listen to me very carefully." He laid his large hand on her head and stroked the shining fair hair tenderly. "As you are aware, Rowell asked for my permission to marry you. I felt obliged to refuse that permission."

Willow's face whitened. She stared at her father disbelievingly.

"But Papa, I love him—"

"I know, my darling," her father said gently. "But

you are forgetting that you are only sixteen. You are not old enough to be certain of your feelings."

"Papa, I shall be seventeen next month!" Willow cried. "And as to being certain of my feelings, I have loved Rowell ever since . . . ever since that summer in England two years ago. I shall always love him."

Willoughby Tetford was momentarily silent. He did not, in fact, question his daughter's feelings, but rather those of her suitor. Even making allowances for the fact that the young man was of aristocratic birth and an Englishman, and therefore a good deal more restrained than he himself in his display of emotions, he was not convinced that Rowell was really in love with his young daughter. Despite his own adoration and admiration for the child, whom he considered unusually pretty and full of charm, he was equally aware that she was very young, unsophisticated, even a little gauche at times. As the wife of a baron, she would be required to undertake duties and responsibilities both in her home and in Royal circles that would daunt many a young woman raised in the right environment. Moreover, she would be living in an alien country among strangers, and the love and support of her husband would be of vital importance.

"Rowell has doubtless declared himself to you," he said thoughtfully. "I suppose I do not need to ask if *you* are quite convinced of his love for you?"

Willow regarded her father from puzzled eyes.

"He has told me many times that he loves me and wants to marry me," she said ingenuously. "What makes you doubt him, Papa?"

For the time being, thought Willoughby Tetford, he would not tell her the most serious cause for doubting Rowell. He would wait and see if the young man returned now to England without renewing his request. If that happened, he would not be forced to disillusion this sweet young girl with the truth. In the meanwhile, he could but stress her extreme youth as a reason for his objections to such a marriage.

But Rowell was not so easily rejected. He counted, quite rightly, on the strength of Willow's love for him—and, not least, Willoughby Tetford's love for his only child. Encouraged by Rowell, Willow urged her father daily to change his mind. She appealed to her mother to speak for her, but Beatrice Tetford would not dispute her husband's wishes in anything; and although she raised no objection to Rowell, she told Willow she must abide by her father's decision.

The summer was nearly over before Willoughby began to weaken. He could not bear the sight of Willow's unhappy, anxious little face regarding him so appealingly. He called her to his study for a second talk.

"I have not made myself a millionaire several times over by keeping my head in the sand," he told her as gently as he could. "And, as it happens, I made inquiries about the Rochfords when we were in England in '89. I regret to tell you, my pet, that the family is in an impoverished state. Their wealth was unwisely invested by Rowell's father, and nothing young Rowell has been able to tell me reassures me that things have improved of late."

Hating to see the shock and dismay that clouded his daughter's pretty face, he added:

"The picture is not entirely black. As I understand it, Oliver Rochford's wife, Rowell's mother, brought a considerable dowry to her marriage, and this very wisely was put into a trust fund for the male child resulting from the marriage. But it cannot be touched by any of the Rochford boys until they reach the age of thirty, and so, for the time being, my dear, Rowell has very little to offer you other than his title."

Surprised but undaunted, Willow could say little other than to declare that she did not mind if she had to be poor so long as she could marry the man she loved.

"But *I* mind very much," her father said, "not because I think you lack the courage and resourcefulness to face a life of poverty, but the circumstances force me to question Rowell's motives for wishing to marry you, Willow. You are my only child and will, when I die, inherit a vast fortune."

Appalled, angry, but above all deeply distressed, Willow said:

"So you don't believe he loves me as he has vouchsafed? Am I so dull then—so plain, so unattractive—that you ridicule the possibility that he might love me for myself?"

Willoughby Tetford was unusually blunt—hurtfully so.

"You are nine years younger than Rowell, Willow, and still very much a child, albeit a very pretty one. But the Tetfords do not begin to be in a similar social class to the Rochfords. One is forced to realize that there must be a great many English ladies of high rank, with all the advantages of their training and upbringing, who would make far more suitable wives for young Baron Rochford than would you, my dear child. Except for the wealth you might offer him, you would be more of a disadvantage to him than an asset."

"What has any of this to do with love?" Willow cried. She was made the more uneasy by her father's words because she had already asked herself those same questions a hundred times and failed to find an answer. Why should Rowell love her? It was not as if he had given her so much as a word or glance of affection when she had stayed as a guest at his home two years ago. His disinterest had been total. It was Pelham who had flirted with her; Toby who had been so kind to her.

"Rowell loves me, I know he does. Please, Papa, I beg you to reconsider your decision."

Willoughby Tetford sighed. He was convinced that such a marriage would not bring his daughter the happiness he desired for her. But perhaps it was never possible for the old to convince the young of the wisdom of experience. They had to make their own mistakes. At least if things did go wrong, it need not be a total disaster. Willow could be brought back to America, where a divorce could be arranged quietly and easily. In two or three years' time, the marriage would either have succeeded or failed, and Willow would still not be twenty—an age at which she could readily find a happier alternative.

"Very well, my darling, you may marry your Englishman, since your heart is set upon it."

Having made his decision, no one could have acted more generously, Willow thought. Rowell expressed astonishment at the size of the huge settlement her father made upon her, insisting that there was no need for it. Willoughby Tetford reassured them that it was but a drop in the ocean of his ever-growing fortune.

"At least it will insure you will not have to live in that poverty you so lightly professed not to mind," he had said, hugging Willow to him.

Although her parents' preference was that the marriage should wait until the following year when Rowell could return to collect his future wife, after further pleas by the engaged couple, it was finally agreed that the wedding could take place in the late fall before Rowell went back to England.

"Marry in haste, repent at leisure!" Willow's mother said tearfully, but Willow was too filled with joy and excitement to let such gloomy forebodings disturb her.

The marriage took place on the last day of October. It was a magnificent, fashionable wedding, marred only by the fact that there was no one present from the Rochford family. Grandmère and Aunt Mildred were too old to travel so long a distance, Rowell vouchsafed, and his brothers must not be withdrawn from their schools and universities; Toby's presence was necessary at Rochford in his absence.

It was arranged, therefore, that Willoughby Tetford's senior partner and close friend, Nathaniel Corbett, should be Rowell's best man. But this was only a small cloud on a day that surpassed Willow's most romantic dreams. She was aware that she looked like a princess in her magnificent flowing silk gown, which was high-necked and had a long train. Her wedding veil of Limerick lace fell in a point over her face and down to her knees, the fullness drawn back from either side with jeweled pins. It was both regal and dignified and yet youthfully virginal. Willow knew that she would never forget the look of pride on Rowell's face as he led her out of the church into the bright sunshine of a perfect fall day.

So great was her excitement and emotion, that afterwards she was to remember little of the huge reception her parents held on the lawn of her home for their many friends. Since most of these were also the new rich who had built for themselves fabulous mansions on Nob Hill, the wedding gifts displayed were numerous and of great value.

"We will need a liner to ourselves to ship so much baggage to England," Rowell chided her gently as he surveyed the glass, china, silver and gold plate that must fill at least a dozen large crates.

Since most of the guests went to the station to see the newlyweds upon their way, there was hardly a passenger on the train who was not aware of the honeymoon couple and who did not remark upon the elegance of the English baron or the youthfulness of his pretty bride. Rowell seemed impervious to the stares and only later referred to the occasion, telling Willow that she must overcome her shyness and ignore the rudeness of the masses.

"Dignity is an important asset," he told her, and she resolved to try hard to behave in a dignified manner, promising herself to restrain her natural impulse to cling to his arm or to invite him to hold her hand.

Willoughby Tetford's private railroad car, bedecked with flowers for the occasion, was awaiting the bridal couple. One of the advantages enjoyed by the very rich, it was only quite recently that Willoughby had bought his own railroad car. He had paid "a modest eighty thousand dollars" for it, he told Rowell, explaining that he used it for journeys to the Kentucky Derby, the Harvard-Yale boat races, the Saratoga horse races, or for business trips to New York.

"You two love birds will be spending your honeymoon on the train," he had said, "so you'll be wanting a little privacy, eh?"

Willow had been sensitively aware of Rowell's embarrassment at her father's somewhat indelicate remark, and she wondered uneasily if the two men she loved most in the world would ever become truly friendly. At best, they tolerated each other for her sake, she thought, as, with a moment of deep sadness, she kissed her parents goodbye. But, as the train drew out of the station, she was happy once more when Rowell praised his father-in-law's thoughtfulness in giving them so pleasant a method of undertaking the six-day journey to New York.

Willow looked at her husband's face with warm content. Rowell showed every sign of being delighted with the comfort of their private railroad car. On his journey to San Francisco in the spring, he had traveled on an ordinary first-class ticket which, while not uncomfortable, had not provided the total privacy or the degree of luxury they were now enjoying. Nearly seventy feet long, their private carriage was ornately furnished with polished mahogany, comfortable upholstered chairs, velvet curtaining, and crystal electric chandeliers.

"Quite like having our own drawing room," Rowell had

commented, looking around him approvingly. The large double bed, discreetly curtained in daylight hours, looked comfortable and spacious, and like the rest of the furniture, was anchored firmly to the thickly carpeted floor.

Apart from enjoying the services of his own valet and Willow's personal maid, Nellie, they also had for their use a chef, steward, porter, and waiter; a spacious saloon; and, not least, their own bathtub.

I am surely the happiest, most fortunate girl in the whole world, Willow thought as the train moved out of the station, and she realized that her marriage was about to begin. She was now Baroness Rochford, wife of the most handsome, wonderful, romantic man any girl could wish for.

It was not until the following day that Willow felt even the slightest sense of misgiving at having left her home. San Francisco already lay many miles behind her, she thought, and soon there would be six thousand miles between her and the security she had known throughout her childhood. There could be no running to her dear, sweet-natured mother for sympathy or advice about her clothes. There could be no depending upon her strong, kind father for guidance and understanding. She had tried so hard these past weeks to forget his warnings that Rowell was influenced by her wealth. In this, he must be wrong in his judgment, she told herself. Rowell had already proved how much he desired her.

Willow's cheeks turned pink at the memory of last night—her wedding night. Rowell had taken a stroll to the observation car while Nellie had attended to her toilette. It was growing quite late when he returned, and by the time his valet departed, leaving her and Rowell alone, she had been tense with nervous uncertainty as to what must next transpire.

Uppermost of her emotions was her shyness, for not since her infancy had she shared her bedroom with anyone—far less her bed. The proximity of her husband's body was both an excitement and an embarrassment, as he had taken her into his arms and begun the strange ritual of married love. It was difficult even now in retrospect to distinguish what had seemed beautiful from what had struck her as immodest and a painful invasion of her body.

Rowell was now engrossed in the reading of his newspaper, as he had been for the past hour.

I love him so much, she thought, as she sat silent in her chair opposite his, staring at his bent dark head. She longed for him to put down his paper and talk to her. There were so many feelings she wanted to share with him, not least her inability to believe in the miracle that had ended with their marriage yesterday morning.

In a little while, the chef would come to inquire what they would like for luncheon. Last evening, they had had a choice of buffalo, elk, antelope, grouse, beefsteak, or mutton chops. Too exhausted by the excitement of the day to be able to enjoy this excellent repast, Willow had watched her bridegroom eat steadily through the large meal. Soon afterwards, Nellie had come to put her to bed.

"Well, my dear, enjoying the view?" Rowell interrupted her thoughts, as at long last he put down his paper and regarded his bride with a speculative stare.

She looked surprisingly young as she sat wide-eyed, gazing up at him, he thought. The tiny frill of her powder-blue Pekin blouse encircled her long, slender neck. From beneath the hem of the dark brown, Empire-styled skirt peeped the toes of her calfskin shoes with their laced fronts and patent-leather tips. She looked even more youthful now than in her wedding gown, he thought with surprise, as he recalled the manner in which he had initiated her into the physical pleasures of matrimony last night. It was a pity that she was so very slender, since it was the truly voluptuous female figure that aroused him most. Nevertheless, the virginal quality of his bride had a different appeal of its own.

"You look charming, my love," he said kindly. "You are quite comfortable, I trust? Not bored?"

"Oh, indeed not!" Willow replied quickly, returning his smile. "After so much excitement yesterday, I am pleased to sit quietly with you."

"Would you have any objection if I take a little walk to the observation car and enjoy a cigar there?" Rowell asked, rising to his feet. "I met a fellow called Paley there last night. Quite an interesting American, I discovered, with a gold mine in the Sierra Nevada foothills, so he tells me. I will suggest his wife pay a call upon you. I believe she is well accustomed to this journey and may be able to enlighten you as to the landscape. She seems a pleasant woman."

It was on the tip of Willow's tongue to profess that she would far prefer to be in Rowell's company, but she bit back the words. Clearly, he wanted to talk to this Mr. Paley on his own and the very last thing she wanted was for her husband to become bored with her company even before they reached England.

Mrs. Paley turned out to be a most excellent traveling companion. An American woman in her fifties, she immediately took the shy young girl under her maternal wing. Her manner was disarmingly frank.

"I understand from my husband that you are on your honeymoon, my dear," she said as soon as she was seated in one of the comfortable chairs resting on the thick piled carpet. "Are you not a little nervous, going to live so far away from your parents in a strange country?"

Willow shook her head.

"I am far too excited to be nervous," she admitted smiling. "Besides, it is not as if I do not know my new family."

She related eagerly an account of her sojourn at Rochford Manor and described her in-laws to her attentive listener.

"Of course, I am quite inexperienced in running so large a household," she confessed, "but Rowell tells me I need not worry, since we have an excellent housekeeper. His grandmother, too, will be there to advise and guide me."

Mrs. Paley kept her own counsel as it crossed her mind that this shy young girl might very easily find herself overwhelmed by the circumstances awaiting her in England.

"I cannot describe to you how beautiful Rochford is," Willow continued. "The house is very old, Elizabethan, and the grounds are truly magnificent. I know I shall be very, very happy there with Rowell."

It was patently clear to the older woman that Willow was deeply in love with her husband. Baron Rochford was certainly quite an impressive figure, she thought, although at first meeting she had not really warmed to his personality as she warmed now to Willow's.

"Your husband is very good looking," she said, "and

so distinguished! But of course, most English gentlemen have that special elegance, do they not? I do admire their perfect manners!"

Willow was enthusiastic in her agreement as to Rowell's virtues. Mrs. Paley then suggested that she and Willow should go to the observation car where, since the windows were not so heavily curtained as·in the private railroad car, they would have a better view of the passing countryside.

They had crossed the Sierra Nevadas during the night, and now, leaving Nevada behind them, the train had gathered speed and was approaching the Great Salt Lake. The countryside was very beautiful, with magnificent mountains in the distance, tall trees growing everywhere. Willow gazed out of the window fascinated by the scenery as the train carried them along the shores of the eighty-mile-long lake. It was a beautiful sight with reflections in the water of the distant mountains and the islands dotted upon its surface.

This first day of their long journey across America was to be the pattern for the remaining five days—only the landscape changing as they went from Utah through Nebraska and on to Chicago. There they changed trains for the remaining nine hundred miles to New York.

Willow tried not to feel hurt that it became Rowell's habit only to spend the mealtimes and the nights in her company. During these past six months she had become accustomed to having him nearly always at her side. But she told herself that she must not be a possessive wife; that Rowell had been a bachelor for a long while, and it might be some time before he acquired the habit of sharing his life with her. It was for her to prove to him that she could be as interesting and lively a companion as Mr. Paley; and, not least, to make herself as pretty and attractive to him as possible.

In the privacy of their large double bed, Rowell became hers alone as he held her in his arms, kissed her, and murmured endearments to her. But it was never long before he fell asleep, and then she lay wide awake, listening to the regular rattle of the wheels on the tracks, trying to keep apprehension at bay.

It was in those long dark sleepless hours that the excitement of her new life waned in the most alarming way, and she recalled once again her father's misgivings as to the depth of Rowell's love for her. Somehow she seemed unable to comfort herself with the reminder that she had no knowledge of what married life ought to be like, or if Rowell's apparent contentment to be in other company than hers was normal in a bridegroom. Her mind conjured up thoughts about the great lovers in the classics, and she realized unhappily that her relationship with Rowell bore little similarity to that of Romeo and Juliet or Orpheus and Eurydice! Real life, she told herself, was probably very different from fiction, and a contented marriage like that of her parents was no doubt the result of a lifetime shared together.

Willow's mother, a strict Quaker, had given her daughter much advice on how to be a good wife, but had given her no inkling of what she should expect within the marriage bed.

"It is your duty as a wife to submit to your husband's demands, whatever they may be," she cautioned Willow. "There may be times when this will be irksome to you, but a considerate husband will make allowances if, for example, you are ill or overtired. But, once having made your vows, child, it is for you to submit to his will in all things. Do you understand?"

Although she did not entirely comprehend these remarks, Willow welcomed her mother's comment. Loving Rowell as she did, she could not imagine that she might ever wish to gainsay him in any respect. Her happiness lay in pleasing him.

Only after the wedding night did she realize what were the "duties" to which her mother had referred. Even now, Willow did not understand why a wife might not want her husband's loving. Her own instincts were such that she wanted to submit totally, to become a part of Rowell. His male body seemed beautiful to her, and only modesty forbade her staring at him or reaching out to touch him; to kiss him. She longed above all to draw him deep into herself, where it felt as if they had become one person and not two.

But perhaps out of consideration for her, Willow told herself, he made no further demands upon her on the second and third nights of their honeymoon, and it was not until their last night on the train that he made love to her a second time.

That evening, he and his new friend Mr. Paley and several other gentlemen were enjoying a game of cards after their dinner.

"And drinking a great deal of brandy, I don't doubt," commented Mrs. Paley as she and Willow sat diligently plying their needles in their embroidery. She looked at Willow surreptitiously, aware how often the girl's eyes turned to the doorway at the far end of the car, obviously longing for her young husband to reappear.

"You look tired, my dear," she said thoughtfully. "Why don't you retire to bed? I shall go and find Mr. Paley and tell him it is high time we retired too."

It was therefore due to the thoughtfulness of her traveling companion that Willow was able to enjoy Rowell's company much earlier than customary. He was in unusually high spirits when he appeared soon after Nellie had completed Willow's toilette. He had had a run of luck and won quite a large sum of money, he told her. When he climbed into bed beside her, his breath smelled of brandy and cigars. He began at once to make ardent advances.

"I fear I have been neglecting you, my beautiful little bride," he murmured, kissing her with considerable passion. "Do you forgive me, my love? You are so soft, so sweet. I am surely the envy of all the gentlemen on the train."

Happily, Willow thought, she had now at long last discovered the lover she had been longing for. Her misgivings vanished entirely as she welcomed her husband's embraces. She felt complimented that he seemed to achieve great joy from their brief union and was lavish in his praise of her before he fell asleep in her arms.

Tomorrow they would arrive at New York's Grand Central Terminal, Willow told herself as she listened to his steady breathing, and the next stage of their journey would begin. They would spend one night at the elegant St. Regis hotel in the city and then they would board the liner that was to take them across the Atlantic to England. Half her honeymoon was over, and ten days from now, she and Rowell would begin their real married life at Rochford Manor.

Willow was still conjuring up memories of that wonderfully happy summer when she had first set eyes upon her adored new husband, when with her arms still embracing him, she fell into a dreamless sleep.

Even in the pouring rain, the rambling old Elizabethan manor house with its red brick and dark oak timbers had a mature beauty that was totally in keeping with the magnificent Kentish countryside. The great lake, covering nearly thirty acres, lay like a vast diamond in the center of sweeping green lawns, reflecting the huge bare oaks, elms, chestnut, and lime trees in its rain-dimpled surface.

"Oh, Rowell, I had forgotten how lovely your home is," Willow cried as their carriage approached the entrance to Rochford Manor. "My home now," she added shyly.

Memories flooded back to the summer two years previous when she had been so very much on the fringe of Rowell's life, never dreaming that one day she would return here, not just as a visitor but as his wife.

"I am so very happy, my dearest," she whispered as she nestled closer against him. He was preoccupied in giving the coachman orders to draw up as near as possible to the great oak iron-studded front door so that they would not get too wet in the driving rain. But their arrival was anticipated, and as the carriage came to a halt, the front door opened and Dutton, the butler, stepped forward with a huge black umbrella.

"May I be the first to welcome you to Rochford Manor, Milady," he said as he assisted her down from the carriage and escorted her to the door.

"Thank you, Dutton," Willow replied, hoping her excitement was not too obvious, and that she appeared cool and dignified as befitted the new mistress of Rochford Manor. But her carefully contrived composure almost deserted her when she saw the long row of servants lined up in the great hall to greet her. Rowell had warned her that, even before she could remove her coat, she must be introduced to the servants who would be arrayed for her inspection.

"Don't shake hands with them," he had directed her when she had pleaded ignorance in these circumstances of the behavior expected of her as his wife. "A smile and a nod will do. You will probably know most of them, for there have been few changes since you were last at Rochford."

She was glad when Rowell came to her side and walked with her down the line of servants—rather like two generals inspecting their troops, Willow thought irreverently, as with difficulty she controlled the nervous smile the idea provoked. She made a determined effort to concentrate as Dutton introduced her to her waiting staff.

She remembered Mrs. Jupp, the cook, a middle-aged, stoutly-built, kindly woman who had sometimes given her a jam tart or a cake when she had wandered down into the huge kitchen on baking day. Mrs. Jupp used to say she needed "feeding up." "Young girls need a bit of puppy fat," she had vouchsafed, eyeing Willow's slim, under-developed body disapprovingly. But now she bobbed a curtsy, and said "Welcome home, Milady!" with all the deference she used to give old Lady Rochford. Gratefully, Willow returned her smile.

She found it less easy to greet with pleasure the housekeeper. Gertrude Spears had been a housekeeper at the manor for more than twenty-five years, and Willow knew her efficiency to be unquestionable. Now in her fifties, she was the oldest member of the staff. She ruled the younger maids and menservants with a rod of iron, and Willow recalled that even the Rochford boys had been slightly in awe of her, although behind her back they had called her "old two-face." They believed that she enjoyed bullying the staff because she herself was harassed by old Lady Rochford to whom she was almost unbearably obsequious. Mrs. Spears wore steel-rimmed spectacles through which she was now peering disapprovingly over Willow's shoulder to where poor Nellie stood hovering uncertainly by the front door.

Rowell had warned her that Mrs. Spears would not take kindly to her bringing her own maid with her from America, far less a foreign girl who would have to be trained to English ways. Willow had been adamant in her refusal to leave Nellie behind, feeling instinctively that she might need one ally in a household that was so long established. Although, as the new mistress of Rochford, it would be her prerogative to approve the selection of her own servants, Rowell had advised her against making any changes.

"The household runs very smoothly as it is," he told her. "Moreover, the organization of so large an establishment will be both strange and difficult for you at first, and you would do well to defer to Mrs. Spears until you have learned our ways. Grandmère places a great deal of trust in her, and so should you."

But Mrs. Spears was not going to be allowed to dismiss Nellie for any reason, justified or otherwise, Willow thought. In a small, firm voice, she said to the housekeeper:

"As you will see, Mrs. Spears, I have brought with me my own maid, Nellie Sinclair. Will you be so good as to give her a room where she will be comfortable?"

The housekeeper managed to hide her surprise. She recalled Willow as a shy, retiring, quiet child very much overawed by the Rochford family, and she had not anticipated that now, still only seventeen, the young lady would be greatly changed. Mrs. Spears had certainly not expected Willow to arrive with her own servant, or to speak in such a determined tone of voice. Bobbing a curtsy, her eyes watched Willow speculatively as she introduced Harold Stevens, the head footman; the parlormaids; the underfootmen; the housemaids; tweeny and scullery maids—thirty in all. Dutton had arranged for the bailiff, grooms, gardeners, stable boys, and other outdoor servants to parade themselves the following morning. Now he dismissed the household staff and said to Rowell:

"Lady Rochford instructed me to tell you that she would like to see you and Milady in her room as soon as you have changed from your traveling clothes, Milord. Miss Mildred is with her. The young gentlemen are shooting at Sir John's, and will be back shortly."

"Thank you, Dutton!" Rowell said. "We will go up presently. Meanwhile, send in tea here immediately for my wife and bring me some mulled wine."

Willow was unaware how tense she had been until the last of the servants had left the hall. Now she relaxed and took Rowell's arm, smiling up at him.

"I hope I did not make any mistakes, my dearest," she said earnestly.

The use of the endearment was still not entirely natural for her, for although she longed to indicate her love for Rowell in every possible way, even after two weeks of marriage she was still curiously in awe of him. Perhaps, she thought, despite her now being the mistress of Rochford, the household would remain the same as in her premarried days. She could not yet take it for granted that Rowell was really her husband and not the romantic dream figure who had barely recognized her existence two years ago.

"You made no mistakes, my dear, but don't be too friendly with the servants. Give them any encouragement, and they'll waste your day with gossip," Rowell replied, moving away from her to stand with his back to the huge fire. Oak logs, some six feet long, burned in the vast inglenook fireplace; but despite the heat they generated in close vicinity, the remainder of the big hall was cold and damp. Willow shivered. She had reminded herself before she left San Francisco that an English winter was very different from the mild winters at home. Nevertheless, she had forgotten how the damp seemed to chill through to the bone despite the warm blue serge traveling coat she still wore.

She was about to join Rowell by the fire, when a gust of cold air swept across the room as the front door opened into the outer hall. The sound of loud male voices penetrated from the anteroom where visitors' cloaks, hats, and umbrellas were kept by Dutton.

"That little Springer bitch of yours is shaping up well, Toby!"

Willow recognized Pelham's voice.

"Toby needs a dog with a good nose if anyone does!" It was Francis' voice now, sarcastic, mocking. "I'm surprised you ever get invited to take a gun, Toby. You miss more than you hit, of a certainty."

Now it was Toby's voice, quiet, unruffled.

"You made up for it, Francis. That was a superb shot of yours! The blackcock must have been nearly fifty yards overhead."

The hall no longer seemed cold and deserted as the three brothers appeared, boots and gaiters covered in mud, shooting coats, breeches, and caps wet through.

Pelham hurried over to Willow, leaving behind him a trail of muddy clods on the parquet floor and Persian rugs.

"Welcome home, sister-in-law!" His voice was teasing

but in his dark eyes there was genuine pleasure. "Sorry we weren't here to greet you!"

"Really, Pelham, you could have all used the garden door and dumped those filthy boots and clothes in the gun room!" Rowell admonished.

Pelham grinned.

"Quicker to come in the front door, my dear fellow," he said. He turned back to Willow. "Let's have a good look at you, Willow. It's two years since I last saw you. That's a long time, y'know."

His eyes traveled from her smart blue Windsor hat with its neat brim and tiny turned back veil, down past her opened traveling coat to her buttoned boots. He gave an exaggerated whistle of approval.

"Well, the cygnet has certainly turned into a swan," he said appreciatively. *Très chic,* if I may say so, my dear. Rowell's a lucky fellow." He walked over to the fireplace and spread his hands to the blaze. "Congratulations, old chap. Between you and me, I never thought you'd pull it off."

Willow, looking at Rowell's face, saw a sudden tightening of his mouth. His eyes looked furious. But then Dutton and a parlormaid arrived with the tea and a steaming silver punchbowl of mulled wine for Rowell and his brothers, and she could no longer see her husband's expression.

Toby came over to her.

"Pelham is absolutely right—you look stunning," he said in his quiet, shy manner. "I can't tell you how happy it made me to hear you were coming to live with us. I hope you'll be very happy, Willow."

"Dear Toby!" Willow said as he bent forward to kiss her lightly on the cheek. "I'm very happy to be here and to see you all again. I can still hardly believe my good fortune!"

"It's Rowell who is the lucky one," Toby replied. He smiled again. "Maybe you have not changed quite as much as your sophisticated appearance suggests," he murmured.

Willow relaxed as she returned his smile.

"These Parisian models I'm wearing are part of my trousseau," she explained. "And you are quite right, Toby

—underneath all the finery, I'm still the same silly young girl you used to know."

"Young—but not silly," Toby replied in the laconic tone that she had almost forgotten was so natural to him.

Rowell came to her side and took her arm.

"It's high time we went upstairs and changed. Grandmère will be waiting for us with considerable impatience, I imagine."

Pelham, seeing the expression of concern on Willow's face, laughed reassuringly.

"The old dragon is temporarily confined to quarters with a bad cold," he said irreverently. "Between ourselves, Willow, I think Grandmère is aping our dear Queen more and more as she gets older. She not only looks like her now, but she has taken to retiring to her rooms on the slightest pretext. She has poor old Aunt Milly running around like a scalded hen!"

He looked quite unperturbed by Rowell's disapproving frown, and winked at Willow. She only just managed to conceal her own amusement from her husband. She had quite forgotten how deferential Rowell always was to his grandmother and how irreverent Pelham could be.

Francis, who had been slouching in one of the leather armchairs with his feet stretched out onto the hearth, now stood up yawning.

"You'll get a good welcome from Grandmère anyway, Willow," he commented dryly. "She is delighted with your marriage!"

At the foot of the stairs, Willow paused to look back at the youngest of the Rochford brothers. Francis' words were an enormous relief to her, for, although Rowell had insisted that his grandmother would have no objections to their precipitate wedding, she had been privately convinced that the mere unconventionality of their quick courtship and marriage would be against the old lady's principles. Moreover, she was well aware how much importance Lady Rochford put on the family line, and had not supposed she would welcome an American "nobody" as a wife for her eldest grandson.

Slowly, she followed her husband up the polished old oak stairs and down the long paneled gallery to the big bedroom that by tradition was always occupied by the master and mistress of the house. It had been empty since the death of Alice and Oliver Rochford and would now belong to her and Rowell.

As Rowell preceded her into the room, she felt her heartbeat quicken. A fire burned cheerfully in the grate, and the quilt had been turned down on the vast four-poster bed. Willow's cheeks flushed a deep pink as her imagination conjured up unbidden thoughts of nights of loving in that big bed with Rowell. Doubtless, in time she would grow used to the feel of his body so close to hers, she thought. But at present, the merest touch of his hand or arm or leg was sufficient to send the hot blood coursing through her veins. She felt very guilty that the marital act itself—which her mother had warned her she might find objectionable, even an unwelcome invasion of her body—was an intimacy she secretly craved. Possibly out of consideration for her, Rowell had only made love to her twice since their wedding night. Although he seemed to fall asleep without the slightest difficulty once his head touched the pillow, she herself could not easily calm the breathless excitement she felt each time Rowell touched her as he turned in his sleep. She longed for him to waken and take her as he had done on that first occasion. Perhaps, now they were home at last, he would do so. She must find some way, albeit with modesty, to let him know that she did not find his attentions unwelcome.

If only she were more voluptuous! she thought sadly as Rowell disappeared with his valet into the adjoining dressing room and Nellie came into the bedroom carrying a copper jug full of steaming hot water. While Nellie removed her coat and dress, she stood patiently, surveying her figure in the tall mirror. Her waist could not be faulted, for it was only a fraction over seventeen inches. Her hips swelled gently and her arms and legs were softly rounded. But her breasts were small and taut. It was only with the help of considerable padding that she could achieve a desirable cleavage when she wore her evening gowns. Nellie forecast that, in time, she would fill out.

"You're but seventeen years of age, Miss Willow," she said comfortingly. "There's lots of girls don't develop as quick as others, to be sure. A bairn or two, and you'll have all the bosom you could want."

But Willow did not want to wait until she had children. She wanted her husband to find her desirable now

—as desirable as she found him. His male body had been both a shock and a surprise to her. Tall, with broad shoulders and slim tapering hips, she thought Rowell beautiful to look upon, although she had seen him naked only once. Since their wedding night in the train, he had disrobed in his dressing room, and always turned off the light before he climbed into bed beside her. Once at the St. Regis in New York she had given way to temptation and allowed her wayward hands to run over his body. On that occasion, he had turned toward her rather than away from her, and after a while, had taken her quietly, quickly, and with seeming satisfaction.

Willow, with her limited experience of married life, had no way of knowing how normal or otherwise it was. For the time being she did not try to analyze her feelings. It was enough for her to accept the miracle of being Rowell's wife; having him always at her side where she could watch his face and listen to his deep voice; and at nights lie beside him. That he rarely kissed her, smiled at her, or spoke to her in loving tones did not seem extraordinary, for she knew that, as a race, the English were said to be reserved, hiding their deepest emotions; that there was a long-established "correct" way to behave, and that keeping to these predetermined rules was more important to an Englishman than expressing openly his views or feelings.

"Don't forget to curtsy to Grandmère when we go in," Rowell cautioned her. "Although you are now mistress of the house, she will expect you to give due consideration to her age."

Willow nodded. One did not easily forget so dominant and forceful a character, and memories of Lady Rochford were still vivid in her mind. She could well recall that even Rowell, the head of the house, was treated by the old lady as if he were a small boy, and that he had always been anxious not to incur her displeasure. Fortunately, thought Willow, the old woman had appeared to like her, and she followed Rowell to her suite of rooms with only a modicum of trepidation.

Grandmère was sitting in bed, propped up by pillows, a lace cap covering her snow-white hair, an embroidered shawl around her plump shoulders. Beside her sat her sister-in-law Mildred Rochford—a thin, stooped woman, with grey straggling hair, a grey dress, a pincenez hanging from a black ribbon around her thin scraggy neck. In her lap lay a copy of *The Times*, which she had been reading aloud to Grandmère. As Rowell and Willow entered the room, she jumped to her feet—large, ungainly appurtenances which somehow seemed not to belong to her—and came toward the young couple, smiling and sniffing.

Willow curbed a smile. She had forgotten Aunt Mildred's sniff. Pelham used to imitate the poor old spinster, remarking quite rightly that she was never without a drip on the end of her beaky nose.

Rowell gave his aunt a quick peck on the cheek and turned to his grandmother, stooping to kiss her outstretched hand.

"I am sorry you are not too well today, Grandmère. It's nothing serious, I hear."

"At my age, even a head cold can be serious," the old lady said sharply. She pushed Rowell aside and peered around him at Willow. "Come here, girl, so that I can get a better look at you."

As Willow made her obligatory curtsy, Grandmère eyed her approvingly. The girl looked charming in her pale green silk teagown. In a year or two's time, when she had filled out a little, she would not be a discredit to the Rochfords insofar as her looks were concerned.

"You've grown very pretty," she remarked in her stilted tone with its faint trace of French accent. "Well, my dear, I have no doubt you will find everything a little strange at first, but you have no need to worry." She held out a small, plump, beringed hand in an imperial gesture to Aunt Mildred. "Fetch me the keys, Milly," she commanded.

While Aunt Mildred hurried to carry out this order, Willow stared around her in surprise. She had never been in Grandmère's bedroom before, and the sight astonished her. It was so very different from the *décor* of the rest of Rochford Manor.

The walls were lined with faded moiré silk, printed with posies of pastel-colored flowers. The gilded rococo doors and wainscot were delicate French design, the chairs and chaise-longue upholstered in pale lavender brocade. On the mantelpiece over the carved marble fireplace was a gold clock under a glass dome. A sketch by Watteau of the *Embarkation to Cythera* hung on one wall. On another was a Fragonard still life of wallflowers, violets, and wild roses. Over Grandmère's bureau was a view of Dijon by Corot.

In her haste to carry out Grandmère's order, Aunt Mildred tripped over a stool near the window, but did not pause to feel for any injury. Hurriedly, she opened the top drawer of a tallboy and withdrew a massive brass ring, heavy with forty or more keys hanging from it. Grandmère took it from her, holding it for a moment in silent thought before she handed it to Willow.

"The keys to every room in the Manor are here, girl," she said importantly. "I have had possession of them since poor Alice died. Now they will be your responsibility, and you must guard them carefully. As Rowell's wife, you are now the Chatelaine of Rochford. It may be customary in England for the housekeeper to have the keys in her possession, but in my country they remain in the safekeeping of the lady of the house. You'll soon find out what each key is for: the still room, the linen room, the gun room, and so on. Always make sure the servant who borrows a key brings it back if you do not unlock the door for them yourself. Mrs. Spears and Dutton may be trusted, but I am not sure about Cook or the head footman, Harry."

Obediently, Willow took the heavy bunch of keys. Silently, she wondered how she could carry such a cumbersome bundle around with her, for it was far too weighty to be put in her pocket. But she did not have the courage to question Lady Rochford.

"You will, of course, call me Grandmère now," the old lady said. "Come closer, child, I have a present for you!"

She reached beneath one of the big feather pillows behind her head and smiled, this time maliciously, at her sister-in-law.

"Milly always wanted me to give this to her," she said, handing Willow a violet-colored leather jewel case. Inside lay a very beautiful emerald necklace. Willow cut short her gasp of pleasure as she glanced anxiously at Aunt Mildred.

"My husband gave it to me on our wedding day,"

Grandmère continued, ignoring Aunt Mildred except to murmur automatically: "Do stop sniffing, Milly! Cedric said it was to be worn by the mistress of the house. I gave it to Alice when she and Oliver were married, but since she died, I have kept it for Rowell's wife. In due course you will pass it on to your eldest son's wife. Do you understand? It is yours for your lifetime."

"Yes, of course, Grandmère, and thank you," Willow said. "It is very beautiful and I will take great care of it."

"Then be off, girl. I have private matters I wish to discuss with Rowell, matters to do with the estate that will not interest you. You may come and see me again tomorrow."

Dismissed in so peremptory a manner, Willow did not think to ask if she might remain. But, as she made her way downstairs, she wondered why she must be excluded from a discussion about the Rochford estate. Rochford was her home now, and anything concerning it must be of interest to her. Without quite understanding why, she felt oddly resentful that her husband should share secrets with anyone other than his wife, even if it were only his old grandmother.

But she did not remain downcast for long. Later, she would ask Rowell to tell her what was said, she decided. Then he would realize that he had not married a stupid girl without intelligence, but a wife who was ready and anxious to learn whatever was necessary to support him, even if it had to do with tedious matters like finance. She knew that Rowell worried a great deal about such things, and her father had warned her that the Rochfords had severe financial worries. Now that she was Rowell's wife, she must learn to lighten that load for him in any way she could. Arithmetic had never been a problem to her, for mathematics came easy, and her governess had described her as a "numerate" person.

Perhaps I really will be able to help Rowell, Willow thought, as her vivid imagination conjured up a romantic picture of herself poring over ledgers and turning to a grateful Rowell with the glad cry that she had finally balanced his books.

She had no way of knowing that, in bringing to the

marriage the huge dowry settled on her by her father, she had already succeeded in getting the Rochford family out of debt.

Chapter Three

November—December 1891

"I HAVE JUST NOW REALIZED WHY GRANDMÈRE RETIRED to bed," Pelham remarked *sotto voce* as he leaned across the ocean of the long Jacobean dining table to speak to Willow. His eyes were glinting mischievously. "She realized that *you* would be sitting in *her* chair at the top of the table!"

He watched with amusement the blush that stained Willow's cheeks. The butler had held this seat back for her, and she had given no thought to the fact that old Lady Rochford may customarily have sat opposite Rowell.

"Forget I spoke," Pelham said contritely, seeing Willow's embarrassment. "I was only teasing you. By the way, you're looking very beautiful, if I may say so."

His compliment was reassuring. She had chosen one of her new Worth gowns. Made of cream-colored surah silk, it had green velvet puffed sleeves with deep lace trimmings at elbows and hem. Around her neck was the emerald necklace Grandmère had given her; on her left hand were Rowell's diamond engagement circlet and her wedding ring. Rowell had merely nodded approvingly when she had shown herself to him in her completed toilette, seemingly more concerned with the set of his own high, tight collar and white bowtie.

Willow was the only young woman at the table, although Aunt Milly had come down to dinner on Grandmère's orders and sat on Rowell's right hand looking thinner than ever in a plum-colored evening gown. The ill-chosen color accentuated her reddened nose and mottled cheeks. A feather boa was draped round her drooping shoulders.

"Is Rupert not back yet?" she inquired in her loud, nervous voice.

"He is still in Bracknell at the home of one of his University chums," Francis said, his tone vaguely spiteful. Rowell shot his younger brother a quick glance.

"Is that friendship not over yet?" he remarked rhetorically. "It's high time Rupert widened his circle of friends. Lord Alfred Douglas is at least two years older than he is. I can't understand what the fellow sees in a nineteen-year-old boy."

"Rupert says 'We share a love of music, literature, and the poets,'" Francis quoted his brother in a wicked imitation of Rupert's rather high-pitched voice. "And besides these common interests," he continued, "our Rupert admires milord's arrogance and independence. His mother, as you probably know, is a divorcee and spoils him—and Rupert too. There is, of course, no Papa on hand to say nay to their various escapades."

Watching Rowell's face, Willow was surprised to see how angry he looked. But he said quite mildly:

"I'll have a word with Rupert when he gets home."

For the remainder of the long drawn-out meal, at which no fewer than six different courses were served, Pelham monopolized the conversation with an account of the trial of the unhappy army officer, William Gordon-Cummings. The trial had taken place during the first week of June while Rowell was in America, and although all details of the scandal had occupied a great deal of space in the English newspapers and been a topic of conversation in nearly every household in the land, Rowell had heard little about its outcome in San Francisco.

A Lieutenant Colonel in the Scots Guards, Sir William had been found cheating at baccarat at a house party at Tranby Croft near Doncaster. The Prince of Wales was acting as banker at the time, and it had proved impossible to keep his name out of the resulting publicity. Not only the Queen, but a great many of her subjects disapproved most strongly of the Prince's gambling—Grandmère most vociferously, Pelham said, grinning. The poor man had been pilloried by the press.

"With the result that the Prince now plays only bridge, although he refuses quite adamantly to give up horse racing!" Pelham concluded.

Willow wanted to know what had happened to the unfortunate Gordon-Cummings, for whom there seemed little sympathy except from Toby.

"The poor devil has been dismissed from the army, of course," Toby told her, "and expelled from various clubs. Socially, he is now *persona non grata.*"

"Rumor has it that he is about to or has already married, a rich American woman," Pelham continued. "Seems to be getting quite a habit, eh, Rowell?"

Willow was about to laugh at what she had assumed to be merely one of Pelham's teasing remarks. But Rowell's face was dark with anger and his voice thunderous as he said:

"Any more of such comments, Pelham, and you may find yourself no longer welcome under this roof."

For a moment no one spoke. Aunt Milly broke the uncomfortable silence with one of her high-pitched nervous laughs.

"Grandmère had a letter from France this morning from Cousin Lucienne. She is bringing Silvie to stay with us over Christmas."

Toby turned to Willow.

"You will like Silvie, I think. She is Grandmère's greatniece. Cousin Lucienne is the niece of Grandmère's brother, if you can work out that complicated relationship. They are entirely French in every way, although both Cousin Lucienne and Silvie speak perfect English. It will be nice for you, Willow, to have a girl of your own age in such a masculine-oriented household."

"Just think," mused Pelham, "Silvie cannot be more than nineteen years old, and yet she is already a widow. Happily, I do not think she can have been very much in love with that German baron Cousin Lucienne persuaded her to marry. He must have been at least forty. Maybe Cousin Lucienne knew he had a weak heart and was quite likely to depart this world prematurely, leaving Silvie his ill-gotten gains."

Francis grinned, but Aunt Milly tut-tutted disapprovingly.

"You wouldn't dare say such things if your grandmother were present," she said warningly. "Besides, Baron von Senden was a most upright man, and his money most honorably acquired by inheritance."

"You will not now lack for interesting things to tell Grandmère when you rejoin her after dinner!" Francis said sarcastically. He, like his brothers, was well used to the fact that Grandmère kept her ear to the ground by means of their spinster aunt. As children, they had never succeeded in keeping any prank from Grandmère's knowledge unless they had been able to keep it secret from their aunt. But Francis did not fear her tittle-tattle as his brothers had cause to do. While they might bring Grandmère's wrath down upon their heads—with the disastrous withholding of their allowances as a consequence—Francis knew himself secure from such retribution. So marked was his resemblance to his father, that Grandmère, who had idolized her only son, had always closed her eagle eye to all her youngest grandson's faults. She spoiled and indulged him and, perhaps most harmful of all, let him know that he was immune from punishment. Even if he were caught red-handed in a misdemeanor, Grandmère excused him on the grounds that he was the youngest, and misled into mischief by his older brothers.

"Is Cousin Lucienne also a widow?" Willow inquired. She had, until now, heard no mention of Grandmère's French relatives.

Pelham nodded.

"She lives with Silvie in a beautiful house in Paris, and although it belongs to Silvie, Cousin Lucienne is still very much head of the household. You will discover, my dear sister-in-law, that Grandmère's side of the family breed very determined women. And how about you, Willow? Are you a very determined woman?" Pelham asked, his dark eyes glinting. "Somehow I think not!"

"On the contrary," Willow replied to his question gravely. "If something is very important to me, then I will not give up until I get my own way." She looked down the length of the dining table and smiled at Rowell. "I have already proved it, have I not, my dearest? Nothing Papa said dissuaded me from marrying you, did it, Rowell? And if Papa had not finally given his permission for our marriage, then I would have run away from home to be with you."

"And found yourself disinherited to boot, I dare say," Pelham remarked too quietly for Rowell to overhear. He stood up, raising his glass. "A toast, I think, to the bridal pair. May they live happily ever after."

"Unlike the endings of those improbable fairy tales Mr. Wilde has been writing," Francis added disparagingly.

At long last, the final course was finished, and Willow and Aunt Mildred could retire to the drawing room, leaving the men to their brandy and cigars. By the time they rejoined the ladies, Willow was white with fatigue, the effects of the day's traveling finally taking their toll.

"Shall we retire, my dearest?" she asked Rowell softly. "I am afraid I shall not be able to stay awake much longer. You too must be exhausted."

Rowell looked down into her small, drawn face. There were dark smudges beneath her eyes, which made them seem even larger than usual.

"I have one or two urgent matters to discuss with my brothers," he said, his tone apologetic. "I'll try not to be too long."

Strangely disappointed, and feeling excluded for the second time that day, Willow said a general goodnight and turned toward the staircase. The long gallery high above her head was lit only fitfully and seemed full of shadows. One of the housemaids went scurrying along the dark passage toward the back staircase, a small ghostly figure half hidden from Willow by the carved balustrade. A door banged, and somewhere a window that had not been properly closed gave out an eerie whistling as the wind soughed its way through an aperture.

Willow shivered, and, gathering up her skirts, hurried up the stairs. Nellie was awaiting her in the bedroom. Lights burned brightly, and in the carved stone grate a fire burned merrily. This room, with its warm brown paneling and thick rugs on the floor, was as welcoming as the gallery had been eerie.

"Oh, Nellie, I am glad you're here!" Willow said as her young maid hurried forward to take her long gloves. "I'm quite exhausted—and you must be, too. It has been a very long day."

"I've put two stone hot-water bottles in the bed, Miss Willow—I mean, Milady," Nellie said cheerfully, her pink smiling face kindly and solicitous. She began to undo the buttons of Willow's gown, chatting as she undressed her young mistress.

"They're quite a friendly lot downstairs," she remarked. "All but the housekeeper. Now, Cook—she is *really* nice—she said not to bother about Mrs. Spears as she'd be bound to be against me, seeing she didn't engage me herself, not to mention me being Irish-American, too. Mr. Dutton's nice, for all he's so proper. He said to be sure and tell him if there's anything *at all* I know about that's not to your satisfaction."

"I'm glad you're settling down, Nellie," Willow answered as the maid removed her petticoat and corselet and began to peel off her silk stockings. "Are you quite comfortable in your bedroom?"

Nellie grimaced.

"It's not too bad, Milady, though it's bitter cold up in them attics. Violet—that's Miss Dodie's maid what I share the room with—she says there are some mornings when she has to break the ice on the water jug afore she can wash. But Mr. Dutton lets us take a hot water bottle up to bed with us, so I'll be all right, Miss Willow—Milady, I mean!"

She drew the thin linen nightdress over her mistress' head, and as Willow seated herself at the dressing table, Nellie began her nightly task of brushing the pale, silky hair which she had let fall from its pins. The French coiffeur on the *City of Edinburgh* had flatly refused to curl it, saying it was far too beautiful. He showed Nellie how to arrange the plaits like a crown around Willow's head—a style that was more sophisticated and flattering than the bun she wore at the back of the crown.

Without ceasing her rhythmic brushing, Nellie continued to gossip.

"We had ever such a good high tea downstairs," she said, sighing reminiscently. "I felt sorry for that girl Violet. She doesn't eat with us, so she missed all the good things. She has her meals with Miss Dodie up in the tower room."

Willow had almost forgotten the existence of Rowell's sister.

"Does Violet have to spoon feed the poor child?" Willow asked compassionately.

"Gracious me, no, Milady," Nellie replied. "Violet says Miss Dodie can manage easily enough with the use of her one good hand. Violet says she's quite clever with it and makes ever such good pictures on the wall—shadow pictures is what she means."

Willow frowned.

"But I thought the child was mentally unbalanced," she remarked. "Making silhouettes requires a certain adeptness, and imagination and coordination."

Nellie sighed.

"Violet says she doesn't think as how Miss Dodie *is* crazed. She says she's a dear little girl and ever so loving. Of course, Miss Dodie's only got Violet to talk to all day long, as she can't read nor write nor sew nor anything. Violet tries to find things for her to do, like holding the wool for winding for her knitting. Of course, it wouldn't do for you to mention it, Miss Willow—I mean, Milady. Violet says Lady Rochford has given orders Miss Dodie is to be kept absolutely quiet—even to keep the curtains drawn—so it wouldn't do for her ladyship to hear what they get up to."

She ceased her brushing momentarily to bend down and whisper:

"Violet said she brings things from home after her day out, like a jam jar with frogs' spawn in it and a box with big black furry caterpillars for Miss Dodie to watch. Gives her something to do, poor little thing!"

Willow knew that she ought not to be listening to Nellie's gossiping, yet how else was she to learn such secrets? she thought. As mistress of Rochford Manor, the house was now her responsibility, and Grandmère had given her the keys. She could not run it properly if she did not know what happened within its walls. The good-natured Nellie was not a mischief-maker, she reassured herself, and allowed the girl to continue with her prattle until Willow's toilette was completed.

It seemed that only Grandmère, the family doctor, and Violet were allowed into Dodie's room. The door was kept locked, and if anyone else wanted to pay the child a visit, they had to ask Grandmère for the key. Her visitors were few, although Toby made a regular nightly call. Violet seemed to think that the child lived for these visits from her brother Toby. Unless he were away from home, he never failed to call in and tell her a story before kissing her goodnight. Pelham too visited his little sister, but less frequently, seeming ill-at-ease in the sickroom. Francis and Rupert went only on Christmas Day and on their sister's birthday.

"Mr. Francis can't stand the sight of her poor arm and leg," Nellie said. "And Violet thinks Mr. Rupert doesn't like it that she looks just like him. He and Miss Dodie both have their mother's blue eyes and the same light brown hair, you see. It sort of makes him feel he might have been the crippled one."

At last, Nellie seemed satisfied with her mistress' hair and, having removed the hot water bottles from the bed, there was nothing more for her to do. Willow sent her off to bed, for the uncomplaining, friendly girl looked as tired as she herself felt as she climbed between the warm linen sheets.

Despite Rowell's assurance that he would not be long in joining his bride, he still did not appear; nor could Willow hear him in the adjoining dressing room. For a long while after Nellie had gone, she lay awake, trying not to wonder why her husband was not as eager to be alone with her in their bedroom as she was to have him beside her. It was their first night as bride and groom in their own home, and his tardiness was hurtful.

In an effort to keep her mind away from such thoughts, she concentrated upon Nellie's account of the invalid child, now lying alone in her sickroom in the west turret. It seemed cruel to leave her so isolated, even though the talkative Violet had said there was an electric bell connected to her bedroom in the attic above, and that if Dodie needed anything in the night, she had but to press the bell and Violet would go to her.

Tomorrow, Willow thought, before I do anything else, I shall go to see Dodie. After all, she is now my sister-in-law—the nearest I shall ever have to a real sister.

Willow had been determined to stay awake until Rowell came to bed, but, to her chagrin, she was so deeply asleep when he climbed in beside her that she did not even stir in her slumber. When she awoke next morning, Nellie was standing by her bed with a breakfast tray, and informed her that Rowell had departed an hour before to see his bailiff.

"And Cook's waiting to see you, Milady, about the menus," Nellie said cheerfully, as she put the heavily laden tray on the table by the bed. "And Mrs. Spears is

waiting for you to give her the linen room key, and Mr.
Dutton wants the still room key and would I tell you it's
urgent!"

"Oh, dear!" Willow cried as she sat up and tried to master her still-sleepy mind. "Find me some clothes while I am
having breakfast, Nellie. I can see I'm going to be kept
busy running this house. You must not let me oversleep
again."

She was indeed far too busy until the end of the morning to keep her self-made promise to visit Rowell's sister.
It was midday before she finally climbed the stairs to the
turret room.

Willow sighed as she took the heavy bunch of keys
from her pocket. There were so many, she thought helplessly, wondering if she would ever manage to find the
right one without having to look at the labels. Only a faint
light filtered through the narrow window at the end of the
little circular landing on which she stood. She moved closer
to the turret casement so that she could more easily read
the writing on the labels. But however carefully she scru-
tinized them, she could find none with "Miss Dorothy"
written on it.

Perhaps the door was not locked after all, she thought,
smiling at her own stupidity in not first trying it. But it did
not open when she turned the handle. With growing nervousness, Willow knocked.

Almost at once the door opened—but only wide enough
for the homely-faced country girl who was Dodie's maid
to peer around it.

"Lawks-a-mercy, Miss—I mean, Milady," she stammered. "I thought as how it must be Miss Mildred."

"As you can see, I am not her," Willow said gently, for
she could see that the young maid was overcome by the
unexpected visitor. "I am your new Mistress, and you, I
imagine, are Violet?"

"Yes indeed, Milady, begging your pardon!"

"There is no need to do that," Willow replied smiling.
"Just stand aside and allow me to come in." She could see
that the room beyond was in semi-darkness, but no sound
came from the interior.

Violet's hand, reddened by years of hard work, tightened on the door handle. Her round hazel eyes were wide
with anxiety.

"I dursn't, Milady, I dursn't," she repeated, looking upon the point of tears.

The poor girl looked so frightened, Willow decided not to press her right of entry, but to go to Grandmère and obtain the missing key.

"How did *you* get in, Violet?" she asked as she turned to go.

"Oh, Milady, Miss Mildred lets me in, and I've to lock up when I leave and give the key back—even if'n it's just to go downstairs for Miss Dodie's meals."

"I see! Well, thank you, Violet. I will see you again presently."

As Willow went carefully back down the spiral staircase, she tried to quell her feeling of growing apprehension. What could be so wrong with Rowell's sister that it was necessary to keep her virtually a prisoner in her darkened turret room? Rowell had mentioned her only in the most casual manner, saying the child was retarded—no worse. Could she in fact be witless, and perhaps dangerously so?

As she made her way along the landing toward Lady Rochford's rooms, she found herself recalling a novel she had read not long ago by Charlotte Brontë. In the book, *Jane Eyre,* the hero had had a wife who was insane. He had locked her away, not only for her own safety, but for the safety of others. Was this why they kept Dodie incarcerated?

She shivered as she knocked on Lady Rochford's door. This time it was not a maid, but Aunt Millie who opened the door to her.

Lady Rochford was seated at her bureau, where she was writing letters. She glanced over her shoulder.

"Well, come in, girl. Don't stand there staring," the old lady said, not unkindly but with a certain impatience.

Willow walked hesitantly into the room.

"I am sorry to disturb you, Grandmère, but I have come for the key of little Dorothy's room."

Lady Rochford's button-black eyes narrowed.

"I am afraid that is quite out of the question, Willow," she said, in a hard, firm voice. "Had I intended you to have it, it would have been with the other keys I gave you."

Willow swallowed nervously. She did not feel able to

argue with Rowell's grandmother, but at the same time, she believed it a matter of principle that she should have the right to go anywhere in her own home, and that she should know exactly how serious was her sister-in-law's condition.

"Soon after I arrived here, Grandmère, you told me that I was to be the new Chatelaine of Rochford Manor," she said. "If I am to be responsible in every other respect, then I feel I must share with you and Rowell responsibility for your granddaughter, too."

Behind her, she heard Aunt Milly sniff loudly. She was not certain if this was in derision at her audacity in standing up to old Lady Rochford, or if it were just her usual habit. Grandmère was looking extremely angry.

"You are far too young and inexperienced to realize the implications involved," she said. "You must take my word for it that the unfortunate child is malformed and certainly no joy to behold. It would serve no purpose whatever, were you to visit her. She is mentally retarded, and I have arranged matters so that she leads a quiet life and is of as little inconvenience as possible to the rest of the household. I must insist that you leave this affair in my hands."

Willow summoned what little courage still remained.

"I would still like to see her, if only once," she murmured.

"Your curiosity does you no credit!"

Grandmère's voice was knife-edged, and tears sprang to Willow's eyes. Her gently-spoken Quaker mother had never raised her voice in such a manner, and not only was Willow hurt by the tone, but by the unfair inference.

"It is not a matter of curiosity, Grandmère, I do assure you," she cried, her voice trembling. "But please allow me to see the child. At least when I have done so, I may understand a little better why she must be kept so carefully guarded."

To Willow's unutterable surprise, the old lady said:

"Very well, go and see her for yourself. But I warn you: you will not be the happier for it. One day, it is to be hoped, you will produce children for your husband, and I can only pray that his unfortunate strain in our family will not be passed down a further generation. Mildred, give her the key!"

Aunt Mildred went to the bureau and took out a large brass key. As she placed it in Willow's outstretched hand, it felt icy cold, and a shiver of real fear ran up Willow's arm and seemed to pierce her heart. Silently, her head bowed, she left the room, her feet taking her slowly but inexorably toward the turret staircase. Her mind teemed with snatches of Grandmère's conversation. If there were truly some dreadful taint in the Rochford family, why had Rowell not told her of it? Might she indeed pass such a thing on to the children she would bear for Rowell? Would they, too, be locked away, prisoners, too grotesque to be seen by the outside world?

Her feet moving ever more slowly, she mounted the stone stairs. Had pride not forbidden it, she would have liked to return the key to Grandmère and never open the door high up above her. She no longer wished to see the poor girl imprisoned there. She wished she were not alone; that she had waited until Rowell could go with her. But she had acted impetuously, and now, unless she were to reveal her fear to Grandmère, she must find the courage to pursue her mission.

She reached the room, put the key in the lock, and turned it.

At first she could see very little, for the room was in semi-darkness. But she glimpsed the outline of a large fourposter bed, heavily curtained, and a shape sitting on a hard-backed chair by the bed. As her vision improved, she saw the maid, Violet, staring at her in wide-eyed astonishment. The girl jumped to her feet, bobbing a curtsy, her movements awkward, her large hands and feet an indication of her farming stock. Normally, such an uncouth girl would have been employed in the kitchens. Willow thought inconsequently. She stepped farther into the room, her eyes turning toward the bed in trepidation of what monstrous apparition she might see there.

After all the terrible sights her imagination had conjured up, Willow could hardly credit her eyes as they alighted on a tiny, frail figure propped into a semi-sitting position by three enormous pillows. Two huge, violet-blue eyes, fringed with black lashes, regarded her with a bright curiosity. This was no monster, no freak, but a normal, if delicate-looking, little girl.

"I'm your brother Rowell's new wife, Willow!" Unconsciously, Willow had lowered her voice to a whisper. "Your name is Dodie, isn't it?" she continued in more normal tones. "I came to say hello!"

Never moving her rapt gaze from Willow's face, the child spoke.

"I know all about you from Violet. She shares a room with your American maid, who is called Nellie. Violet says Nellie is very pretty. She can't be as pretty as you. I think you are the most beautiful lady I ever saw."

Willow only just succeeded in concealing her surprise at what was not only a very lucid little speech, but an endearing one. She moved closer to the bed and sat down on the edge of the white, fringed counterpane. As she did so, she saw for the first time that the child had a withered arm—which she quickly tucked beneath the bedclothes. Her other hand came up to touch Willow's hair.

"It's like silk," she murmured. "It feels just like the silk shawl Toby gave me last Christmas."

Willow's mind whirled in confusion. Grandmère had led her to believe that Dodie was severely mentally retarded, as well as deformed, and yet she had neither seen nor heard one reason for that assessment. It was true that the child's manner of speaking was that of a girl far younger than eleven years of age; but she was perfectly lucid—and surprisingly articulate, if it were true that she seldom conversed with anyone but the maid.

Willow sat down in the chair Violet had vacated.

"How old are you, Violet?" she inquired.

"Eighteen, Milady, cum Michelmas, that is."

"You come from Havorhurst village?"

"Yes, Mum—I mean, Milady!" Violet stammered, overcome by this attention. "Me Dad farms East Meadows, and me Mum looks after the little 'uns."

Violet went on to explain that she had thirteen younger brothers and sisters, and, because she was the eldest of this large family, she had always had to help look after them. Consequently, she had never had time to go to school, and could neither read nor write.

"But she tells me lovely stories," Dodie interrupted loyally, "all about the farm animals and about her family and what is happening in the village. She brings me presents, too. Today she brought me—" she broke off, her pale thin cheeks coloring as she realized that, in her desire to praise her maid, she had all but betrayed her. Her huge eyes filled with tears.

"Well, Violet, what *did* you bring?" Willow asked gently. "I shall not be angry, so you have no need to be afraid."

Reassured by Willow's tone of voice, Violet produced a string of shiny brown chestnuts.

"I thought as how they could learn Miss Dodie to count," she said. "I can't count no more than twenty, but Miss Dodie can't count not even to ten!"

Willow looked back at the little girl. Her initial feeling of astonishment had now given way to one of excitement.

"Would you like to learn to read and write?" she asked gently. "If you could read storybooks it would help to pass the time."

Dodie's face lit with a momentary pleasure, that as quickly as it had come, was replaced by a look of resignation.

"Doctor Forbes would not allow it," she said. "Toby suggested I might be given some picture books two Christmases ago, but the doctor said they would be harmful."

"Harmful in what way?" Willow asked. "Do you have trouble with your eyes?"

"Oh no," Dodie said, clearly surprised by the question. "I can see even better than Violet. Sometimes when she is mending, I thread the needle for her."

"Then picture books cannot possibly harm you," Willow said, anger rising so strongly in her that she found it difficult to keep her voice calm. "I will talk to Doctor—what is his name—Forbes?"

Violet shuffled uncomfortably from one foot to the other, looking so patently unhappy that Willow felt forced to inquire what was wrong.

"Begging your pardon, Milady, but it's Lady Rochford as gives all the orders for Miss Dodie, and if she found as how there were books in here, I'd as like be dismissed. And we need my money bad at home. And Miss Dodie needs me," she added, close to tears.

Willow stood up, her mouth set firmly.

"Naturally, I shall speak to Lady Rochford before I see Doctor Forbes," she said quietly. "That is, if *you* would like me to do so, Dodie."

"Oh, I would, I would," the child cried, so concerned

with the matter that she forgot her hidden limb as she raised both arms toward Willow in appeal.

Willow's heart was stirred by pity. It seemed quite monstrous to her that so harmless a deformity should be the cause of Dodie's segregation from her family. She stood up, her face determined.

"Don't worry," she said reassuringly. "I am certain I will be able to arrange it. And when I next visit you, I want to hear that you have learned all your numbers up to ten!"

Slowly, a smile spread over Dodie's face, filling out the gaunt white cheeks. With renewed incredulity, Willow realized that one day this poor unhappy child might even be beautiful.

"Does the daylight hurt your eyes?" she inquired as she was about to leave the room. Dodie shook her head negatively, and it was Violet who vouchsafed:

"Lady Rochford gave orders, Mum—I mean Milady—that the curtains was to stay drawn at all times."

Willow was deeply shocked. Frail though the child was, there seemed no valid reason warranting her incarceration alone with a maid in this ill-lit sickroom, forbidden even to look at books. What possible justification could her grandmother have for insisting on such treatment? Even if the child were prone to convulsions or fits that were not discernible to a stranger such as herself, there were quite obviously days such as this when the child was lucid and well able to think, speak, and see clearly.

But, although Willow did not lack the courage to return at once to see Lady Rochford, she felt it would be unwise and unfair to Rowell to commence their married life with a serious confrontation with his grandmother. Controlling her impatience, she occupied herself for several days reacquainting herself with the numerous rooms in the manor, with the domestic routine of the servants, and overseeing the unpacking of their wedding presents from the large crates.

It was two days before the wooden boxes were finally emptied and their contents put away. Fully occupied though she was, the memory of the child in the turret room was never far from Willow's thoughts.

There were several occasions when it was on the tip of her tongue to speak to Rowell about his sister. But an inexplicable sixth sense kept her from doing so. She felt instinctively that he would adopt Grandmère's view: that Dodie was not *her* concern. She wondered unhappily if there were a family conspiracy to keep the child concealed. For the time being, she dared not risk angering Rowell. She could not bear his disapproval, and, fearing it, she kept silent.

But, on the fourth day after her arrival, she decided to take up the question of Dodie, not with Rowell but with Grandmère. She would do so casually, on her daily visit to see the old lady; seek her cooperation rather than challenge her opinion.

Grandmère was still confined to her own suite of rooms on the opposite side of the house, and as Willow made her way there, her heart was beating with a mixture of excitement and apprehension.

Grandmère seemed not to have moved since her last visit and was seated at her bureau, still writing letters. Her plump, bejeweled hand clasped a quill pen, which she put down as Willow came forward to kiss her proffered cheek.

"I am sorry if I have interrupted you, Grandmère," Willow said, "but I have not spoken of Dodie since my visit to her, and I thought you might like to know how glad I am you allowed me to see her. I found her a delightful little girl."

She was unprepared for the mask that descended over Lady Rochford's face at the mention of her granddaughter's name.

"Were you blind, then, that you did not see her deformities?" Grandmère's voice was abrupt to the point of rudeness.

"I saw her arm, Grandmère, but I did not feel any horror, only pity," Willow said quietly. "I want to tell you that I think she finds it very tedious lying alone in that darkened room with nothing to do. I believe she is quite well able to appreciate the usual toys other children enjoy. I thought I might go to the village this afternoon and buy her some picture books—unless, of course, you or the doctor know of some reason why I should not do so?"

Despite the tactful manner in which Willow expressed her views, Grandmère's eyes narrowed. Behind Willow's back, she heard Aunt Mildred give a subdued gasp.

"You'll do no such thing!" Grandmère barked. "Doctor Forbes would be extremely angry with you, and so would I. The child is unfit for such pastimes!"

"In what way unfit?" Willow persisted. She was not going to allow herself to be intimidated, although her legs had begun to tremble and her voice was not as steady as she liked.

The tightening of the old lady's mouth was unmistakable, and Willow knew that, despite all her intentions to the contrary, she was about to have a battle on her hands. But it was not one she intended to lose without good reason.

"In what way unfit?" she repeated her question.

Grandmère drew a deep breath, beating an angry tattoo on the desktop with her pen.

"You'd best be seated, girl! You seem to feel obliged to question my authority—something I suppose I should have expected. Obviously, as the new mistress of Rochford Manor, you feel the need to assert yourself. But you are very young—only seventeen, I think—and I did not anticipate that you would consider yourself old enough or experienced enough to question someone of my age."

Willow stood her ground. For all her inner trepidation, she was not going to allow herself to be sidetracked.

"I'm sorry that you have taken my remarks so personally," she said quietly. "I do assure you that I have no wish whatever to assert my authority over yours, as you suggest. I want only to know why Dodie must be kept in such deprived conditions."

"Because the girl is ill!" Grandmère said with surprising violence. "You know nothing of these things—how could you? So perhaps I had better tell you the unpalatable facts, and put an end to this nonsense. My late daughter-in-law, Alice, brought to this strong, virile family of Rochfords an ugly strain of insanity." She looked away from Willow, staring out of the window with an expression of revulsion. "Alice herself showed unmistakable signs of derangement after my poor darling son, Oliver, was killed; and when the girl, Dorothy, was born, the disease manifested itself in full. The poor woman died soon afterwards quite insane."

"But if grief unhinged her mind, that scarcely proves

there is a hereditary strain—" Willow began, but Grand-mère interrupted her.

"There were two other daughters, both of whom died in infancy from brain storms. It is fortunate that this weakness seems only to affect the distaff side of the family. My grandsons, as you know, are all in perfect health. As for Dorothy, Doctor Forbes expected that she would suffer the same early fate as her sisters, but this was not to be the case. Only the most careful nursing and his unfailing attentions saved the girl's life—perhaps not altogether advisedly, since she can never be normal."

"That is a dreadful thing to say," Willow murmured, too shocked to be guarded in her criticism. "Dodie has as much right to live as anyone else."

"But it can never be a normal life," Grandmère said sharply. "She can never marry or have children. That would be to pass on the disease to a third generation—an intolerable prospect."

Willow drew a deep breath as the thought struck her once more that Rowell had made no mention of this hereditary factor; had, for reasons known only to himself failed to warn her that she, too, might have a child that was carrying the disease Grandmère spoke of.

She shivered, putting such thoughts from her mind. She would talk to Rowell himself later about *their* children. In the meanwhile, she was concerned only for Dodie.

"You have still not given me a reason why Dodie should not be allowed picture books and simple toys to play with which would not overtax her. Nor do I see why the curtains should always be drawn in her room. The sunshine and daylight cannot harm her."

Grandmère's mouth tightened.

"Such things could over-stimulate her mind and result in a brain storm," she said. "Doctor Forbes will confirm what I have told you, so I see no point in continuing this conversation. By all means speak to him if you wish, but I suggest that you consult with your husband first. Rowell may not like you, interfering with such long-standing arrangements here at Rochford."

"Very well!" Willow agreed, the color high in her cheeks. She was now convinced that Rowell would support her once she explained to him that Grandmère was over-anxious about her little granddaughter, that she was being overprotective, as was often the case with elderly people. She herself was certain that the cause went no deeper.

But her self-confidence began to wane once more as she left Grandmère's room to go in search of Rowell. The facts old Lady Rochford had given her about the past could not be ignored. She felt a shiver run down her spine that had nothing to do with the chill passages down which she was walking. *Why had Rowell not informed her that his mother had been mentally ill?* Had he been afraid to do so, lest she or her parents object to her marrying into a family with such a serious hereditary trait? If that were true, then it did not show Rowell up in a very good light; indeed, it betrayed him guilty of moral cowardice.

She braced her shoulders. Grandmère had been talking nonsense, she told herself firmly. Or at least exaggerating. That was the only possible explanation. Rowell would not have deceived her on so serious a matter.

Her wish to talk to him at once was made impossible by the unexpected return of Rupert. He was still in his traveling clothes when Willow went down to the hall. His slight figure had a downcast droop. Hearing her approach, he looked up at her, and she was shocked to see that his huge, violet blue eyes were filled with unshed tears.

"Why, Rupert!" she exclaimed in tones that sounded, even to her ears, falsely bright. "We haven't seen each other for nearly two years. You have not changed a great deal. I recognized you at once."

The young man continued to stare at her as he pushed a lock of fine, light brown hair back from his forehead. He seemed to be finding it difficult to speak.

"Luncheon will be served very shortly," Willow tried to fill the silence. "Should you not go and remove your outdoor clothes, Rupert? I will tell Dutton to see another place is laid for you. We were not expecting you back until later in the week."

Now, at last, Rupert seemed able to communicate. With a slight stammer, his words came in a rush:

"I had not expected to return so soon myself. But Alfred . . . that is, my f . . . f . . . friend, Lord Alfred Douglas . he was invited to meet the playwright, Oscar Wilde, yesterday, and since then he talks of nothing else. He had promised to return to Rochford with me today, but now—" He broke off, leaving the sentence in midair. "I . . . please forgive my bad manners. May I offer you my congratulations, Willow. I hope you and Rowell will be very happy!"

The announcement by Dutton that luncheon was served ended Willow's private encounter with Rupert, who excused himself and retired to his own room, stating that he had no appetite. Since no private affairs were ever discussed in front of the servants, it was not until after the meal that Willow was able to speak to Rowell alone in the library. He dismissed her concern for Rupert's obvious distress with a brief:

"It sounds as if he has had a tiff with his best friend. And a good thing, too. I do not care for the way they have been hand-in-glove these past months. Rupert has been far too dependent upon the older boy, and it's high time he made friends of his own age."

But he did not dismiss Willow's account of her conversation with Grandmère nearly so casually. Looking much discomfited, he said:

"I am sure you realize, my dear Willow, that if Grandmère did exaggerate the facts, it was in order to make her point clearly to you. Of course I would have told you when I first asked you to marry me if there had been any such skeleton in our family closet. The facts are simply these: my mother was a somewhat weak character, and her health was never very good. She did suffer depressions, but then so do many women before and after childbirth, and particularly after the loss of a child or a husband. She was certainly not insane."

Willow breathed a sigh of relief. Standing on tiptoe, she kissed Rowell's cheek.

"I am so happy to hear your reassurance," she said. "May I take it, then, that you are in agreement with me about your poor little sister, Rowell? You will tell Grandmère that you consider it in order for Dodie to have some playthings—provided the doctor does not object?"

"My dear Willow," Rowell said coldly, "you have not been in this house for one week, and yet you have already managed to come into conflict with my grandmother. I know you are very young and impetuous, but you could surely show a little more tact in your dealings with her, if only to please me. She has been head of this household for many years, and it will not be easy for her to hand over the reins to anyone as young and inexperienced as yourself."

Willow felt the tears of mortification sting her eyes at Rowell's rebuke. Biting her lower lip, she nevertheless stood her ground.

"I would not have made an issue of a household matter for just the very reasons you point out," she said quietly. "But, Rowell, Dodie is a little girl, eleven years old, and she is lying in a darkened room with nothing whatever to do except converse with that maid who, nice as she seems to be, is nevertheless a farm girl and by no means intellectually very bright. In the brief conversation I had with Dodie, I am quite convinced there is nothing wrong with her intelligence, whatever may be wrong physically."

"I would rather you left such matters in Grandmère's hands," Rowell said evasively. "It is not for you to decide upon Dodie's mental state."

Much as she abhorred the very idea of quarreling with her adored husband, much as she longed to please him and prove herself the perfect wife, Willow could not now shelve a matter that seemed of such importance to her.

"Nevertheless, Rowell, you must admit that it is possible that I could be right, and that Grandmère is being overly protective. It is difficult for you, for everyone in this house, to see Dodie as objectively as I, a newcomer, see her. All of you have assumed, probably since her birth, that she was not entirely normal. But if the child is never given any stimulation, how then *can* she develop normally? Can you not see the logic of my thinking, dearest Rowell? If Dodie appears retarded, then there is every reason for her being so—and those reasons have nothing to do with her intelligence, and everything to do with her upbringing."

Rowell's handsome face was by now reddened with an irritation he made no effort to conceal. His voice was icy as he said:

"I can see that you intend to argue with me, and that distresses me very much, Willow. I had thought you so . . . so agreeable and good tempered."

Hurt by his criticism, Willow tried to take his hand. "Please do not be angry with me, Rowell. I do not want to displease you, and I ask only that you should permit me to speak to the doctor. If he confirms your grandmother's views, then I will say no more about Dodie, I promise you. Will you not agree to so small a request, if it will put my mind at rest?"

Rowell looked relieved.

"I am afraid you will not find Doctor Forbes in disagreement with Grandmère," he said. "He has been our family doctor since '64, and, to my knowledge, they have a strong mutual respect, if not liking, for one another. He attended the births and deaths of the two infants Grandmère spoke of; also my mother during her last days, and, of course, the births of the five of us Rochford sons. He attended us during all our childhood illnesses and he knows the family's health most intimately."

Crestfallen, Willow nodded.

"Nevertheless, Rowell, if by chance he *were* to agree with me . . .?" she asked tentatively.

"Then, in such an unlikely eventuality, it would be up to the pair of you to persuade Grandmère," Rowell conceded. "But I do not want my grandmother disturbed unduly, Willow. She is seventy-one now and entitled to a little peace in her declining years. I would not want her to regret my choice of a wife," he added pointedly.

Willow swallowed unhappily.

"I would not want *you* to regret it, Rowell, not ever," she said in a low, passionate voice. "I love you so much. I do not think you have any idea quite how much I do love you. I would willingly die for you!"

As she flung her arms around him, he held her briefly in his embrace. A wisp of pale gold, silky hair had fallen from its plaited coil crowning her head; her dark eyes were huge, widened as they were in appeal. Her slim young body felt warm beneath his hands, and her delicate lavender scent drifted to his nostrils. He felt a sudden stirring of desire for her and recalled that it was some days since he had enjoyed the sweet freshness of her young body. There was no denying her appeal to his senses at unexpected moments—but far more often this past eight months it was the memory of Georgina's voluptuous charms that had fired his blood. Even six thousand miles away from her across the Atlantic, he had still craved to make love to his mistress. Not even Willow's delicate loveliness and innocent adoration for him had been able to erase Georgina's memory nor arouse in him the same hungry passions.

"I promised Fellows, my bailiff, that I would ride around the estate with him this afternoon," he said gently. "If I do not soon go, it will be dark long before we return. By all means, take the governess' cart or have Peters drive you into Havorhurst to see Doctor Forbes if you so wish. But I do not want to find you in an unhappy state this evening if he disappoints you," he added. He dropped a kiss on her head and smiled. "I have other plans for us this evening, my love."

Willow's happiness was now as quickly restored by his affectionate tone of voice as it had been downcast by his anger. She smiled shyly as she took his beautifully shaped hand and pressed it against her cheek.

"I love you, I love you," she whispered. "You are my whole life!"

"Then you are most certainly doomed," said a teasing voice from the doorway as Pelham came unexpectedly into the room. "No one should ever be *that* important to you, Willow."

Ignoring Willow's gasp and Rowell's grunt of annoyance, Pelham gave her a wicked smile, and, turning on his heel, walked out of the room with the same casual indifference as he had entered it.

Chapter Four

December 1891

"MAY I ASK THE REASON FOR THIS LITTLE OUTING into Havorhurst?"

Willow looked at Pelham's friendly face, and, although she had not entirely forgiven him for his impertinence an hour ago, she decided to confess her true purpose. She could see no disloyalty to Rowell in doing so. Moreover, she was interested to hear Pelham's views about his sister. She was glad now that, having nothing better to do with his afternoon, he had offered to drive her into the village, and she had accepted.

Pelham listened with casual interest to her opinion of Dodie's condition. When she came to the end of her brief account, he shrugged his broad shoulders as he guided the horse past Havorhurst church into the High Street. Although not actually raining, the air was cold and damp, and few people were abroad in the streets.

"Since you have asked my views, I will happily give them," he said in a more serious tone of voice than he usually employed. "I think you may be stirring up a hornets' nest, Willow. Grandmère will bitterly resent your interference, and if, by some miracle, old Forbes were to support you, she will resent that, too. Nor can you expect Rowell to go against Grandmère. He never does. You will only antagonize him, and that is no way to start your married life."

Willow regarded him unhappily.

"But, Pelham, your advice does not give consideration to poor Dodie. Why must she be condemned to what is merely an existence, simply because the enrichment of her life might upset Grandmère and Rowell?"

Pelham looked surprised.

"Do you know, I have never really thought much about Dodie's way of life. It has never been any different that I can remember, and it certainly never crossed my mind that it could be improved." He pulled the horse to a halt outside the doctor's house, and, turning, smiled as he climbed down to help her out of the trap. "Why not wait and see what Forbes has to say," he suggested. "But just don't be disappointed if he confirms Grandmère's opinions."

As Willow was shown into the house by an elderly maid, she tried not to feel further misgivings, now that Pelham had repeated the same warning Rowell had given as to their grandmother's attitude. She was deep in thought, pondering the matter, while the maid went to find the doctor. He now came into the small, rather dingy room that Willow took to be his surgery.

"Lady Rochford! I am indeed honored by your call. I trust that you are not indisposed in any way?"

Willow regarded the man with interest. Although still in

his early fifties, his hair was stone grey, giving him the appearance of a much older man. His side whiskers, too, were grizzled, and his pale blue eyes were half hidden by steel-rimmed spectacles. He was a large-boned, tall man whose physical strength was at variance with an innately weak character.

Like everyone else in the village, John Forbes had been aware for weeks that the eldest of the Rochford boys had married the wealthy young American girl who had been a guest at the Manor two years previously. He regarded the new young mistress of Rochford speculatively. There was no denying her prettiness, he thought. That combination of pale gold hair and dark brown eyes was compelling. Perhaps, if he were to ingratiate himself with her, he might yet find himself invited to the Manor other than for the purpose of treating its occupants. The Americans were known not to be so class-conscious as the British.

"The purpose of my visit is very simple," Willow now told him. "My husband and I feel that we should know more about the true condition of his little sister, Dorothy. Will you be so good as to enlighten me?"

The doctor hurrumphed.

"Ah, yes, little Miss Dodie. She is not ill, I trust?"

"On the contrary," Willow replied. "I found her this morning in quite excellent health—and spirits. I do not wish to question Lady Rochford's views, as you will appreciate, but nevertheless I find it difficult to accept her statement that Dodie is mentally, as well as physically, impaired. Lady Rochford tells me you will endorse her opinion, and I have come to ask you to make the matter quite clear to me. *Is Dodie mentally ill?*"

John Forbes scratched his head, and his fingers tapped nervously on the top of his desk as he wondered how best to extricate himself from the highly embarrassing situation young Lady Rochford had put him in.

"Such matters cannot be answered with a direct 'yes' or 'no,' " he prevaricated. "The child is very retarded; there is no doubt as to that fact. As you know, she has severe physical deformities to her left arm and leg and is very delicate."

"That I do not question," Willow persisted. "But is her mind impaired, Doctor Forbes?"

"One could not expect it to be normal, my dear Lady

Rochford. The degree of abnormality is, of course, open to question. But seclusion, freedom from stress of any kind, plenty of good food and rest—these are natural precautions against any tendency for the brain to succumb."

Willow frowned. She guessed correctly that the doctor was avoiding a direct reply.

"To succumb to *what*, Doctor Forbes?" she insisted.

The man looked at her uneasily. Had she not been told about the weakness in the family, he wondered? As if reading his thoughts, Willow continued:

"I am aware that Dodie's mother had melancholia. I am also aware that there were two little girls who died in infancy. Is this a hereditary weakness or not, Doctor?"

Her companion gave a falsely bright laugh.

"My dear young lady, medical science is not always able to be as precise as you might, in your inexperience of such matters, suppose. We as a profession, are still only on the fringe of the discovery of the workings of the brain. However, it has long been established that weaknesses of this kind are indeed passed down the generations. Naturally, Lady Rochford is anxious—has always been concerned—that her granddaughter should be protected as far as possible from this tendency. I am glad to say that her—our—methods—of treating the child have so far proved very satisfactory."

Willow drew a deep breath.

"Do I understand, from all you have said, that you think a more normal life might be harmful to her? Because I myself cannot believe that it could harm anyone to look at picture books, see the sunlight, enjoy such simple pursuits as threading beads or copying letters. I feel very strongly indeed that the little girl needs occupation, and I would like your agreement that we should at least see how such pastimes affect her. If she were to show signs of stress, then they could be stopped at once."

The doctor walked to the window and stared out into the street. His visitor's suggestion was not unreasonable, he told himself. He recognized Pelham waiting in the trap, but his thoughts were not concerned with that particular Rochford. He would like to get off on the right foot by pleasing the new young Baroness, and, from her earlier remark, it sounded as if her husband supported her view. As for old Lady Rochford—he knew only too well that her main concern was that the unfortunate little cripple should not be on view.

"We do not want all the boys' friends and other visitors to the household to be embarrassed by the child's unfortunate deformities," she had stated bluntly—was it eleven years ago? "It could prejudice my grandsons' chances of making good marriages. We cannot avoid all gossip, but we can at least curtail the details becoming a matter for first-hand knowledge. Let the child remain confined to her own quarters, where she can enjoy every comfort and avoid the indignity of being gawped at by the servants."

The doctor sighed.

"If it is your wish to give the little girl a few playthings, I can see no harm in it," he said now to Willow. "But if there is the slightest deterioration in her condition—"

"But of course, Doctor," Willow interrupted, her heart singing with triumph. "I will take great care that Dodie is not overtaxed, I promise you!"

Her mood of euphoria carried her out to the trap, where, impulsively, she hugged Pelham. He looked surprised when she recounted the discussion. Then he grinned as he handed her up into the trap.

"You are pretty enough, Willow, to have quite seduced the poor fellow against his better judgment," he said. "So where do you wish to go now—the village store?"

With his customary good nature, he waited patiently while Willow went into the little shop which also served as a post office. She and the Rochford boys had come to buy sweets here during that idyllic summer she had spent at the Manor, and the old woman who ran the store greeted her with a beaming smile.

"I'll be with you in just a minute, Miss Willow—I mean, Lady Rochford," she corrected herself quickly. "I must finish serving this gentleman and I'll be right with you."

For the first time, Willow noticed the tall, thin, somewhat untidy young man standing at the far end of the shop. Seeing her eyes upon him, he raised his hat politely. Willow had the feeling that she had seen him before, but, momentarily, she could not remember upon what occasion. He was certainly not one of the villagers, nor a farmer, yet he did not quite have the air of one of the Rochford family friends. His clothes looked shabby, and his light brown hair was badly in need of the attentions of the village barber.

"May I presume to introduce myself, Lady Rochford," he said, stepping forward and smiling pleasantly from large, attractive grey eyes. "My name is James McGill, and I'm the schoolmaster."

Willow held out her gloved hand in greeting.

"I suspect that you have been sent here this afternoon by Providence," she said in her open friendly way. "You see, Mr. McGill, I am here to choose some reading and writing materials for my little sister-in-law—she is eleven years old, but an invalid. Who better than your good self can advise me on the most suitable materials."

James McGill smiled again. He had never been up to the Manor, but he knew all about the Rochford family and had heard about the ailing child. Village gossip had it that the little girl was terribly deformed, and deranged as well. He was surprised to hear of Willow's mission.

He selected on her behalf a slate, chalks, and a picture book or two, while Willow chose some colored beads and a packet of Japanese flowers. These tiny specks of paper had but to be dropped into a glass of water to spread themselves out into little blossoms, which Willow could already imagine Dodie watching with delight.

"Do please call upon me if there is anything in the future you think the little girl might require. If, as you say, she cannot yet read or write, perhaps I could devise some simple lessons for her?" the schoolmaster suggested agreeably.

"That is exceedingly kind of you, Sir," Willow said warmly. She must ask Rowell if she might invite this pleasant young man to the Manor—perhaps even to visit little Dodie with a view to making an assessment of her intellectual capabilities.

But Pelham soon poured cold water on this idea as he drove Willow home.

"Schoolmasters, like doctors and parsons, my dear Willow, are not our social equals. Personally, I would be quite agreeable to talk to such fellows, but you can be assured Grandmère will not receive them, nor Rowell."

"Oh, dear!" Willow said sighing. "I suppose one day I

shall learn all the do's and don'ts I need to know if I am to make Rowell a good wife. You'll help me, won't you, Pelham? I shan't be a bit angry if you point out to me any occasion where I seem to transgress."

Pelham's face softened in a wry grin.

"My dearest sister-in-law, if you really mean that you want my advice, then let me warn you against too impulsive an announcement of your plans for Dodie. Grandmère is certainly not going to like it, and since Rowell inferred that you should mind your own business, your afternoon's work can hardly be expected to endear you to him. Who was it who said, '*Softly, softly, catchee monkey?*' Rowell hates being pushed into anything, so why not be casual and a little vague at first. As for Mr. James McGill, I would not mention *him* at all."

Although Willow, with her quick intelligence, could see at once that Pelham might well be right, the fact itself depressed her. She would have liked it so much better if she could have shared her pleasure and excitement with Rowell and felt that they were working together for the same end—to make his little sister's life happier.

"I love him so much," she spoke her thoughts aloud.

Beside her, Pelham's cheerful face took on a look of sternness.

"I know you do, and although you may have felt that I had no right to speak as I did when I came upon you telling Rowell how you felt about him, I was not joking when I warned you not to let him mean too much to you, Willow. I should really hate to see you hurt."

"Hurt? But why, Pelham? Rowell and I love one another deeply and——"

"And my dear brother Rowell needed money when he married you, Willow. The Rochford's financial affairs have been in a sad way these past two years. I am sorry if I sound cruel, but it is probably kinder to advise you of the truth than to allow you to blind yourself with a great many childish fantasies about love."

Willow's face darkened with anger; her eyes flashed furiously as she said:

"How can you possibly know how Rowell feels about me, Pelham? I think you are jealous of your brother and you want to come between us. To suggest that he married me for my money is a despicable thing for you to do."

Pelham looked down at her with a mixture of pity and irony.

"Jealous I most certainly am, Willow, and I am the first to admit it. Two years ago, when we danced together in the long gallery and I kissed you—do you remember?—I was certain that you were going to grow into the most lovely and desirable of women. Well, you have not disappointed me. Had you returned to England unmarried, I should most certainly have set my cap for you. You will never be entirely safe with me, Willow. I find you far too attractive. But, be that as it may, I am also very fond of you and I would like to believe that Rowell will make you happy. But he does not love you in the way that you so obviously love him. Do not expect it of him, Willow."

But she did expect it, and her mind totally rejected Pelham's horrible suggestion that Rowell had married her because she was rich. He had said he loved her; sworn that he did. He was her husband . . .

Almost as if set upon the task of disproving his brother's warnings, Rowell was at his most affectionate as the family gathered in the big dining room for the evening meal. Grandmère had decided to grace them with her presence, and it was Rowell who eased any possible awkwardness as to who would sit at the top of the table opposite to him by suggesting to Willow that *she* should sit beside him.

"I have barely had a chance to speak to you all day, my dear," he said in an undertone. "You are looking so lovely tonight. That oyster-pink gown is most becoming. I swear, I cannot take my eyes from you."

He continued to pay her small delightful compliments throughout the meal, and Willow felt herself relax. It was as if they were back in the St. Regis Hotel in New York on their honeymoon.

Strangely enough, Willow thought, neither he nor Grandmère questioned her about her afternoon's outing. Remembering Pelham's advice, she herself did not raise the subject. Her overriding concern for the moment was the need to be reassured of Rowell's love. She was very aware of Pelham's eyes turned frequently in her direction, but she ignored him, certain that he was once again teasing, mocking her, and that she need not have taken his words in the trap so much to heart.

Her last doubts vanished completely later that night, for no sooner had Nellie left the bedroom than Rowell appeared in his nightrobe from the adjoining dressing room. His dark, handsome face was softened in a smile as he approached the bed, saying:

"I thought it would never be time for us decently to retire for the night. It would have been unseemly, I think, had I appeared too obviously anxious to take my bride to bed, do you not agree?"

He took off his robe and, still wearing his nightshirt, climbed into the fourposter beside her. For the first time that she could remember, he did not extinguish the light. With one hand he began to stroke the silky strands of her hair, with the other to caress her breast.

"You are very lovely, very desirable," he murmured in a low voice. "And I am well aware that my brothers envy me. I saw the way Pelham was regarding you and I know very well what he was thinking. He was wishing himself in my shoes—the young devil!"

"It may not be proper for a woman to say such things, but *I* think *you* are beautiful," Willow whispered, "and I am very happy that you should find me so."

Rowell did not seem displeased. His breathing quickened and, flinging back the bedclothes, he took hold of her nightdress and impatiently pulled it over her head. She heard his cry of admiration as she was revealed to him, and at the same time, her own breath came in a little gasp of nervous pleasure. Shyly, she became aware that her small pink nipples were fully erect, as if with a will of their own they were demanding the touch of his lips. But it was her mouth Rowell kissed as his hands reached hungrily for the tiny circle of her waist and then moved down to the gentle swell of her satin-smooth thighs.

Instinctively, Willow's hands moved downward to feel her lover's body. She was still a little afraid of this strange symbol of manhood, with its seemingly independent will to enlarge and alter. She knew that it would hurt her when Rowell plunged deeply into her body, and yet still she longed for it. Even after he had withdrawn from her, that longing remained, and it surprised her that at one moment passion could be so forceful and all-pervading, and then as suddenly become motionless, passive, lifeless. She was certain that there must be a great deal more for her to learn about this side of her married life, and that it was only her own lack of experience that left her still needing without knowing what it was she wanted; sad without cause for unhappiness; lonely even with her lover's arms around her.

But this night of loving might be different, she thought, as she felt Rowell's body begin to change; heard his quick excited breathing and knew that very soon now he would search between her legs and find his way into her secret interior. Her own excitement was no less than his, she believed, as she clung to him, her hips moving instinctively in rhythm with him. This time, unlike the previous occasions, she felt a growing sweetness that was part pain pervading her breasts, her stomach, her groin. Her body was reaching, soaring, crying out for Rowell to carry her into the heights to the mysterious magic that awaited them there.

But, suddenly, Rowell's movements ceased. He gave a small groan of pleasure, and his grip upon her thighs slackened. Her sense of loss was like an outrage as the tumult in her veins refused to quieten. She clung to him, near to tears.

"Rowell, Rowell," she cried. "I love you, I love you!"

"I love you too, my dearest," he murmured. "Lie quiet now and let us sleep. You, too, must be tired." With casual kindness, he kissed her gently. Sleepily, he thought with some surprise that his young wife had actually seemed to enjoy the marital act. He had believed this to be uncommon in women who, he had imagined, looked upon their husbands' demands as a duty to be fulfilled. Georgina was different, of course, but then Georgina was not born a lady, and actresses were of a very different breed.

Rowell fell asleep before reaching any conclusion on the matter. His young wife lay awake fighting the threatening tears. She comforted herself with the thought that Pelham had been wrong. Rowell's love for her was as deep and as passionate as a devoted husband's should be. It was her fault, not his, if she were unhappy now when he was so obviously content. He had proved his love for her and his need for her, and it was ridiculous to want more—without even knowing what it was she wanted.

They loved one another in every way, and with that she must be content.

Rowell's mood when he awoke the following morning was benign, if not demonstratively affectionate. He lightly kissed the top of Willow's head as he climbed out of bed.

"Perhaps you would like to ride to the railway station with me after lunch to meet Cousin Lucienne and Silvie," he suggested as he rang the bell to summon his valet. Willow sat up in bed and clasped her arms around her knees.

Her eyes glowing, she voiced her pleasure in the prospect.

"You have many duties to occupy you this morning, I don't doubt," Rowell said casually. His remark prompted Willow to speak of the matter uppermost in her thoughts.

"After I have arranged the menus with Cook and talked to Mrs. Spears about our guests' arrival, I am going to see Dodie," she replied, watching her husband's face anxiously. He gave no sign of disapproval. Willow continued to adopt the vague manner Pelham had suggested as desirable.

"Doctor Forbes seems a very reasonable man," she said. "I had a word with him yesterday, and he voiced no objection to Dodie having a few playthings. What will *you* do this morning, my love?"

"I have papers to occupy me," Rowell answered as his valet knocked on the door. He seemed uninterested in her references to his little sister. "I will see you at luncheon, my dear."

As soon as he had departed into his dressing room, Willow rang for Nellie, her heart singing. She resolved to thank Pelham. However unpleasant he may have been in his references to Rowell, he had certainly been instrumental in helping her gain her own ends regarding Dodie, without need to dispute the matter with her husband.

The little girl seemed quite overwhelmed by Willow's gifts. Starry-eyed, she thanked her benefactor over and over again.

"You must never overtire yourself!" Willow warned the child, watching Dodie's rapt face as she regarded the tiny Japanese blooms opening magically in the water. "You and I share a little conspiracy," she said, "a special kind of secret. One day I want you to be able to learn to read and write, Dodie, but if you become ill, then I shall be forced to take away all your new things. Do you understand? You must promise me you will tell Violet the very first moment you become weary."

"I promise, I promise, I promise," the little girl cried, forgetful in that instant of her withered limb as she tried to fling both arms around Willow. The crippled arm moved only slightly, the tiny hand hanging limp from beneath the over-large sleeve of her nightgown. Pity stirred Willow's heart, but she steeled herself against showing it as she kissed the warm, soft cheek.

Dodie's huge blue eyes were round with excitement.

"Toby said that perhaps one day I might be able to read and write," she breathed the words. Now it was her turn to tell Willow a secret: that she loved Toby best of everyone in the world. "Except perhaps you," she said shyly.

Willow laughed.

"That's only because I have given you some nice playthings," she said. "If I took them all away again, you'd soon stop loving me."

"I wouldn't! I think you are beautiful and I'll love you for ever and ever!" the child cried.

Willow remained long enough to show her how to use the copy-writing book and then hurried back downstairs. Rowell's relations were her first visitors and she wanted to make quite sure that there was nothing lacking in the guest rooms that they might want. Fires had already been lit in each bedroom, and a housemaid was putting warming pans between the sheets. Mrs. Spears had taken care of every detail.

There being still a half hour to fill in before luncheon, Willow decided to pay a visit to Toby. As she had suspected, he was in his laboratory. He immediately set aside the notes he was writing and greeted her with his warm smile.

"This is an unexpected pleasure, Willow," he said as he removed some heavy books from an armchair so that she might be seated. "I rarely have a chance to talk to you except at mealtimes." He dusted the cushions with his handkerchief apologetically.

Willow looked at this strange, unpredictable brother-in-law in surprise.

"But I had imagined you far too busy engaged upon your studies to have time for idle chatter," she said, smiling.

He returned her smile, but his tone of voice was serious as he replied:

"I may not know you very well as yet, Willow, but I do not think you are given to that kind of feminine chatter which, I have to admit, seems a great waste of time —who was at which ball and who wore the latest fashion; who was the belle of the ball and who was the wallflower! No, I have not my dear brother Pelham's capacity for absorbing myself in such trivialities."

"Your work is important to you, I know," Willow said. "That is why I did not wish to disturb you."

"Then I am glad we have this opportunity to resolve the misunderstanding," said Toby quietly. "I am never so busy that I would not welcome an interruption from you."

Willow felt suddenly very relaxed and happy.

"In future, I shall brave the Professor in his den more often," she told him. "I have been wanting to talk to you for some time, Toby . . . about Dodie."

Toby's expression softened and he drew up his chair closer to Willow's.

"Dodie has been telling me how wonderful you have been to her."

"I am far from sure that 'wonderful' is the right adjective," Willow replied with shy pleasure at Toby's compliment. Briefly, she recounted her activities on behalf of the child.

"I fear I am not quite as brave as you, Willow," Toby told her shamefacedly. "I gave up the whole idea of arranging a more normal life for Dodie when I realized what a hopeless battle it would be. I see now I was wrong, and that instead of waiting for Grandmère to give her permission, I should have done as you did and simply acted without her authority. I congratulate you, my dear Willow. And please count on me for any support you may need in future!"

Willow laughed happily.

"I may need your support very soon—but in other matters," she said. "I want to ask you about Cousin Lucienne and her daughter. I know they are Grandmère's relatives and I wondered—"

Toby grinned as he interrupted her.

"I know what you were wondering—whether they would be as severe and overpowering as Grandmère. Well, the answer is 'yes' to Cousin Lucienne and 'no' to Silvie. I am sure that you will dislike the former and love the latter. We all love Silvie. She is very pretty, very naughty, and very amusing. Grandmère gets angry with her, but Silvie simply takes no notice. You will like her, Willow. I am certain of it."

Toby's assessment of her feelings was surprisingly accurate, Willow decided as she became acquainted with her visitors. Grandmère's niece, Lucienne le Chevalier, was a younger edition of her elderly aunt. Sallow-skinned, almond-eyed, she had the same short, plump figure that was common to Grandmère and Queen Victoria. Her dark hair was peppered with grey; her eyes, nearly black, were bright, intelligent, and inquisitive. Insofar as her dumpy figure permitted, she was immensely chic, as indeed was her daughter. Both had brought trunkloads of clothes, nearly all of which were the latest Parisian models. Cousin Lucienne's manner toward Willow was only a little short of patronizing and she monopolized the conversation at mealtimes.

But Silvie, as Toby had predicted, was both beautiful and charming. Although she, too, had the olive skin of her Latin forebears, her complexion was flawless. Her dark, almond-shaped eyes were a great deal larger than her mother's, soft, expressive, and more often than not alight with mischievous laughter.

She was clearly quite impervious to her great aunt's disapproval. During dinner on the first night of their visit, the meal was punctuated with a heated contretemps regarding the little dog Silvie had brought with her from France.

Grandmère had made it a rule that no dogs should be allowed in the house. The labradors and Springer spaniels belonging to the Rochford boys, who kept such animals for shooting, were housed in kennels near the stables.

"My little Bijou is far too small to be a nuisance to anyone, Grandmère," Silvie said firmly when old Lady Rochford asked her to remove the dog to external quarters. "He is a papillon and quite tiny. Besides, he might die of the cold outside."

Outraged, Grandmère turned to her niece for support, but Cousin Lucienne shrugged her plump shoulders helplessly.

"If you cannot persuade Silvie, then I cannot, Aunt Clotilde," she said. In a lowered tone, she added, "Ever since her marriage, the girl has been quite unmanageable. I can do little, I fear. She is independent of me and *hélas, elle le sait,"* she ended in French.

Grandmère snorted angrily. She disapproved most strongly of females being financially independent, especially if they were as young as Silvie.

"You had best find her another husband, Lucienne— and quickly," she said. "That should not be too difficult since the girl has money . . . and good looks," she added grudgingly.

But Silvie von Senden had no intention whatever of putting her widowhood behind her, as she told Willow that night. The two girls sat on the side of Silvie's bed conversing.

"To do so would be merely to put myself back in bondage," she said, smiling. "Now I am free to come and go as I please, buy what I want, even flirt with whom I like, and there is no husband to forbid me."

"But did you not love your husband?" Willow inquired. "Are you not lonely without him? Even after only a few weeks of marriage, I do not think I could endure to be without my Rowell."

Silvie gave a Gallic shrug of her shoulders.

"Ah, Rowell," she said expressively, rolling her "r" in the French manner. "He is very handsome, I admit, the most handsome of all the brothers. Although, Pelham—" she smiled at Willow conspiratorially "—he is much more amusing to flirt with. Rowell is so *serious.* But then he is the eldest and head of the family, so I suppose it is natural. You will be good for him, Willow. It is high time he had a wife and family."

She bent down to pick up the little white dog to which Grandmère had objected so furiously. Laughing, she handed him to Willow.

"Is he not enchanting, *mon petit* Bijou? I do believe I have become more attached to him than to my poor late spouse, Bernard. At least Bijou does not argue with me and he does exactly what I tell him, whereas Bernard could be very stubborn."

Though shocked by the French girl's remarks, Willow was also amused.

"Perhaps you should not have married so young," she said smiling.

Now it was Silvie's turn to smile.

"And who is saying so? Am I not right in believing you yourself are but seventeen years old?"

"But *you* were only fifteen," Willow argued.

"And my husband was in his fifties," Silvie replied, sighing. "But there were advantages, Willow. I shared his bed, but I did not have to make love with him. He was —how do you say in English—*incapable*."

"The word is the same in English," Willow said, shocked once more by this young woman's frankness, yet curious too. She longed to ask if Silvie were still a virgin, but dared not voice so personal a question. Silvie, however, must have read her thoughts, for she said casually:

"I have a delightful young lover in Paris. Mama knows nothing of him, of course, for we keep our meetings secret. He is an actor in the Comédie Française, and she would definitely not approve. But he is very attractive, and although I do not love him, I enjoy very much our afternoons in bed and in his *appartement*."

Silvie might be shocking, but it was quite impossible not to like her, Willow decided. She herself had had a number of friends in her own country—girls of her own age with whom she had exchanged the usual childish confidences. But never had she had a friend like Silvie, who seemed to her the epitome of sophistication. She was flattered that the French girl seemed to like her too. They became close companions, and throughout the ensuing Christmas festivities, Silvie's laughter brought a spirit of light-hearted happiness into the old house.

Though Aunt Milly, Grandmère, and the sour-faced Cousin Lucienne viewed the younger members of the family disapprovingly, Silvie's sense of fun was infectious. Even Rupert came out of his doldrums to help decorate the Christmas tree—a huge fir brought in from the estate by two of the gardeners and placed in the great hall.

Francis, too, responded to Silvie's cajoling and tacked holly and mistletoe to the picture rails.

Perhaps Silvie's greatest triumph was persuading the entire family on Christmas Eve to go to the music room and sing carols to Rupert's accompaniment on the piano. Later, the younger members of the family went to midnight Mass at St. Stephen's, riding there through the frosty night air in two carriages, Silvie's clear voice ringing out over the clip-clop of the horses' hooves.

Snuggled beside Rowell beneath the heavy carriage rug, Willow was aware of an ache of pure happiness. Her heart seemed so full of joy that not even the realization that this was her first Christmas without her mother and father could diminish her content. Rowell held her hand and smiled at Silvie's sallies. And after the service was over, he gave sovereigns to the verger and to all the members of the choir.

Willow longed to be able to tell him about the little Christmas tree she had set up in Dodie's room—on which she had hung two new picture books, a box of wax crayons, and a kaleidoscope. The last had been the schoolmaster's idea, for she had met James McGill a second time in the village, and he had shown great interest in her account of Dodie's progress.

"By next Christmas," Willow had told Toby, "I mean to have Dodie downstairs with the rest of us. You'll help me, won't you, Toby?"

As always, he had promised to do anything he could. Willow's happiness would have been total had it been Rowell who had promised his support. But he seemed to avoid any discussion about his sister, and she felt obliged to respect his wishes. More than ever now, she did not want anything to spoil his obvious contentment with his wife and his marriage. Willow did not intend to tell him until she was absolutely sure, but she was almost certain she was pregnant. It was very, very important to her that Rowell should be pleased. She would be happy to have his child, provided he, too, welcomed it.

Willow had expected to ride back with him from the church, but when she finished talking to the Reverend Appleby, who had cornered her in the porch, there was no sign of Rowell or the four-seater landau. Only Pelham sat waiting for her—in the brougham.

"All the others have gone ahead, Willow," he told her. "They were getting cold, so I told them I would wait for you."

Willow felt a quick shiver of misgiving. Surely her own husband could have waited . . .

"Jump in, dear sister-in-law," Pelham interrupted her thoughts as he stepped forward to take her arm. "And don't look so woebegone. It isn't the end of the world."

As he helped her into the brougham and pulled the rug over their knees, he looked down at her face and sighed.

"You must not blame Rowell for deserting you," he said, shrewdly guessing her thoughts. "If you must know, I am to blame. I persuaded them all to go. I wanted the chance to be alone with you."

Willow was in no mood for joking. She said sharply:

"Don't be silly, Pelham. I know you mean it well, but—"

"But it happens to be true," Pelham interrupted as he searched for her gloved hand. "Frankly, it amazes me, Willow, that you can go around oblivious to the feelings of those poor mortals not within the charmed circle of your love. You notice the merest frown from Rowell, but the looks of hungry adoration I cast continually in your direction you totally ignore. What must I do to show you how crazily in love with you I am?"

Now Willow could smile, albeit disapprovingly.

"I happen to be your brother's wife," she said, "and you should be ashamed of yourself, Pelham, talking in such a manner when but five minutes ago you were in the holy precincts of a church."

"As if that could alter the way I feel about you!" Pelham rejoined. "I know you don't believe a word I am saying. I joke too often, that's my trouble. Willow . . . I have other troubles. May I speak of them to you?"

Willow was glad of the darkness so that Pelham could not see the surprise on her face. She could not remember ever having heard him speak in so portentous a tone.

"It all happened while you and Rowell were in America," Pelham said in a low, tense voice. "I was very stupid: I gambled my next year's allowance and hit a bad streak. I thought I could win back my losses and I signed some promissory notes. Now they have been presented—

and the fact is, Willow, I cannot meet them. My account is already two months overdrawn."

Willow breathed a sigh of relief. Although dismayed by his revelation, a gambling debt was not an insoluble problem. She had been afraid that she might not be able to help him.

"Don't worry about it," she said quickly. "I will speak to Rowell tonight and I know he—"

"You must not mention this to Rowell!"

The sharpness of his tone shocked her into silence.

"Don't you know anything at all about my dear brother?" Pelham said with unintentional cruelty. "He would throw me out of house and home if he but heard the half of my indebtedness. Rowell lives by convention, Willow, by moral rectitude, principles, family honor, and all that. He's so damned controlled he wouldn't allow himself to get into a scrape, even a minor one. And this is a major one. *I signed notes promising to pay money I knew I had not got.* That's how serious it is."

"How . . . how much, Pelham?" Willow asked uneasily.

"Two hundred pounds."

Willow did some quick calculations in her head.

"Eight hundred dollars. That is not too awful, Pelham. I . . . I think I have that amount somewhere in my possession. Papa gave me a bundle of notes as I was getting on the train. He said . . . he said to keep it in case I ever needed money of my own. I . . . I forgot all about it. Will that help you, Pelham?"

"My God, will it help!" Pelham said. "Willow, I hate to take money—from a woman, too. But I must! I swear I will pay back every penny. I swear it on my life. Promise me you will never breathe a word of this to Rowell?"

I can give Pelham the money he needs far more easily than I can give him that promise, Willow thought wretchedly. Why—when all she wanted in the world was to share her life with Rowell—must she have so many secrets from him? Dodie . . . the schoolmaster . . . and now Pelham's troubles.

"Promise me, Willow. I cannot be at peace unless you do."

"Very well, I promise," Willow said.

For a moment or two they sat in silence. Then Pelham said quietly:

"Do you despise me, Willow? I think I would prefer exposure and disgrace to the loss of your respect, your affection."

"Oh, Pelham," Willow said sighing. "We all make mistakes, and you—well, I doubt if with your nature, you could ever stay out of trouble for long. You did a very silly thing, but no, I don't despise you. As to my affection for you, you are Rowell's brother and mine too, now."

"And that is the only reason for caring about me?" Pelham's voice was unexpectedly tense. "You cannot like me for myself, rogue that I am?"

He sounded so young and wistful, Willow laughed.

"All women love a rogue," she said, "or so my father always maintained. So let us remain good friends, Pelham." She was unprepared for the sudden kiss he planted on her mouth. It was not a brotherly kiss, she thought uneasily. But Pelham was smiling again, his old teasing self.

"Just to show my gratitude," he said, and kissed her again, but this time it was no more than a feather-light touch on her cheek.

Chapter Five

December 1891–November 1892

ON CHRISTMAS DAY THE ENTIRE FAMILY, INCLUDING Grandmère, attended church, filling the pews reserved for the Rochford family. The remainder of the day was spent quietly at the manor, the younger members of the family playing whist and then, encouraged by Silvie, enacting charades before an audience consisting of Grandmère, Aunt Milly, and Cousin Lucienne.

Rowell was in the very best of spirits. Since the summer of '89 Willow had not seen him in such a light-hearted mood. Moreover, he continued to treat her most affectionately, congratulating her upon the superb Christmas luncheon which, he said, exceeded Mrs. Jupp's usual excellence.

The festive mood continued into Boxing Day. A number of family friends were invited for the traditional shooting party, the gentlemen arriving after breakfast with their loaders and dogs. In all there were ten guns, Rowell, Pelham, Toby, Rupert and Francis, and five visitors. Rowell's two gamekeepers had promised an excellent day's sport, and by midday, when the ladies drove in their carriages to join the men, Rowell proudly showed Willow the morning's bag laid out for inspection.

Willow was well aware of the methods employed to provide such sport. Young birds were reared in the breeding season especially to enhance the wildlife abounding on the Rochford estate. The guns would be strategically placed behind a hedgerow or copse, and beaters threshed through the trees and undergrowth, driving the game toward the guns. Privately, she thought the sport not a little cruel, although Rowell had assured her that a great many birds escaped, especially if there were poor shots like Toby among the guns. Nevertheless, the morning's tally of pheasants, partridges, rabbits, and hares quite appalled her. She turned away from the sight of furred and feathered corpses with a feeling of nausea.

The floor of the big barn in which the party were to have their lunch was strewn with straw. Servants set up trestle tables and laid out a magnificent cold buffet. But despite their warm clothing, the ladies in particular felt the cold, and Willow's fellow sufferers were more than delighted when she obtained Rowell's agreement that they need not remain, as was customary, to watch the afternoon's shooting.

Later that evening, however, when everyone had departed, he told her not unkindly that she would have to become accustomed to English ways.

"We may very well be invited by the Prince of Wales to a shoot at Sandringham," he told her. "It would not do for you to reveal your disinclination for one of his Royal Highness' favorite sports."

It was his hope to have Willow presented at the earliest opportunity, but early in January the Prince's eldest son, the Duke of Clarence, contracted influenza and a week later he died, despite the doctors' efforts to save him.

Grandmère actually seemed pleased by this unhappy event.

"The boy was uneducable," she said. "He was nothing but a cause for worry and concern to his parents and would never have been worthy to wear the crown of England. His brother George will, on the contrary, make an excellent heir to the throne, mark my words."

The country and the Court went into mourning, and Rowell's hopes of presenting Willow had to be shelved. Willow was not sorry. Doctor Forbes had confirmed that she was pregnant. If not obviously very enthusiastic about becoming a father, Rowell was nevertheless not against the prospect.

"You are a little young yet for motherhood," he suggested. But Willow laughed reassuringly.

"Doctor Forbes says that I am in perfect health."

Nevertheless, she did not want the news made public as yet.

"In particular," she told Rowell, "I do not want Grandmère or my parents told of the forthcoming event. You may think me fanciful, but I would rather wait until nearer my time before informing them, and certainly not until the baby shows."

Clearly, Rowell did not understand why and he merely shrugged away such fancies as part of her condition.

Toby and Pelham were let into the secret and, of course, Willow told Silvie. Silvie professed herself delighted since Willow was so pleased, but she admitted freely that *she* had no wish to bear a child.

"Perhaps I am unnatural and lack the normal maternal instinct," she confessed. "But pregnancy is a tie, and I wish to be free!"

"That is only because you are not in love as I am," Willow argued. "If you were happily married, Silvie—"

But the French girl had interrupted.

"No, Willow! Marriage, too, is a tie, and I wish to be free."

Willow could not understand Silvie's desire for freedom. But at the end of the month, the lively, friendly girl returned to Paris with her mother; Rowell departed to London for a week "on business," and Willow was engulfed by waves of loneliness.

A heavy fall of snow prevented her going out, and

the days spent cooped up in the old drafty house seemed endless as she fretted for Rowell's return. Pelham tried to distract her by explaining to her the intricacies of English politics. He had been surprised to discover that Willow had a quick intelligence as well as a somewhat unusual—for a female—interest in such matters. He described how the Conservatives, now being called the Unionist party, were governing the country. The Marquis of Salisbury was Prime Minister, he informed her. Mr. Gladstone, the elder statesman now aged eighty-two, was leading the Liberal party in opposition.

When she was not in Pelham's company, Willow spent a great deal of time with Dodie. The little girl was trying to copy the letters of the alphabet.

"She's ever so much happier, Milady," the faithful Violet said. "And she's eating more and sleeping better, too."

With Rowell absent, Grandmère never ceased to voice her criticism of the rehabilitation program Willow was employing with her crippled granddaughter.

"Mark my words, Dorothy will have a relapse in due course; then you will see how right I was," the old lady said in cold, disapproving tones.

But there was little Grandmère could do to prevent Dodie's enjoyment of this new way of life, in view of Doctor Forbes' compliance. Realizing that he had antagonized old Lady Rochford, he continued, on his weekly visits, to caution against too much mental activity. But Dodie's starved brain was insatiable.

"I am wondering whether I could persuade that kind Mr. McGill to come to the house for a few hours each week to teach Dodie," Willow suggested to Toby. "He takes such an interest in her progress when I see him in the village."

Toby grinned wryly.

"I doubt Doctor Forbes will support such a venture. And you will have Grandmère up in arms," he warned her. "She has a horror of any stranger seeing poor Dodie! Besides which, McGill is a man. A schoolmarm might have been more acceptable."

"But that is quite ridiculous," Willow argued hotly. "Why should it matter? Violet would be present to chaperon, Dodie. As to the child being seen, her arm and leg may be pitiful to look upon, but she is almost pretty. It is not as if she looks in any degree abnormal, and Mr. McGill is far too nice a man to concern himself with such things."

Toby sighed.

"Sometimes people, especially old people, are irrational," he said. "I know Grandmère is quite convinced that our mother was deranged. I have been reading a great deal lately on the subject." He picked up two large leather-bound books. *The Household Physician,* compiled by McGregor-Robertson and published only last year," he told her, smiling. "In one of these, he makes no suggestion that melancholia is hereditary. As to the two infant girls who died—how could they have been melancholics at that age? I am quite convinced that there is no connection between their deaths and my mother's; and certainly no connection between them and Dodie's unfortunate deformities. One day I hope to prove it."

Willow felt an immense relief, for it had crossed her mind, despite all her attempts to ignore such morbid speculation, that the child she was carrying might not be perfect. If Rowell had any such misgivings, he did not voice them. He returned home at the end of the week in a mood Willow could only describe to herself as vaguely distracted. His thoughts seemed to be elsewhere, and when she questioned him, he told her evasively that he had "certain business worries," and that she must not concern herself with affairs she could not understand.

"Monetary concerns?" Willow asked unguardedly. They were in their bedroom by themselves, Nellie and Rowell's valet both being at tea in the servants' hall.

Rowell stared at his young wife, frowning.

"What put such a thought into your head?" he questioned in a low, vibrant tone. The mood of disquiet which had encompassed Willow this past week now erupted into unexpected defiance.

"You speak as if I were incapable of understanding anything of any import, Rowell. I may be female and young, but I am *not* stupid. I happen to know that your family suffered some kind of financial strain recently, and that the settlement my father made upon me when we married eased that strain. I was just now expressing my concern lest it had not been sufficient to eradicate all the difficulties."

Rowell masked his astonishment with anger. He supposed that his father-in-law must have passed on these facts to Willow despite his assurances that he would not speak of it to anyone. Was it possible, he wondered, that Willoughby Tetford had warned his daughter that he, Rowell, might be marrying her for her money?

"Well, did your father warn you that my motives for marrying you were purely mercenary?" he asked accusingly.

Willow looked at her husband in horrified dismay.

"You should not say such a thing, Rowell, even if you do not mean it seriously."

Rowell's face was stony.

"I asked the question because I wanted a direct anwer," he said coldly.

Willow's dismay turned to an anger born of fear. She could not believe that she was having this conversation with Rowell, whom she loved so deeply and tenderly.

"You have no justification for even suggesting that I have ever questioned your motives for marrying me, Rowell. I have never doubted that you loved me as sincerely as I love you. But now that you have raised the point, perhaps *you* will tell *me: did you marry me for my money?*"

It was on the tip of her tongue to tell him that Pelham, as well as her father, had so accused him, but caution remained uppermost, for she had no wish to cause trouble between the brothers.

But suddenly, to her intense relief, Rowell's face softened and he put his arms around her, saying:

"Of course I did not, my love. But I thought, mistakenly, that you suspected it. After all, Willow, your father was very generous indeed in the settlement he made upon you. There are bound to be those who question the reasons behind our marriage."

"But I am not one of them!" Willow cried, hugging him fiercely. "It may sound immodest of me to take it as fact that you fell in love with me—a young girl without the kind of background desirable in the wife of an En-

glish baron. But I know you would not lie to me, Rowell.
Nor to anyone. I trust you absolutely."

"And you are very sweet and very dear to me," Rowell said, kissing the top of her head. Then, turning, he
walked away from her. He stood by the window staring
down onto the wind-swept garden, his expression uneasy.
He had but recently told his mistress, Georgina, that his
marriage was a perfect success; that Willow was pliant,
agreeable, and adoring and would cause him no difficulties. He did not want a state of affairs where his young
wife felt cheated, neglected, and became resentful and demanding. Until now, his marriage had affected his life
hardly at all, and he had congratulated himself on his
choice of a wife.

Grandmère had been the first to suggest that since
they were in such severe financial difficulties, he must
make an advantageous marriage, he thought. At the time,
he had mentioned the names of several moderately wealthy
young ladies of his acquaintance, but Grandmère had
pointed out very shrewdly that he would not be able to
marry a second time, and that whatever his wife brought
to the marriage, it must be sufficient to see them secure in
the future as well as being adequate to overcome their
present difficulties.

"Then we must look for a millionairess," Rowell had
rejoined wryly.

It was then Grandmère had recalled the Tetfords—and
Willow. When Rowell suggested the girl might be still too
young for marriage, Grandmère had swept the objection
aside.

"With the kind of money her parents have, the girl
will not stay long without a husband," she said flatly.
"And since she is an American, the fact that she is not
aristocracy will be overlooked by Society. Moreover, I recall her as a pretty child. You could do a lot worse, Rowell."

Indeed, he had been more than fortunate, he told himself. The girl had grown into a very attractive young
woman, and although only Georgina, his mistress of three
years, could really stir his senses, he had been surprised
to discover that Willow by no means left him unmoved.
There were times when he had held her in his arms at
the height of their lovemaking when he had quite forgot-

ten Georgina. And now Willow was carrying his child—a son and heir, he hoped.

He was about to turn and smile at her in the friendliest way when his eye was caught by two figures moving arm in arm through the rhododendron shrubbery on the far side of the front drive. Curiously, he watched as they came closer, for they did not have the appearance either of gardeners or laborers.

Willow came to stand beside him, resting her head against his shoulder.

"I think it is Rupert!" Rowell exclaimed. "How strange that he should be out in the garden at dusk with no hat or coat. I do not recognize the fellow with him, do you, my dear?"

Willow followed his pointing finger.

"Is that not Doctor Forbes' son, Adrian?" she asked. "He has been up to the house several times while you were away. I think Rupert said he is trying to mend the Gottlieb Daimler. Apparently he is much interested in motor wagons and has some knowledge of petrol engines."

Rowell looked pleased. Pelham, in one of his typically impetuous moods, had brought back with him, from a visit to Germany, a motor carriage which he swore would transport them all quite safely at four miles an hour. But the machine had never worked and had been abandoned these past two years in one of the loose boxes in the stables. These powered vehicles seemed to be the coming thing—as indeed, Pelham had forecast. In England and also in Europe, various inventors were producing petrol and gas engine-driven motorcycles as well as carriages; and Willow's father had written recently from America about a "gas buggy" he was thinking of buying.

"I am delighted to know that Rupert is harmlessly occupied," Rowell commented. "He has been like a bear with a sore head ever since he lost his friend, young Douglas, to that Wilde fellow. I heard in London last week that those two are forever in each other's company."

He forbore from mentioning to his young wife that the friendship between the young man and the much older playwright was fast becoming a subject for the most unsavory type of gossip. He doubted whether Willow's innocent upbringing would have left her enlightened as to the kind of behavior attributed to Mr. Wilde, who, although a married man, was blatantly adoring of the handsome Lord Alfred. Tongues were wagging.

Rowell was about to turn away from the window when he saw the two figures pause and quite suddenly embrace one another. Shocked, he looked to see if Willow had noticed, but she had now seated herself in a chair by the fire. She looked very pale, and had his thoughts not been angrily concentrated upon his young brother, he might have noticed that she seemed unwell.

"I have something I wish to discuss with Rupert," he said shortly. "If my valet appears, tell him I will be back presently to change for dinner."

For some time now, Rowell had been uneasy about Rupert. There was no question but that the boy was effeminate in his ways as well as in his looks, and he had always appeared uninterested in the opposite sex. One thing was beyond doubt, Rowell thought: he would have no scandals of that kind bandied about in conversation regarding the Rochford family, and the sooner Rupert was made aware of it the better.

He met his brother in the front hall and brusquely told him to accompany him to the library. Rowell's expression left the younger man in little doubt that trouble was brewing and in even less doubt as to the reason. Before Rowell had voiced the first of his insinuations, Rupert knew that it would be a waste of time trying to enlist the eldest brother's understanding. Rowell never saw any point of view other than his own—or Grandmère's. They were two of a kind, ruthless, even cruel, in their single-minded determination to glorify the Rochfords. He hated them both, knowing only too well that neither had any affection for him.

Bitterly, Rupert reflected that Grandmère found it in her heart—if she truly had one—to dote upon Francis. Yet he knew Francis to be a liar, a cheat, and a supreme egotist. Francis, like Grandmère, scorned their dead mother's memory and felt no pity for their little sister, Dodie. His mind was sharp, cruel, and centered entirely upon himself. His favorite pastime was to taunt Rupert or any other human being he believed too weak to stand up to him. Rowell, too, made no attempt to conceal his preference for Francis. Only Toby and Pelham ever showed him, Rupert, a modicum of the affection he craved and even they were usually too busy with their own affairs to notice him.

Rupert's loneliness had been unbearable until he had met Alfred Douglas. Then he, too, had deserted him for someone far more interesting, famous, amusing. Now, at long last, he had found a new friend—Adrian Forbes, and neither Rowell nor anyone else was going to spoil that friendship.

Adrian fascinated him. He was as opposite to himself as another human being could be. Adrian was daredevil, feckless, laughingly independent, full of fun. To his father's disappointment, he had failed to do well at school academically and had declined further education at college, preferring to mooch around in Havorhurst, flirting with the village girls and tinkering with any piece of machinery he could lay his hands on. There was something of the gypsy in his makeup that drew the serious, sensitive Rupert to him like a magnet. Good-naturedly, Adrian seemed not to care about anything but his beloved engines.

"Does our friendship mean nothing to you?" Rupert had asked him that afternoon. Adrian's hazel-green eyes had glinted with amusement.

"But of course, old fellow. I'm really enjoying my days up here at the manor. With luck, we might get that old engine going by the weekend."

With the same casual indifference, he had allowed Rupert to embrace him when they bade one another farewell. He seemed neither to welcome nor object to Rupert's sentimental gestures. Nor did it appear to bother him that Rupert could not invite him into his home.

"Who cares?" he had replied to Rupert's expression of regret. "You can always come to a meal with us, although I don't suppose you'd find much in common conversationally with my father. He's only able to talk about medicine—a dreadfully boring subject."

Rupert now faced his eldest brother with unusual determination.

"You have nothing whatever with which to reproach me—or Adrian," he said when Rowell voiced his objection to his friendship with the doctor's son. "You may think what you like but . . . but Adrian isn't like that. He has lots of girls. He spends most of his evenings with girls. Ask that silly Violet who looks after Dodie. She'll tell you. So why shouldn't I be friendly with him? He may be only a doctor's son and my social inferior, but I don't care. I like him. He's a good sport."

Rowell looked somewhat relieved. Perhaps, he thought, this lad Adrian would be good for Rupert; teach him a thing or two. A few romps in the hay with a buxom Havorhurst girl would do him no harm at all.

"Very well, Rupert," he said. "But take a word of advice from me: chaps like that—any normal chap—won't take kindly to your sort of sloppy behavior. Only Frenchmen embrace one another. It's just not done, d'you hear?"

Rowell returned to his bedroom in a happier frame of mind, but one that was not to last. He found Nellie bending anxiously over the big fourposter bed in which a white-faced Willow lay with her eyes closed.

"Oh, Sir," Nellie gasped on seeing him. "I fear Milady's going to lose the baby. I've sent one of the footmen to fetch the doctor."

Willow opened her eyes and tried to smile reassuringly at her husband. But pain engulfed her and she could only gasp. Nellie began to weep. Rowell looked at the maid with irritation.

"It does appear as if your mistress is having a miscarriage," he said firmly, "but there's no need to carry on as if she were about to die."

His words had the effect of stopping Nellie's tears as she stared back at him unbelievingly. It was beyond her comprehension how he could be so unconcerned about the loss of the coming child—or more importantly, about his wife's suffering.

Willow, too, had heard Rowell's comment. For a moment she ceased to be aware of the waves of pain engulfing her. She could think of nothing but that Rowell did not care if she lost their child.

She held out her hands to him, longing for him to grasp hold of her and share this ordeal with her. But he did not approach the bedside, and the expression on his face was one of irritation.

"I'll go down and see what is delaying Forbes," he said. "In the meanwhile Aunt Milly can attend to you. I dare say she has some laudanum to relieve the pain."

Willow's protest died on her lips. It was not Aunt Milly she wanted, but Rowell, yet he seemed unable to sense her need.

Then pain gripped her once more as if a cruel knife were tearing her body apart. This time she almost welcomed it, finding it preferable to the pain in her heart.

Chapter Six

March 1892–September 1892

THE EASTER HOLIDAY HAD NOT YET BEGUN. FRANcis was still at Eton, Rupert and Pelham at Oxford. When Willow was strong enough to leave her bed, the big house seemed forlorn and quite empty. Rowell departed once more to London, but returned unexpectedly a day later, his manner toward his young wife changed from the dutiful solicitude he had shown through her convalescence to one of attentive affection.

"You have now been at Rochford for nearly six months, my dear," he said one evening. "You must be finding English country life very tedious. I have therefore accepted tentatively an invitation from Lord and Lady Symington to spend a weekend in April at their country house in Buckinghamshire. You will like Esmé Symington. One of her sisters married an American, and I know Esmé is interested to meet you. Theodore, her husband, is an old friend of mine from my Oxford days. Do you feel up to traveling?"

Willow's eyes shone. She ran to Rowell and put her arms around his neck in a childlike hug.

"I am quite recovered," she assured him. "And I would love to meet your friends, Rowell. I must go and talk to Nellie this very minute about my clothes. By good fortune, I have already arranged for that news magazine, *The Queen,* to be sent to me from London, and it is most informative about the latest fashions. I do not want to seem outdated among your friends."

Rowell smiled indulgently, kissing her soft cheek with unaccustomed tenderness.

"You are very pretty, my dear, when your face lights up with excitement. I must try to think up further surprises for you if so simple an occasion can make you so radiant."

They were alone in the drawing room; and with no servants to observe them, Willow sat herself upon her husband's knee, leaning her cheek against his.

How handsome he is, she thought, the now familiar sensation spreading over her body at his proximity. Out of consideration for her condition, he had slept in his dressing room since her miscarriage. He gave no indication now that he wanted her to behave with more propriety.

"You may buy what you need for the weekend," he said, twisting his finger around a strand of her pale gold hair. "The other day I heard a lady saying how very elegant were the new Madame Swaebe teagowns. She is one of the dressmakers under Royal patronage—Princess Leiningen's, I believe. You have but to telegraph to Burlington Street, and I am sure a selection of gowns and costumes would be sent to you on approval."

Willow might have been surprised if she had stopped to consider it—that her masculine-minded husband was concerning himself with feminine matters—but her thoughts were elsewhere.

"I shall talk to Nellie at once," she said. "My wedding trousseau must be quite out of fashion by now."

Nellie was nearly as excited as Willow since she would be going to Buckinghamshire with her young mistress. But she was also a little apprehensive. She knew that visiting servants were always open to criticism by the resident staff and she was still far from faultless as a lady's maid. Not that her young mistress ever took her to task for her shortcomings, knowing as she did before they left America that Nellie would have much still to learn. But Nellie took pride in her mistress' appearance and spent hours talking to Mrs. Spears, who had once been a lady's maid, about the correct toilette for every occasion.

Willow's days were now fully occupied as she and her young maid pored over the illustrations in *The Queen* and made lists of what would be required. The grand total was at last decided upon: a velvet dress for breakfast, three teagowns, and three dinnergowns, since Willow could not possibly appear in the same garment on more than one occasion. She added to the list two tweed coats and skirts for outdoor walks or drives, a "best" hat and a hat suitable for country wear; and finally a mountain of petticoats, stoles, scarves, gloves, and similar accessories.

"Mrs. Spears tells me that as often as not, there is the reading aloud of some books of interest during the evenings and that nearly all the ladies will have embroidery to do, Milady," Nellie said. "She says you will require a large bag to put it in, Milady."

Willow smiled ruefully.

"Then perhaps I shall not enjoy myself in Buckinghamshire as well as I expected, since I do not care for stitching or embroidery," she said. "And while I think of it, Nellie, be sure to pack my ostrich feather fan—and of course all my jewelry. And my very best corsets."

At long last the day came for them to depart. Baron Rochford with his young wife and two servants set out for Tunbridge Wells to catch a train to London, and from there another train to Buckinghamshire. The mountain of luggage seemed enormous, although Rowell gave no sign of surprise. There were two large domed trunks known as Noah's Arks, hat boxes, dressing cases, shoe boxes, umbrellas, Rowell's guncase, Nellie's box with her two clean uniforms and night attire, and the box belonging to Rowell's valet containing his livery and night attire. Seats had been reserved for them on the train, and they rode comfortably to London, where hired hackney cabs took them, their servants, and luggage to Paddington station.

Upon the train to High Wycombe, Rowell encountered several acquaintances bound for the same destination as themselves. Introductions were effected, and he and Willow joined a dozen others in the dining car. From the conversation, Willow deduced that there would be in all some fifty guests staying for the weekend at Symington Hall.

She was not surprised therefore, to see the vast assortment of carriages awaiting the Symingtons' guests: victorias, landaus, buggys, dog carts, traps and flys, and strongly-built wagonettes for the servants and baggage.

When all were loaded with passengers and luggage, the cavalcade set out along the country lane.

Rowell confessed during this last part of the journey that he did not awfully care for Esmé Symington. Willow, however, thought their hostess very agreeable as she greeted her guests warmly on their arrival and had them shown to their room, where a large fire burned a cheerful welcome.

While Nellie and the valet unpacked, Willow and Rowell stood before the flames warming themselves. It would shortly be time for afternoon tea, and Nellie was laying out Willow's clothes—an exquisite rose plush dress with falls of lace and flounces at the neck and wrists. It was the very latest thing in teagowns, so Madame Swaebe had assured Willow, and watching Nellie spread out the layers of the Surah silk skirt, she was happy she had chosen it. Rowell made no demur when she confessed that it had cost her the princely sum of twelve guineas. The color suited her and the style enhanced her figure, he remarked when she presented herself for his inspection. His compliments gave her confidence to face the large assembly of strangers downstairs.

The guests were varied both in age and in social standing, preference being given at every occasion to those of higher rank. But despite the number of people present in the drawing room, the ceremony of taking afternoon tea at the Symingtons varied not at all from that at Rochford Manor, and Willow's nervousness quickly vanished as she enjoyed a muffin, one of the tiny sandwiches, and then a piece of delicious cake cut for her by the maid from the three-tiered cakestand which she carried around to each guest in turn.

Lady Symington sat beside the sofa table and presided over the silver teapot while a parlormaid handed around the milk and sugar. It was a congenial time, everyone discussing quietly the events of the day, the comfort of their train journey, what the weather would be like for the day's hunting tomorrow, as they sipped their tea from fine Wedgwood tea cups. Afterwards, Willow went up to her room to sit and look at the *Illustrated London News,* a copy of which she had noticed when changing for tea. It was pleasant to sit comfortably and rest before it was time to change once more into another dress for the evening.

Nellie was breathless with excitement when she came

up from the servants' "high tea" to dress Willow for dinner. As maid to the baroness, she had been allotted one of the more superior of the servants' bedrooms, as well as being placed next but one to the butler at the servants' table.

"And that's the highest honor, Milady, sitting next to *him*," Nellie said. "He's even grander than our Mr. Dutton, but then he's a lot older and not nearly so nice. All the servants are ever so frightened of him. But he was very polite to me. He called me Miss Sinclair and asked me all sorts of questions about America."

Nellie giggled, her pink cheeks growing even pinker as she confessed:

"I'm afraid I told a few fibs, Miss Willow—I mean, Milady. I said as how yours was a very old, renowned family what had emigrated from Norway to America. I hope you don't mind, Milady."

Willow laughed good-naturedly.

"I don't mind, Nellie, although it is never wise to lie about such things. The Baron has probably already told Lord Symington who my family really are, and if he tells his valet, and *he* tells the butler . . ."

But Nellie was impervious to such warning.

"We'll be gone home before that happens," she said as she took from the wardrobe her mistress' new soft blue satin evening dress. It had contrasting black jet beaded decorations in the lace of the low décolletage and on the hem of the skirt.

When at last Willow's lengthy toilette was completed, she descended the wide staircase on Rowell's arm feeling immensely happy, confident, and content. She had met most of her fellow guests during tea, but several more couples had arrived since then, and Esmé Symington now brought them forward to be introduced. Among them was a strikingly beautiful red-haired woman whose face was vaguely familiar to Willow.

"I do not think you have met Mrs. Georgina Grey," her hostess said, avoiding Rowell's furious glance. "Georgina is a very old friend of your husband's, my dear, and has been longing to meet you."

As Lady Symington moved away, Rowell said in a quick aside:

"Georgina's late husband was a friend of mine, Willow."

So this lovely woman was a widow—like Silvie, Willow thought as she shook Georgina's outstretched hand. She judged her to be in her middle to late twenties. She had a certain presence in her manner and bearing which was only explained when Rowell informed her that their companion had once been on the stage.

Quite suddenly, Willow remembered where she had seen Georgina Grey previously. It was during that summer she had spent at Rochford—at Toby's coming-of-age party, she thought as she tried to recall what Pelham had said about her. Almost in the next instant, she did recall his words: he had said that Georgina Grey was Rowell's mistress.

Color flooded into Willow's cheeks. Although she had been ignorant then, she was now very well aware what the word meant. This woman had known Rowell, her husband, as intimately as she, his wife, knew him. A swift wave of jealousy surged through her, robbing her of speech. Rowell too was silent, but Georgina seemed perfectly at ease.

"I must congratulate you, if belatedly, upon your marriage to Rowell," she said brightly. "No wonder he gave up bachelorhood, my dear. You are remarkably pretty. And that is the most beautiful gown I have yet seen tonight. Rowell, how fortunate you are to have so charming a wife."

A little of Willow's discomfiture left her. After all, she told herself, Rowell was a very attractive man, and it was naïve of her to suppose that he had not had mistresses before his marriage. And she could see why he had been fascinated by so beautiful a woman as Georgina Grey. It was equally clear that he was not at all pleased to see her now. She wondered if poor Mrs. Grey were still in love with him. If so, it must be hard for her to see Rowell married; to have to meet and converse with his wife.

As if to reassure Willow that he had no interest now in his former mistress, Rowell put his arm through Willow's, saying to Georgina:

"If you will excuse us, we should really make ourselves pleasant to Esmé's other guests."

Her gaze riveted upon Georgina's face, Willow saw

a flash of fire in the deep green emerald depths of her eyes. Was it disappointment? she asked herself as they moved away. She could almost feel sorry for the beautiful widow for the abrupt manner in which Rowell had snubbed her. Men were not always very understanding of women, she decided, and could be cruel.

After dinner—a lavish nine-course banquet in the huge baronial dining hall—some of the men went off to play billiards. Others, Rowell among them, sat down to a game of bridge. Georgina Grey made her way to Willow's side and drew her apart from the other ladies who were grouped around their hostess as they took up their embroidery.

"We had so little time to converse before dinner," Georgina said with a friendly smile. "And you looked so lost and lonely when Rowell departed just now with the other card players, I thought you might welcome a friend to talk to."

Willow returned her smile.

"I do feel a trifle odd-man-out," she admitted. "I know so few people in society. I have only been in England for six months and although I have met a number of our neighbors at Havorhurst, I have not yet had the opportunity to meet Rowell's London friends."

Georgina laid her hand on Willow's arm and led her to one of the comfortable sofas by the windows.

"You will soon make friends," she said kindly. "And I hope you will consider me one of them. Now we have the perfect chance to get to know one another better. Esmé told me that you have not been well since Christmas. But you are quite recovered, I see."

"Oh, yes, indeed!" Willow said, responding at once to the friendly warmth in Georgina's voice. Lowering her own, she said: "I was not really ill. I lost the baby Rowell and I were expecting and I was more depressed than ill."

Georgina's smile remained fixed.

"Is that so? Well, my dear, there will be others I do not doubt. Now do tell me how you are managing with that perfectly awful old grandmother of Rowell's—a real dragon, don't you think?"

Willow was momentarily at a loss for words. She did not want to be disloyal in any way to Rowell's family; at the same time it was a relief to know that she was not the only one to think old Lady Rochford awesome.

Georgina laughed.

"I can see you share my opinion of her. Not that I really know her. Having once been on the stage, I am definitely not welcome at Rochford Manor. Did Rowell tell you I was an actress before I married?"

Willow nodded, uncertain of her reply. But Georgina continued:

"I have been to Rochford on several occasions none-theless. But always under an assumed name, of course, and when the house has been so full of guests that the old lady has overlooked my presence. Now, my dear, I am being very remiss in talking so much about myself. I want you to tell me all about you—and Rowell. I don't need to be told that you are quite madly in love with him. That is evident."

Willow felt the color rise in her cheeks as she said shyly:

"Oh, dear, is it as obvious as all that?"

"Even if it is, that's nothing to be ashamed of. You are a very new bride, are you not? You will soon lose that honeymoon look once you have become accustomed to being a wife. Now tell me, my dear, how do you get along with the other Rochford boys? I always think Pel-ham so attractive. He's not so handsome as Rowell, but *very* amusing. He should have been the eldest son. He would have taken his responsibilities so much less seriously than Rowell. I'm afraid that inheriting the title so young has aged Rowell far too soon. He's more like a father than a brother to the family. I know you won't mind me saying this—he is such an old friend—but there are times when he can be quite dull about family duty and all that. Do you not agree?"

Willow was surprised, not only by Georgina's frank-ness, but by the hint of criticism of Rowell. She was also inwardly delighted, for she now felt quite certain that whatever affection had once existed between the two, it was no longer there. As for herself, she welcomed this new friend and later that evening, when she and Rowell were alone in the large double bed, she told Rowell how she felt.

Rowell looked far from pleased.

"What has Georgina been saying to you?" he inquired in a none-too-gentle tone. "I should warn you, Willow, that she is a prattler and cannot be relied upon."

Willow laughed, snuggling closer to him.

"I know you don't like her very much, my love, but really she is quite harmless; I am sure of it. And Rowell, do you know, she also buys her clothes from Madame Swaebe. Now is that not a coincidence? She has told me I have but to ask her and she will advise me of the names of the best ready-made tailors and a good milliner, too. I shall be most grateful for her advice, for I consider her to be quite beautiful and every bit as chic as dear Silvie."

"I would prefer you did not pursue this friendship," Rowell said coldly. "You are too inexperienced to know these things, but Georgina is not a suitable friend for you."

Willow's mouth tightened.

"You mean because she was once an actress and Grandmère will not receive her. But if Lady Esmé invites her here to Symington Hall—"

"That is quite another matter. Esmé has sufficient savior faire to know when she can include Georgina and when she cannot. I have no more to say on the subject, Willow. You are to make it plain to Georgina tomorrow that I have expressed a wish that you should not continue with this friendship."

Willow remained silent. Her pleasure in the evening had vanished and she felt disturbed by the dogmatic manner in which Rowell was exerting his authority as her husband. Surely, she thought miserably, he should allow her to choose her own friends? It had never been her intention to suggest that they receive Georgina Grey at Rochford, but it might have been quite jolly to have met her in London from time to time for a day's shopping and to take tea at one of the new Lyons tea shops, as Georgina had suggested.

The following morning, they were woken by Nellie with tea and a plate of Marie biscuits. Rowell's valet arrived soon afterwards with a small brass pitcher of shaving water and a large enamel jug of hot water for Willow. It was regretted that they could not enjoy a bath this morning, since the three bathrooms were bespoke by other guests.

Rowell said little as they dressed and went down an hour later to breakfast. It was customary, he told her, for them to help themselves, selecting what they wanted from the food kept hot over spirit lamps. There were large covered silver dishes containing bacon and eggs, chops, kippers and a vast bowl of porridge for those who wanted it. On one of the tables were cold platters of ham, grouse, pheasant, gallantines, and a selection of fresh fruit. There were racks of toast and plates of rolls, and coffee, chocolate, or tea to drink.

Georgina Grey did not appear while Willow and Rowell were eating. But when the men departed for the day's hunting, she came downstairs in a long sealskin coat, her head veiled, in readiness for a run in Lord Symington's brand new Daimler motor car. Willow had been invited to join this expedition but Rowell had thought she was not yet strong enough to risk going out in such inclement weather.

For once she welcomed his dictate, for she was in no hurry to speak to Georgina as Rowell had instructed. She considered such a conversation must prove highly embarrassing for them both. She spent the morning in the library. Theodore Symington had a priceless collection of books and Willow appreciated their beautiful leather-bound covers and their variety. She even found a first edition signed by the author, Charles Dickens.

Following upon a lavish luncheon with the other ladies, she spent the afternoon playing whist until, pleading a headache, she excused herself from tea and retired to her room.

Rowell, however, was determined to speak to Georgina since Willow had not. The first opportunity occurred when the day's hunting was over and he found Nellie dressing Willow for dinner. Knowing that his wife would be fully occupied for the next hour, he made his way to Georgina's room.

Doubtless deliberately, Esmé Symington had allotted Rowell's mistress a room on the same landing as himself —a facility he might have welcomed had Willow not been with him, but which under the circumstances, showed Esmé to be either malicious or mischievous. She could be both, he thought with irritation. Her outlook was very modern and she followed the fashions set by the Prince of Wales, thus including quite a number of Jews as well as the new rich in her varied circle of friends.

As Rowell knocked on Georgina's door, he wondered which of the two women had suggested his mistress should be present at this weekend party. It was quite possible they had been in collusion, he decided.

Immediately upon hearing it was Rowell at the door, Georgina dismissed her maid. She was in semi-dishabille and received him in little more than a lace-embroidered chemise. She made no attempt to cover herself with her wrapper. Crossing one long silk-stockinged leg over the other, she smiled at Rowell who was standing in the room with his back to the closed door.

"Well, lover, so you are come at last," she said, her wide red mouth curving into a mock pout. "I thought you were beginning to lose interest in your little Georgina."

Rowell made no move toward her. His expression was inscrutable, but his voice was cold as he said:

"This is no time to play the ingénue, Georgina. I wish to talk to you seriously."

"To *talk*, Rowell? Would that not be wasting what little time we might have for—"

"That is not why I am here," Rowell broke in sharply. "I have come for the sole purpose of warning you, Georgina. If you do or say anything to put my marriage in jeopardy, then you will suffer for it. Do I make myself clear?"

"Oh, perfectly clear, my love—and it must be for at least the tenth time you have so warned me." She turned to stare at herself in the mirror. With studied concentration, she smoothed one delicately curved eyebrow with a fingertip. "I cannot think why you should feel it necessary to keep repeating yourself. I have made myself quite charming to your dear little wife. What more could you ask of me?"

Rowell took a step toward her. His irritation with her was made worse by the fact that she looked extremely desirable in her pose, and that tired though he was after the day's hunting, he would very much enjoy making love to her. And he was certain that Georgina knew it, for she was smiling to herself in the most unconcerned way.

"I don't know what your motive is in convincing Willow that you are her friend," he said angrily. "Had she been less naïve, she would have seen through your overtures long since. Esmé had no right whatever to invite you here the same weekend as she included my wife among her guests."

"Esmé did so entirely to please me," Georgina said airily. "Naturally, I was agog to see the girl you had married. What better way than this, my dear Rowell? The girl is without suspicion. Why are you so worried?"

"Because I do not trust you," Rowell said flatly. "You objected in no small measure when I told you I intended getting married and were furious when you could not talk me out of it. It would be quite within your nature now to try to upset my marriage."

"And do you blame me for it?" Georgina asked. "Don't be such a fool, Rowell. Sometimes I wonder at *your* naivete. Did you not expect me to be curious about the woman who is to share your bed? Did you not even want me to be a little jealous?"

She stood up and walked toward him, her movements slow, graceful, sinuous. She raised her arms and wound them about his neck.

"Silly boy," she said softly. "Who knows better than you how much I love you. At night I am quite desperate with longing for you, my strong, wonderful lover. I have missed you so much, Rowell. That week we spent together was so perfect, was it not? But far, far too short. I need you. I want you . . ."

Her voice was as seductive as her caresses, and Rowell was powerless against them. Since this woman had first initiated him into the varied delights that the female body could offer to a man, he had wanted no other until he had encountered Willow. It had surprised him that the young inexperienced girl he had married could arouse him —if not to the same extent as Georgina—then at least to a degree. But Georgina was irresistible and when she was in the enticing mood she was now evincing, he was defenseless.

As Georgina began to unbutton his jacket, he thought anxiously of the absurd risk he was taking. *Her* maid might be counted upon to be discreet, but if one of the household servants—or worse still, Nellie—were to come to the wrong bedroom . . .

"No, Georgina—" he began, but fell silent as she continued to undress him. Rowell thought briefly of his young wife making herself beautiful for him in the bedroom only a few doors farther along the landing. He was shocked by his own weakness—he who prided himself upon his strength of character, his upright behavior, his observance of the conventions.

Then he stopped thinking as Georgina began to remove her underclothes, slowly, provocatively, dropping each garment at his feet until she stood as naked as he.

Her skin, like that of all redheads, was alabaster white; her breasts were full, and the swell of her wide hips was accentuated by a tiny waist. She had the perfect hourglass figure, marred only by an ugly red birthmark on one thigh. When first Rowell had seen her naked, the mark had bothered him, but now he no longer noticed it. Like a boy with his first woman, he fell upon her with an uncontrollable hunger.

Georgina smiled.

"My darling, my wonderful Rowell," she murmured, and even more softly: "Mine, all mine!"

Willow returned to Rochford Manor in a mood of near perfect contentment. Rowell was in excellent spirits and had been so throughout the long Sunday at Symington Hall. In the morning, they had gone to church and Rowell had actually smiled at her and held her hand during the rather dull sermon.

That the nights had not been quite as loving as Willow had hoped was only the mildest cloud upon an otherwise perfect horizon. She told herself that there were many reasons why Rowell had not wanted to claim his marital rights: out of a mistaken consideration for her health— for she was in fact, quite fully recovered; from exhaustion after the hunt on Saturday; and on the Sunday night because they had a long journey to undergo next morning. She did not let it concern her since he was so particularly loving and attentive in other ways, most especially in company.

It was almost as if he had set out to proclaim to every

one of the Symingtons' guests that he was now a very happily married man.

When finally it was time to bid their host and hostess farewell, the Symingtons professed their disappointment that Rowell would not be moving to London for the Season, as were they. Rowell claimed that he had far too many duties attending him on his estate, but he admitted later to Willow in private that this was only an excuse.

"The truth is, my dear, that we cannot this year afford the lavish entertaining that is required of people in our position," he said.

He did not add that by next year he would have integrated the vast settlement Willoughby Tetford had made upon his daughter with the Rochfords' dwindling resources; and that by then, they might very well be able to enjoy to the full the delights of the London Season.

"We shall have to make do with an occasional day at the races and a night or two in town," he added. "I trust this will suffice."

"Indeed it will, Rowell," Willow assured him. She was surprised that he did not seem to understand that she could be happy anywhere so long as he was with her.

At Rochford Manor, however, minor troubles awaited them and a little of Willow's happiness was diminished. Grandmère had seen fit to visit Dodie during their absence. Finding her with a slight headcold caught from Violet, the old lady had removed all Dodie's books and toys. Willow was greeted by a tearful child who believed her playthings might never be returned to her. Without consulting Rowell or Grandmère, Willow at once returned them. Fortunately for them both, Grandmère saw no necessity to make a further visit to her granddaughter and was unaware that Willow had countermanded her orders. Willow decided to make no mention of the incident to Rowell.

He also faced trouble that spring. Rupert's tutor wrote from Oxford to say that his pupil had been making very little effort at his studies. Rowell was furious, and when Rupert returned for the Easter vacation, there was an ugly scene between the brothers. Rupert promised to apply himself more diligently, but he did little work during the holiday. Soon after the beginning of the summer term, his tutor wrote again—this time to state that in his opinion Rupert stood no chance whatever of getting a good degree.

These unfortunate tidings arrived by the afternoon post and were brought by Harry, the footman, to the veranda where Rowell and Willow were taking afternoon tea. The June sunshine had brought a mass of roses into bloom, and the honeysuckle covering the veranda roof was in flower. Their scent mingling with that of the freshly cut grass had brought about an air of delightful peace and tranquility which, until then, Willow had been enjoying.

Rowell's mood of pleasant good humor changed with alarming abruptness as he re-read the contents of the tutor's letter aloud to Willow in a furious voice.

"But does it really matter, my love?" Willow asked placatingly. "It is not as if Rupert will be taking employment of any kind when he leaves his university."

"That is scarcely the point, Willow," Rowell said bitingly. "That brother of mine is a wastrel, a disgrace to the family. I consider it unforgivable that he has given anyone the opportunity to write such a letter about one of the Rochfords. I shall have to talk to Grandmère about him."

Willow's heart took a downward plunge. She felt intensely sorry for this particular brother. Pelham was able to stand up for himself; Francis had no need to do so since Grandmère would hear no criticism of him; Toby lived in a world of his own. But Rupert . . . he longed for affection and approval and yet always seemed to manage to antagonize his family.

Grandmère was even more put out by the tutor's letter than was Rowell. The two of them spent several hours debating the matter, and when Rowell emerged from Grandmère's rooms, it was to announce to Willow that they had jointly decided to send Rupert into the army as soon as he left Oxford at the end of the year.

"Maybe a year or two in the cavalry will make a man of him," Rowell said. "Grandmère seems to think it might, and I agree with her."

Willow could not prevent the protest that rose to her lips.

"That is surely madness," she exclaimed unwisely. "Rupert is artistic—a sensitive, reserved, shy young man. In the army—"

"And what do you know about the army—or anything else come to that?" Rowell interrupted, his handsome face suffused with anger as he rounded on her. "It's high time you learned a few facts of life, Willow, and then you might be better able to judge whether your elders know best or not. That boy is effeminate. If I don't take steps to prevent it, he'll end up being branded as a sodomite."

Seeing the look of incomprehension on his wife's face, he added less harshly: "Someone whose natural instincts are misdirected—as with that Oscar Wilde fellow who thinks himself madly in love with a boy. God alone knows how such things happen, but they do. And if it's taken to the extreme, it is a very serious criminal offense. *Now* do you understand?"

"You mean there are men who cannot love women as other men do?" Willow asked thoughtfully.

"Exactly!" Rowell replied. "Or to put it more succinctly, they love men in the same way that other men love women."

Willow was effectively silenced. She was not so much horrified as surprised. But nothing, however strange, could alter the fact that the army was no solution for Rupert, she thought. She could not imagine a less soldierly man. She had been brought up on stories told by her father about the courage and bravery of the men fighting in the Civil War. Quite apart from Rupert's character, his constitution, though basically healthy, left him prone to mild attacks of asthma from which he had suffered acutely as a child.

"Do you think the army would accept Rupert?" she asked Rowell tentatively. "He is not very strong."

"Of course they will!" Rowell replied impatiently. "Grandmère knows General Sir William Hackett very well indeed and she is in no doubt that the General will oblige her by taking one of her grandsons into the regiment. You have overlooked the fact that both my grandfather and father were soldiers of considerable distinction. I shall write to the General—and to Rupert—this afternoon."

While Rowell was so employed, Willow went to see Toby.

"I seem to be making a habit of bringing my problems to you," she said apologetically as she finished explaining her concern for Rupert.

Toby waved her apology aside with a smile.

"Your secrets are as safe with me as they would be in the confessional," he said. "But I doubt there is much either of us can do, Willow, to halt any plans Rowell and Grandmère have made. They are a formidable pair when they are united in their opinions and I do not think we would count for much if we tried jointly to oppose them. But once the news becomes general, I will tell Rowell that I, too, consider it madness. You may have to bring up the subject in front of me as it is not Rowell's habit to keep me informed of his plans."

As Toby had forecast, neither Rowell nor Grandmère would listen to his pleas to find an alternative occupation for Rupert. The long summer vacation was fraught with uncertainty while the unhappy Rupert awaited the results of his exams. Willow could not help but be affected by Rupert's obvious dread of the fate that seemed to await him.

"Rowell will not allow me to mention the subject," she said to Toby. "Does it not seem terrible that with this beautiful weather and in this lovely house there has to be such dissension?"

But Rupert was not the only problem to spoil the family harmony. Returning with Rowell from a call upon one of their neighbors, Willow went up to her bedroom to change her attire. Even before she had opened the door, she heard the sound of sobbing from within. To her astonishment, her happy, smiling Nellie was kneeling by the bed, her head buried in her arms as she wept into the coverlet.

Willow hurried to her. She had become deeply attached to the cheerful little maid who waited upon her so tirelessly from dawn till often very late at night. No matter how long and tiring the hours she worked, Nellie never once complained and she made Willow aware that her happiness in life revolved around her young mistress.

"What is wrong, Nellie? Have you had bad news from your family? You must not cry like that. Try to calm yourself and tell me what is the matter."

Nellie's round face was reddened with weeping. Head bowed, she choked on her sobs, unable to speak. When

Willow helped her to her feet and produced a small lace handkerchief with which to wipe her eyes, she finally found her voice.

"It's Mr. Francis, Milady," she gasped. "He must have been drinking too much or something. While you and the Master were out . . . he . . . he . . . caught me in the corridor . . . by the linen room . . . and he . . . he . . ."

Willow's pale cheeks grew pink with anger as she guessed what had transpired.

"He did not hurt you, Nellie? Now you *must* tell me."

"No, Milady, no, not actually," Nellie gasped. "He just caught hold of me like and said how pretty I was and . . . and he tried to kiss me. I told him as how I was a good girl, and it wasn't right of him to take advantage. At first he didn't seem to want to listen and said as how I was being very silly and any *English* servant girl would know as how it was an honor to have a real gentleman pay attention to them. I kept trying to push him away, and then . . . then we heard someone coming up the stairs . . . Mrs. Spears I think it was . . . or maybe Miss Mildred. Anyway, he let me go then but—"

Her sobs broke out anew. "He said he'd have his way with me in the end," she gasped, "even if he had to wait till next vacation. Oh, Miss Willow, Milady, I'm ever so frightened."

"Then don't be," Willow replied, more angry than she had ever been in her life. "I will get my husband to speak to Mr. Francis immediately. You will be perfectly safe under my roof, Nellie, I promise you."

Having sent Nellie to her own room to wash her face and tidy her hair, Willow paused before going to search for Rowell in the library. Now that she was feeling a little calmer, she remembered that Francis was the one who could do no wrong in his grandmother's eyes and that Rowell would never go against Grandmère.

But this was different, she told herself. She was well aware that there had existed the old traditional *droits de seigneur*, but such horrible and unfair customs were not going to be permitted while *she* was mistress of the house. She would make it quite plain to Rowell that it was not Rupert who should be sent away but Francis, if he did not control himself. In this matter, Rowell would not gainsay her.

Only then did it strike her with a cold chill that she had already taken it for granted that she was unlikely to receive the support or reassurances she wanted from the man she had married and whom she loved so deeply.

Then so be it, she decided. She must show no weakness. Her head rose proudly and her mouth set in a stubborn line as she went to find her husband.

Somewhat to her surprise, Rowell, although he made light of the incident, nevertheless agreed without argument to speak to Francis about it. He did in fact warn his brother against any repetition of such behavior and even went so far as to threaten to withdraw his allowance if it should happen again.

Her confidence in Rowell restored, Willow's happiness would have been complete had she conceived another child. But it was not until the following summer that her dearest wish was to be granted.

Chapter Seven

September 1893

IT WAS LATE SUMMER. ROWELL WAS AWAY. AT THE end of June, he had received an invitation from an old Oxford friend to go mountain climbing in the Swiss Alps and had informed Willow that he wished very much to go on this expedition which, regrettably, did not include her.

Although Willow's heart sank at the thought of the two months' separation this would entail, for Rowell's sake she tried not to show it but voiced her approval of the plan. Rowell needed no second bidding. Grateful to his young wife for causing him no feelings of guilt at his desertion of her, he did his best to show his affection the night before he left Rochford.

On that night, Willow now knew, she had conceived a child, and Doctor Forbes had recommended her to rest as much as possible if she wished to avoid another miscarriage. She lay on the long bamboo chair in the shade of the big lime tree overlooking the lake, either reading or talking to Toby. Rowell was still in Switzerland, and Toby must have sensed her loneliness for he often neglected his work in order to keep her company.

The hot weather reminded Willow of that wonderfully happy summer she had spent at Rochford Manor as a child. She often spoke to Toby of those halcyon days, always with a wistful note to her voice.

"Does it not seem strange to you," she remarked to him now, "that I think of them as the happiest of my life? Yet here I am, married to the man I love, soon to bear his child, and for some unknown reason I am sad."

Toby was stretched full length on the sun-baked grass beside her chair, his arms folded behind his head, his spectacles for once not on the end of his nose but tucked away into the pocket of his striped blazer. He looked much younger than usual, Willow thought, watching his long sensitive hand reach out for a blade of grass that had been bleached white by the hot sun, and put it between his teeth. The frown lines on his forehead were gone, and he seemed suddenly a lot younger than Rowell. She had come to think of Toby as the elder brother and had now to remind herself that he was only just twenty-five.

He did not reply to her remark at once but, seemingly, lost in thought, chewed on the piece of grass. Willow smiled as she watched him. Toby always gave the most careful concentration to any problem she took to him—as if he really considered her silly little misfortunes were as important as his work, and no one knew better than Willow how much that meant to him.

"You are the only member of the family who takes my work in the least seriously," he had told her. "But I really do believe it *is* important, Willow. I think I can contribute something worthwhile to medicine if my theories turn out to be sound. I have yet to prove them scientifically of course, but one day I will."

Willow had grown to understand how much of Toby's own self was tied up in his research. It was his life, and he was totally dedicated. It was therefore all the more appreciated by her that he was always willing to set aside that work when she needed his attention. At her request, he had wasted a great deal of time trying to dissuade Rowell and Grandmère from forcing Rupert into the army. Unfortunately, neither she nor Toby had been successful in saving him, for he achieved only a very indifferent fourth-class degree. Rowell and Grandmère had continued to pursue their plans for his future. Grandmère as well as Rowell had written to Sir William Hackett at the War Office. An old friend of her son, Oliver, the General had recommended that her grandson be dispatched to Egypt. He had contacted the British commander out there—a young ambitious Colonel by the name of Herbert Kitchener —suggesting that Rupert might become one of his aides.

"I have read that the fighting with the Dervishes during the Toski campaign was brutal and horrifying," Toby told Rowell in Willow's hearing. "You cannot send Rupert, of all people, out there."

"It is just what he needs to make a man of him," Grandmère reiterated, and Rowell remarked more doubtfully that he did not think there was much fighting in progress at the present, although Kitchener might well be planning to reconquer the Sudan.

Rupert himself had made no attempt to get the arrangement rescinded.

"What is the point?" he had said to Willow and Toby, his eyes downcast and hopeless. "I have never been able to stand up to Rowell or Grandmère. I was utterly wretched at Eton, but they would not allow me to leave. I had no wish to go to Oxford, but they insisted. Rowell simply threatens to cut me off without a penny if I disobey him now."

Willow waited until the white-faced, unhappy youth left for Egypt in April. Then she asked Toby to explain why Rowell and not Grandmère made the ultimate decisions in family affairs.

"It is really Grandmère's doing," Toby told her. "Rowell was only fourteen years old when our father died. Father had stipulated in his will that Grandmère should be our guardian until she thought fit to hand over responsibility to Rowell. She decided to do so when he came of age. Our father had left each of us boys a capital sum that cannot be touched until we reach the age of thirty. The interest from that capital is paid to us at the discretion of our guardian. We are all therefore dependent upon

Rowell's good will until we reach the ripe old age of thirty. Not even Rowell can touch the capital and that is why—"

He had given her a strange unhappy look as he broke off in mid-sentence.

"Why Rowell had to marry someone with money?" Willow said for him. Before Toby could comment, she added reassuringly: "You don't need to feel embarrassed, Toby. Rowell has talked quite openly to me about it. He explained that when he fell in love with me, he did not know whether I had any money of my own. He had no way of knowing that Papa would make a settlement on me, or how generous that settlement would be—so generous that it made it possible for us to marry at once. I am very happy that I have been able to help him and all the family. My Papa has far more money than he knows what to do with."

Willow had been married almost two years now, Toby thought, but she was still not entirely happy. Rowell had no right to leave her so often alone. He had no right whatever to continue his association with his mistress—a luxury he could ill afford in any event. Georgina had insisted upon his buying her a small house in London, and Rowell had virtually to support her. It was quite unfair to this young girl who adored him, and whose fortune, moreover, was paying for Rowell's pleasures.

"I expect it is just your condition making you mopey," he said finally in a comforting tone of voice. "Rowell will be home soon, and then you'll feel much better."

Willow sighed.

"I have no right to be miserable, have I?" she said rhetorically. "In fact, I ought to be the very opposite with so much to please me. It is a tonic merely to think of Dodie, for instance. She is getting on so well now, Toby, I have determined upon making arrangements for the schoolmaster to tutor her. If you agree with my idea, will you drive me to the village to talk to James McGill about lessons for her, Toby? I do not intend to ask Grandmère's permission." She smiled mischievously. "I thought to present her with a *fait accompli*—like last time."

"I'll drive you down this very afternoon if you like, Willow," Toby said at once. "School will be out by four o'clock, and we can tackle McGill together. As for Grandmère, I'll tell her that in your condition you must on no account be thwarted lest it bring on another miscarriage. That should temper her objections!"

Willow's smile faded and she sighed, her eyes suddenly wistful again.

"I am beginning to think Grandmère wouldn't mind if I did miscarry, Toby. She does not seem a bit pleased about the baby. Rowell said she is probably worrying lest I should have a girl. Toby, *there is no danger, is there? I want my child to be perfect.*"

Toby raised himself on one elbow so that he was looking directly into Willow's anxious face.

"I cannot give you proven facts," he said quietly. "But I have been doing a great deal of research on the subject and my honest belief is that there is no connection of any kind between the deaths of the first two Rochford girls, that of my mother, and Dodie's condition. I think the infants may have died of diphtheria—but I cannot prove it. Doctor Forbes insists he made no error in his diagnosis, but frankly, I do not believe him. He is utterly dependent upon Grandmère for the standard of living he enjoys, and I don't think he would admit it even if he believed he had been wrong."

Toby's eyes were thoughtful as he went deeper into his theory.

"As for Dodie, I am very seriously coming to the view that she suffered infantile paralysis soon after she was born. That would explain the arrested development of her left arm and leg. But although Forbes did go so far as to agree I *could* be right, he still insists that her mental development was also retarded. You and I between us, however, are rapidly proving him wrong. It looks as if the intellectual advances Dodie has made in so short a while indicate a quite remarkable intelligence. Now if McGill will agree to come up to the house to see her, as a schoolmaster he can give us an assessment."

Willow reached out her hand and placed it on Toby's arm.

"I don't know what I would do without you, dearest Toby," she said warmly. "I think you are the most wonderful brother any girl could want. I know it is very selfish of me to say so, but please don't fall in love and get married too soon. I'd miss you so terribly if you went away."

Toby's face reddened. He tried to laugh off her compliment.

"I haven't the slightest intention of falling in love—or of getting married," he said firmly. "I'm already married to my work, as well you know, Willow. A wife would get scant attention from me, I fear."

"You underrate yourself," Willow said smiling. "You'd make a very good husband—and a good father, Toby. Dodie worships you. But I don't have to tell you that."

Toby drew out his watch and peered short-sightedly at the hands.

"I think we should start getting ready to go to the village," he said. "That is, if you feel up to it, Willow?"

"I feel very well," Willow replied as her mood changed to one of happy anticipation. "And it is such a beautiful day, I shall enjoy the drive."

The children were leaving the schoolhouse as Toby and Willow arrived in the dogcart at four o'clock. James McGill was still inside the elder children's classroom as they made their way into the small stone building. In front of his desk on the raised dais stood two small figures, that of a boy of about eight years of age wearing old brown trousers and a cotton smock, and beside him a younger girl in an over-large frock almost entirely covering her black stockings and button boots. The schoolmaster was handing them a parcel which the boy took eagerly. He touched his forehead while his sister bobbed a curtsy, and then both children ran out of the side door without noticing the visitors.

James McGill stood up, looking a little discomfited.

"Their father is ill and not able to draw his wages so I've given them a little food to take home," he explained as if caught in some illicit act. He gazed round the empty classroom apologetically. "I'm afraid there is nowhere very comfortable I can offer you to be seated, Lady Rochford."

Willow went toward him smiling.

"I don't think you have met my brother-in-law, Mr. McGill."

The men shook hands, eyeing one another surreptitiously. James McGill had not heard a great deal to the credit of the Rochford brothers and had not taken to the young Baron whom he had met one Sunday at church.

He thought him autocratic and cold in his manner. Pelham Rochford was a more likeable character, he decided, although he had little in common with this typical young blood whose main purpose in life was to amuse himself. But he had heard that Toby Rochford was different from his brothers and an academic like himself.

In a surprisingly short time, the two men became so engrossed in each other's conversation that Willow was almost forgotten. Their quickly ripening friendship pleased her, for she liked and respected both men. She sat quietly listening while James McGill replied to Toby's questions as to what had brought the young schoolmaster, a complete stranger, to Havorhurst.

"I had originally thought of taking a position in a London Board school," James said, "where there was a vacancy for a newly qualified teacher. But I have to confess that I did not have the stomach for it. There were some fifty or sixty children to a class, a horrifying number of whom were from the most wretched homes. They sat huddled on the benches, pale, puny, hungry little waifs, some as young as three years old. I wanted to feed their minds, but I could see that for a great many of them, their first need was to have their bodies fed."

"There is less poverty here in Havorhurst, is there not?" Willow intervened.

"There is more food available in the country than in the cities; and classes are smaller," the schoolmaster said. "Here there is only the occasional child who is really badly in need."

"Then I would appreciate it if you would give me a list of those families who are in dire straits," Willow said. "It is not right that you should have to dip into your pocket to help such children. Were the late Lady Rochford alive, I am sure that she would have concerned herself with such matters, and it will now be my privilege, if somewhat belatedly, to make myself responsible."

"That is very kind of you," the schoolmaster said. He invited his visitors into his house—a small, four-roomed cottage attached to the school. The caretaker, an elderly widow by the name of Mary Gassons who also served him as housekeeper, had prepared a high tea for him. Now, flustered by the importance of these unexpected guests, she hurried off to find the best china and teacloth.

"She's a dear old soul and looks after me like a mother," the young man said, indicating a shabby horsehair sofa where Willow and Toby could sit. The room was littered with exercise and text books which he vainly attempted to tidy away.

"Please do not bother, McGill," Toby said smiling. "Lady Rochford is well accustomed to this kind of disorder in *my* workroom and she already knows the inconvenience that can result from over-zealous tidying."

It was not until after they had enjoyed the simple tea Mrs. Gassons produced for them that Willow and Toby raised the subject of Dodie. James McGill was instantly interested.

"I would be honored to have the privilege of teaching the little girl," he said. "Although I do not have a great deal of free time at my disposal, I could most certainly come for an hour or two several times a week. Does Miss Dodie take to the idea?"

"We have not told her yet," Willow said. "I did not want her to be disappointed if you could not come. But she is hungry for knowledge, Mr. McGill, and you need be in no doubt as to your welcome."

"We will, of course, be offering suitable remuneration," Toby said. He had long since assessed that the young schoolmaster was probably having difficulty in making ends meet on his meager salary. The lack of even the smallest luxury made it obvious that he had no private means.

"We may meet with a slight impediment to these plans," Willow said awkwardly. "I think I have already explained to you, Mr. McGill, that my husband's grandmother, Lady Rochford, is overly concerned about Dodie's health. She may raise objections to her further education. However, my brother-in-law and I are hoping that we can persuade her otherwise."

"In fact, quite determined upon it!" Toby said grinning.

"Then I will wait upon your confirmation," James McGill replied.

As they rode home, Toby made no secret of the fact that he had taken very kindly to the sandy-haired, fresh-faced young schoolmaster.

"He has just the right manner for our Dodie," he said

to Willow as he guided the horse's head homeward. "Too severe, and he might frighten her. He struck me as kindly and unusually refined for one of his ilk."

As they had agreed between them, Willow and Toby did not go to Grandmère with a suggestion but with an announcement that arrangements had been made for Dodie to be tutored.

Grandmère's eyes flashed like two black jet beads.

"I will not have that man in the house, let alone visiting my granddaughter in her bedroom. Such an idea is not only unseemly but most unwise."

Her voice was surprisingly firm for one so elderly. Anger now distorted her face, robbing it of dignity.

Toby stood his ground.

"It may reassure you, Grandmère, to know that we have arranged for Dodie to sit in an invalid chair for an hour or two every day. The chair can be moved to the old nursery schoolroom, where Mr. McGill can work with his pupil in complete propriety. Violet will sit with her."

Grandmère's fury at being challenged was now so intense she could not speak. Aunt Milly hastened to her side as she spluttered into a small lace handkerchief.

"You're making your grandmother ill," she cried shrilly to Toby. "Do you have no thought for her at all?"

Toby's eyes met Willow's. He nodded imperceptibly.

"I am sure Grandmère will feel better once she becomes accustomed to the idea that her granddaughter is really quite a clever child and will benefit enormously from a proper education," he said quietly. "We must move with the times, Aunt Milly, and Dodie should not be bedridden."

"I will never agree to it!" Grandmère spoke for herself. She looked at Willow through narrowed eyes. "This is your doing," she said accusingly. "Toby never interfered before you came to the house. Wait until Rowell returns, my girl. You both seem to have overlooked the fact that *he* is head of this household."

"And are you not overlooking Willow's condition?" Toby asked quietly. "I am sure Rowell, when he hears of it, will be as anxious as we all are to see that she is kept as happy and contented as possible for the next few months. Rowell would be very angry indeed with anyone who upsets Willow unduly."

His words effectively silenced the old lady. She had had a long talk with her eldest grandson before he went to Switzerland, and he had made it very clear to her his concern regarding the Rochford financial affairs. The settlement made by Willoughby Tetford had got them out of debt and would see them through the next few years very handsomely. But Willow's personal inheritance, due to her from her grandfather, would not be hers until she came of age.

"And that is not for another two years, Grandmère," Rowell said. "If by any chance my wife decided to leave me, Willoughby Tetford would make damned sure—begging your pardon, Grandmère—that I never touch a penny of that money. And we shall need it, I assure you."

"Then look to your own behavior, Rowell," the old lady had said shrewdly. Seeing the color rise in his cheeks, she added: "You make a mistake, Rowell, if you think I am ignorant of what goes on just because I never leave the house and because I mix little in society these days. But people talk, do they not, Mildred, and not always discreetly. If you must have a mistress, Rowell, then I should have thought you could do better than a third-rate actress. Your wife is not going to take very kindly to *her* if she finds out. Willow's happiness is your responsibility. You received what you wanted when you married her and now you must make the best of it. Get rid of Mrs. Grey —as soon as possible, for everyone's sake."

Angry but chastened, Rowell had left her room, but his remarks had not gone unheeded. Grandmère understood the meaning and power of money. In this she and Rowell were never in discord.

"Dorothy is not to be allowed out of her room without Rowell's express permission," she said finally to Toby. "Whatever opinions you may hold as to the girl's intelligence, there is no denying her deformities, and you must think of your brothers, Toby—even if Willow does not. Francis will be considering getting married before long. You cannot expect him to invite young ladies to the house with . . . with that kind of thing on view."

Words of protest were on Willow's lips, but she felt the strong pressure of Toby's hand on her shoulder, and her mouth closed. Outside Grandmère's room, he looked at her sympathetically.

"I know just how you were feeling, Willow, but she's too old to change. It would serve no purpose to argue with her. Let us take it step by step. At least Grandmère has conceded Dodie's right to be tutored by James Mc-Gill. That is enough progress for one day."

Willow let out her breath, unaware of how angry she had been.

"You're right, of course, Toby—as you usually are," she said. She linked her arm through his and squeezed it gently. "Let's go and tell Dodie! I'm so grateful to you, Toby, for your support."

He paused, looking down into her bright, expectant face.

"You never put up a fight for yourself, Willow, yet you always seem to be doing battle for someone else. Last time it was for Nellie."

Willow laughed.

"You mean my quarrel with Rowell about Francis! But I had to make a firm stand about that, did I not, Toby? After all, Nellie is my responsibility."

"And you have made Dodie yours, too, and this afternoon you told James McGill you wished to be made responsible for the poor and needy of Havorhurst. Nor must we forget your efforts for poor old Rupert—our only failure to date, I think."

Willow sighed.

"We tried though, didn't we?" Then her face cleared again. "We make a good team, you and I. Is it because we think so much along the same lines, Toby?"

"Perhaps!" Toby said, gently withdrawing his arm from hers. "But you are the one with the courage, Willow. I should have concerned myself with Dodie long before you ever came to Rochford, but I didn't want to become involved."

"You had your work, Toby," Willow said comfortingly. "That takes so much of your time and energy. And I do understand how important it is to you."

"Yes, I believe you do!" Toby said quietly. "I don't think any person could matter as much to me as my research."

But even as he spoke the words, he realized they were no longer true. One woman—a sweet-faced, lovely, loving girl, had come between him and his work, occupying his mind when he should be studying, disturbing his dreams. Unbidden, unwanted, she had stolen into his heart which must remain forever closed to her. Toby had fallen in love with Willow—his brother's adoring and devoted wife.

Willow was unaware of Toby's sentiments regarding herself. But she did know how great was his need for money to buy books, laboratory utensils, chemicals. All too often, he lacked some vital piece of equipment or information he required because he had already spent his monthly allowance. Willow was determined that he should not now be called upon to meet the small remuneration the schoolmaster must be paid. If Rowell refused to give her the money, she thought uneasily—a possibility, if he considered, like Grandmère, that it would be wasted spent on poor Dodie—then she would pay McGill herself. Thankfully, Pelham had recently backed several winners at the races—on which he had placed stakes he admitted were far too high.

"Now I can pay back my debt to you, my dear Willow," he said jubilantly, his eyes teasing as always when he added: "I expect you never thought to see that debt repaid after all this time, did you?"

Willow had received the money reluctantly until he assured her that he could well afford it.

"I am still in funds," he said, "despite three magnificent days in London. I saw Vesta Tilley at the Empire in Leicester Square; *Our Miss Gibbs* at the Gaiety and I took the leading actress, Denise Orme, to dinner at the Savoy. Was I not fortunate, when half London were at the stage door trying to entice her to dine with them?"

"I expect she was overwhelmed by your good looks and generosity," Willow said laughing, for Pelham's high spirits were infectious.

"I'd far rather have taken *you* there, Willow," he said sighing. "As soon as you have produced my nephew or niece, I really do mean to take you up to London. You'd love it, Willow—there isn't another city like it in the world. The flower girls, the buskers, the queues of people waiting to get into the concert halls to listen to Kubelik and Kreisler or to hear Melba or Patti or Caruso sing. Even the poor people queue to get into the music halls where a really cheap seat in the upper circle costs a mere shilling. One might see the Prince of Wales at the Haymarket if there is a French revue on, or one can watch Sarah Bernhardt or Coquelin if you're lucky enough to catch them on one of their seasons in England."

Willow sighed. "I'd love to do and see all those things, Pelham, but most of all I want to go on an underground train."

Pelham laughed.

"Trust you to want to do something different," he said. "Anyway, you'd hate it, Willow. The carriages are filled with horrible sulfurous smoke and you'd be coughing yourself half to death in no time."

"Well at least I have been to Windsor Castle when Rowell took me there for my presentation to the Queen," Willow rejoined, knowing that Pelham had never yet been there. He was curious—as indeed were many others—about the dour Scots gillie, John Brown, in whose honor the Queen had had the drawing room decorated with tartan. Grandmère would not have the man's name mentioned at Rochford, but Willow had often heard the brothers speculating among themselves as how much influence the Scots commoner really did have upon Her Majesty.

"I saw several women on bicycles in Piccadilly last week," Pelham said, grinning. "One nearly fell off when she became entangled with the Rothschild's pet goat. It takes a walk down the street every afternoon despite all the traffic."

"Rowell has promised to take me to London for a long stay," Willow boasted. "So I shall see all the sights in good time, Pelham. We shall stay at Brown's Hotel, Rowell says, and be very comfortable there."

"That will be a change for you both then," Pelham said, an edge to his voice as he walked away from Willow's chaise longue to stare at the gardener pushing the heavy mower over the grass. He loved this house in the summer—in winter too, when there was hunting and shooting to enjoy—but especially on long hot days like this when time seemed to stand still, and the house, sleeping in the drowsy heat, seemed almost to be holding its breath so as not to disturb the peace.

Today, particularly, he felt glad to be home. Perhaps it was Willow, he thought, who made everything seem so perfect. In a long primrose gown of flowing chiffon she looked young, cool, beautiful, with the serenity all women had when they were soon to have a child. Rowell, he thought bitterly, was a damned lucky fellow *and did not know it.* How much longer was he going to let that red-headed Georgina entice him away from his far more beautiful young wife?

I wouldn't let Willow out of my sight if she were mine, Pelham thought as he turned to look once more at the girl beside him. It shocked him slightly that he could still feel desire for her even though he knew she was carrying his brother's child. Not even the dissipations of London had been entirely successful in making him forget Willow. Her pale gold hair and huge dark expressive eyes disturbed him in a way no other woman could.

One day, he thought as he walked away from her toward the house, one day I will have her; make her see that she was wrong ever to love that cold-hearted brother of mine. She needs fun, laughter, happiness, and Rowell gives her none of these. As for passion . . . he preferred not to think about Willow in his brother's arms.

Willow looked up from the tiny garment she was sewing for her coming child and watched Pelham as he moved away from her. Her face softened in a smile. It was lovely to have him home. His mere presence livened the atmosphere and his flirtatious compliments were just what she needed to boost her flagging morale due to her ungainly figure. She did not believe herself neglected by Rowell as did Pelham. She had encouraged him to go on this trip without her. She had told him truthfully that it would make her very unhappy to think that she was the cause of his having to refuse the invitation.

"I am never at a loss for something to do and I have the rest of the family for company," she had assured him.

He had rewarded her unselfishness with the warmest of kisses, and the night before he left he gave her a beautiful gold and pearl brooch which had belonged to his mother. He had given her something even more precious, she thought: the child she now carried with such pleasure.

She looked at the brooch pinned to her lace fichu. Other than her engagement and wedding rings, it was the first piece of jewelry Rowell had ever given her. After the baby was born, he would buy her the locket he had promised—one she could choose herself when they went to London.

She put down her sewing and lay back with her head against the soft cushions, her eyes closing. Deep within, she felt the baby move for the first time. Her hands covered it protectively. For Rowell's sake, she hoped it would be a boy. But she herself did not mind. She would love a little girl with Dodie's violet blue eyes.

I am carrying Rowell's child, she thought. *I must be the luckiest, happiest woman in the world.*

Willow, unlike Toby and Pelham, was blissfully unaware that her husband had taken Georgina Grey to Switzerland in her place.

Chapter Eight

October 1893–March 1894

ROWELL WAS SITTING IN THE LEATHER ARMCHAIR BY the fire in the library while Willow sat at the desk composing a letter to her parents.

Rowell and I hope you will visit us soon and stay for several months. Do you realize that I have not seen either of you for over two years? I miss you so much and wish you could be here for my baby's birth, Mama, but I do understand that Papa is too busy to get away.

Soon after Willow's marriage, her mother had written to say that both she and her husband felt it best to let their young daughter settle down in her new life without parental interference of any kind.

Your father, as you know, was far from happy about your decision, she had said, *and he knows that if he visited you and found you unhappy in any way, he would be unable to stay silent.*

Willow had found it difficult at times to write home in as glowing terms as was necessary to reassure her father. She could not, for example, bring herself to say that Grandmère was like a second mother to her, or that she cared very much for Aunt Milly or her youngest brother-in-law, Francis. She tried therefore to speak only of the good things in her life. As a consequence, her parents were at last writing as if they believed their misgivings were unfounded and that their only child was as contented in her marriage as they could have wished.

Willow ended her letter and took a fresh piece of writing paper from the drawer. This reply would not be quite so easy to compose, she thought with an anxious sideways glance at Rowell. He himself had refused to answer to poor Rupert's most recent letter from Egypt.

"He has only been out there six months!" Rowell had said, tossing the pages into the wastepaper basket with a look of disapproval. "He'll settle down in time."

But Willow doubted it. Rupert's large untidy words were scrawled across each page that she had retrieved. They had been written, she suspected, in a mood close to hysteria.

Colonel Kitchener is a cold, ruthless, single-minded, ego-tistical man utterly dedicated to the destruction of the Dervishes and, I suspect, to re-conquering the Sudan. I do not think he likes me any better than I like him. The heat is unbearable and I suffer terrible headaches and am often ill. The filth of the natives and the squalor of their surroundings appalls me.

I long with all my heart to be home. I think Colonel Kitchener is deliberately giving me the most objectionable tasks because he does not like me. I have a terrible pre-monition that I shall not live long in this horrible country. I beg you, Willow, to plead for me with Rowell. Try to make him understand that I can never be a credit to the Rochfords in circumstances like these . . .

But Rowell, so strong and self-controlled himself, was unable to read between the lines and understand Rupert's despair, Willow thought unhappily. He interpreted his younger brother's letter as one of complaint against minor discomforts. As for Rupert's dislike of Kitchener—that was to be expected, Rowell said. His weakling brother would have little in common with a man of courage and ambition.

Dear Rupert, Willow wrote. *I am afraid that there is no chance at the moment of you being allowed to come home, but Rowell is convinced that given a little more time, you will find life out there less strange and uncongenial. I hope so much that by the time this letter reaches you, you will be feeling much happier.*

In the meanwhile, dear Rupert, I am arranging to send you some medicaments together with a hamper of food from Fortnum's. Toby has recommended an opium compound for your stomach disturbance and Antipyrin and Phenacetin for your headaches. I trust these will arrive in good condition and relieve your pains.

In a very short while now I shall be making you an Uncle. I am keeping very well and so, too, is your sister, Dodie. The schoolmaster now calls three times a week after school has finished for the day and he is teaching Dodie to read and write. She is making most excellent progress and looks forward hugely to her lessons. Toby is designing a special support for her leg which he believes, with the aid of crutches, might make it possible for her to learn to walk. We have not told her yet for fear that Toby's invention will not succeed.

Willow's glance went once more to her husband. Rowell as yet knew nothing of this little secret she shared with Toby. And since neither the servants nor Aunt Mildred were allowed into Toby's laboratory, Grandmère knew nothing of their plan either. Only James McGill knew and had made several useful suggestions to Toby as to how Dodie herself could be taught to adjust the somewhat complicated contraption.

"The child has an exceptional ability to grasp quite new precepts in a matter of minutes," Mr. McGill had said, his pale face lit with a glow of enthusiasm. "I cannot tell you how much I am enjoying teaching her."

Rowell laid down his newspaper and walked over to the library window. He seemed even more restless than usual, Willow thought anxiously. There was little in the way of outdoor activity that he could enjoy while the weather remained so bad, and he was without occupation, unless it was a day when he went hunting or shooting. She herself was no longer able to receive visitors or to go with him in the carriage to call upon neighbors; and Rowell declined to go without her.

He was usually occupied well enough in the mornings giving instructions to his bailiff or talking to the head groom in the stables, but the afternoons dragged, and since he read little but the newspapers, he was very bored. His restlessness made Willow feel guilty and she was glad that Silvie was coming for Christmas, albeit with her less agreeable mother, Cousin Lucienne.

Silvie as always brought a bright festive mood with her. In no time at all, she had engaged even the reluctant Francis in charades, games of whist and Chinese checkers, bezique and drôle. She overruled Rowell's objections to Willow going for short drives with her in the governess cart, insisting that the fresh air would be good for her no matter what Doctor Forbes or Grandmère said.

"You let that husband of yours dictate to you far too much," she chided Willow. "All men are dictators if they are allowed to be so. You must impose your will upon him more often, chérie!"

Willow laughed.

"But it is my pleasure to please Rowell," she protested. "I cannot be happy or contented if he is not."

Silvie gave an exaggerated sigh.

"Then it is your misfortune to love such a selfish egotist as my cousin," she said.

She had brought with her from Paris practically an entire layette for the coming baby and, with her usual thoughtfulness, a quite extravagantly beautiful nightgown for Willow.

"So that you may sit up in bed afterwards looking *superbe*," she laughed. "Then your beloved Rowell will fall in love with you all over again."

But perhaps the most important of all that Silvie contributed to that Christmas was the manner in which she supported Willow and Toby when they suggested that Dodie should be allowed downstairs to join in the festivities.

"Of course she must be with us," she said firmly to Rowell when he forbade any such innovation. "And if Grandmère objects so strongly, then it is she who should remain alone in her suite, not poor little Dodie in her room. There will be no strangers to observe the poor child's deformities which, so far as I can see, is the only reason Grandmère has for objecting to her presence. It is quite outrageous, Rowell. The little girl is *très intelligente*. She is learning by heart some of Mr. Tennyson's poetry and is a *devotée* of Mr. Rudyard Kipling."

Rowell's face reddened.

"I accept that my sister is not so retarded as Grandmère and I had always thought, and that her studies do not appear to have done her any harm, but—"

"There are no other valid 'buts,' " Silvie said equally firmly. "Or is it your pride, dear cousin Rowell, that prevents you admitting that Willow was quite right and you and Grandmère wrong to treat the child as abnormal in this respect?"

"It is certainly not your prerogative to dictate to me in my own home, Silvie," Rowell retorted. "As it happens, I am not against Dodie being allowed to join the family circle for any reason other than that it would upset Grandmère."

"And that is not reason enough to debar a little girl from a more normal life," Silvie said spiritedly. "If you do not support your grandmother, Rowell, she will have to give way; and *that* will not harm her for once in her life."

Dodie was breathless with excitement as Willow sat watching while Violet dressed her for her first descent to the drawing room. Willow had had made for her a lace-trimmed velvet dress the same color as her eyes. To conceal her crippled leg, the dress was ankle length, and the lace ruffles at the cuffs also hid her crippled hand. Even Willow was surprised at how pretty the little girl looked when her toilette was completed.

Toby and Pelham came to carry her downstairs in the wicker invalid chair and added their compliments to Willow's. The child was radiant, and Willow prayed silently that neither Grandmère nor Aunt Mildred would wipe that trusting innocent look of happy expectation from Dodie's face. Fearing either one might well do so, she cautioned Dodie not to expect too much from her grandmother or her great aunt.

"Neither one is given to displays of affection," she said, "and it would perhaps be best you do not address them unless they speak first to you."

Dodie had smiled at Willow, looking quite unperturbed by this warning.

"You do not need to worry about me, dearest Willow," she said. "Mr. McGill has already explained to me that there are some people in the world who cannot help but feel disturbed by nature's imperfections. He said that they do not intend to be unkind, but they cannot alter their innermost feelings. He said I must never mind about my leg and arm because they were imperfections God gave me and He must have had His reasons for wanting it so. I told him about Francis and how he cannot bear to look at me, although you and Toby and Rupert do not mind."

Willow's heart warmed toward the young schoolmaster. He was not employed to give spiritual or moral guidance to this little girl, and yet he seemed excellently qualified to do both.

"Mr. McGill is quite right," she said, adding a last touch to Dodie's shining brown hair, so carefully curled by the willing Violet.

Grandmère did not appear for tea. Dutton informed Willow that her ladyship, Cousin Lucienne, and Aunt Mildred were taking tea in her suite. Silvie was angry, although Dodie's pleasure in everything she saw around her was undiminished.

"It is a deliberate snub to the child," Silvie whispered to Willow. "And yet I still believe Grandmère *will* come down—just to see what we are all up to."

Silvie's guess was correct. At five o'clock, Grandmère descended the stairs. With her portly cousin and stooped sister-in-law trailing behind her, she made her entrance into the drawing room.

Rowell hurried to her side and led her to a chair near to the fire. Dodie's invalid chair was placed beside the big Christmas tree where she could gaze to her heart's delight at the flickering wax candles.

Grandmère's eyes darted across the room to her granddaughter and as quickly away again.

"You may say good evening to your grandmother, Dodie," Silvie said, wickedly determined not to allow the old lady to ignore the child completely. "Perhaps you would like to say it in French so that Grandmère can hear how well you speak her language."

Dodie looked shyly at the forbidding old woman.

"*Bon soir, Grandmère! J'espère que vous êtes en bon santé.*"

"I'm in excellent health, thank you," the old lady replied grudgingly, but in English. Her eyes then turned to Willow. "You look tired," she said. "Should you not be resting?"

Willow tried to believe that the remark was kindly intended, but there was a look in the old lady's eyes which made her words sound more critical than concerned.

She was convinced, despite Rowell's denial, that Grandmère did not welcome the coming of her great grandchild. And now that Willow's time was getting nearer, she began increasingly to worry about Grandmère's belief that a weak strain dogged the distaff side of the family. Not even Toby's repeated reassurances could remove her own nagging fear that she might have a little girl who would die in infancy or who would suffer what poor Dodie had suffered in her young life. She longed and prayed now that she would be able to give Rowell a son.

Silvie did what she could to reassure Willow. She was the only person other than Toby in whom Willow confided her fears.

"I wish so much you were going to be here at Rochford for the birth in March!" Willow said when the Christmas holiday was over and Silvie was packing to depart. "I suppose I am being fanciful but I do believe I am afraid of Grandmère. I know she cannot actually harm me but I feel she threatens me in some indefinable way."

Silvie hugged the younger girl.

"She is a bully, that is all. If you stand up to her, she gives in. If you ask me, the old lady has had far too much of her own way for far too long. Rowell should exert more authority over her."

She hugged Willow again.

"I will try to visit you in the summer," she said comfortingly. "Or better still, you must come to Paris and visit with me. Your baby will be quite old enough to leave by then. We will have a magnificently gay time together. I will pack *Maman* off to the country and we will arrange something to occupy Rowell. Then we will be free to enjoy ourselves, no?"

Willow smiled.

"That word 'freedom' is never far from your lips, is it, Silvie? But I am not like you. For me, happiness lies in sharing my life with Rowell."

"*C'est bien dommage, quand même!*" Silvie said laughing.

The big house seemed very quiet without her. Francis went back to Oxford; Pelham, who had left Oxford, accepted an invitation to go to Egypt with three of his university friends. Like so many of the well-to-do, he planned to avoid the worst of the English winter, staying at Shepheard's Hotel in Cairo and amusing himself with excursions to see the Great Sphinx and the pyramids. But Rowell remained at home and although he spent most days shooting or hunting or paying informal calls upon his neighboring friends, Willow had him to herself in the evenings and was content.

But as February drew to a close, Rowell became increasingly restless. He seemed unable to settle even to reading the newspapers.

"You are not worrying about me, are you?" Willow asked innocently, for she had still another month to wait before the baby arrived.

Rowell had the grace to look ashamed. He was actually worrying about Georgina, whom he strongly suspected of being unfaithful to him. She had complained bitterly to him how bored she was by his continued absence, even though he had explained the reasons for it.

"I don't see why you have to dance attendance upon your wife simply because she is *enceinte!*" Georgina grumbled in one of her lengthy ink-splotched letters. "There is not enough to occupy me looking after this little house. Please come to see me soon, Rowell. I want you so much . . ."

At last Rowell could no longer withstand her pleas or his own hunger for her body. Telling Willow that he really must deal with urgent business affairs in London, he absented himself for two weeks.

"I will be back in plenty of time for the baby's arrival," he promised.

Willow did not try to stop him. In some ways, she was relieved to see him go, for she no longer had to worry herself as to how to entertain him. She had tired more quickly of late and now she sought her bed as soon as the evening meal was over. In her room, the fire blazing cheerily in the grate, Nellie embroidering in a chair by her bed, she could relax against her pillows and enjoy uninterrupted reading of *Washington Square* by Henry

James, a recent publication which Pelham had bought for her in London.

So long as Rowell was nearby when the child was born, she was content to accept his absence now, even though Toby too was away. He had gone to Paris to see the eminent scientist, Monsieur Louis Pasteur, to whom he had written some weeks previously. Somewhat to Toby's astonishment, he had received a letter inviting him to the Pasteur Institute to discuss the subject nearest to his heart —the transmission of diseases.

It was to this domestic all-female household that Rupert Rochford returned in a horse-drawn ambulance from Southampton, where the ship bringing him back from Egypt had docked that morning.

Willow heard the commotion outside her bedroom window and sent Nellie down to investigate. Within five minutes, Nellie was back, her rosy face a strange mixture of excitement and apprehension.

" 'Tis Mr. Rupert, Milady, and he's very ill, and Lady Rochford and Miss Mildred are seeing to him and Cook is giving the driver and the ambulance men some supper. And Mr. Rupert has a soldier with him what Mr. Dutton told me was his batman what took care of him in Egypt. And Mr. Dutton said the soldier said as how Mr. Rupert wasn't sick nor nothing but gone to pieces—his nerves, like."

She paused to draw breath.

"He looked ever so pale when Harry—I mean Stevens, Milady—and that there batman carried him up to his room. And he was crying something awful. And Lady Rochford looked ever so angry. Mr. Dutton says it's the disgrace, you see, though I don't see why it's a disgrace to be ill."

In other circumstances Willow would have dressed and gone downstairs to see what she could do. But she did not feel able in her present state to do battle with Grandmère. Doubtless, it could wait until tomorrow. Maybe Grandmère would decide to send to London for Rowell.

But old Lady Rochford would hear of no such thing.

"There is nothing Rowell can do—or anyone else," she told Willow at breakfast. "I always knew something like this would happen. The boy's a weakling—a disgrace both to his father's and his grandfather's memories. *Dis-*

charged!" She was almost spitting out the words. *"Unfit for active service! It is intolerable!"*

Willow felt a swift surge of anger that was like a physical pain deep within her.

"Perhaps now you will agree that Rupert should never have gone into the army," she said pointedly. "Toby and I did warn you, Grandmère."

But the old lady, accompanied by a fussing Aunt Milly, withdrew from the dining room unwilling to face Willow's accusing eyes.

Doctor Forbes came to see Rupert, but professed himself unable to do much except prescribe plenty of rest, sleep, and good food.

"From what his man tells me, his nerve failed him in a skirmish somewhere down the Nile when they were out on an exploratory patrol," he told Willow. "I fear it may be some time before he recovers. And you, my dear Lady Rochford? You are keeping well?"

"Yes, thank you, but I am tired."

"Naturally," he said soothingly. "Only three weeks to go now, my dear young lady, and then it will all be over."

Three weeks seemed an unendurably long time, Willow thought as she climbed gratefully between the sheets that night. There was a dragging sensation in her lower abdomen, and from time to time she had a niggling pain that kept her from concentrating upon her book.

She was on the point of dismissing Nellie when the first real pain caused her to sit up in alarm. Nellie regarded her attentively.

"Is there something wrong, Milady?"

Willow shook her head doubtfully. It could not be the baby arriving, for it was not due yet. But the pain was very similar to that which she had endured when she had miscarried her last child. She lay back waiting until a second pain engulfed her. Then she said to Nellie:

"I think I am in labor. Go and tell Lady Rochford."

She felt both anxious and elated. Although she dreaded the pain, she longed to hold this baby in her arms. She seemed to have been waiting for it for so long. Soon she would know if it was a boy or a girl . . .

Grandmère came to her bedside. The shawl collar of her heavy satin dressing gown was disarrayed and had obviously been flung over her nightgown in a hurry. Her white hair was still covered by her lace-trimmed sleeping cap. She looked down at Willow speculatively.

"It would seem as if your time has come, my dear," she said not unkindly. "I recall that Alice had that same rosy glow in her cheeks at the beginning of labor. Now, don't worry about anything. Doctor Forbes has had plenty of experience bringing babies into the world and he will be here presently with the midwife. I've sent Nellie to the kitchen to get you some blackcurrant tea."

Willow's labor lasted far into the night. Nellie stood patiently by the bedside wiping the sweat from Willow's face with a wet flannel. Her body was racked more and more frequently by pain and Doctor Forbes' face began to take on a look of anxiety.

"It will be a breach birth, I'm afraid," he said to the midwife, a fat, homely woman from the village who assisted him on such occasions. "Please get my instruments ready at once. I am going to need them."

His anxiety was not unfounded. The baby was finally dragged feet first from its mother's womb—at first by hand, and then when the head appeared, by forceps. It was a mere six pounds in weight and obviously premature. The deep marks of the forceps were indented on either side of its crumpled face, and to the doctor's dismay, there was a light covering of hair on the infant's upper arms and back. It was no fit sight for its mother, and he instructed the midwife to clean it and place it in the basinette in the adjoining dressing room for the time being.

Willow was barely conscious as the doctor delivered the afterbirth and then left his patient to the midwife's care. Nellie had long since been sent out of the room, for the elderly doctor did not consider it proper that a young and unmarried girl should witness the birth. He disregarded Nellie's protest that she had attended the births of many of her brothers and sisters and wished to remain with her mistress. She had been sent to the kitchen and told to wait there for instructions.

The doctor now walked down the landing and knocked on the door of Lady Rochford's room. Aunt Mildred answered his knock instantly. So they had obviously been awaiting his visit, he thought, his anxiety increasing. He did not have good news for the old lady and he dreaded the coming interview.

"Well, what is it?" she asked him. "Boy or girl?"

She was propped up in bed, a small but impressive figure as she gave the grey-haired doctor one of her penetrating stares.

"A girl, I fear," the doctor mumbled. He was very tired and longed to be able to sit down and ease his legs. But the woman kept him standing.

"Continue!" she barked at him. "I can see by your face that you do not have good news for me. There is something wrong with it?"

"Not exactly wrong," the doctor prevaricated. "It is simply that the birth was difficult—a breach birth—and the baby is also premature and so—"

"The child is not perfect!" Grandmère's words were a statement rather than a question. She looked at the doctor's unhappy face and her mouth tightened. "Bring the child here. I wish to see it!"

The old lady was quite well able to visit the baby, the man thought. But it never crossed his mind to argue with her. He went down the landing and opened the dressing-room door. The midwife was still with the now-sleeping patient. Peering into the bassinette, he saw that the baby, too, seemed to be sleeping. Washed and wrapped in a warm blanket, it did not look quite so unsightly as at the moment of birth, but what could be seen of its face still revealed the two ugly weals caused by the forceps. The skin was puffy and wrinkled. Used though he was to such sights, he knew that he would have been hard put to find complimentary words to say about it. It was not a pretty baby.

He lifted the child and carried it from the room unnoticed by the midwife. Outside the door of Lady Rochford's suite, he paused, some strange sixth sense warning him of impending danger. But there was no avoiding this moment, and he knocked on the door for the second time.

The old lady was now out of bed. She came to meet him with surprising alacrity as if she could not contain her anxiety to see the child. As he held it out, she pulled open the blanket. Every muscle of her face and jaw tightened.

"I knew when you told me it was a girl that something was wrong. I saw it in your face. The baby is abnormal," she said sharply.

"But we cannot be sure as yet, Lady Rochford," the doctor argued feebly. "It was a difficult birth, and the child is premature and——"

"And I do not intend to wait until you make up your mind at some later date," the old lady interrupted him. "I can see for myself that it is not a healthy, normal Rochford baby. Do you dispute that view, Doctor?"

"Of course not, Lady Rochford, but after a few weeks, it might——"

"I will not take that risk. *It will have to go!*"

Doctor Forbes stared at her aghast. What could she mean? "Surely not——" So great was his horror that words failed him.

Beside him, Mildred gasped, then bleated:

"No, Clotilde, you cannot——"

"Don't be such a fool, Mildred. I don't mean to murder my own flesh and blood," Grandmère said coldly. She turned back to the doctor. "You must remove the baby at once," she told him authoritatively. "I was afraid something like this would transpire and I have already made suitable plans for this eventuality which I fully anticipated."

"Plans?" the doctor echoed stupidly. Again he felt a premonition of danger. His hands shook uncontrollably.

"Yes, plans! The child is to go to a wet nurse—as far from Havorhurst as possible. *You* will have to arrange that. Its true identity is not to be known, do you understand? You can tell some story—that it is the illegitimate offspring of a well-to-do family, if you like. I shall pay for its keep, of course. Later, when it is old enough—and if it survives—it can be sent to a convent in France."

Both Doctor Forbes and Aunt Mildred were staring at her disbelievingly.

"But the baby's mother . . ." the doctor protested. "And your grandson . . . what would they say about such an arrangement? The mother may wish——"

"The mother will have no say whatever in the matter," Lady Rochford broke in. "She, my son, everyone in the house will be told the child died shortly after birth. Don't you understand, man? You will be doing the unhappy parents—all of us—a kindness. We cannot endure a second time all we have had to suffer because of Dorothy."

She took another quick glance at the baby, and as quickly, averted her eyes again.

"But, Clotilde," Aunt Mildred protested feebly, "even if this could all be done as you suggest, it would be forever on our consciences. It would be a sin."

"Then you will just have to put up with your conscience, Mildred," the old lady said sharply, "because my mind is made up."

"I cannot do it, Lady Rochford," Doctor Forbes burst out. "It would be quite against all my moral beliefs, my code of ethics. Besides, who would believe the child was dead? There would be no body——"

"Nor any need for one. I will arrange for a burial service tomorrow. In the meanwhile, I will tell my son that I asked you to remove the corpse to spare its mother's feelings. She should not be allowed to see such a . . . a hidious result of her labors. All you have to do is remove the child to a foster home, sign a death certificate, and obtain a coffin. That is all."

"It would be denying the child its rightful inheritance," Doctor Forbes found the courage to say. "Nor may it even be necessary, Lady Rochford. As I told you, it was prematurely born, and within a week at most, the downy hair on its arms and shoulders will be gone."

"I will not gamble on so serious a matter," Lady Rochford repeated. "It is best for everyone, including the child, if you do as I say. An idiot in a village community is not unacceptable. In our household, it would be. The child will have a better existence elsewhere."

"I cannot be a party to this!" the doctor cried. "I wish to please you whenever possible, Lady Rochford, but in this, I fear I cannot be a party to what I know in my heart is wrong."

The old lady did not walk away from him nor give any sign of anger. She said quietly:

"I have always rewarded you well for your services and hope that I may continue to do so for many years to come. But I would not be happy with the continuation of our hitherto excellent relationship were you to go against my wishes now, Doctor Forbes. I would, I fear, feel forced to expose your son's misconduct, and that, I regret to say, would inevitably damage *your* reputation. I doubt very much whether you would be able to continue with your practice here—or elsewhere."

"My son!" the doctor repeated with genuine surprise. "I don't understand. What misconduct? He is a little wild, I admit, but he has committed no crime."

"So *you* believe, my poor man. But I do not go around with my head in the sand and my ears blocked as you do. Last summer, when that wretched grandson of mine returned disgraced from Oxford, he renewed his friendship with your son. The Baron did his best to stop it, but to no avail. Both young men were seen in the most unsavory circumstances in my grandson's bedroom."

"You mean they had girls in there? Maids, perhaps?" the doctor asked, duly shocked.

"Far worse than that," Lady Rochford said bitingly. "They had each other, Doctor Forbes. Miss Mildred heard them . . . saw them, in fact."

The doctor's face whitened, and he staggered as if his legs would give way beneath him.

"I cannot believe it," he said. "Adrian is . . . a disappointment to me in many ways, but he is not a—"

"Pederast? Indeed, I fear that he is and that he has corrupted my grandson."

The doctor was silenced by the very sound of the word. Then reason reasserted itself.

"Your grandson is at least four years older than my son. If there was any corruption—"

"My dear doctor, you really are not considering the facts as a jury would see them. Rupert may be older, but he is known universally to be a very weak character. Look at him this minute—a pathetic creature! Your son Adrian at the age of seventeen is far stronger, more mature in every way. Moreover, he has not had the good fortune to be given the moral training and advantages that are afforded all the Rochford boys. The good name of our family will hardly suffer, I think, even if Rupert himself is disgraced."

Nor would it, the doctor thought. He looked helplessly at the thin, unhappy spinster who had, apparently, caught the boys in their criminal act.

"You are sure, Miss Mildred?" he asked.

Her face reddened, her eyelids fluttered, and she sniffed several times before she said:

"I heard them talking . . . calling each other by pet names. Then I heard the kissing, and your son was laughing, and Rupert was—"

"That's quite enough, Mildred. We don't want to listen to the sordid details. Now make up your mind, Doctor Forbes. Are we to protect each other's interests, as indeed we always have in the past, or are you going to force me—for I should be most reluctant—to expose your hypocrisy? For that is what it would be, would it not, if you insist now upon a matter of ethics while overlooking your son's criminal offenses."

The doctor remained silent, trapped by a memory of two events he had almost succeeded in putting out of his mind. On the first occasion, he had noticed Adrian wearing a gold cravat pin and cuff links. Under pressure from his father, the lad had admitted that they were a present from Rupert Rochford. Defiantly, he admitted to receiving other valuable gifts: a watch, a gold-topped malacca cane.

"They are payment in kind for jobs I do for Rupert —for Mr. Rochford!" Adrian had said, flustered by his questions.

"The values are disproportionate," his father had said; but he had let the matter drop since he was tired and very busy. Then he had found the letter in Adrian's desk when searching innocently for a new nib for his pen. At first he had thought it a love letter from a girl until his eyes had caught sight of the signature—*"your ever loving and faithful admirer, Rupert."*

Even then it did not cross his mind that his son was involved in an illicit relationship. Adrian was rough and ready—never dandified unless he was courting a girl. But he *had* suspected him of using the Rochford boy's affection for his own ends—to extort easy money of which Adrian was always in need.

But at the time, it seemed easier to pretend he had not seen the letter. In true cowardly fashion, he had quibbled at the thought of having to take Adrian to task, perhaps even having to confront Rupert himself or, worse still, old Lady Rochford.

Now, too late, he realized that there was no way he could lay the blame at Rupert's door. Adrian was a minor—still under his father's jurisdiction. He himself would never be considered blameless in his failure to control his son, and Lady Rochford might well throw her least-loved grandson to the dogs if it suited her to do so. She had the other boys to prove that Rupert was the rotten apple in the barrel and she might well disown him.

As he carried the still-sleeping child out of the room, his head was bowed in defeat. Despairingly, he asked himself if he could be living in a nightmare; if with a little luck, he might not wake up in a moment and find this was all a terrible dream. But he knew it was no such thing; that he must try somehow to gather his wits together. He must convince the midwife; pacify the mother. A little laudanum as a sleeping draught would at least put off until morning the news he must give his patient.

Then there were the servants to consider. If not Dutton, then a footman would still be awake to hand him his outer garments and open the front door for him. It was fortunate, he thought, that he had driven himself here in his gig. There would be no one to hear if the baby cried on the journey to the village; no one to see where he was going.

But first he must explain to the midwife why he was taking the child out of the house. For a newly born infant —premature at that—to be taken into the night air was madness, unless it were already dead. But in such an event, the child would be left at the manor. His only valid reason for taking it away from Rochford Manor was that time would be saved if he took the baby to the wet nurse rather than having to make two journeys to bring the woman here.

So the conspiracy has begun, he thought wretchedly, as the first of the many lies he must tell came to mind. Even now he was far from certain that he could go through with the old lady's plan, clever though it was. Yet he *must* find the courage somehow. He knew her too well to suppose that she would not carry out her threat to expose Adrian. How deeply involved was his son? he wondered. But he had no time to consider Adrian's part in this at the moment. He must talk to the midwife.

The sleepy-eyed woman was clearly surprised to see the child in his arms and not in the bassinette where she had placed it.

"The infant is ailing, I fear," he said shortly. "It needs a wet nurse immediately if it is to survive at all. Milady will have no milk for several days since it was a premature birth. You are to remain here with Lady Rochford until I call tomorrow. If she asks, you may tell her that in order to give the baby the chance of survival, I am taking it to a wet nurse immediately. But as soon as the patient is awake, I want you to give her a sleeping draught. It is better she remain unconscious for the time being since the absence of her child will certainly distress her. Do you understand me?"

"Yes, sir, and if she asks if it is all right, what am I to say?"

"Be noncommittal. Say I took the baby away before you could see much of it. There is no need to upset her with a description of its deformities!"

As he turned his horse's head down the drive, the infant began to wail—a thin, piteous cry which he knew to be hunger. Perhaps he really was acting for the best, he told himself. The woman to whom he intended to take it had recently given birth to her own child in a village not eight miles from Havorhurst. She was healthy and would welcome the money. If the premature baby had any chance of survival, it might do better in the care of such a woman than in a household where at least one member was intent upon its destruction.

How well conceived was Lady Rochford's plan, he thought bitterly. She had known there was certain to be one or more such women only too anxious to be paid to feed an extra mouth. Seldom a week passed without some farmer's wife producing an addition to her family. Such children came at yearly intervals—their mothers often pregnant before they had finished suckling the last child.

Was the old lady evil as well as clever? he asked himself. Thirty years ago he had been afraid of her and he was still afraid—if not of her, then of the power she wielded.

Thinking back to the birth of the last little girl, Dorothy, he could believe now that old Lady Rochford might have taken similar steps to have *her* removed had the child not seemed to be quite perfect when she was born. The first sign of illness did not appear until she was over a year old, and by then it would have been too late even for Lady Rochford to devise a means of having her spirited away.

The enormity of the crime he was now engaged upon struck him anew. He realized that he had been blackmailed, and his own weakness appalled him. Worst of all to bear was the realization that it was not for Adrian's sake that he was now submitting to old Lady Rochford's will; it was to protect himself. He was fifty-six years old, and if in such scandalous circumstances as would attend his son's exposure, he were to lose his position here at Havorhurst, he could not hope to practice elsewhere without recommendations.

The child's cries intensified, then ceased altogether. Perhaps it had died, he thought, and was horrified to realize that he hoped it had expired. He did not stop to unwrap the bundle beside him. He shivered as the cold early morning air penetrated his warm clothing.

But the chill did not come so much from the elements as from the icy grip of guilt that now and forevermore clutched his heart.

Chapter Nine

March–July 1894

WILLOW WOKE FROM A DEEP SLEEP TO SEE NELLIE sitting by her bedside. An oil lamp glowed dimly in a far corner of the room. The curtains were drawn. There was a tumbler and several bottles of medicine on the bedside table.

"Why, Nellie, you are crying," she said. She wanted to ask why, but her eyes felt heavy and the images in the room blurred. In a chair by the window sat a round, plump woman in a cap and apron whose face seemed vaguely familiar. But as this figure stood up and came toward Willow, her eyelids drooped and she fell asleep again.

When next she woke it was to find Rowell in the chair beside her bed. She smiled at him.

"How wonderful to have you home, my love," she said

drowsily. There was no answering smile on his face as he looked down at her gravely.

"Is something wrong, Rowell?" she asked. She became aware that it was daylight, but that she was in her night-clothes in bed. "Am I ill?" A feeling of anxiety replaced her pleasure in seeing her husband.

"Don't you remember, my dear?" Rowell's voice sounded hushed and strangely compassionate. "You have given birth to the baby."

Instinctively, Willow's hands reached beneath the bed-clothes to feel her stomach. Excitement brought her fully awake as memory began to return.

"How could I have forgotten! Oh, Rowell, where is my baby? Is it a boy? A girl? I remember hearing it cry and after that—" She broke off in mid-sentence, some-thing in Rowell's averted gaze bringing apprehension in place of anticipation. He seemed unable to speak.

"Rowell, it is a girl, isn't it, and you are very disap-pointed. Is that it?" A horrifying thought struck her at the same time as she became aware of a dull throbbing pain between her legs. "There is nothing wrong with the baby, is there?" Her voice rose, and Rowell, frowning, took her hand.

"I am afraid I have unhappy news for you. The . . . the child is dead!"

Willow stared at him round-eyed. She could now recall the agony of the long drawn-out labor, the terrifying pain of the birth itself.

"But I heard it cry, Rowell—"

She broke off, seeing only pity in his eyes.

"I am afraid it died soon after it was born. I'm sorry, my dear. Doctor Forbes did what he could but . . . some-times these things are for the best."

Willow tried to sit up, but she seemed to have no strength in her body. Weakly, she fell back against the pillows.

"What do you mean *'for the best?'*" she cried bitterly. "My baby is dead, and you say it is for the best. Why couldn't Doctor Forbes save it? It *was* a girl, wasn't it?"

Rowell nodded. Willow reached out and grabbed hold of his arm.

"There was something wrong—that's why you won't talk about it. Where is she? I want to see her."

Gently Rowell disentangled himself from her grasp.

"Now, now, dear. Forbes says you must be kept very quiet," he said awkwardly. "I don't think we should discuss the details now, my poor darling. As soon as you are stronger, we will talk about it."

"But I want to know now. I must know. The baby came too soon. Is that it?"

Rowell nodded, relieved that she had given him an acceptable explanation. Later on when she was fully recovered, Doctor Forbes could tell her about the child's deformities. In the meanwhile . . .

"Yes, it was prematurely born," he said. "Now try to sleep, my love. I will send Nellie up to you. I have a few letters to write. I will visit you again later this evening."

She let him go without argument, for he seemed strangely unaware of the pain screaming a protest inside her head. Her baby was dead—and Rowell did not seem to care. He would not even tell her what the baby was like.

Nellie came into the room. Her eyes were red-rimmed. She hurried over to the bedside.

"The Master said you were quite conscious, Milady, so I came at once."

She looked anxiously at Willow's white face. It disturbed her that her young mistress was not weeping, for the Baron had informed her that he had told his wife the child was dead.

"Nellie, is Mr. Toby back from France?"

"Oh, yes, Milady!" Nellie said as she plumped up the pillows behind Willow's head and spooned some water between her lips. "He came back two days ago. You've been unconscious these past three days, you know. The doctor felt it best to keep you under sedation."

Three days! Willow thought. If only she could clear her head so that she could remember what had happened after she had heard the child cry. But it all seemed hazy . . . a jumble of pain, discomfort, strange people bending over her—and Nellie weeping.

"Go and find Mr. Toby and tell him I want to see him," she said. Nellie hesitated, her expression unhappy.

"Doctor said you were not to have any visitors except the Master, Milady."

"I don't care what the doctor said," Willow replied

sharply. "I want to see Mr. Toby now. Tell him not to let anyone see him come to my room. And Nellie, you can stay outside the door while he is here and warn us if anyone approaches. I don't want to get him into any trouble for disobeying the doctor's orders."

Nellie hurried off, willing enough now to do Willow's bidding. She liked Mr. Toby. He was always quiet and calm, and maybe, she thought, her mistress would be the better for a talk with him.

Despite Willow's anxiety to see Toby, she was almost asleep again when he came quietly into the room. She only realized he was in the chair by her bed when she felt his hand on her forehead. Opening her eyes, she looked up into his face and saw both anxiety and compassion there.

"I expect you are still feeling a bit drowsy," he said with an attempt to smile. "Forbes has been giving you laudanum, I gather, so don't worry if you are a little confused."

His voice, his words were reassuring. She tried to smile at him, but her lower lip trembled.

"Toby, I know I can rely on you to speak the truth and *I have to know*. Rowell said my baby died, but he won't tell me why. What was wrong?"

Toby did not look away, although the tortured expression in Willow's dark eyes distressed him immeasurably. He took both her hands in his and held them tightly.

"Unfortunately—and I cannot tell you how deeply I regret it—I was not back until almost forty-eight hours after the birth, Willow, so I can only tell you the facts as they have been told to me. The baby was premature and it was a breach birth—that is to say, it was not in the correct position when you went into labor. Doctor Forbes had finally to deliver it with instruments. It was very weak, and because he knew you would not be able to feed it—because the birth was premature, you understand —he decided its only chance of survival was to put it in the care of a wet nurse."

He paused, unhappily aware of Willow's eyes riveted on his face as he spoke. There was no way in which he could avoid the truth.

"Forbes decided that he might save precious time if, he, himself, took the baby to the nurse, rather than sent for the woman to come here. As it happened, it was probably the wrong decision. So young and weak an infant should not have been subjected to that cold night air. But it died even before he reached Havorhurst, so we have to accept, dearest Willow, that it was not very strong and may well have died even had it remained here."

"If you had been here, Toby, would you have agreed to let him take the baby outside?" Willow demanded.

Toby hesitated. He would not lie to her.

"No, I suppose not," he admitted. "I told Doctor Forbes that I thought he had been wrong, and he agreed it could have been a mistake. But he assured me that it seemed at the time to be the best chance of saving the baby's life. It would have been several hours before the wet nurse could have been brought here to Rochford Manor, and he considered that too long an interval before it received sustenance of some kind."

"Thank you for being honest, Toby. Now I have one more question." Willow's voice was unnaturally calm, controlled. "Was my little girl abnormal in any way, other than that she was premature? Rowell said her death was 'for the best.' What did he mean? I want an answer, Toby."

A deep flush crept slowly over Toby's face. It was very rare that he lost control of himself, but he had been furiously angry with Rowell and Grandmère for making the assumption—totally unjustified in his opinion—that the baby had been deformed. He was even more angry now with Rowell for letting Willow suspect such a possibility.

"There was absolutely nothing wrong with the child that could not be attributable to the method of its birth and the fact that it was premature," he said forcefully. "I questioned Doctor Forbes closely, not only on *your* behalf, Willow, but because as you know, I have strong theories on this hereditary factor that is supposed to affect our family. I do not believe it exists and one day, by God, I'll prove it."

To his horror, he saw that two tears had gathered in Willow's eyes and were now rolling down her cheeks.

"Willow, dearest Willow, forgive me," he cried, as, without thinking, he gathered her impulsively into his arms. Her tears came faster, and soon she was sobbing uncontrollably against his shoulder. He rocked her gently as he might have rocked Dodie, his love and pity for her so overwhelming that words choked in his throat.

"Promise you won't leave me!" Willow said tremulously as her sobs at last began to subside. "I trust you, Toby. I don't seem to be able to trust anybody else. You won't go away again? Promise!"

"Of course I promise. And now you will go back to sleep and get well and strong again. And I shall come and visit you no matter who forbids it." He laid her gently back against the pillows, smoothing the fair hair from her damp forehead. His heart was aching for her. She looked so small, so frail, so bereft.

He remained by her bedside until he saw her eyes close. Then he left the room, shutting the door quietly behind him.

"You're to tell me at once if your mistress wants to see me, or if you yourself are in any way worried about her," he told Nellie. "You understand me? If anything or anybody upsets her, *I want to know.*"

It was a week before Doctor Forbes would give his official permission for Toby to see Willow, although he did see her every day. By then Willow was allowed to sit up in bed, although only for meals. A further ten days passed before she was allowed out of bed for a few minutes, wrapped in blankets; two weeks before she was permitted to dress and spend an hour or two before and after lunch taking little walks around her room.

The services of the midwife, who had remained to nurse her for the first week, were dispensed with as soon as it became clear that Nellie could perform such duties perfectly adequately. Willow had voiced both to Rowell and to the doctor, an unaccountable antipathy to the woman. She refused also to receive a visit from Grandmère. Doctor Forbes had reluctantly dismissed the midwife and forbidden visits from Lady Rochford. The invalid must be permitted a few irrational foibles at such a time, he said apologetically.

Rowell went regularly to his wife's bedside, but never stayed for very long. He seemed anxious to avoid any discussion about the baby, and since this remained uppermost in Willow's mind, conversation between them quickly flagged. She knew he was trying to offer what sympathy he could and tried not to feel resentful when he brought her little gifts which he had especially sent down from London. She told herself that he was very generous and his intentions kindly meant; but nevertheless, she felt bitter that he did not understand why she resented his premise that a piece of jewelry or an expensive ornament could begin to compensate for the loss of her child.

Toby and Nellie seemed to understand her despair far better, although she never cried again in front of either one.

"You mustn't let Dodie know I have told you our secret," Toby said to Willow one day, "but she is trying very hard to walk in my patent contraption. I fear the leather straps chafe her hip where the weight rests and I have had to adjust my design so that there are soft pads where it touches the bone."

Willow was in her chair by the window, a warm rug over her knees. Toby was sitting near her, his long legs stretched out in front of the fire. The room looked warm and cheerful in the firelight.

"You love Dodie, don't you, Toby?" Willow said. "I think you and I are the only two in the family who really do love her."

"I worry about her future," Toby said thoughtfully. "It seems so terrible to me that she will not be loved as other women are. She has grown quite remarkably pretty of late, do you not agree?"

Willow nodded.

"She has turned thirteen, Toby, and will soon be a young woman. Perhaps one day some young man will find her beautiful and overlook her deformities. After all, we don't even notice them."

"But to some she is repugnant," Toby said with rare bitterness. "Francis for one cannot bear to be in the same room with her. And Rupert becomes very distressed if her arm and leg are not concealed."

"How is Rupert? Is he not better?" Willow asked. "Rowell seems to think that as long as he remains secluded in that room of his he will never make a proper recovery."

"Perhaps Rupert does not feel able yet to cope with the family censure he knows will await him. His room is his refuge," Toby said thoughtfully. "At least he is not so often alone now that he has allowed Dodie to go in and read to him. He is teaching her chess, she tells me, and that sounds a big step forward to me. I think Dodie is the only one of the family he can cope with at the moment. He may not feel so inferior with her as he does with adults."

The silence that now fell was a comfortable one as they watched the fire flickering in the grate. Soon Nellie would arrive with Willow's tea, but for the moment, they could count upon remaining undisturbed.

"Toby!" Willow said into the silence. "I have not asked before, but I want you to tell me about my baby's funeral. Was she baptized?"

"Oh, yes, I believe so—else she could not have been buried in consecrated ground. And there was a proper funeral, Willow. The . . . the little coffin was brought back to the house the day after her birth, and the Reverend Appleby was here. I think Grandmère asked that the baby should be named Sophia—or else Aunt Milly chose the name. Grandmère herself attended the funeral service . . . and Rowell, of course."

"But not you, Toby?" Willow asked curiously.

He shook his head, looking suddenly embarrassed.

"I thought someone responsible ought to remain here with you, and with Rupert, of course. There were only the servants and—" he broke off vaguely.

Willow smiled.

"I should have known you were never far away. I remember asking you to promise not to leave me. It seems strange now. I cannot think why I should have felt so afraid; or why, when you were here, I felt safe."

Toby's face flushed but it was not noticeable to Willow, who saw only the firelight reflected upon his cheeks.

"Here's Nellie with your tea!" Toby said, relieved at the interruption. "I must get back to my room, Willow, and do some work."

"Is it going well?" Willow asked. "Your journey to Paris was useful, Toby?"

His face lit up with undisguised enthusiasm.

"Indeed it was! Monsieur Pasteur is President of the Sorbonne and a most remarkable man, Willow. Ever since I read his article in *The Lancet* last year, I felt instinctively that my experiments were running in parallel to his. He has proven a fascinating fact—that rabies is not something people contract out of the blue, but is actually passed via the saliva of a rabid animal to the individual through an abrasion in the skin. Monsieur Pasteur also showed a most flattering interest in my research into the ways by which people catch diphtheria. Imagine, Willow, so great a man taking time to listen to me . . . unknown, unqualified as I am! Yet he treated me as if I were as eminent a scientist as himself."

"Then your research must have impressed him," Willow said. "I have no doubt that one day there will be a Tobias Rochford Institute, and people will come from all over the world to pay homage to you and learn from you."

Toby laughed, pleased by her compliment.

"It is encouraging to have one admirer I can count upon. I am indebted to you for your belief in me, my dear Willow, however misplaced it may be."

But it was she who was in Toby's debt, Willow thought as the weeks passed and life returned once more to normal. He had seen her through the bad, dark days when she had felt she could never come to terms with her baby's death.

Francis returned home for the Easter vacation and left again a few weeks later for the new term. Pelham, who had returned from Egypt, was staying in Oxford for May week.

I wish I could invite you to the Commem ball next month, he wrote to Willow. *Young Francis has fallen crazily in love with a New Zealand girl three years older than himself. She has very advanced ideas on females' being equal in intelligence to males which scarcely pleases Francis. But she is very beautiful and he cannot say her "nay."*

Rowell decided to rent a house in London for the Season.

"You need cheering up, my dear," he said to Willow. "And it will be useful for Pelham and Francis, too. We will take most of the servants with us—other than those required by Grandmère and Aunt Milly . . . and Rupert," he added frowning. "I suppose it is quite pointless to suggest he come to London. Besides, he would hear far too much talk about the Oscar Wilde trial. I have forbidden the subject to be mentioned in this house."

It was difficult to comply with Rowell's wishes. Not only was every newspaper filled with detail about the trial, but their friends could talk of little else, so notorious was the scandal.

At first Willow felt little enthusiasm for removing to London for the Season. She was uneasy about leaving Rupert and Dodie alone with Grandmère and Aunt Mildred. But James McGill was reassuring about Dodie.

"I do not think Lady Rochford will try to dismiss me in your absence," he said. "She has become well accustomed to my regular visits, and I think she is now quite content that her granddaughter is thus harmlessly occupied. Moreover, I make certain that the child and I are never in her way, and so she has had no cause to complain."

But Toby, too, elected to remain at Rochford.

"The London Season would not really give me any pleasure, as well you know, Willow," he assured her. "I prefer country life to city life and, besides, I have more important things to do than waste my time waltzing with simpering young debutantes."

"But you waltz very well, Toby!" Willow laughingly teased him.

"Only with you, Willow, because I know you will be patient if I tread on your toes. Perhaps, just to please you, I will come up for the evening of your birthday."

Rowell was planning an especially lavish ball for the occasion of Willow's twentieth birthday. The large house he had rented in Park Lane could easily accommodate the five hundred guests invited. The Prince of Wales, and, to Willow's great excitement, Princess Alexandra, had already accepted. Rowell considered it quite an honor, for the Princess was becoming increasingly deaf in middle age and less and less inclined to accompany her husband on social occasions. Somewhat to Willow's surprise, he had also sent an invitation to the Countess of Warwick and her husband. Rowell explained that the former Lady Brooke was now the Prince's official mistress and that his wife raised no outward objection to her presence, whatever her private feelings in the matter.

"*I* would not go to any party if you had a mistress

there," Willow argued. She was disconcerted by the look of discomfiture on Rowell's face. Perhaps, she thought, he felt a little guilty that he had once taken her to Lady Symington's country house where his former mistress was present. She had almost forgotten the friendly, red-haired woman who had made herself so charming.

"I do not recall seeing Lady Esmé's name on our invitaton list," Willow remarked. "Should we not include her and Lord Symington?"

With difficulty, Rowell concealed his unease. He had deliberately refrained from adding the Symingtons to their list of guests, for he had not yet forgiven Esmé for inviting Georgina to Buckinghamshire when Willow was with him. Moreover, he had never quite trusted Esmé to be discreet, for he knew her capable of betraying a minor confidence just for the effect her gossip might create. Her women friends were deceived by her air of innocence on such occasions and took it for granted that she had been thoughtless rather than malicious.

With Georgina heavy with child, he feared Esmé might pass on such information to Willow even though he could count on Esmé not to be so ill-advised as to suggest that Georgina's child was his. Esmé, like a lot of his London friends, might guess at the truth but would never dare risk such slander.

"I believe the Symingtons are abroad," he said vaguely to Willow, and the subject was forgotten.

Willow's spirits lifted as soon as they arrived in London.

"Never a dull moment, eh?" Rowell said after the first week rushed by.

Although Willow had not yet enjoyed the experience of a Season in London, Rowell had chronicled in detail what engagements she might expect. From April to the end of July, he had told her, London would be invaded by at least four thousand of the richest, smartest, and noblest families in the land. All would be endeavoring to go to the opening of the Covent Garden opera season; many would be hoping for invitations to the Royal Drawing Rooms at Buckingham Palace. Certainly, everyone would go to the Eton and Harrow match at Lords; to the Henley Regatta; to the weekly "church parade" in Hyde Park; to watch polo at Ranelagh and tennis at Wimbledon; to attend

Royal Ascot and Goodwood races, which traditionally ended the Season.

In addition to these social events there was, of course, the endless round of dinner parties and balls, where eating, drinking, and dancing continued until the early hours of the morning. Theatres, concerts, At Homes and calls, morning rides in Rotten Row filled the calendar for three whole months.

"I am already exhausted and the Season has scarcely begun," Pelham remarked after a particularly late party soon after their arrival in London.

Willow discovered that she had barely sufficient time in the course of the day for the endless change of clothes for varied occasions in her diary. It was often three in the morning before a sleepy-eyed Nellie helped her into bed; and only four hours later, she would be breakfasting before her morning ride in the Row. But the novelty and excitement were stimulating to Willow, who was young enough to show no visible signs of fatigue. Her enjoyment of each occasion showed in the added radiance of her face and in her bright, happy laughter.

Despite his remark to the contrary, Pelham too was inexhaustible. He was much in demand by the eligible debutantes and never without a dancing partner. Yet it seemed to Willow as if he were never far from her side.

"That's because you dance so much better than the other girls," he said laughing as he whirled her around the floor in a waltz or a polka. "Remember the first dance we ever had, Willow, in the long gallery at Rochford? You let me kiss you that night."

"I didn't 'let you,'" Willow protested laughing. "You took me by surprise."

"If you grow any more beautiful, I shall take you by surprise again," Pelham said, a hint of seriousness behind his teasing tone. "It really does amaze me, Willow, that you are still so unaware of your own charms. Half London is in love with you. Even the Prince of Wales noticed you and he only ever notices beautiful women."

Although Willow knew better than to take Pelham's remarks too seriously, his compliments nevertheless reassured her. She had begun to doubt that she was attractive. Rowell had slept in a separate room since her confinement and only very rarely now did he share her bed. He seemed to prefer the card room or the billiard room to the dance floor and although he was an attentive escort when they went out together, he vanished as soon as he saw her in conversation with someone else, and she would not see him again until it was time to leave. It was Pelham who seemed forever at her elbow.

"I like to be seen with the most desirable, intelligent, and beautiful woman in the room," he said smiling.

As the weeks went by, Willow could not fail to realize that in some indefinable way, she *had* grown more beautiful. Marriage, childbirth, or perhaps simply age must have matured her, she thought, for she was now very much aware of the lingering glances of the many men she encountered each day. Even the women complimented her, not least Francis' new amour, Madeleine Villier, whom she and Pelham met one morning in Rotten Row.

"Francis never told me he had such a stunning sister-in-law," the tall brunette said, her eyes running approvingly over Willow's tailored deep blue riding jacket. Made of velvet, it had a small turned-over collar and lapels and fitted tightly over her blouse. The same dark blue was reflected in her wrap-over habit which reached down to her shiny black boots. With her top hat set at a jaunty angle and her blond hair caught back into a tight knot at her neck, Willow looked confident and at ease on her chestnut mare in the bright morning sunshine.

"I knew you were very rich, but not that you were beautiful, Lady Rochford," Madeleine Villier said as they walked their horses side by side. "Do you belong to the Suffragettes? You should, you know. Women like us are needed to show men we are quite as capable as they are when it comes to using our brains. I know you are intelligent. Francis told me his brother has a very high opinion of you—the brother called Toby, I mean, not Rowell. I met your husband last week at Ranelagh, did he tell you? *He* wouldn't know how to appreciate a clever female."

Willow put this rude, critical remark down to feminine spite, for Rowell had taken no pains to hide his disapproval of the outspoken New Zealander and her new-fangled, outrageous views on the equality of women. Only grudgingly did he admit that the girl was very pretty.

"And penniless," he added. "So she won't do for Francis. I suppose she thinks he'd be a good catch."

"Perhaps she doesn't care about money," Willow suggested. "She may love Francis for himself."

Rowell did not trouble to reply.

"I am afraid I have to agree with dear brother Rowell on the subject of Madeleine Villier," Pelham voiced his opinion as the girl rode off with Francis a few minutes later. "Girls like her are not romantics like you and I, Willow. They scheme and plot and work hard to get what they want from life. I know that sort."

"Poor Francis!" Willow said. "I can see he is really smitten."

"Poor all of us who love women who do not return our love," Pelham said flippantly but his eyes were on Willow's face. "One day perhaps, you will feel sorry for me, Willow. Do you not think I am a far more deserving case for your pity than Francis, since I have loved you faithfully for five years?"

"Five years!" Willow repeated laughing. "Faithfully? What about all those girls at Oxford? And that pretty little actress you told me about in London, and Gillian Barratt, that daughter of Sir John's, who never refuses an invitation to Rochford if you are at home—not to mention a dozen others."

"Oh, them!" Pelham said. "You don't think I love any of them, do you, Willow? They are all makeshifts for you."

"One day someone is going to overhear you talking such nonsense and take you seriously," Willow reproved him lightheartedly as they rode out of the park. "Then where will we be!"

But Pelham merely smiled.

"One day *you* are going to take me seriously," he said.

But Willow gave him no serious thought until the night of her birthday ball. Champagne flowed ceaselessly throughout the evening, heightening the gaiety of the occasion.

Enjoying himself hugely and making the most of the excellent food and drink was the portly, genial Prince of Wales. Now in his fifty-third year, the heir to the throne was still highly susceptible to the attractions of any pretty woman who came into his orbit. He was an incorrigible flirt, and the pretty young Baroness Rochford was a new interest. His adored mistress, the beautiful Daisy, Countess of Warwick, was not present at the Rochfords' ball owing to the death of her elderly father-in-law. The Prince liked Americans, especially if they were young and pretty, and Willow's almost white blonde hair and dark eyes intrigued him. He found her shyness novel and delighted to see how easily she blushed when he paid her a compliment.

Willow was at first ill at ease in the company of so illustrious a personage and conscious of the envious eyes of all the women in the room fastened upon her as she sat beside the Prince. But, listening to his friendly, easy conversation, she quickly relaxed and found herself fascinated by his account of the visit he had made to her country when he was but a young man of eighteen.

He quizzed her about her father's railroad interests, sighed over his own impoverished finances, and told her he would ask his wife to invite her to tea at Windsor Castle.

"You'll have to shout—she's unfortunately a little deaf these days—but you'll love her, m'dear. Everyone does, and she'll take to you. She asked me to tell you how sorry she was she could not come after all this evening."

Then sighing, he told her that he'd have to stop monopolizing her and allow her to do her duties as hostess.

"All the men here will be wanting to dance with you," he said, eyeing her with open admiration. "Run along, m'dear, and you have our best wishes for your birthday."

As the Prince of Wales had surmised, Willow did not lack for partners. It was past midnight before Pelham had an opportunity to take her onto the dance floor. Ignoring the onlookers from the seats placed around the ballroom, he held her far too close to him. Willow very soon became aware that it was not unintentional and felt a small shiver of anxiety as she realized that he had had far too much champagne.

When finally the music ended, he continued to hold her in his arms. His eyes were flashing with a strange fire as he looked down at her.

"Come with me," he said in a low, intense voice. "I have something to give you—a birthday present."

Unwilling to provoke a scene in public, Willow followed him reluctantly out of the ballroom and into the conservatory. It was cool and damp, the light casting eerie shadows through the green shrubbery growing there.

"A birthday kiss for the birthday girl!" Pelham said, pulling her roughly into his arms. "I have waited a long time for this."

Before she could protest, he pressed his mouth down upon hers, his arms tightening around her, his heart thudding against the soft curve of her bosom.

Suddenly it was as if she had been transported back five years—to the long gallery at Rochford. As if it were then, the same sensations coursed through her veins. But this time, she thought unhappily, she knew what was happening to her body; knew that she was responding involuntarily to Pelham's desires.

But it was not Pelham she wanted. Her need was for Rowell, *Rowell*. Why was he not here, kissing her with the same violent passion, she thought agonizingly as she tried ineffectually to push Pelham away.

"God forgive me, but you are beautiful," he muttered, drawing his mouth away at last. "Why does it have to be you, Willow . . . my brother's wife . . . whom I want so desperately? For pity's sake, leave him. Divorce him. Run away with me. Are you listening to me, Willow? Do you think I'm crazy? I'm trying to tell you I love you."

With a great effort of will, she managed to speak calmly.

"No, I don't think you are crazy, Pelham, but I am in no doubt at all that you have had far too much champagne. I think you should stay here for a while until you are sober. I shall forget what you said . . . and what you did. *And you must, too.* Lest there be any misunderstanding on your part, I love Rowell very much. I shall always love him. I always have and I always will. Never forget it again, Pelham."

To her unutterable relief, Pelham made no move to stop her as she turned and walked with as much dignity as she could muster, out of the cool, dark room. Her thoughts were in a turmoil, for it seemed as if her mind and her body were two separate entities. She had enjoyed Pelham's kiss; had felt herself responding eagerly to his passion. Yet she loved Rowell!

In the early hours of the morning, when the last of their guests had departed, Rowell came to her bedroom. His cheeks were flushed, his eyes luminous, as he stood by the bedside looking down at her.

"I have received a great many compliments on your behalf, my dear," he said. "Even from the Prince of Wales himself. I must congratulate you on your success. You were unquestionably the most beautiful woman present tonight."

Willow's cheeks turned pink with pleasure at his compliment.

"I am happy that *you* should think so, my dearest," she said softly.

Rowell hesitated and then said tentatively:

"If you are not too tired, I thought I might stay with you for what remains of the night."

Without hesitation, Willow held out her arms.

There was something different about his young wife, Rowell thought as he climbed into bed beside her and switched off the electric light. She had that same breathless, expectant look that he saw so often on Georgina's face when she was demanding that he make love to her. But tonight it was not Georgina who had aroused him. He wanted the woman he knew every other man at the ball had found exciting, desirable—*his* wife.

As Willow eagerly returned Rowell's embraces, she refused to question the reason for the change in her husband. It was miracle enough that he had somehow sensed her own desires, awakened so readily by Pelham earlier that night. As Rowell's kisses became more passionate, she surrendered herself utterly to his need, her own intensifying with every caress, every movement, until she was totally abandoned to the urgent demands of their bodies.

When Rowell had lain with Willow in the past, he had neither expected nor desired from her the inflammatory responses he was accustomed to from Georgina. He was now even a little shocked at the reactions of his young wife. Yet at the same time, he was too deeply aroused to let such thoughts trouble him. It satisfied his pride that she so obviously wanted *him,* and that she seemed impervious to the admiration and flattery even of the Heir to the Throne!

"My darling, my lovely little wife. How beautiful you are," he murmured as he lowered his body onto hers. How tiny and delicate she seemed . . . and yet how strong the grip of her arms around his back, her legs around his thighs.

"I love you, Rowell. I love you."

Her voice as well as her words encouraged him.

Suddenly as he moved deep within her. Willow became aware of a new feeling, so strong, so sweet that she cried out. The wonder increased, spreading with magical beauty over her whole body. She felt Rowell gasp at the same moment as her back arched in final spasm toward him. Her body went limp as he lay motionless above her. Their deep hurried breathing seemed as perfectly synchronized as their moment of pleasure.

Rowell was the first to move. He rolled over on to his back, one arm cradling her head.

"Are you happy, my love?" he asked with soft tenderness. "I was not too rough with you?"

Willow drew a deep breath. There seemed no words by which she could tell him how perfectly happy and marvelously content she felt. Unlike all those other nights when she had been left restless and sleepless, now she was complete; and wonderfully surprised. It was for this that lovers had throughout history risked even their lives to be together; this was what had inspired the great poets, musicians, writers, painters. Now she understood. This night on which she had reached her twenty-first year had also brought her a new wisdom and comprehension hitherto denied her. She understood the beauty, the perfection, of the art of love.

Sleepily, she raised herself on one elbow and covered Rowell's beloved face with grateful kisses.

Chapter Ten

August 1894–December 1895

As soon as the season ended, the family returned to Havorhurst. Even Grandmère seemed pleased to see them, and Dodie was radiant with delight.

"I missed you all so much," she said. "But will you believe it, Willow, Grandmère gave Mr. McGill permission to take me out in the garden to lie in my chair on the lawn. There was so much to see—and to learn about. Mr. McGill is giving me nature lessons."

Dodie was nearly fourteen years old, and already her figure had begun to develop. Willow guessed that along with this new maturity, the girl had also acquired a new set of emotions. The schoolmaster's name punctuated her conversation, and it was plain to see that Dodie had developed a hero-worship for the pleasant, kindly man who was opening up the world for her.

"I am very grateful to you for all you do for Dodie," she said at her next encounter with him. "She is so happy these days and her smile so infectious that I hear even her grandmother succumbed to her charm and allowed her to leave the confines of the house."

The sandy haired, hazel-eyed man regarded Willow seriously as he said:

"Miss Dodie has done much for me too, Lady Rochford. She has made me see the world anew through the innocence of her eyes. In doing so, I have realized how much beauty there is for those who look for it. Do you know, Lady Rochford, I have never heard an unkind word or a complaint pass Miss Dodie's lips. Her body may be crippled, but her spirit is without blemish."

It was not only Dodie's excellent progress that had heartened Willow on her arrival home. At last her parents were making their long-delayed visit.

Now, to Willow's delight, Rowell seemed as anxious as she to make her parents' visit as agreeable as possible. He put himself out to be charming to his in-laws and was gentle and tender to Willow throughout their stay.

"I think you will have to agree now, Papa, that I made the right choice after all," Willow said to him happily at the end of their first week as guests at Rochford Manor. "You and Mama cannot fail to see for yourselves how happy I am and what a wonderful husband I have."

Willoughby Tetford nodded. His manner toward his son-in-law had softened quite markedly.

"I admit that I was overly cautious in my judgment of Rowell," he said without preamble. "We should have visited you sooner, my dear, but your mother and I deliberately did not interfere these past three years. We felt we might unsettle you if your marriage was not working

out quite as well as you expected. But our concern was
clearly not justified, and your instinct was sounder than
your old Papa's."

Her father got on excellently well with all the family,
Willow thought happily. He had brought magnificent presents for every one of them, each carefully selected for the
individual. There was a very handsome pair of Purdey
guns for Rowell.

"Willow wrote that shooting was your favorite sport,"
he said to his delighted son-in-law. For Pelham there was
the very latest design in phonographs and a selection of
wax cylinder records, including the newest tunes from the
latest music hall hits.

"I hear you like dancing," he said with a twinkle in
his blue eyes.

For Francis there was a Kodak camera.

"We read that your Princess of Wales is a keen photographer and thought that this might appeal to you, my
boy!"

For Toby, there was a superb microscope. One look at
Toby's excited face was evidence enough of his pleasure
in the gift.

For Grandmère and Aunt Milly, he had brought Cashmere shawls; for Dodie, a magic lantern, and for Rupert a
Guarnieri del Gesù violin.

"I'm sorry it's not a Stradivari," he said apologetically.
"But I was told this was every bit as good and it certainly
cost as much! I did not give you anything, did I, my
dear?" he said now to Willow. "But your old father has
not forgotten you, as I'm sure you well know. Your present should arrive from London any day now."

His gift proved to be a magnificent painting by Van
Dyke—one of the artist's best known religious works and
of immense value.

"I know you like this sort of thing, eh?" he asked
fondly. "Do very nicely in that long gallery, I should
imagine."

The painting remained unhung while Willow's parents
were in England, for there was so much else to do during
their stay. The whole family, with the exception of Grandmère, Aunt Mildred, and Dodie went to the Goodwood
summer races and enjoyed an exciting Goodwood Cup.
They stayed in a hotel during the three-day meeting, tak-

ing over the whole establishment with their numerous
maids, valets, and coachmen. This outing was followed by
a week in the Isle of Wight for Cowes Regatta. Willoughby
Tetford in particular enjoyed the novelty of sailing in
Rowell's yacht, and returned to Rochford with the declared intention of buying one for himself, possibly on a
par with the Prince of Wales' yacht *Britannia.*

Back at Havorhurst, he and his wife met again all the
old friends they had made in the neighborhood five years
previously. Both Willoughby Tetford and Beatrice, the
quiet Quaker woman whom Willow so resembled in looks,
were popular guests wherever they went; the former for
his enthusiasm for life, for his amusing anecdotes and
keen grasp of financial affairs; the latter for her quiet serene manner which was so much in contrast to her husband's loud, emphatic, extrovert nature.

Strangely enough, Willoughby Tetford showed himself
sympathetically disposed toward Rupert. He went out of
his way to talk to the boy.

"Fighting other men's bloody wars is no more to my
taste than to yours," the American told him bluntly. "In
my opinion, far too much is said about honor and glory
and a damned sight too little about the dirt and agony
and bestiality of it. Let's pray to God there is no more
trouble between our two countries, although I'm none too
happy about this Anglo-Venezuelan dispute. I hope Congress won't interfere or we *shall* be at war with England
again—a shocking prospect."

Rupert's slow recovery was hastened to near normality
when Willoughby Tetford produced as a parting gift to
the family, a shining new French motorcar, a Panhard.
The internal combustion engine placed under the bonnet
was the very latest development of the German inventor
Gottleib Daimler. It boasted sliding gears, a clutch, pedal
brakes, and a foot accelerator.

"You'll probably need a mechanic to cope with the engine," Willow's father said as Rupert, his pale face animated with excitement, walked round and round the car
in silent admiration.

"We'll ask Adrian Forbes to come and help us if we
have any trouble," Willow said, disregarding the angry
glance Rowell shot at her. Despite all that her husband
had said to her, she did not believe there was anything

seriously wrong in the friendship between the two young men. Moreover, she considered that Adrian Forbes, with his happy-go-lucky nature, would be good for the quiet, nervous Rupert.

When her parents returned to America, Willow had time on her hands once more and she decided to invite James McGill to help her hang the Van Dyke and then catalogue the Rochford paintings. Rowell told her there was no comprehensive list of the works of art in the manor and he agreed that since McGill seemed to know a bit about the subject, he would be a good man to employ for the task.

James McGill was pleased to have the employment. The autumn term had not yet begun, and he needed the extra money. He brought Willow a number of books of his own to aid them in identifying the artists. These illustrated editions had been passed on to him by his father who, James told Willow, had been greatly interested in art and might have been a serious collector had he ever been in a position to afford it.

Together he and Willow went down the long gallery and through the rooms inspecting the paintings. As they removed each one from the wall, Nellie followed, dusting behind the frames and wiping the walls where they had hung.

James was soon wide-eyed as he began to realize what a valuable collection the Rochford family owned.

"Many of these are priceless," he told Willow. "They are all originals as far as I can see. Only the Gainsborough in the library is a copy."

Willow thought little about this last observation and only by chance mentioned James' remark to Rowell that evening as they were retiring for the night. Rowell looked at her quizzically.

"The fellow must be mistaken about the Gainsborough. I remember Grandmère telling me when I was a boy that Grandfather gave it to her as a wedding present soon after they were married."

"Then Mr. McGill must be wrong," Willow said. "I'll speak to him in the morning."

But James McGill was adamant. He went back to the library with one of his father's art books and a magnifying glass which he held out to Willow.

"If you care to look at the illustration in this book, you will see that even to the naked eye the two signatures bear little resemblance. This is not the original."

Willow regarded her companion uncertainly.

"But if it is a copy, Mr. McGill, my husband would know. No one would have removed the original without his permission. I don't understand it."

"Excuse me, Milady!" Nellie said from behind her. "Maybe Mr. Francis might know something about it. He was in here one day with Stevens, Milady. Harry was complaining to me that he near broke his back carrying it out to the carriage. You could ask him about it."

Willow felt a shiver run down her spine. Instinctively, she gave no sign of her inner perturbation.

"I'll have a word with Mr. Francis," she said lightly. "Perhaps he sent it away to be cleaned or some such thing."

She knew that James McGill's eyes were on her and her cheeks colored. A sixth sense warned her not to pursue the matter now, but at the first opportunity she spoke to Francis when no one else was present.

"I don't know what you have been up to or why," she said quietly. "But I want the truth, Francis. Where is the original Gainsborough that hung in the library? And why did you substitute a copy without telling Rowell or me your reasons for doing so?"

Francis' face paled and his blue eyes shifted uneasily as he stared down at his feet. Willow, who had never felt able to trust him, was now in no doubt whatever that he was guilty of effecting the substitution.

"I don't see what this has got to do with you," he said rudely.

Willow's anger rose swiftly in her breast.

"It has everything to do with me. You seem to forget that I am Rowell's wife and therefore mistress of this house. I have a right to know everything that happens here, Francis."

"Trust you to notice!" he said furiously. "I don't suppose anyone else in the family would ever have done so. Nobody has ever taken the slightest interest in the family heirlooms until *you* decided to catalogue them. Anyway, who told you *I* had anything to do with the Gainsborough?"

"Nobody told me," Willow replied coldly. "Do you understand what you have done, Francis? You have taken something that is not yours, something very valuable."

His eyes stared defiantly into hers and then lowered. His expression became truculent and he said doubtfully:

"If I admit I took it, I suppose you'll tell Rowell."

Willow looked at her young brother-in-law in perplexity.

"Of course Rowell will have to know," she said. "But whatever made you *do* such a terrible thing, Francis? You must have realized someone would discover the substitution sooner or later."

"In this house?" Francis said sarcastically. "Until you came here, Willow, no one in the family ever noticed what hung on the walls, far less cared what happened to them. That Gainsborough was worth a great deal of money and . . . and I needed it."

Willow was shocked. Francis' voice was in no manner apologetic. He sounded as if he expected her to see the logic of what he had done.

"If you needed money so badly, could you not have asked Rowell for an advance on your allowance?" she asked.

Now Francis' gaze met hers, his expression once again defiant.

"Don't you think I did? But my dear brother was not willing to accommodate me. Oh, not because he couldn't afford to—" he added bitterly, "—but to repeat his own pompous words, because he felt 'obliged for my own sake,' to insist that I live within my means. As if I could manage on two hundred pounds a year with all the expenses I have had of late!"

"Madeleine Villier," Willow murmured, more to herself than to Francis. Now at last she was beginning to understand. She could even feel a small spark of pity for the boy.

"Where is the money now, Francis?" she asked quietly.

Francis looked away, his eyes uneasy.

"It's gone. I've spent it!"

"But you cannot have spent it all!" Willow cried disbelievingly. "On what, Francis? Were you in debt?"

Francis looked away, his eyes avoiding her, his pale cheeks flushed with sudden color.

"No, I wasn't in debt. I bought Madeleine some pieces of jewelry . . ." His voice trailed into silence.

"But Francis, they must have been very valuable. Surely Miss Villier did not accept such gifts? It is not even as if you were engaged to be married!"

Francis' cheeks colored a deeper red. He remained silent.

"Then you must be quite blind in your love for her," Willow said as much to herself as to her young brother-in-law. "You must know in your heart that she is not worthy of your affection, Francis. No well-brought-up girl would consider accepting such presents, let alone gifts of jewelry. She cannot have told that aunt with whom she lives, for of a certainty Mrs. Meadows would not have allowed her to accept them," she added, her mind conjuring up a memory of the elderly lady with a large ear trumpet (for she was nearly stone deaf) whom Madeleine had brought to tea one afternoon in London.

"Madeleine does not consider her aunt has any right to dictate to her how she shall live," Francis said, obviously quoting the girl. "She is twenty-three years of age and she says that now she is entitled to vote on the affairs of her country, she is quite capable of deciding what is best for herself."

"Then she is greatly mistaken," Willow retorted sharply, "for by accepting your presents, Francis, Madeleine has placed herself under an obligation to you, the donor. She could not now object were you to treat her as —well, as a paid mistress. She must know that."

"*She* does not think so," Francis muttered, not without a hint of bitterness in his voice, betraying the fact that he had hoped for certain favors that, minor though they were, she had nevertheless refused him.

"Francis, she cannot love you!" Willow cried. "Do you not see that she is using you? If she really loved you, she would not want you to spend money on her—money she knows you do not have."

"I will have plenty—one day," Francis argued hotly. "And as Madeleine says, why should we not enjoy some of it now when we are still young? I shall be old by the time I am thirty, and Madeleine . . . she may have married someone else by then."

Willow was deeply shocked. Without meaning to betray the true character of the girl he loved, Francis had nevertheless clearly revealed her baseness. The sooner he was rid of her, the better. But how to intervene? she asked herself. Francis would be unlikely to listen to her dictates.

"If Rowell were to hear of this, he would feel obliged to report the matter to Grandmère," she said thoughtfully. "But if it were possible to buy back the Gainsborough . . ."

Francis' face took on an expression first of surprise and then of hope. He had been far more frightened of what might happen than he had allowed Willow to see.

"I could buy it back—if I had the money," he said quickly. "I saw it only last week in the London gallery to which I sold it."

"How much did they give you for it, Francis?"

The pale cheeks flushed with embarrassment, and he paused before he said defiantly:

"Five thousand guineas."

"Five thousand guineas?" Willow repeated aghast. "But Francis, you could have lived in London in the greatest luxury for—" She broke off, realizing that he would never have been able to explain such financial independence.

Francis was silent.

"I *could* raise the money, I think," Willow said slowly. "But before you thank me, Francis, as I see you are about to do, I must warn you that there is a price *you* will pay. I shall expect you to give me your word never to see Madeleine Villier again. It is for your own good, Francis."

Francis' mouth set in an ugly line.

"I will never give her up," he said. "You can't make me, Willow."

"No, *I* cannot force you to act against your will," she replied quietly. "But you must know that Rowell or Grandmère could force you—just as they forced Rupert into the army against his wishes. You would be disgraced, as Rupert was. Moreover, since you have always until now been Grandmère's favorite. I do not care to think of her bitterness toward you if she were to discover you capable of such a dishonorable deed. Perhaps I am wrong now to offer you protection from the consequences of your actions; but I am willing to do so since I believe it in your interests and in the interests of the whole family. In particular I do not want Rowell made unhappy if there is a way I can prevent it. He would be horrified to learn his own brother had stolen from him."

"You would do anything for Rowell, wouldn't you?" Francis said bitterly. "As far as you are concerned, he can do no wrong. But I could tell you—"

"I don't wish to hear your comments about my husband," Willow interrupted quickly, angrily. "I am well aware that you resent the fact that Rowell is the eldest and the heir and can exert control of your life, so you would do better to remain silent upon the subject of your brother. And now I would like your decision regarding the Gainsborough. Am I to give you the money to buy it back?"

There was something in Willow's tone that brooked no argument, and Francis knew it. He was surprised, for he had considered her a rather silly girl who doted blindly on Rowell and appeared to allow Grandmère to control the family without interference—with perhaps the single exception of Dodie. He reminded himself that in this instance too, she had shown surprising determination.

His mind schemed furiously. It would cost him nothing to give Willow his word. He could still see Madeleine —albeit surreptitiously—although Madeleine would not care for a clandestine relationship. She openly admitted that one of the reasons she favored him as a suitor was because his family was so much better connected and socially desirable than her own; and now he would no longer be able to be seen with her in public. But hopefully he could persuade her. At least there was a chance.

"Very well, I will give her up," he lied in a flat, emotionless voice.

Willow, who had not expected him to give way so easily, regarded him thoughtfully. Could she trust him, she wondered? Was she right to be taking matters into her own hands when it was really Rowell who should be disciplining his youngest brother? And this would be yet another secret she could not share with her husband.

Her instinct was overruled by reason and she chided herself for even considering that a gentleman—a Rochford at that—might break his word.

"Then I have your promise, Francis?" she asked.

Looking directly into her eyes and without flinching, Francis gave his word.

A few weeks later, the Gainsborough was back in place, its brief absence explained when Willow said that it had been sent away to be cleaned. James McGill suspected that this was not what had really happened, but other than Willow and Francis, no one but Silvie knew the truth.

"So much money for such a cause!" Silvie remonstrated, when Willow recounted the episode during her Christmas visit.

"But the Rochford family is *my* family now," Willow tried to explain.

Silvie drew a long sigh.

"Cousin Rowell was a very fortunate man the day you agreed to become his wife, Willow," she said quietly. "I wish you luck and happiness in the new year, *chérie*, for you truly deserve it."

But the year of 1895 was not to bring Willow her dearest wish.

"Can there be something wrong with me, Toby?" she asked him on the anniversary of her baby's death. She was making one of her now frequent visits to his laboratory. "Could I have become barren?"

Toby looked at Willow's unhappy face, his own enigmatic. None knew better than he how frequently Rowell was absent from home and he suspected rightly that his brother's behavior toward his young wife was very far from passionate. Pelham had informed him that Rowell was now totally engrossed in his mistress; that he was far more "married" to her than to Willow now that Georgina had borne him a son. The child was nine months old and the house Rowell had bought for his mistress in Chelsea was one of carefree domesticity.

Pelham had been invited to a small card party there by Rowell.

"Georgina has a nurse for the child and is free to enjoy the gaiety of London life with Rowell," he told Toby. "Maternity has enhanced her looks and she is now even more voluptuous than before. Rowell is besotted."

It was a small wonder therefore, that Willow was not with child, Toby thought uneasily.

"You may still be a little below par in health since your last pregnancy," he said in an attempt to reassure her. "Sometimes it can be quite a while before a woman recovers her strength. Don't worry about it, my dear," he added kindly and sought to divert her with an account of the progress he had made in the branch of his work concerning the carrying of diseases.

Willow was able for short spells of time that summer to forget her anxieties while she was in Toby's company. His enthusiasm was infectious, and she shared his excitement when he read in a medical journal that a physicist called Wilhelm Roentgen had discovered what he called "X rays"—as a result of which it was possible to see through the flesh of a body to the bone structure inside.

"This will be of immense service to surgery," Toby said thoughtfully, nearly dropping the spectacles which he had been absentmindedly polishing in his excitement. "Just imagine, Willow, with the use of these rays one could identify at once how badly a bone was fractured and how best to reset it."

Willow was surprised anew at Toby's ability to grasp new concepts and see the implications of the most complicated theories and discoveries. It struck her again how superior was his intelligence to that of his brothers and how truly sad and wasteful it was that he had not been able to enter the medical profession.

It seemed to her the most natural thing in the world to turn to him when she felt in need of advice.

"I treat you like a cross between a doctor and a Father Confessor, don't I?" she chided herself, although somehow she knew that Toby did not mind. "You are exactly the kind of brother I used to dream of having," she continued, "yet it never once occurred to me that one day I would have a brother-in-law to fill the gap in my life. When the day comes for you to marry, Toby, and move to a house of your own, I shall miss you most dreadfully."

"Then I shall have to remain a bachelor, won't I?" Toby said quietly.

Willow shook her head.

"No, you will not, Toby! I forbid it absolutely. You will make the most wonderful husband . . . and father, too. And although it may not be in my own interest, I shall set about finding a perfect wife for you."

"You will do no such thing, Willow," Toby replied vehemently, his face flushing. "I am wedded to my work and that is that."

He did not add that he might have changed his ideas of a bachelor future if Willow had not married Rowell. But such a thought could bring him no pleasure, so he put it quickly from his mind.

"Is it as a Father Confessor or as a doctor that you need me today?" he asked lightly as she curled herself comfortably into her customary chair by the window. She was wearing a very simple pale blue dress with a tight high collar and little pearl buttons. Her hair was caught back with a blue ribbon, and she looked far younger than her twenty-one years.

Although Willow smiled, it faded quickly as she said:

"I am concerned about Rupert, Toby. He must be so very lonely. He seems uninterested in everything but his music."

Toby sighed. His eyes were thoughtful as he said quietly:

"I think Rupert needs to live away from home. Life is never going to be easy for him, since he cannot enjoy normal relationships. He would be far happier were he allowed to continue his friendship with Adrian Forbes, but as you know, Willow, Rowell has forbidden it. Perhaps it would be wrong to allow such a friendship to develop, however discreetly it existed. Certainly the world condemns Mr. Oscar Wilde. But I myself feel sympathy for him and those like him, including Rupert. We cannot help how we are born or how our lives fashion our needs, our loves. I regret to say, it does not always direct us wisely, despite our best intentions."

Willow looked at Toby curiously, her interest aroused by such unconventional opinions.

"Rowell condemns Mr. Wilde quite violently," she said. "He says he should not have transgressed in so terrible a way. But two years' imprisonment with hard labor, Toby! That is a terrible and fearful punishment for so fine and sensitive a writer, is it not?"

"Rowell understands only what he himself feels," Toby said. "And that is a criticism that applies to a great many

other people. It is why he has no sympathy for Rupert or
his particular interests. I have never seen anyone more
carried away than was Rupert the night Rowell took us to
Covent Garden. Yet Rowell was obviously hopelessly
bored by the music."

Fortunately, the two brothers did at least share a love
of shooting, and surprisingly, Rupert, who lacked any real
aptitude for other sporting activities, was an excellent shot.
He seemed to excel himself throughout the autumn, and
as winter approached, Rowell was actually heard to congratulate his younger brother on his exceptional marks-
manship. Unfortunately, unintentionally cruel, he added:

"It's a pity you could not have bagged as many Dervishes in Egypt!"

As Rupert left the room, his mouth a tight, thin line,
Willow sighed. If only Rowell would show more sensitivity,
she thought unhappily, as the comfortable atmosphere that
had prevailed these last few months was once again
charged with tension. Clearly, as Toby now pointed out,
Rowell could not even *imagine* how Rupert felt.

Or how I felt about losing my baby, Willow thought.
Yet Toby had been able to understand her grief and to
offer silent comfort. Was imagination so important then,
she asked herself, in enabling a person to understand their
fellow human beings?

"*C'est tout*—absolutely everything!" said Silvie when
Willow reported Toby's views to her that Christmas.
"Most especially between lovers, *ma chère* Willow. It is
why I am discovering such joy at the moment with my
lover. He is an actor and though penniless and without
much hope of fame, he understands me perfectly and
with great sensitivity, and I adore him!"

"Will you marry him?" Willow asked, laughing at Silvie's extravagant pronouncements. Such outspokenness
from this delightful French girl had once slightly shocked
her. But now she was used to Silvie and considered that
she herself, had become moderately sophisticated in her
attitude to the conventions. Silvie, however, did not agree.

"You are a born conventionalist, *chérie*," she said, hugging Willow affectionately. "Always you think of marriage
—never of love for its own sake."

"Do you really mean love when you speak of it, Silvie?" Willow asked curiously. "Or do you perhaps mean

passion? Is it possible, do you think, to have a perfect rapport with a man when you are making love and yet share little in common with him in your thoughts?"

Silvie glanced at Willow curiously, her eyes speculative as she guessed that Willow's was not a casual question but a personal one.

"I cannot give you an answer, *chérie*," she said. "I do not think that I myself have ever been truly in love with a man . . . at least not to the point where all my senses are in tune with another being. Perhaps were I to find such a man, I might be tempted into marriage again. But until then. . . ."

Willow said thoughtfully:

"Have you no special feeling for Toby, Silvie? The better I have come to know him, the nicer I think he is. I know he is not so handsome as his brothers, but he is so very understanding. He would make a wonderful husband —except that he is so engrossed in his work. It would be so perfect if you and he were to fall in love. I know he admires you."

"Ah, Toby!" Silvie exclaimed. For once she was serious as she said: "I understand very well why you find him so *sympatique*, Willow, but I . . . well, you know me, and although I have a deep affection for him, dear Toby is far too serious for me. I need someone who will laugh with me; dance with me; drink wine with me; make love to me whenever I wish it. And I am by nature *très exigente* —I demand of my lovers constant attention."

She was laughing again as she added:

"You see, *chérie*, I am but a *papillon*, a butterfly. I do not wish to take life seriously as you do. I am selfish and live only for my own amusement."

"Which is all quite untrue!" Willow said, hugging her friend. "You pretend to be frivolous and hide your true kind nature beneath such pretense. I do not think you are so different from me after all."

As if to disprove Willow's opinion of her, Silvie's behavior that Christmas bordered on the outrageous. She flirted amusingly but daringly with Pelham, bringing down the wrath of both Grandmère and her mother, Cousin Lucienne, on their heads.

"Such behavior may be *admissible à Paris*," said Lady Rochford icily, lapsing into French in her anger, "but I

will not tolerate such . . . such *relâchement* of the pro-
prieties in this house."

"They were but cousinly kisses, Tante Clotilde!" Silvie
replied, her eyes widened in innocence although with an
unmistakable twinkle in their brown-flecked depths. "Were
they not, Pelham?"

Pelham attempted to hide his own amusement from his
grandmother. They were most certainly not cousinly kisses.
Had it not been for the fact that it was Willow he really
wanted, he might well have been tempted into an *affaire de
coeur* with Silvie. But it was Willow's slim, delicately
curved body he craved to hold in his arms. He could not
forget that stolen kiss in the conservatory in London. The
subsequent embrace of other women had failed to assuage
his longing for her. He sensed that all was not well between her and Rowell. How could it be, he asked himself,
when Rowell was so often absent? He sensed, too, the
wistful need for love and loving that Willow could never
quite succeed in hiding behind an expression of contentment with her lot.

He himself was more adept at hiding his feelings. He
knew that Willow was totally loyal to her husband, and
that never once had the thought of being unfaithful to
him crossed her mind. Other women might have welcomed
flattery to bolster their egos, but Willow did not want to
know of Pelham's feelings for her. Far less did she wish
to be made aware of her own need and desires.

But he could wait, Pelham thought, as he waltzed with
Silvie or sat close beside her in the carriage or whispered
compliments in her pretty little ear when he passed her
on the stairway. He realized that, were he to engage in a
little nocturnal sortie to his cousin's bedroom, he might
find a welcome awaiting him. But like many others before
him, he did not want what was easily available; he wanted
what he could not have—the inaccessible, unobtainable
Willow.

Chapter Eleven

March–December 1896

GEORGINA WAS ONCE AGAIN WITH CHILD. UNLIKE THE first pregnancy, on this occasion she was far from well. She became increasingly irritable with Rowell and endlessly demanding.

"You are not my wife," he was provoked into reminding her when she complained that he spent far too much time at Rochford Manor and was not often enough with her. "I understand that you are bored and that life is tedious at the moment, but there is nothing I can do about it."

Her unshapeliness offended him. The fact that she was going to present him with a second child born out of wedlock disturbed him only insofar as the extra cost it would involve. The first child, Philip, was now almost two years old and pretty enough, with Georgina's green eyes and red-gold curls. The boy did not look like Rochford. But that was all to the good, since the very last thing Rowell wanted was for his wife to notice the resemblance, were she ever to see the boy, and put two and two together. Willow herself might not consider divorce, but he could well imagine Willoughby Tetford's reactions were he ever to hear his beloved daughter had been deceived.

At least, he told himself with relief, Willow was now twenty-one and a week after her coming-of-age birthday she had received a very large sum of money from her father in the form of shares. She had barely troubled to read the documents relating to this financial benefit, but had handed them over to Rowell. Her total trust in him had aroused a nagging feeling of guilt hitherto unknown to him. Even when he had resumed his relationship with Georgina after his marriage, he had not considered his betrayal of Willow. He had merely been irritated by the knowledge that Pelham and Toby were obviously critical of the amount of time he spent with Georgina; and their

sympathies were with Willow. Grandmère too had remarked that it was high time he produced an heir and that
he was unlikely to do so if he spent so little time with
his wife, he thought uneasily.

This period while Georgina was *enceinte* now seemed
an excellent opportunity in which to spend less time with
her and more with Willow. He knew he could safely leave
Georgina alone in London, certain that she could scarcely
be unfaithful to him in her condition. His mind made up,
Rowell bade farewell to a tearful Georgina and went
back to Rochford.

Unaware of the true reasons why her husband was now
content to remain at home, Willow was, as a consequence,
far happier during the next few months than she had been
at any time since her marriage. Rowell seemed set upon
entertaining her and pleasing her.

He accepted an invitation from Sir Edgar and Lady
Helen Vincent to stay at Esher Place in Surrey so that his
family could attend the racing at Epsom and in particular,
enjoy the excitement of Derby Day. Once again the
Prince of Wales' horse, Persimmon, was running against
St. Frusquin, and it promised to be an exciting race.

The family were pleased not to be traveling on the
roads on Derby Day itself, for it had become a national
holiday since its inception just over a hundred years ago
and it was now habitual for Londoners to stream in their
thousands to the Epsom Downs by whatever transport
they could find. Trains, carriages, dog carts, gigs, bicycles,
and very occasionally a motor-car, wended their way to
Surrey in a never-ending flow. Parliament was deserted,
and in countless numbers, rich and poor alike amassed
on the Downs.

To cater to this vast influx of people, tinkers, peddlers,
gypsies, traders and their like set up stalls around the race
course and sold their wares. Donkey barrows were piled
with fruit, street sellers offered cakes, tarts, gingerbread,
hot eels, boiled puddings and generally did a roaring trade
with the light-hearted, gay-spirited crowds. Punch-and-
Judy shows, jugglers, and organ grinders entertained the
children, and beggars abounded.

Well apart from the masses, the Rochfords watched the
race from the Vincents' box adjoining the Royal En-
closure. They saw the great bay, Persimmon, ridden by

the jockey, Jack Watts, catch up his rival, St. Frusquin, during the last hundred yards of the race. All around them top hats were flung in the air and even the ladies were leaning out of their boxes in their enthusiasm, for the race was so close run that the winner was in some doubt until Persimmon's number went up on the board.

The excitement of the royal win was tumultuous. The crowd, anxious to applaud the winner, broke through the cordon of police surrounding Persimmon, making it difficult for the Prince of Wales to get near his horse.

Pelham was grinning broadly.

"I had a hundred guineas staked," he whispered to Willow, "but don't breathe a word to Rowell, for he certainly wouldn't approve, to say the least, of such high stakes on such a modest income as mine."

When the Prince returned to London to celebrate his popular win, the Rochfords returned with their hosts to Esher Place. Only Toby had not backed the winner, and Rowell was in celebratory mood as they changed for dinner. Throughout the meal, he regaled the company with racing anecdotes, and Willow noticed with pride how admiring were the glances of both the men and women present. He looked princely in his well-tailored black evening clothes, she thought, and although similarly attired, neither Pelham nor Toby could match Rowell's tall elegance and regal bearing.

He is *my* husband, she thought with intense pride, and a surge of impatience swept over her for the night that was to come. In such happy spirits, Rowell must surely come to their bed in the guise of a lover! Her cheeks grew pink as her imagination conjured up a memory of other such nights . . . and in particular that occasion of her twentieth birthday when she had reached the very zenith of pleasure in the act of love. The miracle had not happened since, but she had steadfastly refused to give way to the inevitable disappointment that followed such failures.

It did not matter, she told herself firmly. Marriage was for a lifetime, and sooner or later she would resolve the mysteries of the marriage bed.

But it was not to happen on the night of this exciting Derby Day. The brandy flowed freely after the meal ended, and Rowell was enjoying himself too well. By midnight when the ladies retired, he, his host, and one or two of the other men decided upon a game of cards. Yet another bottle of cognac was brought in by the butler, and it was nearly three in the morning before Rowell retired to bed. By then he had imbibed so much liquor he could barely stand as his sleepy-eyed valet tried to undress him. Willow was awoken by his angry remonstrations from the adjoining dressing room as his servant struggled to remove his patent leather pumps.

Within seconds of climbing into bed beside her, Rowell was asleep, his snores filling the room and keeping Willow awake until the early morning chorus of the birds heralded the dawn.

But her disappointment did not last for long. Rowell awoke in the very best of spirits and informed her that one of his fellow guests had told him of a race that was to be run later in the year—not with horses but with motor-cars —all the way from London to Brighton.

"We will take the carriage to some vantage point en route and watch them go past," he said. "There has never before been a car race to my knowledge. Even Rupert might enjoy such an outing, do you not agree, my dear?"

"Then please, dearest Rowell, could we take Dodie too?" Willow asked, her heart in her mouth as Rowell's expression became doubtful. "Please, my darling. She could be well wrapped up and would come to no harm if the weather is not too severe. I would consider it a personal concession—made to please me, if you would consider it."

Rowell hesitated. Grandmère would not attend such an outing, and if they could keep it a secret from Aunt Mildred, she too could be kept in ignorance. If such an unimportant and inexpensive concession could please Willow so vastly, he thought, then it warranted his compliance with her desires. It was a pity that Georgina's requests, unlike his wife's, so invariably resulted in heavy expenditure on his part. Her dress-making and millinery bills were nearly double those of Willow, and she was forever demanding new furnishings or fittings for the house he had given her. Her latest demand had been for an additional bathroom for the nursery and a second nurse for the new baby.

He made but one further visit to his mistress, in late July, before the child was born. It was not long after the

Prince of Wales' sister, Princess Maud, was married to her first cousin, Prince Charles of Denmark. Georgina had been reading an account of the wedding in *The Queen* and could talk of little else but the unfashionable state of her own wardrobe. Bored by her company and conversation, Rowell promised her a new trousseau after the child was born and hurried back to the peace and quiet of life at Rochford Manor.

A month after the baby's arrival, Rowell felt obliged to visit Georgina again. Carrying in his mind a memory of her heavy with child, a discontented expression quite spoiling her lovely face, he was unprepared for the radiant beauty awaiting him. She greeted him not with complaints but with a passionate welcome.

Rowell's body responded with unexpected swiftness to the invitation in her eyes. Within half an hour of his arrival, he was eagerly removing her striped blue crepon tea gown, unpinning her red hair so that it fell in cascades over her smooth white shoulders, and was soon making passionate love to her in the privacy of her bedroom. He could see no sign of the new infant which Georgina had wisely kept out of his way, well aware of his antipathy to nursery paraphernalia.

Later, when they took tea together in the cozy little sitting room downstairs, the nurse brought the elder child to see his father. The boy had been carefully dressed for this meeting and looked charming in a striped sailor suit with its large flat white collar.

Already in a benign mood, Rowell was suitably impressed by his small son. Georgina, who had been watching him closely, was reassured. Despite his long absence this summer, she knew now that she had her protector safely back in the fold.

But once away from Georgina's physical proximity, Rowell's conscience troubled him anew. But for his marriage to Willow, he thought uneasily, he might have had to sell his best horses, his yacht; certainly, he could not have afforded to keep Georgina in the syle she demanded as a price of her faithfulness to him; he would have had to curtail very seriously his day-to-day expenditures.

Through Willow, he now received a regular income from the shares in America that Willoughby Tetford had given his daughter; and his way of life seemed satisfactorily assured. He must buy a nice piece of jewelry for his wife for the coming Christmas, he thought, on his return to Rochford Manor. They might arrange a big ball for Christmas too, and he would tell Willow she could order for herself a new expensive ball gown for this occasion. She had a childish delight in pretty dresses, and this would please her, he decided. The cost to himself would not be great, and thus he could salve his vague feelings of guilt.

As Rowell had guessed, Willow was delighted by his suggestion that they should throw open the doors of Rochford Manor at Christmas to as many of their neighbors and friends who could attend. Silvie would be with them for the festivities as usual, and when replying to Willow's letter referring to the ball, she said she would bring with her to England one of the very latest creations from Jacques Doucet, the Paris couturier.

Made up in silver lamé, I think, wrote Silvie, *to give you an air of sophistication, ma petite. . . .*

Only the excitement of the car race in the autumn broke the quiet routine of country life—the shooting and hunting days punctuating the calls to and from neighbors and an occasional dinner party as Christmas drew nearer.

At long last December arrived and with it Silvie, enlivening as always the somewhat somber atmosphere of the manor with her laughter.

The promised dress fitted perfectly. Silvie smiled, well pleased with her choice as Willow stared into the mirror, fascinated by her reflection. She embraced the lovely young girl of whom she had become so fond.

"You look like a gorgeous ice maiden, Willow," she said. "Now let me see, *chérie,* you must wear your diamond necklace and perhaps a white ostrich feather in your hair. And here is my Christmas present to you to complete the ensemble, yes?"

She handed Willow a small flat box with the name of one of the big Parisian fashion houses imprinted on it. Inside was the most beautiful fan Willow had ever seen.

"Silvie, it is quite perfect," she gasped, her cheeks pink with pleasure.

"They told me it had once belonged to Marie Antoinette," Silvie said, smiling. "But I doubt that, although they insisted it was old. I simply had to buy it for you because it is such a wonderful match for your dress."

The delicate snow-white Alençon lace from which the fan had been fashioned was exquisitely embroidered with tiny silver sequins in a pattern of butterflies.

"It cannot be more than fourteen years old, since sequins were not introduced before '82," said Silvie, laughing, "but it is still pretty, do you not think?"

"It is very, *very* beautiful!" Willow said happily.

Mrs. Spears engaged a considerable number of extra staff, since every one of the ten guest rooms was to be occupied and some four hundred guests invited to the ball. For days on end, the kitchens were a hive of industry as food was prepared. Huge turkeys and fat geese were brought in from the farms. Whole suckling pigs were roasted on the open spits, their handles turned by two of James McGill's poorest boy pupils who were delighted to have this opportunity to earn a little money. Willow had asked him to make a list for her of those families most in need and had instructed Mrs. Spears to give them employment whenever possible, when such was available.

Housemaids worked tirelessly, sweeping, polishing, dusting. Kitchen maids scoured endless pots and pans until their hands were raw with the hot soapsuds; footmen were kept busy polishing all the silver, and the State banqueting dinner service was brought out and washed. Boys from the village came in to help the gardeners sweep the last of the autumn leaves off the lawns and drives. The head gardener had cut down a huge fir tree on the estate, and the whole household watched as it was carried indoors and lifted into a pewter tub. When firmly planted, it was moved to its position in the hall. There Silvie, Willow, and Dodie decorated it with sparkling tinsel and candles to welcome the guests as they arrived.

In the midst of this well-organized confusion, Grandmère remained aloof in her rooms. Now seventy-six years of age, she suffered in the winter months from severe bouts of rheumatism, and Doctor Forbes was perfoce a constant caller.

On one such of his visits, when preparations for the ball were at their height, he brought news that was far from pleasing to old Lady Rochford—if not altogether unexpected. The country woman Agnes Miller who had been fostering the Rochford child, had recently lost her husband, the doctor related. With five children of her own to support, Mrs. Miller was having to use some of the money Lady Rochford had provided for the care of the little girl to feed her own family.

"I fear the child is no longer receiving the nourishment she needs," Doctor Forbes said nervously. "Is it your wish, Lady Rochford, that I attempt to find a new foster mother for her?"

"No!" Grandmère said sharply. "The fewer the number of people who know of her existence, the better. Besides, from what you have told me, she is beginning to bear a remarkable likeness to her mother, and that too could become a danger if she remains in the vicinity. The coloring is too unusual to go unremarked, I think. No, Doctor Forbes, the time has come to dispatch the child to France."

Aunt Mildred's look of dismay was no less than that of the doctor.

"She is not yet three years old—" she faltered, but was quickly interrupted.

"I have already made inquiries, and the convent will accept orphans after their second birthday," Grandmère said sharply. "The child is to go as soon as it can be arranged. My mind is made up."

Doctor Forbes knew better than to argue.

"I want no hitch in these proceedings, Mildred," Grandmère said later to her sister-in-law. "And do try to stop sniffing and pay attention to me. You are to go to London and engage a nurse to care for the child while she is *en voyage*. I want you to go with them to France and personally see the child into the hands of the Mother Superior of the convent."

"But, Clotilde—" the woman began to protest, horrified anew by such a prospect and already dismayed at having so many ugly memories revived. She had almost succeeded in forgetting the terrible night when Willow's baby had been secreted out of the house and the even more terrible day that followed, when the tiny, empty coffin had been lowered into the grave.

"You are quite well enough to undertake the journey, Mildred," Lady Rochford interrupted firmly. "Seventy-two is not exactly your dotage, you know, and you don't suffer as I do from rheumatism. You may travel first class, of course, on the Channel packet steamer and by rail. I will send a telegram at once to the priest, Father Mattieu, and tell him he is to meet you at the railway station at Épernay. He can then escort you to the Convent du Coeur Sanglant. I will give you a purse with the child's keep for the first year. Thereafter, I will make arrangements for Lucienne to forward my donation to the Convent via Father Mattieu. I want no direct communication with the Mother Superior and *under no circumstances whatever* is she to be told of the child's connections. You will travel under the pseudonym of Miss Beresford and you are to pretend that the child is an orphan and that you are acting for an anonymous benefactor. Now, have you taken in what I have been telling you? You had best repeat it so I know nothing is overlooked. And stop sniffing, Mildred."

"But, Clotilde," Mildred protested once more, "I am certain to be asked by Rowell why I wish to go to France. At my age it is unlikely I would be making such a trip for pleasure."

Grandmère looked momentarily taken aback.

"That is quite astute of you, Mildred," she said, in one of her very rare moments of praise for her sister-in-law. "We shall have to improvise."

Aunt Mildred's heart sank. This would mean more lies, more subterfuge, and create pitfalls in the future if her memory betrayed her.

"I know exactly what we will say," Grandmère announced with complete conviction. "You will be going to London to stay with Grace's in-laws in order to sort out her affairs."

Mildred forgot for a moment that Grandmère's plan was hypothetical. She had never liked Grace. Nine years her senior, her sister had bullied her cruelly in their nursery days, it had been an enormous relief to her when Grace had married one of her brother Cedric's friends and gone to live in India.

But Grandmère's subterfuge was excellently chosen, she now realized. A month ago Mildred had been advised of her sister's death at the ripe old age of eighty-one, and Grace's in-laws had informed them that her personal effects were being returned from India. It was suggested that perhaps Mildred and Grandmère would care to make the journey to London, as they were mentioned as beneficiaries in Grace's will. Not even Rowell would question it if

Grace's affairs were given as the reason for his aunt's absence.

But Aunt Mildred was far less fearful of Rowell than she was of incurring Lady Rochford's displeasure if she failed to carry out her orders. Her horror of the task allotted her increased when she arrived with the hired nurse in her severe grey uniform to collect the child at the railway station at Dover. As the nurse took the toddler's hand from that of Doctor Forbes, who had conducted her there, Mildred was appalled to see the little girl's indisputable likeness to her mother.

"Does she talk?" she asked the doctor nervously.

"My name is Sophia Miller," the child answered, staring up at this strange, gaunt woman with growing anxiety. She had been sufficiently awed already by her ride in the carriage with the stern-faced doctor, and Mildred's thin, unsmiling countenance was far from reassuring. The excitement of the promised "nice visit to the seaside" was fast giving way to a consuming homesickness for the large clumsy farmer's wife whom the child had thought of as her mother. Tears spilled from her large dark eyes, and her tiny red mouth trembled uncontrollably.

The nurse stepped forward and lifted the child into her arms. Too professional and discreet to ask questions, she was nevertheless consumed with curiosity. The little girl's clothes were unmistakably those of a village child; yet Miss Beresford, who had engaged her, was equally obviously a gentlewoman of some consequence. The nurse had been informed only that the infant she was to escort to France was an orphan and would be placed in a convent there. Now it occurred to her that it would have been much easier, far less expensive, and in every way more sensible simply to put the child in an English orphanage. But it was not her place to ask questions. She could only hope that during the journey to Épernay her employer would volunteer information that would satisfy her curiosity.

But Mildred's mouth remained very firmly shut. She scrupulously avoided any contact with the nurse and child, sitting, sleeping, and eating in a different carriage and cabin. Which was doubtless as well, the nurse thought as she tried ineffectually to comfort the little girl, who was now overcome by homesickness and fear of so much that was unfamiliar. The child cried herself to sleep and, but for exhaustion, might have cried all day, too. Only a small china doll given her by a kindly fellow passenger seemed to comfort her, and she clung to it as if for dear life.

Fortunately, the little girl was asleep as they reached Paris and was no trouble as they crossed the city to take the train from Gare de l'Est to Épernay.

The nurse stared out of the carriage window. She had never been to this part of France before, and although in principle she disapproved of foreigners, she was curious to see the countryside.

They were now some few kilometers east of Paris, traveling through the wide expanse of flat, treeless terrain that comprised the wheat belt of Meaux. The dark, plowed fields were dreary and colorless on this cold December afternoon, and the nurse was not impressed. It could as well be the Fens of Lincolnshire, from whence she came, she thought. She was more interested in the heavily wooded country the train next approached as they entered the Valley of the Marne. Now and again she could glimpse the fast moving waters of the River Marne, which ran almost parallel to the railway lines.

An hour and a half after their departure from Paris, she caught sight of the massive limestone cliffs on the outskirts of Épernay. The surrounding vineyards were bare now of their leaves, and rain fell steadily over the valley with a depressing relentlessness.

Her employer spoke no word to her throughout the journey. Mercifully the child was still asleep, but the silence was as depressing to the nurse as the rain; and she settled herself to endure it without complaint since they were so near their destination.

In such manner, the trio reached Épernay where a tall, thin man in a black cassock faded almost to green with age, stood waiting for them on the platform. He spoke only French, and the nurse understood nothing of the conversation exchanged between him and her employer as they drove in a hired carriage out into the bleak countryside. It was growing dark as finally they reached the grey stone walls of the Convent du Coeur Sanglant, some seven kilometers out of the town.

A light flurry of snow was falling, and the convent buildings looked like a fortress, the nurse thought as the iron

gates swung open to allow their carriage to pass through.
The clang of a bell from one of the towers echoed alarmingly in the courtyard, waking the sleeping child, who began once more to cry.

Mildred's impressions were very similar to those of the
nurse. Unlike her sister-in-law, Clotilde, she was not a
Roman Catholic, and even the name of the convent made
her uneasy. The "Bleeding Heart" did not conjure up a
place of comfort and happiness for anyone, least of all
the orphans cared for within these forbidding walls.

She was suspicious of the gaunt, silent Father Mattieu
and uneasy that the hired nurse suspected a conspiracy
concerning her charge. Clotilde must have overlooked the
inherent danger in allowing this stranger to know the
child's ultimate destination. Suppose the woman were to
talk on her return to England? she thought fearfully as
the carriage came to a halt outside the iron-studded doors
of the convent entrance.

An aged nun conducted them to a parlor where a
cheerful fire burned in an open grate. It was clear from
this woman's greeting of Father Mattieu that they were
expected.

To Aunt Mildred's relief, the Mother Superior, when
she arrived to greet her visitors, proved a pleasant surprise. Enormously fat and voluble, she welcomed her
guests expansively, offering them an elaborate choice of
excellent wines and sweetmeats which Mildred had certainly not expected in these holy surroundings. She spoke
excellent English and launched almost at once into a de-
tailed account of the blessings of life awaiting the new
arrival.

It very soon became clear to Mildred that despite the
nun's benign expression, her strictures were almost as un-
remitting as Clotilde's. Her dismay increased as the
Mother Superior elaborated upon the future awaiting the
new "orphan."

"You need have no fear that she will be idle here,
Mademoiselle Beresford," Mother Superior said forcefully. "The Devil is not given time to enter our children's
thoughts, I assure you. They rise at six; the older ones
clean the dormitories, then ablutions until prayers in the
chapel at seven. At eight they take breakfast, wash up
their utensils, and prepare for lessons which begin at

nine and end at twelve. They then have midday prayers —after which the infants may rest on their beds for an hour while the older ones are gainfully employed wherever is most suitable."

"Employed?" Mildred echoed nervously, not so much because she wished to know the daily routine, but because she felt certain Clotilde would expect her to show an interest and might question her on her return.

"We do not believe it is right to allow our orphans to accept charity as a due," said Mother Superior smugly. She poured out a third glass of wine for herself and the silent Priest, seeming surprised when Mildred declined to have her goblet refilled.

"Each child must earn its keep insofar as she can. They do laundry work, cleaning; assist with preparation of the meals, and so on. It is a useful training for them for adult life, and we have considerable success in placing them in domestic service when they are old enough to leave here. Is that not so, Father?"

The Priest nodded his agreement.

"The girls continue their education in the afternoon," Mother Superior went on with her timetable. "After evening prayers, they give the little ones their tea and put them to bed. They themselves eat supper at seven o'clock and may then read or embroider or otherwise employ themselves with a hobby until bedtime at nine. On Sundays and Saints' Days, of course, there are no lessons, and we can enjoy more time at prayer—Vespus, Benedictus, Mass, Evensong, and so on. It is a matter of great pride to me that even our youngest children are in the chapel at least five times on Holy days."

She paused at last to glance for the first time at the exhausted child on the nurse's lap.

"I was told she was quite healthy," she said doubtfully. "She looks frail to me. I trust she is not sickening for some illness?"

"It is just the journey!" Mildred said quickly, in fear lest Clotilde's plans were about to be jeopardized at this eleventh hour.

Making no reply, the Mother Superior rang a brass handbell. A girl of about fifteen in a limp serge dress, starched apron, and black stockings came hurrying into the room. She looked pale and gave no smile as she bobbed a curtsy to each of the people in the room.

"We have a new arrival, Monique," Mother Superior said sharply. "Her name is Sophia Miller, but we shall call her Sophie. Find an empty bed in the infants' dormitory. You had best bathe her first—the carbolic soap, don't forget—and wash her hair. You can give her a glass of hot milk this once. Take her away now."

But as the girl, Monique, tried to obey this order, the child clung desperately to the nurse, who was her last contact with the only home she had known. Despite both Monique's and the nurse's attempts to loosen Sophia's grasp, the small fingers could not be unprised. The Mother Superior stood up. Surprisingly fast for so fat a woman. She stepped forward, whipped out a hand from beneath her white cassock and slapped the child sharply across each clenched fist. The hands dropped instantly from the nurse's cloak, and two enormous tear-drenched eyes stared first at Mother Superior and then at Mildred in silent protest.

Although horrified, Mildred was unable to look away from that small white desperate face riveted upon hers in mute appeal. In an act of compassion quite foreign to her, for she disliked small children intensely, she reached out and took a sweetmeat from the tray. Pressing it into the child's hand, she said quickly:

"There, take that and go with Monique like a good girl."

As the older girl dragged the weeping child out of the room, Mildred's eyes turned to the Mother Superior. There was a look of censure on the nun's face so similar to Clotilde's when she was disapproving, that she nearly apologized for her transgression. Instead, she sniffed twice, blew her nose, and announced that it was high time they were on their way. She sensed that neither the Mother Superior nor Father Mattieu was pleased at this abrupt ending to the visit, but her own fatigue, combined with her distaste for the whole enterprise, gave her the necessary courage to insist that they leave without further delay.

Ten minutes later, the carriage passed once more through the iron gates. As she heard them clang shut behind her, Mildred silently thanked the Good Lord that she was outside them, and that it was Willow's child and not she herself who was now incarcerated in the Convent of the Bleeding Heart.

Her journey home was delayed when bad weather prevented the packet from crossing the gale-swept English Channel. She had perforce to remain at Calais in the company of the nurse for a further day and night—a prospect which ill suited both women. Although the nurse was too well trained to ask for explanations, Mildred was unhappily aware of her silent curiosity. It only increased her own sense of horror when she allowed herself to think of the weeping child.

It was with some relief therefore, that on reaching Dover, she was able to pay the woman and dismiss her. She made her way home alone and unattended to Tunbridge Wells, where she hired a hansom cab at the station to drive her to Havorhurst. By the time she arrived at Rochford Manor, the Christmas Eve ball had already begun. The house was ablaze with lights, and carriages filled the drive the entire way to the lodge gates.

Exhausted, and wishing no part in the festivities, Aunt Mildred entered the house by the garden door and retired hurriedly to her rooms. She was grateful to learn from a footman that Grandmère was laid low with a heavy head cold and had left word that she was not to be disturbed until the following morning.

Downstairs, the reception of their many guests by Willow and Rowell was coming to an end. The orchestra engaged for the night was playing light incidental music by Mozart, Chopin, and Listz as Mildred closed her bedroom door with relief and gratitude at her safe return. Now it changed to music for dancing, although Mildred could no longer hear it. The large hall had been cleared of all furniture to provide a ballroom, and chairs had been placed high above in the lighted gallery. From there, those who wished to watch their more energetic companions could sit comfortably and look down upon the dance floor. Gentlemen began to fill in their names on the ladies' programs, but no couple had yet taken to the floor, as the guests politely waited for their host and hostess to begin the dancing.

Aware of this obligation, Rowell took Willow's arm and led her from the withdrawing room toward the hall. As he did so, he glanced uneasily around him. He had not yet seen Georgina; and Georgina had insisted that she be invited for the occasion.

"It is time your wife acknowledged our relationship," she said. "After all, Rowell, if the Princess of Wales tolerates the Countess of Warwick's presence at her parties, I do not see why your wife should not accept me. You worry too much about her, Rowell. You forget that I have met her and I know her to be the most pliable of creatures. But even were she to object to your having a mistress, you yourself have admitted that she is ignorant of our relationship. Why then should she object to me—one of your old friends—being present at your Christmas party?"

She had argued thus until Rowell had lost patience.

"I will not insult my wife by inviting you to her home," he said. "Such an invitation could come only from her."

At this point in the discussion, Georgina had played the trump card that until then she had kept well hidden. She had a new admirer, she told him, one of the newly-made diamond millionaires.

"He has no title, of course, and he is hardly what you might call a gentleman," she admitted unabashed. "But the Prince has accepted him into *his* circle, and that is quite sufficient to satisfy me. So if you are going to debar me from all the most interesting parties and functions because you are afraid of incurring your wife's displeasure, Rowell, then I do not think I wish to continue as your mistress."

Rowell was unable to ignore her threat, for he knew her to be quite capable of carrying it out. So he had finally agreed that she might attend the Christmas ball at Rochford, but in the company of the Symingtons, and as one of their friends rather than his. Georgina's meek acceptance of this condition left him strangely uneasy.

So far he had not glimpsed her among the other guests, but he knew she must be present—for when Esmé and Theodore Symington presented themselves on their arrival, Esmé had whispered to him how lovely Georgina looked.

"Shall we begin the dancing, my dear?" he asked Willow as they reached the dance floor. "Our guests are waiting for us, I think."

Willow happily allowed herself to be led onto the floor. She knew that she had never looked more beautiful or (which pleased her) more sophisticated than she did this night in Silvie's chosen lamé gown. It was the first really lavish party she had given since her marriage to Rowell, and she was determined that she would not fail him as hostess on the occasion. So far, everything had proceeded without mishap. Those guests who were staying overnight had arrived in time for afternoon tea. Fires burned cheerily in all the guest rooms, and a continual stream of servants went up and down the stairs refilling the copper jugs with hot water. Visiting servants were accommodated in the attic rooms where the order of seniority of their masters was strictly observed, those of lesser status sharing an improvised dormitory.

Now that all the visiting neighbors had arrived, the formal reception was over and the gaiety was about to commence. The orchestra sounded in good heart, and the old manor house echoed to the lively strains of Johann Strauss.

"A waltz, I think," said Rowell, and Willow smiled up at him in happy anticipation.

He was about to encircle her waist with his arm, when from the nearby doorway an imperious female voice carried high above the music:

"Rowell, would you be so kind as to fetch my fan. I think I left it in the drawing room."

Such an uncalled-for interruption would have been acceptable only from someone of Grandmère's advanced years, and even then the command would in all probability have been voiced quietly to an escorting gentleman or attendant servant.

All eyes turned, on the instant, to the woman who had spoken.

Rowell paused as he too looked toward the door as if mesmerized. Willow's gaze followed his. Leaning nonchalantly against the door frame, smiling, was Georgina Grey. She was wearing a startlingly beautiful dress of yellow silk draped with scarlet chiffon; scarlet velvet sleeves ballooned to her elbows, accentuating the whiteness of her skin. Her décolletage was daringly low over her bosom and exposed most of her smooth white shoulders. From beneath the full train of her skirt peeped two scarlet satin slippers with jeweled toecaps. Long yellow suede gloves reached to her elbows, and a high pearl collar was fastened about her throat. Her red hair was brushed back from her forehead and coiled high on the crown of her head *à la Grecque,* a jeweled comb holding it in place. Her pose was theatrical and totally arresting.

Not only Rowell and Willow were staring at her, but so was everyone within hearing distance of her voice. Many of those present knew Georgina Grey was Rowell's mistress and had not been particularly shocked to see her at Rochford Manor. But her deliberate interruption at this critical point of the evening's entertainment was not only a severe breach of etiquette, but an unmistakable challenge to Rowell's loyalty to his wife. No one expected Willow to remain silent. Most held their breath as they waited to see what Rowell—and Willow—would do. Even the orchestra seemed to have quietened, and behind her Willow quite clearly overheard a woman's titter and her aside to her companion:

"What can you expect? She's Rowell's mistress!"

"Testing her powers, I suppose," came the equally audible male reply. *"What effrontery!"*

Color flamed into Willow's cheeks and then receded. She was aware of the rigidity of Rowell's arm beneath her elbow.

No, Rowell, no, she thought, the scream of protest caught in her throat. It isn't true, is it? Don't go to her now. Don't humiliate me. I love you, Rowell. I am your wife . . .

But the grip of Rowell's fingers on her arm slackened, and almost imperceptibly, she felt him move. Oblivious of the hundreds of eyes upon her, she stared up at her husband, silently pleading with him to disregard Georgina's challenge. It seemed to her a lifetime since Georgina had spoken, although it was but a minute before Rowell let go of her arm. He was about to take the first step to obey his mistress' demand when a man stepped forward from the foot of the stairway where he had been standing beside Silvie. It was Toby. Calmly, hurriedly, he walked over to Georgina. He was carrying Silvie's parchment fan.

"Will this suffice, Mrs. Grey? I do agree that it is singularly hot in here. I will ask one of the servants to open a window."

From where she stood, Willow could see the swift flash of fire in Georgina's green eyes as she had perforce to accept the fan Toby was offering her. Then a voice said at her elbow:

"Excuse me, Rowell, but I think Willow has forgotten that she promised the first dance to me."

It was Pelham. Stepping between her and Rowell, he put his arm confidently around Willow's waist; and without waiting for Rowell's reply, he whirled her onto the dance floor. A bright smile fixed upon his face, he murmured in a low voice:

"Whatever you do, don't cry, Willow. Don't let any of them see how you feel. Smile at me . . . that's right. Pretend it doesn't matter . . . because really it doesn't matter, my dearest Willow. My brother was never worth one of your tears, let alone a broken heart."

"But I love him—he's my husband—" Her voice faltered on the edge of the tears that by some miracle still remained unshed.

"But now you know he isn't worthy of your love," Pelham said quickly. "*I* have known it for years, Willow, just as I've known that you should never have married him. You should have married me."

His arm tightened around her.

"Now I have made you smile, because you think I am talking nonsense. But I mean it, Willow. And I'm not the only one who adores you. Toby does, too. Wasn't he magnificent just now? Georgina could have killed him. Dear old Toby! I think he is as much in love with you as I am."

"Oh, Pelham!" Willow remonstrated, smiling tremulously. "I know you are teasing, but I am grateful—to you and Toby. You each proved that you really are fond of me, and that means a great deal to me."

As the dance ended, Pelham guided her off the floor.

"I really meant what I said, Willow. I'm in love with you."

But this time she did not hear him, for against her own will, her eyes were searching the room for Rowell—and for the glimpse of a yellow dress with scarlet sleeves. It was as if Pelham no longer existed.

Had Rowell gone to his mistress' side while she was on the dance floor? she wondered. There was no doubt that Georgina Grey *was* his mistress despite the fact that he had denied it so vehemently when he had encountered the

woman at the Symingtons' house party. Was he being unfaithful to her even then? Had the affair continued these
past five years while she, stupidly, had trusted in her husband's fidelity; in his assurances that he was only going
to London "on business?"

Slowly, relentlessly, memories flooded into her mind.
The night her baby was born—and died—Rowell had not
been with her. Maybe he could have given directives, had
he been there, that would have saved the baby's life. But
all the time, he had been lying in the arms of another
woman . . .

Willow's heart froze still harder as she recalled the many
nights she had lain alone in bed longing for the kind of
love her husband was giving someone else. Naïve, gullible,
she has assumed she was somehow at fault, too inexperienced to attract his attentions. Everyone else—certainly
Pelham and Toby—had known the truth; Francis, too, had
hinted he knew much to Rowell's discredit. She alone had
remained ignorant, trusting, her love for Rowell blinding
her to the truth. He had never loved her. Her father had
guessed it and tried to warn her, but she had wanted so
much to believe her wealth was an unimportant consideration when Rowell had proposed.

Her bitterness was intense as she faced the fact that
she had probably been betrayed not once but continuously since the beginning of her marriage. Yet even now
she could not contemplate so terrible a step as leaving
him. She would not accept defeat so easily. Georgina Grey
might be Rowell's mistress but *she* was his wife, and now
she knew the truth, she could fight her rival for his affections.

I still love Rowell, she thought, even though she knew
with equal certainty that nothing could ever be quite the
same between them again.

Part Two

1897–1905

"Who can foretell what joys the day shall bring,
Or why before the dawn the linnets sing?"

Oscar Wilde, *Ravenna*

Chapter Twelve

May—October 1897

"I T WILL BE YOUR BIRTHDAY IN A FEW MONTHS' TIME, Dodie!" Willow said as they walked very slowly down toward the croquet lawn. "Just think, you will be seventeen, and it seems only a short time ago that you were just a little girl."

Dodie smiled, her astonishingly beautiful eyes lighting up her small, pale face. She was now nearly as tall as Willow, and her figure had filled out to reveal feminine curves of waist and bosom. Had it not been for her malformed arm and the shortened leg which enforced the use of Toby's contraption for walking, she would have been a remarkably attractive young girl.

"Pelham suggested to me yesterday that you might like him to drive us up to London in the landau so that you can see the Diamond Jubilee decorations," Willow continued. "You have never been to London, Dodie, and I do not think such a trip would be too tiring if it would please you."

Dodie's smile faded and her face took on a look of anxiety.

"Oh no, Willow, thank you all the same. I know it is silly of me to think always that strangers are staring at me; and James—Mr. McGill—is always telling me I should overcome my shyness. But I cannot seem to prevent it."

Willow was not altogether surprised. She was well aware of the girl's self-consciousness, but Dodie's use of the schoolmaster's Christian name did engage her attention.

For some time now Willow had suspected that the young girl's hero-worship of her tutor might be changing to a deeper emotion. Moreover, James McGill was calling much more frequently at the Manor to give his pupil extra tutorials, which undoubtedly she welcomed.

Could pupil and teacher be falling in love? Willow

asked herself anxiously. It would not be so surprising if the close proximity these two had shared for the past four years had brought them to a depth of understanding of one another.

It was easy to see why James McGill might love this sweet-natured, innocent girl. But what of Dodie's feelings for the thirty-five-year-old schoolteacher? Although his appearance was unremarkable, his character was far from ordinary. He had shown an unusual sensitivity toward the poor child. His academic teachings had been enhanced by thoughtful guidance on life and people that had helped to give Dodie an understanding of the world beyond her limited existence. But if love had developed between them, it would face terrible opposition from the family.

As if aware of Willow's thoughts, Dodie said now:

"You do like James McGill, do you not, Willow?"

"But of course I do. How could one fail to like so charming a man?" Willow replied truthfully.

Dodie glanced sideways at Willow, her cheeks flushing. "But Grandmère would not allow James at Rochford as a guest, would she? Nor even would Rowell. Does that not seem wrong to you, Willow, that a man is judged on his social status rather than on his merits?"

"Perhaps it does," Willow said gently. "But one has to accept that it is not the English custom to receive those of a lower social standing."

The color in Dodie's cheeks deepened.

"Do you not think that such distinctions of class are becoming outdated now, Willow? After all, the Prince of Wales entertains people the Queen would never receive. Is that not so?"

"So Mr. McGill has been enlightening you about Court behavior," Willow remarked curiously.

Dodie shook her head.

"It was not James who told me. It was Pelham," she said. "James would not speak of such things to me. He will not speak of anything that is important to me—" She broke off as her voice rose in distress.

Now fairly certain as to Dodie's feelings, Willow put her arm around the girl's trembling shoulders.

"Then let us speak honestly to one another, my dearest," she said softly. "You believe that you love Mr. McGill but you are not sure if he loves you. I suspect that he is far too integral ever to take advantage of his position as your tutor to declare how he feels about you."

Dodie's eyes were shining as she stared back at Willow.

"I should have known *you* would understand, dearest Willow," she said. "And believe me, I do not only *think* I love James, I am quite certain of it. I think he cares for me too. But no matter how carefully I pose a question to him that might make him reveal his true sentiments, he manages skillfully to evade a reply that might betray him."

Her eyes clouded with distress.

"He speaks to me of love only in relation to other people. He has told me that it would make no difference to a man who truly loved me that I am so physically handicapped; that one day such a man will come into my life, and when this happens, I must never refuse marriage because of my appearance. James says that true love supersedes everything and that it is a unity of the spirit that unites a man and woman far more forcibly than the mutual attraction of their bodies."

Willow remained silent, too deeply affected by the relevance of the schoolmaster's remarks to avoid their application to herself. She and Rowell shared no unity of the spirit, she thought unhappily.

Since the Christmas Eve ball five months ago, Willow had done her utmost to forgive Rowell. She tried to forget the terrible humiliation he had so nearly inflicted upon her when, but for Toby's presence of mind, she would have been forced to watch her husband leave her side to do his mistress' bidding in front of several hundreds of their guests. Even now the memory was like gall in her throat.

Rowell had made fulsome apologies, of course, and had sworn that he would never see Georgina again. Willow had wanted to believe him. When eventually she welcomed him back into the bed, she sincerely believed that she could put the image of Georgina Grey out of her mind. But the tall, voluptuous redhead had remained in Willow's thoughts like a brilliant ghost and continued to haunt the marital bed.

Georgina had forced her finally to face the truth about her relationship with Rowell. She could no longer tell herself that he had loved her to the exclusion of all others.

She realized that deep within her, she had sensed that all was not well; that Rowell was not proving the ardent lover of her dreams; that they shared very little other than their home—and even that they did not share all the time, with Rowell so often away from Rochford. Only because she had the companionship of Toby, Pelham, and Dodie was she not made far more lonely by her husband's absence.

While shamefaced at first, Rowell had become impatient with her of late, insisting that the affair was over and done with.

But only because he had been found out and not because he himself wished it, Willow thought bitterly. Perhaps also, in part, because her parents were due to arrive next week to spend the Queen's Diamond Jubilee Season with them, and Rowell would not want to incur his father-in-law's censure.

With an effort, Willow set aside her own concerns and turned her attention back to Dodie.

"I wish I could tell you that I might be able to persuade Grandmère or Rowell to allow Mr. McGill to call," she said. "But I think if I were to reveal your feelings to them it might only result in his dismissal; and that would be far worse for you than the present situation where at least you and he can see one another nearly every day. But if you wish, Dodie, I will speak to Mr. McGill and discover his feelings."

"Oh, no!" Dodie cried, grasping Willow's hand in her anxiety. "I do not wish James to know I love him. If he does not care for me, it would be exceedingly embarrassing for us both. Promise me you will not do so."

Willow smiled.

"Of course, Dodie. But I think you may be underestimating James' intelligence. If you regard him with even half the affection that is revealed in your eyes when you mention his name to me, then he must surely have guessed already that you love him! But rest assured that I would speak to him only of *his* affection for *you*. Believe me, Dodie, I would do so with the utmost tact."

Dodie looked at her wistfully.

"Oh I *wish* I could be certain how he feels! Sometimes when he looks at me, I am sure that there is more than mere fondness in his gaze. But perhaps it is only pity, Willow. I could not bear that."

"Then put such a silly notion from your mind," Willow said firmly. "For I know already that James McGill does not so much pity as envy you. He has told me that through your eyes he has discovered the beauty of life unsullied by the world's evils. He holds you in great respect."

As she walked slowly back to the house with Dodie, Willow wished she could consult with Toby before speaking to the schoolmaster. The implications of Dodie's revelations were far-reaching; and she did not feel able alone to take the responsibility of furthering this affair, if such it was to be, between the young girl and the schoolmaster. One thing was certain: that neither Grandmère nor Rowell would ever countenance a marriage. The couple would have no money, and Grandmère would ensure that James McGill was dismissed from the Havorhurst School. The delicate, handicapped Dodie had never known anything but the luxurious seclusion and protection of her home. She would be physically unable to assist James even were he to find other employment. The outlook for them was not happy to say the least.

But Toby had gone to France to visit a certain Pierre and Marie Curie. He had met Madame Curie at the Pasteur Institute on his visit there three years ago. Recently he had had a letter from her telling him of her experiments to discover the reason for the radiation rays coming from a substance called uranium; and he had set off for Paris without delay.

Willow decided to take matters one step at a time. First she must find out how deeply James cared. She decided to call upon him at his house that afternoon.

The schoolmaster was engrossed in correcting a pile of exercise books which he attempted ineffectually to tidy away as his housekeeper showed Willow into the little parlor. Willow tried to imagine Dodie in such a setting and her heart sank as she appreciated how vast was the gap between rich and poor. The entire house could be fitted into the billiard room at Rochford, she thought uneasily.

The housekeeper, Mrs. Gassons, James' only servant, brought in tea and then left them alone together. Haltingly, Willow asked James whether he had grown fond of his pupil over the four years he had been teaching her.

At the mention of Dodie's name, the man's rather plain face became transfigured.

"I admire Miss Dodie more than anyone else in the world," he declared in a low, intense voice.

"Is it no more than admiration you feel for her?" Willow asked quietly. "Forgive me for intruding upon your private affairs, but I have been wondering if perhaps your feelings go deeper than mere admiration. You *do* also feel an affection for Dodie, do you not?"

No sooner did Willow mention the word "affection" than the schoolmaster began to pour out his pent-up emotions to her with quite uncharacteristic volubility.

"I promised myself that I would never tell a living soul of my love for Miss Dodie," he said finally, his grey eyes meeting Willow's gaze with unmistakable honesty. "I know that it is a madness that can bring me no happiness, and far worse, that it might harm the one I love. But reason seems to play no part in my emotions, and each day I find myself more deeply in love. You must wonder at my audacity, Lady Rochford, although I cannot help myself."

He looked at Willow despairingly.

"Had I title or wealth, I could openly declare my love for Miss Dodie. As it is, no one is more aware than I that my lips must remain sealed for ever."

"You know that Dodie returns your affection?" Willow asked quietly.

For the first time, the man's voice was hesitant as he said:

"I fear that may be. My heart longs for her love, but reason tells me that it could only bring her pain were she to care for me. Her happiness is all that matters. Do you think I should leave Havorhurst, Lady Rochford?"

"Indeed I do not," Willow replied without hesitation. "It is you who make Dodie's life so happy. Let us at least discover first if there is a solution to this problem. Have I your permission to speak to my husband and see if he can be persuaded to consider your cause?"

Understandably, James McGill's expression was devoid of hope. His eyes were deeply troubled as he said:

"I appreciate *your* willingness to overlook my shortcomings, Lady Rochford, but I fear the Baron would never permit me to declare myself to Miss Dodie. I do welcome your offer to intervene, nonetheless, since from it I may dare presume that you are not personally shocked by my boldness."

"Of course I am not shocked," Willow replied gently, "for, as I am well aware, it is not always possible to prevent love alighting where it chooses rather than where it is wisest. But I must confess that I am worried. I believe that you love Dodie and that as a mature man, you are quite old enough to know your mind. But whether Dodie is old enough to realize what marriage to a man in your circumstances would entail, is another matter, and one I am sure you have already considered."

James McGill looked surprised:

"Indeed, I have not dared think of marriage to Miss Dodie," he confessed. "Such presumption did not cross my mind. But if such a possibility did exist, Lady Rochford, I swear I could make Miss Dodie happy, despite the fact that I have little but love and understanding to give her."

"I will do what I can to help," Willow replied. "But in the meanwhile, it might be better for you to say nothing of your feelings—or even of our meeting—to Dodie. I do not wish to give her any false hopes for the future."

As she drove home, Willow resolved to wait for Toby's return before she herself took any further action. If she could enlist Toby's support, she thought, and Pelham's too, perhaps Rowell could be persuaded that in a year or two's time, marriage to the schoolmaster would not be so amiss for Dodie. If some kind of financial allowance could be given her, she might then survive on James McGill's very limited salary without undue hardship.

Willow tried to turn her thoughts to other matters. She and Rowell had accepted an invitation to attend a fancy dress ball at Devonshire House early in July and she had yet to choose a costume. Rowell was clearly pleased by the invitation. Most of the prominent members of society would be there, he told her, including the Prince and Princess of Wales.

"Your parents will find such an occasion quite a novelty, I dare say," Rowell commented, anxious as always to impress his wealthy father-in-law.

Willow anticipated the gala ball at Devonshire House with pleasure; but with far greater excitement, she was looking forward to seeing her parents. They were coming to England for nearly six whole months, and by now should already have embarked at New York. But not even this happy expectation could eradicate entirely the unhappy thoughts that had dogged her since Christmas.

The sad fact was, it seemed, she could never count upon Rowell's understanding when it came to matters of importance such as the problem of Dodie and James.

She was worried, too, about Rupert—a problem which should have been Rowell's, but which Pelham had brought to her rather than to his eldest brother. Rupert, he told her, had renewed his association with the doctor's son, Adrian. His valet had seen them together in the boat house, Pelham related.

"Fortunately, the sensible fellow came to me about it. I pay him well to be discreet, so I know we can trust him to keep quiet on the matter, Willow. Damned if I understand Rupert's inclinations," he added, "but Toby tells me this kind of affliction happens more often than one might suppose—accident of birth, or some such, and that Rupert should have been a girl. Rowell isn't going to like it one bit if he finds out."

"Will *you* speak to Rupert, Pelham?" Willow asked tentatively. "As you say, we dare not mention it to Rowell. Bearing in mind his reactions to the Oscar Wilde case, I am in no doubt that he would force Rupert to leave home at once."

Pelham agreed, albeit reluctantly, to speak to his brother, but he had little that was reassuring to report to Willow after he had done so.

"It was damned odd, begging your pardon, Willow," he said, "but Rupert actually seems to love this fellow, Adrian; he cried like a baby when I suggested it wasn't quite the thing to be doing and he'd better stop taking such risks. 'Adrian is all I have in the world to love,' he kept saying over and over again. 'If I cannot go on seeing him, I'll kill myself.'" Pelham frowned. "I know it sounds hellish stupid," he said awkwardly, "but I believe he meant it. What a mess, eh Willow?"

Worried not only for Rupert's moral good, Willow was even more concerned as to what would happen to him were Grandmère to find out the truth. Although the old lady was these days more or less confined to her rooms, now that her arthritis had worsened, she had not lost her determination to keep abreast of her family's affairs. She used Aunt Mildred to spy upon everyone and report to her if anything seemed amiss.

Willow had a certain amount of sympathy for Aunt Mildred, irritating though the pathetic old spinster was. No one in the family liked her, and as Grandmère was getting older, she bullied her sister-in-law more than ever. The thin, stooped, seventy-three-year-old woman seemed always to be cowering in a dark corner, watching, listening —revealing her presence only by her involuntary, nervous sniffs. Her manner with Willow had become most strange. She seemed to go out of her way to avoid any conversation or encounter with her, despite the fact that Willow alone of the household tried to speak kindly to her.

"Perhaps she is aware that you pity her," Pelham suggested. "I do not. She is a mischief-maker, and I hate people I cannot trust."

Hate was a strong word, thought Willow unhappily, but she understood only too well Pelham's revulsion for anyone he could not trust. She minded that Rowell had deceived her far more than she minded his acts of unfaithfulness.

Pelham seemed to regard Rowell's betrayal with equanimity.

"Why do you let his peccadillos upset you so much?" he said. "I know it must be a blow to your pride, but really, Willow, Rowell isn't worth your tears or your heartache. Let him have his precious Georgina if that is what he wants; and you have your lover—me, for instance. You know I have always been crazy with love for you. I wouldn't give a threepenny piece for a dozen Georginas if *you* were available. I could make you happy, Willow, I know it."

It was impossible to be angry with Pelham even when he made such wild and shocking declarations. His dark eyes, so like Rowell's, were always dancing with laughter; his mouth twitching with a smile; his tone teasing but warmly affectionate. There were moments when she almost took his suggestion seriously and considered fleetingly whether she might enjoy having him for a lover. Certainly, she would enjoy being loved, she thought bitterly, for since the rift at Christmas, she and Rowell only very rarely shared the same bed. When they did so, their union was brief, silent, and never, as far as she was concerned, fulfilling.

But Willow knew herself too well to suppose that she could enter lightly upon so intimate a relationship with another man, far less with her own brother-in-law. Silvie might have a nature that allowed her to take lovers, but Willow needed a union not only of the body but of the soul.

Was such a union possible still between her and her husband? she asked herself. Would time heal the humiliation and allow her once more to see Rowell with the same unquestioning, uncritical eyes with which she had come to her marriage nearly six years ago?

Several times, she thought very seriously of leaving him, of leaving England and returning to her parents. She even voiced such thoughts to Toby.

"I am only twenty-two years of age," she said. "Maybe in time I would find someone else—begin my life again. What do you think, Toby?"

He did not answer for some minutes. Then he said quietly:

"I think that if you felt such a drastic step would be right, you would not need to ask my opinion. But since you have asked me, I will say this much. I believe you still love Rowell; that you are angry, hurt, bitter, but underneath all that, you do still want his love."

"Why should I want a man who has betrayed me!" Willow cried bitterly. "He isn't worth my love, Toby."

"Which fact, alas, is irrelevant, since love itself is quite illogical as I see it," Toby replied smiling. "Perhaps if people acted sensibly—which is to say, loved only those who loved them—there would be precious little of the commodity left in this world of ours. So dry your eyes, regain your courage, and refuse to allow Georgina Grey to best you, Willow. Make Rowell see for himself which of the two of you is worth more to him. It cannot be long before he comes to his senses—if he has not already done so. At least he has forsworn Georgina."

As always, Toby's words were a comfort; his advice oddly similar to that given by her father shortly after her parents' arrival at Rochford Manor. While the household was busily engaged packing for their removal to London, her father drew Willow to one side and asked her bluntly whether all was not entirely well with her marriage.

Despite her resolve not to let anything mar his visit, unexpected tears filled her eyes and she admitted finally that her marriage to Rowell was not quite as perfect as she had hoped.

"There is no such thing as a *perfect* marriage, my dear," he told her. "All relationships require compromise. When we choose our partners for life, we accept both good and bad in them. If we all gave up trying to keep our marriages intact the moment something went amiss, we would have a society in which almost as many people were divorced as married—and think what a dreadful mishap that would be!"

So counseled, Willow decided to put the past behind her. She was even happy again as she watched Nellie pack her trunks for London. Rowell, too, seemed in better spirits as they set off with servants, luggage, and carriages for the house he had rented in Park Lane for two months of the Season.

Willow was soon engrossed in the drawing rooms, balls, dinner parties, and ceaseless rounds of calls. Now socially adept, she knew that these so called "morning" visits were to be made between three and six in the evening; that she must leave two cards if no one were at home, with one corner turned down to show it had been left by her in person.

Before long it was the Derby, Ascot and the Gold Cup, and Wimbledon lawn tennis tournament; and at the beginning of July, the long-awaited ball given by the Duke and Duchess of Devonshire.

For some weeks now the family's fancy dress costumes had been completed ready for the occasion. It had been Pelham's suggestion that the Rochfords might go ensemble as King Arthur and his Knights of the Round Table. Rowell approved the prospect of appearing as King Arthur with Willow as Guinevere his Queen. Toby was to be the gallant Sir Galahad, Pelham and Rupert, Lancelot and Geraint. Willoughby Tetford had cheerfully agreed to be King Arthur's father, Merlin. Only Willow's mother had elected not to participate. She was feeling the strain of the endless round of social activities and welcomed a quiet night on her own.

"Have a lovely time, my dear child," she said when Willow called to say goodnight on her way downstairs, "and don't let your father stay up too late or he won't enjoy the polo at Hurlingham tomorrow."

She looked up in quiet satisfaction at her daughter, who was magnificently attired in the robes of a medieval queen. Her simple yellow dress had long tight sleeves and was caught at the waist by a knotted rope girdle. Over it she wore a royal blue cloak trimmed with ermine and fastened at the neck with a large silver clasp. Her hair was covered by a white wimple topped with a tiny gold crown.

"You look beautiful," she said as Willow stooped to kiss her. "Your husband will be no less proud of you than your dear Papa."

Willoughby Tetford, who had deemed himself beyond being impressed by the extravagances of London life, was nevertheless astonished by the magnificence of the historic pageantry awaiting them. All the most influential socialites were present, including the Prince and Princess of Wales. During the evening, Rowell introduced him to Lord Derby, Lord Balfour, and Lord Roseberry, whose wife Hannah was the niece of Baron Rothschild. Pelham introduced him to young Winston Churchill, son of the late Lord Randolph Churchill. Winston was preparing to go to India as a junior officer to help quash the clashes at India's borders. Toby introduced him to the Home Secretary, Herbert Asquith—a brilliant Balliol College classicist and Q.C.

Willoughby enjoyed himself hugely, joining in the dancing with the vigor of a man half his age and showing no visible sign of fatigue as they drove home in the early hours of the morning.

The following day, the newspaper gave much publicity to the Devonshire House ball, comparing it most favorably with the Plantagenet ball given by the Queen not long after her Coronation. The Duchess of Devonshire was said to have provided the crowning effect of the many efforts all were making to give due glory to Her Majesty's Diamond Jubilee. Little else was discussed at the many parties and entertainments they attended throughout July.

In August, Rowell took Willow and her parents to Cowes for the Regatta where Willoughby Tetford was intrigued to learn that the Prince of Wales was trying to sell his yacht *Britannia* for ten thousand pounds. He made up his mind to put in a bid for it, but he was outbid by a Mr. John Lawson-Johnston, the inventor of the meat extract, Bovril. He was disappointed, but compensated by the fact that in the course of the negotiations, he had been presented both to the Prince of Wales and Princess Alexandra.

The family returned home to Rochford to enjoy a quiet few weeks before Rowell and Willow and her parents departed once more, this time to Badenoch in Scotland. After three days watching the games at Braemar, they traveled north to the country home of Rowell's distant cousin who had invited them to stay in his magnificent castle and to shoot over his moors.

Willow as well as her mother was feeling the effects of the hectic Season, and they were glad to leave the men to their grouse shoots while they enjoyed quiet, companionable walks in the beautiful Scottish countryside. Seeing this wild open moorland for the first time, they had ample opportunity to appreciate the grandeur of the rolling hills, the carpets of thick purple heather stretching away into the distance.

Although after six years as the wife of an English country gentleman Willow had learned to appreciate the satisfaction such sporting activities brought Rowell and his friends, it struck her forcibly how sad it was that the wildlife surrounding them must be destroyed in such large quantities. She hated the moment when the gamekeeper's cart arrived at the castle at the end of the day's shoot and the hundreds of limp, dark brown feathered bodies were laid out to be counted and admired by the household.

"I sometimes wish Rowell did not derive such pleasure from killing," she said to her mother during one of their walks beside the nearby Baden Loch. It might have been only her imagination, but it seemed to her that the greater the day's destruction, the more readily Rowell's passions were aroused. She did not care to think that his enjoyment of her body was in any way related to the day's sport, nor could she voice such opinions to her mother, who would have been deeply shocked to hear her speak of such things. Even now, she was looking at Willow disapprovingly.

"No good wife criticizes her husband's chosen way of life," she admonished her daughter gently. "When a woman marries, my dear child, she must adopt her husband's preferences without question. Besides which," she added, "your father is a keen sportsman, as well you know, Willow, and he is beyond reproach."

Willow remained silent, knowing that she could never explain to this good, upright, innocent woman the difference between her father's enjoyment in the sport itself, and the excitement aroused in her husband at the moment of killing. She had been at his side on one unforgettable occasion when a fox had been torn to pieces by the hounds, and although she tried not to think about it, she could never forget the look in Rowell's eyes. She was certain that he actually derived pleasure from the poor creature's cruel death.

Nevertheless, the holiday was a success, and Rowell was in the best of spirits as they bade their host farewell and departed for the train back to London.

They planned their arrival home at Rochford Manor to be in time for Francis' twenty-third and Dodie's seventeenth birthdays. Neither one was awaiting the family's return with bright smiles of welcome. Francis was in a sullen, resentful mood. He finally had had to accept that Madeleine Villier was not going to see him again.

His enforced avoidance of her at all public functions had been a bitter blow to the New Zealand girl, more especially since she had not been asked to many of the parties to which Francis could have gained her an entrée. She soon tired of their secret meetings and when a new suitor appeared on the scene, she wrote a farewell note to him making it clear she did not wish to continue their friendship. She did not, however, return the necklace which had been instrumental in bringing about Francis' theft of the Gainsborough and the subsequent strictures on their meetings.

But Willow was far more concerned about Dodie than Francis. Dodie had clearly been weeping, and despite the fine weather, she was confined to her bed and looked far from well.

"Aunt Milly heard James and me talking in the schoolroom and reported our conversation to Grandmère," she answered Willow's anxious questioning. Her eyes filled with tears. "We were not misbehaving, Willow, I promise you. James would never take advantage of your trust in him, and we have not even so much as held hands. But I was telling him of my feelings for him, and Aunt Milly heard me and reported it to Grandmère . . ."

Willow's heart sank. She could imagine only too well Grandmère's reaction to such a tale from Aunt Mildred.

"James has been dismissed, and Grandmère has threatened to have him dismissed from the school, too." Dodie sobbed. "Oh, Willow, what am I to do? It is all my fault. I have ruined James' life!"

"Nonsense!" Willow said firmly. "And you are to do nothing, Dodie. *I* will speak to Grandmère . . . and to Rowell. We will make sure James does not lose his post. As for his dismissal from this house, it is not the end of the world, my love, for if James cannot come here to see you, there is nothing to prevent your going to Havorhurst to see him, is there?"

Toby was already aware of the situation, having been at home when Grandmère dismissed the unhappy James.

"I have one hopeful suggestion," he said to Willow. "That is to enlist your father's help. He has always expressed a fondness for Dodie, has he not? And Rowell pays attention to your father. If you can persuade both your parents that this may be Dodie's one chance of marriage; that McGill is a worthy enough fellow even if he does have so little to offer her socially and materially, then Rowell may take a kindlier view of the situation. Grandmère may be an old tyrant, but she cannot force her will upon Rowell; and she knows it. Rowell may be afraid of the old lady's tongue—as indeed are we all in this house, but I believe he might prefer her anger to inviting your father's poor opinion of him."

Toby's understanding of human nature was very quickly proved sound. Willow had no difficulty in persuading her father to take a charitable view of Dodie's future. Like many large, strong men Willoughby Tetford was compassionate toward frailty. He was moved by the young girl's unfortunate affliction, and her huge violet eyes held a wistful appeal that he had always found irresistible. He was impressed, too, by her courage, as well as by the remarkable progress she had made since Willow had put an end to her invalid seclusion. Moreover, as a self-made man of humble origins, it was natural for him to champion the young schoolmaster who, like himself, had not been born with the advantages that went with good breeding. He professed himself more than willing to take up Dodie's cause with his son-in-law.

"McGill is old enough and sensible enough to make your sister a good husband," he said to Rowell, coming straight to the point. "And be honest, m'boy, what other chance does the girl have? If she marries this schoolmaster, she'll be off your hands—unlike that poor unhappy Miss Mildred. One spinster in the family is enough, eh?"

As Toby had forecast, Rowell dared not admit to his father-in-law that he was afraid to confront his grandmother with so revolutionary an idea as a Rochford marrying so far beneath her. He himself disliked the idea, but he could see certain advantages.

"I suppose that I shall have to talk to Grandmère," he told Willow unhappily as they prepared for bed. "But I really don't think your father has any idea of how . . . how trying she can be. She is always surprisingly docile in his company. She will blame me, of course, for ever allowing McGill to tutor Dodie. She said it was wrong to employ a man for the task and now she has proved her point! Dodie should have had a governess."

"Oh, Rowell, don't look so miserable," Willow said. "It was not your idea that the schoolmaster should be employed here—it was mine."

Rowell drew a deep sigh that was in part relief. It would make it easier for him if he could lay the initial blame at his wife's door.

"It is all very trying—especially when we returned home from Badenoch Castle in such good spirits," he said in a more moderate tone. "It is most thoughtless of Dodie to upset the household in this manner, more especially while your parents are with us."

Just in time, Willow bit back the retort that rose to her lips in defense of Dodie. Wisely, she made no rejoinder but instead urged Rowell to remain with her in preference to retiring to his dressing room to sleep.

"Stay with me tonight," she said softly. "We can comfort each other, can we not, and try to forget these minor upsets."

Rowell nodded. His wife looked very young and appealing in her freshly ironed, frilled nightgown, her hair falling in soft clouds about her cheeks. Her dark eyes were regarding him with an innocence he only momentarily suspected. It was quite unlike Willow to be devious, he told himself. With typical feminine romanticism she had sided with the young couple, but he did not believe it would have occurred to her to enlist his support through the good offices of her father. Georgina was more than capable of such tricks to get her way, but not Willow.

Reassured, he climbed into bed beside her and as always turned off the light for modesty's sake. Georgina derived great sensuous delight in observing his performance and her own, but he considered such loose behavior would shock his young wife.

He felt the beginning of desire for her slender young body. He could almost feel her longing for his embraces, although he knew it could only be accidental. Well brought up young ladies did not feel bodily desires as did women of Georgina's ilk, he reminded himself. Nevertheless, it was satisfying to know that his wife did not object to his advances and made excellent pretense of enjoying them.

Unknown to Willow, he thought, she had a quite remarkable effect upon men. Not once, but a hundred times, he had listened to his male friends compliment him upon his wife's beauty and charm. It would not be far from the truth to say that Willow had been the rage this Season, attracting even the roving eyes of the Prince of Wales. But fortunately, *he* had his mistress, Lady Warwick, to keep him amused, and Willow was in no danger; nor he himself of losing his wife to the heir to the throne as Mr. Langtry and Lord Warwick had done.

"I am very proud of you, my love," he said as he lifted the hem of her nightgown and drew it unhurriedly over her head. "And I want you to promise me that you will never forget that you are my wife. You belong to me alone—as I now belong to you," he added, pleased that he had finally made the break with Georgina. His marriage must come first, he had told her, and she must no longer depend upon him for anything but financial support. His hands rose higher until they cupped Willow's small, firm breasts.

Father and Toby were right. Willow thought as she

pressed her lips passionately against Rowell's shoulder. I
do still love him.

But perhaps even more important was the renewal of
her belief in Rowell's love for her. "As I now belong to
you," he had said. Now at long last, she thought her real
marriage could begin.

Chapter Thirteen

November 1897–January 1899

WILLOW HAD HOPED TO PERSUADE HER PARENTS TO
stay on to enjoy the traditional festivities of Christmas, but the cold and damp of an English winter
was aggravating the rheumatism which seemed to afflict
her mother more and more often of late; so they had decided to act on Pelham's recommendation and go to Egypt
before returning home to America. To her further disappointment, Silvie was unable to make her annual Christmas
visit to England since Cousin Lucienne was still indisposed.

Willow wished fervently that her new-found rapport with
Rowell had lasted. But their reconciliation was short-lived,
and long before the Christmas festivities, she realized that
he was becoming restless, irritable, and ill-at-ease in her
company. By January he had renewed what he called his
"business visits" to London, and although he denied it,
she was convinced that he was once more seeing Georgina.

In an effort to overcome her depression, she entered
upon a positive orgy of activity, hunting several times a
week with Pelham and Francis; and occasionally, accompanied by Toby, she visited the poor and needy in Havorhurst. She called upon neighbors and had regular At
Homes when her calls were repaid. She drove Dodie into
Havorhurst to take tea with her devoted schoolmaster and
tried not to feel envious of the adoration James could not
conceal from the radiant young girl. Rowell had never—
even in the days of their courtship—shown such devotion.

But despite her many activities, she was often lonely. She should have children to occupy her, she wrote to Silvie, but since the loss of her baby nearly four years ago, she had failed to conceive again. More and more often, she would go out alone and walk to the churchyard to look at the tiny grave with an ache of longing in her heart.

But for Pelham, Willow thought, she might have been overcome by the same melancholia that had afflicted his poor mother, Alice Rochford. Fortunately, Pelham was a persistent and willing escort, and Willow was truly glad of his company. As spring followed the last of the winter months, he persuaded her to go for drives with him in the Daimler—each of such outings proving invariably to be an adventure. He refused to take a chauffeur with him and always tried to effect his own repairs when the engine broke down by the wayside. As often as not, they had to walk to the nearest farm and travel by farm cart back to Rochford Manor. Sometimes it would rain, and they would arrive home in the most undignified manner: soaked to the skin, covered with straw stalks or smelling of turnip tops. Sometimes they would be rescued by a neighbor in a passing landau and driven back in style, and on one occasion by the parson's wife in her gig.

Toby felt obliged to warn Willow that she was being seen far too often in Pelham's company.

"Tongues will wag, dearest Willow," he cautioned her, "if they are not already doing so, which I fear may be the case since Mrs. Appleby called on Grandmère yesterday."

For once Willow resented Toby's interference, however well intended she knew it to be.

"Why should I care about my reputation when my husband has so little concern for it?" she argued defiantly. "Besides, there is nothing wrong in my behavior with Pelham, as well you know, Toby. I like his company. He makes me laugh. As for Mrs. Appleby, I care nothing for her opinion—or Grandmère's."

The anxiety in Toby's eyes disturbed her, and she fell silent for a few minutes. But her bitterness toward Rowell held sway over reason.

"I suppose you're going to tell me that Pelham's manner toward me is not exactly brotherly," she said in a low, angry voice.

"Since you yourself are aware of it, I have no need to say so," was Toby's quiet rejoinder.

"It is hardly *your* business what I choose to do!" Willow declared, perilously close to tears. But Toby would not be drawn into an argument and his ensuing silence unnerved her even more than his cautioning. Nevertheless, she continued to make sorties with Pelham as often as she wished.

In May, the weather took a sudden turn for the better and the temperature rose to that of a midsummer day. During breakfast, Pelham suggested they drive the car to Ashdown Forest and take a picnic luncheon with them.

"We'll *all* go," he said cheerfully, "a happy family party. What do you say, Willow?"

But Francis had returned to Oxford, Rupert had planned a fishing expedition with Adrian Forbes, and Dodie, with Mrs. Gassons to assist her, was taking the barouche to Sevenoaks to buy materials for new curtains for the schoolhouse.

"All the better, Willow. You and I can go alone," Pelham said wickedly when she reported that not even Toby could be persuaded to join them.

Willow hesitated as she recalled Toby's warnings. But Rowell was away yet again, and this time she was in no doubt that he had taken Georgina to the Riviera in his yacht. She herself had pleaded to be allowed to go with him when he first announced his plans to sail to France; but he had informed her that there would be only men on board and that she would feel very ill at ease as the only female. Unfortunately for Rowell, a mutual "friend" had let slip to Willow at one of her At Homes that "Mrs. Grey was abroad somewhere in the Mediterranean." Willow had no proof, but her instinct warned her that Rowell was not being honest when he had explained why she herself could not accompany him. The true reason now seemed obvious.

"You could always divorce him!" Pelham said airily as they drove slowly southward through the Kentish countryside, where the fruit orchards were pink and white with cherry and apple blossom. "Although I suppose a divorce would not be to your advantage. Rowell has control of all your money, does he not, Willow? Even as the innocent party, you'd barely receive enough to live on. You could, of course, go home to your parents."

"No!" Willow said adamantly. "My father would not welcome me. He has already advised me that he considers married couples should learn to compromise and adjust to one another, and my mother is rigidly disapproving of divorce, however extreme the circumstances."

"Did you tell your father Rowell was being unfaithful to you?" Pelham asked curiously.

Willow shook her head.

"No, of course not! But even if he did know of it, I think he would still blame me, and in many respects I *am* to blame. After all, Pelham, it is up to me to keep my husband's interest, is it not?"

Pelham looked at the girl beside him speculatively.

"That theory might hold good had you ever had Rowell's true affection," he said with unintentional cruelty. "But Georgina was already in control of Rowell before ever he married you. She bewitched him soon after he came down from Oxford—and still does. Just as you bewitch me, Willow," he added with a smile.

Willow drew a deep sigh.

"I wish you would not make those kinds of remarks, Pelham, even if they are very good for my morale."

"You do not wish any such thing," Pelham said cheerfully as he steered the Daimler carefully past a huge carthorse pulling a dray-plow.

"Deep down, you would love to throw convention to the winds, Willow, and let me make love to you. But, of course, you will not admit to it because the very idea of taking a lover offends your code of behavior."

Willow resolved not to take his remarks seriously, although for once Pelham's voice had not been mocking and he had sounded quietly in earnest.

As they drove through the tiny village of Hartfield and headed toward the vast expanse of Ashdown Forest, he began to hum the melody of a song from *The Mikado*. With a mischievous twinkle in his eyes, he sang in an exaggeratedly doleful voice:

> *"On a tree by a river a little tom-tit*
> *Sang 'Willow, titwillow, titwillow!'*
> *And I said to him, 'Dicky-bird, why do you sit*

Singing Willow, titwillow, titwillow?'
'Is it weakness of intellect, birdie?' I cried,
'Or a rather tough worm in your little inside?'
With a shake of his poor little head, he replied . . ."

Willow, in a sweet clear voice, joined in the refrain:

" 'Oh, Willow, titwillow, titwillow!' "

Pelham grinned cheerfully as he continued the haunting little song, leaving Willow to complete each verse:

" 'Oh, Willow, titwillow, titwillow!' "

They were both smiling despite the sadness of the tale as he came to the last lines:

"And if you remain callous and obdurate, I
Shall perish as he did, and you will know why,
Though I probably shall not exclaim as I die,
'Oh, Willow, titwillow, titwillow!' "

"You must teach me all the words," Willow laughingly said, as the heather-clad forest came into view.

Pelham stopped the motor car and began to unload the lavish picnic the servants had prepared for them. As they set off in search of a pretty site for their luncheon, the sky was a cloudless blue, larks were singing, and far away a cuckoo was calling. Willow began to enjoy herself. The sun warmed her face and hands and the ground was dry and sandy. Pelham announced himself satisfied with the site he had chosen for their luncheon: a clearing surrounded by pink and mauve rhododendron bushes overlooking a large lake. Huge golden carp were swimming lazily in the shallows among the green leaves of the water lilies. Dragonflies skimmed over the clear water, their brilliantly colored bodies flashing like fire in the sunlight.

"Hungry?" Pelham asked, as he began to unpack the picnic basket.

Willow nodded, surprised by her unexpected appetite.

Soon they were ravenously eating cold roast duck, gallantine of veal, and eggs in aspic. The food was perfectly complemented by some excellent champagne. Pelham had placed the two bottles neck-deep in the cold lake water, and now the wine was nicely chilled as he recharged their glasses at frequent intervals.

Willow was unaware quite how much wine she was consuming. Her overriding wish was to lie back with her eyes closed and rest in the shade of her parasol.

Pelham, too, stretched himself out full length, but with his head propped on one hand so that he could look down into Willow's face. She was only vaguely aware of him staring at her intently and was too sleepy and bemused to worry about it.

"I think I may have drunk far too much champagne," she said drowsily. "I am almost asleep." She yawned with unconscious sensuality and her eyes closed. The man beside her drew in his breath sharply as her beauty stirred his senses.

Pelham had not intentionally brought about Willow's state of semi-inebriation. It had seemed natural enough to fill her glass when he refilled his own, and it did not occur to him until now that she must have drunk almost a whole bottle of champagne while he had finished the remainder. Now he realized that, unaccustomed as Willow was to the consumption of so much alcohol, the wine had affected her far more acutely than it had him.

She opened her eyes and smiled at him in lazy contentment.

"This is all quite perfect, isn't it, Pelham?"

His heart began to hammer in his chest as he watched her breasts rise and fall beneath the thin silk of her white blouse. As her eyes closed once more, the dark lashes lay softly on her cheeks which were unusually flushed. Her lips were open just enough for him to see the pearly whiteness of her small teeth and the tip of her moist red tongue.

"God, but you are beautiful!" he muttered. "Rowell must be out of his mind not to want you. Willow—are you listening to me?"

Her eyes opened and she regarded him with bemused incomprehension.

"Did you know you have a mole on your right cheek? I never noticed it before. If you were a girl, it would make a lovely beauty spot!" She laughed softly, innocently.

"Willow!" Pelham's voice was hoarse as he reached out

and touched her cheek with his hand. "Willow, I'm in love with you. Do you understand me?"

She drew a long, deep sigh and covered his hand with her own.

"You mustn't say that," she said gently. "Dear Pelham, you cannot love me, you know. It wouldn't be right."

Her smile was both vague and unconsciously inviting as she withdrew her hand. She yawned as she stretched both arms above her head.

Pelham had not intended Willow's seduction any more than he had intended giving her too much to drink. But now, suddenly, the years of longing for her welled up inside him in one great crescendo of need, a need he was certain was reciprocated. He had always believed that if Willow once rid herself of her plebeian ideas of right and wrong, she would welcome him as a lover. She was fashioned for man's desire, he thought, and every line of her body demanded love. The very coolness of her coloring was in itself an exciting contrast to the warmth of her dark eyes and that small, red tempting mouth.

"I have waited long enough," he muttered, and bending his head, he pressed his lips against hers.

Only half conscious, on the perimeter of sleep, Willow responded to the kiss. It seemed a natural and pleasurable experience. It was pleasing too, to feel wanted, desired after so many long lonely nights of regret at her husband's absence.

But her initial lack of resistance to him misled Pelham. Encouraged by her seeming acceptance of his advances, he twisted his body violently, so that in one quick motion he lay atop her. He saw her eyes open wide in sudden fear but now he was unwilling to listen to her protests. He was convinced that she desired him as ardently as he desired her; and that her protests were but token, voiced for propriety's sake. He silenced them with kisses that left Willow breathless, her thoughts in turmoil.

Now, too late, her senses returned sufficiently for her to appreciate what was about to transpire. Vainly, she attempted to push Pelham from her, but he ignored her resistance. His hands struggled momentarily with the buttons of her blouse; then impatiently he wrenched it open and reached beneath her thin camisole. A moment later, he was pressing his mouth to her breasts.

"Pelham, no, no," she cried, now frantic with anxiety as she realized how uncontrolled was the force of his passion. "I don't want . . . please, Pelham . . . *please* . . ."

But her words remained unheeded as his hand lifted the hem of her skirt and he began skillfully to remove her undergarments. Willow knew then that any attempt she made to resist him would prove useless. Physically powerless against so strong a man, only her words might have stopped him; but he was deaf to her cries. Her head was spinning and tears coursed down her cheeks as the last remaining vestige of strength left her arms and they dropped helplessly to her sides.

Once again, Pelham misjudged Willow's reactions. As he felt the tension go out of her body, he mistook it for a final acceptance of his advances.

"I want you so much, my lovely, beautiful Willow," he muttered. "Do not be afraid. I shall not hurt you. I love you. Do you understand that? I love you, my sweet adorable Willow."

Willow's eyes closed. She was resigned to the inevitable and expected that she would abhor Pelham's invasion of her body. But as he entered her, not cruelly but eagerly, she was shocked to discover that her body was responding involuntarily to his movements. Her senses reeling, she tried ineffectually to halt her own growing desire.

"No, Pelham, no," she cried out again as her mind protested against such madness. But her lover seemed totally lost to all reason and his movements quickened. Her legs closed around him as now she, too, was lost to reason. She was beyond caring even whether some passerby might come upon them. She knew only that she could not bear it were Pelham suddenly to withdraw from her and leave her so nearly at the pinnacle of completion.

Then, for only the second time in her life, she experienced the full ecstasy of love. It was not by chance, for Pelham had been well aware of what he was doing. He had lain with too many women not to be fully experienced in pleasuring them, and as much as he himself had desired to possess Willow, he had wanted even more for her to discover through him the heady delights of passion.

When at last he rolled triumphantly away from her, believing her as fulfilled as himself, he was horrified to see the tears coursing down her cheeks. Quickly he put his arms around her, trying ineffectually to kiss the tears away. But they only fell faster.

Gently he began to straighten her clothing, watching her face anxiously.

"Did I hurt you?" he asked eventually, unable to bear her quiet sobbing.

She shook her head.

"Then why are you crying?" he asked desperately. "I wanted to make you happy, Willow. I wanted to please you!"

"Oh, Pelham!" Willow cried in despair. "Don't you understand? I did not want that to happen. I did not want to be unfaithful to Rowell—or untrue to my marriage vows. I thought you understood that. Now nothing can ever be the same again between you and me. Our friendship is spoiled for always, and I am as guilty as you."

Pelham stared at her in astonishment.

"But why should anything be spoiled?" he said. "I'll swear on oath that you enjoyed it; that you—"

"That is exactly the problem," Willow broke in, her voice trembling with the intensity of her emotions. "Don't you see, Pelham, I *did* enjoy it even though I knew it was wrong. *You* may think it is reasonable for you and me to become lovers, but I know it could never work. I could not go on being Rowell's wife if I were making love with you in such fashion. I do not love you. I love him."

Pelham released Willow from his embrace and stood up, his eyes angry with frustration.

"This is nonsense, Willow. You know very well that Rowell enjoys the favors of a mistress. Why should you feel obliged to remain faithful to him? I doubt even if he would care that his own brother was cuckolding him, except the blow it would be to his pride if anyone else knew of it. Be logical, Willow. He does not love you—*and I do.*"

Willow too stood up. Her head was swimming and her legs nearly gave way beneath her. She was afraid she might swoon until Pelham, seeing her unsteadiness, lent her his arm for support.

She should hate Pelham, she well knew, for what he had just done to her. But she could not do so, for although he had just forced her against her will, he had done so considerately, with love in his heart.

"Pelham, I don't love you!" she repeated quietly.

For once, Pelham did not regain his customary equilibrium. In the past, after such a statement from Willow, he would have grinned and asked her why she let a lack of love for him bother her. But now his eyes were serious as he said:

"I suppose I hoped that you might learn to love me, Willow. As for myself, I have tried very hard not to fall in love with you. But I have not been able to prevent it and now, after this—" He fell silent for a moment and then added: "Perhaps I should go away. I've thought about it often. I'd quite like to go into the army, despite poor Rupert's terrible experiences. It seems pretty certain there will be a war of some kind in South Africa—the Boers understandably enough don't care for our dominance, especially now that gold has been discovered. Maybe I could forget you more easily if I were to go abroad, far away from you. South Africa might be a solution."

Although Willow's heart sank at such a prospect, for Pelham's cheerful, companionable personality had been invaluable on so many occasions at Rochford Manor, she realized that his suggestion was a sensible one in the circumstances. By taking her in love, Pelham had made it impossible for them to resume their old relationship, and since she was unwilling to further the new one, there seemed little alternative to Pelham leaving home.

"I'm sorry," she said softly. "I would miss you if you went away, Pelham."

"My God, not half as much as I shall miss you!" Pelham cried as he took her into his arms with despairing urgency. "Can you forgive me, Willow?"

"Of course," Willow whispered. "We must both forgive each other, Pelham, for I fear I was not as unwilling as I should have been and doubtless you sensed my need. We must forget it ever happened."

But Pelham knew he could not forget, and a week later, he left Rochford Manor for London. Within a month, he was on his way to South Africa.

Rowell returned home and seemed unusually anxious to make amends to Willow for his previous neglect. He appeared not to notice any change in her, although she felt certain that he must sense her feeling of guilt at her unfaithfulness to him. But Rowell was without suspicion and he appeared intent upon pleasing her. He offered at once to accompany her on her long-delayed visit to Silvie in Paris.

In normal circumstances, Willow would have been overjoyed by such proof that her husband desired her company. But she was now plagued by a terrible suspicion —that she was with child as a result of her brief encounter with Pelham. Although but one month had passed without her customary feminine trouble, she had several times suffered severe bouts of nausea in the mornings. Nellie, who was aware of those occasions, cheerfully informed her mistress that she was almost certainly "carrying" again. Nellie knew how desperately Willow wanted another child and could not understand why her mistress did not now seem better pleased at this likely prospect.

Rowell was both amazed and piqued when Willow told him she preferred to go to Paris alone with Nellie if he had no objection.

"You know I do not approve of much of my cousin's behavior," he said. "I do not consider her a wise companion for you, Willow."

"But we shall have Cousin Lucienne to chaperone us," Willow argued, "and you know that she is quite as strict as Grandmère. I shall come to no harm."

At first Rowell refused his consent. But gradually the advantages to himself prevailed as he realized he could now take Georgina upon the yachting holiday at Cowes which she had been demanding. He need have no conscience that he would be neglecting his wife.

"Very well then, Willow, since you wish it," he said finally. "While you are away, I shall take the opportunity to go sailing."

Willow was too concerned about her own condition to worry that Rowell might be taking his mistress with him.

She needed Silvie's advice; and only Silvie could be relied upon for complete secrecy and for imparting a practical opinion upon her problem.

Willow could not have made a better choice of confidante. Silvie wasted no time in sympathy. Within twenty-four hours of Willow's arrival, she took her to her own doctor. He immediately confirmed Willow's fears.

"So that is that!" Silvie said as she drove a white-faced

Willow back to her house in the Rue d'Artois. "I take it congratulations are *not* in order?"

Willow shook her head, looking at her dearest friend enviously. Silvie was as always the very epitome of chic, in a soft rose-pink silk dress with a narrow belt nipping her waist. On top of her beautifully coiffeured dark hair was perched a tiny straw hat trimmed with the same chenille lace as decorated her dress. It was tilted at a jaunty angle to show the flowers tucked under the brim. She carried a fringed parasol of a deeper shade of pink with which to protect her face from the hot Parisian sun.

Life seemed to hold no heartaches for Silvie, Willow thought enviously. It was free of all the complications which seemed to plague her.

"Do not look so woebegone, *chérie*," Silvie said as they arrived back at the house. "A baby is not the end of the world, *quand même!* You may even enjoy it once you have had it!"

"But, Silvie, you know very well that it is almost certainly Pelham's child," Willow protested. "I am in little doubt of it. How shall I ever find the courage to confess this to Rowell?"

Silvie's expression was almost comical in its dismay.

"But never, *ever* must you consider such a madness," she said. She gave a long sigh. "Only a little innocent like you, Willow, would think of making such a confession. Have you considered the consequences?" she added urgently. "Your husband would divorce you. The courts would condemn you. You would be without husband, home or support for yourself or the child. Pelham would never be able to set foot in his home again and would of a certainty be cut off without the proverbial penny. It would mean disaster for everyone, and you would be totally disgraced and outcast by society."

Willow bit her lip.

"I know! I have thought of it. But how can I do so terrible a thing to Rowell? *I could not deceive him,* Silvie, on so important a matter."

"Can you be so sure it is *not* Rowell's child?" Silvie asked pointedly. "And do not answer that, Willow, for I already know that you cannot be certain since you said that Rowell returned home not a week after your *petite affaire* with Pelham. Besides, *chérie,* is such a deception wrought upon your husband any worse than his deception of you?"

"Georgina Grey!" Willow murmured unhappily.

Silvie's face hardened. She had never expected to be the one to bring such ugly truths home to Willow, but now she realized the necessity of a full enlightenment.

"He may have admitted to his association with Mrs. Grey, but I doubt he has told you of his children *by her,* Willow. He has two, you know—boys aged four and two, I think. I believe there may even be another on the way if there is any truth in the gossip I heard recently."

Such a revelation, coming upon the strain of these past weeks and her own terrible fears for her marriage, was almost too much for Willow's taut nerves to cope with. She remembered suddenly how unconcerned Rowell had been by the death of their new-born child; his seeming unconcern that she had not again conceived. Now she understood why. He already had children denied to her— *Georgina's children.*

Bitterness brought a flood of tears to Willow's eyes. Silvie welcomed them, knowing they would mean a release after the terrible shock she had had to inflict upon her poor friend. She allowed Willow to cry for a short while before she became intentionally brisk.

"Tomorrow we shall go shopping together for some new clothes," she said. "You are to forget everything but that you are with child and that you will return next week to Rochford and tell Rowell the good news. Convince yourself the baby is his, Willow. Meanwhile, we will enjoy ourselves. I have seats booked for a Molière play on Wednesday and for the opera on Thursday. On Saturday we shall be accompanied to the races by my new lover, Jean Lafitte, whom you will find most amusing. Then we will spend a few days at the Château d'Orbais in order that you can pay your respects to Mama. Aunt Clotilde is certain to demand news of Mama, so we cannot avoid this duty. Then we shall return to Paris on Monday, and Jean will take us—heavily disguised of course—to the *Folies Bergère* and to eat in Montmartre. It is time you saw a little more of life than the respectable level on which you live, *chérie.* Then you will go home and wait with happy expectation for your baby to be born."

Silvie made life sound so simple, Willow reflected as

her tears ceased. But she knew that her emotions lay at a deeper level than the French girl's. She feared she would not be able to assuage her own feelings of dishonesty even if Rowell *had* forfeited her allegiance by his behavior. But whichever way her thoughts turned, she knew that Silvie was right; even if she disregarded her own inevitable disgrace, a confession would harm everyone else. She could not go home to America with an illegitimate child, for the shock might kill her mother. The alternative—to let Rowell divorce her, and live alone—was equally impractical since Rowell had possession of all her money and she was unqualified to take employment even if such were available to a divorcee.

"Much as I have longed for another child, Silvie, I could never want *this* baby," she announced sorrowfully.

But it seemed as if Silvie knew her better than she knew herself, for by Christmas, when Silvie arrived with an extravaganza of new clothes for the coming child, Willow had ceased almost entirely to think of its origins and was concerned only with its arrival in two months' time.

Rowell had accepted the news with equanimity, showing neither great interest nor suspicion. As soon as Willow's condition was such as to force her to withdraw from social activities, he made excuses to absent himself from time to time and went to London.

Willow was particularly pleased to see Silvie, for the placidity of approaching motherhood had given way to an obsessive anxiety about the safe birth of her child. She knew she could count on Silvie to give practical advice.

"I must confess I do not understand why you should be so afraid of poor old Doctor Forbes or that miserable old midwife he employs, Willow," Silvie said gently. "But since you have this fear, it would be a simple solution if you were to engage your own nurse, *chérie*. Immediately after Christmas, before I go back to Paris, I will go to London and select a woman of good character and pleasant disposition for you."

"Grandmère will not like it—" Willow began, but Silvie broke in:

"That is of no consequence whatever. It is *your* baby, Willow—not Aunt Clotilde's; and you can rely upon Rowell to support you. Nothing these days, so it seems, is too much trouble for him if it pleases you. I detect a most agreeable change in his manner toward you."

"He is quite convinced this child will be a boy," Willow said uneasily. "He is determined upon an heir for the Rochfords, Silvie. I am praying I will not have a girl."

"Whichever it is, the child *will be a Rochford,*" Silvie reminded her pointedly, adding with a smile: "And no last-minute confessions, Willow—not even if you are dying in childbirth. It wouldn't be fair to anyone, *chérie,* were you to make a deathbed confession!"

Only Toby seemed fully to understand her fear of losing this baby, Willow thought.

"Don't worry," he told her. "I have given you my word I will be at home when it is born. And I promise you I shall watch over it, no matter what orders Forbes gives. You can trust me, Willow."

Toby was one of the few people in the world she knew she could trust, and her fears diminished. But he was unable to understand why she should hold such fanciful ideas that Grandmère and Aunt Milly were putting an "evil eye" upon the child.

"Even if it were possible—and you know such superstitions are ridiculous, Willow—what reason would they have? Besides, Grandmère wants an heir for Rochford as much as Rowell, if not more."

Willow could not explain her apprehension other than to reiterate that it frightened her when Grandmère stared so immutably, and Aunt Milly so assiduously avoided meeting her eyes.

Even had she known the truth of past events, Willow need not have worried. Both Doctor Forbes and Aunt Mildred made it clear to Grandmère that no matter what terrible accident of birth might ensue if this child were another girl, neither would be party this time to its removal.

Grandmère herself was not particularly perturbed by what she called their cowardly assertions. As Willow's time drew nearer, she noted with satisfaction that the mother-to-be was carrying the baby "in front"—a certain indication that it would be a boy, she declared. She was therefore not in the least surprised when Aunt Mildred announced in the early hours of the first day of February that Willow had given birth to a fine, healthy boy.

"Excellent," she said, lying back on her pillows. "Now go and tell Rowell that my mind is made up—the boy is to be called Oliver . . . Oliver Cedric Rochford. And stop sniffing, Mildred. Anyone would think you were not pleased there is a new heir. Yes, Oliver Cedric Rochford —names of which my first great-grandson can justifiably be proud. And tell Rowell to inform Reverend Appleby that I want the church bells rung for five minutes after morning prayers. And send Doctor Forbes to me. I have a little present for him. And Mildred, be sure and keep that London nurse of Willow's away from me. I don't like her. Forbes can bring the child to show me."

Somewhat to Grandmère's surprise, Toby accompanied the doctor when, his attentions to the new mother completed, he carried the baby up to the old lady's rooms.

"I wasn't expecting to see *you*," the old lady said to Toby, quizzing him through her lorgnette. "But since you are here, boy, you can open that bottle of champagne and we'll wet the baby's head. That's what your father did when each of you boys was born. Now let's have a look at my great-grandson."

As Doctor Forbes held out the swaddled child, she peered closely into the small, crumpled pink face. After a few minutes, she put down her lorgnette, apparently well satisfied.

"He's a Rochford, *bien sûr*," she said, her use of her native language betraying her emotion. She looked up at Toby. "Rowell will have plenty to do in the next few days, so you can write to Pelham. Mildred can write to Lucienne. And make sure an announcement is put in *The Times*, Toby."

Toby smiled down at his grandmother. He had never had any great love for her, but it was impossible not to be caught up in her obvious pleasure.

"So you're pleased with Willow for giving you a great-grandson?" he said.

"Willow?" Grandmère frowned. She had given no thought to the baby's mother. "Well, naturally I'm glad she has at last had a healthy child. But not before time. She should have given Rowell a son years ago. Rowell's the one to be congratulated. Why hasn't he come to see me yet?"

Exhausted by all the excitement, she lay back against her pillows, the champagne forgotten as she dismissed Toby with a wave of her hand.

The doctor, escorted by the watchful Toby, carried Oliver Cedric Rochford back to Willow's room and laid him in the basinette close by his mother's side.

Chapter Fourteen

November 1899–December 1900

"I T'S GOT TO STOP, ADRIAN. DO YOU UNDERSTAND ME?" Doctor John Forbes regarded his son across the dinner table, his emotions torn two ways as he noticed for the hundredth time how greatly his only son resembled his beloved wife. Peggy Forbes had died when the boy was born. In all, they had shared less than a year of married life before he was robbed of the woman he loved. The boy Adrian had his mother's happy, laughing nature, her auburn hair and green eyes. It had proved impossible for him, the father, not to spoil this living memory of his adored spouse.

At the age of twenty-three, the lad was quite out of his control. Reckless, idle, unprincipled, Adrian always took the easy way where he would gain most for least effort.

He should have known, the doctor thought now, that his son was once again involved with the Rochford boy. From his moderate earnings he could only afford to give Adrian a small personal allowance, and yet Adrian never seemed short of funds; never came to him for a loan and had appeared perfectly content to drift through the days in the small village of Havorhurst where little happened that could possibly engross a young man of his age. As the doctor's son, he was neither villager nor aristocrat. Like the parson and schoolmaster, Adrian and he himself were looked up to by the one set and down upon by the other, and were socially acceptable to neither.

"Rupert is giving you money, isn't he?" The doctor forced out the accusation with difficulty, dreading the answer he expected.

"So what if he is!" Adrian replied indifferently, leaning back in his chair and puffing smoke from the cigar his father had offered him. "He likes giving me things."

"It is immoral!" the doctor cried, his face scarlet with frustration. "Can you not understand that what you are doing is wrong, Adrian? It is not even as if you have his excuse of not being able to help his nature. You—you could lead a perfectly normal life, yet—" Words failed him. Adrian's broad shoulders lifted in a slight shrug.

"I really don't see why you should bother about it, Father," he said with a casualness that enraged his parent. "I am of age and can do as I please. I am not your responsibility."

"We are all responsible for one another in this world," the doctor said, attempting to keep his emotions under control. "Your shocking behavior has already affected me once in the past with far more serious repercussions than I could ever tell you. I dread such a thing happening again."

For the first time, his son looked interested in the conversation.

"In what way have you been affected, Father? Rupert has never told me anything."

"Rupert—may his soul rot in hell—knows nothing of what happened," the doctor replied darkly. "But I will tell you this much, Adrian—I was blackmailed into doing something so terrible that I will never be able to forgive myself as long as I live. And my everlasting guilt is the price I had to pay to have your unsavory affair with Rupert Rochford hushed up. I will not be put in such a position again, do you hear me? *I will not!*"

Adrian looked at his father's crimson face with genuine curiosity. He had never before heard him speak so harshly. He must ask Rupert what he knew of this unfortunate business. He could only suppose that someone must have seen them together and used the knowledge to blackmail his father. But to obtain what? An abortion, perhaps. Such a thing was by no means impossible, although it would be dangerous for all concerned, especially if it involved a member of the Rochford family. But he could think of none of them who would require an abortion. Young Lady Rochford—whom Adrian thought quite attractive—had just had a child. Could it have been that she had wished to be rid of that first infant which she had had prematurely and which died at birth? Had some other man than the bad-tempered Baron Rowell Rochford fathered that first offspring? The idea was intriguing.

"I do not believe you have been listening to one word I said," his father interrupted his thoughts. "But I am warning you, Adrian, that if you do not desist in this—this terrible practice, then I shall be forced to go to old Lady Rochford and ask her to intervene."

For a moment Adrian felt alarmed. But almost immediately he knew that this was but one of his father's idle threats. The poor old man was terrified of Rupert's grandmother, who was now approaching eighty and looked more like an irascible old witch than ever—or so Rupert told him. Rupert hated his grandmother with a passion equal only to his love for Adrian himself.

Ever since he could remember, Rupert had told Adrian, he had lain in bed in fear of the old lady's nightly visits to the nursery; of the tap of her cane as she marched down the landing; of her face bent over him as she reprimanded him for some new failure to meet her exacting standards. His childhood had been punctuated by visits to the library, where she would rap his knuckles or box his ears and then repeat the punishment if he cried. "You're as weak as that mother of yours whom you so resemble," she would accuse him. "Even your young brother, Francis, is too much a man to cry like a stupid girl in front of me."

Adrian was not greatly interested in these interminable accounts of Rupert's unhappy childhood, but he listened because the outpourings seemed to bring Rupert some kind of relief. Nevertheless, he did feel occasional flashes of sympathy for him, especially since he had obviously been frightened of nearly everything—of the horses he was made to ride; of the kick-back of the guns he learned to shoot; of the dark; of his younger brother's vicious teasing; of losing the use of his arm or leg like his unhappy little sister, and later, of school fellows and masters who invariably bullied him. But most of all Rupert was afraid of his grandmother. The smell of the Eau de Cologne she used was often enough to make him physically ill, he had told Adrian. He hated all women—with perhaps the single exception of his young sister-in-law who was always kind and gentle with him and seemed to understand his nervousness.

"She's a bit like you, Adrian," he said. "She doesn't criticize me all the time the way the others do, or make fun of me."

Adrian did not draw attention to Rupert's inadequacies because he saw little point in it. It was just as easy and a lot more profitable to praise him. Rupert was generous to a fault. He had no need of money, he told Adrian, and he liked giving Adrian presents. It made him happy to do so. And in return, all he asked was the chance to kiss and caress his friend; be caressed by him.

Such affectionate exchanges had to be made in private, of course, but apart from this need for secrecy, it seemed to Adrian to be a lot less troublesome way to amuse himself than tumbling one of the village girls. There was always the fear of getting them pregnant. Besides, such girls could not reward him financially as Rupert did. He now owned a sizeable collection of jewelry and an eighteen-carat gold hunter watch, a gold-topped cane; a large quantity of silk handkerchiefs and cravats on which were his own initials in monogram.

"When I am thirty, I shall come into my inheritance," Rupert often reminded him. "Then I will take you abroad with me, Adrian. We will go to Italy together and see the wonderful art galleries, and to Greece to see the ruins, and you will be my social equal and we shall dine together and live in the same hotels. I'll buy a house for us somewhere warm—in Spain, perhaps, or on the Riviera . . ." His dreams were endless but convincing, and Adrian was quite willing to wait another three years for Rupert to obtain his money.

"I want you to give me your solemn promise, Adrian, that you will not see Rupert Rochford again." His father's voice broke in once more upon his thoughts.

"You know I cannot do that, Father. Rupert would be down here in no time wanting to know where I was," he prevaricated. "Besides, I keep the car in good order for the baron. He relies on me to see that the engine is properly looked after."

"Very well, but you may go to the manor only to see to the car. You must tell Rupert that your private rendezvous must come to an end. Tell him, if you have to, that you have become engaged to some girl. It's high time you did think of settling down, in any event."

But even to the doctor's own ears, his suggestion sounded absurd. Adrian was simply not the type to "settle down" to a life of quiet domestic routine. He was as restless as a gypsy and as unreliable.

"I want your word, Adrian," he insisted, certain of this one thing at least. "The friendship with Rupert must end."

"Oh, very well, Father!" Adrian said, stifling a yawn. He felt cooped up in this small, over-furnished stuffy room. He wished he lived in a large house like Rochford Manor where one could lose oneself in the long corridors and, except for the servants, avoid meeting other people. In his own home he could even hear his father snoring in the next-door bedroom. Sometimes the old man had nightmares and would start shouting in his sleep until Adrian banged on the wall to quieten him.

He went up the following morning to the manor. Rupert became nearly hysterical when Adrian related his conversation with his father and his promise to end their association.

"Everyone wants to separate us," he cried, almost weeping. "Not long before Pelham went off to the war, even he told me I had got to stop seeing you and Pelham never cared much what I did."

"I thought nobody knew about us!" Adrian said doubtfully. "Perhaps I should do as Father suggests and get engaged."

"Engaged?" Rupert gasped, his face white.

"Don't fuss, stupid," Adrian said with a casual shrug of his shoulders. "It would only be to stop any gossip. There's a girl I know—the daughter of the landlord at the Star and Garter. I can fool her, I dare say. In view of Father's lecture, we'd better be careful for a while."

Rupert nodded, his eyes unhappy.

"We'll be having the usual housefull of relations for Christmas, I expect," he said miserably. "It will be difficult to get out much."

"Then we'd best make the most of today," Adrian said cheerfully, and because he knew it would please Rupert, he put an arm affectionately around his shoulders and led him away from the house.

As Rupert had feared, he and Adrian had little opportunity to be together during the Christmas festivities. Not only Cousin Lucienne and Silvie were staying in the house, but there were also a number of Rowell's friends who had been invited for the baby's christening.

Although Willow herself had tried not to indulge her baby son, it was inevitable that little Oliver Rochford would be spoiled. He was so pretty a child that neither Grandmère, his uncles, nor the servants could deny him what he wanted. Fortunately his nurse, Patience Merryweather, lived up to her name, but with a firmness that brooked no interference in the nursery. She was devoted to her ten-month-old charge. Oliver had the Rochford's dark, curly hair and brown eyes, rosy cheeks and a smile that was as impish as his mouth and chin were determined.

Willow knew that, were the little boy in her daily charge, she could deny him nothing. She adored him with a fierce passionate love. Silvie, like all the other females who attended the christening, was enchanted by the child.

"Almost—but not quite—he tempts me to have a baby of my own," she told Willow, smiling.

Dodie, too, doted upon her small nephew, and Willow often caught her gazing at the baby with wistful longing, although she had told Willow firmly that she and James had decided they would never have children.

"I would not dare take so terrible a risk of passing on my deformities," she declared, "even though Toby assures me there is very little likelihood."

On Christmas Day the Reverend Appleby intoned a special prayer for the British soldiers now heavily embroiled in the war with the Boers which had broken out in October. News had filtered back to England of a series of defeats for the British, and the whole village was concerned for the safety of those who were fighting the Dutch farmers in the Transvaal. He made reference to the fact that Pelham Rochford was imprisoned in Pretoria and expressed concern for his safety. But Grandmère was indomitably optimistic that he would escape.

"Pelham is a man of courage, like his father and grand-father," she insisted. "No nincompoop, he," she added spitefully with a sideways glance at the silent Rupert.

Willow wondered how Grandmère could be so devoid of natural feelings of kindness toward her own grandson. Such inhumanity did not bode well for Dodie's future, she thought uneasily.

Nevertheless, after Christmas, Willow took advantage of Silvie's support to try to persuade Grandmère to consider James McGill as a suitor for Dodie. But the old lady, steadfastly refused to give her consent. Rowell insisted that no one should openly defy her.

"I have agreed that Dodie may continue to see the fellow in Havorhurst provided she is properly chaperoned, so I do not accept that there is any need to rush things," he said. "Grandmère needs more time to become accustomed to the idea. It won't hurt either Dodie or McGill to wait a year or two."

Willow suspected that Rowell was hoping his eighty-year-old grandmother would reach the end of her life before a final decision became necessary. He would not be pinned down to making any promises as to when he would raise the subject again and Willow thought it best not to tell him when James and Dodie became secretly engaged at New Year. Dodie now wore the schoolmaster's ring on a gold chain around her neck and had given him in exchange a gold ring with his initials engraved upon it.

Despite the extra calls upon her time since Oliver was born, Willow still found herself missing Pelham's cheerful presence at Rochford. She had worried about his safety, but now that his letters were arriving fairly regularly from the State Schools Prison in Pretoria she felt less anxious about him. He had discovered an old friend, he wrote in cheerful vein, among his fellow prisoners, a war correspondent by the name of Winston Churchill.

Occasionally, when Willow sat in the nursery watching Oliver at play with his bricks, or giving him rides upon his wooden rocking horse, she wondered if Pelham had any idea that her child might also be his. She thought it unlikely he held such suspicion, for he had written to congratulate her when he heard of the birth, ending his letter with the remark:

So you and Rowell finally managed a son and heir

for the Rochfords. Grandmère must be as delighted as you are . . .

Rowell had no doubt whatever that the child was his. He had noticed that Oliver bore a far greater resemblance to him than either of Georgina's boys, who with their long red curls looked remarkably like their mother.

Whenever Rowell thought of Georgina, it was with mixed feelings. Since the birth of their third child, a girl, she had grown far stouter than was becoming to her, and the fashion for tiny, nipped-in, tailor-made costumes and waisted evening gowns did not suit her. At thirty-five, she had just begun to look blowsy rather than voluptuous, and he was no longer quite the slave to her physical charms as he had been. Nevertheless, he did not really want to give up his visits to the comfortable little house in London.

But at the same time, the birth of a legitimate son and heir had changed the focus of his allegiance, for although the toddler held little interest for him at so young an age, he knew it would not be many years before he would want to begin the boy's education. Like all the Rochfords, Oliver must learn to ride; to shoot; to fish; and hopefully, before too long, he could be taught to sail. The Rochford estate would one day belong to the boy, and he must be brought up like his father before him to take care of his inheritance. Oliver would not have *his* financial problems, Rowell thought, since his doting American grandfather, Willoughby Tetford, had settled a vast sum of money upon the boy as soon as he heard of his birth. It was not to be touched until he was of age, of course, but nonetheless it would go far toward helping Oliver to manage the estate.

It occurred to Rowell that it would be an excellent thing if Willow were to have another baby fairly soon. There were far too many childhood sicknesses which could be lethal to a baby of Oliver's age. There should be at least two more boys to ensure the continuance of the family line, he decided.

But despite the fact that Rowell returned to the marital bed and played his part to the best of his ability, Willow showed no signs of becoming pregnant as the new year progressed from spring to summer. It began to irk him that Georgina, whom he would have preferred to be barren, seemed to conceive a child with utmost facility, while his own wife did not.

Willow told him that she herself would like another child as a companion for Oliver.

"Dr. Forbes assures me that there is nothing wrong, and that in time I will conceive again."

"Let us hope so!" Rowell commented tersely.

By December when there was still no sign that she was with child, Willow confided her worries to Toby. He, as always, was her one comfort.

"We've had this conversation before, Willow," he said gently, "after the birth of your baby, Sophia—remember? You came and asked me then if I thought there was something wrong with you—and just look at young Oliver!"

Willow relaxed, smiling.

"You're really fond of him, Toby, aren't you," she said.

Sometimes on clear frosty mornings when the skies were a brilliant blue and the sun shone over the whitened countryside, Toby would take Willow, Patience, and Oliver for drives in the wagonette. He would place the reins in the little boy's hands in such a way that Oliver believed he really was controlling the two huge greys.

"Slacken the reins, coachman," Toby would call out. Or: "Watch Smokey! He's pulling too far to the left."

Helpless with laughter, for she knew Oliver had no knowledge of left or right, far less how to slacken the reins, Willow loved such outings and loved Toby for creating them. It had surprised her to discover that Toby was a born father. He would lift Oliver onto a secure perch among the foliage of the climbing plants in the conservatory and then call out to Willow:

"Have you seen that boy of yours? He has completely vanished. You don't think the gypsies have stolen him, do you?"

Willow, playing her part, would search around her while Toby made wilder and wilder suggestions—a giant butterfly had eaten the boy; a hot air balloonist had landed in the orchard and carried him off in a basket; Mrs. Jupp had put him in the stewpot by mistake and they were all about to eat him for supper—until the small boy could no longer contain his chuckles and would call out: "Mama, Mama! Up here!"

Willow would look up at the glass roof in one direction and then another, but never in the right place until Toby had whisked the child down and set him on his feet behind Willow's skirts.

There were a dozen or more similar games, and soon it was to Toby's tall stooped figure that Oliver ran first when he was brought down to the drawing room. Rowell became irritated by this obvious preference and would order the reluctant child to his side.

"Tell Papa what you have been doing today," Rowell would say. "And stand still when you talk to me, Oliver. And don't pout. Now speak out. I don't want any of that baby talk, either. A train is a train, not a 'choo.'"

"How can I make Rowell understand Oliver is only a baby still?" Willow said despairingly to Toby. "The more angry he becomes, the more reluctant Oliver is to go to him."

"It's just Rowell—his nature. I doubt he could be different even if he wanted. It'll be better when the boy is older."

"Thank goodness he has *you*," Willow said warmly. "I would be very unhappy if I thought Oliver were going to model himself on his father and see life without any sensitivity or humor. He's a happy little boy, and I have you to thank. Rupert is nervous with him and makes him uneasy, and Francis positively dislikes him."

"Which is understandable, seeing that he was Grandmère's pet until Oliver took his place. Do you know, Willow, I think she enjoys it hugely when Oliver stands up to her. She always did admire people who were stronger-willed than herself."

Surprisingly, the child seemed to have no fear whatever of the stern old lady whom he was taken to visit once a day. He treated her more as an equal than as someone to be respected.

"Give that book to me, Oliver! At once now."

Oliver's hold upon the picture book tightened and he stood his ground.

"Grandmère give it back?"

"Very well, but hand it to me at once, Oliver."

To Grandmère's secret amusement, he began to imitate Mildred whenever she was in the room with them. At first, she wasn't aware of the imitation.

"Where's your handkerchief, Oliver? Stop sniffing. Give your nose a good blow."

"Why can't I sniff, Grandmère? Aunt Milly don't blow."

The child was fond, too, of his Aunt Dodie. He seemed as unaware of her shortened arm and leg as he was of Grandmère's age. But most of all, Oliver loved his mother. He would sit on her lap and stroke her hair with his small, sticky hand. He called it "Angel hair."

As the winter weather deteriorated, it became too cold for outdoor activities. Willow often took Oliver up to Toby's laboratory, where the child would for once sit quite still watching Toby at work with his Bunsen burners and glass tubes and bottles. Toby did not mind his chatter and one "why" followed fast upon another.

"Why Uncle call Mama Willow? Why is Nanny Patience? Why aren't me a little girl? Why is Mrs. Jupp so fat? Why hasn't Dutton got no hair on his head? Who is Uncle Pelham? Who are the Boers? What is prison? Is it tea-time yet?"

Occasionally Toby's eyes would meet Willow's as they tried between them to keep pace with the answers.

"He's growing up so fast, Toby," Willow said one day when Patience had taken Oliver off to the nursery for his tea. "Soon he'll be asking questions I can't answer and he'll be going to Eton."

"It's not such a bad place to be!" Toby said reassuringly. "I quite liked it there—and I had a wonderful education. You realize, don't you, Willow, that Oliver is quite remarkably advanced for his age. In part this may be due to the fact that he is so much in the company of adults, but even allowing for that, his ability to put words together, his vocabulary and his intelligent understanding of what is said to him—all indicate that he has an exceptional brain. He deserves a good schooling."

"I know! I am just being selfish," Willow said sighing. "I don't like the thought of his being away from me at boarding school for nine months in the year. Maybe I would find it easier to part with him if I had my little girl."

Toby looked at her curiously.

"You still think of her, don't you?" he said gently.

"She died so long ago, Willow—nearly seven years, yet you still grieve."

"I think I always will," Willow admitted. "Probably because I never saw her tiny body, I never quite believed she died. Perhaps those gypsies you tell Oliver about really did come to Havorhurst and steal my baby."

"Don't talk like that, Willow. It disturbs me," Toby said quietly. "Besides, it is never good to think too much about the past. It's the future that matters. That's why my work is so important to me . . . and maybe one day it will be important to others. I am convinced the time will come when people will look back to the turn of the century and ask themselves how was it possible that we were so ignorant of so many aspects of medicine. I believe that a hundred years from now—maybe even sooner —doctors will understand exactly how our bodies work and why things go wrong; why some people are barren and how to prevent unwanted babies—or even how to insure those that do want them have them," he added, smiling.

"You really do believe these miracles will come about, don't you, Toby!" Willow said.

"And a lot more besides," Toby said quickly. "I think surgeons will learn how to give people new legs and arms, maybe even new skin; and perhaps new lungs and hearts and kidneys, too. Fifty years from now, we won't know the world, Willow. People will be flying around in the skies in air machines, and there'll be so many motor cars on the roads we'll have to put all the carriage horses out to grass."

"Now you *are* teasing me," laughed Willow. "All the same, Toby, I envy you your dreams of the future. I wish you would allow me to help in some way with your work. Ever since you told me about Pierre and Marie Curie, I've thought how wonderful it must be for a woman to work beside her husband, sharing his hopes and tasks and ideas. Maybe I should have married *you,* Toby, and then, when you become famous, I could proudly say I had assisted you."

Toby's head bent further over his work table.

"Maybe it's all for the best that you married your beloved Rowell."

Willow sighed, her eyes unsmiling.

"I know it sounds very disloyal, Toby, but to you I can say anything knowing that you will understand. I don't think I should have married Rowell. He and I really do not have anything in common, or if we do, I do not know of it. After nine years of married life I know no more about him than I did the day I married him. And I have reached the conclusion that there is really nothing more to know."

She looked at Toby's bent head and more to herself than to him, she added:

"With you, it is all quite different. I am always being surprised by you, Toby. You are so quiet people may think you haven't much to say, but I know otherwise. Inside that head of yours is a whole world of fascinating ideas. I do wish you would allow me to work for you sometimes."

It was a minute or two before Toby looked up. His expression was under control as he smiled at her.

"Do you realize that you first offered to help me way back in '89 when you were fifteen years old?"

"Did I?" Willow asked in surprise. "Well, that shows where my latent instincts lie, Toby. I suppose I will get the same answer now as then?"

Toby's hesitation was covered by his movements toward one of his burners. Then he said lightly:

"You've far better things to do with your time than file papers or copy notes for me," he said. "Besides I might never find anything if you were tidying up all the while —and women do tidy things. Admit you long to get your hands on this mess?" Then changing the subject quickly, he added: "By the way, Dodie tells me she is engaged to McGill. I'm glad. I like the fellow. When you next see him, will you wish him well from me?"

Willow nodded.

"I was meaning to talk to you about Dodie," she said thoughtfully. "Would you think it very wrong of me to suggest James write off to the appropriate quarters to see if he can get another teaching post—somewhere far away like Devonshire, for example."

Seeing Toby's puzzled expression, she smiled.

"Not for the purpose of separating them, but so that they can get married," she said. "I don't think Grandmère is ever going to give her consent and I thought perhaps if they were to elope—"

"And what of Rowell? He would never countenance such a step!"

"No, I know. I did not intend telling him. Would that be so wrong. Toby?"

Toby turned away, his eyes unhappy.

"It would be wrong of me to encourage you to deceive your husband," he said. "It wouldn't do *you* much good either, Willow, when Rowell found out. It would only widen the gap between you."

"I would bear that—for Dodie's sake."

"It is a decision you must make for yourself." Toby brought out the words with difficulty. "Perhaps if Rowell were not my brother—"

Willow waited for him to continue, but he remained silent. He seemed suddenly to become very engrossed in his work, and believing herself forgotten, Willow stood up quietly and slipped out of the room.

Only when the door closed behind her did Toby relax his stance. His face was lined with a deep sorrow as his thoughts completed the sentence he dared not voice. If Rowell were not his brother, he would not only have advised Willow to deceive her husband in order to help Dodie, but he would have advised her to leave the man she had married. Rowell, he knew only too well, was not worth one of Willow's tears. He had continued to enjoy the favors of his mistress and now had three children by Georgina, as if she and not Willow were his wife. He was not only totally selfish and uncaring toward Willow, but he was growing ever more narrow-minded and humorless with the years. Pompous, dictatorial, and often stupid, Rowell was as unsuitable a husband for Willow as he was unworthy of her.

His opinion was not biased by the fact that he, Toby, was in love with Willow, he thought. He cared so deeply for her that if he knew she was happily married, he would be content to remain in the background of her life. But he was all too painfully aware of her loneliness; of her desperate need for understanding, kindness, love. He believed it to be something of a miracle that the disillusionments and disappointments she had suffered these past nine years had not made her cynical and embittered. Her sweetness, her unselfishness, her capacity to love, were not diminished by her unhappiness.

There was so very little he could do to improve the quality of her life. He must bear not only the pain of his hopeless love for her, but her pain too, doing what he could to mitigate it. His one release lay in his freedom to love her child—Pelham's child. He was reasonably certain his brother had fathered the boy, although Willow herself had never given him the slightest reason to suspect it. But he had not been blind to Pelham's shamed look when he had returned with Willow from that picnic the summer before last; nor the strange way in which Pelham had suddenly, without warning, decided to leave home and go into the army.

If Toby blamed anyone at all, it was himself for not accompanying them on the picnic. He knew that Pelham had been half in love with Willow for years and that his brother was not so hidebound by morals as was he himself. Pelham had made no secret of the fact that he was attracted by Willow. With Rowell on the Riviera with his mistress, Toby knew he should have realized that Willow might be tempted into unfaithfulness. He had thought of little else while she expected her child.

But he would never question her. The answer did not really matter. He loved the boy because he was Willow's child, a part of her. There had been only one occasion when he had felt bitter—when Oliver had mistakenly called him "Papa." He could perhaps have been the child's father, he thought, if he had gone to America and asked Willow to marry him before Grandmère had put the idea into Rowell's head.

His thoughts went back to the night of his coming-of-age party, when he had watched Willow dancing with Pelham in the long gallery. He had known then that there could never be any other wife for him in the world but her. He had wanted to pull her from Pelham's arms and clasp her in his own. He had wanted, in a totally uncivilized fashion, to fight his brother for her; win her admiration and regard. Yet all he had done was turn his back on them and go downstairs alone.

In retrospect, it seemed now to Toby that that had been the moment when he should have declared himself. Willow had then only a childish adoration for his brother, Rowell, which, as she grew older, turned to a romantic dream. If he, Toby, had written to her regularly after her return to America, he might so easily have changed the direction of her affections. But he had not done so—and now it was too late.

He tried unsuccessfully to shut Willow's face out of his mind as he went back to his desk, finding work, as always, an antidote and a solace to his pain.

Chapter Fifteen

January—September 1901

E VERY CURTAIN IN THE MANOR HAD BEEN DRAWN, and those rooms in use were only dimly lit. Voices were lowered, and even in the kitchen there was no usual exchange of pleasantries between the prettiest maids and the younger male servants. Grandmère had given orders that every member of the staff was to wear black even if it meant working in their Sunday best—an unprecedented idea that had brought home to the younger ones the solemnity of the situation. Queen Victoria was dead.

Only Grandmère and Aunt Mildred were old enough to remember a time when the Queen had not sat on the throne, for her reign had lasted sixty-four years. Although she had been ill for almost a year, her death on the twenty-second of January had nevertheless come as a terrible shock to everyone, not least of all to Grandmère, who was now confined to bed.

Doctor Forbes called every day and showed some concern for the old lady, who seemed pitifully shrunk and to have lost all vestige of her usual fiery spirit. Although this meant a comparative haven of peace for Aunt Milly, the unhappy spinster was quite obviously terrified by the thought that Grandmère might be dying. Without the old lady's monologue of directives, she seemed unable to organize her daily routine and hurried from room to room with head bowed, sniffing and muttering to herself.

Willow tried to reassure Aunt Milly. She herself sat in the chair beside Grandmère's bed for hours at a time in

case the old lady roused herself from her silent apathy and
wished to talk. Such occasions were rare, but when they
happened, Grandmère seemed happy to have Willow
there as she poured out the emotions that were troubling
her.

"This country will never be the same again. Edward as
always a rake—a wastrel and forever upsetting his poor
mother as well as the Government. How can one respect
a man who behaves as he does, flaunting his mistress and
interfering in foreign affairs!"

She seemed troubled, too, by Pelham's continued absence.

"I don't understand it, Willow," she kept repeating.
"Kitchener said the war would be over last summer. It said
in the newspaper that those dreadful Boers have at most
sixty-five thousand men, so why haven't the British con-
quered them long since?"

While it was true it was now a considerable time since
the beleaguered towns of Ladysmith, Mafeking, and Kim-
berley had been relieved, the war still lingered on, even
after Lord Roberts occupied Pretoria in June. Pelham, as
a consequence, was no longer a prisoner, but he showed
no inclination to return home.

"I think he is enjoying himself out there, Grandmère!"
Willow tried to comfort the old lady.

Grandmère snorted.

"I received a letter last week from General Hackett in
which he said Kitchener was far from happy about the
situation. 'The officers of the British Army seem to regard
the war too much like a game of polo,' Kitchener had told
him, 'with intervals for afternoon tea!' It's a disgrace to
this country, Willow, and all Europe is laughing at our
inability to defeat a handful of farmers! I am thankful
Cedric is not alive to know of it—or Oliver."

But for the most part, Grandmère slept. Sometimes she
woke so confused that she mistook little Oliver for one of
her grandsons and called him Toby or Rowell or Pelham.

In view of the old lady's indisposition, Willow did not
pursue her plans to help James and Dodie elope, although
James had learned of a teaching post in Cornwall which
had unexpectedly become vacant. He had written apply-
ing for it and been asked to travel down to the West
Country for an interview.

"It would be quite perfect for Dodie," he told Willow, his grey eyes bright with eagerness. "The climate is far more temperate there, and the little house attached to the school is sunny, warm, and most agreeable."

James had explained at his interview that he was on the point of getting married, and his prospective employer had deemed this an advantage, even when James added that his future wife was not very strong and had a physical handicap.

"So long as your references are satisfactory, Mr. Mc-Gill, the post is yours," he had been told.

Willow had written a glowing report of James, and there was little doubt that her title and signature to this reference were of great influence in assuring James' future.

But when Grandmère fell ill and when Doctor Forbes alluded even to the possibility of her dying, both James and Dodie agreed instantly with Willow that they must take no action that might cause her further distress and perhaps hasten such an unfortunate event.

With typical unselfishness, James wrote to his future employers explaining the position, though it put his new post at risk. Hopefully, he said, he could make himself available for the autumn term if there was the possibility of their keeping the position open for him until then.

Two weeks later, Dodie sought out Willow with shining eyes.

"I told you that they would not readily lose as fine a man as my James," she cried, handing Willow a letter received that morning from Cornwall.

With intense relief, Willow read that the School Board had been able to engage a temporary schoolmaster for the summer term. They were surprisingly sympathetic toward James, commending him for his compassion for his fiancée's elderly relative.

By Easter, although still very weak and frail and confined to her bed, Grandmère was no longer thought to be in immediate danger. She was well enough to start once more to bully poor Aunt Mildred and to make certain her views and criticisms were known downstairs. Scarcely a day went by without some unfortunate servant being reprimanded—a housemaid for not having cleaned the silver well enough; a laundrymaid for not having ironed the frills of her nightgown sharply enough; Cook for a burnt rice pudding. Doctor Forbes' tonics were scathingly rejected as useless, and even the good-natured Patience was told that she was cutting Oliver's curls too short. Rowell was warned that he spent too much time away from home and Willow that it was high time she thought of arranging Mrs. Spear's retirement. She was now sixty-seven and far too slow for Grandmère's liking.

"Grandmère is obviously very much better," Willow told Toby at the end of one such tirade.

"Quite her old self by the sound of it," Toby laughed. "Frankly, I don't agree with Forbes that she was ever in danger. The man fusses too much."

Willow decided to do as the old lady wished and promote the head parlormaid, Janet, to the position of housekeeper. She was thirty-two and had been working under Mrs. Spears for the past five years.

Nellie was delighted, for she particularly liked the Scotswoman who had taken her under her wing when first she arrived at the manor. Moreover, Janet approved of Nellie's engagement to Harry, the head footman. Harold Stevens had always been considered downstairs as something of a "wild one." Although upstairs his behavior was faultless and irreproachable, he flirted outrageously with all the pretty housemaids. He was a frequent visitor to the laundry, which was situated so far away from the kitchens that supervision of the girls' behavior was almost impossible for Dutton, Mrs. Spears or Cook. The grooms and gardeners were also frequent visitors to the rosy-cheeked laundrymaids who worked in the hot, steamy rooms; but Harry, the head footman, held a more exalted position than the outdoor workers and never lacked a willing partner. He had once been severely reprimanded by Dutton, who had espied him carrying a large basket of wet linen down to the washline for a giggling girl whose work he had retarded while enjoying her favors.

But now he was ready to "settle down," and for some while had confined his attentions entirely to Nellie.

Harry's past behavior had been a matter of considerable anxiety to Nellie, who had taken a fancy to him soon after her arrival at the manor. But she had steadfastly refused to permit him any of the liberties he enjoyed with the other girls, and now, at long last, he had decided that she was the right choice for a wife.

Although Nellie was nearly thirty and Harry forty-two, it would be several years before they could be married. But as Nellie confided excitedly to Willow: "It's not as if either of us wants a family, Milady. I had quite enough of little ones around my feet when I was growing up to last me a lifetime. And Harry doesn't like children—too much of a big baby himself, if you ask me!"

It seemed a satisfactory arrangement for everyone, and even Grandmère raised no objections when Willow told her what was afoot.

"When I think of my Nellie approaching thirty, it makes me feel very old," Willow remarked dolefully to Toby. He merely smiled.

"You will never *look* old," he said. "You look no more than twenty-one, Willow, and that is a fact."

"But I feel my twenty-seven years!" Willow replied. "How old do you feel, Toby?"

He looked surprised by her question.

"I never really think about it," he said. "If I think of the passage of time at all, it is only in relation to my work. I am so afraid I will not have enough years to do all that I want."

Perhaps this was the secret of growing old gracefully, Willow thought. Toby had a purpose in life that made every day important to him. Were it not for little Oliver, she had nothing comparable that made her believe tomorrow was as essential as today. It might all have been so different if she and Rowell had truly loved one another. But their relationship had not, as her father had forecast, improved with the passage of time. It remained virtually unchanged, and she knew that with very few exceptions, whenever Rowell was away from home, he was with his mistress and his other children.

Rowell's concern with his other family might have disturbed her a great deal more if Oliver had truly been *his* child, she thought. Her bitterness toward Rowell was tempered not only by her secret guilt, but also by pity. He missed so much fun with the little boy. It was Toby who enjoyed the fascinating mental and physical progress of the growing toddler; Toby who was the recipient of Oliver's adoration and admiration; Toby who enjoyed the fresh excitements of a child's discovery of the world around him.

In July, to Willow's great surprise, Rowell offered to take her to Paris for a month.

"Since you missed seeing Silvie this last Christmas, we might also pay her and Cousin Lucienne a visit," he said.

She was too astonished to comment, but merely nodded her agreement. She was unaware that Rowell had quarreled violently with Georgina and had made what he told his mistress was "an irrevocable break" with her. He had discovered that during his long absence from London while Grandmère had been ill, Georgina had been unfaithful to him. The ensuing scene was still fresh in his mind.

"You have the morals of a kitchen maid," he told her, "and I should have known better than to involve myself with you."

Georgina regarded him uneasily. She had been his mistress for twelve long years, and since his marriage to the American girl, he had been far less readily available to entertain and amuse her. Bored, she had decided to enjoy a brief week in Paris with a French count she had met at the Symingtons. She had believed herself safe from discovery and was unaware that she had been seen in Paris by Esmé Symington. Esmé told her husband, and he had thought fit to report the matter to Rowell.

When Rowell had stormed out of her house to return "for good" to his wife and child, Georgina was not unduly concerned. He had accepted that he must continue to support his children, if not her, and to continue to pay for their home and servants. She could manage well enough when she could attract men like the count who were agreeably generous in their rewards for her favors. Moreover, she had little doubt that Rowell would, as in the past, be back to see her when he had cooled his anger. Although she herself did not fully understand the reason for it, she knew that Rowell was drawn to her like a bee to honey, no matter that his will or his reason dictated otherwise.

Rowell, however, believed his break with Georgina this time to be final. He turned to Willow as much to comfort his wounded pride as in an effort to make something worthwhile of their relationship. In Paris, he took her to the *Comédie Française,* to the Opera, and to the Louvre. He accompanied her to the shops in the Rue Fauberg St.

Honoré and bought her extravagant presents. They sat at the roadside cafés in the Champs Elysées and drank absinthe as they watched the children playing on the merry-go-rounds. He even filled their hotel bedroom with flowers.

He took her one night to *Maxim's,* where among princes, grand dukes, senators, and diplomats they sat listening to the bandsmen in red coats playing light-hearted music for their entertainment. Afterwards, he took her back to their hotel and made love to her with a far greater degree of passion than he had employed since the night of her twentieth birthday party.

Willow was hopelessly confused. She could not understand this metamorphosis in Rowell. She responded passionately with her body, but found herself unable to feel any real depths of love for him in her heart. After their lovemaking was over, as he slept contentedly beside her, she lay awake, trying to fathom why she should feel guilty as well as bewildered. Not even when Pelham had taken her in love had she felt the same degree of wrongdoing as now overwhelmed her. Yet it was her own husband with whom she had shared her body this night, she reminded herself. Her emotions were beyond her understanding.

The dreadful irony of her situation suddenly struck her. After nearly ten years of being an indifferent husband, Rowell had chosen to become her lover, while she, having longed for this to happen throughout those years, now felt only indifference toward *him.*

"If only I still loved Rowell," she remarked wistfully to Silvie.

"I know I shall anger you by saying so, Willow," Silvie said sighing, "but I believe there is little of any import in his head—other than how best to please himself. I cannot think why you ever married him, Willow."

Loyally Willow tried to defend her husband but, in her heart, she knew that Silvie was justified in her comment. Rowell was remarkable for his extreme good looks rather than for the quality of his intellect. As the years went by, they were growing further and further apart. Not even to her beloved confidante, Silvie, could she confess that in her innermost heart, she knew now that it was Toby whose spirit was most akin to her own. She knew, too, that she must curb instantly such betraying thoughts lest they should lead her to believe that she was in love with her husband's brother. He was constantly in her mind nonetheless, and at night she lay awake assessing his character and behavior.

Outwardly, he appeared the most serious of the four Rochford boys, she thought, but his intensity and concentration on his work were misleading, for his sense of humor lurked very close to the surface. Alone with her and little Oliver, he was bright with laughter and fun. The child was attracted to him irresistibly. As was she too, Willow realized apprehensively as she and Rowell returned home to Rochford Manor seeming outwardly reconciled by their shared holiday. She was uneasily aware that it was Toby's welcome which made the manor really feel like home. To find him there, smiling, unchanged, eager to tell her of a new project in his work, gave her an immediate sense of well-being that was frighteningly akin to happiness.

He informed her that Rochford Manor was like a room without a light when she was absent.

"Not even young Oliver could cheer us all up," he added, his lopsided smile belying the seriousness of his tone.

Willow reminded herself that it was Toby's nature to be agreeable to her; to bolster her morale. He had long been aware of her loneliness, and mistakenly she believed his kindness to her to be born of compassion. That it might spring from any deeper feeling, as Pelham had once suggested, was too dangerous a thought to be entertained.

Would Toby *still* think well of her if he knew the deception she had wrought upon Rowell in regard to little Oliver, she wondered. Toby's poor opinion of her would hurt her far more even than Rowell's angry denunciations if the truth became known.

Willow looked down the length of the dining table to where her husband sat talking to Francis. The brothers were discussing the birth of a new foal which had arrived during Rowell's absence in Paris.

"Might make a nice mount for young Oliver in a few years' time," Rowell commented. His expression was benign as he graced the head of the table, his large family grouped around him. His wife was wearing the new midnight blue gown he had ordered for her from Paquin's in

Paris, and looked unusually beautiful. He was at peace with his world—and with his conscience. In his absence Georgina had written no angry recriminations, and for the present, he certainly did not miss her nor regret his decision to break with her.

At the far end of the long table, Willow was deep in thought as a wave of depression settled over her. The years loomed ahead in a long repetitive seasonal pattern: hunting and shooting parties in the winter, the bright empty gaiety of the London Season, the summers at Rochford Manor with the endless round of calling and At Homes, and the never-ending requirement to be constantly changing clothes. How pointless, meaningless, it all seemed!

She glanced around the table and, despite the warmth of the room, she shivered. It was as if she were a ghost sitting there, seeing but unseen. Grandmère was back as usual in her place on Rowell's right-hand side. The old lady was as sharp and critical as if she had never been so ill. Aunt Milly, on Toby's right, looked thin and drawn. Her long neck was flushed a bright red, reminding Willow of a turkey as the poor woman gobbled her food— her one enjoyment in life—with rapt concentration.

I have no right to complain about *my* life, Willow reproved herself sharply, realizing how terribly empty poor Aunt Milly's life had been. She had lived always in Grandmère's shadow with no husband, no children—nothing to look forward to but an old age as Grandmère's companion.

On her far side sat Rupert, silent, morose, withdrawn deep into his own thoughts. Beside him, smiling radiantly, was Dodie whose world was about to expand in a new and wonderful way forever denied her poor spinster aunt. It was August, and at the end of the month, Dodie would leave Rochford to begin a new life in Cornwall with her beloved James. It was high time she saw to Dodie's trousseau, Willow thought. How long ago was it since she herself had chosen so excitedly with her mother her own wedding trousseau? Ten years, almost! Where had those years gone? She was twenty-seven and all she had to show for those years of her youth was little Oliver—her son.

She felt a sudden terrible sense of panic—a longing to

feel part of this room full of people, to belong, to feel that her existence was truly justified. It terrified her to realize that if she had died when her little girl died, everyone at this table would be there exactly as they were at this moment. Only Oliver would not have existed.

Beside her, Toby spoke, his quiet voice penetrating her thoughts.

"I do not know what ghost can be passing over your grave, Willow, to warrant such an expression of despair. Why are you unhappy?"

His voice was so low it was unheard by the others, but his words melted the icy circle that seemed to wall her very self inside her head.

She tried to smile.

"No ghosts and no graves, Toby," she replied hesitantly. "But I will admit my thoughts were not exactly joyful. I was considering Aunt Milly's life . . . and my own. What is the point of our existence, Toby? And the lives of all those other women like us? Aunt Milly is a dependent slave, forced by the circumstances of her unmarried state always to be bound to this house, to Grandmère's side. A paid companion would serve Grandmère quite as well."

"I agree Aunt Milly's life has been wasted," Toby said quietly. "But not yours, Willow. You have only to look at Oliver to know that. And at Dodie! But for you, I doubt my poor little sister would ever have left that invalid room where she spent the first thirteen years of her life. But for your intervention, that quick, intelligent brain of hers may by now have been stultified forever."

He paused while Dutton moved near them to refill their wine glasses. When the old butler was once more out of earshot, he went on:

"And there is Rupert—still deeply embroiled with young Adrian Forbes, I know, but in his right mind and happier than I have ever known him. Had it not been for your intervention with Rowell and Grandmère when Rupert returned from Egypt, I doubt he would have recovered so remarkably from the breakdown of his nervous system."

He looked at Willow's face and smiled.

"Still not convinced, I see! So I will elaborate. Take Francis, for example. He told me how you had raised the money to buy back the Gainsborough—a wonderful gesture of yours, Willow, for the disgrace would have assured his banishment from the family circle, and Francis is so weak and spoiled he would have been unlikely to be able to fend for himself in a hostile world. And lastly, there is me!"

He grinned at her disarmingly.

"You, Willow, have inspired a great deal of the research I have been engaged in regarding the carriage of diseases. Until you came to Rochford, I never questioned the deaths of my two infant sisters—nor even Dodie's handicapping illness. I had grown up accepting them as established facts from the past. You made me see that they might not be facts after all. And furthermore, although I felt sorry for little Dodie, I lacked your courage to alter Grandmère's dictates and do something positive to improve her condition."

"You are very generous giving me credit for so much," Willow replied. "But I do not consider my behavior was ever courageous, Toby. As far as helping Francis was concerned, I acted more from fear of facing Rowell's displeasure than from any real desire to assist your youngest brother."

Toby gave her a long, hard look.

"It is time you stopped belittling yourself, Willow," he said with unusual forcefulness. "It has become your habit to accept Rowell's opinion of you since your marriage to him, yet you must know you are worth so very much more."

Their conversation was curtailed as the footmen served the next course. But later she was given the opportunity to resume her talk with Toby when they found themselves seated in the drawing room apart from the other members of the family.

"You may think I am beginning to sound like one of the new suffragettes when I express my views, Toby," she told him smiling. "But I have been doing a great deal of thinking of late, and I have become convinced that it is a singular misfortune to be born female. From the time of our birth, our lives are so very restricted compared with that of males. A few of us are now being allowed a proper education, but for what end? For what purpose? We are not permitted to make use of our brains in any important field but may only apply our intelligence in the background of family life where, hopefully, we try to raise a more thinking, caring generation for the future. But for those like Aunt Milly who never marry, their lives have no purpose whatsoever."

Despite the seriousness of her tone, Toby laughed.

"I little thought to hear you, Willow, talking like that girl, Madeleine Villier, whom you so disliked!"

"Nor I to hear myself preaching for equality for females," Willow agreed, sighing. "But you cannot know how greatly I wish I had something more in life to occupy me than simple domestic matters." She smiled at Toby to belie the seriousness of her mood as she added: "I know you do not wish me to be involved in *your* work, Toby, but I am quite capable of learning to use a typewriting machine. I am certain I could make an excellent secretary, albeit I am a female."

Toby hesitated. He could understand Willow's need to be involved in more serious matters than the duties of a wife and mother, although it was unusual in a young woman of her age and background. Unfortunately, he was far from sure whether he would be able to continue to hide his true feelings from Willow were he to allow her to share in his work—even if Rowell permitted it. His love for her was both an agony and a joy. He was happy that at least he could watch over her from a distance; be there to comfort or advise her when she came to him confused or in distress. And he could share the child with her, a bonus he had not anticipated.

He was seldom happier than in the company of Willow's child. He could already see in Oliver many of Willow's traits of character, and although he looked a Rochford, by nature he was a sensitive, loving, clever little boy.

"May I take a little time to consider your offer to become my secretary, Willow, if such it was?" he asked, as with an effort he brought his thoughts back to the present. "I must admit I am tempted by the idea, for I do seem to become busier every day that passes. But you are away from home quite often. It may not be altogether practical—" His voice trailed into silence for he knew in his heart that if he were not so desperately in love with her, he would have welcomed Willow's assistance however limited her time.

Willow sighed. She had expected his rejection.

"You are quite right, of course," she said. "For a start, I shall be busy all next week helping Dodie to buy her trousseau. I spoke to Rowell again last night, asking him for the last time if he would approach Grandmère, in the hope that she would give her permission for Dodie's marriage. But Rowell does not want her upset by controversy until she is much stronger. I dared not tell him that the elopement we have planned might disturb her far more. But in my heart I do not believe it will actually harm her, Toby. In fact, when she discovers the truth, her anger may very well be a stimulant, for I think she thrives on dispute!"

Toby grinned.

"I said as much to Dodie and McGill when I took tea with them while you were in Paris. They are both so unselfish by nature I knew they would all too easily set aside their own future if they believed their elopement would have any serious effect upon Grandmère's health. But were that to happen, it would be history repeating itself, Willow. I learned something last week from old Mrs. Spears. She told me a family secret none of us was aware of—that poor Aunt Milly's one and only proposal of marriage was set aside when Grandmère fell ill after the birth of my father."

Willow was intrigued, for as far as she had been aware, Aunt Milly had never received a proposal.

"Her suitor was a middle-aged parson, a widower who was looking for a wife to carry out various parish duties," Toby continued. "He waited over a year for Aunt Milly to give her consent—she was in her mid-thirties by then —but she never did. I suspect that Grandmère, realizing how useful her sister-in-law was, enlisted Grandfather's help in dissuading her from entering the state of Holy Matrimony!" Toby smiled wryly. "It cannot have been too difficult. The parson was not well born and had very little money, whereas my father could easily afford to keep Aunt Milly in the manner to which she was accustomed. In any event, she never had another chance—and that same fate could apply to Dodie if we do not take care. So have no misgivings at this eleventh hour, Willow. I have already told Dodie that she can call upon me for help if she is in need. I came into my inheritance last year, as you know, so I can give her financial assistance if necessary."

Willow nodded.

"I am certain my father would send Dodie money," she said. "Papa never fails to inquire after her in his letters and I know she has his sympathy."

Encouraged and aided by Toby and Willow, the elopement of the two lovers took place at the end of the month as planned. The faithful Violet was to go with them to Cornwall, although they had explained to her that they could afford only the smallest wage. But she insisted she could manage very well on twenty-five pounds a year, and since she would be clothed and housed she would be able to send most of her money home to her mother. She had never been beyond the boundaries of Havorhurst, and the prospect of going to live in the West Country by the seaside was such that she could barely contain her excitement.

Toby and Willow drove Violet and the young couple to the station to take the train to London and only when all three were safely upon their way, did they return to Havorhurst to inform the astonished Mrs. Gassons that her "dear Mr. McGill" would not be returning. For the purpose of avoiding any hint of what was afoot reaching Grandmère's or Rowell's ears, the housekeeper had been led to suppose that the schoolmaster was going on holiday.

Her kindly face lit up with genuine pleasure when Willow announced that the couple were to be married on their arrival in Cornwall and Mr. McGill would be taking up a new post in a seaside village called Porth.

"Miss Rochford is a little saint, if ever there was one," she exclaimed, "and that fond of the Master! I'm ever so pleased for them both, Milady. When you next writes to them, please say as how I wish them every happiness. And don't you worry none about packing up and that. I'll have everything ready when the removals come to collect the Master's belongings."

Four hours after Dodie's departure, Toby and Willow visited Grandmère in her room and confessed that they had participated in the elopement. Willow handed her the letter Dodie had left for her.

I hope you will find it in your heart to forgive us both, dearest Grandmère. James is a truly wonderful man and I love him as dearly as he loves me. I know we shall be happy together, and our happiness would be complete were you to give us your blessing.

"Never! Never as long as I live!" Grandmère stormed, her hands drumming on the table top in impotent fury. "They must be stopped. How dare you both assist in this outrage! Rowell must go after them . . . Send Rowell to me this instant."

But Rowell was somewhere out on the estate and not immediately to be found. Tight-lipped, Grandmère renewed her verbal assault upon those nearest her: Aunt Milly for not having ascertained what was going on beneath her very nose; Willow for having encouraged the schoolmaster to the house in the first instance; Toby for supporting Willow's wishes rather than her own.

"At least Rowell will oppose this disastrous union," she cried. "Why is he not even now following after the runaways? What is he doing that can be more important than rescuing his own sister from that . . . that scoundrel?"

Toby hid a smile as he said calmly:

"I fear Rowell knows nothing of what has transpired, Grandmère. I am sure had he known he would have shared your views and prevented Dodie's departure. But I personally consider it is an excellent match for my sister —quite possibly the only chance she will ever have of living a normal life. James is a thoroughly decent chap and will take care of her to the best of—"

He got no further before Grandmère interrupted him.

"It is not for you to decide what is right and wrong in this household, Toby. I am astounded at your audacity in taking matters into your hands in this . . . this underhand fashion. When Rowell hears of it . . . and where *is* Rowell?" she cried in renewed frustration. "Pottering about with his confounded horses, I suppose. Mildred, have you made it clear to the servants I want him found—*at once.*"

As Mildred hurried out of the room, the old lady swung round and faced Willow, her black eyes flashing.

"You think you have outwitted me, don't you, my girl? But don't you make the mistake of underrating me. You think because you are young and pretty you can twist everyone round your little finger. But I can tell you—"

This time it was Toby who interrupted. In a quiet but threatening tone, he said:

"*That is enough, Grandmère!* Such remarks will not bring Dodie back, and even if you were to succeed this time, I can assure you that she will marry James eventually. You may not want my opinion, but with due respect to you, I intend to say what I have felt for a very long while—that were it not for Willow and her intervention on Dodie's behalf when she married Rowell and came to live here, your granddaughter would still be lying in that room upstairs, a pathetic invalid with a mind so starved of stimuli that she would doubtless by now be the mental deficient you once supposed her. Your bigoted pre-judged attitude to Dodie very nearly resulted in her becoming what you mistakenly thought her. You should now be thanking Willow, as I do, for everything she has done for Dodie."

For once in her life, Grandmère was silenced. Toby was the one member of the Rochford family who had never caused her a moment of anxiety. Quiet, reserved, self-sufficient, he had never come in conflict with her. She had misjudged him, she thought uneasily. Beneath that quiet exterior, he was stronger than Rowell or Pelham. He reminded her suddenly of her dead husband, the General, who had dominated her utterly despite her own strength of character. It was only after his death that she had been able to exert *her* authority upon the household.

But she would not let Toby think he could reprove her, his grandmother, without retribution.

"Leave the room at once," she told him as if he were a small boy. "I don't want to see or speak to you or Willow until Dorothy is brought safely home. I shall send for my solicitor. He will arrange everything."

But eventually she was forced to realize that it was too late to prevent the marriage. By the time Rowell could have caught up with the elopers, the simple ceremony would be over.

"In any event, Grandmère," Toby pointed out, "Dodie is almost twenty-one years of age, and in October she will be beyond your jurisdiction—or Rowell's."

In the end there was nothing Grandmère could do other than to forbid Dodie's name being mentioned again in her presence. Impotent and outwitted, she retired to bed, but as Toby commented shrewdly to Willow, this "relapse" was to impress on the household how disgracefully she had been treated rather than because she was genuinely ill. Doctor Forbes was summoned by Aunt Milly and prescribed a sedative; but Grandmère ordered Aunt Milly to pour it into the commode, for she wished to have her wits about her while "traitors such as Toby and Willow" were intent upon upsetting her.

Rowell's reaction was one of anger with Willow rather than with Dodie.

"You have deceived Grandmère and, worse still, you have gone behind my back," he said accusingly. "You had no right whatever to act without my permission."

Willow had been expecting this outcry and was armed against it. She made no attempt to argue the rights and wrongs of the matter, but stood silent until Rowell left the room and made his way reluctantly to his grandmother's suite.

But although Grandmère sent for her solicitor and tried to have the marriage annulled, this proved impossible.

"So we may congratulate ourselves, Willow!" Toby said some weeks later. "Our Dodie is now Mrs. James McGill. Has Rowell forgiven you yet for your part in the elopement?"

His eyes were gently teasing, and Willow smiled.

"I think he may be secretly relieved that Dodie's future is finally settled," she replied. "Father will be delighted," she added. "He was always much moved by her courage in facing up to her disabilities."

As Willow had guessed, her father's sympathies were entirely with the newlyweds, and some months after hearing the news, he dispatched a very generous check. *To help Dodie off to a good start,* he wrote.

He had planned a further visit to England in the autumn, but the sudden terrible assassination of the American President, William McKinley, early in September, caused him to postpone his holiday.

This dastardly act has had repercussions on Wall Street, he wrote, *and business affairs are likely to keep me somewhat heavily engaged until the new President has settled down. At forty-three, Theodore Roosevelt is the youngest man to hold such high office and although, as you know, he was Governor of New York, he is still somewhat of an*

*unknown quantity as yet. Your dear mother is very
shocked, as is the whole nation.*

But although she, too, had been shocked by the news,
Willow could feel no personal involvement.

"Although I am an American by birth," she told Toby,
"I feel far more deeply involved in England, as if this
were my real home and all of you my real family. Those
halcyon days of my childhood in San Francisco seem to
belong to another life!"

"I'm glad," Toby said simply. "I would hate to think of
your ever leaving England, Willow. I cannot think of
Rochford without you."

Willow regarded him curiously. There was a warmth
and intensity in his voice that took her unawares. Had she
not known Toby's affection for her was no more than that
of a brother, she might have mistaken his words for those
of a lover.

She turned her face away so that he could not see the
swift rush of color that spread into her cheeks. Never,
ever must she allow herself to think such thoughts. That
deep, growing affection she felt for him must never be allowed to develop into anything more; far less must she
permit herself to imagine that Toby, too, felt the same
stirrings of love. Therein would lie tragedy for everyone;
and of all the people in the world apart from little Oliver,
Toby was the one person she would least want to hurt.
Toby was her friend—the most valued friend she had.

I should have married him, not Rowell, she thought
with a terrible sense of despair. For no matter what happened in the future, she could never marry him now.

Last Sunday, sitting in the Rochford pew in Havorhurst
Church, her mind wandering from the dullness of the Reverend Appleby's sermon, she glanced down at her prayer-
book. It was open at the "Table of Kindred and Affinity."
Under the heading of those whom "A Woman may not
marry with," numbered seventeen in the list, were the
words *"Husband's brother."* Fascinated, she had stared at
those words, understanding only too clearly their implication to herself.

Her thoughts had winged back once more to the night
of Toby's twenty-first birthday party; to her own careless
indifference to his feelings as she danced away from him
in Pelham's arms. At that time, Rowell, with his dark good

looks, had appealed to all that was deeply romantic in her; Toby, of the serious, furrowed brow—the quiet, creative, intelligent Toby—had seemed no answer to the childish demands of her heart. Her judgment then had been entirely superficial, and she had never noticed that behind the concealing spectacles, Toby's eyes were infinitely larger, more expressive than Rowell's or Pelham's; that his mouth was gentle, sensitive, kindly, upturning very slightly at the corners revealing the humor lurking behind that serious demeanor. And although he lacked Pelham's flamboyant manner of dressing and Rowell's impeccable tidiness, Toby was tall, lithe and graceful with the most beautiful hands Willow had ever seen.

She had married too young, she thought; before she had had time to grow up and know a man's true worth—or her true self. And now, ten years later, that knowledge had come too late.

Chapter Sixteen

March–August 1902

PELHAM WAS HOME FROM SOUTH AFRICA AND THE war was nearly over. It was almost four years, Willow thought, since he had left Rochford so precipitately, and the memory of that fatal picnic had been pushed to the back of her mind. He gave the family no warning of his return, but simply walked into the house laden with presents for everyone as if he had been absent for only a week or two.

Momentarily, Willow was covered with confusion, unsure how it would be between them after all this time. But Pelham was his old laughing, teasing self. With no trace of self-consciousness, he hugged her briefly, told her that she had grown more beautiful than he remembered and then paid the same compliment to his excited grandmother, lifting the old lady off the ground as if she were no bigger than Oliver.

"And where is the little chap?" he asked cheerfully after he had shaken hands with Toby, Francis, and Rupert. "I can't wait to see my nephew."

When Patience arrived with the small boy, Oliver was instantly at ease in the presence of this new exciting uncle. He was momentarily disappointed that Pelham was not dressed in the red regalia of his lead soldiers and wore only the drab khaki of the modern fighting officer. But when Pelham lifted him onto his knees and showed him his revolver, he was captivated.

Regarding the two of them, Willow was immensely relieved to see that there was no more resemblance between them than between any family relatives. Oliver's curls were a far lighter brown than Pelham's—like his grandfather's, Grandmère often remarked.

Willow was surprised to discover how pleased she was to have Pelham home. She hurried down to the kitchen to arrange with Mrs. Jupp to prepare an extra special meal for his homecoming. Of all the family, only Francis seemed laggardly in his welcome; but then Francis was never happy when he himself was not the center of attention. He had been receiving less and less attention from Grandmère since the advent of Oliver and was becoming ever more surly and ill-tempered as the months went by. He seemed to delight in his old sadistic pastime of taunting Rupert, laughing at his brother's blushes. Both Toby and Willow had several times asked him to refrain from making allusions to Adrian, but Francis merely shrugged his shoulders and said that in a free country, he could speak as he pleased.

The fact that he had still over two years to wait before he could claim his inheritance and leave Rochford was like a thorn in his flesh, an ever-present irritant that required some outlet. His sporting activities did little to engage his sharp mind.

Fortunately, Francis had one new interest: a certain young lady called Annabel. Barratt. The youngest daughter of a well-to-do-family, she lived in a large house near Sevenoaks. Her father, Sir John Barratt, was the M.F.H. of the Glenfield Hunt, and Annabel, at the age of seventeen, had just Come Out, joining the other debutantes in their search for eligible husbands. Francis seemed quite taken with her, and Willow was relieved to realize that he had ceased mourning the loss of the unlikeable Miss Villier.

The Barratt family, like the Rochfords, were removing to London for the Season, which promised to be an exceptionally exciting one since the new king's coronation was scheduled to take place on June 26th. Rowell had rented the usual house in Park Lane, and already invitations to balls and soirées were pouring in from friends. Willow was kept busy replying to them and sending out invitations in return. It always surprised her how many people she and Rowell seemed to know and yet how very few of them she felt were real friends. Her relationships with such people were entirely superficial. Although she followed the custom, it never pleased her that members of society compiled their guest lists from those who were socially advantageous in some way, either by rank or wealth or influence.

By the end of May, all the ministries of Whitehall, the clubs in Pall Mall, the great buildings in the City, and the illustrious private houses in Mayfair and Belgravia were adorned with lavish decorative designs in honor of the coming coronation. Banners and bunting, gaily colored coats of arms and enormous crystal constellations for illumination hung above the Mall and along the processional route from Buckingham Palace to Westminster Abbey. Stands were being built along the way for seating the huge crowds expected on the day. Flags of all the visiting nations were hung from public buildings.

London was rapidly becoming overcrowded as foreign visitors began to arrive and people streamed into the city from the country to see the decorations.

The Rochfords reached London to find the pavements seething with unaccustomed faces, and passage to their rented house in Mayfair was well-nigh impossible. Willow's parents were not with them as had been expected. Beatrice Tetford was ill, the arthritis that had first overtaken her in her mid-forties being now so painful that traveling had become an ordeal. Willoughby Tetford had written to his daughter to say with deepest regret that they could not undertake the journey to England for the coronation as he had hoped to do.

Willow therefore decided to keep a diary in order that her parents—and her mother in particular—would at least feel they had some share in the occasion, albeit at second hand.

Her first entry was dated the end of the month.

"May 31st: We arrived safely in London to hear that the war in South Africa is finally over and peace has been signed. Patience is remaining at Rochford to look after Oliver. Neither Grandmère nor Aunt Mildred is with us, but all the rest of the family is here and we are busy settling in. The house seems quite small after Rochford. Nellie is complaining there are not sufficient wardrobes to hold all my new clothes. Rowell is in excellent spirits and an atmosphere of excitement prevails."

"June 4th: I was too busy making and receiving calls to bring this diary up to date before today. Invitations to parties have been pouring in, and it has taken me all my time replying to them and sending out our own. Today we went to Eton College for the annual celebration of its Foundation Day. Rowell, Pelham, Toby and Francis were like schoolboys again as they greeted all their old friends. Rupert did not accompany us as he did not enjoy his school days. We watched the traditional cricket match and afterwards took tea and listened to the toasts and speeches. We saw the procession of boats and when it grew dark, a magnificent display of fireworks featuring a set piece showing the Eton College Arms. It was most impressive, but quite exhausting and the weather was far from good."

"June 5th: We all went to Epsom for the Derby run. It was cold and wet and everyone but me lost money betting on the King's horse; but I won ten guineas for I backed the winner, Ard Patrick, for no better reason than that it had an American jockey who seems to be known by the strange name of 'Skeets Martin.' The King spoke to Rowell, but Rowell said that he did not seem at all in good spirits."

"June 14th: Today we went with a large party of friends to Aldershot to watch the military tattoo. Alas, it was bitterly cold and wet. The rain drenched all 30,000 troops and the parade ground was a quagmire. It seems the King was unwell, for the Queen took the salute."

"*June 16th:* During the last twelve days, we have attended the opera, the ballet, two receptions, one fancy dress ball, and four dances. We have given two dinner parties and one musical soirée for which we were lucky enough to engage M. Paderewski to play for our guests. When the weather permits, I ride every morning in Rotten Row, which, you may remember, is the custom for all the ladies and gentlemen who can sit a horse! Tomorrow is the start of Royal Ascot which we shall attend."

"*June 23rd:* What should have been a brilliant Ascot was quite spoiled by the fact that the King was not well enough to be present. We still enjoyed the occasion, eating our strawberries and cream and drinking champagne as usual, but everyone is concerned about His Majesty."

"*June 24th:* Unhappily, that concern was justified. Buckingham Palace has announced that the King is seriously ill and the coronation is indefinitely postponed. Rowell said at luncheon how terrible it would be if after waiting so long to be king, His Majesty did not live to be crowned. We are all stunned by this unhappy news."

"*June 25th:* The King has 'perityphlitis' which Toby says is a severe and often fatal inflammation occurring in connection with the appendix. He may be in great danger. Hundreds of the important foreign visitors who came to London for the coronation are now returning to their own countries. The crowds, too, are beginning to disperse. Pelham says that a vast number of tradespeople will be at a financial loss—florists in particular, and those who were said to be supplying 2,500 quails, hundreds of chickens, partridges, and sturgeons to Buckingham Palace to feed those guests who were to have been at the reception after the coronation ceremony. We talk of little but the King's health."

"*June 27th:* Although we are all in low spirits, we went nevertheless to watch the tennis at Wimbledon Lawn Tennis Club. Rowell was most impressed with the standard of play and is talking of having a tennis court made at Rochford. It would make a pleasant change from croquet!"

"June 28th: The King is still very ill. I went with Toby to the Royal Academy to see the Summer Exhibition. I was particularly interested to see the work of my countryman, John Singer—but to be truthful, I was not much impressed by his new painting, a portrait of Lord Ribblesdale. It is sad to see the London streets void of their scarlet stands which have all been dismantled. The lights and coats of arms too, are gone. Pelham returned from tea at Gunters with one of his many female admirers. They were talking to the maître d'hôtel, who told them that they had suffered great losses because of the canceled arrangements. They had contracted to provide one thousand luncheons at the House of Lords and to supply food for 6,000 guests who would have attended the Royal Garden Party. As Silvie would say, *quel désastre!"*

Willow had by now been in London for a month and she was sorely missing Oliver. Rowell was greatly enjoying the sophistication of London life and was disinclined to return to Rochford for the weekend, but Toby had had enough of parties and wanted to resume his work. He therefore escorted Willow home by train where an excited Oliver had wheedled the under-coachman to take him to Tunbridge Wells to the station to meet them. He plied them with questions as they drove home.

Had they seen the King? Was the King dying? Would the Queen cry if he did die? How many soldiers had they seen at the Aldershot Tattoo and were any of them dressed like his toy soldiers? Would he be allowed to play the tennis game if Papa did have a court made for their own use? What was a sturgeon? How could a fish operate on people's bodies to make them well?

Laughing, Toby explained the difference between sturgeon and surgeon and told the little boy that yes, he could cut up bodies if he went to medical school and learned how to do it.

"Grandmère gave me a jig-saw and I'm learning to put the pieces together," Oliver said as they reached the house. "Will you come and see it, Mama? When it is finished, it will be Windsor Castle where the King and Queen live."

Tired though she was, Willow spent a happy half-hour

with her small son before retiring to her room where Nellie divested her of her traveling costume. When she had bathed and changed into a simple housegown, she went to see Grandmère. The old lady had almost as many questions as Oliver. She had never considered Queen Victoria's son a worthy successor to his mother and with an old lady's spitefulness, she now told Willow that in her opinion, it might be to the good if Edward did die.

"And take that smile off your face, my girl," she added sharply to Willow. "I know you young people like him—but only because he is less of a disciplinarian than his mother. Goodness only knows what this country's morals will be like in a few years' time if these libertine ways continue."

She seemed in as good health as her age permitted, and after dinner later that night, Willow inquired of Toby and Aunt Mildred if Doctor Forbes had given any report upon Grandmère lately.

Aunt Milly sniffed—more by habit than from disdain for the doctor's opinion.

"He seems to think Clotilde could last another ten years if she takes proper care of herself," she said. "And I wouldn't wonder either. She may lie in her bed all day like an invalid but she never stops talking."

"Or ordering poor Aunt Milly about, I'll wager," said Toby when his aunt had returned to Grandmère's room. "I suppose she is accustomed to the drudgery of her life by now, but there are times when I do feel sorry for her. She must often wonder why my grandfather's *wife* should enjoy all the cossetting while she, his *sister*, is little better than a paid companion. It saddens me to think Aunt Milly could have married but for Grandmère's selfishness, just as it pleases me to remember Dodie and rejoice that she is so happy."

There had been a regular inflow of letters from Dodie from Cornwall—each one as ecstatically happy as the last. James was loving his new school, she wrote, and in the evenings she helped him to correct the children's written work.

"So we can rest assured we took the right decision when we encouraged her elopement," Willow said happily as she read the latest epistle. Grandmère refused to read these letters and still would not permit Dodie's name to be mentioned in her hearing.

Willow returned to London with an easy mind. She was soon caught up once more in the numerous events of the Season. Rowell was at his best—delighted to have so many amusements at his fingertips and pleased to discover his family so much in demand at parties. He attributed this generously to Willow, who received limitless compliments wherever she went. Even Esmé Symington remarked to Rowell that his wife was one of the most popular hostesses in London and that everyone liked her; that age had added to her charm, and the pretty young girl was now a strikingly beautiful woman.

From time to time, Rowell enjoyed that beauty, although never with the same eager enthusiasm as when he abandoned himself to the delights of a paramour.

Willow recommenced her diary, having posted off to her parents those pages accounting for the month of June. The new page began with a report on the King's health.

"July 5th: There has been an official bulletin saying the King has been operated on and is making a good recovery. We are all rejoicing. Pelham tells me that all the uneaten food prepared for the coronation that might have been wasted has been sent to the Little Sisters of the Poor and to other charities, so many poor people in London will have benefited, for which I am glad."

"July 10th: Together with a large party of friends, we all visited Lords Cricket Ground to watch the match between Eton and Harrow. Pelham, Francis, and Rowell were cheering loudly for their old school, so I was a little naughty and cheered for Harrow! Rowell was very angry. We shall be going to the Regatta at Henley but first we shall enjoy one more night at the opera before the Season ends."

"July 30th: I have been so busy I have had no time to keep up my diary. The King has gone to his yacht on the Solent to convalesce. He was taken on a stretcher by train to Portsmouth, where he embarked. Now that he is so much better, a new date, August 9th, has been arranged for the coronation. Rowell and his brothers went to Good-

wood for the racing but I was feeling too exhausted and declined to go. But I did go with them to Hurlingham Club to watch the polo. Pelham knew a great deal about the game, for he learned to play when he was in Egypt. Last night Pelham took me to the theatre, as Rowell had been invited to a gaming party. With six other couples, we saw *The Merry Wives of Windsor*—a most amusing play with the beautiful Ellen Terry taking the part of Mistress Page. We had supper afterwards at the Savoy."

Although Willow was not a little nervous, Rowell was greatly looking forward to the pomp and pageantry of the coronation of which they would be very much a part. Willow's parents were already aware of their son-in-law's entitlement to be present in Westminster Abbey by virtue of his barony, and Willow had described in detail the robes they would both be wearing.

She wrote now in her diary:

"August 8th: The King has returned from Cowes and seems quite to have recovered from his illness. He is with the Queen at Buckingham Palace, but they are not attending the full rehearsal for tomorrow's ceremony. Our family will be going to the Symingtons' house in Piccadilly to watch the procession from there. Rowell has agreed that we may engage a photographer to take pictures of the two of us in our robes, which I will be able to send to you."

"August 11th: What a magnificent occasion it was! I was so proud to be part of the traditional ceremonial service in the Abbey. The King was in excellent spirits and seemed in no respect overtired by the long day. The crowds gave him rapturous applause, and there can be no doubting his popularity. Tomorrow he is holding an investiture parade of the Colonial troops at Buckingham Palace. Pelham says he is acquainted with several of the officers with whom he fought in South Africa."

"August 13: Today we went to the Oval to watch England play Australia (and win by one wicket) in the fifth Test Match. Like yourself, Papa, I am still not quite conversant with all the rules of this national game, but I en-

joyed the occasion and was pleased we won in this coronation year."

"*August 17th:* Rowell went yesterday to Spithead to see the King hold a coronation review of the fleet. The weather was perfect. Pelham tells me three of the Boer generals were invited but declined to attend. Although former enemies, they have received a most popular welcome. Rowell says the King intends to entertain them on his yacht today at Cowes."

"*August 18th:* The Shah has arrived in England and was met at Dover yesterday by Prince Arthur (of Connaught). The Shah is to visit the King at Portsmouth in two days' time."

"*August 20th:* We had thought to return to Rochford at the end of the week, but Pelham has obtained for us an invitation from Lord Lonsdale to go to Lowther Castle in Cumberland. Rowell has agreed we should accept because he has heard that the pheasant shooting is second to none, although he maintains that the Earl is eccentric to say the least. He is virtually uneducated, having been withdrawn from Eton at the age of twelve, but is a masterly sportsman and a great patron of the sports. I suspect that Rowell's main objection is that he mixed too much and too often with the lower classes in his youth, but Pelham tells me he is highly entertaining. For instance, he drives only yellow cars, and wears yellow buttonholes; his carriages, his servants' livery, even his dogs are yellow! I am most eager to meet him and look forward to our visit, although I have heard his wife, Grace, is delicate and that sadly, she can never give him the son and heir he wants."

"*August 25th:* Oh, Papa, how I wish you were here. The shooting is quite wonderfully organized. A positive army of beaters are employed to drive in the outlying coverts, and believe it or not there are eighteen full-time keepers on the estate; so as you can imagine, there is no shortage of game. The Earl, I think, is more interested in the social aspects than in bagging birds and is an excellent host, but I am still not sure that I like him. I was told yesterday that if he sees that one of his dogs has a greying muzzle he orders it to be shot. He will not tolerate anything he considers inefficient."

"*August 30th:* Tomorrow we leave for home, and I am no nearer deciding whether or not I really like our host. There can be no doubt that he does a very great deal for the sporting world and is endeavoring to improve the status of boxing in this country; he is a great raconteur and by no means unattractive to the ladies; he is flamboyant, a showman, but with a natural courtesy and distinction that cannot be ignored. I think you would like him, Papa, for he is a very generous man like yourself, but Rowell cannot overlook the fact that simply because he has no son to inherit, he is quite indifferent to the preservation of his inheritance."

Willow closed her diary, knowing that there would be little more to relate to her parents now that the Season had come to an end. Her thoughts returned to Rochford and to the little son who would be so eagerly awaiting her return. Toby, too, would be waiting to welcome them home. The thought gave her a warm feeling of pleasure. The autumn months at Rochford were often beautiful, the trees golden, the fruit ripened and ready for harvesting.

"It will be lovely to see Rochford again," Willow said contentedly to Rowell and Pelham, as the train carried them swiftly away from Cumberland. "The hazel trees in the lanes and hedgerows will be thick with nuts and the Kent cobs at the bottom of the garden ripe for gathering. We will take Oliver with us—he's old enough this year— to go nutting," she spoke her thoughts aloud.

But it was not Pelham or Rowell of whom she was thinking, but of Toby, when she used the word "we."

Chapter Seventeen

September 1902–February 1903

FRANCIS WAS IN AN EVIL MOOD. HE HAD THAT VERY afternoon proposed to seventeen-year-old Miss Annabel Barratt—and been refused. Her father had given him permission to ask for his daughter's hand, so her rejection had not sprung from any parental disapproval but from the girl herself. Tossing her long fair curls and pouting prettily, she had declared with youthful frankness:

"If I were willing to marry any of the Rochfords, I would marry Pelham. But not *you*, Francis. You're far too serious. And you do not dance well, either. And you never laugh!"

Bluntly, cruelly, she had not even paid him the courtesy of thanking him for doing her the honor. Despite youth, she reminded Francis of Madeleine Villier, who also did not believe in mincing words—and who also seemed ignorant of how much she could hurt a man's feelings by her so-called honesty.

Francis lay on his bed, his mouth sulky. His eyes narrowed as he speculated upon his ill fortune in finding himself invariably attracted to girls who were pretty enough in looks but totally egotistical by nature. As it was, he had now wasted a great deal of time this past summer paying court to the flirtatious Miss Barratt, he thought bitterly. He had stupidly mistaken her smiles and dimples as encouragement to him, when all the time they had been for Pelham's benefit.

Why must his brother have returned from South Africa at all? Francis asked himself angrily. When Pelham was on the scene, females never noticed *him*. He did not have Pelham's easy facility for light-hearted banter, for laughter, for frivolous amusement. He was too introspective; too intense. And as Annabel had said, he did not dance well!

286

Francis' mouth tightened in something akin to a sneer as he recalled the young girl's barb. Perhaps dancing was not one of his attributes, but that did not detract from his manliness. He had proved himself over and over again with the females he had bedded. But he could hardly indicate such private accomplishments to the girl he had hoped to marry.

It was small comfort that he was not actually in love with Annabel, for if he had married her, the chances were that her parents would have given them a really nice house and estate, and he, at long last, would have been able to leave Rochford. As it was, he would have to endure his dependence upon his family for two long years more. He hated his home—more than ever since the arrival of young Oliver. The way his grandmother doted on the boy sickened him. Toby, too, was forever praising the child's accomplishments and all the servants without exception spoiled him. No one in the house bothered any more about him, Francis. Even Rupert ignored him—the stupid, ineffectual Rupert with his unhappy perversions.

Several times, Francis had considered reporting Rupert's meetings with the doctor's son to Grandmère. But tempted though he had been, the thought of Toby's resultant wrath had made him hold his tongue.

Francis knew that, for all Toby's quietness and solitude, he was a far stronger character even than Rowell. And Francis was further aware that Toby understood *him* all too well. Toby knew when he lied; when he had perpetrated some mischief; when he was in debt. He, Francis, had only dared steal the Gainsborough during his brother's absence from home.

"I don't trust you, Francis, and I never will," Toby had told him not so very long ago. "So mind your step, else you may reckon that you have me to deal with."

Life was singularly unfair, Francis thought, as he rose from his bed and walked over to the window to stare down onto the green sweep of lawns. The autumn leaves had not yet started to fall, but the apple harvest had begun and several of the younger housemaids were returning from the orchard to the house with the handles of their heavily-laden baskets looped over their bare arms.

Among them was Willow's personal maid, Nellie. Francis watched her as she strode with a country girl's wide gait nearer to his view. She seemed to have blossomed in the six weeks since her engagement on coronation day to the head footman. Francis' mouth curved in a brief smile. What a ladies' man Mr. Harry Stevens had been in his day, he thought, pinching the laundrymaids' bottoms, stealing kisses from the housemaids, and even getting one of them pregnant years ago. But now the footman had eyes for no one but dark-haired Nellie Sinclair—and Francis could understand why. The Irish-American girl was like one of the rosy apples she carried—ripe for the picking. It was more than likely she was a virgin still, despite her thirty years, he surmised.

Did she long for the feel of a man's body? he asked himself, his eyes following the buxom young woman as she came still closer. Hunger stirred in his loins as he recalled the occasion when he had caught her alone in the linen room and nearly had his way with her. But she had gone running to Willow, who had soon put a stop to his plans for the girl's seduction.

Would it not be a kind of rough justice, he asked himself excitedly, if now he were to have the girl, rob her of her virginity before Stevens could do so? He had been rebuffed by Miss Annabel Barratt, and it would be some small compensation if he could override another female's rejection of him.

Francis' lips curled in secret amusement. A moment ago he had been excruciatingly bored, but now he was burning with anticipation. He walked over to the fireplace and pulled on the bell rope. A maid appeared and Francis demanded of her that Nellie in person be sent up immediately.

Nellie received the summons uneasily. She had been enjoying the apple picking, which reminded her of the days when as a child she had gathered fruit in the orange groves at home in San Francisco. The sun was warm in the orchard, and she had been happily engrossed in her task. She had no idea why Mr. Francis should want to see *her* for he had his own valet to attend to his needs, and it was not a part of her duties as her young mistress' personal maid ever to serve the young gentlemen of the household.

But Mrs. Jupp told her she'd "best go, and be quick about it."

Francis' bedroom door was open as she approached. Knocking several times and receiving no reply, she peered nervously inside the room. As she did so, a hand came around from behind the door and covered her mouth so quickly that she had no time to scream. From behind her, Francis kicked the door shut and with his other hand turned the key in the lock.

"Are you going to be a nice quiet girl, Nellie, or do I have to put a gag over your mouth?" he asked quietly. The girl's terrified gaze excited him further. "I'm sure you don't want me to hurt you, do you, Nellie," he muttered. "So do as I tell you and you'll come to no harm. Sit down there!" He pointed to his bed.

Nellie glanced around the room with increasing anxiety. The curtains were drawn across the casements, as was customary in summer months, to keep the sun from fading the colors of the carpet. In the dim light, she could make out that the windows themselves were closed. As far as she was aware, all the family were in the garden taking afternoon tea on the lawn. To shout for help would be pointless.

She sat down heavily on the edge of Francis' bed. Her eyes were drawn to his, and she saw the strange, hungry glitter in them and sensed his mood.

"I don't rightly know what you want from me, Mr. Francis," she said quietly, "but lest you don't know, sir, I'm bespoken to Harry Stevens, and servant or no, he'd kill any man as laid a finger upon me."

Francis stood looking down at Nellie's clasped hands. He noticed with interest their trembling. Her full bosom was rising and falling in the most tantalizing way as she drew quick, nervous breaths. The upper curves of her breasts were white and dusted with tiny gold freckles. A lady might have abhorred such marks, but on the servant girl they had an earthy attraction.

"I don't think I find myself particularly frightened by the thought of Stevens' revenging himself upon my person," he said, his voice heavy with sarcasm. "After all, my dear girl, he would have too much to lose, would he not, were he to attack me? And besides, by doing so, he could not give you back your lost virginity. You *are* still a virgin, I suppose, Nellie?"

Nellie made as if to spring to her feet, but with one

lithe movement toward her, Francis pushed her back on the bed. Losing her balance, Nellie sprawled across the coverlet, her cotton skirt riding up her legs to expose her plump, white thighs.

"Please, sir, don't do it," she gasped as Francis fell on top of her, imprisoning her beneath his weight. "Harry and me are going to be married . . . please, Mr. Francis . . . *please* . . ."

But he ignored her cries. He felt no pang of pity as he overcame the girl's fierce struggles to resist him. With quick, precise skill, he unfastened his trousers and forced one knee between her legs. With his hands, he held Nellie's arms pinioned against her sides so that she could neither hit nor scratch him in self-defense.

The smell of her hot, sun-drenched, sweating body aroused in him the deepest of animal inclinations. First he would overpower her completely, he thought, and then he would have his fill of her. Her strong, healthy body, writhing beneath him, added to his arousal. He could now taste the salt of her tears as her head twisted helplessly from side to side in an attempt to avoid his mouth. She succeeded once in biting his arm, but his grip on her only tightened more fiercely as a result.

The sight of his own blood oozing from the scarlet teeth marks on his white skin, reminded him of the girl's virginity. None of the women he had lain with before had been virgins, he thought—not even Madeleine. Now he could learn the delights of being the first man to invade this carefully-preserved cavern of delight.

Nellie was physically strong, but not strong enough to combat Francis' male superiority. He had spent many long hours riding to hounds and tramping the grouse moors, and his muscles were far more powerful than Nellie's. Slowly, her resistance weakened as she became exhausted by her ineffectual struggles. Francis' face and body were now dripping with sweat, which mingled with her own as his half-naked body lay on hers. Sickened, frightened, and in shocking pain, she felt him dive down into her, tearing her apart in a series of agonizing thrusts.

When it was finally over and only the pain remained, she lay still, feeling the hot liquid trickling down between her thighs. She was not aware of the fact that it was her own blood mixed with the horrible product of his body until he flung a towel at her, saying roughly:

"Clean yourself up, girl. You'll ruin that bedcover."

He was still breathing deeply, but the pleasure he had experienced was already dimming as he realized what danger he had put himself in. If the girl told Willow and she reported the matter to Grandmère or Rowell . . .

He pulled on his trousers and walked over to his bureau. From the top left hand drawer, he withdrew a few gold sovereigns, which he threw down on the bed beside the motionless figure.

"That should help you and your precious Harry buy a few things for your wedding," he said. "And I advise you to keep your mouth shut about this—for your own sake as well as mine. Your future husband wouldn't be quite so keen to marry you, I'll warrant, if he knew you were no longer a virgin. And I would make it my business to tell him—and everyone else—that you wanted it; yes, that you offered yourself to me. Old Lady Rochford won't doubt my word. She never did like your mistress bringing you here from America. She thinks all Americans are 'fast,' and I'll tell her she was right. Both you and Stevens would be sent packing, without references, and so much for your future then! Do you understand me?"

Too shocked to reply, Nellie nevertheless understood very well what her molester was saying. It would be his word against that of a mere servant. Only her mistress would believe her, and she would be powerless to help if the Baron were not convinced that she was innocent. The family would doubtless stick together to avoid a scandal and she . . . she and Harry would be the scapegoats.

"Go to your room and tidy yourself up," Francis ordered in a cold, hard voice. "And take care Miss Mildred isn't on the lookout as you go upstairs."

The soreness between Nellie's legs was excruciating as she struggled to rise from the bed. The gold coins fell to the floor with a metallic jingle, but she made no move to pick them up. Watching her, Francis felt a fresh wave of anxiety. He must have hurt the girl more than he had intended. She looked a mess. Anyone seeing her would be inclined to believe *her* story rather than his.

"On second thoughts, you'd best go to your bed and stay there," he said. "I'll tell them you fell downstairs.

Someone else can see to your mistress' dressing this evening. Now pick up that money and be off!"

Obediently, Nellie stumbled toward the door, but she ignored the coins.

Francis' face darkened in sudden anger.

"Pick them up, damn you. Pride is not a perquisite of servants."

But she ignored him, aware despite her pain and fear, that he could not force his hush money upon her.

Francis let her go, his uneasiness increasing once he was alone. He could see only too clearly now that he had behaved with extreme stupidity. He might as well have announced his intention when he demanded that this particular maid be sent to his room when any servant could have attended him. He must think up some valid reason why it had to be Nellie he had needed.

He tried none too successfully to quieten his jangling nerves. An idea began to form in his head. Nellie's engagement to Stevens was general knowledge. He, Francis, might have called the girl to his room in order to give her a wedding present—a somewhat unusual thing to do, doubtless, but just plausible. He could say the money was intended for both servants, but that he had forgotten it was Stevens' day off until after his summons to Nellie. It was partly true, for Stevens had gone into Havorhurst to visit a relative and had asked Rowell at lunch time if he might take the trap.

Slowly, Francis relaxed. He would talk himself out of his trouble if he was calm and convincing. Even if Toby suspected him of lying, there was no proof he had ravaged Nellie—only her word against his that Stevens wasn't the culprit. As for the girl herself—she would recover in a day or two and would soon forget what had happened. Rape was an ugly word but not entirely applicable in this case, he told himself. At the age of thirty, the girl *must* have wanted a man, even if she had so far denied herself such pleasures in order to preserve her virginity.

It surprised him that Nellie had not taken the financial compensation he had offered her—and it angered him. It was as if, even after he had debased her, she had somehow retained her dignity while robbing him of his.

Alone in her attic room, shivering uncontrollably, Nellie felt anything but dignified. She bathed herself from head to toe, not once but twice, in an attempt to wash away the terrible act wrought upon her. She wished herself dead, but it did not cross her mind that she might kill herself, for she knew that would be a mortal sin. But she did contemplate running away. But where could she go? she thought despairingly. Miss Dodie might take her in—in a faraway place called Cornwall.

But Nellie was afraid Dodie would of a certainty write and tell Willow that she had gone to her and why she needed a refuge.

Like squirrels in a cage, thoughts chased one another around Nellie's mind as she curled herself into a small tight ball beneath the cold cotton sheets. Harry—her dearly-loved, strong, handsome Harry would not want her now. He had told her often enough that he had no respect for girls that "did," and that one of his reasons for loving her was that she had "kept herself pure." Even though it was through no fault of hers, she was now sullied forevermore.

Maybe something terrible like this had happened once long ago to poor Miss Mildred, Nellie thought inconsequently, and that was why the poor old lady had remained a spinster. She, like Miss Mildred, would remain unmarried now. She was not even sure if she still wished to be wed—not if a man could inflict such terrible pain on a woman. . . .

Betty came into the room carrying a mug of hot cocoa and a small glass of brandy.

"Cook says as how it'll do you good, Nellie," the young girl said. "We were all ever so sorry to hear you'd fallen downstairs. Mr. Francis said it was a right nasty fall, and if you're not better by marnin', he'll send for the doctor."

Half an hour later, Willow called to see her maid. Nellie struggled to sit up.

"You didn't ought to have come all the way up here, Milady," she cried, shocked by her mistress' unorthodox behavior in visiting a sick servant in her attic bedroom.

"Of course I had to come to see if you were all right," Willow said, leaning anxiously over the bed and staring down at Nellie's white, shocked face. "You haven't broken any bones? Mr. Francis thought not but—"

"No, I've not broken nothing, Milady," Nellie said quickly. "Thank you all the same."

"How fortunate he heard your fall and was there to pick you up," Willow continued innocently. "Are you *sure* you are all right, Nellie? You look so pale!"

"It's just the shock, I expect, Milady," Nellie whispered. "I'll just sleep now, if you don't mind."

"No, of course not, Nellie. And you're not to get up tomorrow until I have given my permission. I'll come and see you in the morning."

She left the room even more uneasy than she had been when she entered it. It was unlike Nellie to be so silent, so quiet, for she was a great chatter and was always laughing, even over mishaps. The fall must have been more serious than Francis had made out. Even he had looked shaken. He had taken the gig and gone into Havorhurst—to see the gunsmith, he had said; but somehow Willow had not believed him. She reminded herself that Francis had never liked illness and that perhaps he wanted to be out of the house for that reason.

But the following morning, Nellie was back at work. Her face, arms, and legs were covered in bruises and she moved stiffly. She refused adamantly to see Doctor Forbes.

"It's just the shock, Milady," she repeated over and over again to Willow. "I'll be all right, truly I will."

Willow herself was not feeling well, although she made no mention of it. She wondered if she could have eaten too much rich food in London and whether this could be the cause of her constant feelings of nausea. It never once occurred to her that she might be with child, for she had almost given up expecting she might conceive again. It was Toby who, seeing her pale cheeks and violet-shadowed eyes, suggested this might be the case.

"Oh, no, I don't think so, Toby—" Willow began; but now that the suspicion was planted in her mind, she knew instantly that Toby was right.

"Are you not pleased then?" Toby asked her when Doctor Forbes confirmed his diagnosis shortly before Christmas. "You have told me so often that you wanted a brother or sister for Oliver."

But Willow, although pleased in one way, could not feel the same unmitigated joy she had experienced when she had been expecting her very first child—the baby girl who had died. In those days she had still been deeply in love with Rowell, and the knowledge that she was carrying a part of him inside her had given her a secret, lasting happiness. Her feelings of guilt while she had carried Pelham's child had often overcome the joy of her approaching motherhood; and now . . . now she was by no means sure that she wanted her husband's baby.

"You must think me wicked and unnatural," she confessed to Silvie that Christmas. "But I cannot even bring myself to tell Rowell the news. At the back of my mind I cannot forget that he has already been responsible for the births of Georgina's three children and that *my* child—this child—will be no novelty to him."

Silvie gave a very Gallic shrug of her beautiful shoulders.

"*Enfin, chérie,* it is a matter of whether or not *you* want another baby. Its father is of no importance, as I see it! So long as it is healthy and you wish it, then it is a cause for celebration."

Willow smiled, envying Silvie her uncomplicated if amoral philosophy for living. It was clearly a satisfactory way of life for her. The young Frenchwoman looked as lovely and as youthful as when Willow had met her for the first time.

"It is love that keeps me young," Silvie said laughing. "*You* should take a lover, Willow. Now that you no longer love your husband, it is the obvious thing to do. If you were not now *enceinte,* I should persuade you to come to Paris with me. My artist, Pierre, has a very handsome friend who would adore you. Perhaps you might even fall in love with him!"

But Willow knew such a thing would be impossible. If she ever allowed herself to fall in love a second time, it would be with Toby. She found herself dreading the thought that one day Toby might marry and leave Rochford. Such an idea was sufficient to strike a chord of icy fear in her heart. But not even to Silvie could she speak of these emotions which she buried deep down within her. She told herself she was content to be the recipient of Toby's brotherly affection; that it was really in the company of the amusing, laughing Pelham that she was happiest.

"What you need, *chérie,* is a good long holiday away from the Rochford family," Silvie announced when the

Christmas festivities were over and she prepared to leave for Paris. "Come and visit me in the spring, dearest Willow. And as you will be quite large by then and not inclined for shopping expeditions and late nights—or lovers," she added mischievously, "we will go to the Château d'Orbais and enjoy the simple pleasures of the country together."

The suggestion appealed to Willow, and she hugged the thought to her as the cold, wet months of January and February kept her confined to the house. Toby was deeply engrossed in his work and she saw little of him. Pelham and Francis spent most of their daylight hours hunting or shooting. Rowell was restless and irritable unless he, too, were preoccupied with a sporting event, and Willow found herself wondering whether he had renewed his association with Georgina—or else were wishing to do so. Now that he was finally aware of her condition, he no longer came to their bed and their communications were on the most superficial of levels concerning such matters as the house or the estate.

Willow now felt the new life stirring within her and she began to look forward to her baby's arrival in June. But first she wanted to visit Silvie in France. Rowell was greatly opposed to the idea.

"There is no question of your traveling in your condition," he argued forcefully.

But Willow made light of such objections, reiterating that the change of air and scenery would do her good and that in any event, it would be warmer and pleasanter east of Paris at the foot of the Côte des Blancs.

"Silvie wishes me to go in April when the spring flowers are at their best," she told her unresponsive husband. "There is no need for you to accompany me, Rowell, since Nellie will look after me on the journey and I shall enjoy every comfort at the Château d'Orbais."

Rowell hesitated. He certainly did not wish to go to France and in any case, he had never really approved of his cousin Silvie or cared for her company. She made him uneasy with her constant teasing, which always seemed to show him up in a bad light. But the real reason why he was reluctant to go abroad was that he had found a new mistress.

Ten years younger than Georgina, Désirée Somners

lived up to her name—she was an actress, available and infinitely desirable. She was not dissimilar in looks to the young Georgina when first Rowell met her, with copper-colored hair and green eyes. As yet Désirée had not made her mark on the stage as a leading lady, but she had been given supporting roles and had appeared in the recent production of *Merrie England*. It was on that occasion Rowell had first set eyes upon her and was surprised by the unusual force of his desire for her small shapely body.

After the play had ended, he had invited Désirée, together with a number of his close friends, to a private dinner party at the Savoy, in one of the special rooms reserved for such purposes. Désirée had responded enthusiastically to his advances and he had discovered himself very much *épris* with the young woman. It was almost as if he had the young Georgina back in his arms, he decided, as he rediscovered the ardent enthusiasm of those earlier years.

It would be very pleasant to take Désirée away on a little holiday while his wife was in Épernay, he told himself. Nice, in the south of France would be very agreeable in the spring. He could take Désirée there on his yacht knowing that he could count upon his well-paid crew to be discreet about the cabin sleeping arrangements.

"Very well, my dear," he said to Willow now. "Since you and Silvie always seem to enjoy each other's company so much, I will not make myself an unwelcome third. If Doctor Forbes agrees that the journey will not harm you, you may go if you so wish."

A few years ago, Willow thought, she would have been silly enough to believe that she had hurt Rowell's feelings by her reluctance to have him accompany her. But now she was cynical enough to guess that her husband had other plans in mind for himself. Mercifully, she told herself, she did not care. After nearly twelve years of marriage, at the age of twenty-eight, she had finally grown up.

Chapter Eighteen

March–June 1903

"**A**RE YOU NOT PLEASED TO BE GOING TO FRANCE, Nellie?" Willow asked. There was something in the droop of Nellie's shoulders, in the expression on her unusually pale face, that prompted the question.

To Willow's consternation, the tears began to run down Nellie's cheeks as she tried ineffectually to fold one of her mistress' evening gowns and pack it into the valise on the floor in front of her.

"Why, Nellie, what is upsetting you?" Willow asked anxiously. "Is it that you will be separated from Harry for the next month?"

The gentleness of Willow's voice was too much for Nellie. She buried her face in her hands and gave way to her tears.

Willow leaned down and helped the weeping maid to her feet. She guided her over to the bed and sat down beside her, putting her arm around her shaking shoulders.

"We have known each other a long time, Nellie," she said quietly. "You were fourteen when you first came to work for us in San Francisco, and I was twelve. You have been my personal maid for thirteen years, and you and I probably know each other better than anyone else in the world knows us. So you should have no doubt in your mind that you can trust me with your confidences. Now tell me what is wrong. Have you quarreled with Harry?"

Nellie's tears ceased as suddenly as they had begun, the enormity of her problem suddenly too overwhelming for tears. She looked at her mistress with stricken eyes.

"I'm going to have a child, Milady!" The words came out in a gasp.

Willow felt a moment of shock followed by one of self-recrimination. She should have guessed. But she had been so preoccupied with her own condition, her own

298

problems, that she had not taken the time to find out why Nellie had lacked her customary bright spirits and healthy energy.

"My dear Nellie, that is not so terrible a disaster," she said soothingly. "We shall just have to hasten your wedding to Harry, that is all." The expression of dismay on Nellie's face caused her to add: "Is that not a sensible solution, then?"

Nellie struggled to find words to express herself. She had made a vow that as long as she lived, she would never reveal the truth about that terrible afternoon last summer in Mr. Francis' bedroom. But she had not then given a thought to the fact that there could be such a horrible repercussion. When she guessed that she was with child as a result of that assault upon her, she had realized that she must still keep her secret. Even if Harry did not take revenge upon Mr. Francis, he would still be given notice by old Lady Rochford or the Master when her condition became known. No matter what *she* said, they would certainly support Mr. Francis' word.

After many a sleepless night thinking about it, Nellie had realized that she would have to run away when she became too large to conceal the truth. Her chances then of finding another post when she was carrying, and without references, were very remote. The small amount of money she had saved toward her marriage to Harry would not last long; nor was it sufficient to buy a passage back to her home in America. She would almost certainly end up in the workhouse.

She had many times considered confessing the truth to her mistress—the one person in the world she was sure would believe her. But when Willow had told her that she herself was with child, Nellie had not had the heart to lay her own terrible problem at her mistress' door. Now, however, she could no longer keep silent, for Willow had ordered her to pack their baggage, as they were to go to France for several weeks.

Between her sobs, she recounted her story in broken sentences. Shocked beyond measure, Willow did not once interrupt her.

"So what could I do, Milady?" Nellie ended, the tears now flowing even faster. "I dursn't tell Harry. Besides, he

wouldn't want to marry me no more now I'm disgraced—
even if I wasn't having no baby."

"Hush now, Nellie!" Willow said, her thoughts racing
as she tried to keep calm in the face of such a terrible outrage. Her instinct was to confront Francis this very instant; to force a confession from him. But Nellie herself
had already considered the consequences of such a confrontation and was shrewd enough to appreciate that certainly Grandmère and almost certainly Rowell would take
Francis' word in preference to Nellie's. They would say
that Harry had despoiled her.

"The first person we must speak to is Harry," she said
quietly. "No, not you, Nellie, but me. I shall tell him what
has happened. I am sure he will understand that it was
not your fault. I believe that he really does love you, and
if he does, maybe this won't affect his wish to marry you."

For ten minutes, Nellie argued stubbornly that Harry
must not be told—for his own sake as well as hers, she reiterated.

But Willow was adamant. She sent the trembling, red-
eyed Nellie to find Harry and tell him that she wished to
speak to him at once in the morning room.

Willow approved of the head footman. He was a pleasant, open-faced, honest man, now in his early forties. He
was an excellent servant and perfectly trustworthy.
Twelve years older than Nellie, he was the ideal match
for her, and when he had first asked for her hand, Willow had been in no doubt that he would make her a good
husband.

"This is to be an informal talk," Willow said as the
head footman entered the morning room. "I am afraid
what I am about to say will come as a shock to you—as it
did to me. But you must try to remain calm for everyone's
sake, not least of all for Nellie's . . ."

She saw the flicker of concern on the man's face. Too
well trained to show any emotion in front of his employers, he was nevertheless unable to hide his anxiety when
Nellie's name was mentioned. He had been worried about
her for some time. She never laughed or joked the way
she used to do; never sang as she went about her work.
And when they walked out of a Sunday afternoon, she refused even to hold his hand, let alone permit him to kiss
her goodnight.

"Reckon as how you've stopped loving me, Nellie," he had finally accused her, and to his consternation, she had burst into tears—his bright, happy Nellie whom he'd never known to cry before.

He was not, however, prepared for the story young Lady Rochford now told him. He was violently angry. Had it not been from respect for his mistress, he might have given vent openly to that raging fury inside him. But out of deference to her, for he knew her to be genuinely fond of his Nellie and a wonderful mistress to all the servants, he managed somehow to control himself.

"So now you know what happened," Willow said gently, "and what is soon to happen as a consequence. Nellie intended to run away from Rochford before the truth was realized—in order to protect your position here, Harry. That should give you some idea as to the extent to her affection for you, since it is easy to imagine what future would lie ahead of *her* if she followed such a plan. Now I need to know how deep is *your* affection for her. Would you still consider marriage to her, knowing that none of this is her fault?"

"I don't know, Milady," Harry cried hoarsely. "I love Nellie—very much. I never wanted no other woman for my wife. But I don't see as how I could live with it—the baby, I mean. I could forgive Nellie, seeing as how it was none of it her fault, poor girl. But I don't know as I could ever look at that child when it was born without hating it with all my guts every time I thought of . . . of its father."

"I understand," Willow said quietly, nervously aware of the violence beneath the surface of the man's respectful tones. "Now it is a question of what is to be done next. But first I must have your word that you yourself will do nothing for the time being—*nothing at all*."

Harry struggled with his bitterness.

"I cannot give you my promise, Milady, much as I'd like to. I couldn't be sure as I'd keep it if I were to come face to face right now with Mr. Francis—"

"I understand your feelings," Willow interrupted. "But if you will make me that promise, Harry, I in return will give you my word that Mr. Francis will be punished . . . perhaps not for this—this outrage, but for another. Please believe me when I say that I know of other circumstances to his discredit which I *can* prove. And I will not now hesitate to reveal them, I assure you."

Harry was silent as his mind raced. He had a very good idea of the circumstances to which young Lady Rochford was referring. He had been the one to carry the stolen Gainsborough out of the house; and although outwardly he was supposed neither to hear nor to see anything that took place among his employers, he had kept his ears open while he went about his duties or stood impassively at attention within a room awaiting a call upon his services.

There had been so many occasions when he, as a junior footman, had been bowled over by what went on within the walls of this great house—more especially in the days when the young gentlemen had been growing up—before Mr. Rowell had brought his young wife home from America. They'd entertained loose women in their rooms; drunk themselves into a stupor; even had a naked belly dancer from Egypt performing on the dining room table while Harry served champagne. Mr. Rowell and Mr. Pelham had been the worst. Then there was Mr. Rupert's goings-on . . . he knew about that, too, poor miserable young devil. And not least, he'd been well within earshot the night Mr. Rowell let his fancy bit attend the Rochford Christmas Ball and humiliate his poor wife in front of all the guests. . . .

"Harry I am waiting for your promise!"

Willow's soft, persuasive voice penetrated his thoughts.

"Very well, Milady, provided I have your word Mr. Francis will pay a proper price."

Toby was aghast when half an hour later, Willow related these events to him before asking his advice.

"I don't see how you can keep *this* from Rowell," he said anxiously. "What a terrible mess, Willow. Poor Nellie. Poor Harry, too. As for Francis—I agree absolutely that he cannot be allowed to escape punishment this time. I suppose you can prove to Rowell that he stole the painting?"

"Without any difficulty," Willow replied. "I have receipts from the gallery where I bought back the Gainsborough—and Francis knows it."

"So we are left with the problem of Nellie," Toby said. "I cannot tell you how sorry I am."

Willow smiled.

"Thank you for not doubting Nellie, Toby. I knew I could count upon your understanding. It has just now occurred to me that Nellie and I are about to leave for France; Silvie will do anything I ask of her, and I could perhaps leave Nellie with her until the baby is born. Afterwards . . ."

"The child could be found a foster home," Toby broke in. "There may even be a family who would adopt it if we could make some financial provision for it. How long before it is born?"

Willow calculated the months. It was September of last year that Nellie was supposed to have "fallen downstairs and injured herself."

"It must be due in three months' time," she said, adding: "That is roughly when Doctor Forbes calculates my baby will be born. My poor Nellie! To think that she will have to endure the pain of childbirth without the pleasure of having a baby to compensate her afterwards. She feels as Harry does, Toby—that she would always hate it. Neither of them even wanted children of their own."

"Francis deserves the very worst punishment," Toby said angrily. "I am ashamed to think that he is my brother. He has always been a rotten apple in the barrel. I blame Grandmère to some extent for spoiling him so terribly when he was young. He never learned that he must be punished for his misdemeanors and as a consequence, he has never had any true understanding of right and wrong. It is the very opposite to the treatment she meted out to Rupert. He was criticized and denigrated frequently without just cause. One cannot be surprised that he now dislikes or, at least, mistrusts all women."

Willow sighed, her eyes thoughtful. Toby had never before spoken on this subject, yet he had clearly given it deep thought.

"And how do you assess Rowell's upbringing by Grandmère?" she asked quietly.

"Rowell might have been very different if he had had the softening influence of a mother's love," Toby replied without hesitation. "As it was, Grandmère raised him with one thought only in mind: that he was the heir to Rochford and that he must be responsible for the safe continuation of the line. Love was not part of that curriculum, and I doubt if Rowell has the capacity to love any person—only this house and all it stands for."

"Then you do not think he still loves Georgina Grey?" Toby shook his head.

"I honestly don't think so, Willow. He finds her attractive—she appeals to that basic need in all men. But I do not think it has ever been more than passion. I suspect that in a strange kind of way he has come closer to loving you than anyone else in the world."

"*You* can say that—knowing all that has happened between Rowell and me?" Willow cried, her eyes bitter.

Toby nodded.

"It may not be the kind of love *you* are capable of feeling, Willow—or I. But in his own way, I think Rowell respects you; and that he is grateful to you for helping him to preserve Rochford. He may not even know it consciously—but I believe he depends a great deal upon you."

Willow walked over to the window and looked down into the garden with unseeing eyes.

"I have thought many times of leaving him—of asking him for a divorce. Oh, I know how great the scandal would be; the disgrace that would follow. I know, too, that life might be very hard for me. But somehow even that seemed better than sharing myself with a husband who I know has a mistress and yet who still claims my body. Do I shock you, Toby?"

Toby's eyes revealed his pain, but he was staring down at his papers and she had no knowledge of it.

"I think I understand your feelings," he said. "It cannot be easy for a woman to continue her marital duty to her husband when there is no true affection between them—or that affection has died. But you are carrying Rowell's child, Willow, and it is perhaps best not to think such thoughts. You may feel very different after the birth of your baby."

Privately, Willow doubted it, but she knew this was not the time to be considering her own unhappiness. First she must try to put Nellie's life in order.

"What is to be done about Francis?" she asked anxiously. "I have given Harry my word that he will not go unpunished, but with Rowell away—"

"With Rowell away, I am head of the household," Toby

interrupted. "Will you permit me to arrange matters with Grandmère, Willow?"

Willow hid her surprise. Toby was unfailingly polite to the old lady, but such verbal exchanges as they made were no more than pleasantries, and as far as Willow was aware, Toby preferred to keep a cool distance between them. But perhaps for the very reason that he did so seldom involve himself in family affairs, Grandmère would now pay attention to him.

"Will you speak to her then, Toby?" she said gratefully, "although I do not want her to know poor Nellie is pregnant. No one must know, not even Rowell. If we are to pursue our plan to have Nellie's baby adopted in France, it is best that we should remain the only ones who are aware she is carrying Francis' child."

Toby nodded. He was not looking forward to his proposed encounter with his grandmother, but for once, his bitter anger at his younger brother sustained him in his determination to see justice done.

As Willow had suspected, Grandmère was astonished when Toby demanded a private interview with her at which not even Aunt Milly was to be present. Concealing her surprise, Lady Rochford sent Aunt Milly upon an errand and invited Toby to be seated. She herself was at her bureau where she had been writing letters—an occupation that usually took most of her mornings. She laid down her pen and turned to face Toby as he pulled up a chair near her.

"Since Rowell is absent and likely to be so for some weeks," he said quietly, "I have taken it upon myself to apprise you of a family matter which must be dealt with at once. It concerns Francis!"

Grandmère's small black eyes narrowed. Not only the serious expression on Toby's face, but her instinct warned her that her favorite grandson was involved in a matter not to his credit.

"Well?" she asked sharply. "You do not need to mince words with me, Toby. What is amiss?"

Despite himself, Toby felt a moment's admiration for the old lady. Whatever else she lacked, it was not courage to face difficulties.

"It has just come to my knowledge—and Willow's— that Francis raped Willow's maid, Nellie Sinclair," he said bluntly. "He had attempted to do so once before, although you were not made aware of it, Grandmère. Rowell reprimanded Francis on that occasion and told him that if it ever happened again, he would send him away from Rochford. Apparently the threat was not sufficient to deter him."

Not even Toby noticed the slight trembling of the old lady's hands, for she quickly concealed them beneath her shawl.

"You use the word 'rape' ill-advisedly, I think," she said caustically. "I do not doubt the girl was willing enough!"

"Then I fear you are wrong, Grandmère, if you will forgive my contradicting you. The girl was a virgin and engaged to the footman, Harold Stevens. Francis forced himself upon her against her will. I am afraid rape is the only appropriate description for his actions."

Grandmère's thin brows raised in momentary surprise. This particular grandson was somewhat of an enigma to her. She had known for many years that she could usually impose her will upon Rowell, that she could dominate Rupert. Pelham was invariably too easygoing to be controversial, and she had always been able to bribe Francis. But Toby, since he had left university, had somehow managed to set himself apart from the rest of the family. He was withdrawn—and a stranger to her. But of late she had sensed his inner strength and judging it equal to her own, she doubted if she could best him in any opposition of their wills.

"The girl is only one of the maids," she said uneasily. "And besides, I imagine we have only her word for what happened? She could be lying."

Toby was prepared for her argument.

"There is no doubt whatever about the truth of her allegations, Grandmère. The only doubt lies in what is to be done about Francis."

"Done about him?" Grandmère repeated, her eyes now flashing. "You are not suggesting that he be forced to leave his home because of this—this transgression with a mere servant?"

Toby remained calm.

"No, I am not suggesting it, Grandmère. *I am insisting upon it.* I think you are overlooking the fact that Rochford is Willow's home, too—and she is quite adamant in her determination that her servants should be safe beneath her roof. Moreover, Nellie is her personal maid, as you know. I think you should have no doubt upon the matter—if Francis remains here unpunished, Willow will leave—and I do not think Rowell would welcome *that* state of affairs!"

Toby's quiet, level tones were having their effect far more certainly than had he shouted or shown his anger.

"We will wait until Rowell returns, and he can decide what is to be done," Grandmère began, but once again Toby interrupted her.

"No, Grandmère, I am afraid it cannot wait so long. Francis' future must be decided before Willow goes to France." Momentarily, his voice softened. "I know you will miss Francis, but it is as much for his own good as for the harmony of the household. It is time he learned he cannot go through life without any consideration for others. A year or two in one of the Colonies would do him no harm. I believe Sir John Barratt's younger brother emigrated to Australia. I dare say it would be possible to arrange for Francis to be sent out to assist him—he owns a sheep farm there, Sir John told me."

"A sheep farm!" Grandmère muttered, her face white with shock. "That is no fit place for Francis."

"On the contrary, Grandmère, since he behaves like an animal, it would do him no harm to have to learn a little farming. With your agreement, I will ride over to the Barratts' house this afternoon and speak to Sir John—although naturally, I will not give him the true reasons why we feel it would be good for Francis to go to Australia."

"First I would like to speak to Francis," Grandmère prevaricated. But Toby would not be intimidated by her furious stare or the forcefulness of her tone.

"Since you are unlikely to be told the truth by Francis, there is little point in discussing events with him," he said with equal firmness. "I am afraid it is too late now, Grandmère, for you to intervene on his behalf. He has behaved disgracefully, and there is no excusing him. I am sure you would not want this whole unfortunate affair made public, but unless Francis is sent away, I myself will not hesitate to make the truth known. I am sure you do not wish that the Rochford good name should be brought into disrepute?"

Beneath such a threat, Grandmère visibly wilted, although she continued to protest that Toby was being unreasonable and far too harsh. She tried alternative tactics.

"I am an old woman, Toby. I might not live to see Francis' return and that would break my heart," she said pathetically.

Toby concealed a smile.

"I have no doubt whatever that you will live at least until you are ninety," he said. "And you do have other grandchildren to console you, Grandmère. You will have to devote your attentions to us instead."

Grandmère did not go downstairs for luncheon. Aunt Milly reported that she was having one of her "turns" and had retired to bed. Willow looked anxiously at Toby, but he smiled reassuringly.

"She is not ill," he told her in a tone of voice too low for Aunt Milly to overhear him. "She is just sulking because she has not been able to have her own way. Don't worry any more, Willow. I will see Sir John this afternoon and hopefully we shall have Francis on his way before the month is out."

Greatly relieved that Toby had been able to convince Grandmère with so little trouble, Willow could now concentrate her thoughts upon the immediate problem of Nellie's condition. At least, she thought, she could count upon Silvie's help. She waited with increasing impatience for April to come.

Silvie was as eagerly awaiting Willow's arrival in France. After spending a night in Silvie's house in Paris, they boarded the transcontinental train next day for the two-hour journey to her country house situated between Épernay and Châlons-sur-Marne on the eastern slopes of the Côte des Blancs.

As the train followed the course of the River Marne, Silvie explained a little history of the Château d'Orbais. It had once been the home of one of the many wealthy wine-growers whose vineyards covered the surrounding countryside, she said, pointing out to Willow the brilliant sea-green of the new spring growth of vine leaves stretching as far as the eye could see. Later in the year, she explained, these bushes would produce the grapes from which the delicious white wine of the Côte des Blancs was made.

"I spent a great deal of my childhood here," Silvie told her, "and I adore the place. Behind the Château is the Côte des Blancs itself, six hundred feet high, and below, the plain is covered with golden corn and ablaze throughout the summer with poppies, cornflowers and marguerites. With your love of Nature, *chérie,* you will appreciate my home."

They were the only passengers to alight at the little station in Épernay, where they found Cousin Lucienne's coachman waiting with the barouche to drive them the seven kilometers to the Château.

The sun was shining warmly down upon them as they rolled slowly along the country road and turned into the drive between two impressive brick columns. The pair of beautiful, wrought-iron gates stood open as the coachman turned the horses into the shady avenue of poplar trees. The rustling of the leaves in the slight breeze, the song of the birds concealed in the foliage, and the gentle scrunching of the carriage wheels on the gravel were sounds that imprinted themselves on Willow's mind as she felt herself relaxing in pleasure against the soft upholstery of the barouche.

At the end of the mile-long avenue stood the Château d'Orbais. Four stories high with a grey slate roof from which dormer windows protruded, the Château was impressive and very French, Willow decided, as her eyes took in the beautifully kept lawns and flowerbeds surrounding the house.

At Silvie's instruction, the coachman drove the carriage round to the rear of the Château, where he pulled the horses to a halt in a large courtyard covered with pale ochre gravel. The three sides of the courtyard that were not part of the house itself were composed of the old wine cellars, few of which were any longer in use, Silvie explained as a footman came running out from the Château to help them alight from the carriage.

Willow fell instantly in love with the interior of the house. The rooms were large and elegant with french windows opening onto the immaculately kept garden. Silvie herself had refurnished most of the rooms with Louis XIV and XV period furniture.

"When my wealthy husband died, poor man, he made it possible for me to indulge my extravagant taste for décor," she told Willow with a smile.

Many of the walls were covered in silk panels and the dining room walls were covered in tapestries from the town of Beauvais, north of Paris, where they were made. A large circular staircase led from the spacious hall to the landing where Silvie conducted Willow to her room.

It seemed to Willow that everywhere in the Château d'Orbais was light, dainty, softly feminine—in total contrast to the somewhat somber dark Jacobean furniture oak paneling of Rochford Manor. Rose colored silk curtains hung either side of the white shutters that had been drawn across the casements of her room to keep out the sunshine. Silvie at once opened them to let in a flood of golden light. The same rose color of the curtains was repeated in the hangings of the four-poster bed; and a huge vase of roses stood on a table nearby.

One of Silvie's maids arrived to conduct Nellie to her room in the attic, and Willow was left alone with Silvie. The two young women smiled at one another as they sat down on the satin-covered chaise longue by the window.

"I am so glad you persuaded me to come and stay here with you," Willow said. "It is all so beautiful, Silvie—and peaceful."

"You are not too tired from the journey?" Silvie asked anxiously, for Willow had now been traveling for almost two days.

Willow shook her head.

"I am feeling surprisingly well," she said, smiling. "If it were not for Nellie's unhappiness, I would be perfectly content." Her smile quickly faded as quietly she related to Silvie the sordid details resulting in Nellie's condition.

"Is there any possibility, dearest Silvie, of Nellie being permitted to remain here until the baby is born?" she asked anxiously.

"Think no more about it, *chérie*," Silvie replied with total equanimity. "You should know without my telling you that I will assist in any way I can. Nothing matters but that you are here and we can enjoy ourselves together."

Silvie's dark hazel eyes sparkled with sudden amusement.

"I would have been *très ennuyer* without your company. I have ended my *affaire* with Pierre and am not yet ready for another lover. I need time to recoup my emotional energies. I, too, need a rest. *Les affaires du coeur* can be very exhausting, and Pierre was becoming far too possessive. I, as you know, must have freedom, else I cannot breathe. If ever I were to marry again, my husband would have to agree that I should live my life entirely as I please and not as an extension of himself. It is strange, is it not, how men do not believe you really love them unless you are prepared to submerge your own identity in theirs?"

Such discussions on life, love, and men took place frequently while the two women went for gentle walks or rode out in the carriage enjoying the spring sunshine. Very occasionally, they paid calls upon Silvie's neighbors. But they avoided the formality of regular invitations, Willow's condition providing an excellent excuse to set aside the At Homes and receptions which Silvie would normally have attended.

Nellie, too, seemed to benefit from the quiet country life. She was befriended by Silvie's enormously fat cook, Marie, who was delighted to have two females, both *enceinte,* requiring her nourishing meals.

Silvie made discreet inquiries in outlying districts about the possibility of finding a foster home for Nellie's baby. Unfortunately, most of the farmers' wives already had huge families of their own and, following an epidemic of typhus the previous year, they did not want any further calls upon their time.

"There is at worst an orphanage not too far from here on the far side of Épernay," Silvie told Willow. "It is run by nuns, and Father Mattieu tells me that in certain circumstances—which I do not doubt means if adequate funds are donated—they will take small babies, athough they usually only take in girls of three years or over."

Willow was uneasy about such a solution.

"I cannot explain why the very idea of an orphanage is abhorrent to me," she said, "no matter how well run the establishment might be. A child needs parents, a home. It needs to be loved."

Silvie shrugged.

"All the same, it is not always possible in this life for

children to have such needs satisfied. Shall we take a drive to the convent tomorrow, dearest Willow? It could do no harm to look at the place. If we find it agreeable, we can call upon the nuns."

It was less than an hour's drive to the Convent du Coeur Sanglant. But they went no farther than the lodge gates. The sight of the great grey stone buildings, the high walls, and massive iron gates locked against intruders—or those wishing to escape, Willow suggested—was more than she could bear.

"Let's go home, Silvie," she said, shivering despite the warmth of the afternoon sun. "I do not think I could bring myself to suggest to Nellie that she leave her baby here— or at least, only as a *very* last resort."

Silvie agreed.

"It is certainly not very prepossessing," she said as she ordered her coachman to drive home. "It has the air of a prison."

There was very little traffic in the quiet country lanes, and neither Silvie nor Willow saw need to caution the coachman to drive more slowly. The horses were anxious to return to their stables and were making good pace in the direction of Épernay when suddenly, as they rounded a bend in the lane, they came upon an overturned farm cart. Willow barely had time to glimpse the frightened face of the farmer before their own horses reared up in fright and the barouche turned turtle, flinging her onto the hard surface of the road.

She felt only a moment of pain before she lost consciousness. When her senses returned, it was to find Silvie, white-faced, bending over her. Behind her stood their coachman and the farmer, staring at her with scarlet sweating faces comic in their expressions of anxiety.

"Are you all right, *chérie? Mon Dieux, quel désastre!*" Silvie cried.

Slowly Willow sat up and, feeling no pain, smiled tremulously at Silvie.

"I am quite all right, I assure you," she said. "I do not think I have suffered anything worse than a bruise or two."

The coachman assisting, she stood up. Her head was swimming, but she felt no other ill effects. Within half an hour, the cart and the barouche had been righted. The anxious farmer was sent on his way with reassurances, and Willow, none the worse for the accident, had regained her color and her composure.

"Nonetheless, we shall visit Monsieur le Docteur tomorrow," Silvie said, frowning, as she helped Willow back into the barouche. "Such a fall cannot be good for you so near your time."

Silvie's local doctor, a delightful tubby little man by the name of Gousse, was instantly reassuring. He could, he said, hear the baby's heartbeat through his stethoscope and even permitted Silvie to put it to her ear so that she, too, could feel reassured.

"Nevertheless, it would be as well to take things very quietly for a day or two," he cautioned Willow, patting her shoulder paternally. "One cannot be too careful, can one, my dear lady?"

Although Willow suffered no after-effects other than slight bruising of her arm and leg where she had hit the ground, Silvie suggested wickedly that they might pretend otherwise and so delay Willow's return home.

"I would dearly love to prolong your visit, *chérie*," she said, her eyes twinkling mischievously, "so let us write to Rowell and tell him the doctor thinks it best you remain in bed for a while longer."

"I am certainly in no hurry to leave," Willow admitted, smiling.

Best pleased of all by this little ruse was Nellie. As her time was approaching, she was becoming less and less willing to bring Francis' child into the world. Both Willow and Silvie were aware of her growing need for reassurance. She was now requesting that they should make arrangements with Father Mattieu to have her baby removed immediately after its birth and placed in the Convent du Coeur Sanglant. She would not be put off by Willow's description of the orphanage, and it was obvious to her mistress that Nellie would never feel any natural love for this offspring of her raping.

"One can hardly blame her!" Silvie said dryly. "Leave the matter to me, Willow, since it seems to upset you so. I will arrange it all."

Perhaps fortunately, Cousin Lucienne was not well enough to leave her bed and she was therefore unaware of the conspiracies being discussed beneath her roof. Doc-

tor Gousse had told Silvie that she must prepare herself
for the worst regarding her mother's condition.

"She is not a young woman, Baronin von Senden," he
said, "and at her age, I cannot hold out much hope of a
full recovery from the tuberculosis afflicting her. She has
refused to go to a sanatorium in the mountains where
there might have been a possibility of a cure. She says she
would prefer to die in her own bed. I do not know if you
yourself wish to add your persuasions to mine?"

Silvie decided against it. She knew how exacting her
mother could be and how she would hate the strange surroundings of the sanatorium.

"Here at least she has her own servants, her own nurse,
her own belongings around her," she told the doctor. "If
such is her wish, then I must allow her to die here where
she is at peace."

The château was large enough for each of the two fac-
tions beneath its roof to remain unaffected by the other.
While the old lady drew nearer to death, Willow and Nellie came nearer to the time when they would bring new
lives into the world. Now in daily attendance upon Silvie's
mother, Doctor Gousse was on hand to keep a watchful
eye upon Willow. He became increasingly anxious about
her condition and confessed to Silvie that he was afraid
that, after all, some damage may have occurred to Willow's baby when she had fallen from the carriage.

"I cannot hear the heartbeat very clearly," he said. "I
fear we must face the possibility that all is not well with
the child. The Baroness should not travel home next
week. The journey might precipitate a disaster."

"Shall I so inform her, Monsieur le Docteur?" Silvie
asked anxiously.

"It could increase the danger if the mother herself is
troubled," Doctor Gousse vouchsafed. "Can we avoid any
details by saying no more than that I am of the opinion
she should rest this last month? Even if all were well, I
could not recommend that she should undertake a long
journey at eight months."

Rowell had by now returned from a very pleasant trip
to the south of France. He was far from pleased when he
received Silvie's telegram informing him that the doctor
had advised Willow to remain at the château until after
the child's birth. But resigned to doing his duty, he tele-

graphed a reply saying that he would leave next day for France. He was greatly relieved when Silvie responded with a second telegram telling him that his arrival so long before the baby was due might cause Willow to suspect something serious was wrong. "We do not wish to alarm her," she added truthfully.

"Please advise me as soon as the birth is imminent," Rowell answered, delighted that he could postpone his visit. Now, in the month of May, he could at least enjoy the start of the Season in London before duty demanded a curtailment of his pleasures.

Willow was feeling far from well. She received with relief the news from Silvie that Rowell had postponed his arrival. She was plagued by a continuous dull pain in her lower abdomen that even Doctor Gousse's sedatives could not ease. Silvie tried to remain cheerful, talking as if she believed all was well, adding to this illusion by going out to buy a layette for the baby.

"What it does not require will do for Nellie's child," she told Willow brightly as she opened box after box of nursery paraphernalia.

But Doctor Gousse was right in his suspicion that all was not well with Willow's baby. On the evening of June 3rd, she went into labor and four hours later, she gave birth to a still-born son.

With tears in her eyes, Silvie broke the news to the exhausted mother. Smoothing the damp hair away from Willow's forehead, she tried to offer comfort, knowing that nothing could make up for this terrible disappointment.

Dry-eyed, Willow lay back against her pillows, her grief and sense of loss too great for tears.

"Perhaps God has been revenged upon me because in the beginning I said I did not want this baby," she said in a small, tortured voice. "I thought I could not love it because it was Rowell's child. But then—Silvie, the day I felt it move inside me, I knew I did want it. More than anything else in the world, I wanted another child, a girl perhaps, to replace Oliver when he goes off to boarding school. Oh, Silvie . . . what am I to do?"

She held out her empty arms in mute appeal, knowing as did Silvie holding her, that there was no remedy. Her baby son was dead.

Chapter Nineteen

June–July 1903

IN THE ATTIC ROOM HIGH ABOVE WILLOW'S BEDROOM, Doctor Gousse was once more involved in bringing a child into the world. As he and the midwife struggled with the writhing woman on the bed, he wondered if this labor, too, was going to end in disaster. He knew already that the unhappy woman had been raped—though not by whom—and that she dreaded the thought of bearing this child. It was not surprising, therefore, that she fought so furiously against its birth. He understood that to Nellie, it must be agonizingly reminiscent of the occasion of its conception. The pain was as cruel, as violent, as unrelenting.

It was nine hours before the midwife offered the wailing baby to its exhausted mother. Nellie turned her face away, her eyes showing her revulsion to it—the living result of her shame.

"We'll try again after she has had a sleep," Doctor Gousse said as the midwife placed the baby girl in the wooden cradle at the foot of the bed. "If it continues to cry, you can give the child a spoonful or two of sugared water."

Wearily, he went downstairs to report the difficulty to Silvie.

"I would be grateful, Madame, if you will do what you can to persuade the young woman to nurse her baby," he said. "But I fear it will not be easy. The child is healthy, *grâce à Dieu*, but I do not like to guess how long she will survive without food."

Silvie was in two minds whether or not to relay this latest misfortune to Willow. By not it was nearly twenty-four hours since Willow had given birth to her stillborn son, and the midwife was talking anxiously about the possibility that she might contract milk fever.

Willow's grief was total. She lay quietly, her eyes

closed, refusing to talk even to Silvie, silently resigned to the midwife's ministrations, uncomplaining, unresisting.

"It is not good for her to contain her grief," the doctor said anxiously. "At least that poor young woman upstairs gives way to her tears!"

"While the poor little mite she birthed starves to death," said the midwife bitterly, for she had a natural love for her tiny charges.

It was Marie, the cook, who provided Silvie with a solution which might otherwise never have occurred to her.

"One mother ill because she has too much milk and no infant to feed; another so sick in her head that she cannot bear to feed her child. It is God's will, Madame la Baronne, that the living baby must be given to Milady to feed," the servant said with a peasant's simple practicality.

Shocked, Silvie informed the woman that such a suggestion was most improper; that it might have been different if Willow's maid were required to succor her mistress' child.

"A lady cannot be asked to wet-nurse her maid's baby, Marie," she said firmly.

Nevertheless, Nellie's baby was slowly starving to death. It was unable to stomach the cow's milk offered by the midwife, and the doctor's inquiries in the neighborhood for a suitable wet-nurse from among the farmers' wives had so far failed.

"There are indeed several women who *have* given birth recently," he told Silvie, "but I dare not give the child to any of them, for they all suffered last year from an infection not unlike typhoid. Their own children may be immune, but this baby would not have the same immunity."

Silvie decided to consult Willow. Where all else had failed, this unhappy news had the effect of stirring her to speech.

"Why ask me what is to be done?" she said bitterly. "Of course I am sorry for Nellie . . . and for the baby . . . but perhaps if it does die it is all for the best since she does not love it."

Until then, Silvie had been entirely sympathetic and gentle with her bereaved friend. But now she was angered beyond caution.

"How can you say that, *chérie?*" she asked accusingly, "You, of all people. Is the gift of life for another so unimportant to you that you can grieve only at *your* loss? I had not thought you so unfeeling!"

Willow's expression changed. She stared at Silvie in sudden shame.

"I do not mean to be cruel," she said. "But in all honesty I cannot bring myself to feel sorrow for anyone but myself, however selfish that may sound. In any event, Silvie, there is nothing I can do lying here in my bed."

Silvie flushed in sudden excitement.

"You could give the baby a chance of life," she said urgently. "You could feed her, Willow, until a wet-nurse can be found . . ."

Willow looked deeply shocked.

"Nellie must be made to feed it herself," she said quickly.

"She cannot—even if she would," Silvie said flatly. "The distress of her ordeal has been too much for her and she has no milk. She will not even see the child. The cradle has had to be removed from her room for fear she might harm the baby."

Willow's face softened.

"My poor Nellie," she murmured.

"Nellie will recover!" Silvie said sharply. "The baby will not—unless *you* help, Willow. Is it so much to ask? You cannot really wish its death for no better reason than that *your* child died."

Willow hesitated before replying, her hesitation long enough to let the astute Silvie know that she had said enough for the time being.

"Think about it for a while, Willow, *ma chérie.* I will come to see you later and you can tell me then how you have decided."

An hour later, with great care, Silvie supervised the midwife while she washed and dressed the baby in fresh clothing. The redness of birth had gone from the tiny girl's face and her skin was a delicate white, her eyes a deep blue-grey seeming far too large in so small a face. Her head was covered by a crown of soft, light brown hair. She was remarkably beautiful.

"Now give her to me," Silvie ordered the midwife, her heart beating nervously as she took the child. "And see that no one disturbs us for at least half an hour. Do you understand?"

Willow was sleeping when Silvie went over to the bedside carrying the child. She called her softly. Momentarily unaware of her surroundings, Willow opened her eyes. Seeing the tiny infant in Silvie's arms, instinctively she lifted her own to receive it. By the time she was fully awake, the baby was in her possession.

"No!" she whispered. "No, Silvie, I don't want it. I don't want this baby. I want my own—" Tears filled her eyes as the infant nuzzled against her.

The baby's instinct was stronger even than Silvie had imagined. Feeling for the first time the warmth and softness of a woman's breasts, the tiny girl turned her face toward the source of life, her little mouth seeking in helpless hunger for the nourishment she needed.

Tears coursed down Willow's cheeks. She looked helplessly from Silvie to the baby and then wordlessly opened the buttons of her nightgown. When she had nursed little Oliver, she had had some difficulty in guiding her swollen nipple into his mouth. It had taken some while before he had become accustomed to feeding from her. But this baby seemed to need no help, as without her assistance, the hungry little mouth found what it had been searching for.

Silvie took pains to hide her satisfaction as Willow became totally absorbed in her task. She walked away and sat in the chair by the window, silent, thoughtful, as Willow eased herself into a more upright position. It was ten minutes before anyone spoke. Then, as Willow removed the baby to her other breast, she said quietly:

"Just this once, you understand, Silvie. I cannot feed the child again."

Silvie made no protest, for Willow's words belied her obvious absorption in her task.

"I understand," she said. "But isn't it a pretty baby, Willow? She reminds me so much of little Oliver. His hair was just that color, was it not? I wonder what *he* would have to say about it if he were here. The child is truly related to him, of course."

Willow nodded, only half her attention on Silvie's remarks. It was quiet in the room, and for the first time since the night she had gone into labor, there was an atmosphere of peace. It was as if she, Silvie, and the baby were cocooned in a world of their own.

"Oliver will be disappointed when I have to tell him there will be no brother or sister after all," she murmured. "I promised him that I would present him with one or the other soon after I returned from France."

"I dare say Rowell may have told him that you would now be bringing a brother or sister back from France," Silvie said casually. "Or perhaps Toby told him. By the way, Willow, there is a letter from Toby. At least, I think it may be from him since the envelope is not addressed in Rowell's writing. Do you not agree that I must now telegraph Rowell? We cannot delay doing so any longer."

Willow looked at her anxiously.

"Oh, no, Silvie, not just yet. A day or two longer will not matter. You know I do not want him here. I need first to . . . to adjust myself. I . . . I don't want to see him yet."

"Very well, we'll wait another day or two," Silvie said, pleased that the conversation had gone as she had hoped. Both she and the doctor had been deeply concerned by Willow's state of mind. Doctor Gousse had spoken only yesterday of the dangers of melancholia threatening Willow as a consequence of the tragic event of her child's death. He was the more concerned because she had already lost one child before this and had also had a miscarriage.

"It is all too easy for women of sensitivity to begin to feel themselves to blame when such a pattern is repeated," he explained to Silvie. "I have known it lead to suicide on one unhappy occasion, and we must take all precautions."

But Willow did not look in the least suicidal at the moment. Silvie thought as she watched her remove the now sleeping child and rock her gently in her arms. On her face was a look of complete tranquility.

"Give the baby to me," Silvie said, going quickly to the bedside. "You've done your duty, Willow, and I don't expect more of you. I am grateful for your assistance."

She was fully aware of the ill-concealed reluctance with which Willow handed the baby back to her. Deliberately, Silvie let its head fall backwards over her arm.

"Do be careful, Silvie," Willow cried instinctively. "Babies have no neck muscles at this age—you must support the head—"

Pretending indifference, Silvie left the room. She returned the child to its cot and went at once to talk to the doctor.

"You may consider my plan immoral when I explain it, Doctor Gousse," she told him quietly. "But I want you to hear me out. I may speak in the certainty that you will never repeat our conversation?"

"It is as if you were in the confessional, Madame la Baronne," said the man promptly. He was nevertheless deeply shocked when Silvie told him that it was her intention to persuade the English Milady to take her maid's baby and bring it up as her own.

"Naturally, Doctor Gousse, I would only encourage this if the Baroness really wishes it. But I think she will. She has a maternal instinct that overrides all others. She wanted her own baby very much and everyone in her family is expecting her to return to England with a child. Nellie's baby could be an excellent substitute."

"But it is the child of her *servant* . . ." the doctor muttered uneasily. "You cannot expect the Baroness to bring it up as her own?"

Silvie drew a deep breath.

"I am as aware of the class differences as you are, Doctor. But *you* do not know who is the father of the child, and I do. I can assure you that this infant has as much right to be brought up as a lady of good birth as—as any other gentleman's bastard."

"But the maid—the real mother," the doctor managed to gasp. "What of her?"

"We will tell her her child died. Nellie will not care—in fact such news would come as a relief to her. She has a fiancé in England waiting to marry her. He, too, will be relieved."

"But her husband—Milady's husband," the doctor stuttered.

"He might also be relieved!" Silvie said quietly.

She was not in the least dismayed by the ease with which she was now misleading the kindly old doctor. Her inference, unmistakably, had been that Rowell was the father of Nellie's baby—a possibility far from improbable —as the doctor would very well know. His only surprise would lie in the fact that Willow was willing to adopt her husband's bastard. But then Willow was not French, and with luck the doctor would shrug off this strange behavior as part of the craziness of the English character.

"Consider my plan carefully, I beg you, Doctor Gousse," Silvie said. "Perhaps it will not be acceptable to the Baroness. I will speak to you again when I have ascertained her feelings."

She realized the necessity for Willow really to want this baby if her plan was to have any beneficial purpose. Willow was still weak after childbirth, and it was important to test her true feelings. Silvie decided to withhold the baby from her when the time for a further feed approached. She sat beside the bed pretending not to notice how often Willow's glance went toward the ormulu clock on the mantelshelf; or how often her eyes turned toward the door when she heard the sound of footsteps. At last, Willow could bear the uncertainty no longer.

"The baby . . ." she said tentatively. "Is she all right? Is she being fed?"

"As far as I know," Silvie replied, deliberately vague. "I think the midwife is attempting to feed her spoonfuls of cow's milk. Maybe the child will be able to digest it this time. On the last occasion she was very sick . . ."

For a few minutes, there was no sound in the room other than the ticking of the clock. Then Willow said:

"There is no question now of the baby . . . dying?"

"I really don't know, Willow. Probably not! But then I suppose if it were to die, it could be all for the best in the long run as you said. After all, what kind of future awaits it in that terrible orphanage?"

At first Silvie could not understand Willow, who began to speak in a deep, husky voice. Then she heard her words, rasped by tears:

"I cannot let it die, Silvie. Please tell the midwife to bring the child to me!"

Steeling her heart, Silvie remained seated.

"But, Willow," she argued, "if you continue to feed it regularly, it could become accustomed to you and then—"

"Bring her to me!" Willow cried fiercely. She pulled back the bedclothes and pointed to her breasts. "I need that baby every bit as much as she needs me!" she cried. "I cannot lie here like this while she struggles for life somewhere else in the house. Bring her to me, Silvie, I beg you."

Silvie needed no second bidding. When she returned with the child, the look of anxiety on Willow's face was enough to convince her as to the future. Her mind resolved, she left Willow alone with the baby and went upstairs to the attic. Nellie was lying with her face to the wall, the tray of food beside her untouched.

"Nellie," Silvie said, her voice sharp but not unkind, "there is no need for you to hide your face any longer. Your baby is dead. Do you understand me? You can get up as soon as you are strong enough and go about your normal duties as if nothing had happened. Your child no longer exists. *You have no baby now.*"

Slowly, Nellie turned toward her visitor, a look of bewilderment on her tortured face.

"Dead," she echoed. "The baby died?"

"I am afraid so," Silvie said firmly. "You had a difficult birthing, Nellie, and although the doctor tried, he couldn't save it. So you must forget all about it. It is as if you never had a child. You must think of your mistress now. She is still very weak after the birth of her little girl and she'll want you near her."

The color was beginning to return to Nellie's cheeks.

"Oh, Madame," she cried, "I'm in ever such a muddle. I thought as how the doctor said the Mistress had had a little boy. But I didn't pay attention, I was that worried. I felt so wicked—not wanting my own baby. Do you think I'm wicked, Madame, being glad and all that it's dead? I couldn't want it, not really, could I?"

"Don't think about it any more, Nellie," Silvie said quietly. "It's all over. Don't even talk about it. No one at Rochford, except your Harry, even knew you were carrying. The Baron didn't, did he? He'll be coming here soon to take you and your mistress home, and I want you well enough to take care of her on the journey. She needs you."

A smile spread over Nellie's homely countenance.

"I'm well enough now, I'm sure," she said. "It was just not wanting to get up and face the world as made me want to stay in bed. But I'm really all right."

"Nevertheless, you are to stay in bed until Doctor Gousse says you may get up," Silvie ordered. She patted Nellie's arm. "I'm glad to hear you are feeling better."

"Oh, Madame, I am that!" Nellie cried. "It's wicked, I

know, to be glad your own child is dead, but I can't pretend otherwise—leastways, not to you, Madame."

So it was resolved—as if indeed it were God's will—Silvie thought as she watched Willow become more and more possessive with her adopted baby. She began to speak to the midwife as if it were her child.

"Isn't it time my baby was fed?" she would ask. Or: "How did my baby sleep last night?"

The doctor looked at Silvie with a certain amount of bewilderment.

"I have to acknowledge that your instincts were right, Madame la Baronne," he said, scratching his head. "Nevertheless, I am far from happy about the deception we shall be practicing upon Baron Rochford. Are you aware that I shall have to falsify the birth certificate and that it is a criminal offense for me to do so?"

"Indeed, I had not considered it," Silvie said truthfully. "Do you think in the circumstances it might be best if we simply forgot the certificate? The Baron will suppose his wife has it in her keeping, and I will tell a little lie to her and say I have it. Between us, it will very conveniently become 'lost.' What do you say, Doctor Gousse?"

"I could still not make my confession on Friday if I am forced to lie to Baron Rochford," the doctor said unhappily.

"Then it is time you took a little holiday, is it not?" Silvie replied smoothly. "It is very pleasant in the south of France at this time of the year. I suggest two or three weeks in Monte Carlo, Doctor Gousse—at my expense, of course. You are in need of a rest."

Doctor Gousse nodded, although his expression remained uneasy.

"But what of the servants, Madame?" he asked anxiously. "It would need but a word from any one of them to your maid . . . to the Baron . . ."

Silvie smiled nonchalantly.

"Was it not you, my dear Doctor Gousse, who warned me about Madame la Baronne's state of mind? I have but to advise the servants that the English Milady is suffering from hallucinations, and that you have intimated it could be harmful to her were anyone to refute her claim that the baby is hers. The maid, Nellie, does not speak a word of French, so communication between her and the servants will in any event be virtually impossible."

With considerable reluctance, not to say apprehension, the doctor was finally persuaded—albeit against his conscience. He did so only because Silvie succeeded in convincing him that her plan was clearly beneficial to everyone concerned.

Nor was Willow easily persuaded.

"I have already practiced one terrible deception upon Rowell over Oliver's birth," she said to Silvie as they walked together around the garden of the château the day before Rowell's expected arrival. She was pushing the wicker perambulator in which the baby was sleeping.

"So then, what is another deception?" Silvie replied. "Must I tell you again, Willow, that the baby *is* a Rochford? Moreover, Rowell is unlikely to concern himself much with a girl. I have heard him say he has no wish for a daughter—only for sons."

"Rowell has been indoctrinated by Grandmère into the belief that the girls of the family are abnormal. At least this will disprove their theory and support Toby's views," Willow remarked thoughtfully.

Silvie nodded.

"If my instincts are right, once they have established the baby's normality they will no longer concern themselves with her. What you must consider, Willow, is that Rowell would never let you keep Francis' child if he knew the truth."

"I could never part with her now. I shall keep her—and call her Alice—after her grandmother," Willow said, her eyes resting lovingly on the sleeping baby. "She is so pretty, is she not, Silvie? I think the name becomes her. Her second name will be Silvie—that is, if you agree."

"You dote upon her, do you not?" Silvie remarked, smiling.

Willow nodded, her eyes serious as she said:

"It is strange, Silvie, but already I am becoming confused as to her real identity. I held my own baby in my arms for so short a while, and now when I look at little Alice feeding at my breast, it is as if I were holding the infant I bore myself. I have to remind myself that she is really—"

"No, do not say it, Willow," Silvie broke in. "You must forget it, as I have. Nellie has no doubt whatever *her* baby is dead and that Alice is your child. Rowell too, will have no doubt—nor Grandmère. Only if *you* have the slightest doubt in your mind that you can love this baby as your own must you reconsider what we are doing. Do you have that doubt, Willow?"

Willow's face softened in tenderness.

"How could I doubt my love for her? She needs me. Last night she cried when I handed her to the midwife. I think she really wanted to stay with me. I am glad the midwife leaves tomorrow. Now I can have little Alice's bassinette in my room."

So the deed was done, Silvie thought, for better or for worse. She had manipulated the lives of three people—Willow's, Nellie's, and the baby's. In time to come, other lives too might be affected. But she could not feel any guilt—only joy at the happiness that was evident. Nellie was up and about again, laughing and singing at her work. She took only a cursory interest in Willow's baby, as she had in little Oliver, and showed no maternal leanings toward it.

Only Rowell showed any degree of displeasure—and that because his wife had borne him a daughter rather than a second son. He paid polite interest in the infant's appearance, agreeing that she was a pretty baby and seemed in excellent health, but he had no real interest in her, as Silvie had guessed. He was anxious to be home.

"You have been away from Rochford over three months, Willow," he remonstrated, "and the servants are getting out of hand. Grandmère is not well enough to deal with them, and they take advantage. Please have Nellie pack your baggage as soon as possible so that we can depart tomorrow."

While her mother was so ill, Silvie could not leave her and return to Paris as she would have wished. She hugged Willow and told her how greatly she would miss her at the Château d'Orbais.

"As I shall miss you, Silvie," Willow said, tears springing to her eyes. "Of course I long to see little Oliver again . . ." and Toby, she thought with a sudden desperate need for the sight of his lopsided, smiling face . . . "but I do so wish you were coming with me, Silvie. You are like my sister now. I cannot tell you how grateful I am . . ."

But Silvie cut short her thanks.

"It is enough for me that you leave happily," she said simply, as she waved goodbye to her visitors from the platform at Épernay.

The train gathered speed and the baby began to cry. It was as if she too were sad at leaving the kind-hearted Frenchwoman who, unknown to her, had given her a new life, a devoted mother.

"Hush, my baby!" Willow crooned as she cradled the child. "We are going home, my little Alice."

Bored with the train journey, Rowell watched Willow, who was annoyingly engrossed in her new offspring. He had considered her behavior little better than a peasant's in her insistence upon overseeing every detail of Oliver's care. But then he was apt to forget his wife's origins, he reflected dourly. Willoughby Tetford, for all his wealth, was a self-made man, and but for his good fortune in investing in the American railroads, would have remained on the level of the lower middle classes.

Nevertheless, the man had managed to produce a daughter with all the outward appearances of a lady of considerable quality, Rowell thought. His wife's gentle refinement both of speech and manner were assets he admitted were over and above those financial assets for which he had married her. She was remarkably beautiful —but in a cool, dignified, introverted way that could never fire his blood as did the common little Miss Somners—and the brazen Georgina.

Were a man's sexual appetites a matter of habit? he wondered, remembering the waitresses, chorus girls, and housemaids he had enjoyed in his youth before he met Georgina. Yet, if Pelham found a young woman amusing, it mattered not to him which class she came from! Only his brother Toby seemed unusually fastidious in his tastes, for he never took advantage of the maids and certainly never hung around stage doors as did he and Pelham in their younger days.

Toby was the fellow who should have married Willow, Rowell thought with a sudden flash of intuition. They were two of a kind—intellectuals who read books for pleasure and concerned themselves with such causes as the exploitation by industry of the poor. Willow was forever busying herself with the sick and needy in Havorhurst, when in her position, she might have been enjoying herself as did other wives of their acquaintance. As for Toby—he was ridiculously obsessed with his desire to discover some secret of medicine that would cure the world of its ills.

Rowell sighed. The train was nearing the outskirts of Paris. He would have to summon porters to carry all his wife's and infant's paraphernalia to the fiacres and then transport the two women and the baby from one station to another. At least he had cabins reserved for them all on the Channel packet and Peters would be waiting with the carriage at Dover. Hopefully the man would have the good sense to bring the wagonette too, to carry the mountain of luggage his wife seemed to have felt necessary to take with her to France.

"Can't you stop that child crying?" he said coldly. "The sound is disturbing to a degree."

Willow looked up, her face impassive.

"Only if I feed her, Rowell. She is hungry."

"Then she will have to wait," Rowell retorted, flushing. "I have no wish to witness such a task. You should find a wet-nurse for it, Willow. I should have thought you would have more consideration for your figure!"

Willow opened her mouth to reply, but closed it swiftly. She would not engage in argument with Rowell in front of Nellie, even if Rowell had not the good manners to refrain from criticizing her in front of a servant. Besides, she thought, his opinion was really of little consequence. He could not forbid her to feed her own baby if she so wished.

She rocked the baby gently in an effort to still its cries. As the child drifted into a light slumber, Willow sighed. She must try not to resent Rowell's attitude to this new arrival in his family. No matter how unimportant to her the fact that little Alice was not his child, the truth was that she could not expect *him* to feel any natural bond of parentage. That she herself felt deeply maternal toward the child—and Nellie not at all—could not alter the truth. Alice was now *her* baby, *her* responsibility, and if Rowell disclaimed her, she must never hold it against him.

Never mind, little Alice, she thought. Oliver and Toby will love you just as I do.

Of that there was not a single doubt in her mind.

Chapter Twenty

July–December 1903

WILLOW'S RETURN TO ROCHFORD MANOR WITH THE
new baby passed almost entirely without notice,
for during Rowell's brief absence from home, the
unhappy Rupert had tried to end his life.

Grandmère was beside herself. From the tirade with
which she greeted them, it was immediately obvious to
Willow that it was not grief she felt at this near tragedy,
but anger at the scandal which had only just been averted.

Putting the baby Alice in Patience's care in the nursery,
Willow changed hurriedly from her traveling costume into
a comfortable housegown and made her way to Toby's
laboratory, knowing that she would receive a coherent
and factual account of events from him.

Toby's kindly face was lined with anxiety as he pulled
out a chair for her and made her comfortable.

"I could make very little sense of Grandmère's tirade,"
Willow said quietly. "But I did gather that Rupert is out
of danger—that he is not going to die?"

Toby frowned.

"He'll be all right, Willow—physically, that is. But I
am far from sure about his mental state. As you can
imagine, he must have been in a pretty desperate frame
of mind to have attempted such a thing, and I see no solution to his problems."

Willow bit her lip.

"But why did he do it, Toby? What happened? Had it
to do with Adrian?"

Toby nodded.

"I blame myself for not keeping a closer eye on Rupert
while you were away, Willow. Apparently, sometime during the early spring Adrian's fancy was taken by one of
the village girls. Rupert found out and, at first, did nothing but mope and write pathetic letters to Adrian begging

him not to desert him. But he never posted the letters or
the dozens of copies of Oscar Wilde's poems he clearly
intended to send Adrian. Then two days ago . . . it happened."

He looked at Willow anxiously, uncertain whether to
tell her the whole unsavory story. But he realized that
sooner or later she would be certain to learn the facts and
he preferred that she hear them accurately from him.

"Rupert tried to hang himself," he said quietly. Hearing Willow's gasp, he added quickly:

"By a stroke of good fortune, his valet went up to his
room to collect a coat that needed cleaning. He was able
to cut Rupert down before . . . before it was too late.
Forbes was sent for, and apart from considerable bruising
around Rupert's throat and a temporary loss of speech,
he is none the worse for his ordeal. Understandably, the
terrified valet rushed off to tell Dutton, who at once informed Grandmère. So it was she who went first to Rupert's rooms and found the letters which she read and
passed on to me with instructions to burn them. Old
Forbes and the servants have been sworn to secrecy. The
doctor is sixty-five years of age, you know, and the shock
was pretty great for him, too—Adrian being his son."

"Poor man! But most of all poor Rupert," Willow said
softly. "He must have been suffering untold unhappiness
to go to such lengths."

Toby sighed.

"Grandmère is insisting Adrian be sent away from Havorhurst. She was silly enough to tell this to Rupert, and
he has made no secret of it to me that if Adrian goes he
will try again to put an end to his life."

"Is Adrian Forbes in love with the Havorhurst girl?"
Willow asked thoughtfully.

Toby shook his head.

"You would not suggest such a possibility if you knew
him better, Willow. I went down to see him to find out for
myself what was afoot, and the fact is I am appalled by
the young man's fecklessness. He has not the slightest regard for the girl concerned. He amused himself with her
because he was bored. The clandestine nature of his meetings with Rupert were, so he said, a great nuisance, but
more importantly, Rupert had been promising him for
years that when he obtained his legacy at the age of thirty,

he would take Adrian abroad to begin a new life together. Adrian knew Rupert had had his thirtieth birthday last December and he did not believe him when he said it would be at least six months before he could realize the actual capital due to him from the trust fund. He thought Rupert was deceiving him. So he went with the girl partly to spite him. All one can say to Adrian's credit is that he did seem somewhat shaken by the results of his casual disregard for Rupert's feelings. To tell you the truth, Willow, I think he was also flattered."

"Does that mean he is still prepared to go away with Rupert?" Willow asked doubtfully.

Toby nodded.

"As far as I can see, yes! But I am really far from certain, Willow, if this would mean ultimate happiness for my unfortunate brother. I have seen some of those letters Rupert wrote; they are revealing of two things: a deep capacity for love and a desperate sensitivity. Adrian will never be capable of understanding or returning that love. He is willing to be 'bought' by Rupert in a manner one can best describe as that of a gigolo—if you know what that is, Willow?"

Seeing her look of incomprehension, he added gently:

"It is a male prostitute—one who sells his body for monetary reward. Adrian is quite open about his desire to live as a gentleman of leisure, without the necessity to work. Rupert can provide that life. It is the limited degree of affection Adrian can give in return that disturbs me. I doubt it has any depth."

"So what is to happen?" Willow inquired anxiously.

"Pelham and I talked it over in Rowell's absence and decided we must jointly make funds available at once to Rupert until he can claim his own money. It is up to Rupert then whether he wishes to pursue his original plan to take Adrian abroad. Adrian has agreed to wait until Rupert has recovered for a final decision to be made. He has nothing better to do in any event, as he admitted quite shamelessly. If they *do* decide to go, Pelham will arrange it—without Grandmère's knowledge, of course. As far as Rowell is concerned, it is up to you, Willow, to tell him if you think fit. Rowell cannot prevent Rupert's leaving now he has money of his own. I myself feel it might be best if he does go. I see no other future for him."

"I will go and talk to him," Willow said. "He must be so unhappy."

For the first time Toby smiled.

"He is fond of you, Willow. Perhaps you can gain his confidence better than I," he said quietly. "Incidentally, it's good to have you home—although I wish it could have been in happier circumstances."

The curtains were drawn in Rupert's room. He was lying in bed, his face chalk-white, his neck swathed in bandages. Between his hands he held a small book which he had been reading before Willow came in. As she went over to the bed and bent down to kiss his pale cheek, his blue eyes filled with tears.

"So they have told you of my latest disgrace," he murmured brokenly.

"You must not think of it as such," Willow said firmly. "But you must never do so terrible a thing again. However painful, life is the most precious gift we ever receive, and we must live it as best we can."

Wordlessly, Rupert handed her the book he had been reading, opened at a marked page.

Willow sat down in the chair beside him and began to read. It was a poem by Oscar Wilde called *Roses and Rue*. Her own eyes filled with tears as they skimmed the lines.

> *Could the passionate past that is fled*
> *Call back its dead,*
> *Could we live it all over again,*
> *Were it worth the pain!*

And farther down the page:

> *And your eyes, they were green and grey*
> *Like an April day,*
> *But lit into amethyst*
> *When I stooped and kissed;*
> *And your mouth, it would never smile*
> *For a long, long while,*
> *Then it rippled all over with laughter*
> *Five minutes after.*

Rupert was dry-eyed now as he took the book from her and said:

"Adrian's eyes were green and his laugh—" He broke off abruptly, and then began to quote more of the poem from memory:

> *But strange that I was not told*
> *That the brain could hold*
> *In a tiny ivory cell*
> *God's heaven and hell.*

"Oh, Rupert!" Willow said in a whisper. "Please try not to feel it all so deeply." She smiled tremulously. "Your brother Pelham once said to me: 'No man is worth all your love, Willow!' And I think he was right. No one is worth your whole life, Rupert. You must try to remember that in the future."

To her surprise, Rupert nodded his agreement.

"Lying here these past few days, I have come to terms with the truth, Willow. I can never, ever be as I would like it. As Wilde says in another of his poems, *'I shall weep and worship, as before.'* Adrian will never love me and I know it—but I have to be with him. Toby has said that Adrian is still willing to go abroad with me, and that is my one hope of happiness. So please try not to think too badly of me after I am gone, Willow. I know the others will despise me—or most of them—but I would not want to forfeit your regard."

Willow stood up. She was still holding the book in her hands.

"May I keep this," she asked, "as a memento of you, Rupert? But also that I may reach a better understanding of . . . of others. We are all apt to condemn what we do not understand. And if you will do so, please write to me. I shall think of you often and pray for your happiness."

Two weeks later, Rupert left Rochford Manor. Rowell, far from being angry, was delighted when he read Rupert's farewell letter.

"He asks for my forgiveness," he told Willow scornfully. "Is he really too stupid to understand how relieved I am to be rid of him? He has never been anything but a worry, and this last episode . . . well, as you know, my dear, I was deeply shocked to say the least. He could have brought disgrace on the whole family if the truth had become public knowledge. Thank heaven we have reliable servants who won't gossip."

"Do you not feel a little sad for Doctor Forbes?" Willow asked. "After all, he has lost his only son. I doubt that either Adrian or Rupert will ever return to England."

"And a good thing too," was Rowell's terse comment. "There's a new generation growing up under our roof, Willow, and it's up to all of us to set a good example. I wouldn't want Oliver modeling himself on Rupert—and that's a fact."

Rupert's name, like Dodie's, was henceforth never mentioned in Grandmère's presence, according to her instructions. The old lady seemed satisfied with her new great granddaughter, but showed none of the interest she had evinced—and still did, in Oliver.

"We must take care the boy does not become spoiled by her as was Francis," Toby said caustically to Willow. "I sometimes think Grandmère should have been told of Francis' theft of the Gainsborough. Had she known, she might be less indulgent with him."

Francis had been dismissed from the house last month, but not in exactly the punitive manner Willow had hoped. Grandmère had enlisted Rowell's support for her favorite grandson, and it had finally been decided that she would pay for Francis to go on a world tour, balking Toby's arrangements to send him off to Australia to fend for himself.

"My plan is more befitting a gentleman—a Rochford," Grandmère defended her wishes. "After all, he did no worse than rape one of the maids, and there was no need to treat him as harshly as Toby suggested."

So while Willow was in Épernay with Silvie, a triumphant Francis departed upon an expensive and highly interesting and fashionable trip around the world.

He knew nothing therefore of Rupert's affairs or of Grandmère's bitter rejection of her grandson when she discovered he had finally escaped from the confines of his home and would never again be required to listen to her ceaseless recriminations. Francis would not have cared any more about Rupert's happiness than he did about Nellie's, Willow remarked to Toby as Nellie began to make preparations for her wedding to Harry at the end of the summer.

"It is almost as if she had never had a baby," she added, hearing Nellie's bright happy laughter and observing her complete return to her normal smiling self.

"Yet I cannot be so certain Harry has forgotten," Toby said uneasily. "He seems quieter, more watchful. I sometimes wonder if he hates all the Rochfords now."

Seeing Willow's look of dismay, he smiled.

"I dare say I am only imagining it," he added reassuringly. "I am sure they are going to be very happy, Willow."

Nellie and Harry were married quietly in St. Stephen's church at the end of September. Rowell had agreed that they might live in one of the tiny two-roomed cottages on the estate.

The entire indoor and outdoor staff were allowed to attend the simple service, and most of the occupants of Havorhurst village were outside the church to throw rose petals and rice and to wish the couple good fortune. The ceremony was followed by a party in the servants' hall, but there was to be no honeymoon, since both Nellie and Harry had decided to save their money for the following summer when they planned a week at the seaside in Brighton.

"The bride looked radiant, did she not?" Toby commented later to Willow with a smile. "I was obviously quite wrong in thinking that Harry bore a grudge over the past. He was in every way the proud and doting bridegroom."

With Nellie safely married, Willow's thoughts returned once more to her own life. It was now three months since she had brought Alice back from France, and still she felt intensely uneasy about the deception she, with Silvie's help, had perpetrated upon all the family. She had no regrets about the substitution of the baby girl for her own dead son. Little Alice was growing more beautiful every day and was, so Patience said, the most contented baby she had ever cared for. Willow was fascinated by the infant's perfection. Her eyes were changing from blue to a deep grey which she supposed would become dark brown like Oliver's as she grew older.

The little boy, now four and a half years old, was no

less doting than Willow and was enormously protective toward the baby. He sensed that his great grandmother was not interested in his sister and asked continuously why Grandmère did not wish to see Alice every day as she did him. Willow had finally to tell him that Grandmère preferred little boys to little girls, but that Alice was far too young to mind and he must not be upset as everyone else in the house loved the baby very much.

"Uncle Toby loves her," Oliver agreed, "and Uncle Pelham; but Papa does not like babies, does he? Nanny says he'll love Alice when she grows big and pretty!"

He showed no sign of jealousy of the new arrival and seemed delighted that there was another child in the house.

As far as Rowell was concerned, Willow thought, she need have no fear that he suspected Alice was not his child. He had shown as little affection for Oliver and, like most fathers, he was uninterested in the affairs of the nursery. Nevertheless, her conscience troubled her in that she was not only deceiving her husband, but the trusting, honest Toby. When he remarked that the baby bore little resemblance to her, she felt herself blushing with secret guilt.

"She has the Rochford coloring, does she not?" Toby said innocently. "But I think she might have been prettier still if she looked like her Mama!"

Willow had been determined that she would never tell Toby all that had transpired at the Château d'Orbais. Silvie had advised her in the strongest terms never to mention the truth to a living soul.

"The fewer people who know, the safer for all of us," she had cautioned.

But now, with Nellie safely married and Alice accepted unquestionably by the family, Willow was overwhelmed by longing to share her secret with Toby. Although in one way it was no true concern of his, she hated the feeling that she was concealing something from him; it made her reluctant to be in his company and at times, it brought about a strained atmosphere whenever they were alone together. No longer preoccupied with Nellie's wedding, she found the silence that fell between them increasingly unbearable.

"Walk with me down to the lake, Toby," she said suddenly, her mind made up. "There is something I must tell you."

The autumn leaves were already beginning to fall from the trees and carpet the lawns as they made their way through the rose garden and past the still colorful herbaceous borders. Haltingly, as they walked, Willow recounted the details of the weeks she had spent at the Château d'Orbais. Toby listened without interrupting. The part that Silvie had played in this near-tragedy soon became clear to him. Perhaps even more than his cousin, he could appreciate the effect it must have had upon Willow to lose her baby. He recalled the intensity of her grief when the infant, Sophia, had died. Nevertheless, he was momentarily shocked when Willow confessed that little Alice was not her child but Nellie's; that she had adopted as her own the daughter of a servant.

But then he remembered that the baby was also his brother's offspring and therefore a true Rochford. As such she was no less entitled to be raised as a member of their class than those offsprings of other similar liaisons. He himself knew of gentlemen who had had associations with actresses or governesses and raised their children to a higher position. Was not Rowell himself intending an Eton education for Georgina's two sons?

"At first I thought only to save the baby's life," Willow spoke softly beside him. "She was virtually starving to death. I kept thinking how my own first baby had been so desperately in need of a wet-nurse, and that had one been immediately available, she might never have died. It was my duty, I thought. And then . . . Toby, as I held her in my arms, it is as if my baby had not died. Can you understand this? I had no time to consider Rowell or that what I was doing might lead eventually to my deceiving him. The future did not cross my mind."

She paused briefly and then continued:

"By the time I did consider the consequences, I knew I could not be parted from Alice. Silvie pointed out to me that no one need know of the substitution—not even Nellie if we told her her child had died. Silvie made it all sound so simple—and she was right—*it was*. No one questioned it. Even *you* did not doubt that Alice was mine."

"Then why have you told me now, Willow?" Toby

asked angrily. Did Willow have no idea of the anguish such confidences caused him? No matter how derogatory the opinion he held about her husband, Rowell was his brother, and his loyalties were inevitably divided, albeit in Willow's favor. But he could not divorce himself from his love for her, and the opinions she demanded of him could never be totally unbiased. He was torn in two; by the longing to be able to help her and by his inability to do so. He wished desperately she had not felt compelled to make this last confession.

"There was no need to tell me about Alice," he added quietly. *"Why me, Willow?"*

Willow's cheeks flushed a deep pink.

"Do you remember saying to me last week that by producing so perfect and healthy a girl, I had finally disproved Grandmère's theories about there being a fault in the distaff side of the Rochford family? I found it impossible to meet your eyes, Toby. I felt so terrible, I wanted to weep with shame. You are my dearest friend, and I should never have lied to you about Alice."

It was a full minute before Toby could bring himself to speak. Then he said softly:

"I understand and I do not condemn you in any way. But of course my theories are not altered by these facts. Alice still has a Rochford for a father." He was moved by the look of intense relief on Willow's face. Despite his attempt to control his feelings, he was unable to keep the tenderness from his voice. "I do not believe any harm has been done, and certainly not to Rowell. Silvie was right when she said that the advent of a daughter will not affect his life in any way. One day Alice will marry and leave home and that will end his responsibility for her. As for supporting her in the meanwhile—well, it would be ridiculous not to admit that Rowell has grown very wealthy entirely due to the financial advantages *you* brought to your marriage, Willow. And a great deal of the benefit goes to support Georgina and the three children she has borne Rowell. It seems to me to be only fair that you should keep the baby you love."

"I want to believe that very much," Willow said quietly, her eyes full of unshed tears. "But it was not my intention to try to settle any scores with Rowell, Toby. I have learned to accept that my husband has what amounts to a

second wife and family. I am not the only woman who
has to live with such knowledge and I do not imagine that
I will be the last. Regretfully, I cannot bring myself to be
as magnanimous as our dear Queen Alexandra and invite
my husband's mistress to my home! She is a remarkable
woman, do you not agree, to make a friend of Mrs. Keppel? I doubt if there is anyone in England who does not
admire her for behaving with such understanding and dignity."

"The Queen is doubtless very well aware of the beneficial influence Alice Keppel has upon the King," Toby
said sardonically, "and is unselfish enough to accept the
relationship, perhaps knowing that it doesn't undermine
her husband's love for her. As for Georgina—she is not
another Mrs. Keppel, you know, and lacks even a modicum of her breeding, tact, and diplomacy. Besides, it is
my belief that Rowell is tiring of the pretentious Mrs.
Grey."

He made no mention of the fact that Pelham had seen
Rowell with another, younger woman who was certainly
his new mistress. From all accounts, the girl was little
better than a harlot, and it shocked Toby every time he
stopped to consider that his eldest brother actually preferred such company to that of his own enchanting wife.
Willow seemed to grow more lovely every year. Her contentment with her new baby and her delight in young
Oliver had removed that wistful anxiety that had once
seemed to haunt her, and serenity suited her cool, fair
beauty.

"You are happy now, are you not, Willow?" he asked
anxiously.

With a childish gesture he found endearing, Willow
crossed her fingers superstitiously.

"I hardly dare to admit to happiness lest fate overhear
me and decide to bring some new misfortune upon our
family," she said, smiling.

It seemed as if her words were prophetic, for not a
month had passed since Nellie's wedding before the Rochfords were faced with a major tragedy.

Rowell, Pelham, and Toby were in the front hall where
they had just returned from a day's shooting. It was the
first day of November, grey and chill, and a huge log fire
had been lit for the returning sportsmen. Pelham was re-

counting to Willow the size of the day's bag when suddenly young Oliver, unaccompanied by his nurse, came hurrying downstairs. He ran to his father and began to tug furiously at his sleeve.

"Papa, Papa—" he cried breathlessly, but before he could continue, Rowell sharply removed the small boy's hand and said:

"You do not greet grownups and interrupt their conversation in such an ill-mannered fashion, Oliver. Go back to the nursery this instant."

The boy hesitated, his face betraying both fear and anxiety.

"But, Papa—"

This time Rowell's voice was even sharper as he said angrily:

"Are you deliberately disobeying me, Oliver? Are you suddenly deaf that you did not hear my command? *Leave the room this minute.*"

The child's eyes filled with tears. Scarlet-faced, he turned in appeal to his mother. It was not Willow's custom ever to countermand Rowell's orders to Oliver no matter how greatly she might disagree with them. But now not only Oliver's precipitate behavior, but the strange look on his face caused her to say to her husband:

"Let us hear what he has to say, Rowell. I feel it may be important." Without waiting for his agreement, she turned back to the child. "Now tell Mama what is amiss, Oliver."

"It's Grandmère!" the boy gasped. "Her and me were playing draughts and I was winning and she just suddenly went to sleep and wouldn't wake up to finish the game. I shook her and shook her, and Aunt Milly came in and shook her too, but she just *won't* wake up and Aunt Milly said to come and fetch Papa."

For a moment, no one moved. No one spoke. Then all three brothers made a simultaneous dash for the stairway. Willow remained still, her arm now comfortingly around Oliver's shoulders.

"Is Grandmère dead, Mama?" he asked tremulously in a hushed voice. "She couldn't be dead in the middle of playing a game, could she? *Could* she, Mama?"

"I don't know, darling. Perhaps it *could* happen like

that," Willow said gently. "After all, Grandmère is very old, you know."

"But I don't want her to die," Oliver said, the tears now spilling down his cheeks. "I want her to go on playing games with me and telling me stories about Great Grandfather Cedric and the battles he fought and—"

"Willow!" Pelham's voice from the top of the stairs interrupted the child's tearful flow of words. "Will you send Peters to fetch Doctor Forbes immediately. It's very serious . . ."

In deference to the small boy, he did not continue. But shocked, Willow understood his meaning: Grandmère was either dead or dying. She herself had never felt any real affection for the autocratic old lady—as, strangely, did Oliver—but the thought of her no longer ruling the family from her rooms upstairs was unimaginable.

Later that evening, Toby told them that Grandmère's death must have been almost instantaneous.

"Her heart would have simply ceased beating," he said quietly to the silent shocked trio who had gathered in the drawing room. "We must all realize that from her point of view, it was a wonderful way for her to go. There was no long, drawn-out illness, no pain. It is Aunt Milly we must feel sorry for—she is beside herself with grief."

"As indeed I am, Toby," Rowell said quickly. "You talk as if this were not as great a shock for all of us as for Aunt Milly."

Toby looked at his brother wryly.

"I do not doubt it, Rowell, but we are all young enough to be able to cope with sudden death and Aunt Milly is not."

Willow went up to sit beside the poor woman's bedside. Doctor Forbes had given her a sedative, but she seemed unable to cease her hysterical reminiscences, her memory carrying her back to her youth when, as a child, she and Cousin Lucienne had been bridesmaids at "Clotilde's wedding to poor dear Cedric. That was sixty-five years ago," she wept. Without really seeming to know who Willow was, she confessed her terrible feelings of bitterness toward her sister-in-law for preventing her marriage to "that dear, dignified man, Percival Tomlinson," the Parson who had proposed to her; but over the years, Clotilde had convinced her that the right decision had been made.

"I owe her a lifetime of comfort!" she cried, breaking into painful sobs. "And I never had the chance at the end to thank her."

It was all Willow could do to remain silent. Aunt Milly's "lifetime of comfort" had been one of virtual slavery to a self-centered, domineering old woman with an iron will. Aunt Milly had had no life. She had merely existed in Grandmère's shadow.

She did her best to comfort the poor woman who seemed totally bereft.

"It's partly because she has no one now to direct her," Toby said shrewdly. "Every thought, every action has been dictated to her by Grandmère for so long that she cannot think for herself. You may have to be very positive with her, Willow, until she recovers her own will again."

Not only the family, but the entire village attended old Lady Rochford's funeral five days later. Curtains were drawn across windows in even the smallest cottage and lowliest farmhouse. Rowell had sent several telegrams around the world in the hope of reaching Francis, but they all knew he would be unable to return to England in time for his grandmother's burial. Dodie and James were also telegraphed, but Willow advised James not to bring his young wife on so long and distressing a visit. But he made the journey, regardless of the fact that the old lady had totally disapproved of his marriage to her granddaughter.

"I always understood her feelings toward me," he told Willow. "Lady Rochford was a Victorian and she could not easily relax her strict standards. I felt I must pay my respects, and Dodie wanted me to do so."

The arrangements for the funeral occupied so much of Rowell's time that it was not until after it was all over that he fully appreciated the genuine grief he felt at his grandmother's passing. Though she had never loved him as she had loved Francis, they had had much in common and had always understood and respected each other. He felt weakened by her going and turned to Willow for comfort. She was surprised—and not a little disturbed—by the fact that on the very night of the funeral, Rowell came to their bed with a most unusual impatience to claim his marital rights. It seemed wrong to her that after the day's solemnity, his thoughts should turn to bodily pleasures. She felt that his desire to enjoy such earthly passions somehow showed a lack of respect for Grand-mère's spiritual being.

It was almost as if he were seeking to establish his own existence; his vigor; his youth and entitlement to life, she thought unhappily as she complied with his wishes. Row-ell had, in fact, been brooding over the finality of death. His urgent demands upon his reluctant wife seemed some-how to verify his place among the living. Afterwards, he slept soundly, the sad gravity of the day momentarily for-gotten.

But by morning Rowell was once more plunged into a silent gloom which deepened further when a telegram ar-rived from Épernay. By strange coincidence, Cousin Lu-cienne had died on the day of Grandmère's funeral.

"Of all the inconsiderate times for her to die," he ex-claimed with total illogicality. "Now I suppose we shall all have to go to France for *her* funeral. As head of the fam-ily, I shall be obliged to go. It is most inconvenient," he repeated. "As if I had not enough to do here seeing to Grandmère's effects."

To Willow's dismay, he retired to the library, where in-stead of answering the many letters of condolence that were beginning to pour in by every post, he solemnly drank himself into a stupor. It therefore fell to Willow to dispatch a telegram to Silvie saying they would arrive as soon as possible and sending their love and sympathy.

"I am sure there is no need for *you* to go, Willow," Toby said with an anxious look at Willow's white, ex-hausted face. "Pelham and I will accompany Rowell. Be-sides, someone should keep an eye on Aunt Milly."

"But I know Silvie would like me to be with her," Wil-low sighed, "and Patience can watch over Aunt Milly. Doctor Forbes says there is nothing seriously wrong with her that time and rest will not put right."

Two days later, Willow with her husband and two brothers-in-law arrived in Paris.

Silvie had had her mother's coffin transported to Paris for the funeral, since she had expressed a wish to be bur-ied beside her husband's grave in Fontainebleau. Com-pared with Grandmère's funeral, that of Cousin Lucienne was a quiet affair with only a few relatives and close friends in attendance. Silvie, who had been expecting her mother's death for some while, was dry-eyed as the coffin was lowered into the grave.

"I am sad, naturally enough, but pleased that she no longer suffers," she told Willow. "By the way, Doctor Gousse sent his very warmest regards when he learned that I would be seeing you today."

Seeing the color rise in Willow's cheeks, she added quickly:

"Have no fear, *chérie*. He is absolutely to be trusted, I assure you. Quite apart from his fondness for *me*, he thinks you are the most beautiful woman he has encountered—and for a Frenchman, that alone is enough to guarantee his allegiance!"

Despite the gloom and sadness of the past few weeks, Willow had to smile. The remark was so typical of Silvie.

"I shall come and stay with you as soon as I have sorted out Maman's affairs," Silvie promised. "I long to see little Alice again—not to mention your handsome little Oliver."

True to her word, she arrived in England a month later. By then Aunt Milly was once more downstairs, but obviously still unable to grasp that Grandmère was not about to call her for an errand. She seemed permanently to be listening for the old lady's commands and was most at ease when Willow asked her to perform some little task. It was as if the habit of obeying were so strongly ingrained that she needed—as Toby had forecast—to be given instructions.

Silvie was still in mourning, as were all the Rochfords, when they sat down for dinner on the evening of her arrival. There was a fashionable cut to her black moiré silk dress.

"I had a *couturière* from Worth run it up for me quickly," she said in reply to Willow's compliment upon her appearance.

"And most becoming it is, too," Pelham commented with an admiring glance at his pretty cousin.

Aunt Milly sniffed disapprovingly as she listened to their badinage. But after the meal, the talk reverted to more serious matters as Silvie turned to Rowell, saying:

"Even with the assistance of my accountant, I have had quite a task clearing up Maman's papers. You must be finding it even more exacting sorting out Aunt Clotilde's affairs, Rowell."

He nodded.

"Old people seem to collect such a mountain of trivia," he complained. "Yet one dare not dispose of it without careful regard lest it should have some importance."

"And one cannot always be sure what *is* of importance," Silvie agreed. "Last week, I discovered that every year Maman has been sending to Father Mattieu, our priest at Épernay, the princely sum of two and a half thousand francs. That, I suppose, is about a hundred guineas. It seemed most strange to me, since Maman had no great liking for the man; so I went to see him and do you know, Willow, he refused to tell me why she gave him these regular payments. He said he was vowed to secrecy and all he was prepared to tell me was that it was for charitable purposes. His manner was most disagreeable. It is not as if I had been suggesting Maman was keeping him in champagne, *nom de Dieu!*"

Her quick, bright laughter was silenced by a strange strangled voice from the opposite side of the room as Aunt Milly said:

"Did he tell you nothing more?"

Such was her tone that all faces were turned to regard her. She was scarlet and her hands were flapping in agitation.

"Why no, Aunt Milly," Silvie said. "As I told you, he was sworn to the secrecy of his profession. But I went to Maman's bank, where I discovered that this same sum of money had arrived every year for the past six years from a Miss Beresford from England. As it was sent by post, they had no idea who this lady might be."

Her voice trailed into silence as Aunt Mildred's face drained of color. She gasped several times as if trying to draw breath and her hands clutched at her chest. She remained thus in rigid immobility and then with a crash she fell to the floor before anyone could reach her.

Toby was first at her side. He opened the high whalebone lace collar of her black evening dress and waved his hand in front of her face.

"Open the windows," he ordered. "She needs air—quickly!"

As the footman rushed to do his bidding, he felt for her

pulse. His face when he looked up at Willow was filled with anxiety.

"Someone must fetch Doctor Forbes. I think she is having a heart attack!"

But for once Toby's diagnosis was not entirely correct. Aunt Mildred's heart had been unable to bear the strain of her fearful anxiety. Not only had Silvie's words brought back in horrifying clarity the part that she, as Miss Beresford, had played in the baby's abduction, but she had thought for one unbearable minute that her guilt was about to be exposed. Her heart had momentarily failed, and Aunt Milly was now severely paralyzed by a stroke.

Chapter Twenty-one

December 1903–July 1904

THE LONDON SPECIALIST CALLED IN BY ROWELL TO attend Aunt Mildred informed them that she was suffering from an apoplectic condition from which it was possible she might not recover. Although she remained in a coma for nearly two days, however, her condition improved sufficiently for her to be given nourishment. By January she was pronounced out of immediate danger, although the specialist could give no assurance that she would ever recover her speech or senses. Such movements as she could make appeared to be little more than involuntary twitchings of her head and limbs, and to all intents and purposes, she was paralyzed. She now had both a day and a night nurse permanently in attendance.

Willow forced herself to sit with the poor woman for at least an hour every day, although Aunt Milly gave no sign of recognition. One side of her gaunt face was twisted grotesquely in a downward droop and her eyes seemed incapable of focusing, making it difficult to assess whether or not she comprehended what was said to her. Occasionally she gave an animal-sounding grunt which bore no relation to speech and which the nurse told Willow was no more than the passage of air through her larynx.

For once, Toby had few reassuring words to offer Willow.

"It is impossible to be certain how much Aunt Milly understands—if anything at all," he said. "But these are early days, Willow. It is only a month since she suffered the seizure. The specialist said he has known cases where, after a great many months, a patient regained some faculty. But equally he warns Aunt Milly might never do so."

Nevertheless, Willow felt a strange compulsion to visit the pathetic invalid every day. Despite the fact that the day nurse believed her patient incapable of understanding Willow read aloud from the newspapers and talked of current events without even knowing whether Aunt Milly could hear her.

"I had a letter from Father this morning," she said one afternoon to the motionless figure in the bed. "Mother is a little better, but still in some pain. Father says he is considering offering money to the Wright brothers to help them develop their flying machine. Oliver was tremendously excited when he heard Father's news that they had managed to fly their machine six hundred feet through the air just before Christmas. Oliver is determined one day to fly in such a machine . . ."

But it was difficult to maintain monologues such as these, and she found it easier to read items from the newspapers. Hoping it would be of interest to Aunt Milly, she read aloud an article about the doctor's widow, Mrs. Emeline Pankhurst who was now trying to gain support in London for the Women's Social and Political Union she had started in Manchester. The article was far from supportive of this new development of women's suffrage but it did agree that it was unfair that fathers of illegitimate children should not be held responsible in any way for their offspring.

"It says here, Aunt Milly, that if an unmarried mother's baby dies of starvation or from exposure, the mother can be hanged for murder, yet the man responsible for the baby's existence bears no culpability. I'm sure even Grandmère would have believed that wrong, do you not agree?"

There was no flicker of response from the invalid.

"I am afraid the nurse is right, and Aunt Mildred has no grasp of the meaning of such accounts," Willow was obliged to admit to Toby as the winter months of January and February gave way to spring. "Sometimes I wonder if there is any point in my visiting her day after day. I know Doctor Forbes and the nurse think I am wasting my time."

But Toby encouraged her to continue.

"One day there may be some slight indication she understands," he said, "and then perhaps we shall be able to discover why she was so shocked by Silvie's conversation last Christmas. I must confess that although I have thought about it as often as you, Willow, I can see no connection between Cousin Lucienne's affairs and Aunt Milly's sudden attack of apoplexy, yet what else could have accounted for it?"

Rowell refused to enter into such discussions, which he considered a waste of everybody's time. He had long ago made clear his antipathy to the sick room and to any form of illness. He paid only the briefest of visits to his aunt and at the beginning of May he expressed his intention of going to London for the Season. Willow dissuaded him from renting the Park Lane house again for their joint occupation.

"I feel I should not leave Aunt Mildred," she explained, much to Rowell's annoyance. He could see no reason for his wife's constant attendance upon the sick woman while he was paying the wages of a day and night nurse.

"You and Pelham could stay at your club," Willow suggested. "I know Toby is intending to remain at Rochford this summer and Francis is not yet home, so to take so large a house for two people would be unnecessarily extravagant, would it not?"

Rowell at once saw the advantages of his wife's proposal—and not only the financial ones. If Willow remained at Rochford, he would be free throughout the summer to escort Désirée where he pleased without having to concern himself with his wife. He therefore planned to go to London with Pelham at the end of the month.

On the day prior to Rowell's departure, Willow sat reading *The Times* to the sick woman. She was recounting how Pelham's former fellow prisoner of war, Winston

Churchill, now a Tory member of Parliament, had crossed the floor to the Liberal benches. Suddeny she broke off, her heart beating in excitement, as she saw Aunt Milly's arm lift and then fall back on the coverlet.

"Aunt Milly," she said breathlessly. "Can you understand me?"

Again the hand moved fractionally in what this time seemed an unmistakable gesture of assent.

Willow turned sharply and called to the nurse who was sitting by the window crocheting.

"Go and find Mr. Toby," she ordered her. "Ask him to come here at once—as quickly as he can!"

It did not occur to her to send for Rowell, whom she knew to be now engaged in a discussion with his valet concerning the packing of the clothes he wished to take with him to London.

Rowell was therefore unaware of the disturbance at the other end of the landing, or of Toby as he hurried into Aunt Milly's bedroom in answer to Willow's summons.

Willow greeted him with controlled excitement.

"Aunt Milly moved her arm," she told him. "It was a definite signal, Toby."

Smiling at Willow, Toby bent over the invalid and asked softly:

"Do you know who I am, Aunt Milly?"

For the third time, the paralyzed woman indicated that she understood what was said to her.

Toby turned back to Willow and drew her away from the bedside so that they could not be overheard.

"It would seem you are right about her," he said quietly. "But we must be careful not to overtax her at this early stage. If her brain is now beginning to recover, it will be best if her return to normality is gradual and with no undue strain."

He went back to the bed and asked gently:

"Is there anything you want, Aunt Milly? Food? Drink?"

This time there was no obvious response. Willow looked anxiously at the white, twitching face.

"Is there anyone you wish to see?" she suggested.

Now Aunt Milly's hand moved . . .

"Rowell?" Willow inquired, but there was no response. One by one, Willow listed the names of all the family, but there was no further indication of understanding from the sick woman.

"I think we should let you rest now, Aunt Milly," Toby said authoritatively. "After you have had your luncheon and a little sleep, Willow or I will come back. In the meanwhile you must not worry about anything at all. Now that we know we have the means of communicating with you, we will be able to make life a lot easier and happier for you."

Willow was by now impatient to share the news of Aunt Milly's progress with Rowell. Eagerly, she made her way down to the dining room for lunch where he awaited her. Toby followed more slowly, for he was anticipating his brother's disappointing reaction to their news. As Dutton began to serve the meal, Rowell listened to Willow's account of his aunt's miraculous progress with skeptical eyes.

"I cannot see that it will make much difference to Aunt Mildred even if she does fully regain her speech, which in any case I doubt," he said dourly. "The specialist made no bones about the fact that she will be bedridden until she dies. Besides which, when did Aunt Milly ever have anything of import to say, even in her normal condition?"

Toby was unable to conceal his look of irritation at Rowell's failure to appreciate what even one tiny spark of progress must mean to the paralyzed woman upstairs. Scornfully, Rowell rejected Willow's suggestion that Aunt Milly was clinging to life with such stubborn determination only because she had something of importance she wished to impart. Although Toby would not encourage her in this conviction, neither did he gainsay her. Doctor Forbes, on his evening visit, opposed in most forcible terms her assumption that they had discovered a reliable method of communication with the patient. In a surprisingly emphatic tone of voice, he advised against any further attempts to question Aunt Mildred.

"You may well be adding to the poor lady's stress," he said sharply. "We have no way of knowing if her brain is functioning normally, and it is a possibility I myself very much doubt. What you consider to be her 'replies' may have no relevance at all to your questions."

"I suppose he *could* be right," Toby admitted later to Willow, his voice doubtful. "However, we can easily put Aunt Milly to the test, Willow. For example, I could ask her, do I have blue eyes, or is her name Dodie? If she understands that her answer should be in the negative, she will *not* respond. But if we ask her if her name is Mildred, she will move her arm or her hand in assent as she did this morning."

Willow gave a long sigh of relief. Without realizing it she had been holding her breath in her anxiety. She did not try to rationalize why it was so important to her that she could communicate with Aunt Milly. It was an instinct so strong that it refused to be quashed by reason.

"I myself am totally convinced she has something important she wants to tell us," she commented to Toby, as disregarding Doctor Forbes' wishes, they paid a last visit to the sick woman's room before dinner that night. Toby put an arm around Willow's shoulders and gave her a brief, reassuring hug.

"Don't worry about it. We'll soon find out."

Within ten minutes they had established to their mutual satisfaction that the paralyzed woman did clearly understand the simple questions they were asking her. Toby dismissed the night nurse from the room.

"Aunt Milly may not feel able to respond freely in front of an employee," he remarked quietly to Willow. They sat down either side of the bed and Toby began asking the questions he knew were on Willow's mind.

"Is there something you want to tell us, Aunt Milly?"

There could be no doubting her assent. He continued in slow measured tones. Had it to do with Grandmère? This time the movement of Aunt Milly's hand was less obvious. Toby frowned as he glanced at Willow.

"Perhaps Grandmère is only part of it," Willow suggested hesitantly. At once there was a definite response. Willow smiled.

"With a little patience, Aunt Milly, we shall soon be able to discover what is worrying you."

For half an hour they continued to ask questions they hoped would be relevant. Did the problem concern Rowell? Pelham? Francis? Rupert? Dodie? Aunt Milly herself? Only to the last of these names did she give any positive response.

Toby looked at Willow, his eyes nonplussed.

"It obviously concerns something that happened in the past between Aunt Milly and Grandmère," he said. "But however are we to establish one incident from their life-time of shared activity?"

Willow glanced at the woman lying prone in the bed. She thought she could feel the desperation in Aunt Milly's faded blue eyes as they gazed into hers; but reason cautioned her that it might only be her imagination.

"Is it something that happened long ago, Aunt Milly?" she inquired.

"Obviously yes!" Toby remarked as he watched the response. "Twenty years ago, Aunt Milly? Longer? Ten years?"

This time they could be certain Aunt Milly was trying to give a positive reply as her fingers twitched restlessly. But a moment later, her mind seemed to be wandering again.

Toby stood up.

"I think we have done enough questioning for one day," he said to Willow. "We'll pursue it tomorrow, Aunt Milly. Meantime, you must not worry. Have a good night's sleep and we can 'talk' in this fashion tomorrow. We will soon discover what it is you want to tell us."

But Rowell continued to remain indifferent to Willow's excitement when she related the details of their visit to his aunt at dinner.

He was serving a large capon which had been cooked by Mrs. Jupp à la Royale—a recipe much favored by Rowell, who particularly enjoyed the ragôut of cocks' combs, truffles, button mushrooms, and ham, in its rich velouté sauce.

"What Aunt Milly thinks important is probably not so at all," he said discouragingly as Dutton put Willow's plate in front of her. "Something trivial she forgot to do for Grandmère which is preying on her mind, perhaps. I doubt very much, in view of the limitations of Aunt Milly's existence, that she can have any major transgression on her conscience," he added sarcastically. "She was not exactly a *femme fatale*, eh, Pelham?"

Pelham grinned, but nevertheless agreed with Toby and Willow that on occasions, even the most unlikely people were discovered to have committed extraordinary indiscretions.

"Rowell *may* be right," Toby cautioned Willow when, after an early luncheon the next day, Rowell and Pelham departed for London. He and Willow were taking a short walk down to the lake. "I myself do not have your total conviction that Aunt Milly has something vital to tell us. As Rowell says, when one considers the life the poor old soul led, the 'disasters' in it were trivial to a degree."

Willow sighed as the first drops of rain forced them to hurry back indoors.

"I know I must sound unreasonable," she admitted with a wry smile as Dutton closed the front door behind them and they made their way upstairs. "But call it 'woman's intuition' if you like, Toby. I cannot explain it—but I feel it—a strange desperate urgency imprisoned inside Aunt Milly's mind . . ." She broke off and then, after a moment's hesitation, she continued almost inaudibly:

"Ten years ago, Toby, almost to the very month, my baby girl was born and died. Is that too much of a coincidence or could it be relevant?"

Toby's eyebrows lifted in speculation, as they walked slowly along the gallery.

"I had forgotten how long ago that was, Willow. I suppose it *is* just possible that there is a connection. But I cannot see how Aunt Milly would have been involved that night."

He looked at Willow's cheeks, flushed now with excitement as, having crossed into the east wing, they opened the door of his laboratory. It was the one room in the house where they could talk undisturbed by visitors and unattended by servants. Closing the door behind him, he put his hands on her shoulders and said gently:

"Please don't build any hopes of learning something new about that tragic night from Aunt Milly. I know she and Grandmère were the only members of the family in the house when your baby was born, but even had there been any mischief intended—and I can see no reason for it—Doctor Forbes was in attendance upon you and would not have allowed any harm to come to you or the baby."

"Then why was he so anxious we did not question Aunt Milly? He did his best to stop us, Toby, don't you remember?" Willow cried.

Toby nodded.

"Yes, but he may have been quite genuine in his belief that it would be too much of a strain, upon her, and that her brain is incapable of reason. Forbes is an old man now, Willow, and even when he was in his prime, I never did have a high opinion of his ability to diagnose."

He became suddenly conscious of the fact that his hands were still holding Willow's shoulders and that his grip had strengthened. Willow, too, became aware of it and as he let his arms fall hurriedly to his sides, she felt her heartbeat quicken. Her senses were already acutely activated by the excitement of their conversation. Now she was a helpless victim to the rush of emotions that surged through her. With no thought for the consequences, she flung her arms around Toby's neck and pressed her cheek against his.

"Toby—oh, Toby," she cried, "please hold me! I need you so much I—"

She broke off as Toby abruptly drew his face away from hers. He stared down into her eyes with a look of despair in his own. It was, she thought, as if he were reading her very soul. She could hear the swift thudding of his heart as clearly as she felt the pounding of her own. Her whole body was trembling violently as she clung to him.

For a brief moment it seemed that Toby was going to speak. But instead, he let his arms enfold her totally, and bending his head, he pressed his mouth to hers.

I love him! I love him! I love him! The words, unspoken, raced through her mind as her body responded to his kiss. At long, long last, she was where she needed most of all to be—in his embrace. Here was safety; happiness; a joy almost beyond bearing.

As their lips parted, they stared once again into each others' eyes. Still no words were exchanged, as with a despairing cry, Toby drew her fiercely back against him. Willow could feel now the full force of his desire as he kissed her again and again until she felt as if her body had melted into his. Then only did he release her, leading her to her customary chair by the window.

He walked away from her and sat down heavily in his own chair by the table where he worked. By putting these few feet of distance between them, it was as if he had established their separateness.

But he can never do so, Willow thought as her heart ached with the terrible pain of understanding. We are one person, Toby and I—part of each other. I know exactly what he is feeling now, because I, too, feel the same.

"You know that I love you, don't you?" she said simply. He smiled at her, his eyes filled with a deep tenderness.

"Yes, I know, Willow. Just as you know that I love you. I have loved you for years, Willow—ever since you were a little girl of fifteen and first came to Rochford."

Willow nodded.

"I only discovered *my* love for *you* after my visit to Paris three years ago," she said. "But it must have lain there in my heart long, long before that, Toby. I have always taken it for granted that I could come to you for comfort whenever I was in trouble or distress. I did not associate my need of you as friend, counselor, adviser, comforter, with the emotion of love. I believed for a long while that I loved Rowell. I confused love with passion, adoration. But real love is different, isn't it? I know now that it is far, far deeper than any passion. You are like another part of myself, Toby, a necessary part without which I am never quite complete."

Toby's face clouded with pain.

"You must not say any more, Willow. To admit to such feelings between us can only strengthen the barriers that will always keep us apart. We can never marry—you and I. You are my brother's wife . . . and there is nothing either of us can do to right that wrong. The mistake was mine—in ever allowing it to happen."

"No, Toby. I *wanted* to marry Rowell. I thought I loved him. Perhaps those feelings I had for him might have deepened into something worthwhile had he—" She broke off, knowing instinctively that Toby would not want to hear her being disloyal to Rowell, however little the regard he had for his eldest brother.

Toby drew a long, painful sigh.

"We must never, ever give way to weakness again, Willow—for our own sakes as well as others'. If we are to continue sharing our lives in this house as in the past, it can only be as brother and sister. It is not going to be easy to regain that relationship, but it is the only one possible for us."

Tears filled Willow's eyes as she nodded helplessly.

"I understand, Toby. However difficult, I will try never to show my love for you again; never to speak of it. I do not know if it will be the harder because we have opened our hearts this once. I do know I can never be anything but happy in the knowledge that you love me—selfish as it is for me to feel so. You would make such a wonderful husband . . . and father. I have said before that you *should* marry, Toby, and have children of your own."

"And I have told you before that *your* children will suffice me very well. I love young Oliver only a shade less than I love you! And I am already little Alice's slave—"

He broke off as he became aware of the tears running down Willow's cheeks. He made as if to go to her, but quickly curbed the impulse.

"Please don't cry, my very dearest girl," he said, his voice almost a whisper. "To tell you the truth, your unhappiness is the only thing I cannot bear with fortitude. Believe me, Willow, if I thought it would make things easier for you, I would willingly leave Rochford. You have only to say—"

"No, Toby, no!" Willow broke in with an attempt to smile through her tears. "And I promise you on my word of honor that I am not crying from unhappiness. It was just that your love for Oliver moves me very deeply. You are always so good to him and he is devoted to you. I think it would break his heart if you were to leave Rochford. It would certainly break mine."

"Then I stay," Toby said firmly. "But this is the last time you and I are ever alone in this room, Willow. You may visit me here sometimes with Oliver, if you so wish. But I do not think I could answer for myself were we to continue to spend long hours alone together here as we have in the past. In the company of others, it will be far easier for us to restrain our inclinations to be close to one another; to use endearments; to speak our true thoughts. Nor must we ever tarnish our love with feelings of guilt. As things are now, we have nothing with which we need reproach ourselves and I want it to remain so—as I know you would, too."

Toby is right—as always, Willow thought, but not without a momentary bitterness. All around them people were engaging in romantic intrigues. Many married men like Rowell had mistresses; many women like Silvie took lovers. The morality insisted upon by the late Queen was observed only outwardly—and hypocritically. Society did as it pleased without sign of guilt. The only guilt, as far as Willow could see, lay in being found out.

But her bitterness did not last, for she knew that she, no less than Toby, wanted to be able to hold forever to her heart the thought of a perfect love between them, neither clandestine nor incestuous. Limited although love between brother and sister-in-law might be, it would be above recrimination: a love that she could admit to in years to come to her children without shame.

"I do understand—and agree with all you say," she told Toby quietly. "But since this is a kind of ending in a way, dearest Toby, I cannot leave without a farewell embrace."

She rose from her chair and walked over to him. As he stood up, holding out his arms to her, she saw tears in his eyes. Then his mouth came down to hers. She allowed herself one bitter-sweet moment of abandonment to the forces of passion within her, knowing that henceforth they must be controlled. She kissed him fiercely, longingly, allowing him to know how intensely she wanted so much more than that kiss. Just this once she thought, I shall give way to weakness. Toby would have to be strong for them both. Given her way, she would let him take her; offer to him in body as well as heart.

She could not know how nearly Toby succumbed to the temptation she presented. He was burningly aware of the racing of her heart, of the rise and fall of her breasts, of the sweetness of her breath on his cheek. Beneath his hands, her warm, soft body molded itself against him and the pain of his longing for her became unbearable.

Roughly, he pushed her away from him.

"You would regret it—as much as I," he reminded her as he walked to the door and held it open for her. "And I will never do anything, my dear love, that might one day cause you unhappiness. But I do love you. Never, *ever* doubt it."

There was nobody about as Willow went slowly downstairs. One of the footmen on duty in the hall told her that Patience had taken the children for their afternoon walk. The big house seemed empty but for the servants. Francis was still upon his travels; Rupert, no one knew where. Doctor Forbes had had no letter from Adrian and had told Willow that he wanted none.

"As far as I am concerned, my son is dead," he had told her in much the same tone as Grandmère had used about Rupert when he departed.

Willow glanced at the grandfather clock in the hall. It was nearing time for afternoon tea. At five o'clock Doctor Forbes would pay his daily visit to Aunt Milly.

Willow paused, the strangest of feelings suddenly coursing through her veins. She calculated that by now Aunt Milly would have wakened from her afternoon nap; that she might even at this moment be waiting for Willow to come and talk to her. It could be that this very afternoon, Willow thought, she would find the key to the mystery of Aunt Milly's secret. And even if nothing were discovered, a visit to the poor old lady would keep her mind off Toby . . .

Following her impulse, Willow made her way back upstairs and along the landing toward Aunt Milly's rooms. She paused outside Grandmère's adjoining suite. It was now empty of all her possessions and was bare but for the dust-sheeted furniture. Her clothes had been sent to the poor and needy and except for the jewelry and valuables she had distributed in her Will among the family, her remaining trivia had been given to the servants.

Grandmère had made no other bequests except to the faithful Doctor Forbes, to whom she had left a velvet casket. Aunt Milly had handed it to him on the old lady's written instructions. It was securely locked and no one had been told what was in it. The doctor himself made no reference to it and gave a noncommittal reply when Rowell had asked him if Grandmère had adequately acknowledged his services.

"Frankly, I am surprised the old girl left him anything at all," Rowell had commented later to Willow, "bearing in mind that it was Forbes' son who ran off with Rupert!"

Willow moved on and opened Aunt Milly's door. She could hear the bright professional chatter of the day nurse as she went in. She was sitting by the bed crocheting, as was her wont during the long hours of attendance upon her undemanding patient.

"If you would care to go to the housekeeper's room and have your tea there, I will sit with my aunt," Willow told the nurse who quickly took advantage of the offer.

Willow sat down in the vacated chair and held Aunt Milly's hand.

"Would you like me to read to you?" she asked. "No? Then shall I ask you some more questions?" This time, there was a movement of assent. With a stab of excitement which she tried to subdue, Willow said:

"Toby and I were trying to work out what might have occurred ten years ago to cause you distress, Aunt Milly. The only thing we could think of is the death of my baby girl. Could it possibly have to do with that?"

She felt a moment of anxiety as the pathetic old woman gave a sudden ugly gasp. Her lower jar dropped and saliva ran from between her lips. From deep within her throat came yet another noise.

She was trying desperately to talk, Willow realized. The drooped side of her face seemed to be even more distorted.

"Don't try to speak, Aunt Milly," she said, wiping the cracked lips gently with the linen cloth that lay on top of the sheet. "Just lift your hand if you can when you wish to answer 'yes.' I am here to help you in any way I can. Are you sure that you want me to continue with my questions?"

Willow had no way of knowing the frantic struggle that was going on inside Mildred's head as she fought helplessly against the paralysis that gripped her body. Ever since her attack, she had known that it would not be long now before she followed her sister-in-law to the grave. But unlike Clotilde, she was terrified of dying with such a terrible sin lying upon her soul. She was convinced it was God's punishment when, believing herself about to be exposed by Cousin Lucienne's daughter, she had been so smitten by guilt that she had had a near fatal apoplectic fit. God wanted her to lie here in silence reflecting upon her crime so that when He finally sent for her, she would have repented her sins and confessed them. But while she was by now more than ready—in fact, desperately eager —to confess and make what atonement was possible, how could she do so while the power of speech was still denied her?

Willow's kindness to her was like another thorn in the crown of thorns she felt she was being asked to wear. The poor young woman who had suffered so cruelly through her, Mildred's, actions, was now her one hope of redemption. It was to Willow she must confess; to the one she had sinned against.

Mildred had long since ceased to fear Willow's condemnation. She wanted one thing only: to be free of her guilt so that she might die in peace. There could be no worse pain, she believed, than the burden of sin she now carried.

As Willow's questioning began once more, she brought what last vestige of physical strength she possessed to control the slight movement of her arm. The questions were growing nearer and nearer to the truth.

Had some harm been inflicted on the baby? By Doctor Forbes? By Grandmère? By Mildred herself? Had any one of them killed the child—even accidentally? If not, had its death been due to negligence?

If only I could explain, Mildred thought in helpless frustration. Willow's questions all related to the baby's death. How could she, Mildred, possibly indicate that the baby—the child—was still alive!

Willow was feeling the same terrible sense of frustration. The first heady excitement of discovering that Aunt Milly's problem had in fact to do with the baby's death was now giving way to misgivings. Perhaps after all, Aunt Milly had nothing of real import to tell her; perhaps the poor old spinster was simply feeling regret that she had not shown Willow greater sympathy when her baby had died. Remembering those past terrible months, Willow could not recall one occasion when Aunt Milly had expressed a single word of sympathy. If anything, she had avoided Willow in a most unkind manner, leaving the room when she entered it, cutting short all conversation.

By now Willow had been in the room over half an hour. At any moment, the nurse would return from her tea and Doctor Forbes would arrive. Yet she could think of no other question to ask, since Aunt Milly had made it clear that the baby had not been harmed.

More to herself than to the motionless woman in the bed, she said:

"There is nothing else I can think of to ask you, Aunt Milly—unless it is whether Grandmère wanted my baby to die?"

Astonished to see Aunt Milly's immediate response,

Willow's heart missed a beat. Hurriedly, she voiced another question.

"She wanted my baby dead—but she did not harm her. But what else could she have done? Aunt Milly, my baby *is* dead, isn't she? You would know if she was not. *She is dead, isn't she?*"

There was no movement. Desperate for an answer, Willow bent closer over the bed. Had Aunt Milly fallen asleep or was she indicating a negative reply?

"Aunt Milly, you must answer me," she cried, shaking the poor woman's inert shoulders in her desperation. "Is *my baby alive?*"

She just had time to see the certain movement of Aunt Milly's hand before Doctor Forbes spoke from the doorway. She had been too engrossed to hear the door opened.

"Lady Rochford, what are you doing to my patient?" The doctor sounded very angry, and Willow stared back guiltily as she realized that she had quite unconsciously been using force upon the helpless old woman.

"I'm sorry, Doctor Forbes, but you don't understand," she cried. "Aunt Milly has been answering some questions, and I have discovered something of immense importance." She looked up into the old man's stern, unrelenting face. "It's about my baby," she said urgently. "She isn't dead, Doctor Forbes. Aunt Milly has just said so. Old Lady Rochford had something to do with it, though. I don't yet know what happened. *But my baby is alive.* I think Aunt Milly has always known it, and it has preyed on her mind all this time—being unable to tell me before she dies . . ."

She caught hold of the doctor's arms, her movements unconscious in her extreme excitement.

"Why don't you say something, Doctor? Have you not understood me? Don't you see that it all makes sense? Grandmère always believed there was something wrong with the girls in the family. She must have thought there was something wrong with *my* baby and so—"

"Lady Rochford, I am sorry to be so rude as to interrupt you, but in my professional capacity, I am bound to say that I fear you are hysterical. *I must ask you to leave the room at once.* Poor Miss Mildred is a very sick woman, and this kind of behavior can do her nothing but harm. As for your statements—I can only say that I am deeply sorry for you. I believed that you had long since recovered from your grief over the child who died."

Willow stared into the expressionless blue eyes, her own brilliant.

"But she didn't die! Aunt Milly said—"

"Your aunt is incapable of speech, Lady Rochford. Such movements as she may give can be—and I don't doubt are—entirely involuntary. Moreover, I have already explained to you—and to your husband—that she cannot be pronounced to be in possession of her faculties, mental or physical."

Willow's cheeks burned with angry color.

"You may not think she knows what she is saying, but *I* do. I don't believe now that my baby did die and I never shall until it is proved to me. I never saw her poor little body, and now I know why—*there never was one!*"

With remarkable strength, the doctor prized open Willow's fingers which were still grasping his arms. His voice was knife-edged as she stood trembling slightly, staring up into his eyes.

"You seem to have forgotten, Lady Rochford, that while *you* did not see your child's corpse, *I* did. The infant lies buried in Havorhurst graveyard, and I myself put her body in the coffin. I am sorry to have to upset you, but there is nothing more to be said upon the matter. Despite anything this poor sick woman may have led you to believe, your child—unquestionably and *legally*—is dead."

Chapter Twenty-two

August 1904–March 1905

ROWELL HAD RETURNED FROM LONDON IN ILL HUmor. Désirée, having sworn a hundred times that he was more important to her than anything else in the world, had secretly signed a contract to go with a theatrical company to the United States for a year. There was nothing he could do to prevent her leaving, for she had presented him with a *fait accompli*. Furious and frustrated, he had left her without saying goodbye and certainly without a handsome farewell present.

Still nursing his badly wounded pride—for he had thought himself adored by the faithless little schemer—the very last thing he wanted was trouble at home. But for once—and to his surprise—Willow refused to have the discussion of her private concerns postponed to an occasion he considered more convenient.

"I have already waited six weeks to talk this matter over with you, Rowell, and I will not wait longer!"

White-faced, but with a determined set to her mouth, Willow was not to be ignored, and Rowell was uneasily aware of it.

He was sitting in the library, the whiskey decanter conveniently placed at his elbow, *The Times* perforce lying idle in his lap as he stared up at his wife. He had not immediately noticed her appearance since his arrival home shortly after luncheon and now he felt a swift surge of approval at the picture she presented. She was wearing a pale blue and white striped Jacconet afternoon gown. She had a wide white sash around her waist, and the fresh white lace of the collar was caught in a pretty blue enamel brooch at her neck. Her hair was swept off her forehead and arranged in a thick coil threaded with a dark blue ribbon. It framed her oval-shaped face. Her dark eyes were brilliant with some inner excitement which seemed to enhance their size and beauty.

"Very well, my dear. Be seated and we will talk over your problem," he said in kindlier tones. "Would you care for any refreshment?"

Willow shook her head and turning, told the attendant footman to leave the room.

"What I have to say is confidential," she informed her husband. "And it is not just *my* problem, Rowell, it is ours. It concerns our child—the little girl I bore ten years ago. Rowell, I am now absolutely convinced that our baby Sophia did *not* die. Aunt Milly has indicated it as definitely as she has been able to indicate any established fact. Moreover, I am convinced that Doctor Forbes knows what did happen to the baby and that he is terrified of what we will find out. I must insist that you talk to him, and if he will not confess the truth—whatever that might be—then we must take some other action to ascertain the truth."

Rowell drained his glass and put it down on the sofa table with an angry thud.

"What nonsense is this, Willow? You know perfectly well that I have the death certificate, and that the child was buried in St. Stephen's graveyard. I really cannot—"

"Rowell, I know what I am saying and believe me, I am perfectly within my right mind. Something happened that night—something probably Grandmère and certainly Aunt Milly knew about. It is my intention to find out the truth and nobody, not even you, Rowell, is going to prevent me. I hope I make myself clear. If you will not aid me, then I shall proceed on my own."

"Proceed to what, may I ask?" Rowell inquired coldly.

"I will petition for a Faculty!"

Rowell's mouth fell open in astonishment as he heard Willow's words. He was not himself entirely sure what this legal phraseology meant, but judging by the emphatic tone of his wife's voice when she had made her pronouncement, she did. It would appear she really was in earnest and this was no passing whim.

"I mean what I say, Rowell. If Doctor Forbes will not tell me what happened, I want the baby's coffin disinterred. Only proof that she lies buried there will silence my doubts."

It was Toby who had found out for Willow what procedure would be required if the coffin were to be lifted from the ground and its contents inspected. He had understood Willow's terrible uneasiness of mind and although he did not share her conviction that some mischief had been perpetrated and that the child really was alive, he did agree that until she was convinced otherwise, there could be no peace of mind for her.

"And if Rowell will not agree to an investigation?" Willow had asked him.

"I honestly do not know the answer to that, Willow. I am far from sure that a woman could petition for a Faculty against her husband's wishes. But let us face that when and if we come to it. We must just await his return."

"I am quite sure this whole unhappy business is a storm in a teacup," Rowell said now, but his tone of voice was less emphatic. "But since you are so determined, I will speak to Forbes."

"Thank you, Rowell!" Willow said. "But I wish to be present when you do so. I have a right to know what he says, although I do not think it will be much."

"Nonsense, my dear. He is the only one who can give us every detail of the night's events—and if he cannot, then I shall want to know the reason why."

"You will talk to him later this afternoon—when he calls to see Aunt Milly?" Willow persisted.

Rowell frowned. He did not like it when a female put pressure upon him in such a fashion. He had been accustomed to it from Georgina, but not from Willow. Nevertheless, he said now:

"I suppose since you insist, I will have to do so or I shall have no peace at all." He noted the softening of Willow's expression and his mood of irritation was once more replaced by admiration. His wife was a remarkably pretty woman, and—as Esmé would say of a woman approaching thirty—in her prime. Willow had not aged with childbirth as had so many of his friends' wives. Her body was still as slender as that of a young girl's—as slim as Désirée's, when he came to consider it. If he could but teach his wife some of Désirée's tricks for pleasuring a man, he might not wish to stray so far from home, he reflected.

Into Rowell's mind came memories of past nights of love shared with his wife. There had been one or two occasions when she had come near to shocking him with her responses. Perhaps he had been silly to discourage her. If he were to indicate by some means or other that he enjoyed a really passionate woman . . .

"Come here, my dear," he said, holding out his arm. "I gave you but a peck on the cheek in the hall on my arrival. Now that we are alone—"

Willow felt her heart miss a beat as she took a reluctant step forward. She had not failed to hear the change in Rowell's voice nor to notice the look in his eyes. But the very last thing in the world she wanted was her husband's loving. Any response she made would seem a betrayal of that deep, genuine love she had shared so briefly with Toby. Moreover, she had little doubt that Rowell had returned from London with the taste of his mistress' kisses

still on his lips, her perfume still clinging to his clothes—
as had Georgina's so often in the past.

She shuddered uncontrollably as Rowell's arm drew her
to him.

"Come now, what prudery is this?" he asked softly.
"There is no servant present . . ."

He pulled her down upon his lap, and his excitement,
heightened by the several glasses of whiskey he had just
consumed, dulled his perception. Feeling Willow tremble,
he gave a small cry of pleasure.

"So you do want me," he said triumphantly. "I know
when a woman is eager for love—as you are, my pretty
little wife."

His hands reached for her breasts, cupping and squeez-
ing them through the material of her dress despite her attempts to struggle free. She turned her face aside as he
tried to kiss her but his mouth fastened on her neck, and
she could feel his hot breath on her shoulders as he pulled
her dress open and down over her upper arms.

"No, Rowell, please . . . not now, not here . . .
please . . ."

Not in the least angry, Rowell withdrew his mouth. He
was smiling.

"Very well, my love. We will wait until we can enjoy
ourselves in bed tonight with a great deal less restriction.
You can dismiss Nellie this evening. I, myself, shall have
the pleasure of undressing you. What do you say to that,
my dear?"

I cannot—I cannot, she thought as silently she rose
from his lap and straightened her dress. It is my duty to
do as he wants—but I cannot. I do not want him near me.
I do not want him to touch me.

But greater even than her repulsion was her need for
his good will. Hating herself, she bent and kissed his
cheek in simulated affection.

Later that evening Doctor Forbes stood before Rowell
in the library and steadfastly refused to change any of the
declarations he had made ten years previously.

"You saw no reason to question my actions then, Lord
Rochford," he said, white-faced. "Why should you doubt
me now—just because an insane old lady has put some
crazed notion into your wife's head?"

Rowell looked at the frail old man contemptuously. He

had never much liked the family physician, but had accepted that Grandmère would have no other medical man in the house. He blamed Forbes in part for his young brother's downfall. It was still like a thorn in his flesh every time he thought of a Rochford going so far off the rails as had Rupert. In the year since Rupert had left home, Rowell had readjusted his thoughts and now managed to convince himself that it had not been his brother who was the corrupter. He preferred to consider that Adrian Forbes was the miscreant who had led Rupert astray. His father should have kept better control of him, Rowell now told himself.

"I do not care for your reference to my aunt as 'an insane old lady,' Doctor Forbes," he said coldly. "I happen to agree with my wife that Miss Rochford does understand many of the questions put to her. And as far as the dead child is concerned, I am told she is quite adamant that the baby did *not* die."

The doctor's hands were trembling so violently he clasped them together in an effort to control their movement. But he did not waver in his reply.

"Your grandmother saw the child's body," he insisted. "Your aunt may not have done—I cannot remember if she was present when I brought the coffin to the house before the funeral. The baby died while I was trying to deliver it safely to a wet nurse. That is all I can tell you."

"Why was the wet nurse not brought here to the baby?" Willow demanded. "What possible justification was there for taking it out into the cold night air and putting it at risk in such a fashion?"

"It could not have survived much longer without nourishment—"

"That is not true," Willow broke in, for she was remembering Nellie's baby—her little Alice—who had lived more than twenty-four hours before she had taken her to her own breast. "I know for a fact that newly-born babies can survive quite a while."

The doctor's mouth was working furiously and his faded blue eyes blinked rapidly.

"Your baby was premature, Lady Rochford. It was a difficult breach birth and the infant was underweight, sickly . . ."

Afraid lest Rowell was going to accept this reply, Willow caught hold of his arm.

"Rowell, I don't believe it. I never have and I never will. Please . . ."

Mentally, Rowell shrugged. Left to himself, he would be more than prepared to take the doctor's word. After all, what difference could it all make now—ten years later? But his pretty young wife was appealing to him with a great fervor. It would not be such a bad idea to indulge her if to do so would put him in her good graces. He had been somewhat neglectful of her over the years to say the least—and now that he was nearing forty years of age, it was about time he started to put his house in order. Besides which, he thought, an inquiry would certainly inconvenience the doctor and repay him with a certain rough justice for not having kept a stricter control upon his perverted son.

"I fear I am not satisfied with the facts you are now presenting to me," he said pompously. "My wife is perfectly justified in stating that the child's body should have been shown to her—or, if she was not well enough, shown to me."

"You did not ask to see it—" the doctor attempted to speak, but Rowell interrupted him.

"The coffin was closed by the time I arrived home. I had no reason then to request that it should be inspected by me. But now that my aunt has assured us the baby did not die, I have no alternative but to pursue the matter."

"You must do as you think best . . ." the doctor murmured, his body drooping in unexpected acquiescence. He knew the Rochfords. Rowell was like his grandmother —stubborn as a mule once his mind was made up. Fortunately, it was highly unlikely that permission would be obtained for the body to be exhumed. After so long a lapse in time, no coroner would want the task of viewing such remains, even were he to suspect that the baby *had* died a violent or unnatural death—for which no evidence existed. The only coroner he knew to have been involved in such a case had told him that he had evaded a similar exhumation on the grounds that after so long a time, there would be a danger of infection to those performing the task.

Rowell was now beginning to enjoy himself. He fancied

that he knew quite a bit about English law—especially relating to the affairs of his estate. He had had on one occasion to give evidence at the trial of a common poacher and had been complimented by the magistrate for his lucid, informative, and damning summing-up of the man's character.

"Leave this to me, my dear," he told Willow when the doctor departed. *"You* have no need to worry about the legalities. *I* will talk to Toby—he has a level head on his shoulders—and we'll soon have this sorted out."

To Willow's relief Toby had the tact to allow Rowell to believe that his own interpretation of the intricacies of the law originated with Rowell. When her husband joined Willow in their bedroom later that evening he was in good spirits. Willow was already undressed and in bed, thus avoiding the possibility Rowell had mentioned earlier of allowing him to disrobe her.

"What I shall now do," he told her, "is to instruct our solicitor to prepare a petition to send to the Chancellor—the Bishop's Chancellor. Toby thinks he knows the fellow—a gentleman by the name of Matthew Maybury who lives in Canterbury. You, Forbes, and I will doubtless be questioned and may be required to give verbal evidence if the Chancellor requests it. Old Reverend Appleby may not be well enough to put in an appearance, but he can give his evidence by affidavit, I dare say. What we're after is a Faculty enabling us to have the body disinterred for the purpose of identification or to ascertain that there are human remains in the coffin—"

With no sensitive regard for Willow's shudder of distaste at the thoughts he was evoking, he continued in such vein until he was halted in his account by his valet, whom he then preceded to his dressing room. Willow could hear him talking to the servant through the half-open doorway She knew by the heightened level of Rowell's tone that he had been drinking heavily throughout the evening. In such state, he was either violently aggressive and abusive to the servants or fulsome in his praises of their virtues.

When at last Rowell reappeared, every nerve of her body was taut with apprehension. She knew that his bonhomie might change when he finally fell on top of her and discovered himself too drunk to be able to fulfill his desires. At such moments, he would invariably blame her for his own shortcomings.

But tonight, his mind had clearly been diverted from his afternoon purpose. He lay with his head on the pillow beside her, his arm across her waist but his mind still fully preoccupied with legal niceties. He was still expounding his themes when his voice trailed into silence and was followed almost instantly by loud, persistent snores.

Unable to sleep with this disturbance, Willow slowly eased herself from beneath his arm and slid out from under the sheets. It was a hot, sultry August night. Barefooted, without even a wrapper, she tiptoed over to the open windows.

The garden was brilliant with moonlight. A heavy dew lay over the lawns, which glittered with a thousand tiny sparks as the moon's rays reflected on the dewdrops. In the far distance, beyond the dark looming shadows of the trees, she could see the silver shimmer of the lake. Her body seemed to be on fire. As she covered her breasts with her hands, they seemed to be burning hot beneath her palms. She wanted . . . what was it she wanted, she asked herself? She wanted . . .

Her eyes closed and she leaned forward until her forehead touched the cool glass. How impossible it was proving to keep her word to Toby, to forget what had happened between them! How right he had been not to allow them to pursue their need for one another beyond a kiss, an embrace, for now her memories were like needles in her mind, forcing themselves upon her consciousness despite her determination to forget.

Where was Toby now? she thought with a deep ache that seemed to encompass her whole body. In his room asleep, perhaps, his dear, funny face relaxed in slumber, Was he dreaming of her? Or was he awake, wondering as she was, how love would be between them? No, not love, but passion—a fierce wild abandonment of desire; that was how it would be between them. And afterwards, she would hold him, kiss him, stroke his cheek, tell him how terribly, agonizingly she loved him.

Somewhere down in the avenue of trees, a barn owl hooted. Willow's eyes opened and she shivered. There behind her in the big marital bed lay her husband, snoring still, impervious to her true needs, her true self.

Why did I ever marry Rowell? she thought. How could I ever have wanted him in the way I now want Toby? But it had never been quite like that. She had wanted Rowell to love her; to need her; to admire her; to show her affection. But with Toby it was different. It was she who wanted to give herself to him; enfold him; make him part of herself.

She thought of Silvie's caution regarding her future were she to ask Rowell to divorce her. It had been unlike Silvie to give any counsel against freedom, yet she had taken great pains to stress the disgrace for a woman that inevitably followed divorce; the social ostracism; the financial problems. Now her situation was even more in favor of her remaining with Rowell than when Oliver was born. She had two children to consider. One day Rochford Manor would be Oliver's, and she could not take it upon herself to deny him his birthright.

Willow drew a deep sigh as she closed the windows reluctantly and returned to bed. She tried to find the oblivion of sleep, but now she was haunted by renewed doubts as to the past.

What reason could Aunt Milly have for reiterating that the baby had not died? Was she in fact trying to say that someone had killed it? Such an idea was really not credible unless, through neglect, the baby had been allowed to die. If only Aunt Milly could speak—tell her in words what had really transpired that night. As for the disinterring of the coffin—it would be an ordeal almost beyond her bearing. But if the little casket did contain the body of a newborn female infant, it would at least prove her child was not somewhere in this world alone, and unprotected.

During the following week, Rowell asked her the same questions she had asked herself. Why was she so convinced that she felt it necessary to demand the unnatural process of exhumation—and after so long a passage of time?

"From what my solicitor tells me, it is highly improbable my petition for a Faculty will be granted," he told her truthfully. Seeing her look of dismay, he added: "Nevertheless, I am pursuing the matter as I promised you. But do not build any hopes on its success, Willow, for I fear you may be disappointed."

Willow went in search of Toby.

"Is it true you know the Bishop's Chancellor?" she inquired. "Can you bring any personal influence to bear upon him, Toby?"

Toby frowned.

"I can try, Willow. I knew the fellow briefly at Oxford. But I think a great deal may depend upon what credence he places on your evidence—and that of Doctor Forbes. I agree with you absolutely that the doctor gives the impression that he is not telling the truth. Rowell showed me Reverend Appleby's deposition, and that throws very little light upon the matter since he, like yourself, never saw the body in the coffin." He paused before adding thoughtfully:

"Nor, indeed, did Rowell. And we have only Doctor Forbes' word that Grandmére looked into the coffin before it was sealed. None of the servants did so, although Nellie told Rowell that she had asked if she might see your baby but was refused permission to do so. The midwife has also been questioned and she has no further light to shed on that day being, so she says, in constant attendance upon you. I suppose we may hope that the Chancellor will accept that there is room for doubt in the light of Aunt Milly's implications."

When Silvie arrived for her annual Christmas visit, she could offer little more assurance than Toby.

"Tyrant though she was, I cannot believe Aunt Clotilde would condone any act of violence, *chérie,*" she said. "She was not an evil woman even if she was very far from saintly. I have to say I believe the baby did die, Willow—albeit from neglect."

As forecast by Rowell's solicitor, Mr. Bartholomew, the Chancellor, rejected his petition. Willow was on tenterhooks as Rowell hesitated in his acceptance of this rebuff. But he finally agreed to request an appearance before the consistory court, where his appeal would receive a hearing.

Feeling himself challenged, he said:

"Since we have started this unhappy business, we may as well go through with it."

Willow was genuinely grateful to him. But with Christmas over, she became increasingly impatient for Mr. Bartholomew to complete the preparation of the petition and for Rowell to make an appointment to see the Chancellor.

She continued to spend several hours a day with Aunt Milly, but no matter how ingeniously she worded her questions, she was unable to obtain any further detail from the sick woman as to what had transpired that night so long ago. There were times when it was painfully obvious that Aunt Milly's movements were totally disconnected and unintelligible as to their meaning, and on such occasions, her heart sank as she recalled Doctor Forbes' warning that the old lady's mind was too confused to be considered reliable. She was terrified lest the Chancellor feel there was insufficient evidence to justify the issuing of the Faculty.

"Am I being horribly morbid, Toby?" she asked as the second week of January passed by with still no apparent progress made. "Do you think it unnatural of me to want my baby's grave disturbed for no better reason than to put my mind at rest?"

Toby regarded her drawn face and longed to bring back serenity and happiness to it.

"I do not think you are being morbid," he said truthfully. "If there is even the smallest doubt that the baby did die, then you should leave no stone unturned to discover the truth. But it worries me that you may feel bitterly disappointed if your fears prove unfounded."

"I am prepared for that," Willow said. "I think I might even welcome it. In my heart of hearts I suppose I myself do not believe any crime was perpetrated. Logic tells me I have no real reason to question the known facts, and yet every instinct tells me I must pursue this now that Aunt Milly has renewed my fears that all was not well."

"When you give evidence at the consistory court, you might do better to sound *totally* convinced," Toby cautioned. "Do not voice any doubts, as clearly there will be plenty of those circulating already."

It was six long weeks before at last the day set for the hearing of Rowell's petition arrived. Toby's words rang in Willow's ears as she rode with Rowell and their lawyer to Rochester in the landau. The Reverend Appleby and Doctor Forbes followed behind them in a second carriage. The court was sitting in the consistory chapel of Rochester Cathedral, and Mr. Bartholomew now advised them that the Chancellor would be present, together with the Bishop of the Diocese, the Archdeacon, and the Registrar who was an ecclesiastical lawyer.

Staring at Mr. Bartholomew's round pink face, Willow thought how much younger he looked than his contemporary, Doctor Forbes. The lawyer, in his late sixties, was still actively engaged in legal business, but the doctor had a new young assistant, Doctor Rose, and since the contretemps with Rowell over Aunt Milly, he had ceased to attend the Rochford family. It was therefore several months since Willow had last seen him, and she had been not a little shocked by his appearance when they gathered at Mr. Bartholomew's office before setting out for Rochester. The old doctor was obviously nervous, and the few necessary replies he made to the solicitor had been stammered and unnaturally hesitant. Perhaps this would go in their favor, Willow thought, for it seemed unlikely that he would give the court the impression of being a self-assured man.

Her instincts were justified. It proved a simple matter for Mr. Bartholomew to establish that the doctor's behavior on the night of the baby's birth had been irregular to a degree. Doctor Forbes' reiteration that he had acted under Grandmère's instructions and at all times with her agreement was clearly disapproved of by the court. The responsibility was his and his alone, the Registrar pointed out.

The elderly vicar was shown to be equally vague about events, and he, in his turn, finally admitted that he had simply complied with old Lady Rochford's instructions—which had been to arrange the child's funeral as speedily as possible.

Rowell was not required to give evidence, having been absent on the night in question; but Willow was invited to do so. Despite her inner trembling, she managed to appear calm, rational, and completely logical in her summing up of the events which led up to their petition.

"Despite those instincts I have already told you of that something was amiss that night, my Lord," she concluded, "I did accept that my baby had died and been buried in St. Stephen's graveyard. I would not have pursued the matter further had it not been for the positive assertion of Miss Mildred Rochford that my child did not die. I know you have affidavits from my aunt's day nurse and from Mr. Tobias Rochford that they are in no doubt Miss Rochford does comprehend and acknowledge a large part of what is said to her. Doctor Forbes' assistant, Doctor Rose, has also signed an affidavit to this effect."

Her voice gained conviction as she added:

"So I am not alone in this belief that my husband's aunt understands me and knows what she is trying to say when she gives signals of assent. She is obviously not far from death, poor woman, and I cannot believe she would be untruthful at such a time in her life. I believe she is trying to rectify a wrongdoing of which she is cognizant. With all my heart, I beg you, sirs, to allow the Faculty, so that the truth may be established once and for all."

"Can you suggest any reason why any persons or group of persons should have removed a live child elsewhere and then deliberately deceived you and your husband into believing it to be in the coffin, Lady Rochford?"

Willow had been prepared for such a question by Mr. Bartholomew.

"Yes, my Lord, I think there was a reason. My baby was premature and sickly. There had already been three previous cases in my husband's family of females who were not entirely healthy—two infants who died in 1864 and my sister-in-law, who suffers from a deformity of her arm and leg. I think the late Lady Rochford may have feared a repetition of this and that she decided it would be for the best if the baby was removed elsewhere at birth."

For a moment, there was total silence in the court, and then the doctor was recalled for further questioning. His face was as white as paper as he reiterated his former evidence. He was reminded that he was on oath, but he would not alter his evidence in any way.

"As indeed he dare not," Mr. Bartholomew remarked as they drove home an hour later. "To do so would insure his being struck off at the best; and at worst he would be accused of the crime of kidnap—among other misdemeanors."

"But now that the Chancellor has agreed to issue the Faculty, nothing can stop the disinterment, can it, sir?" Willow said. "When the coffin is opened, the doctor will surely be found guilty if my baby's remains are not there?"

"Guilty of what, Lady Rochford? The body, if proved

other than that of a female infant, could have been substituted by someone other than the doctor himself. If there *is* no body, it could have been stolen by others. After so long, it would be virtually impossible to prove that Doctor Forbes was involved in a conspiracy."

"Unless he were to confess!" Willow said.

"Assuming there is anything requiring a confession," Rowell pointed out, but not unreasonably. "This is pure speculation, my dear, and I suggest we cease all discussion upon the matter until after the disinterment."

Willow was barely able to contain her impatience as week followed week with still no date set for the exhumation. The Chancellor had been called away to another diocese and was busy with other matters.

"He will issue the Faculty in due time, Milady," Mr. Bartholomew said with typical lawyer's disregard for urgency.

It was six weeks to the day and one week short of the eleventh anniversary of her baby's death that the small group of people gathered in St. Stephen's churchyard to establish the identity of the body in the tiny coffin buried there.

Willow herself was not in the group gathered around the Rochford family gravestones. It was four in the morning and the rain was falling in a steady downpour as the local police officer directed the grave diggers to commence their grisly task. Rowell and Toby stood a few yards away from the canvas screen that had been placed around the tiny grave to ensure privacy. Willow sat alone in the dark interior of the landau at the entrance to the graveyard huddled in her thick wool coat, her hands buried in her sable muff and the carriage rug tucked around her legs. Neither Rowell nor Toby had wished her to come.

"If you cannot sleep, my dear," Rowell had said, "then please wait in the library until we bring you news."

But Willow felt impelled to go at least as far as the church and would not be gainsaid, even when Toby reported the miserable cold wet weather attending the ordeal.

"There is no point to your being nearby," Rowell said irritably.

Willow sighed as she huddled deeper beneath the warm rug. Rowell was justified in his comment, she thought.

Nevertheless, she had felt driven by some inner compulsion to be here, although she could neither see the group nor hear their voices. The only sound was the restless stamping of the horses' hooves as they lowered their heads against the driving rain. Peters, the unhappy coachman, was a dark shapeless hump beneath the heavy oilskin he had pulled over his head and shoulders.

Willow shivered as the wind rocked the carriage lanterns flickering in the darkness. What would be the outcome of this dawn vigil? Had Aunt Milly been confusing her baby with another? With Dodie, perhaps? Old people —even those who had not been stricken by apoplexy— often became very confused in their memories. Yet even as recently as the previous day, the poor unhappy woman had continued to lift her hand in assent when Willow asked for the hundredth time: "Did my baby live, Aunt Milly?"

Now that the Faculty had been granted, and in a sense victory achieved, Rowell had lost all real interest in the proceedings. Having gone so far as to issue the petition, he had felt obliged to prove that he was justified in demanding the disinterment; but never at any time had he been convinced in his own mind that there was need for identification of the small corpse. He was certain that the skeleton of the infant would be discovered within the next half hour and he was now waiting impatiently for the unpleasant task to be completed so that he could return home to a hot breakfast and warm fires.

Beside him, Toby too was silent, but his thoughts were on the woman in the carriage. Like Rowell, he was certain there was nothing untoward to be discovered this day and he feared the effect such an anticlimax would have upon Willow.

Her belief in Aunt Milly's sanity worried him a great deal, and although he did not entirely decry the instinct she insisted was driving her on to the truth, he knew from books he had read that some women had great powers of self-delusion. It was far from unknown in medical circles that females could so wish themselves pregnant that they could actually show physical signs of being with child.

He glanced at his elder brother who, despite the solemnity of the gruesome occasion, was now engaged in a lively conversation with the pathologist who had come down from London to pronounce on the remains. Toby sighed. Rowell was an enigma to him. It was as if they had both come from different planets rather than from the same parents. His brother, he thought, was not a bad man—merely totally egotistical and lacking in understanding of those unlike himself. It surprised Toby that he had supported his wife in her obsessive desire for an inquiry into the past, and he was forced to the not very kind conclusion that Rowell had actually welcomed it as a diversion. The real reason for it seemed totally to have escaped him.

The two rubber-caped gravediggers suddenly put down their spades, and at a nod from the police constable, knelt down on the rain-soaked soil and drew up the small coffin. The pathologist stepped forward, his galoshered shoes squelching in the wet muddy puddles. Toby closed his eyes, knowing how terrible the contents of that coffin might be after so many years. He had had no obligation to be here at all, although he had never considered remaining absent. If anything were amiss, Willow might need his support.

"For God's sake, Toby, come and look at this!"

It was Rowell's voice, oddly excited. He was looking down at a small dark object the pathologist was holding in his hands.

"A confounded brick! So m'wife was right after all. Who in the name of heaven would have suspected such villainy!"

Willow did, Toby thought, as horrified, he too stared at the brick which had been used in place of a body to weight the coffin. All along, Willow had known with that feminine instinct of hers that something was wrong.

"This is now a police matter, Milord," the constable said to Rowell. "I shall be making a report to my superiors for 'tis mighty clear things are not what they should be, for sure."

"I too will make a report, Lord Rochford," the pathologist said as he handed the brick to the constable and instructed the gravediggers to close the empty coffin. "You'd best put the soil back in the grave or we'll have the whole village agog with speculation," he said sensibly.

The look of excitement had left Rowell's face and he now turned anxiously to the constable.

"I don't want a word of this getting abroad," he said sternly. "If the press get hold of the story, we shall have no peace at Rochford Manor. Keep your mouths well shut, all of you, and I'll see to it that you don't suffer for it!"

"Nasty business, to be sure," the pathologist said as the three men made their way back to the waiting carriages. "I little expected to be dealing with a brick in place of a corpse."

Rowell looked anxiously at Toby.

"Damned if I know how to tell Willow. It's a pity she left the house. There's no knowing how she's going to take this news."

But Willow surprised him by her calm acceptance of the facts.

"It does not surprise me, Rowell," she said quietly as she made room for him and Toby beside her and beckoned to Peters to drive home. "I have believed for some time that my child is alive. Now Doctor Forbes must be made to confess the truth. If our daughter is alive, I shall find her."

"You cannot count upon Forbes' confessing, my dear," Rowell said warningly. "If he was involved in this—this mischief, he'd be a damned fool to admit it. He gave evidence to the consistory court under oath. At the very least, he'd suffer a term of imprisonment for perjury which would mean his incarceration for what's left of the old fellow's life. No, I doubt we'll get much out of him."

"I am afraid Rowell is right," Toby agreed quietly. "Our only hope of finding out the truth is from Aunt Milly. We'll just have to broaden the scope of our questions until we gain some clue from her."

Willow nodded. Now at least she had some justification for the long hours she spent with the sick old lady attempting to read her mind. Now she could begin again from a known fact. Since the baby had not been buried, she must have been removed elsewhere. It might take time, but if she had to go through a list of every village, every town, every city in the country, she would find out sooner or later.

She managed somehow to smile at Toby as he assisted her from the carriage. He held the umbrella over her head as Dutton opened the front door. The grandfather clock in the hall was striking six o'clock. A housemaid was on her knees by the grate adding logs to the newly-lit fire. A footman came hurrying forward to take their wet clothes and umbrellas. From the servants' passageway through the green baize door came the sharp appetizing smell of frying bacon.

Toby took her arm and led her to the fireside where flames were licking the dry logs. Sensing her impatience, he said in a low voice:

"It is still too early to call upon Aunt Milly. We will go see her after we have had some breakfast. A hot meal will be good for us all."

Willow nodded, not surprised that Toby had sensed her desire to hurry upstairs to the sickroom. But before she could make any reply, there was a sudden flurry of white in the long gallery. The night nurse in her starched apron and cap was leaning over the banisters.

"Milady, Milord, I think you should come quickly to Miss Rochford's room," she called down in urgent tones. "She has had another apoplectic seizure. Would someone notify the doctor, please?"

Willow's legs seemed to have no strength left in them as Toby and Rowell between them half carried her upstairs. Once again, her instinct was so overpowering that she did not need to be told what she would find when she entered the sickroom. The one person in the world who might have helped her find her lost daughter would never talk again. Aunt Milly was dead.

Part Three

1905–1910

"And soon the grass with brighter flowers will blow,
And send up lilies for some boy to mow."

Oscar Wilde, *Ravenna*

Chapter Twenty-three

March–April 1905

"I UNDERSTAND EXACTLY HOW YOU FEEL, WILLOW, but Rowell is right—there is nothing more he can do. There is nothing any of us can do," Toby said.

It was a bitterly cold March day. A blustering northwest wind beat in gusts against the window panes of the manor house and whistled between any crack it could find in the old oak frames. Despite the huge log fires blazing in all the rooms, the house was full of drafts and everything felt damp to the touch.

Willow shivered. The weather was in keeping with her mood—alternatively violent with the pent-up frustration of inactivity, and silent with a hopeless depression.

The family was in mourning for Aunt Milly. The usual round of winter social events was therefore denied them, and Rowell had already made clear to everyone that there would be no removal to London in May for the Season. Immediately after Aunt Milly's funeral, Pelham departed for Egypt. Willow did not blame him, for there was nothing he could do to assist in the attempts to unravel the mystery of her missing baby.

Rowell was leaving the whole affair in the hands of a Scotland Yard detective, but as the kindly officer had pointed out, there was very little hope of discovering the truth. Grandmère and Aunt Milly—the only two people to see into the coffin on the day of the funeral other than the doctor—were both dead. And Doctor Forbes stuck rigidly to his story throughout a series of grueling interviews by a number of senior officers. Suspicion clearly lay at his door. But as he pointed out repeatedly, he could not be held responsible for what happened after he had delivered the coffin containing the body to Rochford Manor. Any number of people could have tampered with it before the funeral.

His manner was far from reassuring. His trembling hands and white sweating face gave every indication that he was not telling the truth; but since it had all happened so long ago, there were no leads to be followed up, and the police could make no accusations against him. No one came forward with new evidence. The midwife, now retired, had been questioned once more but had nothing to add to the statement she had previously given—that the baby was alive, if weak, when it was removed from the house, a fact confirmed by the butler who had let the doctor out of the house and watched him place the bundle beside him in the gig.

"It is best we should all now forget the whole unfortunate business," Rowell said. He resented Willow's implications that his grandmother had wished the baby harm and the slur this cast upon the family name.

He might have been more critical of his wife if he did not in fact share her conviction that Grandmère was quite capable in those days of taking matters into her own hands and dealing with them as she thought fit without informing anyone—even him.

As far as his first-born child was concerned, he himself had no special feelings regarding it. It was as if the baby had never existed. He would infinitely have preferred that it was well and truly buried and could be forgotten. He did not share Willow's obsessive desire to discover its whereabouts and he found his wife's company depressing. Moreover, he was anxious to supervise the refitting of his yacht at Cowes. It was not therefore from altruistic motives that he suggested it might do Willow good to pay a visit to Silvie.

"You always enjoy her company, and the change might cheer your spirits," he said as March gave way to April.

Willow realized that Rowell wished to put the exhumation out of his mind and that he did not like to be reminded by her of the resultant enigma. Only Toby appeared to understand her passionate need to know the truth—however terrible. Nevertheless, he, too, thought it advisable that she should go away for a while.

In Silvie also there was a deep vein of compassion, despite her avowals that she lacked all the normal maternal instincts. She hugged Willow warmly as she welcomed her to her charming, elegant little house in the Rue d'Artois.

"I can appreciate your restlessness, *chérie*. Nevertheless, life must go on and you cannot live in the past," she advised.

Willow nodded.

"You are right, of course, Silvie, and now that I am here with you in Paris, I shall do my best to forget that terrible dawn in the graveyard and poor Aunt Milly's death."

Silvie eyed her friend speculatively. Willow had lost an alarming amount of weight, and her skin was as pale as a camellia petal. But not even the violet shadows beneath her eyes could detract from her increasing beauty.

"My dearest Willow, it is time you reconsidered many aspects of your life," she said gently. "Has it not occurred to you that you are now thirty years of age, which in my opinion is very much a halfway mark. One first becomes attractive to the opposite sex at about fifteen. One ceases to have the same desirability at forty-five, even though some women are still beautiful at that age."

Willow smiled at the seriousness of Silvie's tone. It was much like that of a parent addressing a young child.

"So . . . I shall be old in another fifteen years' time," she said, smiling. "What of it, my dear Silvie?"

Silvie hunched her shoulders in an expression of exasperation.

"Do you not realize that you are wasting your life?" she asked rhetorically. "You have a husband who rarely comes to your bed and yet you have never had a lover—not even one!"

Willow sighed.

"I have been unfaithful to Rowell once," she reminded the French girl, "with Pelham—even if I did not exactly intend it."

"*Mon Dieu, mon Dieu!*" Silvie cried, throwing up her hands in despair. "I am talking of a real *affaire du coeur, chérie*. It is not I, as you seem to suppose, who is unusual in taking a lover whenever I so desire. Most married women do the same—albeit with discretion, *ne'est ce pas?*"

Willow smiled again.

"But I do not desire any man," she said, adding, "Except one . . . and he is forever beyond my reach. So there it is, Silvie . . . *tout simplement*," she added hoping to make Silvie smile. But Silvie's look of concern deepened.

"He is married—this man you love?" she inquired.

Willow clasped her hands together in sudden nervousness.

"No, not married," she replied softly, shaking her head. "I suppose I may as well tell you, Silvie, for you will prize my secret from me sooner or later. For some time now I have known that it is Toby who means more to me than anyone in the world. Do I shock you, Silvie?"

"Shock me—*mais pas du tout!*" Silvie said. "Moreover, I can fully understand why you should fall in love with him. He may be far too serious to please me, but you, *ma petite,* look always for the deeper meanings of life, do you not? You are two of a kind, and I recognized this long ago. But I was hoping that you would not see dear Toby's affinity—nor, indeed, become aware of his immense charm. That shy smile of his is most attractive, not to mention the intensity of his eyes when he is talking of his dreams for the future. One has the feeling that Toby desires for mankind a world where medicine can cure all ills —even broken hearts, perhaps!"

She sat down beside Willow and put her arm around her shoulders.

"Last Christmas I could not fail but notice how often you looked toward him; how your voice softened unconsciously when you spoke to him; how your face lit up when he spoke to you. But do not look so frightened, *chérie*— no one else would have noticed. But I, being a woman too, and so anxious always about your happiness—well, I keep my eyes very much open."

Willow sighed.

"Well then, you may as well know, Silvie, that Toby loves me too, but we have promised one another never to speak of our feelings. If the truth became known, he would certainly leave Rochford, which I could not bear," Willow said in a low, passionate tone.

Silvie was momentarily silent. Such a love was certainly doomed. Toby could never marry his brother's wife even were Rowell to divorce her.

"I am so very sorry," she said gently. "You must try to forget these feelings, Willow. They cannot bring you happiness."

"I know, I know!" Willow cried. "And I have tried so

hard to fight them. But it seems as if I am not in control of my heart, my thoughts. There are times when I am sitting in a room with Toby listening while he talks and suddenly I am not listening any more, I am thinking: 'Suppose he walks toward me and takes me in his arms . . .' My knees tremble with a desire so strong that I think were Toby really to come toward me, I would fall into a swoon —or worse still, I might throw myself into his arms."

Willow's face was softened with love as she added:

"At night, I often dream that Toby is kissing me, touch-me—even that he is making love to me. I wake with such a sense of loneliness that it is beyond description. I long for morning so that I can dress and go downstairs and at least be able to sit at the breakfast table and see him there. It is a terrible torture—and a sweetness too, for I am never happier than when I am in his company."

"My poor darling," Silvie said. "But how can you bear such frustration? I do not think it can be good for you, *chérie*. The more I consider it, the more certain I am that you must take a lover—and do not look so horrified. I do not mean for love or for marriage, but so that you may for a little while enjoy the pleasures of being a woman. It appals me to think that after thirty years of life, you have known only two men and one of those intoxicated when he made love to you! No, *chérie*, it will not do. You are far, far too lovely for so much beauty to be wasted."

Willow's tense expression relaxed once more into a smile.

"You make it all sound so simple, Silvie. But I dare not put my marriage at risk for so frivolous a pleasure— if pleasure it would be; and I am far from certain of that. I can think of no man with whom I might wish to share my body."

Silvie laughed mischievously.

"As to the risk to your marriage, you can trust me to arrange a rendezvous with total discretion. As to the man —I found the perfect lover for you years ago: that friend of Pierre's whom I see quite often in Paris. He is most charming, very nice looking, terribly poor, and an artist. Moreover, he is still unmarried and lives alone in a large studio in the Rue de la Planchette. I would happily have enjoyed *une petite affaire* with him myself, but alas, I am not his type. He tells me I am too flamboyant and extroverted. He says he likes women who are quiet and secretive; who do not reveal their inner selves. Now that is a description of you, dearest Willow."

"But even were he to admire me, you could not be certain I would admire him," Willow laughed.

"Let me be the judge," Silvie cried vehemently, surprising Willow who had not until then taken their conversation very seriously. Now she realized Silvie was in earnest.

"I could not enter into the spirit of such a meeting," she said firmly. "It might be different were I to meet someone —a stranger perhaps, neither of us knowing who the other was. Maybe then I could overcome my shyness, my reluctance, and that ingrained sense of conventionalism for which you so often chide me."

"Ha!" Silvie exclaimed, her eyes sparkling. "That is exactly the cause of your trouble, Willow, and I have the perfect solution. I shall arrange a rendezvous, and you and Pierre's friend shall both go incognito. I will explain that you do not wish him to know your real name. He can call you . . . why, yes, he can call you 'Juliet' and you shall call him 'Romeo,' and then, if you do not like each other—or if the evening is not a success—why then, you will never meet again."

For the next three days, Willow prayed that Silvie would forget this wild, impetuous plan to which somehow agreement had been forced from her. She told herself that Silvie could not hold her to her promise since she had not meant it to be taken seriously. She hoped Silvie would forget the whole improbable scheme, for she herself had regained a sense of reality—and more important than that —of morality.

But then she recalled the week preceding her departure to Paris when Silvie's letter arrived, saying how delighted she would be to have Willow stay with her. Rowell had been unable to hide his satisfaction.

Willow's heart had hardened in sudden cynicism. His sudden concern for her was so out of character that she could not do other than suspect—wrongly, as it happened —that Rowell intended an assignation with Désirée Somners. Doubtless, he imagined that she, his wife, knew nothing of his new mistress, far less her name. She had never told him of the revelational letter she had received from Georgina Grey on the subject of her successor. It was locked away in a box. Too distressed to reply, Willow had hidden it in her dressing-table drawer, somehow unwilling to consign it to the fire as it deserved.

I do not expect you, Lady Rochford, to hold any feelings of sympathy for me, Georgina had written. *But everyone speaks of you as a person of great kindness, above all toward those in hardship. I am therefore appealing to you on behalf of my children. I understand it is already known to you that your husband is their father. But since his attentions have been engrossed by that vulgar little actress, Désirée Somners, he has neglected the innocent children he fathered.*

I realize that your husband has many calls upon his time and that it may not be convenient for him to visit our children. But it is not right that they should suffer financial hardship as well as his neglect. He ignores the fact that we are in dire straits and I am sure you yourself, would not want . . .

Willow had read no further. Sickened though she had been by this past relationship that had wrought such havoc on her own marriage, she had nevertheless come to terms with it, realizing that Rowell had entered into it long before his marriage; and that in a strange way, Georgina Grey had prior claims upon him. But Désirée Somners was inexcusable on every count. It was not even as if she were someone Rowell could love and respect or a worthy rival for her husband's affection. Willow had made discreet inquiries and learned that his new mistress was little more than a cheap chorus girl whose mother had been a woman of the streets and whose father was unknown.

She was convinced that he was taking Désirée with him to Cowes and she could not forget his look of relief when she had said quietly: "Very well, Rowell, I will leave for Paris tomorrow."

On the fifth day of Willow's visit, Silvie announced that the assignation was made. Disregarding her dismay, Silvie ignored all her protests. She would brook no refusal from Willow, she insisted, and she was holding her to her promise. The proposed rendezvous would take place in the utmost secrecy, she said; therefore, she would not employ her own coachman but hire a fiacre to take them to the restaurant where they were to meet Pierre and his artist friend.

"I would never have agreed to go with you if Rowell had not made it so clear to me that he welcomed my absence," Willow said bitterly but with truth as she awaited with increasing nervousness the arrival of the fiacre that evening. "That I am going with you tonight is, I fear, as much to revenge myself upon him as to please you," she added wryly.

Silvie laughed.

"Your reasons do not concern me, Willow. It is enough that you are coming with me—and you look quite, quite beautiful, *chérie!*"

Willow was wearing an apricot cream silk dress. Much plainer than was the current fashion, it molded her figure down to below her hips, where it flared out into layers of tucks and flounces. That morning, Silvie's coiffeuse had come to the house to wash and arrange her hair. It shone a pale light gold, "like a shaft of morning sunlight," the hairdresser had exclaimed poetically to her beautiful English client.

Willow was silent as the fiacre drove down the cobbled back streets toward the Left Bank. The pavements were glistening from an earlier shower of rain. Here and there a chestnut tree glowed pink in full blossom. People were hurrying home from work or making their way toward tables and chairs outside the bistros and cafés on the sidewalks. The soft spring air was tinged with the faint blue smoke of roasting meat, of garlic, of Paris itself.

Suddenly, Willow was overcome by the magical expectancy of this single moment in time. It was as if she were fifteen years old, on her way to her first ball, nervous lest she might not attract a young man and that her dance program would remain empty all evening; yet confidant deep down inside herself that she did look pretty; that her dress enhanced her figure, and that she was about to meet the romantic beau of her dreams.

"I swear that you look nearer twenty than thirty!" Silvie said beside her. "Is this not amusing, *chérie?* The moment before the night begins is always the most perfect—for one can still believe it will be the best night of one's life!"

Willow smiled, not a little surprised to discover Silvie's emotions so akin to her own.

But that brief moment when all her senses seemed heightened by pleasurable awareness vanished as the cab drew up in front of a small, crowded restaurant. A wave of nervousness overcame her. In a daze of confusion, she was conscious of two men coming toward the fiacre; of one paying the driver; of the other putting a hand beneath her elbow and leading her into a small, dimly-lit room. A waiter guided them through the noisy crowd of people to a small table in a quiet alcove.

Willow supposed that it was Silvie's friend, Pierre, who was taking control of their seating and that the man who sat down beside her was her unknown escort. She could not find the courage to look at him, but he sounded perfectly at ease as he said in English:

"Good evening, Juliet!" His voice was strongly accented, but soft and tinged with humor. "Am I permitted to say that even dear Silvie's most glowing report of your beauty falls far short of the truth."

Willow looked up hesitantly into a pair of eyes so deep a blue that they reminded her of the gentians growing in the rockery at Rochford. The Frenchman was far from unattractive, she decided. His nose was long and straight, his mouth full-lipped above a small dark beard. His hair, also dark, was lightly flecked with gray and was longer than was conventionally fashionable. Otherwise, the only hints he gave that he was an artist were his black fluttering tie worn *à la Lavallière* and the yellow gloves, which with his black velvet hat and walking stick, he had handed to the waiter.

His smile was warm and friendly, lessening his first attack of nerves.

"I will confess that I arrived here a most unwilling accomplice to Pierre's little ploy," he continued as Silvie and Pierre settled themselves at the table, talking animatedly to one another as if their companions did not exist. "I did not care at all for the idea of spending my evening in the company of a strange English lady who would not even reveal her true name. But now I am most grateful to both Pierre and Silvie for arranging this little dinner party. I am enchanted to meet you, Madame."

"And I to meet you, sir," Willow replied shyly, but with genuine pleasure. She confessed her own aversion to Silvie's proposal that she should rendezvous with a stranger. Her companion laughed and suddenly she was perfectly at ease in his company.

The business of choosing dishes from the menu momentarily interrupted the conversation. The careful selection of a well-balanced meal was taken with utmost seriousness by Willow's three French companions. With much encouragement and advice from their waiter, a perfect repast was ordered: soles poached in Chablis and garnished with oysters and prawns, to be followed by boned quails *en croute* filled with *foie gras* and accompanied by a sauce of truffles and mushrooms and served with tomatoes and croquettes. These superbly cooked dishes were rounded off by a concoction of *marrons purées* and freshly whipped cream, and the whole meal was to be accompanied by excellent red and white wines followed by iced champagne with the whipped chestnuts.

The conversation was animated and general as they ate, but as the last of the dishes was cleared away, Silvie and Pierre began a heated discussion between themselves. Willow's vis-à-vis turned and smiled at her, a gleam of amusement in his eyes.

"Our very good friends will be bitterly disappointed if we do not play the parts they have so carefully designated for us," he said in an undertone. "We are expected, I think, to fall instantly in love and to want that love instantly satisfied."

Willow laughed softly.

"I admit that would be Silvie's plan for me," she said. "But alas, I am not as free in my thinking as is my very dear friend."

Her companion nodded.

"Nevertheless, we could arrange that they are not disappointed. If you would agree to come to my studio to drink coffee with me now, however innocently we behaved when we arrived, they would suspect the worst. We should make them happy, and I would be delighted to entertain you in the most respectable of ways, if that is your wish. It is entirely as you please, Juliet."

The excellent meal, the easy conversation, and above all the constant flow of champagne had brought about a feeling of euphoria that Willow found confusing. She had comforted herself before leaving Silvie's house with the thought that she was committed to no more than a meal with her unknown escort. Despite her desire to be revenged upon Rowell, she had had no intention whatever of becoming involved, however casually, with a stranger. But now Rowell seemed to belong to another world, and she, his wife, to have been left behind in England with him. Here in Paris was an altogether different young woman —Juliet, who was enjoying the society of a charming man. In the most sensitive and subtle of ways, he had advised her that he found her desirable.

She was perfectly aware that if she agreed to go with him alone to his studio, he would be justified in supposing that she was prepared for a great deal more than coffee! To go unchaperoned to this man's rooms so late at night was to invite his further attentions. Yet she was excited rather than frightened by the prospect of being alone with him in his studio. Somehow she could not imagine that this Frenchman would, like Rowell, sit in an armchair and read the newspaper while she was observing him over the coffee cups. The thought made her laugh:

Beside her, her companion said softly:

"In repose, your face seemed to me more lovely than any woman's face that I have yet seen. But now, when you smile . . . you are even more beautiful. Why do you smile so seldom, Juliet?"

"Perhaps because I do not have anyone around me to make me laugh," Willow said. "But you are too flattering, monsieur. I am far from sure that I can believe such compliments."

"I do not know how much Silvie has told you about me, Juliet," he replied, "but so that we may understand one another, I will assure you of one thing—that I never tell lies—not even in kindness and far less in flattery. You may believe, absolutely, anything I say."

Willow nodded. There was something strangely reassuring in his declaration, and she was suddenly confident that she could believe in his sincerity.

"Very well. I will accept your invitation to take coffee in your studio," she said quietly.

Half an hour later, having made their farewells to a delighted Pierre and Silvie, they were climbing the stairs to the studio on the fifth floor of a big house of *appartements* not far from the restaurant.

"Will you tell me if you expected me to return here with you?" she asked curiously as her companion opened the door and removed her sable evening cloak.

She glanced around the huge room, her eyes taking in the disorder of canvases stacked haphazardly against the walls, the smears of paint on the bare-boarded floor, the huge low untidy bed with its duvet pulled back as if the occupant had just arisen. Above their heads, the glass of the slanting roof was hazing the mass of stars in the night sky. Her surroundings were so strange that she might be in another world, she thought.

Her companion took her gently by the shoulders and turned her around so that her gaze now rested on him.

"I will answer your question truthfully," he said. "Before I set eyes on you this evening, I was wondering how I could avoid inviting you to come home with me, as I did not think I would find you attractive. I was quite embarrassed by the prospect. I had supposed that Silvie's friend would be like her; or, since I was told you were married, that you were a bored wife seeking a new excitement. I know now that I was wrong. I was not in your company ten minutes before I realized two things: first, that I was very, very attracted to you; second, that encounters of this nature were quite foreign to your normal behavior. I am right, am I not?"

Willow nodded, surprised that he had seen beneath the surface of her casual conversation at the restaurant.

"I will not ask all the questions that seethe in my head," the man continued. "I was told by Pierre of the conditions under which you agreed to attend this party and I accept that I shall never know you except as 'Juliet.' Perhaps there will come a time in the future when you will tell me your real name and all about yourself; but now I honor my promise to Pierre and Silvie not to ask questions. I am grateful that the Fates have sent me 'Juliet,' albeit only for a few hours. Will you have coffee now? I do make an excellent brew—or would you prefer some wine? Or a little Cointreau with your coffee?"

"A liqueur with coffee will be very agreeable," Willow said as he went toward a curtained alcove. She heard him fill a kettle and the pop of a gas jet bursting into flame. There seemed nowhere to sit that was not covered with tubes of paint or rags or brushes. Smiling, Willow walked across the room and sat down on the bed. She was surprised to find she was quite unafraid. She liked her companion very much—just as Silvie had forecast.

Clever Silvie! Willow thought. Was it because she, too, was a female that she had guessed so accurately how wonderful it would be for her, Willow, to feel a woman again; how much she had needed to hear the warmth of desire in a man's voice, to feel her body's response to the gentle weight of his hands on her shoulders, even to know that he wanted to make love to her.

By the time her host returned with the coffee and liqueurs, she had tucked her feet under her and was leaning in a relaxed manner against the tapestry that covered the wall behind the bed. They smiled at each other as he put down the tray and sat down beside her.

"You are not cold, my Juliet?" he asked softly.

She shook her head. The large studio had retained the warmth of the spring sunshine that must have shone all day through the sloping glass roof.

"It is true that you make good coffee," she said. "Do you cook for yourself, Romeo?"

He smiled at the use of his alias.

"I think I am too old for such a name," he said. "Moreover, *I* have no need to hide my true identity from *you*, so please call me Maurice from now on. And yes, I do often cook for myself although there is a *femme de ménage* who comes in several times a week to clean and sometimes she cooks a meal for me."

"You are very thin, Maurice," Willow said maternally. "I do not think you eat enough!"

Maurice laughed as he took Willow's hand and raised it to his lips.

"That is the first really personal remark you have made to me," he said. "Am I too thin then to please you, Juliet?"

Willow shook her head.

"No, I do not care for fat men," she replied. Maurice was still holding her hand and she was so conscious of this first physical contact between them that she barely heard his voice.

"It will sound banal if I tell you I want to paint you," he was saying. "But any artist would want to do so. You are in every respect so unusual—your coloring, your expression. But no matter, Juliet, even if you will not sit for me one day, your image is imprinted so clearly on my mind that I shall be able to paint you from memory."

"Is it true all artists fall in love with the woman they

portray?" Willow asked in sudden curiosity. "Silvie tells me it is so."

Maurice sighed.

"I cannot speak for others, but I have thought myself in love many times, but never I think, very seriously, as some men love. I dare say I am too selfish—too absorbed in my work to want that distraction. Unconsciously I avoid too deep an involvement. But it is not always easy . . ."

"I know someone else who feels as you do," Willow said, her heart suddenly aching with longing for Toby. "He also has work that comes before anything else in his life. In other ways too, you remind me somewhat of him."

Maurice took the empty coffee cup from Willow's hand and put it down on the tray. Turning to look at her, he said firmly:

"I will not permit you to think of this man tonight, Juliet. You are here with me, and I will not allow you to be sad. Your eyes are full of unshed tears. They are still beautiful, but not so beautiful as when you smile."

He leaned forward and touched her lips with his. For an instant, Willow felt herself tense. Then with a small sigh, she leaned toward him and his arms encompassed her swiftly in a warm embrace.

"You have no need to fear I will do anything you do not wish," he murmured against her ear. "But I hope so much you will not deny me yourself. I want you so much, so *very* much, my lovely Juliet . . ."

Willow made no attempt to restrain him as he began expertly to unfasten the buttons on her dress. He seemed in no hurry, and as he drew the garment down from her shoulders, he paused to cup her breasts in his hands. But then he brought his mouth down on hers, this time in a determined, hungry kiss that took her by surprise. She felt her body arch toward him. As his tongue explored her mouth, her nipples stiffened beneath his palms and a slow warmth spread along her thighs.

She was suddenly impatient to be free of her restrictive clothing. That impatience increased as slowly, calmly, he continued between kisses to undress her. As if of their own volition, Willow's hands lifted and she began to unfasten his coat. She felt no shame at her brazenness, no sense of wrongdoing.

Soon she lay naked before his gaze. Soon, he too had

removed the last of his clothing, and her breath came in short quick gasps as she became fully aware of the urgency of his desire for her. Unbidden, memories flashed through her mind of the cold dark nights when Rowell had climbed into bed beside her and made the first tentative approaches to her. She had only once seen her husband without clothing—far less any other man—and now she stared curiously at Maurice as he stood naked beside the bed. His eyes were a brilliant blue as he looked down at her.

"You are very, very beautiful," he said, his voice low, intense.

"And you are beautiful, too," she replied in innocent surprise. "I had not imagined that a man's body could look so—so desirable."

Maurice concealed his own surprise at this unconscious revelation of her inexperience. He now realized the limits that her husband must have put upon their married life. What kind of man, he wondered, could possess beauty such as this woman's, and not be overwhelmed with passion and the desire to see her; to be seen by her? Was the man a prude? Or merely ignorant about females and the fact that they too could feel desire; enjoy a man's loving?

"We will not waste one moment of this magical night," he said, kneeling beside the bed. "We will savor each minute to the full, and it will be as if only you and I exist in the whole world."

All shyness and the last vestige of apprehension vanished, Willow held out her arms. She was aware of a wonderful sense of freedom that she had never before experienced. She did not have to concern herself with tomorrow; or even with this man's approval of her. She could do as she wished, as her body dictated, with no fear of seeming wanton, unconventional, unladylike. After tonight, they would never meet again—unless she wished it. For the moment, it was as he had said: they were the only two people in the world.

For Maurice, it was as if he were initiating a virgin into the delights of love. He was quickly aware that Willow knew very little indeed about the workings of her own body, let alone of his. With a rare understanding and sensitivity, he guided, controlled, led her to a point where it seemed to her that the very sweetness of her desire had become a torment.

But still he would not hurry the conclusion. His mouth covered every part of her body with kisses. Then, with delicate precision, he lowered his body and they became as one person, their movements perfectly synchronized.

Rivulets of sweat ran between Willow's breasts and mingled with that of her lover. Her pale gold hair was tangled about her face, and impatiently she brushed it away so that she could return Maurice's kisses. Somewhere deep within her head, her mind told her that this must indeed be a dream. Awake, she could never have conjured up such depths of sensation as her body was now experiencing. It bore no relation whatever to married love, she thought: to the brief frustrating encounters with the man she had married. *But it should have been like this with Rowell!* All the time, deep down within her, *this* was what she had wanted, needed. Now at long last, she understood her body.

When finally Maurice brought them both to a simultaneous release, Willow fell back against the cushions, a long, long sigh of content welling up from within her as the sweet throbbing of her body spread over and through her. Her lover bent over and gently touched her cheek with his lips.

"*C'était bien, non?*" he inquired in his own language.

"Very, very good!" Willow said, smiling. "I am so glad I met you, Maurice—so grateful too. You have taught me much."

"It is I who am grateful," he murmured. "I am so happy, and yet I cannot help but be sad, too. Am I wrong in fearing that you are not going to let me see you again after tonight?"

Willow was astonished by her lover's perception. Until he voiced the words, the decision had lain only in her subconscious.

"How did you know I would not want to see you again?" she asked.

In the semi-darkness, he smiled wryly.

"Perhaps just because it was so very good," he said. "You would be afraid that next time it might not be so perfect. You would not want to risk that disappointment. If we never met again, our night together will remain a memory of perfection, untarnished, romantic, a dream."

"You are very wise, Maurice, and very, very understanding," Willow said, pressing a kiss into his palm as he lifted his hand to caress her cheek. "But there is more to it even than you suspect. I am afraid that I might all too easily become addicted to such . . . such passions as you aroused in me tonight—just as an opium eater bcomes addicted to the drug that brings him pleasure. And I cannot remain in Paris. I have to go home . . . to my children," she added. "I love them both very much."

Maurice gazed down at her sadly.

"But you may return to Paris one day in the future? To see your friend Silvie, perhaps? You must promise me that you will have her notify me if you do. I could not bear it if you were in my city again and I did not see you."

"Then I will promise," Willow said tenderly, "although by then you may have another woman in your life and you might find me a great inconvenience!"

"That could never happen," Maurice replied fervently. "I shall be searching for you in all women from now on, my lovely Juliet. Something of you will be in every portrait I do in the future. Perhaps I myself do not want to see *you* again. I too might become addicted and I fear that could be the beginning of the kind of love which, as you know, I have forsworn." He drew a deep sigh before kissing her tenderly.

"When this night is done we will part, my unknown Juliet. But for the moment, I cannot bear the thought. Come back into my arms so that I can hold you close for a little while longer."

Dawn was breaking when Willow's lover escorted her in a fiacre through the deserted streets to Silvie's house. Both horse and driver were as sleepy as the occupants, and since no one was in a hurry, the horse was allowed to plod slowly over the cobbles. Willow was half asleep as she lay with her head cradled against Maurice's shoulder. The conflict of happiness and sadness was overwhelming, and she shut her mind firmly to everything but the sound of the horse's hooves, the occasional cough of the cab driver and Maurice's slow, steady breathing.

Far away to the east, the first rays of the sun streaked the sky with a delicate orange. A solitary bird sang half a melody as if it too were not fully awake. A milk cart passed them, the horse fresh from its stable, snorting in the cold morning air as it clip-clopped cheerfully from house to house.

"Alors, M'sieur, M'dame, nous sommes arrivées!"

The driver's hoarse voice stirred Willow into wakefulness. Maurice's arm tightened around her and he kissed her with a sad tenderness.

"I will not say goodbye, Juliet. It is *au revoir*, is it not?" he asked urgently.

"Au revoir then, Romeo!" Willow said, trying to ease the moment of parting for both of them. But as one of Silvie's sleepy-eyed servants opened the front door and with no visible sign of surprise let Willow into the house, she knew that in this moment of parting she was deceiving Maurice. Even if she came to Paris to stay with Silvie, she would not see him again as she had allowed him to believe. Her conscience would not permit it. It was not that she felt even a small vestige of guilt toward her husband. It was because she knew now as she climbed the stairs and entered the sanctuary of her bedroom that it was not Maurice's body that she had craved so violently. He had been but the recipient of all the pent-up love and longing that she felt for Toby. Her lover's kisses and caresses had been Toby's. Her need had been for him and not for the man in whose arms she had lain.

Her last thought before she fell into an exhausted sleep was that she did not regret the night's events. Her one and only regret was that it had not been Toby's arms enfolding her, his hands touching her, his eyes gazing into hers as she gave herself to him with all the love that tragically could never be his.

Long before Willow was awake, a delivery boy brought to the house a huge bunch of scarlet roses. Silvie took the flowers to her shortly after Nellie had carried in her breakfast.

"It would seem you have made a conquest, *chérie!*" Silvie remarked with a smile.

Willow drew a deep sigh.

"He wishes to see me again—but I cannot do so, Silvie," she said quietly. She attempted to explain her feelings, but she could see that Silvie did not entirely understand them.

"Tu es folle!" Silvie said. "First you cannot be unfaithful to your husband, now you cannot be unfaithful to Toby because you love him."

"I could not lie to Toby, Silvie. He knows me so well I think he would soon guess if I had a lover. As for Maurice, it would not be fair to him either."

For once Silvie did not make light of Willow's arguments, but said thoughtfully:

"In some ways I wish I could fall in love in such manner. If ever I did feel as deeply, I would marry if the man were free to marry me."

Willow remained in Paris a further three days during which she did her best to forget her night with Maurice. She was unaware that he stood for several hours in the shadow of the doorway of the house opposite to Silvie's, waiting to catch a glimpse of her. Up to the moment when he saw her carriage leave, laden with luggage, he continued to hope that he might see her again. When he realized there was no longer any possibility of it, he returned to his studio and began to paint a portrait of the woman he still knew only as 'Juliet' from memory.

Chapter Twenty-four

April 1905–April 1906

WILLOW AND NELLIE ARRIVED HOME TO FIND ROCHford Manor in a turmoil. To their astonishment, Rowell himself opened the front door as the carriage drew up outside.

His brows were drawn over his forehead and his breath smelled strongly of whiskey as he took her elbow and guided her indoors.

"So you got my telegram then?" he said tersely.

"No, I received no telegram," Willow replied. She sensed Rowell's tension and said anxiously: "Is something amiss, Rowell?"

"Amiss!" Rowell was choking with anger. "There has

been a major disaster, Willow—and I'm damned if I know what to do about it."

He made no apology for swearing, but hurried her into the library and, again to her surprise, instructed Nellie to remain outside the door and on no account to move from it. There was no footman in attendance.

Rowell went directly to the decanter and poured himself a drink.

"You'd better sit down," he said to Willow. "This is going to come as a shock to you."

"But what on earth has happened, Rowell?" Willow asked as she removed her gloves and hat and sat obediently in the chair opposite Rowell's. "What is this all about?"

Rowell tossed back his drink and then turned to look at his wife.

"I'll tell you what it is all about: Francis came home two days ago. I was in London. Toby was ensconced in that confounded laboratory of his, and Francis thought he had the house to himself. He rang the bell and Stevens answered it."

Willow felt her heart plunge and her face whitened.

"Harry," she whispered.

"Yes, Harry. As far as I can gather, Francis was stupid enough to start taunting him—'How's that pretty little piece of skirt you fancy, Harry?'—that kind of remark. At first Stevens said nothing, but Francis was not going to dismiss him until he knew he'd got a rise out of him. It seems he bore a grudge against Stevens for his dismissal by Grandmère three years ago and he resented his still being in our service."

"Francis bore a grudge against Harry!" Willow protested. "But it should have been the other way round!"

"Which it was!" Rowell said bitterly. "Stevens had every reason, I suppose, to hate my unfortunate brother, and Francis was a fool to taunt him, I'm not denying it. Nevertheless, Stevens went too far."

"Too far?" Willow echoed stupidly. "What do you mean, Rowell?"

"Stevens hit him. The fellow insists he only intended to shut Francis' mouth and stop his speaking about—well, about the pleasures of Nellie's body—that sort of thing.

Toby believes Stevens, but I'm not at all sure Stevens didn't mean to do it."

"To do what, Rowell?" Willow almost shouted in her fear and frustration.

"Kill him, of course. Francis died last night. Hit his head on the marble surround of the fireplace and fractured his skull. Toby sent for me at once, but by the time I got home from Cowes—well, the poor chap was already dead. So the fact is, Willow, Stevens killed him."

"Oh, my God!" Willow whispered as she tried to control the horrified thoughts circling in her brain. She could feel no personal regret at Francis' death. She had never liked him, and after his treatment of Nellie, she was delighted when he was sent away from Rochford. But that he should die in such circumstances shocked her deeply. Poor Harry! But even more so, *poor Nellie.* What would become of them both now?

"It was an accident, Rowell!" she cried. "You said so yourself. It couldn't be called murder, could it?"

Rowell refilled his glass and began to pace the room.

"Damned if I know. I suppose it would be termed manslaughter if the facts came out. And they would come out —if there were a trial. Stevens would blow the lot, and then what kind of reputation would the Rochfords have? I simply will not countenance it and I've told Toby so. First rape, and then murder in retribution—it doesn't bear thinking about. If the papers got hold of the story—"

"Does anyone know—other than Toby and Harry?" Willow asked.

Rowell shook his head.

"Not yet! Toby had the presence of mind to tell Doctor Rose and all the servants that Francis had tripped and fallen. There'll be a post-mortem, I dare say. We might be able to hush it all up, if Stevens keeps his mouth shut. But for the present, the stupid oaf has taken leave of his senses—says he's glad he killed Francis; that the world is better off without him, and that he doesn't care if he hangs for it. Toby seemed to think he would calm down, especially once you and Nellie returned. I sent you a telegram to Paris, but I suppose you were already on your way home when it arrived."

"Where is Harry now?" Willow asked.

"Locked in the cellar," Rowell answered grimly.

"Thought it wouldn't hurt him to cool his heels in there for a bit. Thank God Grandmère isn't alive. It's about the only good thing I can think of."

Certainly, Rowell was not thinking with any sadness of Francis' death, Willow decided. He seemed concerned only for the effect this terrible event might have upon the family name. That his young brother should lose his life at the age of thirty-one appeared not to disturb him—if indeed he had given it a thought.

"Is Pelham still in Egypt?" she asked.

"As far as I know, yes," Rowell replied. "Toby saw no point in bringing him back to this—this *débâcle;* and nor do I. We've got to sort it out between us somehow."

"I'll have a word with Toby, shall I?" Willow said. "Then perhaps I could talk to Harry. I think he'll listen to me. I am sure I could persuade him for Nellie's sake, if not his own, to keep quiet about the accident. But first I must break the news to Nellie before she hears any gossip about Francis' death from the other servants. I'll take her up to my room and tell her to remain there until after I've spoken to Toby."

Although Willow had vowed never again to go alone to Toby's laboratory, the gravity of the present situation put all other considerations out of her mind. Toby looked surprised as he opened the door to her, but his face immediately softened into a smile of welcome.

"I had not expected you back so soon, Willow," he said. The smile left his face as he added: "It is a shocking state of affairs to which you have returned."

Willow went to her chair by the window, curbing the longing to be in Toby's arms; to touch his cheek. Somehow, her experience in Paris with Maurice had only increased her need for the man she loved.

Resolutely, she put such thoughts from her.

"At least Rowell seems to be taking the tragedy relatively calmly," she said.

Toby sat down at his table, his brows drawn together in a worried frown.

"Twenty-four hours ago, Rowell was swearing that Harry must hang for Francis' death. It was all I could do to calm him down and make him see reason. It is perhaps fortunate for us all that Rowell's first concern—as always

—is for the family reputation. It comes even before vengeance."

"But it *was* an accident?" Willow asked. She was relieved when Toby nodded.

"I had a long talk with Harry and I am in no doubt that, although in one sense he did want to kill Francis, in actual fact he intended only to stop his talking. I gather Francis was deliberately and sadistically taunting him, knowing the man could not answer back without fear of losing his position. He continued doing so until finally Harry could stand no more of Francis' insults—he even went to the horrible lengths of describing his own enjoyment of Nellie's body. So Harry hit him—a single blow to the jaw that sent him over backwards. It was a pure accident that as Francis fell, his head hit the marble surround."

"What are we going to do, Toby?" Willow asked. "Harry cannot go on working here at Rochford as if nothing had happened. Besides, there is Nellie and her feelings to be considered."

"The two of them will have to leave Rochford—hard as that will be for you, Willow," Toby said thoughtfully.

Willow drew a deep breath.

"Perhaps we should send them both to America—to my parents. Mother was always fond of Nellie, and Father would be delighted to have an English butler. Nellie could be reunited with her own family."

Tobby nodded.

"Now that would be a perfect solution, Willow. Rowell will be pleased to see the back of them—and they can make a fresh start in a new country. Will you put the suggestion to Harry and Nellie? After all, the man may not wish to go, although I think he is in no mood to argue. He is, quite naturally, frightened of the consequences of his actions—even although he still insists he doesn't regret hitting Francis."

Willow sighed.

"It seems somehow as if this family is dogged by misfortune," she said ruminatively. "My baby . . . Grandmère's and Aunt Milly's death . . . Rupert . . . and now Francis."

Toby heard the note of despair in Willow's voice and said quickly:

"That is looking at the bad side only, Willow. We have our share of good luck too. Pelham returned safely from the war. Rupert survived his attempt to end his life. You have two beautiful children who have both survived their infancy. I myself have been fortunate enough to make excellent progress with my work. Not all the Rochfords are doomed, you see!"

His wry affectionate smile warmed Willow's heart. Nevertheless, her eyes were wistful as she said:

"When I came to Rochford as a bride nearly fourteen years ago, I imagined everything would be quite perfect—all of us happy and united and successful. I suppose that was unrealistic. Life is not meant to be perfect."

"Perhaps not for us all," Toby argued quietly. "But it is for some. There was a letter from Dodie while you were away, and she sounded radiantly happy with her beloved James."

"But even for Dodie there are some imperfections," Willow reminded him. "She would dearly love to have a child."

Toby's expression changed to one of excitement.

"And that may yet be possible," he said in a low intense voice. "I am trying to establish that there is no hereditary weakness in the family, Willow. I dare not say too much lest I am proved wrong—but we could be on the brink of a discovery about the carriage of diseases that would prove my theories. I truly believe it is only a matter of time before I can do so. Recently I have been reading about some work done by Professor Leoffler in Frankfurt, and there is no doubt that certain bacilli can be transmitted by someone who does not himself show any outward symptoms of a disease."

His face glowed with excitement as he pushed his hair impatiently away from his forehead. "Don't you see what this could mean, Willow?" he continued, his voice intense. "The bacilli on which the professor did his experiments concerned diphtheria, and years ago Dr. Forbes admitted to me that when the two Rochford babies first fell ill, he believed they had diphtheria. He rejected the diagnosis then because he knew that neither infant had had contact with anyone suffering from the disease."

Toby took off his spectacles and polished them absentmindedly before replacing them. His mind was clearly engrossed in his subject.

"But just suppose, Willow, that someone in the house harbored the bacilli—even Forbes himself, for example. That would explain why both babies became ill simultaneously for no apparent reason. I am endeavoring now to discover the whereabouts of the nurse in charge of the children at the time. All I have found out so far is that she was called Irene Barton, and Dutton thinks her home was in or near Brighton. She must be nearing seventy now, so I am praying that she is still alive. I have written to various officials who are trying to trace her for me. If she should prove to be a carrier of the diphtheria bacilli . . ."

Willow was at a loss for words as she realized the implication of Toby's words. If Toby was proved right in his theory, it would disprove once and for all Grandmère's insistence that there was a strain of mental instability in the female family line. She stood up, staring at Toby as he continued:

"And there are even further implications, Willow." His voice was now quiet and firm with conviction. "Ever since you first came to Rochford and insisted that Dodie was mentally as normal as you or I—and proved it—I suspected that Forbes' diagnosis of hemiplegia was unfounded. I think she was suffering from infantile paralysis. I have now read a great deal on the subject, and had Forbes not been influenced by Grandmère's obsession, I do not think hemiplegia would have occurred to him. Infantile paralysis is a far more likely cause for Dodie's underdeveloped limbs."

Willow had no difficulty in following Toby's analysis. There could have been no connection between the infants' deaths from diphtheria and Dodie's illness nearly twenty years later.

"No wonder you are so excited, Toby," Willow said. "What marvelous news this will be for Dodie if you prove your case."

Toby smiled and then suddenly the enthusiasm was wiped from his face as he said apologetically:

"I have no justification for feeling so happy at a time like this. But I forgot momentarily about my poor brother's death. I cannot pretend any great personal grief, since

Francis and I were never close. But the fact remains that he was my brother and had as much a right to his life as you or I."

"We cannot bring him back," Willow said quietly as she prepared to leave the sanctuary of Toby's room. "So it is best to think of the living now, Toby. I will go and talk to Nellie . . . and Harry."

To remain here with Toby was to court disaster, she thought, for she longed to run to him and hug him. Moreover, she had left the anxious Nellie in her room, and however much she dreaded the prospect, Nellie must now be told of the disaster that had taken place while she was in France.

Nellie's first reaction was one of deep shock. When Willow was finally able to reassure her that *she* was in no way to blame, her tears were renewed for Harry. These, too, ceased falling when Willow told her that "even the Master admits Harry was put under the greatest provocation."

"You must never think of it as anything but a terrible accident, Nellie," she said. "And that is how the family intend to deal with it."

Albeit reluctantly, Rowell agreed to the plan to dispatch Harry and Nellie to America as soon as possible. He resented the fate that the man who had killed his brother —however accidentally—was not going to be made to suffer unduly for his crime; but he was aware of Willow's devotion to her maid and her immovable determination that Nellie's life should not be ruined. It was Francis' behavior which had been the initial cause of all the trouble, she kept reminding him, and he could not deny it.

The decision made, the unhappy pair were booked a passage without delay. Willow telegraphed her parents, and within two weeks of Francis' funeral, Harry and Nellie were packed and ready to leave for San Francisco.

Tears were pouring down Nellie's cheeks as she bade her mistress farewell. There were tears in Willow's eyes too, as she forgot protocol and hugged her faithful servant in silent misery.

"I shall miss you very, very much, Nellie—but you mustn't worry about me," she said. "Lily will look after me."

"I know, Milady, but Lily doesn't know your likes and

dislikes as what I do and my place is with you, Milady—"

"No, Nellie—it is with Harry," Willow said firmly.

Nevertheless, although Lily proved an efficient and nice-natured maid, Willow realized that Lily would never be anything more than a servant, whereas over the years her faithful Nellie had become her confidante and friend.

She tried to settle down once more to the quiet routine of a summer at Rochford. The family were now in mourning for Francis as well as for Aunt Milly, and callers were few. Rowell was increasingly restless. Désirée was still in America where, so he had been told, she was the toast of the town wherever she performed. To add to his discomfort, he was being besieged by begging letters from Georgina. Her count had deserted her, she told him, and she was living in very impoverished lodgings in a seedy northern suburb of London. It was not Rowell she wanted but money.

The elder boy, Philip, was now eleven years old, and Rowell was paying wholly for his schooling. He had arranged to pay the fees directly to the school—having discovered that money he had sent to Georgina for the purpose, she had been using for herself.

In her fortieth year, Georgina had become fat and slovenly, and Rowell, no longer in the least attracted to her, made no bones about his disinclination to offer her any financial assistance.

I pay for the children's upkeep and education, he had written. *And I suggest that you call upon your other protectors for maintenance for yourself, as I do not consider I am in any way responsible for you . . .*

He turned his attentions to his legitimate son. Young Oliver was now six years old—a strong, sturdy little boy of high intelligence and cheerful, happy disposition. He seemed to lack all fear and was always ready to enjoy a new adventure. His good looks and high spirits endeared him to everyone, and now that Rowell could converse with him, he was beginning to enjoy the small boy's company.

"It is time he learned some real horsemanship," he told Willow. "That old mare, Buttercup, is far too fat for him —and too slow. I intend to let him ride Starlight in future."

Willow's heart sank. Starlight was a four-year-old Arab

colt standing over thirteen hands. He was not only too large but far too spirited for so young a child.

"Rowell, Oliver is only just six. I do not think—"

"I am not concerned with your opinion, my dear," Rowell broke in coldly. "As all women do, you mamby-pamby your son. You don't want another Rupert in the family, I imagine?"

Willow's cheeks flared an angry pink.

"Rupert's troubles did not derive from an excess of love," she said pointedly, *"but rather from a lack of it."*

But Rowell's mind was made up, and a delighted Oliver was taken down to the stables to try out his new mount. At luncheon, Rowell announced:

"The boy managed remarkably well on our ride this morning. Your worries were quite unnecessary, my dear. Starlight behaved himself—as I was sure he would, riding alongside my hunter."

Rowell's favorite mount was a six-year-old thoroughbred. Half English, half Arab, it was a massive, impressive looking animal, beside which the chestnut colt, Starlight, was dwarfed. Willow tried to forget her misgivings, telling herself that Rowell was considerably more knowledgeable than herself on the subject of horses and that doubtless he knew very well that Starlight could be trusted when in the company of his own hunter.

Toby made no comment other than to warn Willow not to voice her anxieties again.

"To do so would only make Rowell more determined," he said. "He would regard your warnings as a challenge he must disprove. At least he's showing interest in the boy, Willow—and he *is* fond of him. I don't believe he will take undue risks."

Willow tried not to worry as the summer months passed by and autumn approached. By then she had received word from her parents that Nellie and Harry had arrived safely and were settling down very well. Nellie was unable to write, but Harry had penned a short note in a childish scrawl thanking Willow for all she had done for them and promising to take care of Nellie and her parents. They, of course, knew nothing of the events which had led up to Nellie's return to America and neither had questioned Willow's explanation that Nellie wished to live near her family again.

Francis' name was never mentioned at Rochford except once, on Pelham's return from Egypt. Pelham was told the full story, and like Rowell, showed little regret at his younger brother's demise.

"From all accounts, it was entirely his own fault," he said. "Francis always went too far. There were no happy mediums with him, poor fellow."

He was not home for long. One of his many friends invited him to go salmon fishing in Scotland, and he left Rochford not more than a fortnight after he had returned there, promising to be back in time for Christmas.

Silvie wrote to say that she would not be with them as usual for the festivities.

I have a new lover, chérie, she wrote to Willow, a Russian Count who has invited me to go with him to India, of all places. I have never yet been there but the prospect of the hot climate appeals to me as much as living in the palace of an Indian Rajah. Will it interest you to hear, I wonder, that I ran into Maurice last week? He could speak of little else but you and took me back to his studio to see the most wonderful portrait he has done of you. I had quite a job to persuade him to sell it to me but finally he did so and it has pride of place in my drawing room where everyone who sees it remarks on your beauty. Maurice has captured quite wonderfully well that wistful expression you so often have . . .

Willow was glad that at least she had been instrumental in bringing the charming Frenchman inspiration for his work. She sent him no message in her reply to Silvie, not wishing to give him any false hopes that they might meet again. She remembered him with warmth and pleasure and still felt no regret at her single night of transgression, least of all when she submitted to her husband's occasional demands upon her. There were times when she questioned whether Rowell would care very much if she failed in such wifely obligations; but always her sense of duty prevailed, and closing her eyes and her mind to what was happening, she endured his brief caresses and kept her innermost self separate and withdrawn in a world of her own.

True to his word, Pelham came home for Christmas. Despite Rowell's insistence that the family should remain in strict mourning, Pelham disregarded this and booked seats for a matinée performance at the Duke of York's theatre of Mr. James Barrie's popular new play, *Peter Pan*.

"I hardly think anybody can be shocked by the Rochfords' appearance at what is after all a play for children's enjoyment," Pelham quashed Rowell's objections. "It was the most remarkable success last winter, and if you don't wish to come with us, that's your loss. I shall take Oliver and Willow."

Willow enjoyed the charming story of the "boy who wouldn't grow up" almost as much as the six-year-old Oliver, and Pelham volunteered to see the play a second time if it was still running when Alice was old enough to understand it.

Dodie and James arrived the following day. It was Dodie's first visit to Rochford Manor since her marriage. Rowell had given way to Willow's pleas to permit his sister to return home with her husband for the vacation, and Willow was overjoyed to see them. Though still unable to walk without crutches and Toby's iron support, Dodie surprised everyone by the remarkable progress she had made toward complete independence. Her bright, happy laugh could be heard everywhere around the house.

"Were it possible for me to bear James a child, there would be no happier woman in the whole world," she confided to Willow. "As it is, I can love your two adorable children instead."

Oliver was now of an age to be wildly excited by the advent of Father Christmas—a part played excellently by Pelham in red cloak and white beard. Little Alice, now two and a half years old, was somewhat overcome by the occasion and stayed close by her mother as the bearded "stranger" handed out gifts.

The child was growing very pretty. She seemed to have inherited the French blood of her great grandmother and bore a marked resemblance to Silvie—a fact quickly observed by Pelham. The little girl responded to his gentle teasing and was amusingly coquettish with him. Laughing, Pelham declared that she was like her French cousin in this respect also.

As far as Willow could see, her small daughter was as opposite as was possible from either of her two real parents. Her nature was gentle and loving and without even a hint of the egotism normal in infants of her age. She adored her brother and would willingly hand over to him whatever he demanded—even her favorite china-faced doll. She reminded Willow a little of the sweet-natured Dodie. Unlike Oliver, she never threw a temper tantrum or burst into tears of ungovernable rage when she was thwarted. Oliver was a fiery, passionate little boy who had difficulty in controlling himself—but as Toby pointed out to Willow, it would have been unnatural for so clever a child to be docile.

"It is a pity James does not still live near enough to tutor him," Toby said with a friendly grin at his brother-in-law.

Before she returned to Cornwall, Dodie spoke briefly to Willow on the subject of the missing baby.

"I do not suppose it will help to solve anything, dearest Willow," she said, "but James thought I should repeat to you what Violet once said to me. It seems that on the night your baby Sophia was born, Violet heard the commotion and came to my room to ascertain that I was not in need of anything. She remained with me until dawn and was on her way back to bed when she saw Doctor Forbes come out of Grandmère's room with Aunt Milly. Violet swears he was carrying the baby in his arms. I do not suppose this has any significance, but it does indicate that Grandmère was involved, or at least consulted—Aunt Milly, too."

Willow bit her lip, her eyes filling unexpectedly with tears.

"I do not want to speak ill of the dead, Dodie, but in my heart I am convinced Grandmère was responsible for everything that happened that night. Doctor Forbes would not have dared remove the baby without her authority. I believe she wanted my baby to die . . . or at best, to disappear. We shall never discover what happened to her."

"Oh, Willow," Dodie cried. "I feel so sorry for you! But maybe she really is dead, although they did not find her . . ."

"I try not to think about it," Willow said. "I have Alice now and, of course, Oliver."

Nevertheless, as March approached, her thoughts as always went back to the child she had lost, and her mood of depression deepened. She was not sorry when Rowell departed to London for a few days.

"At least I don't have to worry about Oliver's riding Starlight when Rowell is away," she told Toby ruefully.

But Rowell was back by the end of the month and as the weather improved in the early weeks of April, he renewed his young son's riding lessons.

"Papa is teaching me to jump." Oliver announced in a fever of excitement. "But Starlight was naughty today and Papa says I must be very firm with him."

"The colt's a bit frisky after the winter," Rowell admitted. "Don't fuss, my dear."

But Rowell had underrated the pony's strength. Riding farther afield one morning than was customary, Starlight suddenly took it into his head to bolt. He had caught sight of an unfamiliar white farm dog which had been hunting in the spinney they were passing. As the mongrel darted out from the trees, the colt bounded forward and Oliver lost his grip on the reins.

Had Oliver been able to keep his balance longer, Rowell might have caught up with the pony on his far faster thoroughbred, but Starlight was already more than two lengths ahead when he swerved suddenly to one side and the boy was thrown from the saddle.

White-faced, Rowell and the groom riding behind quickly dismounted and bent over the small inert form lying crumpled in the long, wet grass.

"Come on, old chap. You're not badly hurt. Just winded . . ."

Rowell's voice trailed into silence as he realized that the boy was quite unconscious and could not hear him. Oliver's riding hat had fallen off, and there was an ugly gash on his temple from which blood was oozing slowly. Sickened and thoroughly frightened, Rowell turned to the groom.

"Help me back into the saddle and then lift him up to me. I must get him home quickly," he said. "Then ride ahead of me and get the doctor—*at once*, man. Never mind the colt. You can send a stable lad to round him up later."

The slow walk back to the manor seemed interminable to Rowell. The boy's unconscious body was surprisingly heavy as it lay across his lap, the small tousled head cradled in his arms. The child's eyes remained closed, and Rowell was filled with dread that he might be taking home a corpse. Illness of any kind unnerved him and he was far from sure whether the movement of his horse was doing further damage to the injured child. He steeled himself to face Willow's accusations—justified, it now seemed.

But Willow had no concern other than for the child as Rowell carried Oliver to his room. Dismissing Rowell with a word, she helped Patience undress the small unconscious figure and pull the bedcovers over him. The wait for the doctor seemed endless, although he arrived within fifteen minutes of the groom's summons. His examination was careful and thorough.

"He's badly concussed," he announced to the silent Willow. "I cannot say how serious it is. There are no bones broken so far as I can tell."

He removed the pillow beneath Oliver's head and rubbed his limbs vigorously. There was no sign of improvement.

"I'm afraid there is very little more that I can do for him," he said.

Willow stared at the young man disbelievingly.

"But you must be able to do something, Dr. Rose!" she cried. "He can't just be left unconscious—"

"It could be some hours, Lady Rochford, or even days, before he comes out of the coma," the doctor said. He forbore to add that it could very easily be never. It was shock enough for any woman to see her child in such condition. The boy's skin was pale and cold, his breathing scarcely perceptible. The danger lay in the possibility that the coma would last so long that his young patient would die of starvation rather than from any injury to the brain.

"Perhaps you would care to send for Dr. Gornway who attended your aunt after her stroke," Dr. Rose said. "He is undoubtedly the best brain specialist in the country. But to be honest, Lady Rochford, I do not think he could be of much assistance until the boy recovers consciousness."

Stunned by shock, Willow watched as Patience, obeying the doctor's instructions, put hot stone water bottles at Oliver's feet and around his small body. Only when the doctor had mentioned Aunt Milly's name had it occurred to Willow that Oliver's injuries could result in paralysis.

Such a thought was unbearable, and she turned quickly away from the bed.

"I will of course remain here with the child for as long as I can," the doctor said reassuringly. "He may regain his senses at any time. He must be kept very quiet if he does. He may vomit. If he becomes excited, you must apply iced cloths to his head. You will need a trained nurse. Perhaps your husband could make arrangements?"

Dazed, Willow went downstairs to find Rowell, but her thoughts remained with the little boy and as quickly as possible, she hurried back to his room. There was still no sign of his recovery. Patience had returned to the nursery to give little Alice her tea. Doctor Rose was looking anxiously at his watch.

"I shall have to leave presently, Lady Rochford, to go to my evening surgery," he said apologetically.

"I will stay with my son," Willow said quickly. She bent over the bed and smoothed the dark hair from Oliver's forehead. His skin was cold and clammy, and she felt a fresh wave of fear sweep over her.

"He isn't going to die, is he, Doctor Rose?" she whispered.

The young man cleared his throat and in falsely brisk tones announced that concussion was quite a common result of riding accidents and he had not yet come upon a case that had proved fatal.

But downstairs where Rowell awaited him in the library, he admitted that prolonged coma could result in death.

"There is no way we can feed an unconscious patient," he explained. "But let us hope the boy will have come out of the coma long before lack of nourishment becomes a serious factor. He is a strong, healthy little boy and a slight tumble should not have too serious consequences."

Rowell looked away uneasily.

"It was hardly a 'slight tumble,' Doctor. I'm afraid the boy fell rather heavily, head forward. It was a miracle he didn't break his neck!"

"Yes! Well, we must hope for the best, Lord Rochford. I have left a sedative for your wife. I fear she is deeply shocked."

He did not add, seeing the half-empty whiskey decanter, that there was obviously no necessity to leave a sedative for the boy's father. As he left the house, he sighed, wondering what demon of bad luck sat on the baron's shoulder. He knew, of course, all about the exhumation. Then there had been Miss Rochford's stroke and her death, and then the unfortunate accident to young Francis Rochford. But he did not himself much care for the haughty cold baron, and his sympathies were directed more toward the man's beautiful wife. Everyone in Havorhurst loved her, and even old Doctor Forbes, who was strangely bitter about the Rochfords, spoke well of her.

The poor old man had had no word from his absent son and was too proud to ask the Rochfords if they had heard from Rupert. Since the exhumation, the elderly doctor had ceased to practice and had handed over entirely to his new young assistant. Peter Rose was well aware of the rumors that had circulated in the village about his predecessor's part in affairs leading up to the consistory court inquiry; but no one seemed to know the exact facts of the matter, which remained a mystery. He himself saw no reason to let the past concern him.

It was four long days and nights before Oliver showed any sign of coming out of his coma—and then the periods of consciousness were so slight that the nurse was only able to spoon a few drops of chicken broth between his lips before he relapsed once more into unconsciousnes.

The specialist, Mr. Gornway, could offer Willow little positive reassurances. Although Oliver did have further brief periods of consciousness, they were always short-lived and the little boy had lost an alarming amount of weight.

"I fear it is just a matter of 'wait and see,' Lady Rochford," he told Willow.

Willow believed she was at the end of her powers of endurance as she kept a ceaseless vigil by Oliver's bedside, leaving his room only to snatch a hurried meal or a few hours' sleep at night. Sometimes Pelham came to sit with her; sometimes Toby—but never Rowell.

"Try to understand, Willow. He must be feeling even worse than you or I, having been responsible for the accident." Toby reminded her.

"I know, Toby," Willow said. "That is why I have never reproved him for putting Oliver at risk despite my warnings."

But Fate had yet a further blow in store for Willow. At luncheon on Wednesday, 18th April, a telegraph boy rode up to Rochford Manor on his bicycle. In his excitement, for he knew the contents of the telegram, he ran to the front door and was nearly turned away by Dutton. However, upon hearing the lad's breathless account, the old butler allowed him to remain on the doorstep as he hurried to the dining room.

Rowell picked the paper up from the silver salver Dutton held out to him. Telegrams were not usually harbingers of good news, and he opened the envelope with trepidation. His face whitened as he read the few brief words and he glanced quickly at his wife's pale face and away again.

It was damnably back luck, he thought, on top of everything else . . . but he would have to tell her. Dutton was standing beside him presumably waiting for an answer. Willow and Toby were both staring at him, waiting for him to speak. He would have to tell them. . . .

"I'm sorry, but I'm afraid I have bad news," he said. "It seems there has been a very bad earthquake—in San Francisco. The telephone system is out of order and the only news from the city is coming by Morse code from a telegraph operator." He looked at Willow's horrified face and added quickly:

"Your father's senior partner in New York, Nathaniel Corbett, received the news of the 'quake but there is no word as yet of your parents, my dear. They may be safe. We shall have to wait and see."

He did not add that the telegram stated the whole city was now on fire. For a short while longer Willow could go on hoping that her parents had survived. However bad the earthquake, *there must be survivors,* she told herself. It was inconceivable that both her beloved parents were dead.

Chapter Twenty-five

April—May 1906

"I WILL TAKE THE NEXT TRAIN TO LONDON," ROWELL said. "It will be far easier to obtain information about the earthquake if I am at my club. Meanwhile I'll dispatch a telegram to your father's colleague immediately, asking him to keep in constant touch with me there. As soon as I have any definite news of your parents, I will return. Hopefully that will be later tonight."

It seemed a sensible decision. From his club, Rowell could contact the newspaper offices and other likely centers of information.

"Try not to worry, Willow," Pelham said, as an hour later Peters drove Rowell to the station. "It may not be so serious an earthquake as the telegram indicates. News quite often becomes exaggerated and distorted in the excitement of the moment."

But it was mid-morning the following day before further news arrived in the form of a lengthy telegram from Rowell. It appeared that the disaster was far worse even than they had feared. Fires were raging all over San Francisco. Water and gas mains had fractured, and it was nineteen hours before the first relief train had arrived with food and medical supplies for the survivors. The general situation seemed chaotic and the fires were out of control. First estimates seemed to indicate that there were at least a quarter of a million homes destroyed. There was still no news of Willoughby and Beatrice Tetford.

Willow tried to remain calm as she maintained her vigil by Oliver's bedside. But her hands were trembling uncontrollably as she said to Toby:

"I have been praying to God, Toby, that if He will not spare my parents' lives—then at least will He spare Oliver's. Do you think it wicked of me to try to bargain with God at such a time?"

"Wicked or not, it is a very human thing to do," Toby said gently. He glanced down at the unconscious child and tried to hide his misgivings. The boy was continuing to lose weight and still there seemed no prolongation of the brief periods when he was conscious enough to be given nourishment. Doctor Rose had informed him privately that Mr. Gornway was very concerned. Patients coming out of a coma usually continued to progress toward full consciousness, the specialist said, and Oliver's relapses could be due to some kind of pressure on the brain. He had spoken of having the child's skull X-rayed, but at the same time feared lest the journey to London to a hospital equipped with the new machinery might cause further and fatal injury.

Toby could see all too easily the terrible strain this uncertainty was having upon Willow. She had lost almost as much weight as the boy. He knew she slept very little at night, refusing the sedative Doctor Rose had prescribed for her so that she could make frequent visits to the child's bedroom. Although there were now two nurses in attendance upon Oliver day and night, Willow was never out of the room for very long. Now, to add to the terrible strain was the strong possibility that her parents had perished in the earthquake. Other than to remain at her side, there was nothing he could do to lighten the load she carried.

Rowell did not return home until Saturday afternoon. As the family gathered around him in the library, he spoke in solemn tones as he informed them that there was still no word of Willow's parents.

"It is, of course, far too soon to discover names of survivors," Rowell said quietly. "The most recent telegram I had from Mr. Corbett said the city was a heap of smoldering rubble. But as you can imagine, reliable news is obtainable only from the relief trains via Los Angeles."

He made no mention of the fact that while in the city he had heard rumors that fortunes had been lost by the banks, most of which were no more than heaps of stones. Willoughby Tetford had once told him that he had over a million dollars in bonds in one of the San Francisco banks, although the bulk of his wealth was lodged in New York.

"I feel it incumbent upon me to go at once to America,"

Rowell announced. "If your parents have survived, my dear, they may be in desperate need of assistance; and if not . . . well, there will doubtless be a great deal that requires my attention."

Willow stared at her husband in bewilderment.

"But Rowell, you cannot leave England *now,*" she protested. "Not while Oliver—" Her voice broke and her eyes filled with tears.

"Surely it would be better to wait until we have more definite news about Willow's parents," Toby said quickly. "After all, Rowell, it seems from what you have told us that it will be some time before any kind of order is restored to the city."

Rowell glanced at his brother, frowning. Did Toby not appreciate the fact that Willow was almost certainly her father's sole heir, and that he, Rowell, must be on hand to safeguard her interests?

"All the more reason that I should go personally to San Francisco," he said. "Someone will have to insure that . . . that burials are decently carried out or . . ." he added quickly as he saw the effect of his words on Willow . . . "or to arrange medical care or even simply to remove those who have survived to a safe place."

"There will be officials sent in to see to such matters," Pelham said flatly. "I agree with Willow that it is far more necessary that you should remain here with her."

"I did not invite your opinion, Pelham, so kindly refrain from interfering in what does not concern you," Rowell said angrily. Pelham shrugged his shoulders and quietly left the room. He was followed a moment later by Toby who, much as he longed to remain by Willow's side, felt acutely that he had no right to interfere, as Rowell had pertinently reminded Pelham.

Willow stared at her husband helplessly.

"Do you realize, Rowell, that Oliver could . . . could die . . . and you . . ."

"Now, there is no need to be so pessimistic, my dear," Rowell broke in firmly. "Gornway himself told me it could be weeks before we can be sure one way or the other what will happen. Besides, there is nothing whatsoever I can do. The boy has the best medical care available, and that is what matters."

"No, Rowell, you must not go!" The words were

dragged from Willow. "Suppose Oliver regained consciousness and asked for you."

Rowell turned away from the look in Willow's eyes. He still felt uncomfortably guilty about the boy's accident—not the less so for the fact that Willow had made no accusations against him. Nevertheless, he had no doubt where his responsibilities now lay.

"I am surprised you show so little anxiety for your parents, my dear," he said, as he went over to the decanter and poured himself a drink. "But I suppose it is natural for a mother to put her child first. I, as your husband, must set aside emotion and consider other responsibilities —such as your future and the children's. Your father is an exceedingly wealthy man, and it is befitting that I should have your interests foremost in mind since you yourself show so little concern for finance."

As Willow continued to stare at him in shocked disbelief, he was momentarily conscious of a feeling of shame. It was quickly subdued as he once again justified his desire to make certain that Willoughby Tetford's fortune was not lost among the rubble.

"Your father has no son to take over at this time, and I consider myself, as his son-in-law, obliged to offer my assistance. Frankly, it surprises me you question my decision."

"My father has friends, bankers, business colleagues, to mention but a few of the many hundreds who will go to his assistance, Rowell. They cannot all have perished and certainly not the directors of T.R.T.C., who like Mr. Corbett are based in New York. I see no necessity for you to go immediately. At least wait until Oliver is out of danger. You owe him that much."

Rowell drained his glass and replaced it on the side table with an angry thud.

"Kindly allow me to be the judge of what is right and what is wrong," he said coldly. "I do not need you to tell me my duty, Willow."

"Do you not, Rowell?" The quiet chill of Willow's voice surprised her as much as it did him. "Then perhaps you and I will never agree on the subject, for as your wife, I certainly do not accept that your first duty has always been toward me. Your mistresses have had precedence, I think, on very many occasions."

She watched as Rowell once more lifted the decanter and poured himself a drink. She expected a furious rejoinder, but Rowell said calmly:

"You are obviously overwrought, my dear, and I shall discount this moment of hysteria. On your way out, will you instruct the footman to replenish this decanter. I have told the man twice I expect it to be kept full at all times."

Slowly Willow turned on her heel and walked out of the room. If there had been any love left in her heart for Rowell these past few years, it was now gone completely. He is a stranger to me, she thought as she made her way back upstairs to Oliver's room.

A further telegram arrived from New York that evening. This time it was brief and unhappily factual: Willoughby Tetford, his wife, and several of his servants had perished in their home. Willow now had to face the fact that not only her parents, but in all probability, Harry and Nellie too were dead.

"So that ends any further discussion regarding my proposed journey," Rowell said flatly as he read out the telegram to his stunned audience. "It must now be as obvious to all of you as it is to me that it is my duty to go as soon as possible. I shall leave in the morning."

As happened so often, Willow turned to Toby for comfort in the anxious days following Rowell's departure.

"I condemned Rowell totally when he left," she said as they walked in the garden side by side after a recent visit to Oliver. "I could not bear the thought that he was putting money before his own son. But I know he does not love Oliver to the same degree as I do. Perhaps he lacks paternal instinct."

"Rowell is not a demonstrative sort of fellow—especially with children," Toby said thoughtfully. "And to be honest, Willow, you cannot blame him altogether. It is not customary for fathers to concern themselves with children who are still in the nursery—at least, not in this country and not among our class. You perhaps compare Rowell's attitudes with those of your father toward you when you were Oliver's age—and that is hardly fair to Rowell."

Willow sighed, some of the tension relieved by Toby's words.

"You always succeed in balancing my point of view with your logic," she said, smiling. "Whatever would I do without you, Toby! It may shock you to hear it . . ." she added quietly, ". . . but I had been considering very seriously asking Rowell to divorce me when he returns from America. Ironically, Rowell himself gave me the notion when he reminded me that I am almost certainly Papa's sole heir. He has told me that he estimates Papa's fortune to be well in excess of three million dollars. Therefore he would have all the money he could want for Rochford and himself, and if we were to be divorced, he could make financial provision for me without a modicum of hardship."

Toby did indeed look shocked.

"You would leave Rochford?" he asked. "Go back to America?"

Willow sighed again.

"I don't know, Toby. I could not leave at all unless Rowell agreed to let me have the children. But don't let us even think about it, for you have made me realize that I have no real justification for breaking up my marriage. I know Rowell genuinely believes he is acting in my best interests and it would be wrong for me to hold this visit to America against him. I wonder if he is worrying about Oliver?"

"Of course he will be," Toby said quickly.

But in point of fact, Rowell had other far more pressing matters to keep him awake at night.

Upon his arrival in New York he went immediately to Wall Street to the head offices of the Tetford Railroad and Transportation Corporation. This vast fourteen-story building was the heart of the complex of companies owned by Willow's father. Over the years he had increased his railroad empire by shrewd investment in refrigerated cargo, mail transportation, warehousing, and more recently in the manufacturing of electrically run cable cars and subway track.

Willoughby Tetford's senior partner and lifelong friend, Nathaniel Corbett, awaited Rowell in an impressively large office, guarded, somewhat to Rowell's surprise, by two female staff he assumed to be secretaries. Mr. Corbett greeted him politely but not entirely warmly.

"It is a sad occasion for our second meeting, Lord Rochford," he said, offering Rowell a chair. He was in full mourning and looked with disapproval at Rowell's spotted bow tie. "I would also like to express my regret that Lady Rochford cannot be here with you. She telegraphed me, you know. How is your little boy?"

Rowell studied the American critically. Like Willoughby Tetford, Nathaniel Corbett was a self-made man in his mid-fifties, of sturdy build and humble origins. It was never easy to establish the social class of an American, Rowell thought, but fifteen years ago he had decided that Corbett was no gentleman and he saw no reason now to change his mind, despite the ostentation of his surroundings. In fact, they were much too ostentatious. An ugly modern chromium cabinet stood across one corner of the room, and a hideous orange jardinière on a marble plinth graced another. His vulgarity, like the Tetfords', was as painfully obvious now, Rowell decided, as when he had had to suffer his services as his best man at the wedding. He had aged noticeably since then, and there was no sign of the blustering joviality he had shown on that occasion. Rowell decided to cut short the formalities and get down to the business in hand.

"As far as I am aware, Mr. Corbett, my son is still suffering from severe concussion," he said briefly, crossing one leg over the other and flicking an imaginary piece of dust from his lapel. "Now about my father-in-law's estate, sir . . ."

The grey-haired man sitting opposite the English baron was careful to hide his sense of shock. It was not yet thirteen days since the earthquake; the bodies of the Tetfords —his dearest friends—had not yet been recovered as far as he was aware, and their son-in-law wished primarily to discuss business! Willoughby, by the look of it, had correctly assessed the man his beloved daughter had married, he thought.

"I have sent one of the directors to San Francisco—a very capable man by the name of Barry Adams," he told Rowell. "He telegraphed me two days ago to say that the situation is still chaotic. It may be some time before he discovers exactly how Mr. and Mrs. Tetford died." He added quietly: "Your visit to New York may be a little premature, Lord Rochford, since we cannot have the will read until we have certificates of death."

Rowell gave an impatient sigh.

"I am well aware of that, Mr. Corbett. Nevertheless, as

Mr. Tetford's senior partner and friend, you must have some clear idea of what plans my father-in-law made for the corporation in the event of his death. He was not exactly a young man, and I imagine he would have made provision for his possible demise."

"I suggest we postpone this discussion until after Mr. Tetford's last wishes are formally made known," his partner said coldly. "As you will appreciate, Lord Rochford, I have a very great deal of extra work requiring my immediate attention. If you would care to come and see me in a few days' time—"

"I have not come all the way to America to cool my heels or to amuse myself in New York, sir," Rowell rejoined angrily. "Be so good as to tell me what is taking your fellow in San Francisco so long to verify the facts. You say he has been there a week already?"

"That is so. Perhaps you would care to go there yourself, Lord Rochford? It might help you to appreciate the underlying difficulties. Mr. Adams has made use of Mr. Tetford's private railroad car, since we doubted there was hotel accommodation of any kind available. You may make use of the car, Lord Rochford, if you so wish."

"I shall do exactly that, sir," Rowell said. "In the meanwhile, please send my wife a telegram telling her I have left for San Francisco, but hope to be back in New York shortly."

His tone of voice was that of a man addressing a servant or an employee, and Nathaniel Corbett only just succeeded in guarding his tongue. Like it or not, he reminded himself, Lord Rochford was the husband of his dear, deceased friend's only child, and he would accord him the deference he demanded for that reason only.

Rowell wasted no time in New York. He was impatient to know the contents of Willoughby Tetford's will, and if death certificates for him and his wife were necessary, then he himself would make sure they were quickly made available to the lawyers.

He took the train from Grand Central Terminal and five days later, after changing trains in Chicago, they shunted slowly into the blackened ruins of the burned-out city.

Conditions were far worse even than Rowell had imagined and somewhat chastened, he began to appreciate why

Mr. Corbett's underling, Barry Adams, was taking so long to complete the necessary formalities. Twenty-eight thousand buildings had been destroyed. Rescue workers were still searching among the blackened rubble for bodies. The military had set up tents to house the homeless, and there was a vast encampment in Golden Gate Park.

The Palace Hotel, like so many of the buildings, was uninhabitable, and Rowell was grateful to have the comfort of his father-in-law's private railroad coach in which to reside. He was shocked to discover that at least five square miles of the city had been totally incinerated. The business center had ceased to exist. Tracks were being laid down the streets toward the bay so that trains could carry the truckloads of rubble and debris down to the harbor and jettison their contents into the water.

There was no transport available, and Rowell was obliged to go on foot to Nob Hill to see what had become of his father-in-law's mansion. Tired, begrimed, and not a little shocked by the terrible devastation, he there encountered Mr. Corbett's junior director, Barry Adams. This stocky, ginger-haired gentleman of about Rowell's own age was supervising a small group of workers who were sifting among the blackened rubble that had once been a magnificent house. Upon hearing Rowell's name, he immediately accorded him the deference that had been markedly absent in Mr. Corbett's manner. Rowell cut short his effusive greetings with a curt demand for information.

"I am glad to tell you, my Lord, that order is beginning to come from chaos," Mr. Adams said pompously as he took in Rowell's air of authority and importance. "The bodies of your relatives were recovered some while back, but it was not until three days ago I was able to arrange for their burial, according to their wishes, in their home town cemetery in Los Angeles. Fortunately, Mr. Tetford had told Mr. Corbett where—"

"You have death certificates for the deceased, I presume?" Rowell broke in curtly.

The man nodded, no longer certain that he liked this cold, austere Englishman who spoke so impersonally of his late relatives.

"I have also seen to the burial of the servants who died with them—a Mr. and Mrs. Stevens," he continued hurriedly. "Mr. Stevens came from England, but his wife's family arranged for both bodies to be buried in the same grave in their local churchyard. I trust I did right to permit it?"

Rowell nodded disinterestedly. Looking around him, he could see that the part of the house still standing was so badly gutted by fire that there was little hope of anything being retrieved undamaged.

"It is to be hoped that Mr. Tetford was fully insured," he commented wryly as he and Mr. Adams began to make their way back to the comparative luxury and cleanliness of the railroad car.

His companion nodded none too happily.

"From the inquiries I have so far made," he said, "the insurance companies are making no immediate payments even though some people are destitute. We shall fight them, of course, but they are claiming that the earthquake was an act of God, not covered by the policies."

It was not until both men were refreshed by a hot bath and enjoying dinner that Mr. Adams referred once more to his late employer. "A very fine gentleman, Mr. Tetford," he said. "He will be of inestimable loss to the corporation. You, my Lord, will wish to go to Los Angeles to pay your respects, no doubt?"

Rowell motioned to the steward to replenish his glass and then said:

"I see little point in delaying my return to New York. The Tetfords were, as you doubtless know, my wife's parents, not mine. It would serve no useful purpose for me to visit their graves."

Mr. Adams looked uncomfortable, but managed to hide his disapproval as quickly he changed the subject.

"You must be anxious to know the details of what happened to your wife's parents, my Lord," he said, surprised that Rowell had not already asked for them. "I have spoken to some of the servants who survived the disaster, and it seems that when the house first started to shake, most of those inside ran out into the open. But your mother-in-law, Mrs. Tetford, was bedridden with arthritis and refused to allow herself to be moved. Mr. Tetford then refused to leave without her—and so did the maid, Nellie. *Her* husband would not leave her, and so all four of them remained together. A further tremor brought down a part of the house, but not the wing where they resided. But by then the fires had broken out all over the city and the wind was spreading the flames rapidly toward the house."

Rowell looked momentarily shaken by this grim story. "Surely at that stage Mrs. Tetford agreed to be moved?" he asked.

"Yes, sir, she did, realizing by then that it was their only hope of survival. Mr. Tetford's valet—a devoted and faithful fellow—returned to the house in the hope of saving them, but they had left the decision too late and all five were burned to death—a terrible state of affairs."

Rowell nodded vaguely, his mind now concentrated upon the fact that Harry Stevens could never trouble him again. That was one saving grace in this *débâcle,* if the least of them, he thought.

He felt a sudden glow of excitement at the prospect of the future. Life would be very greatly enhanced back in England once the Tetford empire had passed into Willow's hands. The Rochfords would be one of the richest families in the country, and with a little care and thought, Rowell surmised, he should have no difficulty in gaining an entry into the King's close circle of friends. He, Rowell, would enlarge Rochford Manor to nearly double its size and add to the stables. He could buy the best bloodstock in the world, and in a year or two's time, it could well be the Rochford colors that were carried to victory in the Derby, the St. Leger, the Oaks. . . .

Rowell returned to New York in excellent spirits, the death certificates of his parents-in-law safely in his coat pocket. He had reserved a suite of rooms for himself— the very best—in the St. Regis Hotel and he was pleased to be back in a city where the dreadful smell of burning was mercifully absent.

Refreshed by a good night's sleep, he presented himself early next morning at the office of Mr. Nathaniel Corbett. In his hands were the death certificates, which he handed over triumphantly to the man sitting opposite him.

"You will now be so good, sir, as to telephone Mr. Tetford's lawyer and request him to come here immediately and read my father-in-law's will," he said authoritatively.

Somewhat to Rowell's surprise, for he had feared that

the lawyer might have other engagements and be unavailable at such short notice, Mr. Corbett at once agreed to his demand. Unknown to Rowell, he had already been informed the previous evening by Barry Adams that Lord Rochford would be making such a request first thing in the morning and he had made provision for the request he anticipated would be forthcoming. Unlike Rowell, he himself was already fully aware of the contents of Willoughby Tetford's last Will and Testament, for his old friend had discussed his wishes many times in the past and Corbett was one of his executors.

It was but half an hour's wait before the lawyer arrived. A thin, shaggy, unprepossessing little man, he was nevertheless an important personage in the corporation and he, too, was an executor.

"It would have been preferable if your lady wife could have been present, Lord Rochford," he said with a slight bow to Rowell. "However, Mr. Corbett tells me that you are representing her, since your son's unfortunate accident may preclude her coming to the States for quite some time. Please accept my sympathies, my Lord."

Rowell curbed his impatience as the lawyer began to fumble in his portfolio. Finally he found the relevant documents, and readjusting his gold-rimmed spectacles, he began to read:

"*I, Willoughby Joshua Tetford, being of sound mind . . .*"

Rowell listened with increasing impatience as the lawyer read out the lengthy list of minor bequests to his household servants and to the long-serving employees of the corporation; to his Presbyterian church and in acknowledgement of his wife's Quaker faith, to the Society of Friends. There was a much larger bequest of half a million dollars to his lifelong friend and business partner, Nathaniel Corbett, who was to succeed him as chairman of the corporation. Corbett and the corporation lawyer were to be his executors. His house and its contents he left to his wife or, if she predeceased him, to his daughter, Willow Ann Rochford, to be used or disposed of at her discretion.

"They were last valued at a sum well in excess of a million dollars, but we will have to wait and see what can be reclaimed from the insurers. At the moment they are denying liability," the lawyer said, with an anxious look at Rowell's stony face.

Now at last the lawyer began to read the long and complicated paragraphs relating to the disposal of Willoughby Tetford's vast empire. As the lawyer's voice droned on, Rowell was unable to conceal his disbelief and mounting anger as his father-in-law's intent became clear to him—*he would be prevented from touching one penny of Willoughby Tetford's fortune.*

Once the executorship was completed, the lawyer intoned, the net proceeds were to be handed over, lock, stock and barrel, to a Trust Corporation, where a board of directors headed by Nathaniel Corbett would be set up to administer the estate according to Willoughby Tetford's wishes. The capital was to remain untouched until it passed to Willow's surviving children in equal shares when they reached their majority. No distinction was to be made between male and female. In the meanwhile, an income was to be paid to his wife and daughter, the amount to be determined totally at the discretion of the trustees, according to their needs. Any income not so released was to be accumulated and to pass to the children as an accretion to their capital interest.

"It is insupportable that a board of trustees should be the judge of my wife's requirements," Rowell broke in furiously. The lawyer ignored him. He proceeded to relate the complicated clauses whereby Willoughby Tetford's major shareholding in the Tetford Railroad and Transportation Corporation was to be held by the Trustees until the residuary beneficiaries obtained their vested interest.

"I will be sending a copy of Mr. Tetford's will to Lady Rochford," Nathaniel Corbett said as the lawyer's voice finally ceased. "And of course we shall keep your wife fully advised with regard to the situation in San Francisco, although I fear from what Adams tells me, very little will be retrieved. I hope that once your son has fully recovered, my Lord, Lady Rochford will be able to make the journey to New York so that we may apprise her in person of some of the more complicated issues involved. It will, of course, be well over a year before we can hope to complete the winding up of her father's estate and for the Trust Corporation to begin operating. She can have every confidence that we shall all of us act at all times in her best interest."

So Willoughby had once again proved a highly shrewd judge of character, Mr. Corbett thought, as he looked away from the ugly disappointment that marred the handsomeness of the aristocratic Englishman facing him.

No longer able to control himself, Rowell now sprang to his feet, his face ashen.

"This is ludicrous," he said furiously. "Do I understand from this that my wife has no control whatever over the Tetford Corporation—or indeed, the capital?"

Nathanial Corbett's expression was impassive as he replied quietly:

"That is so, Lord Rochford. Mr. Tetford did not consider his wife or his daughter in any respect knowledgeable enough about business matters to handle such complex affairs—nor, indeed, to be interested in doing so."

"But *I* could—" Rowell broke off, his face turning a fiery red as he realized he had fallen into a verbal trap set for him by Corbett. It had already occurred to him that his name was markedly absent from his father-in-law's will and that the huge fortune he had been anticipating had been most astutely tied up so that he himself could not lay hands upon it. It was an intolerable insult, and the two men in the room with him were equally aware of it.

Momentarily he wondered whether Willow, too, had known of her father's intent, but he quickly rejected the supposition. Willow had never been in the slightest interested in money and had what he considered to be a reckless disregard for the importance of wealth. Absurdly romantic, she set far greater store on the trifling emotions of love, kindness, charity, and the like. She was too ignorant, in his opinion, to grasp that wealth was the very basis of security and that nothing was more true than the old proverb: When poverty flies in the window, love flies out the door!

"I must on my wife's behalf insist that you make every immediate effort to ascertain that the insurers pay in full for the Tetford's house and possessions," he said, tight-lipped. "My father-in-law would certainly not have wanted his daughter to be left penniless."

"Penniless, Lord Rochford?" Nathaniel Corbett repeated dryly. "But surely as your wife, sir, she does not lack for any luxuries?"

"Of course she does not, sir!" Rowell snapped angrily. "But as a beneficiary of such a vast fortune as her father's she is entitled to a great deal more than I, alas, can give her. I hope that as one of the executors of her father's will, you will see that she receives her full dues."

Nathaniel stood up, a half smile on his face.

"You may be assured that I shall at all times have her interests first to heart," he said emphatically. "Mr. Tetford was not only my partner and employer but he was also my dearest friend—as indeed, Mrs. Tetford was my wife's. I have had the pleasure of knowing Lady Rochford since the day of her christening, and you need be in no doubt that I will act on her behalf as if she were my own daughter. You will perhaps convey these sentiments to her on your return, Lord Rochford? You will be leaving for England shortly, I do not doubt?"

Rowell stood up, gathered his light tan suede gloves, bowler hat, and ebony cane from the coat stand and turned slowly to face the man to whom Willoughby Tetford had seen fit to hand over the power that should have been his own. There was no reason why he himself should not, at very least, have been made an executor in place of the nondescript little lawyer, he thought furiously. As for the Trust Corporation eventually to be set up, he could see no chance that he might be appointed one of its directors. At the most, he could expect through Willow to receive the insurance company's compensation for the house when and if they settled the claim; *and* an indeterminate sum from the dividends from Willow's shares in the Tetford group of companies. It would be a paltry sum at best in view of what might have been realized had Willow inherited the corporation.

Such was the violence of Rowell's frustration and disappointment, he decided to walk back to his hotel. His route took him along Broadway. Lost in thought, he paid no attention to the hoardings outside the theaters or to the people jostling him on the pavement. A woman came out of the doorway of a theatrical agency and was nearly bowled over by the swift-moving Rowell as he strode past her.

"Well, of all the surprises! If it isn't Rowell. *I can't believe it!*"

Halted in his tracks, Rowell found himself gazing into the green eyes of Désirée Somners. She had a black peau-de-soie mantle, trimmed with frills of kilted chiffon carelessly dropped over an aquamarine colored tailor-made costume. With a jabot of cream lace at her throat and a frothy tulle and feather Watteau hat perched on her chestnut hair, Désirée looked theatrically stunning. Rowell was momentarily speechless.

Smiling coquettishly, Désirée said. "You *are* going to invite me to lunch, aren't you, darling? We've such a lot to talk about."

Rowell's hesitation was momentary. He had not forgotten his resolve never to speak to the little minx again, but now, staring at her delightful, friendly, pretty little face and hearing her bright caressing voice, he was newly enchanted. Besides which, he had nothing better to do with his time, and Désirée would provide a sympathetic ear to an account of his morning's disappointments.

Désirée, too, was at a loose end and nursing a disappointment. Over luncheon she informed him that she had been engaged to play the lead rôle in a theatrical production in San Francisco. The play was expected to be a smash hit and had been booked for several months. The earthquake had brought such plans to an abrupt end, and here she was in New York, temporarily without work despite the fact that she had made quite a name for herself during the past year in America. She went on to relate her successes.

"So you see. Rowell, I was proved right in my instinct to come to the States, although it meant I had to leave *you*. I knew that if I told you of my plans beforehand you would never have allowed me to come here. I never stopped loving you, but I simply had to find out if I was a good actress—prove myself, as it were. It was always my intention to come back to England and see you again . . . there was no other man for me. . . not ever. I wanted so much for you to be proud of me, Rowell."

Rowell was only too happy to be persuaded by her that she was telling him the truth. Not only did it assuage his masculine pride—badly damaged by her abrupt departure —but it left the way open for a very enjoyable holiday in New York. Désirée, it seemed, was very much free and at his disposal. He would, of course, have to find a less fashionable hotel for them to reside in. Désirée would doubtless find a discreet place for them to go. It was finally agreed that both would return to their present abodes to pick up their possessions. Désirée would call for him at the St. Regis later that afternoon.

Rowell was only momentarily halted in his plan when he was given a telegram on his return to his hotel.

Mr. Gornway deeply concerned about Oliver. Please return. Very anxious. Willow.

It sounded ominously as if the boy were going to die, he thought as he made his way up to his suite of rooms. Perhaps he should return home at once now that there was no genuine need for his remaining in New York. On the other hand, his presence at Rochford could not alter the inevitable. He could do nothing to assist the boy. A day or two longer could not really affect the ultimate outcome, especially since it would be the best part of a week before he could reach home.

He telegraphed Willow saying that he would return as soon as possible, but that he was having difficulty in obtaining a passage at short notice. When Désirée called, his valet had completed his packing and Rowell was waiting with impatience for the pleasurable dalliance to come.

At Rochford Manor there was an atmosphere of jubilation. Not long after Willow had been advised by Mr. Gornway that Oliver's condition appeared critical, his periods of unconsciousness suddenly decreased. Now, a week later, although he slept a great deal, his coma was a thing of the past. Exactly five weeks and one day after his riding accident, Mr. Gornway pronounced his small patient out of danger. Good careful feeding, bed rest, and tonics would soon complete his recovery, the specialist told an ecstatic Willow.

"A wonderful homecoming surprise for his father, eh, Lady Rochford?" Mr. Gornway said, smiling.

Willow nodded. She looked pale and tired but inordinately happy.

"I know this news will take a great weight off his mind. You see, he blamed himself for Oliver's fall—quite wrongly, of course. Thank you so very much, Mr. Gornway."

Later that afternoon as Willow and Toby took tea in the library, Toby glanced at her radiant face and said cheerfully:

"I think we should be celebrating with champagne rather than tea."

Willow laughed.

"I cannot wait to see Rowell's face when I tell him the good news. I have been thinking about him a lot and I am convinced that one of the reasons he went to America and has been so dilatory in returning was because he could not bear to see Oliver at death's door. I know he blamed himself. I am so relieved and so happy I hardly dare admit to it aloud lest I tempt the Fates."

Toby forced a smile.

"There is really nothing that can happen to mar this present joy," he said comfortingly. "So make the most of it, Willow. It's good to know when one is happy and fully able to appreciate it."

But Toby would not have dared to tempt the Fates had he been able to envisage how short-lived Willow's happiness would be. They had barely told the footman to remove the tea things before old Dutton came in carrying his silver salver. On it lay a letter with an American stamp. It was postmarked New York and addressed to Willow in a handwriting unfamiliar to her.

"It isn't from Rowell," she remarked as she took the paper knife from Dutton and slit open the envelope. "It is probably another letter of condolence from one of poor father's colleagues." She had been kept busy answering many such letters for the past two weeks.

But this one came from her mother's old friend, Angela Corbett.

I have prayed for guidance from the Lord before finally deciding that it is my duty to put pen to paper, she wrote. *The last thing in the world I want is to add to your many burdens and I am aware that you must still be suffering great grief at the loss of your parents and enduring great anxiety at your son's health. Nevertheless, my dear, I have to tell you that I am afraid your husband has been behaving in a manner that can only be called reprehensible . . .*

The word was underlined several times. Willow's heart plunged and her cheeks whitened as she read on:

Despite the fact that your husband is in mourning and that his child's life hangs in the balance—or so Nathaniel informs me—Lord Rochford was twice seen by mutual friends of ours and your parents in the company of a woman who can most certainly not be called a lady. She is an English actress with a doubtful reputation who calls herself Désirée Somners. Our friends mentioned the matter to us as they were offended on your parents' behalf and of course, Nathaniel and I are deeply concerned for you.

The relationship may be perfectly innocent, in which case Lord Rochford will be able to satisfy you on this score. But it cannot be called less than tasteless for him to be seen alone with such a woman in public places in a city where your father was so well known. Your husband's title automatically attracts interest and gossip and it can only be a matter of time before the Press become aware of this undesirable association. Nathaniel wished to approach Lord Rochford but I persuaded him to allow me to write to you instead . . .

Silently, Willow handed the letter to Toby. When he had time to read it, she invited no comment but said quietly:

"I could forgive Rowell for going to America when his son lay at death's door. I have already forgiven him his mistresses; his indifference to me; his lies and deceit. But this I can never forgive, Toby. It is not that he is enjoying once more the pleasures of Désirée Somners' physical charms, but that he has chosen to do so in preference to hurrying home to his son's bedside. That is intolerable."

She looked up at Toby, her eyes dark with unshed tears.

"I have thought about it often, Toby—and always rejected the idea—but now my mind is made up. I am going to ask Rowell for a divorce. I can now afford to support myself—and the children. I shall leave as soon as Oliver has recuperated."

Only then did she give way to the threatening tears. Not trusting himself to go near her, Toby sat rigid in his chair. Willow's pain was his sorrow; but his suffering, though for different reasons, was greater even than her own.

Chapter Twenty-six

June–September 1906

"HAD I NOT GIVEN WILLOW MY WORD NEVER TO REveal her identity to Maurice, I would be inclined to show him this," Silvie said, holding up a letter she had just received from England. Her ex-lover, Pierre, gianced up at the portrait of the beautiful girl hanging over Silvie's drawing room mantelshelf.

"Perhaps it is better for Maurice not to know anything more about her," he said. "As the mysterious, unattainable love of his life, she is a continuing inspiration to him. He has now painted eight pictures of her, and they are so good the Elysée Gallery has offered him an exhibition."

Silvie sighed.

"I do not know what will happen to my poor darling Willow. She was once so in love with Rowell. Small wonder she wishes to divorce that callous cousin of mine. She should have done so years ago."

Pierre smiled.

"You were always the advocate of freedom, dearest Silvie, no matter the rights and wrongs of the matter. But most women—and your friend may be one—prefer the married state to any other."

Silvie shrugged her shoulders expressively.

"Alas, that is true even if they are married to the wrong man. As for my cousin Rowell, he has shown himself unbelievably heartless. It is no longer a matter of *if* Willow divorces him but of *when* she does so. At the moment her late father's affairs are in such confusion that it could be a year or more before she can hope to realize enough money to live on. Meanwhile, Rowell has control of all her possessions. I shall, of course, offer to lend her money, but I doubt very much that she will accept it. She says quite adamantly that she will not put her children at risk until she can be confident of a secure future for them."

"So she is remaining under the matrimonial roof for the time being?" Pierre inquired.

Silvie nodded.

"I shall tell her to bring the children to Épernay for a long holiday. The atmosphere in that house must be unbearably depressing. It seems Rowell has gone to London to enjoy the Season by himself since Willow has declined to accompany him. She will not leave the child. Thank heaven little Oliver is making such a steady recovery."

"You will not inform Maurice if your friend agrees to visit you?" Pierre asked curiously.

Silvie shook her head.

"Not unless she wishes it. A lover is not always the solution to every unhappiness, *mon ami,* and perhaps for the moment Willow is better without any further complications in her life."

"And Maurice can work without distractions," Pierre agreed. "If he continues in his present vein, he will end up as famous and successful as Lautrec and Degas—and *you* will be responsible, my feckless Silvie, by providing his inspiration! Will you permit the two of us to take you to dinner tomorrow evening, or are you otherwise engaged?"

Silvie's face relaxed into a smile.

"I am not seeing my Russian, if that is what you meant, Pierre. My affair with Sergie is over. But I *am* otherwise engaged. My English cousin Pelham is coming to Paris for a few days, and I shall be fully occupied finding amusements for him. He is as insatiable as I in his search for pleasure."

As Pierre left Silvie's house and walked through the streets to the Rue de la Planchette where Maurice had his studio, he felt a moment's regret at the cruelty of nature. The woman he had just left had once been an outstanding beauty. She was still immensely attractive, but he had today glimpsed for the first time the tell-tale signs of age marring the perfect contours of her face. Silvie was still not midway through her thirties, but she was beginning to put on the extra weight so common in Latin women once they left girlhood behind them. These indications of aging in Silvie were still slight enough not to be noticeable to the everyday observer, but Pierre's keen artist's eye had seen the truth beneath her careful *maquillage*. Her profile lacked the perfect, flawless lines depicted by Maurice in his portrait of 'Juliet.'

Pierre hurried his pace. He had news for his artist friend: news that might be of great interest to Maurice. He, himself, was excited at the possibilities opened up by his recent discovery of a new model for him.

The studio was in its customary state of confusion, the disorder unnoticed by Maurice as he stood brush and palette in hand, working furiously at a canvas on the easel. He nodded absentmindedly at Pierre, indicating with his head a half-empty bottle of wine on a table laden with tubes of paint.

"Put down your brushes, *mon vieux*," Pierre ordered as he helped himself to a drink. "I want your full attention."

Maurice's eyebrows raised questioningly.

"It is important, then?" he inquired as he continued painting.

"It could be," Pierre said mysteriously until his friend laid down his palette.

"Well, what have you to tell me?" Maurice asked as he too poured out a glass of wine and seated himself on the bed beside Pierre.

Pierre grinned.

"I went last night to *Le Ciel Rouge*," he announced portentously.

"So?" Maurice prompted as Pierre paused. *Le Ciel Rouge* was a moderately high-class brothel in the Rue Steinkerque occasionally frequented by his friends, and much patronized by tourists because of its reputation for cleanliness.

"So . . . Madame Lou-Lou has a new arrival—a child of twelve!"

For one of the few times in his life, Pierre saw shock on Maurice's face and he laughed.

"Do not look so horrified, *mon ami*. I am not suggesting that you are a cradle-snatcher. Besides, *la petite* is not yet one of Madame's girls. She is the new *fille de salle*."

Maurice sighed, concealing only with difficulty his impatience to return to work.

"Then how does all this concern me?" he inquired.

"Because I think you might wish to see the child—possibly to paint her," Pierre announced.

"To paint her? Is she so beautiful then, this youthful *fille de salle?*"

"On the contrary. She is a skinny little gamine, gauche, all arms and legs and no figure." Pierre was now enjoying himself as he noted Maurice's increasing curiosity.

"Then why should she interest me? Or Madame Lou-Lou, come to that? Most of the maids she engages are trained for less innocent purposes than serving drinks, *n'est ce pas?*"

"A purpose doubtless Madame has in mind for this child," Pierre agreed. "But what will interest you, my dear Maurice, is the girl's face. It bears the most extraordinary likeness to your Juliet. The bone structure is identical and so is the hair coloring—although she has very blue eyes—almost violet in tone. The resemblance did not strike me immediately, indeed, not while I was at *Le Ciel Rouge*. It only occurred to me this morning when I stood looking at your portrait of Juliet in Silvie's house. I had to come immediately to tell you."

Maurice looked doubtful.

"I sometimes question whether you should be an artist at all, Pierre. Your powers of imagination might be better employed as a writer. How could a *fille de salle* in a Paris brothel bear even the slightest resemblance to my beautiful Juliet?"

Pierre grinned.

"I know it sounds improbable. Nevertheless, it *is* so. I beg you most earnestly, Maurice, to come with me now to *Le Ciel Rouge* to see for yourself. If you do not agree with me, I will stand you lunch at *Le Jardin de Paris.*"

Maurice laughed.

"Very well, since I am hungry, I will accept your invitation. I warn you, though, that I shall order all my favorite dishes, regardless of cost—*grenouilles, venaison, rhum babas,* and of course, champagne . . ."

But two hours later, neither Pierre nor Maurice was sitting in *Le Jardin de Paris.* A satisfied Pierre had returned to his own studio, and Maurice was furiously at work. On a chair with her head turned fully to one side, her cheap dress covered by a colorful Indian shawl, sat Madame Lou-

Lou's new *fille de salle*. She was plucking nervously at the fringe of the shawl with small, thin hands.

"Stop fidgeting!" Maurice ordered. "And don't keep turning your head to look at me when I speak. I don't want to see your eyes—only your profile!"

His excitement was so intense that he had so far given no thought whatever to the child he had just brought home in a fiacre from *Le Ciel Rouge*. Madame had been none too willing to allow the girl out of the house. It was only through the invocations of his friend Pierre—a favorite client of Madame's—that she had finally accepted that Maurice wanted nothing more than a model to paint.

"She will be back in two hours," Pierre had promised, "and my friend is willing to pay the same price as he would pay for the services of Yvette or Babette."

Madame had succumbed to this generous offer. Her huge, heavily painted face and vast bulk had quivered with amusement as Pierre reminded her that not all men wanted the same thing from a woman and that artists were primarily concerned with their art and only occasionally with women.

"Not that the girl can be called a woman, eh?" Madame enjoined, her scarlet mouth grimacing as she prodded her silent little *fille de salle* on her flat chest. She glanced down at her own enormous pendulous breasts and sighed.

"I shall keep *la petite* Perle a virgin until she has something in addition to offer my customers," she said. "Meanwhile, she's a good little worker, and you're not the first one, Monsieur Pierre, to see her potential. There was a titled English milord here last night who, drunk though he was, remarked on the girl's unusual coloring. So take her if you wish, but she must be back by six, *hein?* And in the same condition, please!"

Two hours, Maurice thought. It was not enough. He must somehow arrange with Madame to have the girl for longer periods of time.

"Tell me what you do at *Le Ciel Rouge?*" he said abruptly. "How long have you been there? Is Perle your real name or one Madame has given you?" he added with a smile. All Madame's girls were provided with names she considered exotic when she took them into her *maison*. Many went on to become *cocottes de luxe*—mistresses of rich old men who purchased them from Madame.

"My real name is Sophie," she said. "Sophie Miller. In my last job where I was a *fille de service,* I was just called Miller. But Madame says I must now call myself Perle. It is a nice name, do you not agree?"

Maurice ignored the question as he pondered her reply. She did not talk like a servant. The reason became clear when she went on to tell him that she had spent the first eleven years of her life in a convent.

"I hated it there," she said flatly. "Sometimes we were punished even when we had not done wrong—as a warning," she added bitterly. "All the girls who were old enough had to work very hard—not just at our lessons, but cooking and cleaning, even those who were not on charity. And all of us—even the little ones—were forced to attend the services in church. We went five times on Sundays. We were nearly always cold—and hungry."

"You are an orphan then?" Maurice asked as he outlined the shape of the girl's head. As Pierre had told him, the hair coloring was the same almost-white gold as Juliet's had been, and he was fascinated by the similarity.

Sophie nodded.

"I have no parents; but the priest, Father Mattieu, used to bring money for my keep from a distant relative. He would never tell me the name of this relation, and Mother Superior said I must stop asking and thank God that I was not on charity. But then suddenly the money ceased to arrive and Mother Superior said she could not keep me any longer at the convent and I must go out to work."

"So you became a *fille de service?*"

"Yes, Monsieur—for a Monsieur and Madame Grimaud in the Rue de la Paix. They ran a *maison de modes* and had a large *appartement* over the shop."

"You liked it there?" Maurice asked, more to keep the girl still than because he had any great interest in her pathetic little story.

Sophie's thin, angular face softened in a sudden smile.

"At first I did. It seemed so wonderful to be in a real home after the convent. I had my own little room in the attic. Cook—the only other servant the Grimauds kept—slept next door. She was strict, but kind enough so long as I did my work well, and she seemed quite satisfied with me. Madame Grimaud was satisfied too, at first, but then Monsieur Grimaud began to pay me attention. I do not know why, because I know I am not pretty, and Madame Lou-Lou has since explained to me that men like women with full breasts and rounded hips. But Yvette said Monsieur Grimaud was probably a pedophile."

Despite his free and easy life as an artist, Maurice was shocked by the word falling so casually from this child's lips. Although she was still by some miracle a virgin, it seemed she had already acquired the vernacular of the prostitutes with whom she now lived.

Mistaking his silence for lack of understanding, the girl said:

"I too was unaware that such people existed, Monsieur, but it is a fact that there are men who can only enjoy themselves with children. Is that not strange? Fifi says I will discover that there is no end to the variations of preference men have. I do not think I would like to lie with old men, though. I hope it will always be young men who will want to pay for me. Yvette says it makes no difference, and all that matters is that one's clients are rich. Then you may be given presents—although Madame Lou-Lou does not like it. She takes all the money the girls earn and then pays them every week what she thinks is fair. Yvette is saving up to get married. She is engaged to a farmer in Provence."

Maurice did not pause in his painting—time was too precious. Soon he would have to return the girl to the brothel. Provided he could not see her eyes, it was not difficult to imagine that it was a young Juliet posing for him; that Juliet had once looked like this girl. The line of the cheek, the curve of the chin, the delicate bone structure were all similar.

Sighing, he laid down his brush and told Mademoiselle Perle she could move now if she wished. He felt a moment's disappointment as she stood up, for the resemblance to his Juliet was instantly gone. The thin, angular arms and legs and awkward stance bore no likeness to the beautiful, graceful, mysterious woman who haunted his dreams.

Maurice took off his paint-smeared smock and felt in

his trouser pockets. He produced a ten franc coin which he handed to her.

"I will give you another one each time you come to pose for me," he promised. "But you had best not show it to Madame Lou-Lou lest she appropriate it for herself!" Or suspects me of having used her precious Perle for other purposes, he thought grimly.

The girl became a regular visitor to the studio. Madame Lou-Lou, having carefully cross-questioned Sophie after her first visit, seemed reassured that Maurice had no ulterior motives. She was well-satisfied to be paid for the child's time which meant, virtually, that she was having her services as a waitress for nothing.

Sophie was happy enough to be employed as a model. She thought Maurice a trifle eccentric in his desire to draw and paint her, but it satisfied her ego and put up her standing with Madame's girls, who had considered her unlikely ever to provide them with much competition, even if in the future her figure blossomed with maturity.

Maurice began to take an interest in the child and encouraged her to chatter freely while he worked. She told him how one of the street girls, called Blanche, who went quite regularly to *la Maison Grimaud* to buy hats with an admirer, had suggested to her that she was overworked at the *modiste*'s.

"There's no future in a dump like this," she had said to Sophie. "You should apply for the job going at Madame Lou-Lou's. She's looking for a new maid and you would have better prospects there!"

Maurice had joined with Sophie in her self-deprecatory laughter when she told him that she had asked Blanche if Madame Lou-Lou's was also a *magasin de modes*.

"I did not know then that there were houses that catered for men's needs," Sophie said simply. "I realize now how ignorant I was a year ago when Madame Lou-Lou engaged me. Yvette has since explained everything to me. We were not told about such things in the convent. There we were not permitted to talk about men or love or having babies. And books which mentioned these subjects were not permitted, even if they were classics. I read quite a lot of books when I was at Madame Grimaud's."

Sometimes Maurice listened to her chatter, sometimes he was too engrossed in his painting to do so. Her mixture

of innocence—purity even—and her bordello language
and aspirations intrigued him. She spoke a great deal on
the subject of her virginity and could not wait for the day
when this precious asset might be surrendered.

"You are eager to lie with a man?" Maurice asked
curiously as he tried a third time to capture the delicate
lines of the tendons of her neck. "You think you might
enjoy what the other girls do?"

"Of course not! I have seen them at work and they
look so silly—the men even more so than the girls. But
I should earn money."

She looked expectantly for the small tip he always gave
her, and if he forgot it, she reminded him. Madame,
aware of his growing dependence upon his young model,
put up her price. He paid without argument, for the number of canvases was mounting steadily.

By mid-summer, Sophie, now quite at home in the
studio, announced proudly that she had at last entered
the ranks of womanhood and that Madame was pleased
because she was beginning to develop a *poitrine*. Surprised,
Maurice noticed the two small jutting breasts and slight
rounding of the hips. He had been concerned only with
the girl's face and her manner of holding her head, which
was so reminiscent of his Juliet. He had never attempted
to draw her body.

"Last night an Eastern gentleman tried to buy me,"
Sophie continued proudly. "Yvette told me. But Madame
refused, even though he offered a very high price. I am
glad, because I would like my first one to be young and
handsome like your friend, Monsieur Pierre. Yvette says
Madame is surprised men even notice me yet because I am
so thin. The English milord I told you about said he would
come back in a year or two's time and look out for me.
Do you think I might be beautiful one day, Monsieur
Maurice?"

"No, I don't!" Maurice said, laughing. She turned her
head and pouted at him.

"*You* never go to *Le Ciel Rouge*, do you?" she asked
curiously. "Do you not like women? Or have you a mistress
of your own?" When he made no reply, she added mischievously: "Perhaps you are one of those Yvette told
me about who prefer men?"

Maurice was saddened by the slow but steady loss of

the childish innocence he had first remarked in her. There was little in her conversation now to remind one of her strict convent upbringing—except the paradoxical perfection of her accent. She spoke the words of a *poule* in the tones of a lady, and the combination was both amusing and sad.

He was, however, unprepared for and totally *bouleversé,* when on calling for her one afternoon at *Le Ciel Rouge,* he found himself confronted by a slim young woman with brightly henna'd hair.

"Mon Dieu!" he cried aghast as he realized it was Sophie standing before him with an expectant smile on her face. The beautiful pale gold silky sweep of her hair was gone. There was now an ugly red concoction piled on top of her head making her look like a vulgar street walker. Her face was heavily made up, her mouth absurdly enlarged into a scarlet gash.

"What is the matter? Don't you like my new coiffure, Monsieur Maurice? Yvette—"

"It is an outrage!" Maurice interrupted, his face white with anger. "I cannot paint you like that. You look—"

He broke off, grabbed her unceremoniously by the arm, and dragged her out to the waiting cab. During the brief ride to the studio he neither looked at the girl nor spoke. Not a little frightened by his manner, Sophie for once was also silent.

In the studio, Maurice instructed her curtly to stand with her back to him by the bed, place one foot upon it and lift her skirt so that he could see all of her buttoned black boot, her black stocking, and the red garter above her knee.

"Now turn your head toward me," he commanded in a tight, hard voice. "And think of all the money you will earn with your harlot's looks and ways!"

He painted feverishly, his picture slowly coming to life. This time it was no head and shoulder portrait of a strangely beautiful girl on the threshold of womanhood, porcelain skin, delicate blue veins, fragile bones. This time his picture resembled *Cha-U-Kao,* one of his late friend Toulouse-Lautrec's paintings, of a girl dressed as a clown, fastening her corset. It had the same bold disregard for convention, for propriety.

Maurice had never before painted a picture so swiftly.

Still in the same mood of intense anger, he scrawled *La Perle* across the top and signed his name below. Then he laid down his brush and felt in his trouser pocket for some money. He flung the coins down on the table.

"That's ten times your usual tip," he said coldly. "Now go back to your brothel where you belong. I shall not need you again."

Open-mouthed, the girl stared first at him and then at the money.

"I don't understand," she said. "What did I do wrong, Monsieur? Why are you so angry?"

"You've made it impossible for me to paint you again," he replied tersely. "And worse even than that, you have made it impossible for me to paint *her*."

He rifled furiously through the pile of canvases and selecting one of Juliet, he placed it on the easel.

Misunderstanding him, the girl said:

"You can paint whom you please—I'm not stopping you." Her blue eyes flashed with sudden fire and her head lifted proudly on her small shoulders. "I thought you liked me, Monsieur Maurice. Well, I don't want your money. I'll make *much* more than you can ever give me without your help or your silly paintings. And to think that I had made up my mind to let you be the first—even if you couldn't afford it!"

She burst into tears, but brushed them angrily away; and before Maurice could stop her, she had fled down the rickety wooden stairway. He heard the front door bang as it closed behind her and from his window he could see her small henna'd head, far below, disappearing around the street corner.

An hour later, Pierre found him slumped in front of his latest portrait, the paint still wet and glistening. Pierre stared at the painting in astonishment and then said slowly:

"It's very good, Maurice—you've caught the avaricious look of the harlot exactly; and yet the innocence of youth is still there despite the wanton manner in which you have posed the girl."

He was less complimentary when Maurice related events to him.

"You were very cruel," he told his dejected friend. "She's only a child and I think she had become very fond of you. You were the first person other than her precious Yvette ever to take an interest in her."

"Well, I cannot forgive her, however unreasonable that may sound to you," Maurice replied. "Don't you see, Pierre, that everything is ruined now. In the strangest way, Perle and Juliet had become one person—it was as if I had recaptured Juliet—only twenty years younger. Now I cannot remember either of them as they were. I see the red hair, the scarlet lips, the painted cheeks—the depravity. It is as if my love itself had been despoiled."

"You are talking nonsense, my friend," Pierre said. "And I am not in the very least surprised. You have been working without pause for nearly a year and what you need is a good long holiday."

Maurice shrugged.

"It will do no good," he said, sighing. "I shall never paint either of them again!"

"Then you will paint someone else," Pierre said sensibly. "Now what will you do with this painting—*La Perle,* you call it? It should fetch a few francs, I think. It is really remarkably good."

"I shan't sell it," Maurice replied stonily. "I shall give it to Madame Lou-Lou. You can take it to her for me and she can hang it in the salon. It will be a good advertisement for her, and for Perle."

"So!" Pierre exclaimed as he patted the dejected Maurice on the shoulder. "You are filled with resentment because your little model has finally forced you to see her as she is and not as a reincarnation of your precious Juliet. And all to the good, I say. What is more, you will agree with me when you are once again of sound mind. Come, *mon vieux,* I will treat you to dinner at *La Nouvelle.* I owe you that since it was I who foolishly introduced you to the source of all this trouble."

For the first time, Maurice smiled.

"I don't really regret it," he admitted. "I know I've done some of my best work lately. But you are right—I want to forget that child now and Juliet. I give you my word I will not mention either of them again. Will that content you, Pierre?"

Back in *Le Ciel Rouge,* Yvette was comforting the sobbing girl in almost the same words.

"Forget your artist, *ma petite,*" she said. "No man is worth a woman's tears!"

"But I loved him," the girl wept. "Truly I did, Yvette. I did not realize how much Monsieur Maurice mattered to me until he told me he never wished to see me again."

Not even to Yvette, who came close to being the only mother figure she had ever known, could Sophie confess that she had seriously contemplated offering the artist her precious virginity. She had decided to make him this gift not because she wanted to put their relationship on such a level, but because it had been stressed so often at the brothel how prized her virginity would be. It was all she had to give. Monsieur Maurice, she had decided, might not be as young a man as she had hoped for, but he was clever and nice-looking and very much a man of the world. His studio, with its strange smells of linseed oil, paint, and turpentine had become a kind of home for her.

Yvette was offering her a handkerchief and telling her to stop crying.

"First love is always the most painful," she was saying. "But you are very young, Perle, and there will doubtless be others. Besides, this work we do here is sometimes the easier if one is not in love. I know my André resents my profession despite having agreed with me that it is the only way I can earn money for my dowry quickly. I believe he sometimes thinks I enjoy those men who pay for my body," she added, sighing.

She looked down at the girl and her face softened.

"I tell you what, *chérie,* you can have that Japanese kimono of mine you so admire . . . the yellow one with the red embroidered butterflies. Will that cheer you?"

Sophie flung her thin childish arms around the buxom, heavily painted young woman and hugged her.

"You're the kindest, most wonderful person in the whole world," she declared, the tears drying magically on her cheeks. "I shall pray for you every night, Yvette—two Hail Marys', and more if I don't fall asleep."

Momentarily, anyway, Monsieur Maurice and his cruel rejection of her was forgotten. She had made up her mind never to think of him and never, ever to fall in love again.

Chapter Twenty-seven

July—October 1906

WILLOW'S CONSCIENCE WAS TROUBLING HER. ROWELL had been in London for the whole of July and August and she had basked in lazy contentment at Rochford with Toby, Pelham, and the children. Every day had seemed to be sunny and warm, and Oliver had at last regained his color and his lively spirits. They all but lived in the garden which was ablaze with colorful flowers.

Pelham had built for the boy a house in the branches of the large lime tree overlooking the lake. While they picnicked on the lawn beneath it, Patience keeping an ever-watchful eye on little Alice, Oliver ate voraciously in what was now known as "My House." The novelty had greatly increased his appetite which had been so sadly lacking during his convalescence.

Now his two uncles played endless games of cricket and croquet or went fishing with the child without fear of overtiring him. Quite often Willow joined in their games, and the garden was filled with laughter. Her happiness was marred only by thoughts of her parents' and Nellie's untimely deaths. She was in frequent communication with Nathaniel Corbett and, punctiliously, she signed the various documents he sent her, confident that she could leave all business decisions safely in his hands.

Rowell had left her in no doubt of his angry disappointment at the terms of her father's will. Indifferent now to his moods, his abuse of her beloved father could not hurt her, and she remained coldly indifferent to his tirades. She, in turn, had left him in no doubt that she considered their marriage to exist in name only; that she could never forgive him for his behavior in New York or for his indifference to his son. She had even mentioned the possibility of divorce to him, but he had refused to listen and strode out of the room to pack his trunks to go to London. She was happy to see him go.

Between them, Pelham and Toby made certain that she was never alone long enough for her grief for her parents to overwhelm her. Pelham in particular was in high spirits, the reason for which Willow was aware, for Silvie had written to tell her that when Pelham visited her in June, they had greatly enjoyed a brief affair that went beyond the bounds of flirtation.

"Is it not surprising, Willow, after all these years . . ." she wrote.

"We get on amazingly well together," was Pelham's comment to Willow. "I had been accustomed to sharing Silvie's company with all the family at Christmas time and I had no idea she could be even better company in her own home. We had tremendous fun together in Paris. By the way, I saw that portrait her French artist friend painted of you—and I must say he has caught an amazing likeness. I wanted to meet the fellow, but he had gone off to Italy with a friend of his, another artist."

"You did not tell me you had had your portrait painted, Willow," Toby remarked, "or that you had met any of Silvie's artistic set!"

It was intended only as a casual rejoinder, but Willow's cheeks suffused a deep guilty pink and she was certain that Toby had noticed her blushes. Although he made no further comment, at the first opportunity that they were alone she felt impelled to say:

"I shall never love anyone but you, Toby, no matter how you may suspect the contrary."

The unexpectedness of her declaration caught him unawares and defenseless. He took her hand in his and pressed it to his lips. It was the only physical exchange of love between them during that long hot summer, and yet there was not a moment when Willow was in his company that she was not deeply and painfully aware of him. Sometimes their eyes met over Oliver's head or as they passed some object from one to the other. Each time, Willow felt her heart leap and the expression in Toby's eyes revealed his corresponding awareness of her.

It surprised both of them that the happy-go-lucky Pelham did not sense the tension between them. Unlike Toby, he was quite openly affectionate with Willow, occasionally kissing her cheek and often putting an arm around her shoulders and hugging her affectionately. Willow knew that such exchanges would have been impossible between her and Toby, but never an hour passed that she did not long for them.

At least Toby had his work to divert *his* thoughts away from her, she told herself, unaware how often he escaped to his laboratory merely because he dared not trust himself in her presence.

Toby now lived in an agony of uncertainty about the future. He could think of little else but that if Willow carried out her intention to divorce Rowell, perhaps go to America, he might never see her again. Yet at the same time, he debated with himself whether this might not be the only solution for them. If the present situation continued much longer, he was not certain if he could answer for himself. His longing to touch her, hold her, was becoming obsessive. He was grateful that his brother, Pelham, was always a third in their small group.

Like Willow herself, he dreaded Rowell's return to the family home. But not even Rowell's absence could ensure absolute freedom from tension or distress. One sunny afternoon toward the end of August, Willow was called indoors by Dutton to receive an unexpected visitor. It was a young gentleman, Dutton told her, who would not give his name. The old butler described him as "modestly attired but well-spoken, Milady, although somewhat nervous," thus increasing Willow's curiosity as to who her visitor might be.

The servant's description was accurate, Willow thought as Dutton showed the young man into the drawing room where she had said she would receive him. As the butler left the room, closing the door behind him, her visitor approached hesitantly and made an awkward little bow. Willow judged him to be somewhere in the region of twelve years of age. He was a tall, thin boy who was clearly outgrowing his clean but shabby Norfolk jacket and knickerbocker trousers. He had short-cropped, red-gold hair and green eyes with which he was now anxiously regarding her. His voice, when he spoke, although still that of a young boy, was husky with nervousness.

"Your servant, Lady Rochford!" He inclined his head with old-fashioned formality over the hand she held out to him. "I did not give your butler my name, Milady, lest it should cause you any embarrassment in public. I am Philip Grey."

For a moment, Willow regarded her visitor uncomprehendingly. As far as she was aware, she had never met him before. But as if reading her thoughts, he said quietly:

"My mother is Mrs. Georgina Grey!"

Color raced into Willow's cheeks and receded as swiftly, leaving her very pale. She was both angry and distressed. She would not have received him had she known his identity . . . and yet now he was here, looking so young and defenseless she could not bring herself to have him shown the door.

"Please believe me, Lady Rochford, I would not have come here unless I had been quite desperate," the boy said, obviously speaking with an effort. "To be frank, Ma'am, I have nowhere else to turn."

"Has your mother no relatives?" Willow asked with difficulty.

The boy blushed.

"An aunt, Ma'am, a Miss Augusta Fry, who lives in Northumberland. But many years ago—when she heard of my birth—she closed her doors to my mother. Mama did write to her when first she . . . she fell upon hard times, but my great aunt did not reply, and Mama says she will never relent."

"Then you had best be seated," Willow said quietly. Surreptitiously, she searched the boy's face for a likeness to Rowell but could see none. He was remarkably like his beautiful mother. One day he would be an exceedingly handsome man. She noted the nervous twisting of his hands as he tried to conceal their trembling from her, and her pity was stirred. Philip Grey looked and sounded as desperate as he had declared himself to be.

"Suppose you tell me what has brought you here—to *my* house," she added pointedly.

There was a sudden glint of tears in the boy's green eyes but his head lifted proudly.

"I have not come to beg, Lady Rochford. I have come here as a last resort in the hope of borrowing money. It is for my mother. She is very ill—possibly even dying. She will not hear of my leaving school to take care of her. I am old enough to find work, to earn money—but my father has threatened to disown me if I leave school and Mama says I would be one more mouth to feed if I did so."

Now all but overcome by emotion, he looked down at his hands and in a quieter voice, said:

"You cannot know what it is like, Lady Rochford, for us to see our mother starving. We cannot even send food home from our schools. All I can hope to do is to work hard so that when I have passed my examinations I can obtain a good position. I am good at mathematics and I could perhaps gain employment in a bank or as a shipping clerk. As soon as I am earning, I would pay back any money I borrowed. I swear it on my mother's—my sister's—lives, Ma'am."

Willow bit her lip, too astonished to formulate a quick reply.

"Have you not asked your father to help you?" she inquired. But even before the boy spoke, she knew what the answer would be. She was not fully prepared, however, for the bitterness of the boy's reply.

"I have done so many times, Lady Rochford. But I will never do so again as long as I live. I hate him for letting my mother suffer. I even prefer to beg your assistance than to ask him again for help!"

Pity was once more foremost in Willow's heart as she stared at Rowell's eldest son. For all his youth, Philip Grey had both dignity and pride, and she could imagine what it must have cost him to come to her today. She dared not think what retribution would follow were Rowell ever to hear of it.

"You know my husband is in London?" she asked.

Philip nodded.

"I see! Then you have been discreet as well as courageous in coming here today. Perhaps you will now tell me of your mother's condition since you say she is in such sore straits."

Georgina, it seemed, had contracted a disease, the shameful nature of which she had refused to tell her son. He knew only that there was no known cure for it, and that the doctor had said she might die. They had moved into the cheapest lodging house in a street that was close to being a slum. The dirt was such that the boy refused to describe it to Willow. Four other families lived in the house, Irish immigrants who were as often as not drunk, and Philip's seven-year-old sister, Jane, had been molested not once but several times. The charitable societies that had been formed to help gentlewomen in distress had refused help to Georgina as soon as they discovered her past reputation and that her children were bastards. The religious societies had been even more condemnatory. Only the Salvation Army had offered help of any kind, but it was only a fraction of what was needed by way of food and medicine for his mother.

Willow stood up and pulled on the bell rope. When one of the footmen appeared, she instructed him in undertones to have a lavish tea sent in for the visitor and for a hamper to be prepared for him to take away with him when he left.

"Now, Philip," she said as the footman departed, "let up consider this loan you have come to negotiate. I am prepared to lend you money because I believe you are honest, and because I believe your need is genuine. But I will do so on one condition only."

The boy jumped to his feet, his pale face flushed with hope.

"I will fulfill any condition you name, Lady Rochford," he cried.

"Then it is that the loan shall not be repayable for fifty years."

Philip frowned, his green eyes widening questioningly.

"But that would mean . . . in fifty years, Lady Rochford, you would be dead and even I too might be dead. I would be sixty-two!"

"That is a chance we shall both have to take then," Willow said, smiling despite the gravity of the occasion. "But if you *are* still alive, and can afford to repay me, then I should like you to give the money to Salvation Army."

She turned hurriedly away from the look of relief mingled with gratitude in Philip's eyes. She instructed him to make himself comfortable while she absented herself for a little while. She made her way to her bedroom and taking a key from her purse, unlocked a drawer in her dressing table. She withdrew from it several small leather jewel boxes. One contained an emerald necklace, another a diamond and ruby pendant, the third a sapphire ring and brooch. All these pieces of jewelry had been given to her by Rowell, and her mouth twisted in a bitter smile as she reflected that she would never wish to wear them again. It seemed a perfect solution that they should be sold to pay Rowell's dues; to honor his responsibilities.

She put them carefully in a small shoebox and then sat down at her Davenport desk. Withdrawing a piece of crested writing paper, she wrote a few lines, signed the brief note, and put it in with the jewel cases in the box. Her face was quite calm and expressionless as she went back downstairs. She put the shoebox down beside the boy.

"You must take these to a good London jeweler," she said, "to someone who can be trusted to give you a fair price for them. I have put a note inside declaring that they are mine and that I have given them to you to dispose of for me. The jeweler may be surprised, but he will not refuse you. Now please enjoy your tea. I have already eaten."

It did not escape her notice that tears of relief, or perhaps gratitude, were sliding down the boy's cheeks.

"I have many calls upon my time, so if you will excuse me, I must leave you now. Ring the bell when you have finished your tea. My coachman can drive you to the station."

As Philip jumped to his feet and fought for words, she smiled at him with difficulty.

"I shall take your thanks as said, Philip," she forestalled him. "I do not suppose you and I will meet again, but if you are ever in serious need, please write to me. And you may tell your mother that if one day my own son grows up to have as much love and consideration for me as you have shown for her, then I will be proud of him."

It was inevitably to Toby she related the sad story about the boy's visit to her. As always, he listened quietly, not commenting until she had poured out her heart to him.

"You have done all you can, Willow—all the boy wanted," he told her. "More would have put him under an unbearable obligation. I suppose, since he is Rowell's son, he is also my nephew. But don't grieve over him, Willow. I will keep an eye on the situation—from a discreet distance, of course. Pelham and I between us will make sure the children do not starve—or the mother."

Willow was far from certain as yet what her financial circumstances would be when her father's affairs were finally sorted out. Mr. Corbett wrote regularly to her, assuring her that she had no need to undertake the long journey to America unless she so wished; that such documents as immediately required her signature he would continue to send by the postal service. Understandably, he made no reference whatever to Rowell's meetings with Désirée Somners. Willow, after a great deal of thought, had replied to Mrs. Corbett's letter, exonerating Rowell insofar as she could. Désirée Somners, she told Mrs. Corbett, was a protégée of theirs and it was at her own request that Rowell had entertained her while he was in New York.

She was far from certain whether Mrs. Corbett or her husband would accept so unlikely an explanation, but not only her own pride but her concern for the family good name prompted the lie. Rowell was not the only Rochford, and any scandal attaching to the name must reflect on innocent people such as Toby, Pelham, and her children. She felt obliged to protect and succor those beneath her roof for at least as long as she remained the chatelaine of Rochford Manor.

I am as much trapped here as if I were a rabbit in a snare, she thought with a shiver of apprehension. The bonds of marriage were after all too strong to be lightly discarded; her involvement in this family too great to be suddenly abandoned. She had vowed "for better or for worse"—and a deep-rooted core of obligation was making it impossible for her to ignore what she felt to be her duty. The Rochford inheritance was Oliver's, rightly or wrongly, and obligation for his future, too, lay heavily upon her shoulders.

Rowell returned briefly to Rochford before departing once more for the grouse shooting in Scotland. He behaved as if there had been no rift between him and his wife, and ignored the fact that Willow had firmly closed her bedroom door to him.

His attitude to Oliver during his sojourn at home was in Willow's opinion, nothing short of extraordinary. He was determined that Oliver should be made to ride again and not be permitted to give way to what he considered was an irrational fear of horses.

"It is inconceivable that a Rochford should not ride," Rowell stated flatly. "You are not considering his future, Willow. Why, he would be unable to hunt! No, he must be put back on a horse immediately."

He himself carried the screaming boy down to the stables and held the struggling child in the saddle.

"Bit too soon after the accident, don't you think, Rowell?" Pelham said as the boy's screams became more and more hysterical. "Give it a month or two longer, eh?"

But Rowell, feeling his judgment challenged, would not retract his commands—Oliver was to be put on the mare for not less than half an hour every day.

"That is an order," he said, and one he personally saw was carried out until he departed for Scotland.

Willow wrote to Mr. Gornway, who replied in the strongest terms, saying that any violent exercise was inadvisable and must on no account be undertaken for at least a year after the accident. But the damage was done. Not only did Oliver develop a marked stammer, particularly in the presence of his father, but he also began walking in his sleep.

"Try not to worry. He will grow out of both habits," Toby tried to reassure Willow.

By no means convinced that it was the riding that had brought about these developments, Rowell nonetheless allowed himself to be persuaded by Willow that Oliver should not, for the time being, be sent away to boarding school. He agreed that he could be tutored by the Barratts' governess—an excellent teacher engaged by Sir John and his wife to educate their two youngest children. The Barratts' house was but seven miles distant from Rochford Manor, and Peters would drive him there each day.

Now, however, all the children were enjoying their summer holidays, and both Pelham and Toby encouraged Willow to accept Silvie's invitation to take Oliver and Alice to Épernay for the few remaining weeks before the September schooling began.

Silvie's letter made it clear Willow need have no fear that events which took place when she was last at Épernay would be remembered by her staff. Marie, the cook, had died last year and none of the other servants had ever fully understood what happened to the babies, she wrote. Thus reassured, Willow agreed to go.

"I shall personally escort you there," Pelham said, "since Silvie has included me in her invitation. You, too, Toby."

But Toby professed himself too busy, and finally Willow and the children departed for France with Pelham, Patience, Lily, Pelham's valet, and a mountain of luggage. The good natured Silvie welcomed them with cries of pleasure, many kisses, and a whole host of invitations.

"We shall be very gay and amuse ourselves well," she said with a sideways glance at Pelham. "Now that the trains are so much faster, we can enjoy a few days in Paris, too. Willow, you are too thin and too pale, whereas I—I am putting on weight far too quickly."

"But becomingly, Silvie," Pelham said with an admiring glance at his cousin's rounded figure. He had been quite astonished on his previous visit earlier in the year when Silvie responded to his advances. But it was an agreeable surprise. In bed, Silvie had proved herself an enthusiastic participant, but unlike the other females of Pelham's acquaintance, there were no emotional repercussions on the following day. With a carefree immorality, she indulged her appetites, openly acknowledging her intentions to enjoy herself how she pleased.

She amused Pelham with risqué accounts of her past lovers, their successes and their failures, and above all, she made him laugh. Her total independence and self-reliance were in a way, a challenge to him.

Silvie was far too experienced to be unaware of the reasons for Pelham's pursuit of her.

"He has always been able to take any woman he fancied," she told Willow soon after she had arrived at Épernay. "With his looks and charm, they all succumbed without a fight. So now I make certain that *I* am not always attainable."

Despite herself, Willow laughed.

"And what will you do, dearest Silvie, if he becomes your slave?" she enquired.

Silvie shrugged her elegant, plump shoulders.

"Pelham will never be any woman's slave—or not for long. He is a born philanderer—but so am I, Willow. I have been considering quite seriously the prospect of marrying him. We would suit one another very well, provided Pelham agreed that I had as much right to 'a philander' here and there as he, a man, would have. Pelham would make an attractive escort, a delightful husband in many ways. And I can give him the money he needs—by no means an unwelcome alternative to youth. And he has always had a great love for France, which is fortunate since I do not think I would care to live in England. How would you feel, *chérie*, if I were to become your sister-in-law as well as your cousin by marriage?"

Willow was delighted by the prospect—and not a little envious of the couple's obvious happiness. The Château d'Orbais rang with laughter, and even the servants were affected, and smiled and sang as they went about their work.

Three weeks later, the day before they were to return to England, Silvie and Pelham became officially betrothed. Silvie gave a gala dinner party at the Château d'Orbais to celebrate the occasion.

"I would have invited Pierre and Maurice," she whispered laughingly to Willow. "But they went off to Italy to paint and heaven alone knows where they are now."

Which was perhaps as well, thought Willow. Her loneliness was often intolerable—the more so since she was unable that holiday to ignore the physical exchanges of affection between the newly-engaged couple. There was sufficient fraternal likeness between Pelham and Toby for her to be reminded far too often of the man she loved, and there were times when her body ached for him as fiercely as her mind always craved his companionship.

She tried not to think of Toby with some other woman, although in her heart of hearts, she did not believe he was always celibate. He was quite often away from Rochford on some mission or conference concerning his work, and she deliberately refrained from questioning him on his return as to where he had stayed, whom he had met. But the thought tormented her in the darkness of the night and left her weak with jealous yearnings to be in the place of those other women he must need and enjoy from time to time. She chided herself for such base imaginings, but still could not prevent them from eating into her mind.

With Pelham married to Silvie and living in France, there would only be her, Rowell, and Toby left at Rochford, Willow thought uneasily. With Rowell away so frequently, it would leave the two of them more and more often alone together. This past summer had only been made possible by Pelham's presence helping them to keep at arm's length. Perhaps after all she would pursue her plan to divorce her husband—or to ask him to divorce her. Perhaps if she could offer him suitable financial recompense, he could be induced to allow her to go away with the children. She could not leave without them.

Money meant power and influence to Rowell, she reflected, and was more important to him than anything else in the world. She would write to Mr. Corbett on her return home and ask him how large a sum of money she could raise if she needed it.

Some three weeks later, she penned her query to Mr. Corbett. He replied to her letter with commendable promptness.

I deeply regret that it is still too soon to give you figures of any kind since we are nowhere near achieving probate. The affairs of T. R. T. C. are extremely complex and your father had many ancillary interests. Nor are we any nearer achieving a positive decision from the insurance company regarding your father's house and private possessions.

Before putting any project before you, I would like to remind you that your father and I started out as partners thirty-six years ago and it was entirely due to his foresight and business acumen that I am now an exceedingly wealthy man in my own right. I am therefore eternally in your father's debt. You, my dear child, were his greatest concern, particularly since you left the States, and I gave him my solemn undertaking that I would hold your interests to heart no less than if you were my own daughter.

Having said as much, may I please place such resources as I have personally available entirely at your disposal?

There was more in similar vein, but although Willow was greatly touched by the offer, she knew that she could never accept it. She would not begin a new life indebted to anyone else—even if that person was her father's oldest and dearest friend.

"Please put all such concerns from your mind, dear Mr. Corbett," she replied by return of post. "I am in no pressing need, I do assure you . . ."

Having given her reply to one of the footmen to hand to the postboy when he called, she felt a sense of relief. The decision to proceed with a divorce was once again postponed until some other time. Whether she wished it or not, she could not leave Rochford yet.

I am both cowardly and cruel, Willow told herself as she watched Toby walking across the lawn toward the house, Oliver skipping happily beside him. I am cowardly because I cannot face life without Toby; cruel because I am the unwitting barrier between him and some other woman's love.

There were tears of mortification in her eyes as she made her way upstairs to her bedroom. Once there, she dismissed the waiting Lily and alone went to her dressing table and withdrew from it the heavy bunch of keys. One by one she touched each of them with thoughtful concentration. Grandmère's rooms. Aunt Milly's, Francis' —all were now locked, the unmade beds and furniture covered with dust sheets, redolent with the smell of mothballs. Rupert's room was also dust-sheeted and locked, his books, violin, stacks of music, and childhood treasures carefully wrapped in paper and stored away in cupboards by Toby and herself. Would there ever be word from Rupert? she wondered. Had Adrian been able to give him some small measure of happiness? Would she ever know?

The key to Dodie's turret bedroom she held for a long time as her mind swung back over the fifteen years since she had first visited the pathetic little invalid in the darkened chamber. For Dodie at least, she, Willow, had found the key to happiness when she had forced Grandmère to unlock her door and allow the imprisoned butterfly to emerge. But it was not so for herself, Willow thought. From the time of her arrival here as a young bride, it was almost as if a key had been turned upon her and the freedom she had known as a child had thenceforth been denied her. She was a prisoner at Rochford— Rowell's prisoner, perhaps? Or Toby's? But for Toby, might she not have escaped long since? If so, then it was love that was really her jailer.

Chapter Twenty-Eight

January–April 1907

"**S**O MY DAYS ARE NUMBERED, EH, ROSE?"

The younger man remained silent. Poor old Doctor Forbes had asked for the truth when he suggested he should examine him after Christmas. While he could not lie, neither could he bring himself to tell the man he had less than six months to live.

John Forbes leaned back, resting his head against the worn brown leather of his wing chair. He puffed at a long stemmed briar pipe. Occasionally he coughed, but he did not allow the pipe to go out.

"You ought to stop smoking, sir," Peter Rose said, but without authority, for he knew that this was one of his senior partner's palliatives to the pain that from time to time engulfed him.

"No point trying to prolong my life now," John Forbes said with a dry smile. "And to tell you the truth, young man, I shall not be sorry to go. I've led a pretty useless life one way and another, and what with my son leaving the country . . . well, there are no grandchildren to look forward to, are there?"

It *had* been a useless life—wasted, he thought. All those high hopes and aspirations of his youth were ground down under the heel of that evil, domineering old Frenchwoman at Rochford Manor. Bitterly the dying man recalled how he had let old Lady Rochford influence him from his earliest years in practice. It had begun so long ago, in the year 1864, when those two infant girls had died. If he had not been so afraid of incurring her wrath by confessing his mistaken diagnosis, he might never have fallen under her domination.

Before he died, he thought with sudden conviction, he would write a letter to Tobias Rochford, telling him about those deaths. Rose had told him of the work Tobias was

464

doing researching the causes of diphtheria. Rose himself had been most impressed by the progress being made in the Rochford laboratory and he knew of Tobias' search for the nurse, Irene, whom he was convinced was a carrier.

Forbes himself thought this theory a bit unlikely. But he fully understood the young man's compulsion to disprove his grandmother's insistence that there was a strain of insanity in the female line of the family—which brought to mind the surviving daughter, Dorothy. He had almost certainly been wrong about her, too. Infantile paralysis was not only an obvious diagnosis but a perfectly reasonable one for her condition—and yet he had let that wicked old harridan convince him the girl was just another mentally handicapped female with physical deformities in addition. But for young Lady Rochford's intervention, the poor child might have remained a bedridden invalid all her life. *He* would not have had the courage to rescue her.

And now death was looking over his shoulder. Would Satan be waiting to greet him at the gates of hell for his part in the abduction of the Rochford baby? he wondered wryly. If so, then old Lady Rochford would be standing close by the devil's shoulder. Maybe if he made a clean breast of affairs, he could cleanse his soul. But *even now* he lacked the courage, although he had nothing more to lose. It really made very little difference whether he died here in his own home or in one of his majesty's prisons, he reflected. But what he could not face, were he to confess, would be young Lady Rochford's eyes when she learned the truth about her missing baby.

For the thousandth time, he pondered on the fate of that unwanted child. With both Lady Rochford and the Comtesse le Chevalier dead, he doubted very much that the payments for her upkeep at the convent were still being made.

What fate awaited the child of charity? he asked himself anxiously. In this country, at best it would be a life of drudgery in domestic service. Or it might mean an apprenticeship to a modiste. He had once in his student days been called to the bedside of such a girl. She was lying in a tiny airless cubicle in one of the attic rooms above the shop, literally worn out by overwork. From one of the other girls he had learned that they began their day plying their needles at six-thirty in the mornings and were often still kept at their tasks till midnight. There had been as many as sixty-two women and girls in a room allowing only one hundred and fifty cubic feet of air. No aristocratically bred girl could survive such conditions. Those girls who did survive rarely escaped from this bondage.

Forbes allowed his eyes to close as pain momentarily overrode all other thought. Although still not quite seventy, he was so thin and frail that he looked nearer ninety. His body was failing fast, but his brain would not be stilled.

Perhaps, he thought, he would die the easier if he were to make sure that the Rochford child was at least alive and living in not too terrible circumstances.

I'll go to France, he decided, before it is too late. He knew very well the nature of the disease that was killing him and that he could not afford to postpone such a journey too long. If he did not delay within a day or two he could be in Épernay where the *Convent du Coeur-Sanglant* was doubtless still opening its doors to orphans.

By now Peter Rose had gone out on his rounds. When he returned he would ask him to make train and packet reservations for the journey to France. He'd say he needed one last holiday before he died. He would ask for a booked passage to Paris only. From there he himself could buy a train ticket to Épernay—for it would not do to let Rose know his ultimate destination.

When his young partner returned, Forbes was asleep. Peter Rose stood looking down at him with professional regard. He had given the old man six months—but now he doubted very much whether he'd last that long. It might be nearer three, he thought, as gently he shook the sick man into wakefulness and told him that it was time for afternoon tea.

Rowell had been out hunting with Pelham and Toby and it was not until tea-time that he returned to the manor to find Willow awaiting him. As he let his valet pull off his mud-spattered boots and loosen the cravat at his neck, he felt a healthy weariness which was quickly replaced with a strange excitement as his young wife came into the room. It was rare these days that she approached him and it had gradually come upon him that in fact she always went out of her way to avoid him. At first he had been unaffected by her cold indifference. He suspected that she still nursed a grudge against him for spending that week in New York with Désirée. He hoped that she would, like other wives, come around to accepting his infidelities.

But Willow's attitude had remained unaccepting, and he had been far from pleased when he returned from the grouse shooting in Scotland to find himself still locked out of her bedroom. Only on such terms, she told him in a cold hard voice, was she prepared to continue with the marriage.

Rowell had laughed off her statement, but it had nonetheless caused him a few wakeful hours. Throughout their marriage he had only very occasionally felt any real stirrings of desire for his wife, but he was accustomed to taking her as and when he wished; and he was now in two minds whether or not to force her to comply. The reason for his hesitation was that he sensed she might pursue her threat to divorce him. He believed that it could not be long before Willoughby Tetford's affairs were settled and that Willow would begin to receive some benefits—albeit not the millions he had anticipated. He himself had invested a large part of the Rochford resources very heavily in those American companies that his father-in-law had praised so highly. Now, unexpectedly, his stockbroker had told him that the country seemed to be heading toward some kind of financial crisis.

An excellent day's hunting had helped to put such unwelcome thoughts from his mind and now, as his wife approached him, he felt an unaccustomed stirring in his loins. She was looking startlingly beautiful, he thought, his eyes traveling from her smooth head to her small protruding bosom and from thence to her tiny waist and the swell of her hips. She still had the figure of a girl—despite the children she had borne.

"Rowell, I have received a telegram from Mr. Corbett. I think it is important and that you may wish to read it."

Her voice was quiet and unemotional.

"Well, let me see it then," Rowell said not ungraciously. He took the telegram from her and read it first hurriedly and then word by word, his heart sinking as the

impact registered fully on his consciousness. His stockbroker had been right—there was a major panic on Wall
Street. Corbett and his fellow directors were watching
the position with great concern and, with the rest of the
country, were praying for a halt to the frightening slide
in prices.

"There's nothing *you* can do about it," he said to Willow, not without a degree of satisfaction. Had his father-
in-law seen fit to make him a director, he would already
have been on a boat for New York. "You'll just have to
sit back and see what Corbett is made of. One thing is
certain—it is no concern of mine. Your father made it
clear he did not wish for my involvement."

Briefly, the hot color flared into Willow's cheeks and
as quickly receded. In a way, she could understand
Rowell's frustration—for had he not married her for her
money? It must have been a bitter pill to swallow when
he learned that the vast fortune would never be hers or
his but would pass to the children. Now it seemed possible that she might not receive even a small income from
the trust.

Within the next few weeks, the situation worsened and
Rowell warned Willow that they might have to consider
making economies.

"I invested quite a lot of money in American companies of which I had heard your father speak well," he
admitted. "We may be in for a rough ride, my dear. I may
have to sell the yacht to tide us over some temporary
embarrassments."

"Oh, Rowell, I'm sorry!" Willow said with genuine
regret. "But I'm sure we'll manage," she added optimisti-
cally. "I could make some domestic economies if I tried.
The waste of food in our household is quite shocking.
I will talk to Cook tomorrow."

Rowell quickly covered Willow's hand with his own,
imprisoning it there. Willow had still not invited him into
her bedroom, and on the two occasions when, embold-
ened by alcohol, he had made half-hearted attempts to
force his way in, she had not even replied to his en-
treaties. He was astonished to discover himself more and
more obsessed with the need to win back her regard
and re-establish himself as her husband. This was the first

real sign she had given of softening her attitude toward him.

"I fear that our marriage may not always have been quite as perfect as you would have wished, my dear," he said. "I may not always have been . . . well, quite as considerate as I should. But my affection for you—and, indeed, my regard is in no degree lessened by the passage of time. I want you to know that."

It was perhaps the nearest Rowell had ever come to speaking of love, and Willow could not prevent the bitter reflection that it had come too late. Such a statement from her husband ten—even five—years ago might have made so much difference to their marriage.

"Let us not speak of such matters," she said. "There are some things better left unsaid between husband and wife, and I have no desire to recriminate." *I too have not been blameless,* she thought.

Twice, she had deceived him in a way that still troubled her conscience—first with Oliver, which may have been a lesser transgression, since she had not invited Pelham's advances. But in substituting Nellie's baby for her own and pretending to Rowell the child was his . . . that had been deliberate. She did not regret it, but it made her less condemnatory of Rowell than she might otherwise have been.

Rowell glanced sideways at his wife's beautiful profile. He hoped that she had given up any crazed notion to divorce him. Since she had welcomed him home from New York with such cold accusatory words as she gave him Mrs. Corbett's letter to read, there had been no further mention of her leaving him. He had complied with her request to have her bedroom to herself and since then, he had not spent a great deal of time in her company. There were those who were beginning to remark how seldom the Rochfords were seen together these days, but fortunately the boy's prolonged illness and the Tetfords' sudden death had afforded him good enough reasons to quieten gossips like Esmé Symington.

But now Willow was no longer in mourning, and it was time they rejoined society as a couple, he decided. This seemed the right moment to tell her so.

Instinctively, Willow rejected such a proposal. She had no wish to be in Rowell's company or to rejoin society and its wild search for amusement. But even as she opened her mouth to decline, a kind of despair made her hesitate. If her financial position were now such that she could not leave Rowell, then her life with him had to continue.

"A little holiday together might do us both good," Rowell was saying persuasively. "We could go abroad for a week or so, my dear, go to Deauville for the racing perhaps."

With a sigh Willow realized she could not go on burying her head in the sand at Rochford Manor, nursing her love for Toby and living for the pleasure of every moment she spent in his company. The strain on them was already beginning to tell. During her Christmas visit Silvie had warned her that soon even others less perceptive than she would not fail to feel the tension between Willow and Toby when they were together in the same room.

"It is like being close to an electric spark," said Silvie. "Even my short-sighted darling Pelham has guessed you two are in love."

Willow therefore agreed to consider Rowell's request that she accompany him to Deauville. She decided to ask Silvie and Pelham to join them too—their company at least would insure a happier holiday. Willow tried not to feel bitter toward Rowell because his need of her had come too late in their marriage for her former love for him to be revived.

A severe bout of influenza had laid Dr. Forbes low for the whole of February, and Dr. Rose had forbidden him to attempt to visit France until the spring. Even now, although it was April, he was feeling far from well.

The Channel had been choppy, and in company with many other of the passengers, he had been seasick. The train journey into Paris had seemed endless, and now he had finally arrived at the Gare du Nord among a seething crowd of tourists and visitors, he felt almost too exhausted to find one of the blue-bloused porters to take his luggage to a fiacre.

When at last he was seated in the hired cab, he ordered the *cocher*, in his white patent leather tophat, to drive him to a reasonably priced hotel he knew in the Rue St.

Honoré. Then only did he relax against the upholstery. The sunlight was streaming through the green leaves of the trees lining the *grands boulevards*, and despite his exhaustion, the old man felt a surge of excitement mingling with nostalga stir the blood in his veins. He breathed deeply, his highly attuned senses catching the very smell of Paris—the flowers, the freshly baked bread, the drains —and everywhere the restless movement of people circulating in the streets.

As they drove down the Champs Elysées, the sight of the great Cathédral de Notre Dame filled him with sadness. He had come to Paris on his honeymoon—a week of perfect happiness that he was never to know again. Nine months later his young wife, Peggy, had died in childbirth, leaving him to care for the child conceived in this city. He remembered how he and his bride had held hands in front of the tiny flame burning before the tabernacle in the Cathédral. How sincerely they had both prayed to a God who, he had afterwards thought bitterly, must have been laughing at him, knowing His intention to remove the only person in the world who mattered to him.

On the following morning, only partly refreshed by an uneasy night's sleep, Doctor Forbes took the train to Épernay. Watching the passing countryside, the old man pondered on the possibility of there being a life hereafter—a heaven where he would be reunited with Adrian's mother, Peggy. It was only this faint hope that sustained him now that he stood on the brink of departure from a world which had fallen so far short of his expectations. He was half hoping that at the convent, in the presence of so many holy women who had dedicated their lives to God, he might find reinforcement for his flickering faith.

But the Mother Superior of the *Convent du Coeur Sanglant* was soon to dispel any such illusion. The pious charity of the nuns, it seemed, had lasted only so long as old Lady Rochford's payments for the child had continued. Within a few months of her death and that of Comtesse le Chevalier, the eleven-year-old girl had been sent off to Paris to work for a *modiste* as a *femme de ménage*.

Doctor Forbes was rendered momentarily speechless

when he was so informed, unable to grasp the concept of a Rochford working as a skivvy for a lower middle class family. But the Mother Superior had no such qualms.

"We train all our girls for domestic work," she said. "If they are neither lazy nor immoral, they can be sure of their keep and a roof over their heads for the remainder of their days."

She was perfectly willing to supply Doctor Forbes with the address of the *magasin de modes* where the little girl, Sophie Miller, had been sent. It was a respectable household run by a God-fearing, hard-working French couple, she told him.

Somewhat relieved, Doctor Forbes took the return train to Paris. He was once again feeling ill and decided that since he was in no real hurry, he would delay his visit to Monsieur and Madame Grimaud until the following day.

But Madame Grimaud was even less reassuring than the Mother Superior. The girl sent her by the convent had proved far from satisfactory, she stated. At first all had been well, but then Miller—she called all her servants by their surnames, she told him—had attracted the attention of one of their regular clients, a young woman with a dubious reputation.

"*Une cocotte de luxe*," she whispered with a sideways glance at her elderly English visitor to be certain that he understood her meaning. "She enticed my girl away, and I had had to pay the convent good money for her. Mind you, I made sure that I was repaid—every sou; and I have refused to serve that *cocotte* since, even though she was a good client. I know her sort. When she isn't too busy selling herself, she earns money procuring young girls for the Paris brothels in the neighborhood. So I don't doubt that is where you'll find Miller—and she won't be much like a convent-bred girl if you do find her, that's a certainty!"

Doctor Forbes' hand clutched at his heart, where he felt a sudden agonizing pain. Realizing her visitor was far from well, Madame Grimaud fetched him a chair and a glass of water. When he had recovered a little, he asked her to be good enough to describe the girl to him. Madame Grimaud gave a grudging picture of her former employee's appearance.

"A skinny little thing, Monsieur, but I suppose some might think the girl pretty—or at any rate, unusual. She had rather remarkable fair hair—so pale a gold that it was almost white—and exceptionally large, deep blue eyes. She was fine boned for a servant girl—not nearly as strong as one would desire for her ilk. She was quiet, well-spoken, and well-mannered, as one would expect of a convent-reared orphan. But they are all the same, these girls—they want the luxuries and the easy life money can buy, and no sooner do they see a way of getting it than they're on the streets. No morals, no gratitude . . ."

If Madame Grimaud were right Dr. Forbes thought, Baron Rochford's daughter was now working in a Paris brothel. It was a fate far far worse than any he could have imagined. Had he foreseen the possibility, he might never have set out on this journey.

But once more back in the sanctuary of his respectable hotel, he knew that he could not now let the matter rest. If the girl *was* in a brothel, then he had to find her, rescue her. But he knew nothing more than the name of the young woman, Blanche, who had, according to Madame Grimaud, enticed her maid away from her. He might ask the help of the police, he thought, but at once rejected the idea. The police would want him to declare his own interest in Sophie Miller, and that he could not do without revealing her true identity.

He decided to spend the afternoon resting on his bed. Even if he did not sleep he hoped to regain sufficient strength to go out that evening to do what must be done —make a tour of the brothels in the neighborhood of *La Maison Grimaud*.

Country doctor though he was, he was not so naïve as to be unaware of what went on in the big cities after nightfall—the crime, the perversions, the bestiality. He knew that no matter what a man lusted after, it could be bought if he had the right sum of money in his pocket. Like any other commodity in Paris, this girl, too, could be bought.

As he dressed himself slowly and meticulously in a clean white shirt and dinner jacket, John Forbes considered his own meager wealth. He had never spent the money with which old Lady Rochford had rewarded him throughout the years—payments made in return for his silence, he now admitted openly to himself. It had all been put aside for Adrian—but now, as far as he was concerned, he no longer had a son.

The boy had never written to him since the day he had left the country with Rupert Rochford. The thought of Adrian's involvement with Rupert was unbearable to him. Brought up himself by strict Victorian parents, he held their rigid views on sexual morality. There was therefore now nothing in the world that would have persuaded him to set out upon a round of the Paris brothels other than his own relentless conscience and his ceaseless feelings of guilt toward the child he had helped to abduct.

The *cocher* of his fiacre had no such qualms. With a grin, he listened to the elderly Englishman's halting attempts to explain in French where he wished to go and nodded. Yes, he knew the district. Yes, he knew of several excellent houses thereabouts, all of whom employed young girls—if that was Monsieur's particular pleasure, he added with a knowing wink. Certainly, he would be prepared to wait outside the brothel while Monsieur surveyed the goods within, and if Monsieur could not at once find what was to his choosing, then he would conduct him elsewhere.

"My time is yours, Monsieur," he said, having long since espied the thick wallet his customer had concealed in his coat pocket.

It was not yet eight o'clock when the *cocher* pulled up his horse and climbed down from his box, his shawled coat hanging almost to his feet. Still grinning, he opened the door for the old man and helped him out of the fiacre. Doctor Forbes went up the steps of the house the driver was indicating and forced himself to pull the bell. The door was opened by a manservant, but as Forbes was ushered into the hall, a thin white-faced woman dressed in black bombazine came hurrying toward him. Her hair was knotted in a chignon on top of her head and her eyes darted swiftly over her customer, assessing his wealth by his attire. There was no doubting she was the Madame, her visitor thought, his courage ebbing fast.

Her smile was grotesque, and Dr. Forbes drew back.

"*Entrez, entrez, Monsieur,*" she said quickly. "You will join me in a little drink, I hope? It is early yet, but soon there will be many others here. In the meanwhile, a little drink, some music perhaps and, of course, the girls . . ."

Forbes had already decided that his best chance of finding Sophia Rochford was to pretend that a very young girl of her particular coloring was his personal fetish. To admit his real reason was almost certain to insure that the girl would not be produced for his viewing. Now, with red-faced embarrassment, he told the Madame his preference was for an adolescent girl, perhaps even a virgin; and he gave Sophia's description as outlined by Madame Grimaud.

Although she had no such demoiselle to offer him, the Madame insisted that he see one or two of her younger girls. At her summons they came running into the room. They were preceded by a servant carrying a bottle of champagne lying sideways on a bed of ice in a silver bucket.

The girls were in evening dress, one in blue and the other in orange, their dresses cut so low that their nipples were exposed. They wore high-heeled shoes, and the split skirts of their dresses revealed long, slender, silk-stockinged legs. Behind them was an effeminate-looking young man who seated himself at the piano at the end of the long salon and began to play a polka.

But as the girls came hurrying over, smiling and coquetting, Doctor Forbes stood up.

"I regret that they are not to my particular taste," he said, drawing out his wallet. With unaccustomed firmness, he cut short Madame's insistence that she had other girls to interest him—if not to his exact choice of coloring, alas, then of many exciting varieties.

Paying her liberally for the wine he had not drunk, Doctor Forbes managed to make his way out into the street where his *cocher* was patiently awaiting him.

He made visits to three other similar houses before finally he was ushered by Madame Lou-Lou into the salon of *Le Ciel Rouge*. Once again wine was brought to him instantly, and while he listed his requirements, Madame smiled and swayed her vast bulk before him, assuring him that she could supply whatever he wanted.

Her salon was a long room, like the first he had seen, but the center was bare of furniture, the floor polished in readiness for dancing. Comfortable chairs and sofas were grouped by the walls, and palms in ornate pots separated one group from another and provided a modicum of privacy. The atmosphere was redolent of cheap perfume and the tobacco from the customers' cigars. There were already a dozen or more couples in the room, either dancing or entwined upon one of the sofas.

"Yvette!" she called sharply to one of the girls passing by. "Call La Perle. I want her here at once."

Madame Lou-Lou turned back to Doctor Forbes.

"You are fortunate, Monsieur, to have come to my house. *J'ai exactement ce que vous désirez. Ma petite Perle* is one of my most prized *enfants* and will suit Monsieur to perfection."

How fortunate, she thought, that the child had been so insistent upon allowing the henna rinse to grow out of her hair.

"Perle?" Doctor Forbes repeated, his hopes falling as swiftly as they had been aroused by her comments.

"You do not care for the name, Monsieur? Then you must call her by whatever name pleases you, but I think when you see her, you will agree that it suits her. Her skin, her fair hair, her—"

She halted her long list of attributes as the girl herself came slowly across the room toward them. Once again Doctor Forbes felt a stab of pain in the region of his heart; but this time it was caused by excitement. There could be very little doubt that he had found what he was looking for. Despite her shockingly immoral attire and painted face, the young girl was sufficiently like her mother for him to be convinced that this was Baroness Rochford's daughter.

"She will do," he said abruptly. "I wish to talk to her!"

"But of course, Monsieur. A little talk, a dance perhaps, and soon the appetites are whetted, no? Perle, take Monsieur to a table. José, Monsieur's champagne to accompany him, please."

Sophia surveyed the elderly Englishman and tried to hide her disappointment. Yvette had told her that the older the clients were, the richer in all probability. But this one looked neither rich nor imposing. She caught Madame Lou-Lou's dark beady eyes upon her and smiled quickly as she linked her arm through that of her client. She felt him tremble at her touch and judged that the old man was nervous.

"Some are!" Yvette had told her. "They don't like to think they are buying you—they want to pretend you really fancy them, so *you* have to pretend."

She sat down opposite the elderly man, allowing the slit of her bright yellow skirt to fall apart and show a yellow satin garter as Yvette had taught her. Her legs were still too thin and despite the fattening foods Madame Lou-Lou insisted she eat, she lacked the rounded fullness of the other girls. There was music playing in the background and two maids were busy serving drinks.

"I used to serve drinks when I first came here," Sophia told her silent companion as Marie deposited the champagne on the table. "But it is much more interesting talking to customers. You are English, Monsieur? You must be lonely so far from home."

At last Doctor Forbes found his voice.

"I do not wish to talk about myself, my dear, but you. I want first to know how old you are," he said in a low, intense voice.

Sophia hesitated. Yvette had warned her that some men felt guilty if a girl was very young, while others liked them to be still children. But Madame Lou-Lou did not cater for those who preferred really young children still wearing childish clothes and playing with toys.

Unsure of her customer's preference, Sophia pouted prettily, playing for time.

"How old would you guess me to be, Monsieur?"

Doctor Forbes did a quick calculation.

"Thirteen?" he said. Thirteen years ago, this painted child was the innocent babe he had pulled from her mother's womb.

"Now that is exceedinly clever of you, Monsieur," Sophia said brightly, wondering how he had guessed so accurately. "Thirteen and a half, to be exact."

Bit by bit he prized her story from her. She was an orphan, she told him. She had been raised by the nuns in a convent in Épernay and had left there to work for the owner of a *magasin de modes* in Paris.

"Madame Grimaud did not like me—I think because her husband was always watching me," she told him. "Do *you* think me pretty, Monsieur?"

Doctor Forbes tried not to feel shocked by the girl's obvious expertise as she pursed her small rosy lips in a childish moue. Despite her extreme youth, she was already a practiced harlot.

"Were you called Sophie—Sophie Miller before you came here!" he asked in a small, hard voice. "Was it the Madame who changed your name to Perle?"

Now it was the girl's turn to look shocked—and frightened.

"Are you a friend of Monsieur Grimaud?" she demanded anxiously. "If so, I assure you Monsieur, that he and Madame were fully compensated by Madame Lou-Lou after I had left their employ. My papers are all in order and I have registered with the Préfecture and got a card. Madame will not keep girls who do not attend for medical visits twice a month."

Doctor Forbes hastened to reassure her that he was not there to check up on her. His hands were trembling with excitement.

"I am here only to make certain that you are the person for whom I have been searching," he said.

"You have been looking for *me*?" Sophia asked, wide-eyed. A strange expression crept over her face. "You have not been sent here by . . . by a certain Monsieur Maurice . . .?" Her voice trailed into silence.

"By nobody of that name—or any other," Doctor Forbes said, dashing the girl's hopes.

In the year since the artist had left Paris, Sophia had not forgotten him; and while with one half of herself she hated him and could never forgive him for his rejection of her, there still remained the secret, childish adoration for him she had once had.

Nor had she forgotten her desire to give herself to him. But after the humiliation and pain of her first submission to another man's invasion of her body, she had put firmly from her mind any thought of love in connection with the act. She readily adopted Yvette's philosophy that her task was to exploit men's lusts and not expect to enjoy the encounters; to reap the rewards in the form of money, no more. Love did not enter into the transaction.

The elderly Englishman had fallen silent, but now he was beginning to talk to her again in his bad French.

She tried to understand him, but feared she must have misinterpreted his meaning when he stated that he knew who her parents were and that she came of a titled English family; that he was here to rescue her; if necessary to take her back to England where he would find her respectable employment. Her real name was Sophia —not Sophie, he insisted. She had the blood of the English aristocracy in her veins and could not be allowed to remain in a brothel.

Sophia was fascinated, and immensely intrigued. Although she suspected this might be a fairy-tale spun by a drunken old man, nevertheless, it was interesting to speculate that she was well-born, a lady even. She had often wondered why she was not like other girls, other servants. The cook at Madame Grimaud's had nicknamed her *la Duchesse* because of her small delicately-boned hands and feet, and because of her long slender neck and the way she held her head. And, of course, like all the other orphans at the convent, she had woven dreams of rich titled parents who would one day come to rescue her after discovering the terrible misunderstanding that had led to her supposed orphaning.

Doctor Forbes was peering into Sophia's face with great intentness.

"You cannot remain here," he reiterated. "Although I am not at liberty to reveal the names of your parents, I do know that such a way of life for their daughter would be intolerable to them. You must come home to England with me, Sophia. I will find you respectable employment."

The daydream had gone on long enough, Sophia decided. Of course she could not leave *Le Ciel Rouge*— nor even wished to do so if it meant returning to a life as a maid to someone like Madame Grimaud. She told Doctor Forbes so bluntly.

"I am happy here, thank you all the same, Monsieur. I earn good money and the other girls are my friends. If I am not to be reunited with these people you say are my parents, I have no wish to go to your country. Besides, Madame Lou-Lou would never permit it. I am very popular with her customers, and when I am older—"

"I will buy you from Madame," Doctor Forbes cried, his anxiety mounting as the girl spoke. With an effort, he lowered his voice. "I have money, Sophia. I could arrange suitable employment for you—perhaps as a governess in a titled household. You might eventually make a good marriage to someone nearer your own station. You cannot remain here."

For half an hour he talked to her, painting as rosy a picture as he dared of the future awaiting her. Sophia became increasingly interested as finally she was convinced of his sincerity.

"You mean I might even have my own servant? A horse and carriage? A house of my own?"

"They are all possible, Sophia. It might be necessary to train you first to speak and behave as a young lady—but that would not be so difficult since you are French—or have been brought up as such. I would have to find a lady to sponsor you; to take you under her wing and launch you in society. But there *are* such—widows and the like—ladies of good birth and lineage who have need of money. Besides, what future can you hope for in a place like this?"

A protector such as she hoped to acquire might tire of her, he argued. As she grew older, she would begin to lose her beauty. A husband would support her for life—be obliged to do so.

Sophia's blue eyes began to sparkle. The sheer adventure of the enterprise caught her imagination. But why, she inquired, could Doctor Forbes not reveal her true parentage. Was she illegitimate? Why did they not want her back? Were they dead? These questions he refused to answer.

Confident that it would not be long before she could prize the facts from him, Sophia agreed that he might speak to Madame Lou-Lou to inquire if she were willing to sell her.

"You might do best if you tell her that you want me for your mistress," she advised seriously. "Madame would not be swayed by reasons of morality, nor by your story of my titled parents, which in any case you refuse to substantiate. Men do buy girls for mistresses, however, although she will not sell me cheaply, Monsieur."

Sophia's estimate of her value to Madame Lou-Lou was not inflated. For half an hour Madame refused even to consider a price for her Perle.

"There is something special about *la petite*," she told

the doctor. "Not long ago there was a French artist who wanted her for his model—and only Perle would do. He paid full price for her although he left her a virgin. And before that there was a titled English Milord who noticed her even though she was only employed as a maid at the time. He said he would return for her when she was older."

"Name any price, Madame, within reason," Doctor Forbes argued stubbornly. "I am determined to have her."

Madame calculated shrewdly. The girl had already cost her ten thousand francs—Madame Grimaud's price for the sale of the twelve-year-old virgin.

But the girl had been working for a year now and was showing no signs of filling out as Madame had hoped. Her Perle could well turn out to be one of the scraggy ones whom most men would not look at. It was all right while they were still children—children were always wanted—but Perle was getting older.

"I would want paying in Napoléons," she said, eyeing the old man reflectively. "Five hundred, Monsieur—no more, no less."

She was rarely surprised by the behavior of any man, but now this thin, frail old man astonished her. He had not, after all, even sampled the girl as yet! But without hesitation he said:

"Very well, Madame, five hundred Napoléons. But you must realize that I do not have that sum of money to hand. I shall have to return to England and gather my resources. It may take a week or two."

Madame smiled.

"You may take as long as you wish, Monsieur. I assure you I shall not part with her to anyone else—not even to Milord Rochford if he should come back for her."

Doctor Forbes' hand went yet again to his heart. His face whitened alarmingly and he gasped for breath. Madame regarded him uneasily. Once before in her long career, she had had an old man die of a heart attack on the premises, and such unfortunate occurrences caused trouble with the Préfecture de Police and gave the house a bad name.

"Rochford?" Doctor Forbes stuttered. "You are sure of the name?"

Jealousy—that's all it was, thought Madame, relaxing.

The old man did not want competition. She wondered if she could still up her price.

"But certainly, Monsieur. Milord Rochford has often visited us in the past—a most charming gentleman. 'Lou-Lou,' he always says to me, 'you are more beautiful than ever. Give your greatest admirer a kiss!' Of course, Monsieur Pelham is not always sober and on the last occasion he was here, he could not enjoy himself with the girls even though I had offered him any one of his choice quite free. But that is men, *hein*? There is no explaining their natures. But he was not too drunk to overlook my little Perle—she was serving drinks then—and to remark upon her. 'There is something about that girl . . .' he kept saying, and when his friends took him away, he vowed he would be back for another look at her and swore he'd be sober next time. So you see, Monsieur, you are not the only one who has taken a special fancy to the girl. My price remains six hundred Napoléons and that is my last word."

"Six hundred! But Madame, you said five—"

"Oh, no, Monsieur, you must have misunderstood my language. I said *six*, not *cinque*. But I am sure you will have no difficulty arranging the money."

Doctor Forbes was silenced. The news that Pelham Rochford had been here and seen Sophia had been almost too much for his sanity. Pelham could not have known that the girl was in reality his own niece—how could he? Yet he too had been struck by Sophia's likeness to her mother and been drawn to her because of it. It could only be God's mercy that had not brought him back long since to buy the girl's favors.

"Six hundred Napoléons, Madame," he said. "It is agreed?"

Madame smiled. She had not expected him to refuse. She had seen that look in a man's eyes many times—a look that betrayed him a slave to his desires. For six hundred gold pieces, she would have given him Yvette, too, had he bargained with her.

"There, Monsieur," she said, holding out her hand. "The contract is agreed! As soon as you have the money, the girl is yours."

Trembling so violently he could scarcely move, the doctor stood up. Then, without a farewell glance at

Madame or Sophia, he staggered like a drunken man out of the salon.

Sophia, who had been watching from a distance came running after him.

"Monsieur, you are not leaving?" she asked, her small painted face a mask of disappointment.

Doctor Forbes paused.

"I shall be returning to collect you, Mademoiselle, in a few weeks' time. Madame has agreed to sell you to me," he added. "But I must first go back to my home in England to find the money. I do not carry so vast a sum on my person."

Sophia's blue eyes sparkled and she clapped her hands in childish delight.

"Then you are to pay a very large sum for me? I am worth so much?" she inquired.

The old man nodded. Despite his increasing feeling of ill health that was overriding all other thought, he was appalled anew that a Rochford should value herself in terms of money. But the fault was not the child's, it was his, he told himself. But for his complicity, she would not be here, but living like the Baroness' other little daughter, Alice, in the comfort and security of Rochford Manor.

"I had almost forgotten," he said, feeling in his breast pocket. "I have a present for you."

Sophia gave a little gasp of pleasure as he withdrew a large gold locket and handed it to her. He could not tell her, of course, that it had once belonged to her paternal grandmother, Alice Rochford, and been handed to him by her great grandmother, old Lady Rochford, as a gift for services rendered. Even now, thirteen years later, he could remember the look of contempt in her black beady eyes as she had put the box of trinkets on the table before him.

"These belonged to my daughter-in-law. Since I consider she brought only bad luck to this household, I do not wish to keep them. You can sell them. They should fetch a guinea or two. Doubtless you could do with the money."

As she had guessed with her usual shrewdness, he had needed money. But although he had sold one or two of the less personal objects, he had been unable to bring himself to sell the locket. Inscribed on the inside were the words 'To Alice from Oliver, July 12, 1862,' and beside it was a tiny faded sepia photograph of a young man with Dundreary whiskers and a drooping mustache.

The fact that both parties were long since dead did not change his reluctance to dispose of so personal a memento for the few pounds it might realize. Now, all these years later, he had decided before leaving England to give it to the child he believed to be still in the convent. The locket would be a link with a past unknown to her, but its inscription sufficiently indeterminate that it could not lead to any investigation into her origins.

To his discomfort, the child now flung her arms around him and hugged him with childish delight as she plied him with eager questions. Who were Alice and Oliver? Who had suggested he bring her such a gift? Was it *really* *true* that she was the daughter of titled English parents? Was the locket real gold?

He cut short her inquiries. The Alice and Oliver referred to on the locket had been dead many years, he told her. He did not know what the date July 12th 1862 commemorated, he added truthfully, and he could tell her nothing more about her parentage.

"Be a good girl now until I return for you," he said, realizing as he voiced the platitude how absurd it was enjoining a young prostitute to behave herself.

Sophia released him from her embrace, her eyes shining.

"I shall watch out for you every single day, Monsieur," she said. "Promise that you will not forget me!"

Forget her, thought Doctor Forbes bitterly as the *cocher* drove him slowly back to his hotel. As if he had been able to forget her for one single night since the day of her birth . . . the tiny Rochford baby he had ruthlessly driven away from the house she could never be allowed to see again.

Chapter Twenty-nine

May—October 1907

FOR THE FIRST TIME IN THIRTY-FIVE YEARS, DOCTOR John Forbes was happy. He was sitting on deck on the packet steamer heading for Calais. The Channel was like a mill pond and the sun was dancing on the calm green surface of the water. The white chalk cliffs of Dover had already receded beyond the horizon, but the French coast was not yet in sight.

He drew out his gold watch and glanced at the face. In another hour and a half he would be on French soil; by teatime he would be in Paris. His excitement mounted.

Down below, in the cabin he had booked lest he felt seasick, but had not after all needed, was his valise in which was safely locked the six hundred Napoléons he intended to take that night to Madame Lou-Lou. He was booked into the same hotel where he had resided last time he was in Paris, but with an additional room for his young "niece." Before this day was over, little Sophia Rochford, or Sophie Miller as she was known, would be out of that house of immorality and safely under his guardianship. The relief of knowing it was all arranged was intoxicating.

But this was not the only reason for his wonderful feeling of well-being. He knew now that he must confess in full his part in the conspiracy to abduct the baby— and take his punishment. It would not be so terrible a price to pay now that he knew his days were numbered. He realized he would almost certainly die in prison—but he had reached the conclusion that it mattered not one whit to him where he died. All that mattered was that when he did so, he would be absolved from his guilt and could hope to be reunited with his beloved wife.

He realized that the child could not immediately be reunited with her family lest the shock prove too much

485

for poor Lady Rochford. In time Lady Rochford would have to learn of her daughter's past; but first Sophia must be made to understand that her family might find it impossible to welcome as a daughter a girl newly arrived from a brothel. He must persuade her to conceal those unsavory details at least until she was re-established within the family circle. The girl was intelligent and would see for herself that she must set aside once and for all the ways of a prostitute and revert to the pure, chaste way of life taught in her convent.

A few months in the establishment for young ladies to whom he had written would, so the headmistress replied, work wonders with girls from any background. She could show him the most excellent references from families who were trying to better themselves and who had entrusted their daughters to her care. The results were remarkable—even with those poor girls who were not by birth well-bred and refined in speech and manner . . .

A smile flitted over Doctor Forbes' gaunt face as he tried to envisage the headmistress' reaction if he were to deliver Sophia to her in her split-skirted canary yellow dress, her small pointed breasts almost certainly partially exposed. He must buy for her a navy blue alpaca dress, with a prim white organdy bow at her neck.

A nurse passed his deckchair, a child either side of her holding dutifully to the folds of her black cloak. The smaller of the two, a little girl, was prettily dressed in an embroidered, full-skirted pink coat with a velvet Peter Pan collar, the older child a boy, in a neat sailor suit with a straw boater perched on his long fair curls. As Doctor Forbes watched, the boy ran suddenly to the side of the deck and leaned perilously over the railings.

"Look, Nanny, I can see land. Is it France? Is it Calais? Are we nearly there?"

Doctor Forbes felt the child's excitement surge through his own frail body. Eagerly, he made as if to rise from his deck chair, but as he did so a pain so swift and terrible tore through his chest, that he fell back gasping. A second pain followed almost at once—this time beyond bearing. His body slumped over the side of his chair, and as the children's horrified nurse hurried over to him, she realized that he was already beyond her help. Doctor John Forbes was dead.

Despite the Captain's discreet inquiries, no one on board seemed to know the frail old gentleman who had died so suddenly at sea. His identity was established from his passport and his body was carried to his cabin by two stewards, one of whom, less honest than the other, volunteered to sit with the dead man until the ship docked and the authorities could be called on board.

No one was ever to discover that in the half hour before the packet reached Calais, the steward located the key of Dr. Forbes' valise on the body. When carrying the old man's luggage to the cabin at Dover, his sharp ears had detected the jingle of metal and he had guessed there was money within. But he had not anticipated such a fortune as met his eyes when he unlocked the dead man's case. Not only were there silver coins, but gold too. The temptation to steal them was too great to be resisted.

When Dr. Forbes' effects were inspected by the French police at Calais, he was assumed to have had in his possession only the few thousand francs they discovered in his wallet—the sum he had in fact set aside to pay his hotel and lodging.

After the French doctor had formally pronounced the old man dead, the cabin was sealed and the body returned to England on the next home-going packet. By the time it reached Dover, Doctor Rose had received the telegram sent by the Calais police to Dr. Forbes' address advising of his sudden death. It was Peter Rose therefore who, after the requisite postmortem in a Dover hospital, arranged for undertakers to bring his colleague's remains back to Havorhurst for burial. As far as he was aware, the old man had no relatives other than the son he had disowned, and he felt obliged to offer this last assistance.

Rowell and Willow were in Deauville with Silvie and Pelham, where they were attending the racing and enjoying a few days' holiday. It fell to Toby therefore, to attend the simple burial service in the village church. A man of his own age, Rose had often assisted him in small matters relating to his work, and Toby felt it only kind to walk with him beside the coffin, since there were no other mourners.

"Of course, Forbes was dying anyway," Peter Rose said to Toby after the coffin had been lowered into the grave. "I reckoned he had only a few months to live at best.

What I cannot understand is why, in such a precarious state of health, he should decide to go to Paris again. He went last month, you know. His behavior was very strange, to say the least. He made several trips to London after his visit to France, and I know for a fact that he was keeping a large sum of money in the house which he told me was 'for another holiday.' But on what could an old, sick man spend such large sums? He was no gambler —in fact, he was rather straitlaced."

"Perhaps he had located his son," Toby suggested, "but was unwilling to talk to you about Adrian in view of the lad's relationship with my brother, Rupert. But if you *should* discover among Forbes' papers any reference to my brother's whereabouts—or Adrian's, I'd appreciate it if you would tell me."

Peter Rose nodded.

"Of course I will. But I was never really close to him, you know. I don't even know if he took all that money with him to France. It was not found on his body, but neither is it in the house. It's a bit of a mystery. The old fellow did not encourage any intimacies. But he was kind to me in his way. He has no relatives and has nominated me as one of his executors."

After the funeral, Mr. Bartholomew announced that Dr. Forbes had revoked his will after his son's departure abroad and made clear his wish to disinherit Adrian. He had made a second will leaving his house and all his worldly goods to his young partner. Dr. Rose was to dispose of his effects as and how he thought fit.

On her return from Deauville, Willow took the news of Doctor Forbes' death with quiet resignation.

"Any hope I might have had of discovering my baby's whereabouts is now buried with him," she said to Toby, adding wistfully: "I suppose there is no chance that he left a letter among his effects that might throw any light on the mystery?"

"None at all, Willow," Toby was obliged to tell her. "Peter Rose went through every drawer and every paper most meticulously. There was surprisingly little memorabilia for an old man—but then of course, he knew he had not long to live and perhaps cleared his own papers in anticipation."

Willow tried to forget her disappointment. She had

other more urgent worries to concern her, for Nathaniel Corbett had written to her reporting that the country was now in a period of recession and that there was great anxiety on Wall Street at the alarming manner in which the market was falling.

I fear the corporation is seriously affected, he wrote, *and although there are others far worse affected than ourselves, the position is nonetheless causing us much concern—particularly as I can see no immediate prospect of any halt to the slide.*

Rowell was barely able to conceal his own deep anxiety when Willow showed him the letter. He had already been advised by his stockbroker of the seriousness of the crisis on Wall Street and now it was confirmed at first hand. He dared not tell Willow how heavily he had invested in the United States and how precarious was his own financial position. He did suggest that perhaps they should make further economies.

"We will not do the Season in London this year," he told her. "I shall confine myself to attending only the race meetings."

Seeing the look of surprise on Willow's face, he added quickly:

"What happens on Wall Street can happen on our Stock Exchange. It is sensible to prepare for such eventualities."

"I am certain I could make greater economies here at Rochford," Willow offered. "We really do not need half so many servants as we employ. Twenty-five indoor servants to cater for the three of us and the two children does seem an unnecessarily large number."

Rowell was pleased with his wife's compliance. His humor of late had been good, particularly since their visit to Deauville. He had enjoyed the racing and the light-hearted amusements of the fashionable French seaside town. Furthermore, he had put himself out to be agreeable and attentive to Willow and had seemed intent upon assuring her comfort and entertainment. Nor had he made any but the most casual attempt to share her bedroom, seeming to take for granted her refusal to resume their marital relationship. He had slept in the adjoining dressing room without argument.

Nevertheless, Willow sensed that he would not continue for much longer to forgo his rights. Her own attitude of mind was one of resignation to her marriage, but she believed this was only possible so long as there was no exchange of intimacies between her and the husband she had ceased to love. Instinct warned her that from time to time Rowell wanted a great deal more from her than token affection. She would find him staring at her, eyes narrowed, cheeks flushed, with a hungry gaze that was unmistakable in its intent. At such moments, she thought with bitter irony how greatly she would prefer him to have a mistress to satisfy his needs.

On two occasions during the holiday at Deauville, Silvie had spoken seriously to Willow about her future.

"You have made up your mind to remain with Rowell?" she asked. "The idea of divorce is forgotten?"

Willow nodded, her eyes uneasy as they avoided Silvie's direct questioning gaze.

"I know mine is far from being a perfect marriage, but it is tolerable," she said thoughtfully. "Rowell respects my wish for the privacy of my own bedroom and . . . and I believe he really is trying in his own way to make amends for the past."

Silvie sighed.

"I have noticed a marked change in his attitude toward you. I would not be surprised if you told me that at this late stage of your marriage, your husband had suddenly discovered himself in love with you. I have seen him watching you, Willow, with a most possessive look in his eyes. Could it be that he has turned hunter now that you have virtually put yourself beyond his reach?"

Willow shivered.

"I don't know, Silvie, and I really do not want to think too deeply about my relationship with Rowell. I am certain of only one thing: that we can never be lovers in the way that you and Pelham are. I think you two are going to be ideally happy together and I am so very pleased for you both."

"And Toby?" Silvie asked quietly. "Do you still love him as much as ever, Willow?"

"As much, if not more—and as hopelessly. I think Toby feels the strain just as I do. Shortly before we left England, he had begun to pay attention to Oliver's new governess—an intelligent, pretty girl whom the Barratts engaged to tutor their two youngest ones. I try not to think about it, but in my heart I know she would be good for Toby."

Willow made a determined effort that summer to avoid Toby as much as possible. She adopted a distant manner which she hoped would lead him to suppose that she and Rowell had become reconciled during their holiday together in Deauville. But fate seemed disinclined to make it easy for her, for in July she received astonishing news from Silvie, which she could share only with Toby. They were united briefly by their pleasure on learning that Rupert was well and happy at last, despite the fact that Adrian had deserted him some two years previously. Pelham and Silvie had encountered Rupert quite by chance in Frankfurt, where he was now living with a charming, erudite German Count by the name of Maximillian von Krege.

He is divinely good looking! Silvie wrote, *and obviously deeply devoted to Rupert. Rupert said I might tell you and Toby, but forbade me to pass on news of his whereabouts to Rowell. He has promised to write to you . . .*

In the past Willow would have enjoyed a long talk with Toby about his brother, but now she deliberately cut short any lengthy discussion they might have had about Rupert. Putting this new secret they shared firmly out of her mind, she gave an informal dinner party to which she invited the young governess, Stella Menzies.

Soon afterwards, she arranged a day's outing to watch a tennis tournament in Brighton, during which she made certain that Toby and Miss Menzies were seated as often as possible beside one another.

"Doing a little matchmaking, eh, my dear?" Rowell asked that night as he took her downstairs for dinner. "And not a bad idea, either. It's time old Toby found himself a wife. The girl's not unattractive and would suit him very well."

To hear Rowell express her own beliefs brought a swift pang of sorrow and pain to Willow's heart that was almost unendurable. Fortunately, Rowell did not detect the brittleness in her tone of voice when she replied quietly:

"Yes, I too think they are well matched. Stella is charming as well as pretty."

"But not nearly as beautiful as you are, my dear,"

Rowell said, taking her arm and pressing it against his side.

Willow allowed her arm to remain linked through his as they made their way into the dining room. She had a part to play if her plan for Toby's future was to materialize, and that part demanded that she let Toby see her contented at Rowell's side. Fortunately for her, Pelham's lighthearted banter and excellent good spirits made it possible for her to laugh and joke as if she had not a care in the world.

Silvie had arranged to be married quietly in Paris during the first week of October. Only members of the immediate family were to be invited, and Willow and Rowell were to give a big reception for the newlyweds at Rochford at Christmas. Silvie and Pelham, meanwhile, planned to have a party in Paris soon after their honeymoon in Biarritz for all Silvie's French friends.

"Both Pelham and I prefer a small family affair to a large, formal wedding," she told Willow. "After all, I have already had one of those when I married poor Bernard in Dresden."

For the ensuing three weeks before Silvie's wedding, Willow kept herself busy supervising the sorting and packing of all Pelham's belongings for shipping out to France.

"You are the most dreadful hoarder I ever came across," she chided him as she came upon a cricket bat he had had in his school days, a half-filled album of foreign stamps, books that belonged in the nursery. A delighted Oliver was the recipient of such boyhood treasures, although he refused to be consoled at the approaching departure of his Uncle Pelham.

"You shall come to Épernay every summer and holiday with us," Pelham promised. "To Paris too, if you like."

"Perhaps you and Tante Silvie will have a little boy of your own by then," Oliver said glumly. "Then you won't want me!"

"Don't you believe it," Pelham said with a wink at Willow. "I do not think your Tante Silvie will wish to be encumbered by the patter of tiny feet—and I know I won't."

"What is 'encumbered'?" Oliver inquired, his interest diverted, and was sent off by Pelham to look the word up in the dictionary.

Although Rowell grumbled that they were off to France on the very day the pheasant shooting season began, he was in good humor as he, Pelham, and Toby escorted Willow across a calm Channel and made their way to a hotel in Paris not too far from Silvie's house. He was quite looking forward to being Pelham's best man and fussed unnecessarily about the safety of the mountain of luggage they were bringing with them, not to mention the number of servants—three valets and Willow's maid, Lily. The perfect weather, however, was not conducive to anxiety and would, they all hoped, last until the wedding on the following day.

October 2nd was indeed like a midsummer's day. The blue sky was bright with warm sunshine, and that afternoon, half Paris seemed to make the same decision to walk along the boulevards or crowd into the *parcs* and *bois*. The tables on the pavements were full, and every street was brilliant with color, the ladies having adorned themselves while they still could in bright summer dresses and hats. Many carried gaily patterned parasols to protect them from the sun's rays.

Jostling their way along the Boulevard Saint Germain came two colorfully dressed young girls on either arm of a somewhat shabbily attired, thick-set, perspiring young man. Although both girls were quite remarkably pretty, he was not walking proudly with a smile on his face. In an ill-fitting suit, his Sunday best, he shuffled along with the ungainly strides of the farmer that he was. His name was André and he was the fiancé of the taller of the two girls, Yvette. He was hot, tired, and very thirsty and longed for a glass of cider or cold white wine. But the girls were chatting animatedly across him, exchanging remarks about the other ladies' dresses and hats and seemingly oblivious of his presence.

When at long last they were to his relief about to seat themselves at a café table, Yvette suddenly stopped and pointed to the opposite side of the street.

"Look, Perle—a wedding," she cried. To André's dismay, he was forced to postpone his longed-for drink for a further period of time while the two girls stood and gaped at the crowd outside the church. He drew a deep sigh of exasperation. Only twice a year could he afford to make this trip from his farm into Paris to see Yvette, a labor of love indeed, for he hated the noisy bustling city, and moreover the journey was costly.

He had hoped to have Yvette to himself, but today she had insisted upon bringing with her her new friend, Perle. He acknowledged grudgingly that the girl was pretty, but he himself was not interested in her. She was far too small to make any farmer a good wife, he considered. Dressed all in blue to match her eyes, she looked like a little china doll, and he could not imagine her helping with the harvest or rounding up the cattle, far less treading grapes with those tiny, blue-slippered feet.

At least his Yvette had sturdy hips and strong legs and arms and hopefully would bear him some strong, healthy sons.

Totally oblivious to the discomfort of their male companion, Yvette and Sophia were staring in envious wonder at the bridal couple now appearing on the church steps. Although there did not seem to be as many people in the group as might have been expected at a society wedding, they were in no doubt that this was a fashionable and important occasion. The bride's fairy-tale gown of palest pink silk flowed into a small train at the back. The sleeves were tight to her elbows and then flared out in a deep fall of lace. She was carrying a bouquet of pink and white carnations. Covering her dark hair was a matching pink picture hat, from which floated a froth of tulle veiling. She was smiling up at her groom: a tall, magnificently dressed man in a silk-faced frock coat, grey waistcoat, and striped trousers.

Behind them were grouped three other gentlemen and a remarkably pretty woman in a cream-colored organza dress embroidered with tiny yellow and blue flowers. She too was wearing a large hat, made of a fine cream straw with a deep brim shading her face and pale blue ostrich feathers curling down one side.

"I wonder who they are!" Yvette remarked, sighing as she attempted to reckon up in her mind how much the bride's outfit must have cost and whether she would be able to afford to have a dress made like it when eventually she married André.

But Sophia was not listening. She grabbed Yvette's arm and cried in a low excited voice:

"Yvette—that's him. The bridegroom. That's him!"

"What in heaven's name are you talking about?" Yvette asked.

Sophia's face was now bright pink.

"The bridegroom!" she gasped. "That's the English Milord who came to *Le Ciel Rouge* and took notice of me—the one who promised he'd come back for me."

She took a step toward the edge of the pavement, but Yvette caught hold of her arm before she could go any farther.

"Are you quite crazy?" she demanded, realizing that the younger girl was about to cross the road to speak to the Englishman. "Haven't you any sense of propriety at all? Why, even if it is the English Milord, which I doubt, you can't talk to him. You never *ever* recognize a client out of the house, Perle, unless he first speaks to you, and most particularly not if he is with a lady. As for this one . . . with his bride . .!" Her voice registered her shock, and Sophia stood back, her whole body drooping with dejection.

"I'm sorry, Yvette. I didn't think . . ." she murmured.

Unrelenting, Yvette turned to André and hurried her two companions away from the church to the coffee house farther down the street. As they seated themselves at a table, the church bells rang out and could be heard quite clearly from where they sat. Yvette noticed the tears gathering in Sophia's eyes and said:

"There's no need to be upset, Perle. No harm done. Besides, I'm sure you couldn't recognize your Englishman after so long—eighteen months, isn't it?"

Sophia's mouth curved into a defiant pout.

"It was him—I *know* it. I'd never forget him . . ." Her voice trailed into silence as she saw Yvette's disbelief. Yvette turned to her fiancé.

"Proper little storyteller, this one," she said, not unkindly. "First she has us all believing an English Milord fancied her; next it's a famous artist who's going to make a Mona Lisa of her; then she tells us she's really the long-lost daughter of an English aristocrat! Had us all convinced for a while, too."

Sophia's head suddenly lifted and the blue eyes flashed.

"It's true, Yvette. The old man said so. And I have the locket to prove it . . ."

"The locket!" Yvette said scornfully. "What does that

prove? Nothing, I keep telling you. He could have bought it in any old shop and just told you that cock-and-bull story about your relatives. I don't believe a word of it. If he'd meant it, he'd have come back for you—and you know it!"

Sophia had no answer. Six months had passed, and the old man had not returned. Even Madame Lou-Lou had told her to forget about him and put her mind to her work.

"Men are all the same," she had said. "They'll tell you any story that they think will impress you—though why that old man should spin such a tale, I can't imagine. But one thing's for sure, *ma petite* Perle—there are always plenty more where that one came from."

Angrily, Sophia brushed away the single tear that had managed to escape and was rolling down her cheek. Yvette could say what she liked—it *had* been the English Milord outside the church! And Madame could say what *she* liked, that old man had *not* been lying to her.

One day, she thought, one day before I'm much older, I'll find out once and for all who I really am.

Chapter Thirty

December 1907–July 1908

IT WAS NOT ONLY A RELIEF TO WILLOW, BUT TO TOBY too, when Silvie and Pelham arrived at Rochford for the Christmas season. He was as deeply in love with Willow as he had ever been, but there was now a constraint between them which he believed was deliberate and of her choosing. It seemed to him that she went out of her way to indicate how much improved was her relationship with Rowell, who, surprisingly, showed none of his usual enthusiasm for hurrying off to London without her.

Toby made a conscious effort to be happy about it for Willow's sake, although the logical workings of his mind gave the lie to what his eyes were seeing. No one knew better than he how little two such disparate human beings had in common, and although he could very easily understand how Rowell might have fallen belatedly in love with his wife, he could not imagine how Willow could still retain any illusions about her husband.

Since Willow's happiness was more important to Toby than his own, he decided that he could best contribute to the success of her marriage by simulating a far greater interest in the young governess, Stella Menzies, than actually he felt. He made no attempt to refute the suggestion when Silvie and Pelham accused him of flirting with the girl; and he tried to look pleased when Dodie, who was home with James for Christmas, told him she was convinced that Stella Menzies was already enamored of him.

"Now that Pelham is so happily married, it would be quite perfect if you too, dearest Toby, were to settle down," she said affectionately.

Toby tried to hide the pain that followed Willow's comment as she added to Dodie's persuasions:

"Yes, indeed, Toby—it is high time you had a loving wife!"

But he had not the slightest intention of marrying Stella Menzies, and as the new year gave way to spring and they were more and more frequently paired off at parties, either by Willow or the Barratts or even, upon occasions, by neighbors, Toby made up his mind that the situation must be made clear to the girl herself. Stella Menzies was nearing twenty-seven, and Grandmère would have described her at that age as "on the shelf" and "destined to spinsterhood." But she was still pretty enough —with her light colored, soft brown hair and hazel eyes— to attract a suitor, and Toby was the first to admit that she would make some man an excellent wife.

By the beginning of the summer, Toby had still not raised the issue, but knew he could no longer avoid doing so since everyone was now making it quite clear that they were expecting him to announce his engagement. One warm day in early July he drove over in the gig to pay an informal call upon Stella.

He had no difficulty in engineering a private meeting with her, for the Barratts welcomed his attentions to the young relative. Sir John himself now suggested Stella should leave her young charges in their mother's care so that Toby could take her for a drive.

As soon as they were away from the house and driving along one of the leafy lanes that criss-crossed Sir John's large estate, Toby reined in the horse and turned to the young woman sitting silently beside him. She was wearing a pretty green flowered Jacconet dress with a neat lace collar. The brim of her Leghorn hat hid her face from him as he turned to look at her. He felt a moment of deep anxiety, fearing that she was under the misapprehension that he had brought her here in order to propose marriage to her. He drew a deep breath and said:

"We have spent quite a little time in one another's company of late, Stella, and since we are both unmarried, I am afraid this may have led many people to speculate as to our relationship . . . that is to say, there may be those who have been wondering . . . whether we might feel more than mere regard for one another."

He looked quickly away as he saw the blush rise in Stella's cheeks. But when she spoke, her voice was calm, quiet, and level-toned.

"I understand exactly what you are trying to say, Tobias," she informed him. "We may indeed be the subject of romantic gossip. I myself feel that it is the greatest pity that a man and a woman cannot be good friends without that friendship being immediately misconstrued."

Toby only just succeeded in withholding his sigh of relief.

"I was afraid lest you should have imagined—not unreasonably, I assure you, that my sentiments toward you were more than those of a mere friend."

To his surprise, the girl laughed softly.

"I must admit I have asked myself several times what were your intentions. But now that you have brought up the subject, Tobias, I welcome this opportunity to speak to you quite honestly—at least, regarding *my* feelings. May I do so?"

"I would be very pleased indeed if you would so enlighten me," Toby said genuinely.

"Then I must tell you that I do hold you in the highest regard. You are one of the kindest, most intelligent, and likeable of companions I have had the good fortune to meet. But alas, my heart is no longer my own, Tobias, and however misguided its direction, I cannot alter it."

"You are in love with someone else?" Toby asked, unable to hide his astonishment. "I must be very blind not to have noticed—"

"Indeed you are not, Tobias, for you are the only person who knows of it—not even the man concerned is aware of how I feel. You see, I happen to know that he loves another and is betrothed to her." She paused, her eyes suddenly sad. "Since you are my friend—and I trust I may so call you—I know I can rely on your discretion. The man I so favor is well known to you—Doctor Rose."

"Peter Rose!" Toby echoed. "I did not realize you knew him."

"Socially, no, but he has been to our house many times this past year to attend to the children during their attack of the measles. On one occasion, I had to call at his home to collect some medicine and he invited me to stay and take tea with him."

She smiled at Toby's astonishment and then continued:

"I expect you would—were you less well-mannered— like to tell me now how stupid I have been to let myself fall in love with a man who is already affianced to another. But, alas, Tobias, not even those females such as I who claim to have a little intelligence, can always control the waywardness of their hearts."

"I am the very last person to call you silly," Toby said quietly. "For I too am in love with someone beyond my reach. That is what I wished to tell you today—that my heart is not mine to offer you as I feared you might be expecting. So we are two of a kind, you and I!"

A grin suddenly spread over his face.

"It has both its tragic and its comic side, do you not agree," he said, "all Havorhurst linking us together, and both of us secretly in love with someone else!"

He reached for her hand and pressed it in a warm gesture of affection.

"Do you know, Stella, I am really sorry! I find myself liking you even more than I did before. I had not thought of it until now, but it occurs to me how excellent a wife you would make for a doctor. I cannot believe that Peter Rose has not also considered it, despite his betrothal."

"His engagement is of many years' standing," Stella

said quietly. "Even if Doctor Rose were to have thought a little about me—and I do not think he is entirely unaware of my existence—then I have no doubt he would honor his obligations to his fiancée."

Toby sighed.

"Yes, Peter is not the kind of man to go back on his word. I'm sorry, Stella, for you would have been well suited." He released her hand and added thoughtfully: "So now we must find a satisfactory way to silence the gossips. I cannot tell my family that you love another, for they would instantly ask me who was the lucky man. And I would not wish to reveal the fact that I too love another. How then shall we resolve our problem?"

"Would it not be simplest to say that you suggested marriage to me, but that I rejected your proposal on the grounds that I would not care to share my home with your family? After all, it is true that Lady Rochford would remain mistress of Rochford Manor even if I went there as your wife."

"But we could leave Rochford—" Toby began, but Stella interrupted him.

"I know it is not much of an excuse. Any girl truly in love would disregard such a minor consideration, besides which, Lady Rochford is quite charming and in other circumstances I would be more than happy to share my home with her. As for living elsewhere, Tobias, no one would consider it in the least extraordinary were you to refuse to leave the laboratory you have been at such pains to furnish at the manor."

Her mouth curved in a humorous little smile.

"So . . . *you* will not remove; and *I* will not share my home! Provided we both stubbornly maintain these reasons to all who may question them, we cannot be doubted."

Toby looked at the girl with admiration and not without amusement.

"I never doubted your intelligence, but now I must applaud your ingenuity," he said. "If we follow your excellent plan, we can perhaps continue as friends—and I would dearly like to remain your friend, Stella. To some extent at least, we can console each other since we are both recipients of each other's unhappy secrets."

"It will be an excellent relationship," Stella agreed. "I have so often bemoaned the fact that young men are not encouraged by society to enjoy platonic friendships with the opposite sex."

Toby nodded thoughtfully.

"That is true, more is the pity. We men are reared to think of females as wives, mothers, mistresses—never as individuals in their own right. But perhaps the new generation will grow up with more enlightened ideas. My cousin Silvie, who you met at Christmas, is already a firm believer in the equality of the sexes. And although it goes against the grain, my brother Pelham has accepted this novel idea. They seem very happily married, too!"

"But those days have not yet come when everyone thinks as liberally as your brother and his wife," Stella reminded him, "so perhaps we had best return to the house before my kind relatives begin to fear you have abducted me!"

The result of that afternoon's talk with Stella Menzies was such as to relieve Toby's mind and to lift his spirits so markedly, that in the ensuing weeks Willow could not ignore the change in him. She attributed it to the astonishing new relationship that seemed to be developing between him and the young governess. Although Toby had informed her that Stella had rejected his proposal of marriage, he did so so cheerfully that she was convinced this was but a temporary refusal, and that when he proposed a second time, Stella would almost certainly accept.

In the meanwhile, Toby continued to be a frequent caller at the Barratts' and always asked that Stella be invited if they gave a luncheon, tea party, or dinner at Rochford.

Willow tried very hard to be happy for his sake. In an effort to put all thoughts of him out of her heart, she opened her bedroom door once more to Rowell, who now showed himself as eager a lover as once he had been indifferent. But she deeply regretted this loss of her privacy, and the nights she shared with him were as unsatisfactory for her as they were satisfactory for her husband. It was inevitably a matter of endurance and never one of pleasure. The only relief lay in the fact that Rowell did not seem to expect her to enjoy their lovemaking—in total contrast to the Frenchman, Maurice, she thought wryly. *He* had been determined that she should derive as much pleasure as he.

Silvie had informed her at Christmastime that Maurice and Pierre were back in Paris after their long holiday in Italy. He had a new model—an Italian girl—who shared his studio and whom he now painted with the same feverish intensity as he had once painted her, Silvie said. So that episode of Willow's past was now dead, she thought wretchedly—as dead as Toby's love for her. In one way her day-to-day life was made easier as both tried to avoid encountering one another around the house. When they did so, their conversation was as impersonal as between any other members of the family.

The news from America was still far from good. Continuing their plan to economize, Willow and Rowell did not rent the house in London for the Season but remained at Rochford. Occasionally, they attended a race meeting or went to London for an evening at the theater or to a dinner party.

Willow herself went to London for two days during the summer holidays to give Oliver a special treat. They were to go first to the science museum in Kensington, and then to Madame Tussaud's to see the waxworks.

Willow booked a suite of rooms for herself, Oliver, Lily, and Patience at Brown's Hotel, and it was there, in a quiet corner of the lounge, that she received a second visit from young Philip Grey.

He had written to her the previous week requesting the meeting as a matter of some urgency, and afraid lest he was in further difficulties, she had replied telling him he might call upon her in London.

Philip had grown taller in the two years since she had last seen him. His voice was deeper too, but he was otherwise unchanged. He bowed over her hand with the same careful formality he had shown on their first meeting, and begged her pardon for taking up her time.

"I have not come on this occasion to ask your assistance," he said, a slight blush staining his fair cheeks. He sat down on the chair Willow indicated and continued quietly: "I wanted to set your mind at rest, Lady Rochford. That is to say, I wanted to tell you that you need never concern yourself with me or my family again . . ."

Haltingly, he managed to explain that he and Rowell's other two children were cutting themselves adrift from their father—a break that was intended to be permanent.

Georgina had died last month, and as a result, their great-aunt had assumed responsibility for them. Philip's brother and sister had already gone to Northumberland where she lived, and he was following on a train that very evening.

"My great-aunt is going to send us to schools in the north of England," he told her, "and we shall be living with her during our holidays. I understand she is a very wealthy old lady and that she can well afford to bring us all up as she thinks fit. But in return, she is demanding that we have no further contact with our father."

A price that Philip obviously felt able to pay, Willow surmised, for he had little love left for the man who had treated his mother so shamefully.

"I felt obliged to tell Great-Aunt Augusta the truth about these last few years," he continued. "She at once insisted that I should call upon you and return the money that you so very generously made available to us in our need. I have not forgotten that our agreement was that it should not be repaid for fifty years . . ." he managed to smile as he said these words . . . "but my great-aunt wishes us to begin our new life with a clean slate. Would you therefore permit me, Lady Rochford, to give you this?"

He drew out a pigskin wallet from his pocket and removed a banker's note which he handed to Willow.

"That is the sum the jewelry realized," he said anxiously.

Willow nodded, her eyes filling unexpectedly with tears.

"Please say no more, Philip. I understand your great-aunt's sentiments and I appreciate your coming to see me. I am glad your future is now so happily resolved and I am sure you and your brother and sister will settle down very well in Northumberland."

The boy stood up, his movements awkward but his head still proudly erect as he said:

"One day I hope to be able to repay my personal debt to you, Lady Rochford. You see, quite apart from the money, your readiness to assist me on my last visit to you, meant a great deal more to me than you may have realized. I had been in such dread of coming to see you, and you . . . you made it so simple. Because of you, I was able to bring some comforts to my poor mother before she died, and for that I shall always be in your debt. My

great-aunt said she considered you to be a true saint—
in view of the circumstances—and that I must never
forget, if I am losing my faith in humanity, that people
like you do exist. And I *shall* never forget you, Lady
Rochford—not even when I'm fifty!"

When Willow looked up, Philip had gone. She sat for
a long time attempting to sort out her emotions. No one
would blame her, she thought, if she were to hate the
boy who had just left her. Not only was he her husband's
bastard, but the son of the woman who had undermined
her marriage even before it had begun. She could not be
sorry that Georgina Grey was dead, but equally, she
could not bring herself to dislike Philip.

Unbelievable though it was, his compliment lifted her
spirits and renewed her self-esteem at a time when she
was beginning to lose it. Rowell's new-found love for her
was, she well knew, only superficial, its nature entirely
physical. He knew nothing of her innermost thoughts,
nor concerned himself with her true feelings. To try to
rebuild her marriage on such shallow foundations seemed
absurd, and yet there was no alternative other than to end
it. If Toby were to marry Stella and move out of Rochford, the prospect of a future alone with Rowell for the
next thirty years until she died was dismaying—yet still
she felt compelled to try to create a serene and contented
home for her children.

She returned with a happy but exhausted Oliver to find
Toby awaiting her with undisguised excitement. Even
before she had removed her hat and gloves, he caught
hold of her arm and hastened her into the library where
he could talk to her undisturbed.

"I have something of the most immense importance to
tell you," he repeated not once but twice. Willow's heart
sank. She was convinced that he was about to inform
her that he had proposed once more to Stella Menzies
and that the girl had accepted.

"I have been to Brighton," Toby announced in a low
intense voice. "And Willow, *I have finally found Irene!*"

For a moment, Willow's relief was so intense that she
did not register the implications of his pronouncements.

"Irene?" she echoed stupidly.

Toby caught hold of her arms and whirled her twice
round the room.

"*Yes, Irene,*" he all but shouted. "Do you remember that article in the *Medical Annual* stating that diphtheria could be carried by a person with no external symptoms of the disease? I knew when I read it that the infants' nurse, Irene, could provide the proof I needed to establish that the Rochford baby girls could have caught diphtheria. And Willow, I now have that proof. She is a diphtheria carrier. Not proof enough to satisfy the scientific world . . ." he added quickly, "but I shall do that very shortly. I've already begun tests. But I have no further doubts—and you won't either once you hear what I have to tell you."

Willow all but fell into a chair as the trembling of her legs became too much for her to continue standing. She wanted both to laugh and cry. Toby's excitement was so overwhelming that she longed to throw her arms around him and share his joy at closer proximity.

Toby's mood would not allow him to remain still. He paced the room as he talked, stopping only occasionally to make sure that Willow was following his feverish, disconnected sentences.

Slowly, Willow began to understand what he was telling her. The nurse, Irene, now lived with her married sister in the little town of Rottingdean, near Brighton. Over the years since she had begun work as a children's nurse, the unfortunate woman had gained a thoroughly bad reputation. As she moved from one place of employment to another, her previous mistresses referred to the death or deaths of offspring while in Irene's care. The number of deaths became too many to be coincidental, and the poor woman was eventually refused a post because she was thought to be a harbinger of bad luck.

"I spent several days with Irene," Toby related. "At first she was unwilling to talk about the past but gradually she realized that I was trying to put an end to the stupid superstitions that had grown up around her. One of her mistresses had even accused her of 'putting the evil eye' on her child. But Willow, the child died of diphtheria. *All the children who died in Irene's care, died of diphtheria*—just like the infant Rochfords, Barbara- and Josephine, way back in 1864."

He paused only to draw breath and then went on:

"Shortly before my mother offered the poor woman

employment all those years ago, Irene herself had had diphtheria. She recovered and seemed to be in excellent health. But we now know that she still carried the germs of the disease within her and that at any time, she could pass on that infection just as if she were still smitten with it. As you know, in every town and village there is an epidemic sooner or later, just as there are outbreaks of measles or whooping cough, so no one ever attributed the cause to Irene."

He smiled briefly at Willow before continuing:

"As you can imagine, a mother whose child had died usually dismissed the nurse afterwards; so Irene was never long enough in any household for it to be realized that nearly all the children put in her care were affected by the same disease. Children born later to those families—such as me and my brothers and Dodie—had different nurses. But it was never Irene's fault—for she was quite unaware that she carried the bacilli. Even when three of her sister's children died, no one suspected, for there was already an epidemic in the village where she lived."

Now he finally stopped pacing and stood staring down at Willow with an anxious look in his eyes.

"I was not intending to mention the fact to you for fear of causing you any distress," he said quietly, "but not very long before his death, I received a letter from old Doctor Forbes. In it he confessed to me that he believed he had wrongly diagnosed the Rochford infants' illness and that he felt the cause of death should have been given by him as 'diphtheria.' He further stated that he believed he had failed correctly to interpret Dodie's illness which was, he was later convinced, more likely to have been an attack of infantile paralysis. He could not prove the facts one way or another, but felt I should know of the possibility of his errors before he died."

"Why did you not tell me of this when you received the letter?" Willow demanded, her face ashen.

"Because I was convinced that you would feel Forbes' admission of guilt in those two instances reaffirmed your conviction that he was somehow involved with your baby's disappearance," Toby replied truthfully.

Willow's eyes narrowed.

"And *you* do not think so, Toby?"

"Perhaps! I am not certain. I wrote back to him thanking him for his letter and assuring him I would treat the contents entirely confidentially. I hoped that would give him confidence in me if he had further confessions to make."

Willow drew a long breath.

"Perhaps that was wise. But now we will never know. It is all too late."

"At least he has helped make retribution where Dodie is concerned," Toby said gently. "There is no reason whatever why she should not have the child she wants. Is that some consolation for you, Willow?"

Willow attempted a smile.

"Yes, I suppose it is. You will write to her and James, of course. And your discovery about Irene lifts one worry from my shoulders, too. Neither Alice nor Oliver can pass on insanity when they have children of their own. Nor you, Toby, when you marry."

He ignored her last remark and turning away, he said abruptly:

"You must be tired after your journey and be longing to change your clothes. I must not take more of your time—but I wanted you to know the good news before anyone else, Willow. You have always given me so much encouragement in my work."

Once again, tears stung Willow's eyes as she heard his tribute—no less than Philip's and yet worth so much more to her coming from Toby. Her love for him was like a dull, stabbing ache in her heart.

Rowell received the news of Toby's discovery with skepticism.

"It all sounds a bit far-fetched to me," he said as he and Willow had breakfast together the following morning. "Odd fellow, Toby! You can never be sure what he's really made of. Take that girl at the Barratts'. I was sure he'd found himself a wife at long last. Dare say he scared her off with all that paraphernalia he's got in that laboratory of his. It wouldn't surprise me if the whole lot blew us all sky-high one of these days!"

But he had other matters on his mind of far greater importance to him than his brother. He wanted to begin Oliver's riding activities again. Willow's face paled.

"Rowell, you promised you would set aside such plans for one year. You cannot go back on your word. His stammer is still quite bad, and Patience tells me he continues to suffer terrible nightmares and walks in his sleep."

Rowell's face darkened.

"I have never agreed that the boy's unfortunate habits are connected in any way with his being put up on the mare. That was some idiotic new-fangled notion of Gornway's to which you and Toby subscribe but which never convinced *me*. The longer you leave it, the worse it will be when Oliver does have to sit a horse again. Fear is something we all have to overcome."

Controlling herself with an effort, Willow said quietly:

"Rowell, I am holding you to your promise that Oliver need not ride for a year. If you were to go back on it, I would feel very bitterly toward you—very bitterly indeed. And that would be a pity, would it not, when our marriage has seemed of late to be on a far happier footing? Whenever possible, I am anxious to concede to your wishes, day and night, and I would appreciate it very much if you would in this instance concede to mine."

Rowell did not miss the particular emphasis she gave to the words "and night." He was perfectly willing to give her her way on this occasion if it meant guaranteeing his right to share her bed whenever he wished.

"Very well, my dear, since it is so important to you," he said as he put down his knife and fork and picked up *The Times*.

Willow stood up, laid her napkin down on the table and quietly left the room. As slowly she climbed the stairs, she reflected that there had been very many times when she had submitted to her husband's embraces for other reasons than love—from duty, from loneliness, from a desire to make her marriage happier, and even once, long ago, because she had wanted him. But never before had she submitted to him to gain her own ends.

She did not regret selling herself. Such was her love for her children that she would do so again—as often as she believed their welfare demanded it.

Was Silvie right after all, she wondered as she opened the door of her room and stood looking at the great double bed? Did all women use their feminine charms to get what they wanted from men? Was it after all by such a worthless yardstick that men measured love?

With a small bitter smile twisting the corners of her mouth, she sat down at her little mahogany bureau and began writing a letter to her friend.

Chapter Thirty-one

March 1909–April 1910

YVETTE WAS LEAVING LE CIEL ROUGE, AND MADAME Lou-Lou was giving her a farewell party before the house opened for the evening. Everyone, including Sophia, had bought presents for Yvette's bottom drawer, for she was to marry André on the first of May. There was champagne to drink, and Charles, the pianist, had offered his services free and was now playing all the girls' favorite melodies and songs.

Everyone was a little drunk, and sentimental tears were shed by the older girls who had given up any hope of making marriages themselves.

"I am not at all certain that I shall like having babies every year," Yvette confessed to Sophia. "Moreover, I shall miss the companionship here and most of all, I shall miss you, *chérie!*"

Privately, Sophia had long ago determined that she would never marry a farmer. When she married, it would be to a rich, titled man who would give her a big house and servants and wardrobes full of beautiful clothes—in fact, she intended to make the kind of marriage Doctor Forbes had suggested to her. But she had not voiced these aspirations since the day she, Yvette, and André had seen the English Milord at his wedding and Yvette had decried the old man's promises.

There had been several occasions since then when Sophia had considered selling the locket Dr. Forbes had given her. But no matter how greatly she had desired the money for a new dress or hat, she had not yet been able to bring herself to part with the gold trinket. Apart from its possible—if unlikely—links with her unknown family, Madame Lou-Lou always drummed into the girls that gold was the most precious of all commodities, since unlike paper money it seldom lost its value.

Several of the girls were now imitating the dancers at the nearby *Moulin Rouge*, performing the can-can with an obscene abandon. They skipped, pranced, and tossed up their petticoats as Charles pounded out a furious *galop* on the old piano. Grabbing Yvette's hand, Sophia dragged her onto the floor, and they joined the dancers while Madame's huge bulk wobbled in her armchair as she sat applauding them.

The sadness of Yvette's impending departure was momentarily forgotten as they pirouetted and gyrated and the pins fell from their carefully arranged hair so that it tumbled around their bared shoulders and bosoms. Some of the younger girls attempted to hold their ankles and lift their legs above their heads—a feat which seemed easy enough for the professional dancers, but which had Madame's girls falling on top of one another as their shouts and shrieks of laughter filled the salon.

When the dancing ended, Madame ordered more champagne. The servant who brought in the new bottles of wine informed her mistress that there was a knife-grinder in the street outside demanding to know if they had work for him. Madame promptly ordered him to be brought into the salon, where the disreputable, dirty old fellow was seated at a table as if he were an important customer and given a drink.

The girls crowded around him and began to tease him, their mood of frivolity infectious as each in turn paraded before him as if he had been a king. Each tried to outdo the other in their vociferous claims to give greater, more unusual, more exotic pleasures than her neighbor.

The poor man's astonishment caused them to laugh the louder; but gradually the champagne began to take its effect and soon the illiterate old fellow was on the dance floor, his gaucherie forgotten as he began to dance, his shirt-sleeves rolled up to his elbows, in his dirty black waistcoat and baggy grey trousers. His bewhiskered old face split grotesquely by a grin which spread his mouth from ear to ear, he made the most of a day that he was well aware would never be repeated.

Encouraged by one of the girls, he even had the drunken temerity to invite Madame Lou-Lou herself to dance with him. But though willing enough, the old lady's legs would not support her. Somebody had found the knife-grinder a top hat left by a customer and unclaimed, and he was now made to dance with Yvette, in whose honor the party was being given.

When finally the old man collapsed in a stupor in the middle of the dance floor, Madame ordered two of the waiters to carry him out into the street. The girls sat down, their arms around one another as Charles began to play a ballad well known to all of them called *A Saint-Lazare*. A sentimental song with a plaintive melody, it told the story of a streetwalker who worked for the man she loved rather than for her own gain but ended up in prison for being without her card from the *Préfecture de Police*.

Tears began to fall as they joined with Charles in singing the last verse; but Sophia remained dry-eyed. She could see no reason for pitying the girl who had brought about her own downfall, or at least so far as Sophia could see. To sell oneself in order to pay for a man's vermouth-cassis, hair pomade, and other such luxuries struck her as ridiculous. She would do no such thing, she vowed silently, and she would take care never to fall in love, if love brought with it such folly.

But by now it was time for the party to end. The salon, Madame Lou-Lou reminded them, must be cleaned and the girls' clothes changed in readiness for the early customers. Business was business when all was said and done, and *Le Ciel Rouge* had never yet opened its doors late.

Sophia followed Yvette up to the tiny room they shared on the fifth floor, helping to carry her many wedding gifts. While Yvette packed them carefully one by one into her valise, Sophia went to the drawer where she kept her most prized possessions and drew out the locket. For the hundredth time, she looked at the inscription: *To Alice from Oliver July 12, 1862*. Who in fact were they, these unknown people? The old man had told her they were both dead. One jeweler to whom she had shown the locket had told her it was eighteen-carat gold and worth quite a large sum.

"I can always sell this, and then I would have the money to take the train to visit you in Provence," she said thoughtfully to Yvette as their impending separation seemed suddenly to be painfully close.

The older girl paused in her packing and turned to look at Sophia.

"That is a kind thought, *chérie*, but you are growing so pretty these days, I swear it will not be long before you find a rich patron and have plenty of money. Next year you will be sixteen and in your prime." She continued to stare at Sophia as if seeing her for the first time. "It is quite remarkable how you have blossomed out," she said. "And even stranger is the way you have developed. I know we all tease you when we call you 'La Duchesse,' but it's true that you do have the look of an aristocrat. You have such tiny bones compared with the rest of us and your neck is so long and thin and your skin—"

"You are beginning to sound like Madame Lou-Lou," Sophia broke in laughing. She felt suddenly overwhelmed by emotions—sadness at the impending parting with Yvette, but also of happiness. The party had been such fun, and Yvette had just told her she was not only beautiful but that she had class, too.

In a moment of impulsive generosity, she tossed the locket to Yvette.

"Catch—and it's yours," she cried. The gold pendant soared through the air which was redolent with the smoke of the Turkish cigarettes Yvette favored. But Yvette's hands were grasping a china vase Babette had given her, and she was unable to put it down quickly enough.

Uncaught, the locket fell to the floor at her feet. Both girls stood staring down at it. The spring had been knocked open, and the tiny miniature and its frame had become dislodged from the inside.

Simultaneously, they knelt down to retrieve the pieces which, though separate, appeared to be undamaged.

"No harm done," Sophia said as she sat back on her heels. "It was silly of me to throw it. We can stick it together again, Yvette."

She broke off as she noticed for the first time that

there was writing of some kind on the back of the little oval photograph. Faded with age and distorted by the glue which had hitherto held the picture in place, the tiny letters were barely distinguishable.

"It is in a foreign language, I think," Sophia said frowning, as she handed it to Yvette for her opinion. One by one, Yvette spelled out the letters: "*Alice and Oliver outside St. Stephen's, Havorhurst on their wedding day, June 1862.*"

Yvette shrugged.

"It means nothing to me," she said. "Perhaps they are English words. Why not take it along to Nicole? She used to work for a modiste in London before she was sold to Madame Lou-Lou. Perhaps she will translate it for you."

Wordless with excitement, Sophia raced along the landing to Nicole's room. The English girl was lying on her bed, a wet cloth over her forehead, groaning.

"I shall never be able to work tonight," she moaned. "And they say champagne does not give you a hangover!"

But at Sophia's urging, she sat up and took the tiny photograph from the girl's hand. She deciphered the faded writing and translated it without difficulty.

"Do you know this St. Stephen's, 'avor'urst?" Sophia asked breathlessly. "Oh, please try to remember, Nicole. Did you ever hear of such a place in England?"

"St. Stephen's is undoubtedly the name of a church, but Havorhurst, Havorhurst . . ." Nicole repeated slowly. She shook her head, groaning once more as she did so.

"I regret no, Perle. Is it so important? I will try to remember when my head is clearer."

"I don't know if it is important or not," Sophia said truthfully, her excitement suddenly subdued. "It could be. It depends to some extent whether this 'avor'urst is in England or in some other country."

Nicole groaned again.

"I would imagine, since the words are English that it *is* in my country. Havorhurst sounds English. Now off you go, Perle. My head hurts far too much to talk any more."

Yvette was interested in Nicole's comments, but not over-encouraging.

"It would cost a very great deal of money, *chérie*, to go to England. And who knows, were you to discover this "avor'urst' and even that you have relatives there, who is to say if they will make you welcome?"

"You mean because I am *une cocotte*?" Sophia asked rhetorically. "But my relatives need never know my profession. The old Englishman told me there was an establishment in London where I could be sent to learn to speak and act as a young lady of good family."

Yvette shrugged.

"It is your decision what you do with your life, *chérie*. You could face many disappointments and spend good money to no purpose."

"I will think about it," Sophia said as she began to undress. "Maybe I will not go to England after all."

But the words were spoken only to save further discussion. Her mind was already made up. She would ask Nicole to teach her the English language. At the same time, she would save up—no matter how long it took her to do so—the necessary amount of money to pay for her passage to England and to support herself while she searched for the unknown " 'avor'hurst.' " Her quick mind had already assessed that churches kept records, and if she paid the priest, he would look up those records for her and find out the *nom de famille* of the Oliver and Alice who were married there in the year 1862.

With a secret smile upturning the corners of her mouth, she pulled the canary yellow dress over her head and surveyed herself in the mirror. This was her lucky dress—the one she had worn when the old man had first recognized her. He had known her identity—she was convinced of it. Now it was only a matter of time before she too discovered who she really was.

When Willow placed the tiny, fair-haired girl in Dodie's outstretched arms, she could not help but remember yet again the night of the birth of her own little daughter. But her sadness did not last long, for Dodie's radiant happiness embraced them all.

"James and I have already decided upon a name," Dodie told Willow. "We shall call her Alexandra after our dear Queen." The smile on her tired, flushed face gave way to a moment of anxiety. "She is quite . . . *quite* perfect?" she asked for the second time.

"She is absolutely perfect!" Willow said with conviction. "Shall I send James in to you now?"

Leaving the small bundle safely in her mother's arms, Willow left the room to tell the waiting James that his worries were over and that his wife and baby daughter were thriving.

Downstairs in the tiny living room, Violet was hanging baby garments to warm before the fire. Red-cheeked, cheerful as ever and totally devoted to her mistress, Violet was speechless with pleasure at the safe arrival of Dodie's baby. James had decided they could now afford to employ the services of a local girl to do the rough cleaning and Violet was to be the baby's nurse.

"I'll tek care of it, Milady, like it was my own," she assured Willow.

"We owe so very much to you," James had paid tribute to Willow. "Dodie and I have often discussed how barren our lives would have been had you never married Rowell and gone to live at Rochford. I doubt if I would ever have married—and Dodie would have continued to lead the life of an invalid. We can never, ever thank you enough."

Remembering James' words as she fell wearily into her small bed, Willow found comfort in the thought that her own marriage had been worthwhile for the happiness it had brought the devoted couple, even if she herself had not found the happiness she had hoped for. Just before sleep overtook her, she recalled Grandmère's words when she had handed her the keys of the big house: *"You are now the chatelaine of Rochford."*

With the confidence of extreme youth, it had not then occurred to Willow how onerous those tasks might prove upon occasions. Yet had she the chance to go back in time and refuse them, she knew she would not do so. There were, after all, many compensations, of which Dodie's baby and James' happiness were not the least.

Willow remained in Cornwall until the end of the month. By the time she returned to Rochford, she had been absent in all for five weeks and Rowell had become increasingly restless. Toby was currently visiting the University of Heidelberg, and with no one but Patience and the children in the house, he decided to go to London. But there too, he found little to amuse him. The King was still in Biarritz, and the Season had not yet begun. Fox hunting was over, and although Rowell was invited by a friend in Buckinghamshire to go otter-hunting for a week, he was by the middle of April once again cooling his heels at his club. A chance meeting with his old friend, Theodore Symington, resulted in a bachelor night on the town. They were quickly joined by two young actresses they encountered at the stage door of the Tivoli Theatre, and for the first time since his week in New York with Désirée Somners, Rowell broke his vow to be faithful to his wife.

The two men decided to enjoy to the full the informal pleasures of London life and gave themselves up whole-heartedly to the debaucheries so readily available. Having enjoyed themselves to the point of satiety, each returned home, promising to meet again the following month to repeat their activities.

Not unexpectedly, Rowell showed little interest in Dodie's baby when Willow returned from Cornwall, his only comment being that it was a pity Dodie had not given birth to a son since it was the only child she was likely to have.

Again, not unexpectedly, he declined Silive's invitation to go to Épernay with Willow for the two months of the children's summer holidays.

"It would mean missing Henley, Cowes, Goodwood, the Eton and Harrow match," he said bluntly. "You go if you wish, my dear, but I shall not accompany you."

"Good!" Silvie said bluntly when Willow and the children finally arrived at Épernay in July. "We always have much more fun without your brother, do we not, Pelham,"

It was an idyllic holiday for Willow. Pelham enjoyed his role of favored uncle and Silvie was an amusing and exciting aunt whom Oliver, and little Alice in particular, adored. She spoiled both children, insisting that they be allowed to eat with the adults and remain up until all hours as did their French counterparts. She invited neighboring children to play with them and arranged informal luncheons and parties for Willow.

"Never a dull moment with my dear wife," Pelham said, laughing. "She may exasperate me at times, Willow, but she never bores me. My life with her is as uncon-

ventional in the extreme as life at Rochford in Grandmère's day was rigidly controlled. I am even learning
the atrocious language," he added, smiling.

Only once was Pelham serious. It was on the night
before Willow was due to return to England. Walking
with her in the garden in the soft twilight just before darkness fell, he linked his arm in hers and said:

"Very occasionally, my thoughts go back to the past,
Willow. Those days at Rochford when you first went to
live there now seem so very long ago. Yet I have never
forgotten how madly in love with you I was and how
jealous of Rowell. I often meant to thank you for the
sensible way in which you coped with my adolescent
desires. Somehow you succeeded in turning me down flat
without destroying my ego!"

He turned to look at Willow's profile, a soft creamy
white in the shadows.

"You are still very beautiful, you know," he said quietly.
"Were I not in love with my mad, adorable Silvie, I
would still find you very desirable. Rowell is a damned
lucky fellow, and I agree with Silvie, he doesn't deserve
you."

Willow was relieved that he made no reference to
Toby. But he did allude to her friendship with Silvie.

"I have often thought that, but for you, my dear, Silvie
and I would not be married," he remarked thoughtfully.
"Silvie says she would never have continued those visits
to Rochford every Christmas after her mother died had it
not been for you. She is devoted to you, Willow, and
knowing how you looked forward to her visits, she resolved to bring a little fun into your life at least once a
year."

"In which she succeeded very well," Willow said, smiling as she recalled some of the Christmases they had all
shared.

"I doubt if I myself would have kept in touch with her
had it not been for those visits," Pelham said. "So in a
way, dearest Willow, we both owe our happy marriage to
you. Does that please you?"

It was seldom Pelham ever spoke in a serious vein,
and Willow was moved by his declaration—the more so
as Silvie had said much the same thing the day before.
Such tributes as theirs, James', and Philip Grey's helped

restore her belief that her existence was not entirely meaningless, pointless—a belief that had been seriously undermined when she suspected that Rowell had a new mistress.

She returned to Rochford restored in health and spirits. Toby too had returned—from Heidelberg, where he seemed to have spent the most exciting and enlightening few months in the company of several learned professors and two scientists. Listening to his eager account of his activities, Willow found herself losing the thread of his conversation. She was watching the changing expressions of his face as he frowned in concentration or leaned forward with brilliant eyes to emphasize a point. Occasionally he would lean back in his chair sighing with regret that he himself knew so little and had so much to learn from these great men he admired.

I will never love anyone with this same intensity, she thought. It mattered not the least to her that Toby was nowhere near as handsome as Pelham. The lines on his face had deepened with age, and she realized with a sense of astonishment that he was already in his forties. Tall, thin, angular, he still seemed to her like an overgrown schoolboy, his clothes never quite fitting as they should, his bowtie a little askew within five minutes of his valet tying it properly for him. He was lacking all vanity, his mind engrossed with the miracles of life that were so much more important to him than his appearance.

But the intimate happiness Willow felt at this reunion with him was short-lived. At dinner on the following evening, Toby returned from a visit to the Barratts with the news that Stella Menzies had bought a typewriting machine and was teaching herself to use it.

"She can already type far faster than I can write," Toby informed Willow, "and she has most kindly offered to make neat copies of all my Heidelberg notes. Am I not fortunate?"

He has quite forgotten, Willow thought, that once many years ago I begged him to let me become his secretary. Wryly, she considered that not only was Toby fortunate, but so too was Stella. She would now be able to assist him in his work, as so often she, Willow, had longed to do.

Rowell returned from London in time to join Toby in

the annual cricket match played on Havorhurst village green. When the five Rochford brothers were boys, they had been the mainstay of the team when the Gentlemen played The Rest. Now there was only Rowell and Toby left, Peter Rose, two of the older Barratt boys, Sir John, and a few other members of the local gentry to make up the eleven.

To Oliver's delight, his father put up a creditable performance, scoring a half century and taking five wickets. Willow, with all the other ladies, including Stella, served tea to the players and watched the match from the shade of the pavilion while the villagers sat on the grass with their children urging on their team.

It was a beautiful warm September day, the blue sky cloudless, the swallows wheeling over the soft red roof of St. Stephen's, which overlooked the green, as they prepared to migrate. The highlight of the day came for Oliver when old Sir John professed himself unable to run and Oliver was allowed to run for him. Partisan though they were, the villagers were happy to applaud the small boy who one day would be their landlord and control their lives and fortunes.

Although few had any particular liking for the present Lord Rochford, they respected him and they loved his wife. There had always been Rochfords at Havorhurst, and to the villagers the affairs of the family were their concern, too.

Rowell was by no means displeased with his small son's popularity that day. Nevertheless, he raised once more the question of his being sent away to Eton in the New Year.

"Being tutored by a governess in the company of four girls is really highly unsuitable for the boy," he professed as the old butler served dinner to them the night after the cricket match. Now almost seventy, Dutton was soon to be retired, but for the time being, doddery though he was, he would not allow even the senior footman to serve his master at table.

"Stella is an extremely able young lady," Toby said quietly. "I have seen her syllabus and I consider her pupils are receiving quite as good an education under her tutelage as they would at a school."

"I do not dispute your young lady's efficiency," Rowell

replied with a knowing grin at his brother. "But there are other factors to be considered. Oliver should be learning cricket, football, boxing. He should be mixing with other boys of his own age."

Willow remained silent. She realized that any objection she raised would only harden Rowell's resolve if his mind really were made up. And Oliver himself was beginning to request more masculine activities. He had heard of the new Boy Scout movement and had asked if he might join. He wanted, too, to learn about aerodynamics—a subject outside Stella's capabilities. He was determined to be a pilot when he was grown up, and Bleriot's extraordinary achievement in flying his machine across the Channel in July had fired his interest still further.

To Toby's amusement, the boy had read what little was written about flying in his *Chambers Encyclopedia*. Although this was a comparatively new publication issued in 1906, it was already quite out of date, Oliver pointed out. It stated that "it is difficult to believe that any mechanism, however beautiful in design, can effectually take the place of that which is associated alone with the breath of life!" This, Oliver said, showed how ignorant people were on the subject of flying machines.

"Which goes to show how amazing are the advances in recent years in this field as well as in medicine," Toby told the boy. He spent the remainder of the afternoon helping Oliver to construct a flying toy propelled by twisted strands of India rubber. It became Oliver's dearest possession, not even supplanted by the beautiful new bicycle his father gave him that Christmas, nor by the watch his Uncle Pelham brought him from France.

On New Year's Day it began to snow, and the children were able to enjoy the delights of tobogganing. In mid-January the lake froze, and traditionally, all the villagers were free to enjoy it. It was still the school holiday, and the Havorhurst children as well as the Rochfords made the most of it. Since there was no hunting while the ground was so hard, Rowell, too, was content to amuse himself on the ice. But although after the thaw, hunting was renewed, the season was soon over. He became increasingly restless, and by the end of April, Willow guessed that he was planning to go to London. She raised no objection, for she now knew that she was always far happier at Rochford without him.

On the morning of his proposed departure, Rowell was delayed when one of the carriage horses was discovered at the last moment to be lame.

"Why do you not drive to Tunbridge Wells Station in the Daimler?" Willow inquired, for the car lay idle most of the while now Pelham had left home.

"I'll not take the risk," Rowell said irritably. "Besides which, with the new speed limit of twelve miles an hour, I'd certainly miss the 11:20 train and have to cool my heels waiting for the next one."

But the delay turned out to be longer than was expected, and by the time the landau was ready, Rowell was red-faced with impatience.

The coachman, Peters, was now almost as old as Dutton. As he set off down the drive at a leisurely pace, Rowell called to him angrily:

"Get a move on, man! What are you dawdling for? I shall miss my train."

But even though the two big greys picked up speed, as they drove past St. Stephen's Rowell noticed that it was already ten o'clock. He shouted again to Peters.

"What's the matter with you, for heaven's sake? Don't you realize I'm in a hurry, you old fool?"

Peters grunted and increased the horses' pace, but only marginally. He knew these lanes like the back of his hand, and they twisted and turned like a corkscrew. It wasn't safe to drive fast along them. They were barely wide enough for one carriage, let alone two, and it was impossible to see around the corners if anything was coming in the opposite direction. His fear for his life—and for the horses, was greater than his fear of his master, whose ill temper he knew well enough.

Rowell's patience snapped before they were a mile out of Havorhurst village.

"Pull them in!" he shouted. "I'll drive myself."

Shaking with anger, he alighted from the carriage and climbed into Peters' seat. He'd ruin his grey kid gloves, he thought, but it was a small price to pay. He was meeting Theodore Symington for luncheon at the Café Royal and he had no intention of missing the appointment.

He flicked the whip across the backs of the pair. Immediately, they surged forward and broke into a fast canter. Peters gripped the seat as sweat broke out on his forehead and on the palms of his woollen-gloved hands. This was madness. If a carriage were coming toward them they would never be able to stop in time . . .

But it was not a carriage which was to halt their mad dash through the countryside. As they raced through a hamlet and rounded a bend on the outskirts, a small child ran suddenly out of the door of a farmstead into the road. The child was in pursuit of a kitten, which managed to reach the opposite side of the road in time. But the child did not. Almost before Rowell was aware of what was happening, the hooves of one of the horses bowled the child over beneath the hooves of the second animal. Terrified, the great beast reared, the landau lurched over to one side, flinging its occupants into the road. Then it righted itself and the horses bolted off down the lane.

Rowell was first to regain his senses. The child was never to do so. As its mother came screaming into the road to lift the crumpled body, no one could have been in any doubt that it was dead.

Rowell forced himself into a kneeling position. His head was swimming and he felt sick with shock. He looked round and saw the prone body of the coachman lying on the grass verge. He crawled toward him on his hands and knees and discovered that the old man, though badly cut about the face, was still breathing.

The distraught mother now came screaming over to the two men. She was clinging to the lifeless little body in her arms.

"You've killed her. *You've killed her*. May God forgive you, for I never will. It's murder. I heard you. You were going too fast. And now you've killed her. Murderers! Murderers!"

Horrified, he realized that everything the woman was saying was true. They *had* been going too fast—and as a consequence the child was dead. But it had been an accident—a simple accident—not *murder* . . .

By now two farm laborers had arrived on the scene. They stood staring at the group, their eyes sympathetic as they looked at the mother and condemnatory as they looked at Rowell and his coachman.

"We saw you go by," one of the men muttered. "You was going too fast, sir."

"Killed her—that's what they done," the other said.

With difficulty, Rowell rose to his feet. His head was now beginning to clear and he was uneasily aware that there were two witnesses who would bear out the woman's story. There was no way by which he could avoid the intervention of the police—for the child was certainly dead. If he were accused at the inquest of being responsible for its death, his good name would be gone for ever. He might even be charged with . . .

It was at that juncture Rowell decided he would on no account put the Rochford name at risk. The two farm laborers had been at the far side of the field a good hundred yards from the road, he thought. While they may have been near enough to see the carriage go by, they would not be able to swear on oath which of the two men was driving. They, like everyone else, would take it for granted that the coachman would have been in the driving seat. The woman had only heard, not seen them. It would be his word against Peters' . . . and by the look of it, the unfortunate old fellow might not live to tell his side of the story.

Rowell straightened his back and looked at the laborer nearest to him.

"One of you had better ride into the village and fetch a doctor," he said. "My coachman needs attention. Don't just stand there—" he added, his tone gaining authority. "And one of you see if you can round up my horses. You'd better bring a policeman back with you from the village."

He turned to the woman, who was now sobbing uncontrollably as she rocked the dead child in her arms.

"Take her indoors," he said. "I am very sorry this has happened. But you will be well compensated, I assure you. My name is Rochford, Lord Rochford from Havorhurst. This is all most unfortunate. I had only just told my coachman he must slacken speed if he didn't want to lose his job—then the child ran out . . . most distressing."

No one questioned his remark. Peters was now regaining consciousness and moaning. By the look of it, he had a broken arm, but was not after all about to die.

Rowell went over to him and helped him into a sitting position.

"You're all right now, Peters," he said calmly. "The doctor's coming and you'll be well looked after. Pity about what's happened. Doesn't do to go too fast down these country lanes."

He saw the look of confusion in the old man's watery blue eyes and went on in a voice loud enough to be overheard:

"The fact is, Peters, I really should have let one of the younger men drive me. I've been promising myself these past two years I ought to retire you. Not far off seventy, are you? Well, there's a nice little cottage empty not far from Havor Wood. Time you and your wife retired there, don't you think? You're due a good pension."

It was not until the following day that Peters was well enough to appreciate exactly what his master had been talking about after the accident. He was now in bed in his flat over the stables, his arm set in a splint, his wife sitting anxiously by his side when, to his astonishment, young Lady Rochford called to visit him.

"I wanted to be quite sure you were all right, Peters, and not in need of anything," Willow said as his flustered wife showed her into the tiny bedroom. She sat down in the chair beside the bed, her eyes pitying as she looked at the old man's face, now blue with bruises and patched here and there with painful-looking grazes.

"I be all right, Milady," Peters said as tears filled his eyes. "It was good of you to come." His voice broke. "It's just that . . . that I can't help thinking about the poor little mite and the poor mother . . ."

"You must try not to blame yourself too much," Willow said. "I know my husband feels partly responsible for the fact that you were driving too fast. He means to speak up for you at the inquest."

The old man's tears ceased as he stared into Willow's face.

"But, Milady, t'weren't me as was driving the carriage. T'was the Master. He wouldn't let me drive no more, seeing as how I was going too slow for his liking. So he took my place and . . . and that's when it happened."

For a moment, Willow felt too sick to speak. All night long, Rowell had paced the bedroom floor, telling her over and over again how the accident had happened. She had pleaded with him to try to put it out of his mind, but he had seemed unable to do so. She had attributed his almost fanatical concern to shock—and yet somewhere in the recesses of her mind, she had felt a deep uneasiness. She knew Rowell so well—knew instantly when he was lying to her, but until this moment she had not fully realized that he had been lying about the accident.

But he could not lie on so important a matter, she thought. Peters must be confused. Or perhaps she had not heard him correctly.

"Tell me again, Peters—exactly what happened," she said gently. "You've no need to be afraid. I will help you. Just tell me the truth."

Peters drew a long shuddering sigh.

"I baint afraid, Milady, only sad for that there woman and the poor little mite. I'll never forget her face as long as I live." And he went on to explain how Rowell had insisted upon driving himself.

By the time she left Peters, Willow was in no doubt whatever that she now knew the truth. The old man's sincerity was beyond question, his account simple and obvious. It was just like Rowell to lose his temper and take the reins from the stubborn coachman who had refused to hurry. He never liked being thwarted. And then, she thought . . . then he must have panicked when he found the child was dead . . . seen a way to put the blame on his servant.

No, she prayed, please God no! Rowell will have thought better of such a dreadful, cowardly, despicable action by now. It was just the shock of the moment.

Slowly, her feet dragging, she went back into the house. Rowell was where she had left him—in the library, drinking whiskey. His cheeks were flushed and he did not even show her the courtesy of rising as she went into the room.

Before words could form themselves on her lips, Rowell spoke.

"I suppose you've been listening to Peters' side of the story," he said truculently, his voice slurred. "And now you're on your high horse because I mean to let him take the blame. Well, I can tell you this much, Willow, I have no intention of being pilloried for a paltry accident."

"Paltry!" Willow echoed, her face chalk-white. "Rowell, a child died because of you. That is bad enough. But that you should let Peters be held responsible when—"

"Don't be a fool!" Rowell interrupted rudely as he poured himself another whiskey. "They won't do anything to him. He's an old man, and I shall insist it was an accident; that if he'd been a bit younger, he could have stopped the horses in time. It's high time he retired anyway. I'll let him have the cottage down by Havor Wood and give him a decent pension. A bit of gossip won't hurt him, whereas it would ruin us."

"Ruin us?" Willow said stupidly. "You mean socially, Rowell? Do you really think *that* would matter to me when it is a matter of your honor at stake? You cannot mean it—not you, who have so often preached the importance of the Rochford good name—to me, to Rupert, to Pelham, even to Francis! And only yesterday you were preaching to Oliver about the necessity for a Rochford to show courage. Where is *your* courage now, Rowell?"

"Don't you start preaching to *me*!" Rowell shouted. "You've had far too much of your own way ever since you came to this house. I've been too weak with you— that's what's wrong. Well, I don't need a woman to tell me what I will and will not do."

"I am not telling you what to do, Rowell," Willow said quietly. "I am asking you, begging you even, to do what you know in your heart is the *only* honorable thing you can do. It is for your sake, don't you see? Even if the whole world believes you innocent, *you* will know you are guilty. I will know it. Peters knows it."

"Well, no one else is going to know it," Rowell said violently. "You were willing enough to cover for Stevens when he killed Francis. Why should you balk at doing the same for me as you did for a mere servant?"

Ignoring his last remark, Willow made one last effort.

"Rowell, I would stand by you throughout any unpleasantness that might come of your confession of guilt. I swear it on my children's lives. I won't say a word of reproach if we are ostracized—nor even if you were forced to go to trial and were publicly accused of the child's death. I would prefer any such indignity to the knowledge that the man I had married was a coward."

Rowell looked up from his now empty glass, his dark eyes burning as they stared into hers.

"Then the sooner you get used to the idea, the better," he said. "As far as I am concerned, Peters was driving the landau, and it was Peters, not I, who killed that child."

Chapter Thirty-two

May 1910

A WEEK LATER, ROWELL AND TOBY ARRIVED HOME from the inquest and joined Willow at luncheon. They were in excellent spirits.

"The verdict was 'accidental death'," Rowell said with a sideways glance at Willow's pale face. "So you have nothing more to worry about, my dear. Peters will not have to go for trial."

Willow remained silent. She could not believe that Rowell imagined the coroner's verdict would alter her opinion of his behavior. She had refused to go with him to the coroner's court which had been convened in the local schoolhouse in Havorhurst.

Toby was surprised by Willow's silence. He was unaware of the true facts of the accident as he said innocently:

"I cannot tell you how magnificently Rowell spoke up for Peters. You really should have been there to hear him, Willow. I am convinced it was entirely due to the speech he made in Peters' defense, that the coroner found in the poor old man's favor. Rowell even went so far as to insist that if anyone should be held responsible for the child's death it was himself; that, preoccupied with the business affairs that necessitated his journey, he had not noticed until too late how fast they were traveling and that he had failed in his responsibility to slow Peters down."

Willow put down her knife and fork. Toby's ignorance

of the truth and his praise of Rowell only increased her horror. Unaware of her inner feelings, Toby continued:

"Rowell went on to say that Peters was one of our oldest, most trusted servants; that there had even been occasions when you allowed the children to travel to Sir John's without their nurse, confident that Peters would take the utmost care of them. It was a masterly speech, Rowell. It made me proud to be a Rochford."

Rowell helped himself to some more vegetables and motioned to Dutton to replenish his glass of wine. His face was flushed.

"We can now forget the whole unfortunate business," he said. "I've told Peters he can have the Havor Wood cottage and I'm pensioning him off. Jackson can take over as coachman."

Excusing herself on the grounds that she was not feeling very well, Willow left the room. Dismissing Lily, who was in her bedroom, she locked herself in and sat down at her bureau.

On the desk lay a small bundle of letters from Nathaniel Corbett. The most recent—which she had received the previous day—confirmed one he had written a month earlier. The recession in America was over, and although the economy had not recovered as totally as Mr. Corbett had hoped, there was a seventy-two-percent improvement.

I am therefore able to inform you that the trust now has funds available for distribution and you will shortly receive a letter asking you to advise the Trustees whether you wish the money to be sent to England or prefer that it should be banked here in your name . . .

Willow drew a long, deep breath. Before the accident, she would have had no hesitation in having the money sent to England. But now . . . now it was as if fate were helping her to make the decision she knew in her heart must be made—to leave Rowell and return to her homeland.

For a long time she remained motionless, staring with unseeing eyes at the objects in the room. For nineteen long years she had lived in England; thought of herself as English; raised two children who had no knowledge of her country. To remove them to so different an environment was to cause a complete upheaval in their lives. Oliver, in particular, would be leaving his heritage behind him. But they will adapt, as children do, she thought.

But could *she* readjust to that old life? San Francisco had been rebuilt. Perhaps a new and thriving city was the right background for the new life she must make for herself and the two children. But it would not be easy. And worst of all, she would be putting six thousand miles between herself and Toby.

For the hundredth time Willow considered the alternative—to remain here at Rochford as Rowell's wife. For the hundredth time she knew that it was no longer possible for her to do so. Rowell had forfeited the last vestige of respect she had ever had for him, and now she despised him. She did not want Oliver to model himself upon such a father; to grow up like Rowell with values and morals so superficial that they were little more than thistledown when a cold wind blew.

This afternoon Rowell was going to Lewes to look at a foal; Toby was going to London and would not be back until late; Patience was taking Oliver and Alice to a children's birthday party at the Barratts'. She would be quite alone in the house except for the servants. This too seemed like the hand of fate, for now she could arrange for Lily to pack her own and the children's belongings unobserved. She had been waiting only for the result of the inquest before putting her plan into operation, hoping that despite everything, Rowell might still find the courage to tell the truth. But that had not happened, and now she must go as quickly as possible—before circumstances made her change her mind.

There were still one or two letters to be written before she left—to Dodie, to Rupert—whose last cheerful letter from Munich still lay unanswered in her bureau drawer. But most important of all was the letter she now began writing to Toby—a letter she intended to post when she reached Dover.

By the time you read this, I shall be on my way to France. She paused to still the trembling of her hand.

I will remain there for a few days until I can book passage for the children and myself to America. I am asking Rowell to divorce me but even if he refuses, my resolve to end our marriage will not be changed.

Perhaps you will think me a coward for finding myself

unable to say good-bye to you in person. The truth is, dearest Toby, that even the thought of saying farewell to you tears my heart to pieces. My affection for you throughout the long years we have known one another is no less now than it has ever been. It is at least some small consolation to me to know that your future happiness seems certain. Stella will surely change her mind once she hears that I have left Rochford and she knows that she would be the new chatelaine. I pray that you will both be very happy.

I would like to reassure you with regard to my own future. Mr. Corbett has written to tell me that my father's company is back on its feet and that there is money available for my needs and the children's. We shall go to San Francisco where I still have many friends.

You may wonder why, after waiting so long, I have suddenly come to the conclusion that I must go away. If I tell you that Rowell himself admitted to me that he, and not Peters, was driving the carriage when the accident occurred, you will understand. Will you be so good as to make certain that Peters does not suffer further after I am gone. Terrible though it must sound, I cannot trust Rowell any more to fulfill his promise to give Peters a good pension.

I shall write to you, dearest Toby, and I hope that you will keep in touch with me . . .

Dry-eyed, Willow laid down her pen. Her heart was now like a stone in her chest and she felt icy cold as she began to move unhurriedly and like an automaton. It was as if some voice inside her were giving her directions. First, ring for Lily. Tell her to pack only those clothes necessary for a sea voyage and a simple day dress to wear in Paris; no furs, no jewelry other than those items she had brought with her as a bride; no books, no ornaments; no mementos except the photographs of the family that were locked away in her bureau . . .

Willow looked up as her maid came into the room. She must now perforce tell Lily the truth—that she was leaving Rochford and England forever.

"It is entirely up to you, Lily, whether you wish to come to America with me," she told the astonished servant. "I shall not consider it a disloyalty if you prefer to remain in your own country," she added, trying to soften the shock to her gawping maid.

But Lily had grown to love her mistress almost as greatly as Nellie had once done and she recovered quickly from her initial surprise. She did not hesitate in her decision.

"I'll come with you, Milady," she said without hesitation.

"Then you will have to be *very* discreet, Lily," Willow warned her. "You are the only person as yet who knows of my intention to leave tomorrow. Not even Nanny is aware of my decision, and I do not yet know if she will wish to go with me. If she does not, you may have to help me care for the children on the voyage as I will not have time to engage another nurse."

"Nanny will come with us, sure as ducks is ducks, Milady," Lily said quickly. "There isn't nothing in the world would part her from Master Oliver and Miss Alice!"

Silently, Willow prayed she was right. The children adored Patience and would be far less disturbed if she went with them.

Efficient as always, Lily made short work of packing those items Willow required. The trunks were carried downstairs by two of the footmen, who were told to put them in the loft over the stables "for storage."

Less easily, Willow tried to decide what Lily must pack for the children. Warm clothes and nightwear, but what of Alice's dolls' house? Which of her many beloved dolls? Was there room for Oliver's toy flying machine, for his animals? They would have to leave behind his bicycle. But she would buy him another, once they found somewhere to live . . .

Only as she stared around the nursery did Willow's eyes fill with tears. This large, comfortable, homely room with its gas fire and fender, its scrubbed wooden table on which the children had their meals and painted and wrote and did their jigsaws, was filled with memories. She had enjoyed so many happy hours with them here. In one corner stood the dappled grey rocking-horse that had once been loved by the five Rochford boys, its mane woefully thin now, the paint scuffed where the feet of three generations of children had kicked its sides . . .

While Lily packed, Willow wandered through the open door into the adjoining night nursery. Patience's full-sized bed and the two smaller ones where Oliver and Alice slept were neatly made, their counterpanes snow white. In a far corner stood the old wooden cradle on its rockers, half covered with a dust sheet but still used by little Alice as a cot for her dolls. Beside each of the smaller beds was a table with a nightlight for Oliver, who still woke screaming from his bad dreams, though less often now.

Willow's heart hardened. It would have been only a matter of time before Rowell demanded that Oliver should be made to ride again. Now that would never happen.

One of the young maids knocked on the door to tell Willow that afternoon tea was ready. Willow glanced anxiously at the nursery clock. Half past four. It would not be long now before Rowell was back; and only an hour before Patience would return with the children.

"Bring tea up here," she told the maid. "Lily and I are sorting out the children's unwanted clothes and toys and we don't wish to be disturbed."

It was after five when the footmen carried down the children's trunks and put them with Willow's in the stable loft. The new coachman, Jackson, drove Lily into Havorhurst to dispatch a telegram to Silvie. It was fortunate that Silvie and Pelham were in Paris and not somewhere abroad, Willow thought, since it would be far easier and happier for her to stay with them than in a hotel while awaiting passage to America.

She heard Rowell return, watching from the landing as he went straight into the library. He would be making for the whiskey decanter, she thought. He had been drinking heavily ever since the accident and every night he had to be helped to his room by one of the servants. From her own room, she heard his shouts and mumblings, for he always became alternately aggressive and maudlin when he was drunk.

If he was drinking from now until bedtime, it would be the same tonight, Willow thought, but without rancor. It was perhaps easier for her to spend this last evening with Rowell if he were not in one of his pleasanter moods. She wanted nothing to undermine her determination to go.

Slowly she made her way along the landing to Toby's laboratory. Although she had never before entered his rooms without being invited, she now took the bunch of keys from her waist and unlocked the door. It was growing dark and the room was filled with shadows. If she half closed her eyes, it was not difficult to imagine Toby's figure stooped over his table deep in concentration.

She walked over and stood behind his empty chair, her hands reaching out as they had so often longed to do, to touch his head.

"Oh, Toby, Toby," she whispered, the pain all but unbearable as the poignancy of this silent parting from him tore at her heart. Had he been here now, she knew she might all too easily falter in her plan to leave on the morrow. His laboratory was so much an intrinsic part of him that it seemed as if he must be here—by the window, perhaps, staring into the garden? Or over by the cupboard while he searched among his piles of papers for something he needed.

She tried to imagine Stella here in this room, standing where she now stood behind Toby's chair. Could Stella ever love him as she, Willow, did? Would she be gentle, caring, understanding, loyal? Would she give him children? Would Toby take her in his arms and hold her as he had once held her, Willow? Would he kiss Stella's mouth, her eyes, her hands? Would he feel that same torment of desire that had nearly overcome them both on that solitary occasion when she, Willow, had been in his arms?

Such thoughts were intolerable, and she pushed them swiftly away. It was Toby's happiness she must put first—not her own.

At the other end of the landing, Patience had returned with the children and was putting them to bed. Both were a trifle overexcited, and as always at such times, Oliver's stammer was worse.

"I could give him a little laudanum to help him sleep," Patience suggested when Willow entered the night nursery. She kissed both children goodnight and went back to her bedroom to change for dinner. She decided to wear a primrose chiffon Empire gown. It had an underskirt made of satin and was trimmed with cream *guipure* lace, and had been made for her holiday in Deauville. It was the last time she would ever wear it, she thought as the dinner gong sounded, and picking up a cashmere stole she went downstairs to join Rowell in the dining room.

Rowell was in a truculent mood. The foal had not come up to his expectations and he felt his afternoon had been wasted. He criticized the entrée and had the veal returned to the kitchen to be served "at a decent temperature, if you please—not stone cold." Since Willow drank only a glass of red and a half glass of white wine, Rowell drank the remainder.

"If I don't empty the bottles, the servants will," he said loud enough for old Dutton to hear him.

He followed up the meal with two double brandies, and by nine o'clock Willow could no longer make sense of his muttered rejoinders. She laid down her tapestry work and announced that she was retiring to bed.

Rowell looked up, his cheeks flushed by alcohol, his eyes brilliant but unfocused as they roved over her body.

"Not a bad idea of yours," he said with a leer. "I'll come with you. Nothing else to do, anyway."

Willow blushed, but made no relevant reply.

"I dare say you will want a last nightcap," she said quietly. "I'll go up now."

"Don't go yet, my dear. Come over here," Rowell mumbled, holding out one arm. "Come and have a drink with me."

"No, Rowell, I'm very tired," Willow replied as she made her way toward the door. "I'll see you in the morning."

She hurried out of the room before he could make any further suggestions. Rowell watched her go, his fuddled mind trying to puzzle out her words.

"See you in the morning," she had said. But he wasn't going to wait till the morning to have what he wanted.

"Can't have understood me," he muttered aloud. "Should have made it clearer. Never know what's what—these females!"

With Désirée, he thought confusedly, misunderstandings did not occur. She always knew what a man wanted, and, what was more, she could make a man want it even when he thought he was too tired.

Too tired, indeed! He'd show that cold-blooded woman upstairs how to overcome tiredness. Time she learned a trick or two. He'd soon put an end to her nonsense.

For half an hour he remained in the library drinking, but he did not lose sight of his purpose. For once he did not call for a servant to assist him upstairs, but made his own way up and lurched along the landing to his wife's bedroom. He could see no light shining from under the door. Trying the handle, he rattled it several times before reaching the conclusion that it was locked.

Until now, Rowell's mood had been comparatively good-humored. But the moment he discovered himself thwarted, his mood changed to one of anger. Beating his fist on the door, he shouted furiously:

"It's Rowell, your husband. Open the door this instant!"

Upon receiving no answer, he banged even louder.

Hearing his raised voice, and afraid lest he might wake the whole household, Willow slipped her peignoir around her shoulders and went barefooted to the door. It was her intention to try to calm Rowell with soothing words; to urge him to go to his own room where a comfortable bed awaited him. It did not cross her mind that she was in any danger.

But Rowell was far too drunk to be deterred by words. Shoving the door open with his shoulder, he pushed past his wife, catching hold of her arm as he did so. He then dragged her forcibly across the room and pulled her down on top of him as he fell onto the bed.

For the first time in their marriage, Willow felt physically afraid of Rowell. She had seen him drunk on many occasions, but there was usually a servant with him, and when she had made clear her unwillingness to let him into her room, he had always lost interest in his purpose and allowed himself to be led off to bed.

"Not going to take no for an answer tonight—" Rowell was muttering as he attempted to pull the Japon dressing gown away from her shoulders. "You're m'wife, dammit, Willow, and you'll do what I want for a change—"

The écru embroidery on her gown ripped suddenly as she tried unsuccefully to pull away from Rowell's embrace.

With a triumphant laugh, Rowell rolled over on top of her and began kissing her neck. As Willow's hands rose to protect herself, he caught both her arms and held them pinioned at her sides. His breath reeked of whiskey fumes and his eyes were glazed; but his body seemed to have lost none of its strength.

Willow stifled a scream as she fought furiously to free herself. His weight was so heavy on her chest that it was all she could do to breathe.

"Wanna a little fight first, eh?" Rowell muttered. At that moment, her nightgown fell from her shoulders and her beautiful firm breasts were fully exposed to his gaze.

"God, but you're beautiful," he cried hoarsely, his eyes traveling swiftly down to her smooth rounded stomach. Breathing heavily, he began to struggle with one hand to undress her fully. His fingernails, as they tore at her clothing, now clawed into her flesh, and Willow was no longer able to prevent a scream from passing her lips. Mistaking that cry for one of pleasure, but forgetting that he was still fully clothed, Rowell began to move on top of her in preparation for the imminent pleasures he was anticipating.

At that moment, the door opened and someone came into the room.

Willow was the first to see the small figure in striped pajamas standing at the foot of the bed.

"Oliver," she gasped.

Still unaware that he had been interrupted, Rowell paid no attention.

"Rowell, let me go, *let me go*," she cried in a fierce desperate voice. "It's Oliver. He's sleepwalking! Please let me get up."

But now the child was awake. He was staring in bemused amazement at the scene in front of him. The sight of his mother's naked body with his father astride her was terrifying. He could hear his mother pleading to be let free, see his father continuing, so he thought, to attack her. Horrified, he called out in a thin nervous stammer:

"L . . . Let her go!"

Now at last Rowell realized that the boy was in the room. Furious at the interruption and still half drunk, he staggered off the bed and confronted the terrified child.

"Get out!" he shouted. "Don't you know you're not allowed in here—not *ever*! You'll be punished for this, my boy—severely punished. Now get out of here!"

He lifted his hand as if to strike the child, but before

he could do so, Willow caught hold of his arm and held on to it with all her remaining strength.

"Oliver was sleepwalking, Rowell. He didn't know where he was. Don't touch him. I forbid you to touch him."

Rowell pushed her brutally aside.

"You've namby-pambied your son long enough. It's time he learned a few lessons." He struck Oliver across the face. "Now go to your room. Tomorrow morning at nine sharp, you will come to my study. Six of the best might knock a little sense into that blockhead of yours!"

Although Oliver's eyes had filled with tears and one hand was lifted to cover his stinging cheek, still he made no move to leave. He stood staring uncomprehendingly from Rowell to his mother.

Despite every instinct demanding that she do so, Willow dared not go to her son lest she increase Rowell's uncontrolled venom. She said in as quiet and level a tone as she could manage:

"Go to bed now, Oliver. I am quite all right, I promise you. Find Patience and she will give you something to help you sleep. Off you go now, like a good boy."

Wordless, Oliver turned and ran out of the room.

As the door closed behind him, Willow turned to face her husband, her eyes glittering contemptuously.

"If it is still your intention to rape me, Rowell, then you had best do so now and be done with it. If not, then kindly leave my room."

Rowell stared at his wife's white, furious face uneasily. The interlude with Oliver had partially sobered him, and he was no longer so sure of himself. There was a dangerous look in Willow's eyes—in the tense rigidity of her stance—that he found unnerving. "Rape," she had said. It was an ugly word. Surely she knew he was not going to *rape* her? He had only wanted . . .

"Well, can't you make up your mind?"

Her voice was icy, scathing, somehow ridiculing him. His mood became sullen.

"One of these days you'll regret playing Miss High-and-Mighty with me," he muttered stupidly, the threat momentarily restoring his ego. Then quite suddenly, he forgot altogether the purpose of his visit. What he wanted most in the world was a drink. Where in the devil's name was his valet? he wondered. What did he pay a houseful of servants for if not to be ready to cater to his needs?

Without even a backward glance at Willow, he went to the door and, opening it, shouted his valet's name down the corridor. Willow heard the servant open the door of the dressing room and Rowell's angry demand for the whiskey decanter to be brought up to him at once. Without so much as a backward glance in her direction, he stumbled along the landing, and she heard the dressing room door crash noisily behind him.

Willow pulled her nightrobe around her and somehow found the courage to leave the comparative safety of her room. The floor was cold beneath her bare feet as she hurried down the long dimly-lit gallery toward the nursery suite. The day nursery was in darkness, but the door of the children's bedroom was ajar, and she could see the flickering golden glow from the nightlights. She paused, uncertain whether her unexpected presence might disturb the frightened child still further. But then she heard the soft lilt of Patience's voice humming a lullaby and she knew that she was not needed after all.

Reluctantly, she left the familiar security behind her and hurried back along the landing. She paused outside the door of Rowell's dressing room. She could hear his slurred, angry voice remonstrating with his valet, followed by the creak of the bedsprings and a moment later by drunken snores. She hurried into her room and, closing the door behind her, turned the key in the lock with trembling fingers. She stood with her back to the cold mahogany, shivering uncontrollably.

As if she were trying to comfort someone else, she whispered over and over again:

"Don't think about it. Tomorrow you will be far away and this will all seem like a bad dream. Don't think about it."

But it was not a dream, and she had yet to remove herself and the children safely out of the house which never again could she call her home.

It was seven o'clock in the evening, and twilight was falling when Sophia set foot for the first time in Havorhurst village. Lights were burning cheerily from the small mullioned windows of the Havorhurst Arms, and she decided that she might as well take the advice of her driver and alight there. Hopefully, the landlord would provide a meal as well as information on how to find the priest of the local church. She reminded herself that in England such a man would be known as the Parson or Vicar.

Paying off the driver of the motor taxicab which had brought her from Tunbridge Wells railway station, she reflected that her small hoard of money was disappearing alarmingly quickly. Fortunately, she had been befriended aboard the packet steamer crossing the English Channel by two middle-aged Yorkshiremen. Although she had understood little of their strange dialect, they had paid for her lunch and when they landed, invited her to take tea with them in a pleasant sea-front hotel in Dover. They would have paid for her to stay at a first-class hotel for the night had she not had to decline the invitation, being anxious to reach her destination without further delay.

Sophia sighed as the taxicab drove off down the single unlit street. She was unaccustomed to country villages, and Havorhurst struck her as a poor sort of place to live. Dover had looked far more exciting with its bustling pavements, its masses of sailors, and exciting-looking shops strung along the edge of the vast ocean she had seen for the first time in her life that very morning. She bent down and picked up her valise and pushed open the door of the inn with her shoulder.

A dozen male faces turned to stare at her in astonishment. Pewter mugs brimming with ale were left standing on the wooden tabletops, brier pipes were removed from below the mustaches as all conversation ceased.

Aware of the sensation she was creating, Sophia smiled. Madame said it was a sign of beauty if one could turn heads in one's direction. She reached up to touch the red ostrich feather on her new black straw hat, smoothed the tight-fitting waisted jacket of her scarlet traveling costume and took a step forward so that her beautiful new red patent leather boots would show beneath the folds of her long skirt.

"Good night!" she said politely in Nicole's best English. "I wish please to meet with Mister the Parson and have conversation, and afterwards to eat the dinner."

The silence that had fallen was now broken by several

guffaws, and then a buxom woman appeared from a back room carrying two pint-sized beer tankards, a clean white apron around her waist, her fair hair tied up on top of her head in a bun.

"You be a foreigner, dear, surely," she said, knowing very well that no English lady would have entered the village pub—not even with a male escort. Yet the girl looked as if she had class.

"I am a French girl seeking my relations in your village," Sophia said calmly.

There was a further silence before the villagers' natural hospitality asserted itself. A place was made for her on the oak settle by the inglenook fire in which several large logs blazed, heating the kettle hung on a hook over the flames. A glass of cider was brought to her, and the questions began.

In her halting English, Sophia explained that she did not know who her relations were—only that they had probably lived at one time in Havorhurst. Heads were scratched while thought was given to the matter. No one seemed to think the foreign girl's relatives could still be in the neighborhood.

"I've known everyone 'ereabouts these past fifty yearn," said the landlord. "B'aint been no one new 'ere, not since Doctor Rose come."

Over another beer, it was agreed that Sophia's plan to see Parson offered the best chance to find her forebears.

"If 'e don't find your folks, you cum back 'ere, dear," said the landlord's wife kindly. "Appen we can fix you up with a bed for the night, surely."

Two of the younger farm laborers, red-faced and grinning sheepishly, offered to accompany Sophia to the vicarage, but she had long since assessed their social standing and considered that she might make a better impression on the all-important parson if she were alone.

Leaving her valise in the care of the innkeepers, she set out on foot toward the village church. A boy on his bicycle nearly fell off his machine as he turned to gape at this stranger. Only very rarely was a new face to be seen in the High Street, and certainly no one as colorful and striking as Sophia in her scarlet costume and plumed hat, a beacon even in the gathering dusk.

Sophia was unprepared for her welcome at the vicarage.

The elderly maid who opened the door to her gasped and tried to close it before Sophia could walk past her.

"The Reverend is busy, Miss. He wouldn't want no strangers visiting at this time of night," she blurted out, her face a mask of disapproval.

"I do not wish to see no Reverend," Sophia said in as imperious a tone as she could muster. "I wish to see Mister the Parson or Mister the Vicar, if you please."

While the maid hesitated, a bald pink head appeared around the door of a room on the right of the long, ill-lit passageway.

"Who is it, Polly? What is going on?"

As Sophia stepped forward under the single light bulb, the late Reverend Appleby's successor came out to meet her, his spectacles slipping to the end of his sharp beaky nose as he peered down at the small figure in front of him.

"Who are you? What do you want?" he asked, uneasily aware, as his maid had been, that it was not only by the color of her clothes but by the paint on her face that his visitor could best be described as "a scarlet woman." He hoped very much that no one had seen her approach the vicarage at this time of night—for goodness only knew what his reputation would be worth hereafter.

Perplexed, but still undaunted, Sophia explained her mission.

"It is my desire that you look this night at the book of records, if you will be so kind, Monsieur," she ended her explanation. "I am come the very long way from France and now I am much fatigued and wish quickly to be with my relations."

"I fear it is much too late to look at any records tonight, young lady," the vicar said sternly, backing away from Sophia nervously. "The register is locked up—and in any event, it is in the church. You can come back in the morning at a respectable hour—if you insist," he added unhappily.

Sophia's blue eyes flashed.

"It is not yet begun, the night," she pointed out. At Madame Lou-Lou's they would be only now opening the doors to the first customers. Suddenly, she smiled. "Do not be afraid, Monsieur," she said. "I am not the poor girl. I can pay you well, see?" She reached in the purse dangling from her wrist and drew out several gold coins. "It is enough, no?" she asked with growing confidence. Yvette had told her that money could buy anything— anything at all, provided one offered enough.

The vicar looked even more shocked.

"Surely you are aware, young lady, that it is an insult to try to bribe a man in my . . . my position." Encountering Sophia's wide-eyed, innocent stare, he was suddenly afraid that he had misjudged her. "Tomorrow—if I am able to be of assistance to you—by all means you may make a donation to charity," he added. "We have a Poor Box in the vestry—"

Sophia shrugged.

"I pay whatever you tell me," she said simply. "But I will not leave 'avor'urst wizout the knowledge I seek."

"Tomorrow!" the vicar said nervously. "Come back tomorrow."

Sophia continued to stare for a moment longer at the vicar. His black cassock was green with age and frayed at the hem. The few strands of grey hair he still possessed fell untidily across his pink pate. His expression was even less congenial than that of Father Mattieu of whom he reminded her. Sophia felt a moment's regret that, true to Madame Lou-Lou's prognosis, she had never developed the full rounded figure so desired by men. Years after she had left the convent, she had recalled the familiar lustful look in Father Mattieu's eyes when he had patted in a most undignified fashion the older orphan girls on their rounded buttocks. Yvette had agreed that not even *les religieux* were above the call of the flesh. Were she, Sophia, more voluptuous, perhaps she might have received a more helpful attitude from this gaunt old man.

Sighing, she shrugged her slender shoulders and turned away. It was growing late and she was tired. Perhaps it would be as well to stay the night in the friendly *auberge* and begin her search next day.

The vicar watched her leave his home with a combination of relief and guilt. This was no time of night for any young woman to be walking alone in the darkness. There were no less than eight empty rooms in the large, cold vicarage, and he could have offered her hospitality. But he dared not do so, fearing lest next morning the milkman or the postman or any one of his female parishioners might see her leave his house and wonder . . .

But before his conscience could overcome his reluctance, Sophia had flounced out of the house and was picking her way down the graveled driveway in her high-buttoned boots.

In Paris, she thought, the streets were paved and fit to walk on. Her misgivings about Havorhurst increased—and were intensified when the well-meaning landlady, only just hiding her intense curiosity, conducted Sophia to the room where she was to spend the night.

Sophia eyed with disdain the faded wallpaper, brown in places from great patches of damp. At Madame Lou-Lou's, the wallpaper was brightly colored and renewed every second year. The brass bedsteads were polished to a high shine, and magnificent satin covers and plump pillows graced them. There were warm rugs on the floors. She looked down at the bare boards beneath her feet and at the faded chenille bedcover apprehensively. She was sure that the sagging bedsprings would give way beneath her and wondered uneasily if there would be bedbugs in the flock mattress. Madame would never have permitted such a sorry state of affairs.

"You'll be right as rain here, m'dear, surely!" the landlady said, blissfully unaware of Sophia's comparisons. "When you've unpacked and tidied yourself, you cum back downstairs and I'll have a nice hot supper for you."

The inmates of the Havorhurst Arms watched approvingly when Sophia finally tucked hungrily into the huge plate of rabbit stew the landlady put before her. They noted the dainty manner in which she cut the meat into small portions and placed them carefully in her mouth. They nodded approvingly when the landlord produced a bottle of wine—French wine, he informed Sophia proudly —that he'd kept for just such a special visitor as herself. Sophia gave him her warmest smile, aware that here at least she had made a conquest.

It was nearing nine o'clock when a place was made for her once more by the fireside and the entire room entered into a prolonged discussion on the mystery of Sophia's relations. It was only when the landlord called that it was "closing time" that they reluctantly departed for their

own homes, delighted to have such an unusual bit of
gossip to relay to their waiting wives.

The Havorhurst Arms had not yet changed from the
use of oil lamps to the new electricity, and as the landlord
handed Sophia a candle to guide her up to bed, he gave
her a long, searching look.

"You do surely resemble me of someone," he said,
scratching his head. "I can't say exactly as who it might
be—but I'd 'ave bet a pound to a penny I'd seen you
somewheres afore if I hadn't of known you'd never been
in England afore today."

But now Sophia was feeling the effects of the long day's
travel, and she was too tired to pursue the matter. Bidding
her host a polite "goodnight," she retired to bed.

Early the following morning, a bowl of porridge—
which she had never tasted before—followed by a large
plateful of ham and a mug of hot sweet tea, put fresh
heart into her. With a cheery wave to her hosts, she set
off once more for the vicarage.

But although the news had not yet reached the Havorhurst Arms, it was already spreading quickly through the
village—the King was dead. Housewives scrubbing their
doorsteps hurried inside to draw their window curtains,
children were called in from play, and Sophia passed
down the High Street almost unnoticed. Even before she
reached the vicarage, the church bells began their mourn-
ful tolling, and Sophia's heart sank. Maybe after all, this
was not going to be the day she had longed for, worked
toward, for so many months. Maybe the shabby old
parson would be kept busy ringing his church bells and
have no time to show her his records . . .

Her fears were justified, for although the vicar was not
himself employed in ringing the bells, he was busy at
his house writing a special sermon for the sad occasion of
the death of the monarch. Sophia had perforce to wait in
the darkened parlor until at long last he was prepared to
take her up to the church. But her spirits lifted once more
in hopeful expectations as he took the great duty register
from its cupboard and began turning the thick yellow
pages backward to the year 1862. It was cold in the
vestry, and the dismal tolling of the bells high above their
heads echoed forbiddingly around the stone walls. Sophia

realized that the vicar's mind was on other more important matters and that he glanced only fitfully at the names and dates as his finger ran down the yellowed pages.

At first, it seemed as if at this eleventh hour, her hopes were going to be dashed. The vicar announced that if there were no "Alice" or "Oliver" mentioned on the page, there was little point in looking further. Tears of disappointment filled her eyes, but were still unshed when she saw the man pause, peer more closely at the writing and then at her.

It simply could not be so, he was thinking. This painted French Jezabel could not possibly have connections with the Rochford family. Not even if she were one of the young gentlemen's by-blows. But then, as he looked at Sophia properly for the first time, he took in the extraordinary pale gold of her hair, the line of cheek and chin, and his heart missed a beat. There *was* a family likeness—unbelievable though it might be—to young Lady Rochford. And he recalled now a story about his predecessor, the Reverend Appleby—being called to give evidence at a consistory court regarding a missing child.

"Well, Monsieur le Curé?" Sophia reverted to French in her excitement. "Is it that you think you have finded my family for me?"

The man hesitated. By all means, let the girl make her own inquiries up at the manor, but he was not going to put his foot in it by taking her there, lest he was mistaken in imagining the likeness. Had she been less garishly attired, less obviously the kind of woman she was . . .

"These could be the people you are searching for," he said evasively. "There was a wedding performed in this Church in 1862 between Oliver Rochford and a lady named Alice. The Rochford family live in the manor house about a mile out of the village. They own most of the land around—and the village, too."

Sophia's violet blue eyes danced with excitement.

"But it is they, of a certainty," she exclaimed. "I thank you, Monsieur. With all my heart, I thank you." She plunged her small gloved hand into her purse and drew out double the number of coins she had intended to put in the Poor Box. "It is a miracle," she cried, pressing the coins into his hand. "I have prayed to the Virgin Mary, and she has answered my prayers. Please thank her for me, Monsieur. I will light many candles for her when I return to Paris."

It was only as she hurried back to the Havorhurst Arms to collect her portmanteau and pay for her night's board and lodging that Sophia realized she might never go back to Paris now. Her relations—*her real family*, were but a mile away.

Her mood of euphoria was in no way diminished when the landlady informed her that there were no such things as hired motors or even horse-drawn fiacres to be had in Havorhurst; and that most folk went on foot.

" 'Tis but a mile up the road to the manor, m'dear," she said, and glancing up at the sky, added: "Since you've got no waterproof coat, p'raps you'd best borrow my old cape. The hood will protect your pretty hat if it rains."

Sophia hesitated. She had no wish to spoil the effect of her new outfit by covering it with the dusty old cloak the woman was now handing to her. But then she remembered the hard work she had to do to earn the money to buy these new smart clothes for her English visit. She took the cloak, knowing full well that she could discard the ugly garment before she reached the manor; that in her smart new regalia, she could not fail to create a good impression. She could disregard Yvette's warning that she might not be welcomed. Nicole had taught her not only the language but many other useful English customs— how to hold her teacup with her little finger pointing outwards; how to say "Pardon" if one sneezed; to refer to the main salon as "the parlor"; and never, ever to sit on a gentleman's knee. There were many more such cautions, which Sophia had memorized, and she was perfectly confident that she could now behave as befitted a real "lady."

As she waved farewell to her kindly landlady, she turned her pretty head and nodded gracefully as she set off down the road.

"Ta, ever so," she said sweetly in perfect imitation of her teacher, Nicole. She was rewarded by the landlady's wide, beaming smile.

* * *

It was the seventh of May in the year 1910. Willow woke from a fitful sleep to dark grey clouds and the threat of rain. Lily brought in her breakfast tray on which lay *The Times*. The newspaper was black edged, and the headlines in black ink announced that King Edward VII had died just before midnight.

The King's death was not unexpected. A medical bulletin issued by Buckingham Palace two days previously had stated that he had bronchitis and that his condition was causing serious anxiety. Nevertheless, Willow was both shocked and saddened by his passing, as indeed would be the whole nation, the newspaper stated. It carried two long articles on his life, his reign, and his death. Although his son, now George V, was generally liked, his people had loved the pleasure-seeking boisterous King.

"The Master gave instructions for all the curtains to be drawn," Lily informed her. "And Mr. Dutton has instructed us all to wear black—" She broke off, looking at Willow's bruised white face curiously. "Will—will we still be leaving, Milady? His Majesty being dead and all?" she asked tentatively.

Willow hesitated, but only for a moment, before she nodded her assent. Not only was it impossible for *her* to remain a further night under Rowell's roof, but she feared for Oliver, lest Rowell decided to carry out his threat to thrash him. And not least of all, if she lost her courage now, she might never again raise it sufficiently to walk out of her home, her marriage, the life she had led for the past nineteen years.

She had spoken to Patience after she had kissed the children goodnight the previous evening, and the nurse had not hesitated in her reply. Oliver and Alice were her children, and as long as they were alive, her place was with them, she said reassuringly.

"Go and tell Nanny to dress the children as if for a carriage ride," she ordered the waiting Lily. "And warmly —I think it is going to rain. And tell Jackson to have the carriage ready in an hour—and the wagonette. The trunks can be loaded at the last minute. Jackson need not be told that he will be driving us to Dover."

Leaving her breakfast untouched, she climbed out of bed. Her body ached with stiffness, and there were big red weals on her skin where Rowell's nails had raked her.

She walked slowly to her mirror and understood then why Lily was staring at her. The bruises on her cheekbones were painfully obvious. Sending Lily about her tasks, she tried ineffectually to cover the tell-tale marks with powder. But she soon gave up the task and began to dress herself without Lily's help.

Lily returned almost at once to her mistress' room. Her eyes were anxious.

"Nanny says Master Oliver is not very well, but she's dressing him all the same, Milady. She says as how he's a bit feverish and won't talk to no one, not even to Miss Alice."

"A ride in the fresh air will be good for him," Willow replied evasively.

As soon as her toilette was completed, she sent Lily to get ready for the journey, then went along to the nursery. Alice came running to her side.

"Where are we going, Mama? Nanny says it's a s'prise! Why must I wear this horrible black dress? I don't like it, Mama. I want to wear my blue one."

Willow glanced over the child's head at Oliver. The boy was standing silently by the window, staring down into the garden. He avoided her eyes when she spoke to him, and she was momentarily overcome by the enormity of what she was about to do. This was Oliver's house, Oliver's heritage. One day he would be Lord Rochford— and this house, this estate would be his to pass on in due course to his children. Was she right to take him away? Quickly she took his hand in hers.

"Come, my darling, we're going out in the carriage." She looked questioningly at Patience. "Everything ready?" she asked. Patience nodded, and the small group left the nursery and proceeded downstairs.

Rowell was in the library, his thoughts entirely preoccupied with the news of the King's death. He could remember little of the previous night, although he had a vague recollection of a quarrel with Willow, who had been objecting to his sharing her bed. Such had been his state of inebriation that this morning he had totally forgotten Oliver's untimely interruption.

He glanced at the clock over the mantelshelf. It was ten

o'clock. He was surprised that Willow had not yet come downstairs, although from time to time she did take breakfast in bed. He wanted to discuss with her the plans that must be made to go to London next week for the King's funeral. Being one of the peers of the realm, he would officiate on this, as on any other state occasion, and it was his wife's duty to accompany him.

He rang the bell and asked the attendant footman where her Ladyship was.

The servant had already heard gossip of last night's debaucherie from Rowell's valet, but his face was impassive as he replied tonelessly:

"I believe her Ladyship has ordered the carriage for half past ten, Milord. I understand she is going out with Nanny and the children for a drive."

Rowell frowned.

"Going out," he repeated in astonishment. "Doesn't she know the King died last night?"

"I believe she does, Milord. Lily took up the newspaper with her Ladyship's breakfast," the servant replied, his voice still as expressionless as his face.

Rowell rose to his feet, and pushing past the footman, went out into the hall. High above his head, he saw Willow and the children with their nurse coming down the long gallery to the head of the staircase. He noted that they were indeed dressed in carriage clothes and his face darkened. This was no proper occasion to be paying calls or going for a joyride. Had Willow lost all sense of propriety?

He waited until they had descended the stairs and without preamble, said:

"Please cancel whatever plans you have, Willow. I do not wish anyone to leave the house today. You are aware, I believe, that the King is dead?"

Willow turned to Patience.

"Take the children out to the carriage," she said quietly. "Wait for me there. I will not be long."

She waited until they were gone before she turned to face Rowell.

"I think it would be best if we were to go into the library," she said quietly, and as Rowell opened his mouth to speak, she added firmly: "I do not think you will wish the servants to overhear what I have to say."

Rowell's head was throbbing. Instinct warned him that trouble was brewing, and he decided not to dispute Willow's suggestion. He allowed her to precede him into the library, where he sank gratefully into his chair. Willow remained standing by the door.

"I am leaving you, Rowell," she said in a quiet emotionless voice. "I do not intend to give you my reasons—there are many—and I am sure you know most of them anyway. I would like you to divorce me, but even if you will not, this will not prevent my going."

Speechless, Rowell stared up at his wife's pale face. Her dark eyes looked enormous, and the tell-tale bruises were clearly visible on her cheeks. He could remember now striking her—pushing her aside when the boy had interrupted them. He thought he now understood what she was about. She had voiced her protest in the form of a threat to leave him. He was now expected to apologize, to put matters right.

"Of course I shall not divorce you," he said as he stood up to confront her. "You are my wife. Your place is here with me. If I upset you last night—"

"I am formally renouncing my responsibilities, both as your wife and as mistress of this house," Willow interrupted. She took the heavy bunch of keys she had intended to leave in the hall and laid them on the table beside the whiskey decanter. Quite irrelevantly, she observed with relief that the footman had remembered to refill it—an omission that always caused Rowell acute irritation. But it was no longer a matter with which she need concern herself, she thought with astonishment. As she had just informed Rowell, Rochford Manor, its servants, the running of the great house, and Rowell's wishes, were no longer her concern or her responsibility.

"You are obviously not well," Rowell said with a sharp look at her tense face. Even now he did not take seriously her announcement that she was leaving him.

Willow nearly smiled.

"I am perfectly well and perhaps for the first time since I set eyes on you twenty-one years ago, I am in my right senses. I do not love you, Rowell, and I do not wish to remain here as your wife. I am going back to America with the children."

Now Rowell could no longer discount her intentions. Willow was neither out of her mind nor hysterical but in deadly earnest. His face darkened.

"I suggest that you think twice before you walk out of that door," he said warningly. "For if you do, Willow, you will never be allowed to come back. As for taking the children with you—that is something I can and will prevent."

Willow drew in her breath sharply. For the first time, her face betrayed emotion.

"I am taking them with me," she said. "It is not as if *you* want them, Rowell. You don't like Oliver and you have never taken the slightest interest in Alice. Let me have them and—" she paused only for the fraction of a second before she continued: "—and I will see to it that you are well compensated. My father's companies are once again doing exceedingly well. I have been advised by Mr. Corbett that I can draw on as much money as I want. I will arrange for you to benefit in that I shall make no claim upon you for myself or for the children, and I will make over to you my own shares in the corporation."

Rowell's mind had cleared. While Willow was speaking, he began to understand very clearly just how important the children were to her. He had but to insist upon his right to keep them and he could keep her, too. Money would not compensate for her loss. Perhaps it was true that, years ago, he had married her not from love but because he had believed her to be an heiress. But now he wanted her for herself. Not only did he abhor the thought of the gossip once it became known that his wife had left him, *but he did not want to be alone in this great house without her*. She had run his home even better than had Grandmère in her lifetime, he thought. She was the perfect hostess, beautiful, intelligent, popular . . . and he still found her desirable.

"Go if you wish," he challenged her in a low, harsh voice, "but you will not take the children with you, Willow. Leave me and you leave them too."

It had long ago crossed Willow's mind that Rowell might try to use the children to bargain with her, despite the fact that he had little love for either of them. She had prayed that he would not do so, counting upon his disinterest in them. For his sake, for hers and for the children's, she had sworn to herself that she would never reveal their true parentage. But now if Rowell insisted, he would leave her no alternative. She could not go without them, and Rowell knew it. She made one last attempt to persuade him, sinking her pride to plead with him.

"Please let me have them, Rowell. I will bring them up as you would wish. I will see that they write to you—even that they come and visit you when they are a little older. No one knows better than you how precious they are to me. Let them come with me, I beg you."

"No!" Rowell's voice was like a whiplash. "And if you thought I would consider such a thing, then you really have lost your senses. They are my children—Rochfords—and they stay here with me."

Willow bit her lip, unable for a moment to say what must be said. She saw Rowell's eyes watching her, a look of triumph already there as he congratulated himself on winning the day.

He thinks I will stay, she thought in detached surprise. He really has no idea how impossible he has made it for me to do so.

She looked directly at him, her hands clenched at her sides.

"Rowell, they are *not* your children!"

She saw his eyes narrow and then bore into hers in disbelief.

"What new nonsense is this? Of course they are mine—Rochfords, both of them," he said uneasily.

"Yes, Rochfords," Willow said quietly. "But you are not their father."

"Then who the devil is?" Rowell cried, his face scarlet, his hands flailing.

"Do you really wish me to tell you, Rowell? I will, if you insist."

"I damn well do insist!" Rowell shouted, overcome by a terrible fear that Willow might be telling the truth.

"Then you force me to confess that Pelham is Oliver's father, and Alice is the child born as the result of your brother Francis' attack upon Nellie."

For a moment there was a stunned silence. Then Rowell shouted:

"I don't believe it! You are lying!" Her gaze was unflinching, and he suddenly realized that she would never lie about such a matter. "Even if it is the truth, those children are mine in law," he added violently.

"I would go personally to court to dispute such a claim," Willow rejoined quietly. "And although it might be difficult for me to prove that Pelham was Oliver's father, I would have no difficulty in proving that Alice was Nellie's child. I am sure you would not welcome the publicity that such a case would be bound to arouse, would you, Rowell?"

She thought for one moment that he would strike her, but instead he began to rant at her, abusing her with all the gutter adjectives he could think of. She waited, her head high, until his vituperative tirade finally came to an end. Then she said:

"As you say, Rowell, I have not been blameless these past years. But when I came here as your bride, I loved you; I respected you; I wanted no other man for my lover. You were my whole world. Even when I found out about Georgina and later, about the children that poor unfortunate woman bore you, I forgave you. No wife could have been more determined than I to make our marriage work. It was my over-riding concern to do so while yours was to find pleasures elsewhere—outside your home. Let me speak," she added as Rowell made as if to interrupt her.

"It is the last time I shall ever talk to you, so please hear me out. Twenty years ago, you came to America and swore to my father that my happiness was the only thing in the world that mattered to you—but it never did matter—never! I do not think you know what it is to love, Rowell. Perhaps you never will. But fortunately I no longer care. I am thirty-six years old, and have possibly thirty years of life left to me. I intend to live those remaining years not as *you* wish, Rowell, but as *I* want. I am tired of being your wife; tired of marriage. From now on, I intend to be myself just as you have always been yourself—only I hope that I shall be able to live with more dignity than you do and with a sense of honor that is not hypocritical nor set aside as soon as it is tested." She looked at him pityingly.

"I could even now forgive you for those pains you have inflicted on me throughout our marriage, but I could never forgive you for what you did to your servant. I'm going now, Rowell, and I don't want ever to see you again."

As she made to leave the room, Rowell attempted to grab her arm, but she twisted free. Her eyes were filled with scorn as she said:

"Even were you to detain me now by force, it would be only a matter of time before I did go, Rowell. You could not keep me a prisoner here and you could not watch me all the time. I would leave at the first opportunity."

Rowell's arm fell to his side. Now at last, he recognized defeat. Not that he would let her get away with this, he thought furiously as the door closed quietly behind her. He would get in touch immediately with his London solicitors. He would find a way to get those children back once and for all. They were legally his. No matter what it cost, he would have them taken from her. He would let her go now, believing she was safe; that she had scored a victory over him. She would find out soon enough that it was only the start of the battle— a battle that in the end he, Rowell Rochford, was bound by law to win.

Willow stepped into the carriage where Patience, Lily, and the two children sat awaiting her. Behind was the wagonette loaded with their trunks. Jackson closed the door and climbed up into the driver's seat. He touched the whip to the horses' flanks, and minutes later, they were bowling down the long gravel drive.

Staring out of the window, Willow's thoughts winged back to the day when she had come up this same drive as a bride, full of hope and full of love for her young husband. Now she was leaving everything she had dreamed would bring her happiness.

Gusts of rain were sweeping across the emerald green lawns. The leafbuds on the great horse chestnut trees lining the drive had not yet opened and the dark, heavy branches swung menacingly in the wind. The lake looked cold and bare, its surface ruffled and broken into a thousand pinpoints by the heavy rain.

Looking backwards toward the house, Willow's eyes went unwittingly to the closed casements of Toby's laboratory and were suddenly filled with tears.

Beside her, little Alice clutched her hand:

"Look, Mama, there's somebody coming up the drive," she said in her small clear voice.

Willow's gaze followed the child's pointed finger. Now she too saw the short, slight figure, huddled deep into a brown mantle, her head protected by the hood from the driving rain.

" 'Tis a girl coming to apply for the laundrymaid's job, I daresay," remarked Lily. "I heard as how one was wanted."

"She'll be half-drowned by the time she gets to the house," said Patience.

"Mama, can we not stop and give her a ride back to the house?" little Alice inquired anxiously. "It is such a long way for her to walk. Please, Mama?"

Willow closed her eyes as if to shut out the clamor of voices. Neither the child nor the servants could know that her courage was fast evaporating. If she were to go back to that house—to catch sight of Toby, she might never again find the courage to leave. It would take the laundry girl but a short while more to walk to the manor and she would not be much wetter than she was already.

"Do you wish me to stop, Milady?" Jackson called down from his box.

"No, drive on," Willow said sharply.

There could be no going back.

As the carriage swept by, the Honorable Sophia Rochford's cloak was bespattered with muddy water. She paused, turning to stare after the disappearing carriage.

"*Merde alors,*" she swore with a Gallic shrug of her shoulders. "If that is a sample of my relations, I'd as soon not know them!"

She was cold, tired, and the landlady's cloak had not prevented her getting drenched to the skin. Despite the fact that Nicole had assured her she could expect sunshine and good weather in England in the spring, the skies had darkened and the landlady's forecast proven when a positive deluge of rain poured from the leaden skies. Within minutes, the rough surface of the lane leading to

Rochford Manor was a quagmire of mud which had ruined her new boots. Moreover, two farm carts had passed her by without stopping to offer her a lift.

In the year since the locket had revealed the first real clue to her background, Sophia had never lost the total conviction that it was her destiny ultimately to be re-united with her family. Neither Yvette's warnings nor even Madame Lou-Lou's threats not to allow her back in *Le Ciel Rouge* if she went to England, had weakened her resolve. Nor had she yet permitted her disappointment in Havorhurst itself to dismay her more than momentarily. She would have liked her relations to be living in an amusing place like Dover, but philosophically resigned herself to the fact that one could never have all one's heart's desires. It was but a small disappointment in the light of her discovery that her family were, as the old doctor had said, titled, wealthy, and important.

But now as she stood watching the carriage disappear through the gates of the drive, her spirits flagged for the first time. Was it after all possible that she would not be made welcome? That she would not even be recognized as a Rochford? The locket proved nothing, as Yvette had pointed out, since the old Englishman might just as easily have presented it to *her*. Sophia had only his word that it had belonged to *her* relations and she had already ascertained from the landlord of the Havorhurst Arms that the elderly doctor had died some three years ago. He would not be available to speak for her even if he were one and the same man she had met at *Le Ciel Rouge*. She did not even have proof of *his* identity.

The rain was easing slightly, although now the gusts of wind stirring the bare branches of the trees were gathering momentum. Sophia shivered. Her legs ached and she felt a great longing for the bright lights and warm familiarity of *Le Ciel Rouge*. It had seemed this morning an exciting adventure to be alone in a foreign country, but now she longed for the sound of a French voice; for the girls' friendly banter; for hot coffee and croissants.

She turned now to stare once more up the drive. Although the outlines of the manor were blurred by the rain, its size and beauty were discernible, and Sophia was impressed by its grandeur. Moreover, the big house no longer seemed so far away.

She hoped very much that not all the occupants had just swept by her in the carriage. A great many people must live in so large a mansion, she decided. Someone would be there to receive her. It might be only a matter of minutes before she came face to face with the parents she had never known.

Resolutely, she stepped forward. The courage that had sustained her during the many privations at the convent, the drudgery at *La Maison Grimaud*, the long hours and poor pay at Madame Lou-Lou's, now returned. With the same hope of fulfillment that had once guided her mother in the same direction, Sophia walked toward her future.

At almost the same moment, Toby left his laboratory to hurry downstairs. For once, he did not stop to close his door. From his turret window, he had seen Willow climb into the carriage beside Patience and the children. But for the fact that the wagonette was behind them, piled high with trunks, he might not have given the small party a second glance. Now he was filled with terrible misgivings as he rushed past one of the maids and down the stairs.

The big house was hushed, only a halflight creeping through the curtained windows. A portrait of the late King now hung over the empty fireplace in place of Grandmère's portrait, the carved gold frame draped in black crêpe.

Toby could see no sign of Rowell, but one of the footmen informed him that the baron was in the library. Toby pushed open the doors. Rowell was slumped in his chair, a half-empty whiskey glass in his hand.

"Where has Willow gone?" Toby asked without preamble.

When Rowell did not reply, he walked over to his brother's chair and said in a sharper voice: "Where's Willow?"

Rowell grunted, slumping deeper into his chair.

"Gone," he muttered.

"For heaven's sake, Rowell, pull yourself together," Toby almost shouted. "Gone where?"

"Left me!" Rowell muttered. "Going back to America. Taken the children with her, rotten little—"

The sharp sting of Toby's hand on his face prevented

Rowell from uttering the degrading name he intended to use. He stared up at Toby in astonishment.

"What's all that about?" he said, his speech slurred. "I'm telling you, Toby, she's no damn good—never was. Good riddance, I say!"

For a few long moments, Toby stared down at his brother, his eyes filled with pity and disgust.

"You never did realize what a wonderful woman you married, did you?" he said. "You never noticed how unhappy she was when you failed to give her any love, any understanding. She was just someone you wanted from time to time when you had no one else to amuse you; someone to run your house for you; entertain for you. You were never really her husband, Rowell, and I'm not in the very least surprised to hear that she has finally had enough of being your wife."

As Toby paused for breath, Rowell's expression changed from that of astonishment to disbelief.

"Well, who would believe it! *You* were in love with her," he jeered. "All the time you, Toby, were secretly in love with my wife. And I never guessed. None of us ever guessed. Is that why you never married? Is that the real reason why you haven't married that pretty little governess of yours? Because you wanted *my* wife!"

Toby was once more quite in control of himself.

"Just for the record, Rowell, you may like to know that Stella Menzies is going to marry Peter Rose. Rose's fiancée wrote to him a week ago calling off their engagement, and he rushed straight round to the Barratts' and asked Stella to marry him. I am telling you this before I go, lest you were hoping that I might provide a new chatelaine for Rochford Manor."

Rowell looked up, his reddened eyes narrowed in bewilderment.

"Before you go?" he echoed. "Go where, Toby?"

"To America, of course. Where else?"

For a moment, there was total silence in the room. Then Rowell said:

"You know, don't you, that even if I divorced Willow you can never marry her?"

Toby nodded. Although his eyes were sad, his face was suddenly bright with happiness.

"There are other things in life besides marriage," he said. "I can take care of Willow, Rowell. And I can give her the one thing that you could never give her—"

As he reached the doorway, Toby turned and, looking over his shoulder, he added softly:

"—I can give her love."

Epilogue

THERE COULD BE NO SIMPLE, CONVENTIONAL FUTURE for Willow's sixteen-year-old daughter, Sophia Rochford. Half aristocrat, half commoner; half English, half American, raised in a French convent and trained in a Parisian brothel, her destiny leads her to the brink of tragedy and into the many pitfalls of love. Happily reunited with her father, she believes mistakenly she is secure as the new chatelaine of the Rochford Manor. But Rowell's promises are not to be fulfilled. As a consequence, her hatred of him and the other men who have betrayed and used her is to come near to destroying her. Her determination never to be hurt again is to conflict violently with her passionate need to love and be loved.

In Volume II of the Rochford family saga (now in preparation), Sophia's life unfolds during the years from 1911 to 1918. Inevitably and far from happily, she is reunited with Willow, Toby, and the Rochford children, Oliver and Alice. The threads of her life become entangled with those of Rupert, her half-brother Philip Grey, Dodie and James; and with the artist, Maurice. She meets Pelham and Silvie Rochford and is reunited briefly with her friends in *Le Ciel Rouge*.

Her wild escapades lead to an enforced unhappy marriage to a Hungarian count older than herself, and she finds herself fighting a strength of will surpassing even her own. Her passionate resentment of his dominance is to lead her into extremes of outrageous behavior that are to come near to ruining her life. It is finally the discovery of her love for one man that is to halt her on the very brink of disaster.

Acknowledgments

I WOULD LIKE TO THANK THE FOLLOWING PEOPLE FOR their assistance in providing research material:
The staff of the Institute of Bankers, the British Institute of Radiology, the Westminster Medical Library; Croydon, Sevenoaks, East Grinstead and Edenbridge Public Libraries; Mr. Recorder M. J. W. Marsh for advice on legal matters; Mr. J. W. West (Midland Bank Trust Company); the staff of the Haywards Heath and Edenbridge branches of the Midland Bank; the Manager of the Duke of York Theatre; the Royal College of Physicians; Mr. S. Moseley (Chairman of Marsh Green Village School Managers); Dr. John Bishop Harman.

I would also like to express my appreciation of the patience and efficiency shown by my research assistant and secretary, Penrose Scott; my gratitude for the hard work and dedication of Wendy Rose, who typed and re-typed with untiring enthusiasm. I wish to thank Joy Tait for her editorial assistance and encouragement; Phil Garside for continuity checking; Maggie Duffy (San Francisco) and Lilias Atkinson for their contributions.

Finally, I would like to thank my family and my housekeeper, Mrs. Greensmith, for putting up so uncomplainingly with this author's odd hours, odd moods, and detachment from normal family commitments. *The Chatelaine* may be my story, but it could not have become a book without the help of all those who contributed and nursed it into life.

Ballantine's World of Historical Romance...